Love Me Do,

A love story;

Interspersed with some *Lyrics*,
Representing the principal *Themes*.

IN NINE PARTS,

BY Jonnie Comet.

Comprising an early *History*,
of two Young People *in love*,
Including all *Trials* and *Entanglements*, thereof;
Over the span of some *Sixteen Months*.

Surf City Source
New Jersey
AD 2025

Love Me Do;
the novel

* * *

Sixth, 'Reunion' paperback edition, August 2025

Edited by Melissa Stockhart
with Jayne Christopher and Victoria Macintalk

In memory of original editor Colin Bunge, MArts,
St John's College, Cambridge University,
1958-2024

Made on a Mac
Typeset in 11-pt Baskerville

Cover artefacts from the Author's archives
Layout by Surf City Source

Published by Surf City Source media group
New Jersey
www.surfcitysource.com

ISBN 978 0692268896
16 14 12 10 8 7 9 11 13 15

Printed in the USA

No *Microsoft* products were used
in the successful preparation of this manuscript.

* * *

Twenty years after

preface to the *Third* edition, of 2010

Not long ago I was teaching an 11th-year literature class in which *The Great Gatsby* was assigned; and as with every other time I have read that book since my own 11th year my thoughts returned to *Love Me Do*. It may seem heady for any author to compare himself to the unparallelled Scott Fitzgerald; but surely the literate reader will recognise the similarities between that book and this one. In truth *Gatsby*, with its heart-rending portrayal of fatally unrequited love, was my first singular inspiration to write in the first instance; and that central theme, of self-reinvention, self-determination and a constant Platonic striving to reach an unreachable star, has been a form of motivation to me all my life.

Certainly Jon is to Gatsby as Jeanne is to Daisy– the gentle, insecure, idealistic 'young roughneck' determined to deserve the one whom he has always held as a precious princess in his heart whilst being so unwilling to rush in like a fool in love that even a kiss might be both too earthly and too out-of-reach. If Jay has placed Daisy on a pedestal, so has Jon placed Jeanne. The difference is that in *Love Me Do* no great irreparable mistakes are made– nor have ever been made– and all remains as optimistic as was that great wide future when Jay Gatz saw Dan Cody's yacht for the first time. What is love without optimism anyway?

Appropriately, Gatsby's demise comes because he commits no unselfish, heroic sacrifices to truly merit his princess– for of what worth is a princess on a pedestal if her pure-of-heart champion will not aspire to ascend and meet her there? I confess a Romantic bent in this regard, that I never cared for the *noir*, nor even the fatalism of the gothic, being essentially a moralist now as when I conceived and began this book over 35 years ago. There is no darkness or hapless tragedy here. There is only a moral, as all fables must have.

If *Gatsby* is an allegory, then *LMD* might be its counterpart in realism; and so we shall let the realism in *Gatsby* have its counterpart in the allegorical elements of *LMD*. (Look for them– they are everywhere.) Where *Gatsby* is succinct, almost (but not quite) to a fault, the saga of Jon and Jeanne is saturated in detail (almost, but not quite, to a fault). But it is a saturation in syrup and icing, meant to give a reader the full dose and then some of what he or she seeks in this story to begin with. Delve into this book, live it, love it, dream it, drown in it, as though it were your first love-at-first-sight and first kiss all over again; let it be for you the sweet romantic evening that should never end, lest, in good time, it inevitably shall– as we have seen:

'I am afeared,
Being in night, all this is but a dream,
Too flattering-sweet to be substantial.' – *R&J*; II, ii, 141-143

I once fielded a question about the genesis of some scenes in this book and upon reflection realised that those passages which may seem most surreal are in fact those that most accurately represent the original inspiring events. Nothing the students in *LMD* do is patently unlikely; indeed its author witnessed (and instigated) events such as these (and many more) whilst living through the very generation that *LMD* depicts. Since this book was envisioned in the early 1970s as a collection of vignettes of 'typical' high-school life, many of the details as to hairstyles, fashions, entertainment and music, and especially attitudes about school, drinking, drugs, sex and life in general, are historically authentic precisely because they were written at that time.

This leads to the other question I have got most often about this book: was there a real 'Jeanne'? As to the answer I can only offer this axiom, endued to me by a beloved professor in literature: that to an author there is no true 'fiction', only a well-rendered and reordered relation of the writer's own reality. Any 'fictitious' character tends to be an idealised edition of some true-life inspiration; that is only the nature of fiction and of authorship. So yes; there was a real 'Jeanne' –or, I should say, she still remains in her perfect Platonic conception; for such love as what one must be capable of in order to write such a paean as *LMD* does not fade with either distance or years but exists in the realm of the Ideal and for all time.

Tennyson has said it is better to have loved and lost than to have never loved at all. If this author has loved, he has not lost; for this book has been both labour and fruit of that love.

The new Surf City Source edition is dedicated with fond and abiding admiration to my daughter Mary, born only half a year before this book was completed, yet who eerily enough in her innocence, gentle heart and even appearance has grown up the most perfect embodiment of 'Jeanne' for her own generation. May you find your own 'Jonathan' one day, sweet child; and may you never settle for less.

– Jonnie Comet   afloat; November 2010

* * *

A message, from the Author:

I am grateful to the following for encouragement, criticism, and profound inspiration. Whether you know it or not, you have helped make this story what it is: a labour of love.

Instructors who piqued my interest in writing
and shaped my 'colloquial' style:

Mr *Williams*, 6th year ('I'm from Missouri; you have to *show* me');
Mrs *Beverly*, whose favourite author was Pearl S Buck;
Sarah *Cohen*, thanks for the lessons in casual teaching;
Jeff *Romm*, a Beatles fan if ever there were one;
Bob *Seiler*, a lifesaver at lifesaving;
Bob *Nimmer*, for grading my writing and not my grammar;
Mrs *Carrides*, you knew these characters before anyone;

and most specially
Art 'Onkel Wini' *Winiarski*, you're unforgettable and you know it.

Others of whom I was so fond,
and whose influence was felt throughout this writing:

Christine ('call me "Chris" ') *Cerce*;
Robert *Imhoff*– no; I never forgot ya, bro';

The insane geniuses of Mr *Allen's* draughtsmanship class:
Francis 'Jimmy' *Connor*, Pat *Donnelly*, Alfred *Walthour-Dove*, Jerry *Gardner*, Maury *Groves*, John *Hamilton* and Mike *Wayne*;

Mark *Bosch* (I *still* tell people about the night you banged out 'While My Guitar Gently Weeps' on Debbie *Nissman's* piano);

Michelle *Baderak*, for encouraging me to become a literature teacher just to spite Mr *Heckman's* disdain for my attitude;

Carl Haugneland;
Walt Koenig;
Elly Curtin;
Rich Ciccotosto;

All the JFK cheerleaders;

my cousin *Anne-Bone*;

Rino;

The Beatles, for the impact their work left on me;

and

the *real* 'Jeanne', for unending flights of fancy.
You listened to all my stories and told me I should write a book.
Sorry if it's later than you expected; but here it is,
and it's dedicated
to you.

– Jonnie Comet   New Jersey; May 1990

Have you ever seen me;
Have you ever known me;
Have you ever loved me;

As I have loved you?

* * *

Love Me Do.

by Jonnie Comet

Chapter 1

Deep in love, not a lot to say

Wilshire, Connecticut
September 1973

Beth heard it first. 'There he is now,' she said, glancing up at the ceiling.

Her mother stopped chewing to pause for a second. When she recognised the ringing of the alarm clock above Andy Kim singing 'Rock Me Gently' over the radio, she made a nod and then she finished her bite of toast. 'There he is now,' she agreed, and took a wee sip of coffee.

The tone of the ringing above stairs changed as the button was pushed in. Quite abruptly the sound stopped. Beth went back to the cooker to check on the eggs. Two minutes later her twelve-year-old sister Eve shuffled wearily into the kitchen. 'What's to eat?' she asked in a sleepy voice, still trying to tuck in her striped t-shirt.

'Eggs,' said Beth, and then smiled. 'Take it or leave it.'

Eve sighed. 'Well; given *that* choice....' She dropped into a chair across the table from her mother. Beth delivered to her a fried egg on a dish and set it next to the fork she had set out. 'What's this? –only one?'

'One is enough,' Beth replied, and returned to the cooker.

'"One is *enough*"? Hey; Mom–'

Her mother looked up at her. 'One is enough. You only have half a day; you'll be home for lunch.' She took a quick look up at the wall clock and, leaving the folded newspaper on the chair, disappeared into the next room.

'*Jeez....*' Eve cut open the egg with the side of the fork and took a hungry mouthful.

Beth paid the dissent no mind. She was her mother's daughter, light-haired and fair of face, with a gentle, peacekeeping demeanour. However she resembled her father in physique, lightweight and disproportionately slender. Eve was just the opposite, with what would soon be a buxom figure like her mother's and the dark hair and sun-blessed complexion of her father. She favoured the Italian side in temperament, quick to emotion and slower to reason. The two rarely found any common ground. Beth would never go in for Eve's boyish shenanigans, and Eve had little patience for the polite formality with which Beth addressed even her own siblings; their incompatibility was a source of constant strife within the household.

Andrew came down, still combing out his long brown hair. He was often accused of being vain, but the proof of his attention to his appearance was in his wealth of female admirers; still not yet fourteen, he had already made a name for himself in the junior-high-school set as everyone's favourite playboy. Beth got up at once to serve him his egg; and he sat down without a word of thanks and delved in hungrily. 'One is enough,' Eve reminded him.

Beth scowled at that. 'Diggit,' Andrew said sarcastically, wiping his forehead clear of the hair for the tenth or twelfth time this morning. 'Some kinda starvation diet, and doo.'

'You're both a pair of ingrates,' Beth told them irritably, and sat down to finish her own breakfast.

'Thanks for the compliment,' Andrew retorted, not looking at her. 'It's not every day that you get compared to a manhole cover; you know?'

Eve laughed with him. It was already 7.10; and the oldest of the brood had not yet come down. 'I thought his alarm clock went off,' Eve said. 'That dude could sleep through an earthquake.'

'Diggit,' Andrew mumbled.

Beth let out a sigh. 'I'll get him,' she volunteered, and stood up. 'It's a tough job; but somebody's got to do it.'

'Better take a weapon,' Eve advised, as Beth ascended the back stairs.

'"One is enough",' Andrew mocked her. 'She never cooks enough. As if the rest of us are on diets too.'

'Diggit,' Eve agreed, and stood up and went round into the kitchen. 'As if she even needs one. Wanna bowl of Quisp?'

'Diggit.'

Beth ignored them and pushed open the door to the room above the kitchen. It emitted its characteristic squeak and stopped halfway open, blocked by some stack of books or magazines. An Alpine range of laundry, some soiled, some fresh from the washing, rose above the desk, dresser and chairs. Musical instruments and stereo components and automotive parts and boxes of tools formed an obstacle course to make the Marines tremble. The dark brown drapery was drawn tight against the bright morning sun. Beth gasped in the hot, humid air as she swam her way through the clutter to the bed in the far corner.

Jonathan Christopher Cavaliere, the Younger, was visible only as a lump beneath the thick wool blanket that even in summer he kept tucked into the sides of his bed. 'Hey,' she called, like a yachtsman requesting permission to come aboard; 'are you up yet?'

Jon did not stir.

She sidestepped his prized electric bass guitar leaning precariously against the foot of the bed. 'Jon,' she said, a bit firmer, 'it's time to get up.'

No response came from the lump in the blanket.

'Jon,' she sang gently, reaching over to rock him a little, 'you'll be late....' All this was to no avail. She took one step back and announced in a loud voice, 'We have to leave for school in twenty minutes!'

The lump rose straight up at the sound, to settle down again bent up in the middle. Beth peeled back the blue blanket and the sheet to reveal her elder brother, in a black t-shirt and his underpants, with his face in the pillow and his rump in the air.

'Get out of bed,' she commanded playfully, 'because I want to be able to clean up the kitchen after you eat.'

Slowly he lifted his head and winced at her from beneath a tousled mop of light-brown hair. In a hoarse morning voice he asked, 'Surely you're not implying that I'm a slob about eating?'

She smiled, although disgusted to survey the disorganisation about her. 'Well; maybe not just about *eating*....'

'What time is it?' he croaked.

She looked towards his night-table but could not locate the clock amid the clutter. 'About quarter after,' she said. 'We have to leave by twenty-five of. Split sessions this year, remember.'

His reply was to drop face-first into the pillow with a groan.

'So what are you gonna wear today?'

'I don't know,' came the voice from the pillow.

'Where's all that clean stuff I brought up here yesterday?'

'Around,' said the pillow.

She looked about and recognised a few remnants from the clean laundry, including a pile of neatly ironed and folded shirts and a few pairs of bright-white tube-socks. 'Jon, I can't believe you! How can you just throw this stuff around, when it took me all day yesterday just to make sure you and your brother had stuff to wear to school.... This whole room is a disgrace!'

He looked up then and asked, 'You didn't make French toast down there, did you?'

'Argh!' she growled, and stomped out.

Down in the kitchen her father had come out and helped himself to an egg from the pan. The morning paper ranged over half the table and across from him Eve and Andrew crowded next to each other, munching on their bowlfuls of sugary Quisp cereal. Beth passed by them without comment and collected their dirty dishes for the dishwashing machine. Since her mother had resumed teaching another season, fifteen-year-old Beth assumed all the morning kitchen duties for the school year, a responsibility she took on willingly and with great diligence and patience.

Eve got up to carry her bowl to the sink, having finished the cereal ahead of Andrew. Her father took one look at her and said, 'So is that what you're wearing to school these days? Dungarees? You look like your family can't afford to keep you in clothes.'

Eve made a little laugh. 'It's what everybody wears now, Pop.'

'Everybody's a slob,' lamented her father, disappointed.

Above stairs the water ran. 'Good,' said Beth, mostly to herself; 'that'll be him now. I want him to eat and get out so I can clean up this kitchen.'

Mrs Cavaliere reentered, in a blue jacket and pleated white skirt, smelling of Chanel's Number Five. 'Okay, gang, I have to get going; it's my first day too. Beth, sweetheart, you will straighten up this zoo?'

'Yes, sure, Mom.'

'You're a sweet child, honey; I don't know what I'd do without you.' She caught her daughter by the back of the neck and planted a kiss on her cheek. 'And Eve is going to behave like a young lady today. No detentions on the first day of junior high.'

'Diggit,' Andrew mumbled, and then got up with his empty bowl.

'She won't even dress like one,' complained Mr Cavaliere, 'so you'd expect her to act like one? Look at your sister, there—'

'Oh; come on, Pop,' Eve laughed; and Andrew did too. 'At least I'm *normal*.'

'*Normal*,' her father scoffed, and then was silent.

'To each his own,' Mrs Cavaliere philosophised, and gave the other two each a kiss on the head. 'Well, family; I'm off,' she said cheerfully, and met her husband's kiss then. 'Have a good day, all!' She went out the kitchen door and down the stairs to her newly-washed maroon Volkswagen.

Jon came down then, in one of the silk-screened t-shirts he and Eve had designed and a pair of well-worn bell-bottomed jeans, and sat down in the chair opposite his father. 'Hey; how come you got me up so late? Dag; it's practically seven-thirty.'

'Your alarm went off half an hour ago,' Beth told him. 'You got yourself up so late. Just remember you have to give me a ride today. There's no way I'll make it on time *now*.'

'Aaaaaaah....'

She stood there glaring at him with the turner in one hand and her other hand planted upon her hip. The apron completed the impression of domestic authority. 'Are you going to eat this last egg?'

'Naah; I don't want nothin'.'

Without looking up from the paper, Mr Cavaliere sighed and said, 'I hope you realise that when you say "I don't want nothin'" it makes you sound like you never went to school, so cut it out.' Still not looking up he said, 'You eat something.' He gestured to Beth then. 'Give him the egg.'

'Aaah; I'm not hungry in the morning.'

'Don't go off to school without breakfast. Most important meal of the day, man.'

'Dag! I'll be home for lunch!'

'Eat the egg. To Beth he said, 'Give him the egg.'

'Aaah; I hate eggs.'

'Eat the egg. Gives you protein. Eggs have everything.'

'Yeah; right. Cholesterol....' Jon grimaced as Beth chiseled the egg out of the pan onto his plate.

'*You* don't have to worry about cholesterol.' Mr Cavaliere turned a page.

'Just how you like it,' Beth smiled. 'Almost-burnt.'

'I do *not* like them "almost-burnt",' he told her.

'Yeah; well; whenever you fry eggs, they all seem to turn out that way,' she teased.

'Just *eat* the *egg*, man,' Mr Cavaliere pleaded painfully, his patience waning.

'Yeah, yeah....' Jon cast one look at the egg on the plate and abruptly got up.

'*Now* what?' Beth glared at him.

'I need a *fork*, you know.'

She whirled about in the kitchen, snatching a fork out of the drawer and turning it to him prongs-first. 'I oughta let you have it in the *gut* with it, Ingrate. And you expect me to cook?'

He swiped the fork out of her hand with a smirk and stalked back to his seat. 'Hah!' he scoffed. 'No, Mister Bond. I expect you to *die!*'

'Daddy,' Beth whined, 'he's being obnoxious again.'

Mr Cavaliere stood up, brushing his thick black hair off his forehead, and winced at his eldest son. 'Man; I wish you could just be a little less boisterous in the morning; Christ....' He gathered the paper off the table and left.

They both watched him pace out of the room, hearing him go up the front hall steps. '*That's* what you are,' Beth said then. 'Boisterous.'

'Boisterous,' Jon laughed. 'Like you didn't *even* start it. So let me just eat this; will ya?'

She swung shut the door to the dishwashing machine with a sigh and left him alone to his breakfast.

A familiar thumb stuck out into the Parkway traffic, and Jon geared down and stopped at the kerb. 'Holy shit,' he said to his sister; 'look who it *is*.' He unlocked the rear door with the electric lock switch and called to his old friend. 'Yo, dude!'

'Hey, dude,' Mike Jolson called in, as he hurried to get in behind Beth. 'No way; this ain't even the *same car*?'

'Hell yeah,' Jon smiled proudly, jamming the stick into first and putting his foot down. 'Where you *been* all summer, man? Me and Holloway worked for like four months on this bitch.' He shifted into second. Beth gasped with the acceleration. 'Just got it on the road last week.'

'Shit....' Mike looked about at the beautiful white upholstery and soft grey carpet. 'No, man; we were in Hawaii till about two weeks ago. My mom's cousin's wedding, so....' Mike's mother was pure Hawaiian, the war bride of an Army truck driver called Albert who had shortened his surname from Jolonowicz upon his enlistment for Korea.

'You lucky son-of-a-bitch.' Jon sped past an old Mustang convertible full of schoolgirls and put the stick back into fourth, at about sixty, whilst his sister gripped the sides of her seat with anxiety. He was happy to show off the car, especially to a friend of such long standing. The two had met during eighth year, when the Jolsons had moved to Lake Drive from Delaware and Mike's sister Dawn had become infatuated with her sixth-year classmate, Andrew Cavaliere. Mike and Jon became fast friends and spent half of junior-high school sharing jokes and playing silly pranks, a classroom activity neither of them had yet outgrown. There had once been a formidable clique of them who had all grown up in the same neighbourhood and gone through most of the last six or eight years of school together. Now in high school, tastes in music, selection of girlfriends and other diverging interests had separated all but about five of them. Mike played billiards at the bowling alley, drank beer and experimented with narcotics, whilst Jon, eschewing the petty theft and vandalism recently pursued by some of the old crowd, remained sentimental at heart and still enjoyed the more childish antics of days gone by. He had been getting considerable exercise all summer, working outdoors with his father on construction sites; though Mike had always been reed-thin, these days he was looking even more so by comparison.

'So,' Mike said in the car; 'Jenkins says you're on the swim team again this year.'

'Huh? Oh; yeah.... I was like the third guy picked this time.' He chuckled a little, knowing that some boys would think that a subject for boasting. 'I must be getting good.'

'Rah, rah,' Mike said, to tease.

'Hey dude,' Jon told him; 'shut *up*. Swimmin' ain't no rah-rah sport like basketball, and doo. I only joined 'cause I wanted to get good at it. It's not like I'm gettin' a jacket out of it, or let alone a letter....'

'Rah, rah,' Mike teased, and laughed.

'Yeah; well; don't be such a dope addict.'

They both laughed at that; though sometimes Jon worried that such might already be the case. He turned right at Chester Pike and joined the block-long queue of cars waiting to enter the schoolyard gates. Proud of the new car, Jon waved to two leggy sophomores and allowed them to cross ahead of him. They each gave him a shy little glance and trotted past, with Jon and Mike smiling at their short skirts and their disorientation on their first day of high school.

Beth would get out in front of the building; it was her first day too and she had no designs on tardiness whilst parading the shiny new hot rod round the school driveway. Jon and Mike, the juniors, felt differently.

Mike stepped out and got into the front seat when Beth had gone. 'So,' he said; 'I take it you put that four-speed in; right?'

'Of course,' Jon said, and patted the console-mounted gear lever. 'Took a while gettin' used to clutchin' a big car, too. Like I've driven my dad's trucks, you know; but like this clutch is set up really light. Holloway wanted it like that.'

'I know what you mean,' Mike laughed. 'Me and that ol' Comet have been through like three clutches together.'

'Shit,' said Jon. 'That's just you beatin' on it.' He raised the volume of the stereo then.

They rounded the first turn, where the lane came parallel with the front wing of the school building. Mike had noticed how Jon had let the car ahead go a little farther on, opening the distance between the two cars at the first of the tarmac speed-bumps that punctuated the schoolyard's driveway. 'So what size *is* this motor?'

Jon smiled. 'Four-twenty-seven, four-bolt mains. The original block. Only now it has two AFBs, ten-to-one pistons, and a five-hundred-lift cam.'

'So,' Mike said casually, disregarding all that; 'I s'pose it catches rubber, then?'

Jon laughed a little and leaned back with confidence. 'All gears, dude.' The front wheels rolled gently over the bump; and Jon brought the car to a stop with the rear tyres perched at the crest. Out the window a few girls caught Mike's eye and he waved to them nonchalantly as though he always attracted attention from pretty girls. They pretended to ignore him, actually more interested in the car itself and its driver.

The car ahead went round the corner of the school building. Jon floored the throttle, lifting his left foot a half a second later. The engine ran up and then caught the clutch, and, as those twelve-inch-wide tyres screamed and the heads turned, Jon, an old friend and a new car roared off towards the back of the building.

Steve and Holly had met up with Bobby and the four girls just inside the schoolyard and walked with them as they started in through the rear parking-lot. Anne and Debbie were enthralled with disputing the new season's television programmes, and the boys stood and talked about cars. As for Jeanne, her thoughts were elsewhere. She sat upon her notebook amidst the dewy grass with her legs together to her right and her new yellow dress flowing out about her like the petals of a flower about their pistil. The ruffled cotton dress was very pretty, soft, feminine and wonderfully flattering to her figure. Bobby Crocker had told her she looked very nice; but she knew an old friend like Bobby would always say nice things about her. Just four days ago she had a wave set into her hair and the blond bangs curled out from her temples and away from her eyeglasses, feathering back down past her shoulders and flicking up just below her collar. The other girls had all said they liked the style; but Jeanne had expected to hear such good friends say so. Unfortunately the opinions of her friends fresh from ninth grade were not what she wanted to hear today. This would be her first day in high school.

She would be one of the youngest students in the sophomore class. To appear fitting as a potential date for some upper-class boys was her biggest concern this morning. As Debbie had said, it would indeed be exciting to date a few juniors or even seniors, perhaps even those with cars of their own. But there was one boy in particular whom she could not get out of her mind.

I just hope, she thought, that *he's* still around. If he is, I hope I get a chance to run into him today. Or, better yet, maybe *he'll* run into *me*. She got a shiver down her spine at that thought and began to feel nervous again. It seemed that feeling nervous was one of the things she did best. I just want to *see* him, she thought anxiously, nearly ready to pray for such a thing out loud. I just want to see what he's like. I want to see him around, and have him see me, and maybe like *see* him seeing me.... He was always so cute and so nice and so cool, and I just know he still is; and God, I only hope that being a junior now hasn't turned him into some kind of snob.... And if he says like even *one word* to me, just *one*, oh, God, I *promise* I'll make the most of it. I *swear* I will. And then maybe....

It came round the rear of the school building, moving at a mere walk as though the slow procession of cars bringing students in to the schoolyard were truly a parade. Jeanne stared at it, marvelling at how the early-morning sun glinted off every corner, framing it in a wet silvery haze and leaving the car's outline indistinguishable in the reflection. Sparks of platinum sunlight flickered off each of the chrome-plated spoked wheels and reflected in the hundred or more spellbound eyes.

The boisterous bass rhythm rolling out under the car made it ominously obvious that this was no car to be underestimated. Music blared out all the open windows; Jeanne recognised it as The Raspberries' 'Go All The Way'. The white vinyl roof added a touch of luxury whilst the black kick-panel, black bonnet and blackout grille set it off as a definite hot rod. Upon recognising the bold white monogram on the quarter, she suddenly felt her heart leap.

In twelve-inch balloon letters, it proclaimed: *JCC*.

Excitement ricocheted through her entire body and left it tingling. Goosepimples sprouted up all over as she gazed fully entranced at the beautiful silver car, visions of dreams-come-true racing about in her head.

The wide white-lettered tyres rolled gently to a stop beside a brown-haired boy standing by the edge of the lane, about thirty yards from where Jeanne sat demurely on top of her notebook in the grass. She saw the driver smile beneath that shaggy mop of almost-blond hair and she was sure that, even from behind those sexy mirrored sunglasses, he looked right at her, if only for a second.

The brown-haired boy in the dark-green body-shirt conversed with him for a third of a minute; and then the driver behind gave a short 'peep' on the horn. At this he laughed, and Jeanne could just hear him over the music and the rumble of the dual exhaust.

Suddenly the engine ran up loud and deep; and with a deafening thunder the car rocketed off ahead, viciously spinning the fat rear tyres for thirty yards up the driveway.

Bobby Crocker whirled about on his feet. 'Jesus *Christ*!'

Staid, conservative Steve only stood and stared silently, hiding his wince of distaste, as the silver Chevrolet charged into the car park and was whipped into the far aisle. His younger sister Anne found the words: 'What the *hell* kinda burnout—?'

'*Damn*!' swore Bobby Crocker, watching the car disappear into a parking slot well back in the aisle. 'Whose car *is* that?'

'Shoot if *I* know,' Steve confessed, looking hard at his sister with a new wariness.

'I think Richie DeMarco just lost the "Class Hot Rod" award,' their friend Holly giggled.

'Damn,' Bobby said again, as the fragrances of sweet perfume and a wet summer dawn were violated by the odour of burning rubber; 'whose car *is* that?'

'Yeah,' mushed Debbie. 'I've got to *have* him!'

Anne and Holly laughed at that. But Patti, sitting on her own notebook in the grass with Jeanne, only smiled. 'Your guess is as good as mine,' she said quietly, looking at Jeanne with a secret ripe on her mind.

Jeanne only turned shyly away and pretended not to have noticed a thing. She knew they all thought of her as having a crush on Jon Cavaliere; but not since she had last seen him, from the snack bar at the bowling alley as he had been entering the billiards room one summer evening, had any of them said anything to her about it. At times during the last school year she had wondered if it were really that way herself; but now, seeing those familiar initials on the side of that car, her mind was raving excitedly all over again: *Wow!* Jon Cavaliere has a hot rod!

Her first semester's schedule in high school called for US History 1 for first period. Fortunately all the first day's periods were shortened to just fourteen minutes each, to allow for the extended homeroom session to schedule and acclimatise the tenth-grade newcomers. The teacher, Mr Morris, merely took attendance, gave a brief synopsis of the course and then turned over the remaining five minutes for the students to become acquainted. The two boys in front of Jeanne took up an avid discussion of cars and Jeanne, easily bored with such talk, turned a disinterested ear and awaited her next class.

But she had to perk up when she heard one of them say, 'So, man; you see Cavaliere's bolt this morning?'

'What; *Cavaliere's* got a car now?' The second laughed. 'What next?'

'No, dude; you shoulda *seen* it. Says he just rolled it outa Holloway's shop last Tuesday. It's a four-twenty-seven, man, with a four-speed—'

'A *Chevy* four-twenty-seven? What is it, an SS Chevelle?'

'Naah. No *way.* No, man; it's a Caprice. A 'sixty-eight Caprice, four-door hardtop. Beautiful piece, too. You shoulda seen it.'

'A four-door *Caprice*, with a *four*-speed? Get out.'

'Diggit, man; you shoulda seen the wicked patch he laid with that thing. And there it is, man, an M-twenty-two rock-crusher in there, with the bucket seats— Aw, man; it was *nice.* He was showin' it to some of the dudes before the bell and I took a look at it. It's got two four-barrel Carters on an Offy intake, three-seventy-three Posi, Hookers; you know, all the nice stuff. And inside, it's like a Caddy, man; power windows, power seats, factory air….'

'Yeah? What's the outside look like?'

'I can't believe you didn't *see* it, man. It's silver, right; but a real light kind of silver, with about fifty coats of pearl lacquer, it looks like. It's got a white roof, and like maroon pinstripes, and a black SS hood, and it's got chrome Cragars, and oh yeah; it says "Spellbinder" across the front of the hood, in maroon paint.'

Spellbinder, Jeanne thought. Is that what he thinks of himself now? I can't believe he could be so conceited already; I mean: he was always so nice, just a year-and-a-half ago…. But isn't that what he said, that time? —'If you can do it, *do* it'? Sure he did. Jeanne remembered the day as if it had been yesterday. There were certain memories like that,

that would never fade. Well, she decided; if Jon Cavaliere can bind me
into a spell, I guess he has the right to call himself a *spellbinder*....

By fourth period Jeanne was losing all interest in high school as a
new social experience and renewing more interest in Jon Cavaliere as
an old flame. For her fifth she was scheduled for English Composition
in Room 148. The teacher introduced herself as Mrs Irene Hampton.
Her kind, motherly looks fit her well; for she was determined to know
all the students by their faces as soon as possible. She suggested that
they each call out their first and last names in turn, beginning by the
door and proceeding round the room towards the windows. Debbie
and Jeanne were fortunate enough to have seated themselves over
along the windows so, as Debbie. whispered, 'we don't have to feel
stupid first.' A perfect thirty students was enrolled; and this method of
attendance consumed about half the allotted fourteen minutes.

'Jeanne Banfield,' she had announced, modestly batting down the
amorous stares from the boys in the room. She would say she despised
her reflection in the mirror, with the orthodontic braces on her teeth
and one pair of eyeglasses or another since fifth year; but in junior-
high school Jeanne had been the centre of attraction among the boys.
Her Danish side had blessed her with a pristine complexion and an
abundance of rich blond hair; and whether due to her friendly nature
and the way she would happily chat away an entire class period with
even a casual acquaintance, or to something about the way her figure
had begun to blossom beautifully, the opposite sex were drawn to her
as if by magnetism. She was reluctantly becoming accustomed to the
attention in recent years, and even her closest friends were not immune
to feeling a little envious now and then.

Now, she was only anxious to move on to her next and last class and
to get through the day. Composition was not her pet subject; she had
selected the class last spring only at the prodding of Debbie who was
overly extroverted and would enjoy reading her works aloud, no matter
how naïve her viewpoints. Jeanne knew she could never bring herself
to be so bold. In fact if not for Debbie's constant enthusiasm about
everything, she might well have sought the counsellor to transfer to
something less demanding, perhaps a poetry course.

With but a few minutes left to the abbreviated period, the door
opened.   In wandered none other than the 'spellbinding' Jon
Cavaliere, wearing a t-shirt with some surrealistic superhero design on
it and the mirrored sunglasses set up on his hair.   He carried no
notebook, slouching on his hands in the back pockets of his faded
jeans, a casual, uninhibited lope to his walk.

The teacher smiled up at him. 'Hi,' she said cordially. 'Get lost?'

'Uh, no,' he said, scanning the room for familiar faces; 'not so...
unfortunate. Sorry I'm late.' He shuffled to a stop beside the teacher's
desk and looked right at her, charming her instantly with a dimpled

smile.

The teacher actually needed a moment to collect herself. 'Okay, well… and your name is–?'

He looked down at her roll book then. 'Cavaliere.'

She consulted the roster. 'Ah, yes,' she said. 'And the "J" is for–?'

'*Jon*,' he told her. 'Well– "Jon", as in "Jonathan".'

'All right,' she said, and stood up to introduce him. 'Class, this is Jon Cavaliere.'

He turned then, facing the entire class, and realised he was onstage. 'So hey, people,' he said with a smile; 'what's goin' down?'

Some laughed, more than a few able to welcome the levity as a release from the tediousness of their first day back in school. 'Nothin' much,' drawled a tall, thin lad with long hair from the very back of the room, and Jon started down the aisle towards him.

'Hey, dude,' he said; 'so are we out to make this a jammin' class; or what?'

'If you can do it, do it,' said the long-haired boy.

It had occurred to the other students that there were in fact no empty seats down the aisle he had chosen; but then the late arrival singled out a short, slight boy at the end of the third row and tapped on top of his desk. 'Do you mind?'

'What?' asked the boy nervously.

'I noticed a very prime piece of real estate in the front of that next row, that I thought you might be interested in.' Again came that smile, so genuinely enchanting that no-one could feel intimidated.

Yet as the self-conscious sophomore gathered his folder and textbooks and got up to move, the rest of them looked on in silent amazement. He marched straight up to the empty seat by the door; and when they looked back at the place he had vacated, Jon was sighing in exaggerated comfort with his feet up on the book-basket under the student's chair in front of him.

Incredible, thought the teacher, without a word to say. It's those dimples, Debbie thought, and fantasised about giving him a fond pinch. If you can do it, *do* it, thought Jeanne; and her insides quivered like gelatine. *Forget* transferring out, she told herself. I'll make this class my favourite one if it *kills* me! Turning to his mate then, Jon asked aloud, 'So what's up Barry?'

People laughed. 'Nothin' much,' the long-haired Barry said as before, cracking a rare smile.

'Hey,' he whispered to the girl just to his right, indicating the teacher; 'what's her name?'

'Hampton.'

'Yo, Miz Hampton!' he called out, and waited for her to look up. The others quieted. 'So what's this class about?'

A girl just to Debbie's right spoke up then. 'About thirty feet square, and ten feet high,' she said.

The class welcomed the humour. 'Oh, *jeez*,' complained Jon, overemoting in feigning exasperation; 'now Cindy's on the level of *Mad* magazine....'

'It's English Composition,' smiled Mrs Hampton, not ruffled in the slightest; 'and it's just that. Compositions in English.'

'Ah, good; I don't habla any 'Span'yole.' Still he smiled. 'So what kind of compositions?'

'Oh; essays, things like that. You'll be reading up on various topics and doing written arguments, and we will debate issues sometimes....'

'Yeah; all right.... Any fiction, stuff like that?'

'Yes.' She addressed the class. 'As I said before, we will be doing plenty of essay writing and proving points and things like that, but we will also of course be doing a good bit of purely creative writing as well, short stories, poetry, narratives, drama—'

'*Drama*?!' Jon spoke up. 'Hey; I ain't up for writin' any more *whole plays!*'

The teacher laughed. 'Why; have you written any drama before?'

'Aaah; I had to do one last year,' he told her. 'You know, rewrite a half-decent short story into a skit the whole class could put on; you know, stage directions, and doo.'

'Really?' Mrs Hampton was impressed.

'Yeah; well; it's not as easy as it sounds. After that I'm due for a coronary—'

'Well,' she said; 'what we'll be doing is really just a dialogue of events. I like to call it drama because that's what it resembles most, a one-act play.'

'Oh,' he said. 'Sounds cool enough.'

The girl next to Debbie turned about and said to him, 'Yeah; well; that's easy for *you* to say.'

'Oh; and don't Chubs got the humour today, boy!' Again the class laughed. 'Yo, Cindy, you know what? The *devil* made me do it!'

At that Cindy shrieked aloud and put her face down in her hands, laughing in terrific embarrassment. The teacher frowned. So did everyone else. 'What does the *devil* have to do with—'

'Aaah; it's an inside joke,' Jon said. 'Involving a hot dog, a math book, and chocolate milk.... Too gross to go into.' A few others laughed.

'Are you two friends, then, by any chance?' she asked either of them.

'No *way!*' insisted the girl called Cindy, who was by now quite red. 'I never saw him before in my *life!*'

'Hi, there, Cindy, old pal,' Jon called over to her; 'aren'tcha glad you've known me since *fifth grade!*'

At this the class howled uproariously, nearly drowning out the bell to dismiss the period. 'You know *what?*' Debbie sided to Jeanne, as all rose from their seats. 'That's *him*! The one at the lake, who—'

'Don't say it,' Jeanne told her quietly. 'I don't think he wants to remember.' It hurt her to have to admit that. 'That was so long ago....' Boy, she thought then, is it *ever*.

* * *

'Well,' said PJ cheerfully, deliberately bumping Jeanne in the elbow with her armload of books; 'so what do you think of high school so far? Split sessions are nice; huh? Getting out at quarter after twelve....'

Jeanne had a pretty smile, despite the braces that might have hidden her teeth. She hated them but, oddly, the boys seemed not to mind. 'Oh; it's all right....' Together they both laughed. 'Actually you know I think it's fantastic!'

'Yeah,' sighed PJ; 'and after only one week.... So many boys, and only three years left....'

The two of them laughed again. 'Patti says one of the juniors on the football team has asked you out already.'

'Yeah; well; if you can *do* it....' PJ laughed, enjoying it when she joked about herself. Actually she was quite pretty, short, slender and modestly shapely like Jeanne, with long straight blond hair and bright, happy blue eyes. Her buoyant personality made her a favourite in any group of teenagers. 'I suppose you've heard that Debbie and I are in the same gym class?'

'Yes,' said Jeanne.

'Well; so why do I have to hear it from her that Jon Cavaliere is in your English class? Come on; who is it you're dealing with here?'

That was PJ's style of teasing: blunt and to the point. Jeanne had known her since the Banfields moved to the Old Mill neighbourhood at the start of fourth grade; PJ knew her as well as anyone did. But Jon Cavaliere as a topic of conversation had never been easy for her. 'Uh, yeah; he is.'

'I think his car's fantastic,' PJ said. 'Of course, *he's* pretty fantastic too!'

Jeanne smiled, hoping to look as though she had no real feelings on the subject either way, even if PJ would never be fooled by her façade. Inside she wanted to say, God, he's *more* than fantastic. He's *gorgeous*. And one of these days, I'm gonna get to tell him that....

They had both heard the sound of someone calling out in the schoolyard behind them, repeating the same announcement over and over like a pavement vendor. But neither of them had paid much attention to what was being advertised until quite suddenly Jeanne was grabbed by the arm. Whirling about she came face-to-face with

Christopher Santana, the newly-elected junior-class president, in dark green Levi's and a pale grey striped body-shirt, who extended to them two mimeographed sheets of paper.

'Rock concert, tomorrow, at the Hill,' he said again, and then jogged away.

They both watched as he caught the next two girls in the parking-lot to deliver the same message; and then Jeanne and PJ turned their attention to the papers he had left with them.

Jeanne's eyes grew wide as she read the bold block lettering:

> Dudes and Ladies: There will be a Rock Show at the Hill in
> Wilshire Park, Saturday, September 10th, at 12 noon.
> Don't miss this Premiere Showing of a New Act.
> Produced by Dave Holloway and Chris Santana.
>
> A splendid time is guaranteed for all.

She looked up, for the moment feeling like the victim of some silly and embarrassing practical joke. Yet most of the other people on their way out of the schoolyard were carrying or reading the same papers, and not one of them looked to know any more about it than she did. PJ looked up too and, as they rounded the corner of the athletic field fence where the driveway led out to Atlantic Parkway, they saw Chris Santana break into a run. Incredibly enough, he darted straight out through the traffic and over the grass median. One second later Jon Cavaliere's silver car shot in from nowhere, its left rear door hanging open. Chris dove aboard. Even before the door closed the tyres were spinning on the tarmac, and the silver hot rod was gone and away towards the east end of town.

'Wow,' said Jeanne quietly.

'What was *that* all about?' PJ wondered.

'I don't have a clue,' Jeanne said honestly.

'Who's Dave Holloway?' PJ wanted to know. 'I mean: like I know Chris Santana, because *everybody* knows who *he* is, but—'

'It's very strange,' Jeanne said, as though to herself; and then PJ looked at her.

'What do *you* know about it?' she asked with a smile, always wanting to be in on all the secrets.

'Nothing at all,' Jeanne said, sounding deathly serious. 'I just wonder…. Oh; I'm sure I'm just imagining things. It's nothing.'

'Like what?'

But Jeanne would not volunteer her thoughts. Surely they would seem too silly anyway. 'Never mind,' she said, and felt as though she were blushing bright-red.

'Well,' said PJ then; 'I say we show up at the park tomorrow and find out. Then we'll know if your hunches are right. That is, if you ever tell me what they are....'

Jeanne knew her friend was only being curious.   PJ Carson was many things, and adventurous and inquisitive were both PJ high on the list.   PJ had sat next to her in that physical-science class they had shared in seventh grade, that seemed so long ago.   PJ had been the one who had seen the look come over Jeanne upon meeting eyes with Jon Cavaliere for the first time.   There had been a glow about both of them that moment that perhaps only PJ would ever really comprehend.   Since that day, PJ had been the only one in whom Jeanne confided with the whole secret.   It was something far too deep inside to be shared with anyone else.   The meaning would only be wasted on those who only knew secondhand.

* * *

She had never thought herself adventuresome.   But, for the same reasons that she would not have gone with anyone else, Jeanne went along with PJ to the park the following morning.   Twelve o'clock seemed very early for a rock-and-roll show; yet Jeanne felt as though the day were half gone when they arrived.   Gnawing at the pit of her stomach was a worry that exactly what she wished would be exactly what would happen; and she was nearly praying aloud to delay the inevitable.   It might have felt infinitely better to simply avoid the whole thing and to never know for sure.   Somehow not knowing for sure all this time had not seemed so bad, compared to what might have happened if she had known beyond the shadow of a doubt.   For now, it was a decision that did not have to be made; and Jeanne had become comfortable in the interim of indecision.

PJ certainly felt adventuresome today, dressed in tight-fitting denim shorts and her black Alice Cooper concert t-shirt, with that wide Panama hat and those mirrored sunglasses.   She could really look a sight when it moved her.   Jeanne was only amused by her, although half the other people at the park had dressed similarly; this was still the summer.   But deep inside she felt terribly queasy, convinced that someone was about to play a sinister trick on her.

Excitedly PJ pranced up the tree-lined driveway of the park, trying to get out past the woods to their left for a good look down at the hill.   The little roofed platform at the base of the hill was often the stage for performances; even the local repertory theatre put on productions there during summer evenings.   The police department managed a fireworks demonstration on Independence Day, and for the Wilshire Summer Festival there were jazz concerts and magic shows; and all depended on the little open-sided pavilion across the little manmade pond from the grassy knoll that was known as the hill at the park.

'Will you come *on*?' PJ scolded her. 'You're walking too slow! We have to find a place to watch! It's after twelve already!'

'Oh,' Jeanne said, trying to sound as though nothing really mattered; 'come on, yourself. We'll get there whether we run or not.'

'God! —Jeannie, sometimes I think you're the slowest person on earth!' She trotted ahead a little as though she could see through two hundred yards of trees from that much further along.

Suddenly the sound of an electric guitar sliced through the woods, as loud as though it were right in front of them. Jeanne looked up, starting to run; but PJ, last year's star sprinter, was already fifty yards ahead. A drum banged, and then there were other instruments; and just as the singer began she cleared the line of trees and gazed headlong down at the pavilion, past several hundred people already gathered; and her mouth dropped open in sheer surprise.

She squinted in the sun, trying to recognise the foursome in the shade of the pavilion. The boy singing was a complete stranger to her, tall and lanky, in long jeans and an open black shirt, his long brown hair often in his eyes whilst he played sporadically on a rather small black guitar. His voice was thick with throat distortion; this was his first number today and yet he sounded like a fifteen-year-old with a cold who had stayed up too late at night smoking cigarettes. Somewhere, though, there was great passion in the voice, singing John Lennon's 'Revolution' from five years ago.

The musicians were all very capable at their instruments. The singer performed a guitar solo, really just a barrage of sustained notes, distorted by the meaty tone of the amplifier. Behind him a boy at the drums straddled a high stool. He looked no older than fourteen; without a shirt, his thin arms and flat chest made him look still younger. He tended to overplay a bit but sounded quite competent. His hair, although somewhat mussed, was cut in sort of a Beatles style, and his eyebrows were dark and straight and made him look a little like Ringo Starr, or even George Harrison.

Jeanne did not recognise the drummer. She looked hard at the other guitar player who stood towards the centre of the stage, just to the right of the one who sang. Something in that serious expression looked distressingly familiar, and she could not take her eyes from him until she had placed it. His hair was perhaps the shortest of the group, the dark-brown locks parted in the middle of his forehead. No sweat had yet stained his light-blue t-shirt; for he stood still whilst playing, unlike the others who bobbed about animatedly. His red mahogany guitar caught a reflection once and the glare stung Jeanne in the eye; it was a beautiful guitar, brilliantly polished. She thought about a boy who might polish such a nice guitar with great pride, like some boys her brother knew who would wax their cars every afternoon. Her brother used to make jokes about people who polished their cars too often, because it could rub away their paint. Jeanne thought she had heard a joke about someone polishing a guitar too much, so that the finish might wear off, and slowly it began to come to her. She had seen the boy with the mahogany guitar play before. In fact, it had been right to her.

The chords to 'We've Only Just Begun', The Carpenters' latest hit, had not been so simple for two thirteen-year-olds to learn. The song was not even a good choice for one guitar, even by experienced musicians. Yet it had been what they had been 'messing around with', as her classmate had said, and the job had only been to transpose piano chords into G for the guitar. But his friend had been the one to do it. 'He's the star of the music class,' Jeanne had been told. 'If it can be written, he can figure it out.' This had been met with modesty and some embarrassed teasing; and, though everyone in the class was very impressed with the boys' apparent talents, the two boys bantered back and forth until the joke came out. 'You know,' his friend had said, 'I just figured out why you *really* stand out in that ensemble class. It's that stupid guitar. The way you polish it, they can't *help* but notice you.'

Right then Jeanne realised why the boy in the pavilion with the polished red guitar looked so familiar and then why she had felt so uncomfortable about coming to see the rock-and-roll show, the premiere showing of a new act, and why she had worried about someone playing a joke on her. If Chris Santana, before he had leapt into that silver car, had known just who had received his leaflet and for whom they had been distributed, then maybe it was not so hard for her to put her feelings of apprehension together with the possibility that there had been a design behind her coming to the park today. And, as that thought slowly began to take hold, she turned her gaze from the boy with the polished red guitar to the last member of the group, at the far left end of the stage.

He looked cute, in white jeans and a black t-shirt. The high-heeled shoes made him look taller than he really was. His hair looked to be the closest to assuming some predetermined style, although down to his eyes in front and still longer in back. In the bright sunlight it looked far blonder than in the fluorescent light of the classroom. His guitar was jet-black, polished almost like a mirror, with bright chrome hardware and white plates for the controls and below the strings. Jeanne noticed his guitar went the other way; he was a left-handed player. He stepped up to the microphone to sing 'Day Tripper' and for a second, as on Tuesday, he seemed to be looking straight at her. Jeanne felt a jump inside then, just as she had all the other times before, and wished she had been able to know, beyond the shadow of a doubt, that from behind those mirrored glasses he knew exactly why she was staring straight back at him. A shiver shot down her spine and left her insides tingling wildly.

PJ turned and said something about going down to be closer to the stage; but they were already so close that the volume of the PA made little else audible. Jeanne just stood there, dumbfounded, whilst she entertained another fantasy from long ago come alive. She had always dreamt, since that special day in science class, that he might grow up to become some famous actor or rock star, with long hair and a fancy hot rod, and though all the girls would want him only she would ever have him. It had become so gripping a faery-tale that she would lapse in and out of attention in school, just living out yet another wonderful part of it over again. Now, only one part of the story had not yet come true; and her heart hammered in her chest to think that it might just take place today. She closed her eyes and tried to imagine how it would come to pass.

'Day Tripper' was over; and he turned and said something to the tall boy who had sung earlier. Someone tossed him a can of Coca-Cola and he opened it, deliberately spraying some of the audience with the soda. There were laughs even at that. He turned and said, well away from the microphone, 'So; how does it look?'

'It was Santana's fliers,' said his mate. 'Dude was on the stick. This crowd's a surprise to me too.'

'So what's next?'

'Hell if *I* know. Hey– let's introduce people now.'

'No, man; you wait till the end, remember? Otherwise they forget who we are.'

'Naah.... That ain't always true. I say we let 'em know who to remember.'

'All right; let's do it.'

They were both satisfied for the moment; and so the tall guitar player stepped up to his microphone. PJ tapped her arm whilst Jeanne and several hundred others looked up at him. '*Jeannie!*' she said excitedly, keeping her voice quiet in the hush of the crowd on the lawn. 'Do you know who that *is*? God; isn't it *fantastic?*'

'All right,' the tall one with the black guitar was saying. 'Just to let you know a little about the group and ourselves. Behind me is Mr Richard Denning on the drums, and our lead guitar player, Bob Prescott, and then of course over here, the one and only Jon Cavaliere.'

The crowd responded with applause, but Jeanne's mouth had dropt open in supreme surprise. Suddenly a daydream had come true, beyond the shadow of a doubt. Jon smiled and said into his own microphone, 'And of course to the far end of the stage, your emcee for the evening, and mine too, the illustrious Dave Holloway.' He waved his hand back towards his partner, as the crowd applauded again, and said, 'A little bit of rock and roll for ya.' With that the band launched into The Rolling Stones' 'Jumpin' Jack Flash'.

Wow! Jeanne thought. Jon Cavaliere has a rock group! *Wow.*... The thought took a few bars of the song to settle in, until Jon was leaning into his microphone to sing a high harmony over Dave's lead vocal. But she had heard those introductions; and she could not mistake those adorable dimples. *Wow!* she suddenly wanted to yell out loud. It's really *him!* This is *fantastic!*

The band on the stage played a few more upbeat numbers, things like 'Saturday's Alright For Fighting' and 'We're An American Band'. Jeanne absorbed everything she saw and heard, standing five yards deep in the crowd separated from the stage by the reflecting pool, her eyes wide open as though hypnotised. The music was good, punchy and quick, full of life and enthusiasm. There were no evident mistakes and they all sang exceptionally well; but Jeanne was not a music analyst. She could only think of how exciting it was that her fantasies were really coming true. Soon she could imagine Jon Cavaliere singing on million-selling records with his famous band, touring all over the world and growing richer and more popular by the minute. It was all just wishful thinking, and she probably knew that; but throughout the set she was convinced it would all come true some day.

Jon crossed the stage after 'Takin' Care Of Business' and spoke with his good friend Bob Prescott. Like Jeanne and PJ, Bob had never forgotten that rainy day in eighth grade when he had intruded upon Jon's physical-science class with his acoustic guitar whilst the regular teacher was out. It had turned out that Mrs Sheridan, the substitute, was a friend of Jon's mother; and so no-one would complain when the door was shut for the two boys to entertain the class with a few sing-along numbers. The culmination of the show, for that was just what it had become, was Jon's quiet solo vocal of Paul Williams' 'We've Only Just Begun', with Bob's gentle guitar accompaniment.

Not yet fourteen, with only three years' formal guitar instruction behind him, Bob had already been a talented arranger, deliberately using easy chord inversions to give the well-known pop ballad a very sentimental country-and-western feel. The class had been very sincere in their applause. Even Mrs Sheridan was impressed; and she told Jon after the period that she would look forwards to sitting in for any of his other teachers in the future, just to see what other 'pleasant shenanigans' he might attempt.

Jon had always felt that the success of that little impromptu revue had all been due to Bob's participation. In truth the concept had been entirely his own idea, and he had shared it with Bob only on the condition that its premeditation would always remain a secret. It simply could not be made known that Jon Cavaliere had arranged to serenade a seventh-grade-girl right in class, least of all one with braces on her teeth and glasses and such skinny legs.

These noble intentions, however carried out, were the type of thing Jon would only ever share with Bob, his blood-brother and dearest friend. They had met in the summer they were both five, when Bob's family had moved into the neighbourhood, and had walked to school together on their very first day of kindergarten, proud to use the 'buddy system' by holding hands when they crossed the streets. By now, their relationship had gone beyond mere words and so they never spoke of it, satisfied just to take each other for granted as friends to last a lifetime. Words would only get too emotional and corny anyway.

'So do you think she's here?' Bob asked him during the break.

Jon wiped some sweat off his forehead and set his sunglasses up in his hair again. 'Aaah; I don't know. Probably not. This is probably all just a big waste of energy.'

'I doubt that,' Bob said seriously. 'I saw Carson, and a few others of that crowd. She's here. We just don't recognise her, not being in school clothes, you know. Now if she was in a bathing-suit–'

Jon smiled wryly at him, recalling the same fateful incident at the borough swimming lake. Even after two whole summers and a year between, during which he scarcely saw her at all, that memory alone could still bring chills down his spine and then profound embarrassment immediately after. He turned away for a sip of Coca-Cola. 'Dag; some secret agents *we'd* make. *"Get Smart"*, and doo.'

'Hah!' Bob laughed aloud. ' "Right, chief!" ' They both laughed.

'All right,' Dave said, as Ricky Denning sat down at the drums again; 'we got an audience here. Let's play something.'

'Right, chief,' Jon said, as Bob had, and he and Bob laughed.

Jon started 'All My Loving,' singing as though he loved every word of the song, making no errors in the bass-guitar part and scanning the crowd through the mirrored sunglasses for that one person whom he had wanted most to see him play today. He was thankful for Dave and Chris insisting that their act practise so long before appearing in public; for it gave him great confidence in his performing ability, even to where he could think of other things whilst singing and playing. If she *is* here, he supposed, who would she be with? PJ Carson? *That* would be fitting…. Bob played the brief guitar solo, effortlessly as always, and Jon stepped back from the microphone to give him attention. It was a consideration Dave had taught them all to have for a soloist; and Jon had never been one to hound the spotlight. In fact he had never played before such a large crowd in his life; it was a sobering thought. But, as though on a rollercoaster ride, the apprehension was exhilarating, as though he were flirting with grave danger. Any obvious mistake here might well spell the end of the ride, yet it was thrilling to risk coming so close to catastrophe.

But so far there had been not a hitch; and Jon was very pleased with how well they were received. After all everyone loved a free rock-and-roll show, the better the show, the better the bargain. He stepped up to the microphone at the close of Bob's solo and right then he saw her, and he had to sing the opening line again whilst looking straight at her. She was cute, in a pink cotton tubetop and short white cutoff denim shorts, staring right back up at him as though spellbound. With her hair up off her neck she looked about eleven; and he remembered that it had been before her twelfth birthday when he had first met her and had first admitted to himself that he was crazy about her. Since then they had both grown up in many ways; but, in one way, he had always remembered her as being the same cheerful, sweet, ladylike little girl she had been that first day. The sunglasses had indeed saved face for him then; for, with that thought on his mind, he would never have wanted her to see how he blushed at the sight of her.

Dave sang The Beatles' 'Rain', as he liked to do the John Lennon numbers. Jon sang Badfinger's 'No Matter What' and 'Baby Blue', and he and Dave alternated lead vocals on the Doobie Brothers' 'Listen To The Music'. Jeanne shivered with delight. Jon was truly amazing, a talented star on the stage and yet special only to her, because long before the cheerleading squad, before his car, before the title of Wilshire Junior High South Prom Princess 1973, and before this band, there had been a sweet, special relationship only the two of them would ever know or care to remember.

And so, after the afternoon had gone past eighty-five, and the Coca-Cola had run out and the equipment was packed into Dave's old van and Mr Cavaliere's estate car, Jeanne and PJ and everyone else walked home, sighing with the heat and satisfied that the free rock-and-roll show announced in the schoolyard had been as good as they all had hoped, or even better. Jeanne would not remember Ricky Denning splitting a drumstick to pieces on the wing-nut of the ride cymbal, or Dave Holloway kicking over a can of soda on the stage, or Jon Cavaliere slipping in it as he stepped back from his microphone, or even Bob Prescott having to bluff his way through the lyrics of Harrison's 'What Is Life'. How fallible the band had really been was of no consequence to her, and she revelled in her memory of Eric Carmen's chorus, as sung so unforgettably by the one and only Jon Cavaliere:

'Baby, let's pretend that tonight we'll live for ever;
If we close our eyes and believe, it might come true;
Baby, let's pretend that we'll always be together,
But for now just let me spend the night with you....'

For weeks afterwards it was the only dream she had.

* * *

Chapter 2

Making each day of the year

Mrs Hampton was excited about receiving the completed papers. For the last three years she had been giving the same assignment first in her Composition 1 classes. 'You must be able to know what your feelings are before you can use them to write. What better place to start than with a piece about yourself? Convey your opinions about yourself, the way *you* see you, but nothing really heavy– it's not an autobiography. If you were to describe the person you are, say– if this would be an article in *Life* magazine about you– how would you want that article to read? Then *that's* what you write.'

She never expected the students to live up to her hopes. They were, after all, taking a composition course to learn how to compose; there would be plenty of misspellings and grammatical errors and surely most of them would be hopelessly embarrassed by having to exploit their own feelings of self-worth for a school assignment. But Mrs Hampton would later admit she had not wholly prepared herself for what she received in her fifth-period class.

Jon Cavaliere turned in a wonderfully interesting article about himself, the car enthusiast and sailor, musician and composer, designer and artist, writer and humourist, done completely in the third person, as though his inferences and suppositions had been drawn from first- and secondhand information by an objective observer and not himself. Nowhere was the egotistical bragging of an academic apple-polisher, nor was there any of that common adolescent tendency to be self-critical. It might have been easy to accuse him of cheating by way of a ghostwriter; but there it was, exactly what she had always hoped to receive, neither too brief nor too lengthy, three sides of beautifully hand-lettered manuscript.

She was eager to show the paper round the teaching staff, and those familiar with Jon's legendary classroom prowess congratulated her on the luck of the draw that had sent him under her tutelage this term. He was, as one colleague put it, 'that student you always hoped to get but never thought you would.' Another warned her, 'Beware of his classroom cutting-up. They will always laugh along with him, like when he compares the word "composition" to "compost".' But it was widely agreed amongst the faculty that, as a junior, Jon's writing was probably already on a collegiate level and that his further education should be assured at all costs. The attractive young comedian with the exceptional IQ began to look more and more like a true diamond in the rough. Mrs Hampton thrilled to the challenge: a poor teacher might lose influence over the whole class, but a good teacher would make him shine.

* * *

Jeanne and Patti and PJ were the final three girls named to the Wilshire High School junior-varsity cheerleading team for the 1973-74 school season. The selection had not been very difficult. Rather, the politics of teachers, coaches and parents had essentially kept the other ten positions on the squad promised to those juniors who had been on the team as sophomores and a few who had narrowly missed varsity. Jeanne and Patti and PJ, then, displaying their exceptional abilities from having been so well-coached on the freshman squad in junior high, surpassed all the sophomores and juniors at the tryouts and were signed to complete the roster straight away.

Jeanne was overjoyed to have made the squad. Perhaps the notoriety of the high-school cheerleading team, which obviously made starlets out of all its members, would fortify her characteristic sociable spirit. She had always been very popular with the boys, although never completely understanding why; yet there was one who actually seemed to avoid her and would have to be brought round. Though in a way it distressed her, it was also a challenge. They had never truly dated, though she had always dreamt that they should; and so with jitters inside she cherished those vivid recollections of what past they did share. She had sat ahead of him in that physical-science class; and he would tease her because her hair fell all over his desk. But it was his hair that she loved, long and buoyant, the envy of every girl to whom she pointed him out. She had liked to call him 'Jonny', at first just to tease, because he had said no-one else ever called him that. She had lent him a pencil once, one of her father's good draughtsman's pencils which had found its way into her notebook at home; and when he forgot to return it she was too embarrassed to apologise to her father for having lost it whilst secretly pleased that the boy she liked so much now had something of hers.

But it was the afternoon spent riding about the shopping arcade on his chopper bicycle, over two years ago, that was still one of her favourite memories. At times she could still hear him laughing in front of her and feel the air pulling back her hair. Her stomach swayed and leaped with the bumps and turns; and she could still lose herself for a minute or two, happily reliving it over and over in her mind. Though school would recess for the summer just a few weeks after that, and she would hardly see him at all the following year, the impression of the hair-raising ride, with her arms so desperately and devotedly wrapt about him, would remain as clear as that May afternoon sunshine in her heart.

Debbie and PJ often teased her about it, especially in the few weeks following the concert on the hill. It was meant only to be playful and well-intentioned prodding; but Jeanne never responded well to being pushed into taking decisions. She felt confident she would arrive at her own conclusions and that, given time, she would be perfectly able to woo herself a boyfriend. It was just that the timing had to be right.

Debbie Blake was something of a tomboy. As children Jeanne and Anne might have played with fashion dolls; but Debbie had been out building tree-houses and playing football with her three brothers. Now, at the start of tenth year, boys were suddenly the only thing on her mind, no longer as teammates or scrimmage partners but as objects for impetuous crushes. Much of the muscle she had gained running about with the old gang had diminished as her figure became more feminine; and boys who thought her unappealing even last year now sought dates with her quite ardently. But, despite her new status as a young lady, Debbie would always remain sweet and sentimental at heart, like the happy child she had been when they had first met; and that endeared her to Jeanne the most.

Jeanne had never been a tomboy. In fact she had a lifelong reputation of being about the most ladylike, even girlish girl any of her friends knew. So, in the new social scene of high school, she found herself at the centre of boys' attention and with quite a few of the girls' envy. To most she seemed to represent the best blend of all that was both astral and approachable, neither too lofty nor too familiar. She was pretty, but not voluptuous. She was ladylike, but not richly glamourous. Her family were neither wealthy nor miserable. Her grades were good but she was not consistently on the honour roll; and though agile and healthy she was not known as an athlete. To shallow boys she was a trophy worth stealing; to the best of them she was a princess worth deserving. Yet through it all she never seemed to fall into egoism or pride, considering herself merely a nice and artless girl growing up in a busy and complex world.

Youngest of her group of friends, Jeanne turned fifteen on 12 October; and her mother had arranged for several of the crowd to come by that Friday evening for a celebration. Mrs Banfield was always very thoughtful about such things and never overbearing; and the young people all enjoyed her hospitality. Everyone brought a gift; and Jeanne wanted for nothing all night.

Steve Marlowe actually had bought her a very nice mohair sweater. Jeanne was touched by his thoughtfulness; but then their two families had known each other since the Banfields first moved to the Old Mill neighbourhood from California. In fact Steve's sister Anne had been the first friend young Jeanne had met in the fourth grade. PJ and Patti and Debbie had all come round a few days later, and with that she had been admitted to a very close circle of confidantes who would soon come to share sentiments and secrets.

But though Anne always listened sympathetically and Patti was full of wisdom beyond her years, PJ Carson was the only one in whom Jeanne confided her deepest, most private thoughts about Jon Cavaliere. Ever since that day he had serenaded her in science class, Jeanne had harboured a boundless infatuation for the long-haired, babyfaced boy with the dimples in his cheeks. He seemed to have a natural charm that affected all females, teachers and students alike; and Jeanne fell into a weak-kneed swoon at the mere sight of him in the corridors. It had been a whole year since she and Jon Cavaliere had been in the same school for the same session and already her fantasies were going full-steam-ahead again. And only PJ fully understood why.

'Shame he doesn't know your address,' she teased, looking over the birthday greetings Jeanne had set atop the television console. 'I bet he might've sent you a card. Even if he only signed it "From a Secret Admirer".' She giggled.

'Oh; stop,' Jeanne said, and got a little red. The boys and Debbie had begun a rousing cards game in the dining room and fortunately none of them thought to listen in.

'I still say, that time at the lake, you should've sent him something,' PJ said. 'But, it's never too late. You could still write him a–'

'Oh, PJ, that was so long ago…. He doesn't even remember.'

PJ looked at her and suddenly felt very sad. 'I can't imagine that he would ever *forget*, Jeannie. It's not exactly–'

'You don't believe it yourself. I mean: like he totally ignores me in the halls. He's even in my English class, but….' Jeanne was saddened to have to admit it. 'I guess maybe that's it, then. He doesn't *want* to remember.'

'No, no; don't say that…. I'm sure that he's just being shy.'

'Shy? No; he's not shy. He comes in to class and rearranges people. He cracks jokes out loud with teachers he's never met before. That's not shy. He's just being himself; and that includes *not* being friends with *me*.'

'Jeannie, you've been saying this for two years. Have you ever actually gone up to him and said something?'

'Oh…. What would I say though?'

'I don't know; just say "Hi". It doesn't matter what you say. He couldn't help but like you. God! –last year they elected you Prom Princess, Jeannie. The most popular kid in school. You can't say he wouldn't notice you–'

Patti came out of the kitchen where she had been talking with Mrs Banfield. 'So; what's happened to the party, kids? Aren't you celebrating with us?'

'We're talking,' PJ said.

'Oh. Well; the boys want to play Yahtzee; and we want a few more people. Come on out, and we'll play.'

'Patti,' PJ said, 'wait. Maybe we could ask you.'

'No, PJ,' Jeanne began; 'I don't think–'

'Sure,' PJ assured her; 'Patti will know. So Patti. What can the cutest kid in school do, when she's crazy about some guy, and he won't talk to her?'

Patti smiled at Jeanne with that knowing look. 'Well,' she said, not unfamiliar with the subject at hand; 'in this case, it might be a little different. From what you've told me, he seems to be very popular. I would only suggest that you speak to him first. If he's as popular with everyone else as he seems to be, then there's almost no chance he'll be cold to someone new. If he hasn't talked to you yet, then maybe it's just because he hasn't thought to yet. You know; because he knows so many people already. But I would never say he'd reject you, Jeannie.'

'See?' PJ smiled, putting an arm across Jeanne's shoulder. 'It'll just be a matter of time.'

'Exactly,' said Patti. 'If it's going to happen, then it will, Jeannie. I'm sure he'll get his nerve up and speak to you. It'll just be a matter of time, as PJ said.' They both stood there and smiled at Jeanne who looked no less anxious. 'Now let's go out and play Yahtzee with these people.'

Jeanne did have faith in Patti's wisdom. They all tended to look up to her, though she was really no older and had no greater experience. Some certain grace and reserve about Patricia Louise Harper just made her seem far more mature than her peers. She was indeed a beautiful girl, with her fair Welsh features; and that regal strawberry-blond hair all done in waves and curls looked like delicious icing atop a perfect peaches-and-cream complexion. At fifteen she had a lovely hourglass figure, able to wear the tightest jeans and the shortest miniskirts with enviable *élan*, driving the best of her friends to jealousy over the eye attention she received from the opposite sex.

But despite a weakness for the latest fads Patti was basically conservative in nature; and a large part of her wardrobe was fine Scottish wool skirts and Shetland sweaters. Older men tended to ogle her approvingly and, if at times she were not mistaken for being five years older, it was at least assumed she was part of some aristocratic old British peerage. The impression was not deceived by an adorable lilt of the Queen's English and sentences so perfectly structured that to some classmates she came off as a grammar exercise read aloud. Her mother, the daughter of a United Nations envoy, had been born in Cardiff, and her father was a diplomatic attaché with the US Navy; young Patti and her elder brother Bruce had been raised in the cradle of etiquette and social graces.   As a teenager she possessed great compassion and her sage advice came from sincere understanding and a philanthropic desire to help others.   To the other girls she was a great font of optimism and common sense; and they all sought her as a seer to cast light upon their muddled predicaments.

The game of Yahtzee was but a muddled memory to Jeanne by the end of the night.   Debbie ran out before ten, claiming she had to catch *Love, American Style* on television at home; it was like her to occasionally shuffle priorities.   Perhaps she never assumed it would be preempted by some special report on the Vice President's resignation. PJ and Anne kept up a silly banter about the sexiness of blowing on the dice at every turn; but it wore on everyone by about their eighth throw each.   Jeanne's brother Curt rang from Kings Point with his birthday wishes, and her mother came out to call her to the phone. Steve got up to speak with him too; the party had begun to break up by then anyway.   Soon Jeanne was bidding everyone a fond farewell, knowing she was bound to see them all again within two days if not sooner.   The question of how to reacquaint herself with Jon Cavaliere reiterated itself in her mind a thousand times before she fell asleep; and in the light of morning she could recall only her oracle Patti acknowledging that it would all be a matter of time.   That seemed to rest best with her, and Jeanne was relieved to resign herself to patience. All things would come to pass in time.

* * *

The song of the pneumatic wrench carried out into the quiet street. Dave's Aunt Audrey had apparently gone out in the Cadillac and so Bob parked his father's Malibu at the kerb.   He walked up the clean-swept gutter to the driveway, never even considering pounding straight across the well-groomed lawn.   People could say what they wanted about the advantages of such an unrestricted lifestyle; but since his father had left him in her care Dave Holloway had been very doting to his godmother, particularly when it came to the upkeep of the rambling old Victorian mansion he now called home.   She in turn delighted in his company but, of course, most women did.

The wrench whined again.   Bob smiled at how out of place it sounded in the lush, sedate environs of the country-club neighbourhood.   But for as long as he had known Jon, and especially since the two of them had begun associating with Dave and Ricky, unusual juxtapositions had become a way of life.   It was not often that such intense creativity and clever, witty expression found such deep roots in boys of such youth.

Bob often said Jon was the one with all the talent but, when asked,

Jon would insist that just the reverse was true. Bob was probably a bona-fide musical prodigy; although the greater part of his training was on one instrument, he had learned it thoroughly and successfully. There were those in the local music scene who would attest that, even as a sixteen-year-old playing in the garage, Bob Prescott was a more masterful guitarist than half the professional rock-and-roll musicians in the area. His restrained and meticulous approach to playing made all his solos letter-perfect; he possessed exceptional skill at orchestral arranging and yet enjoyed playing in a small outfit where his resources were challenged all the time. Jon spoke highly and proudly of his best friend. He remained convinced that Bob's very professional nature was a prime ingredient for their band's ultimate success.

But such back-patting was the norm among the modest boys of this circle, so unlike their teenaged peers in their lack of egoism or pretentiousness. All of them were self-effacing to the point where, to their public, their personal accomplishments were virtually enshrouded in mystery, none of them more so than Jon. Bob was one of the privileged few to know Jon's real worth. Heavily influenced by both his parents, Jon might only have been expected to rebel. His mother, modest and benign, had come from a well-to-do family of the Philadelphia Main Line and never considered herself a tradition-breaker for marrying into the working-class nor for taking a mere teacher's position at Lakeside Borough Elementary School. Jon's father, a decorated flying ace in the War, passed up the Army's offer of a free university education to pursue his love of carpentry and founded his own general contracting business. Bob knew both of Jon's parents well and accepted them as they were, quietly amused with their disdain at their son's interest in rock-and-roll music as a career choice. He knew the rebellion was merely being passed along from parents to offspring. It was really the natural order of things for, in a family of nonconformists, the bucking of all forms of tradition was tradition itself. Probably Jon did not even realise that. But for Bob such insight had come with the responsibility of being blood-brother and soulmate.

He ducked under the half-open garage door and stood up inside the warmth of Dave's shop. In the corner the ever-present radio, energised with the lighting switch, articulated Dobie Gray's 'Drift Away'. Jon's silver-and-white Caprice rested in the middle bay with its front wheels up on ramps about a foot high. Two sneakers stuck out from beneath the left front wing. The wrench ran again. Bob smiled again and said, 'Hey; what's happening?'

Jon recognised the voice as well as he would that of his own mother. 'Hey, bro'. What's up?'

'So what is it you're attempting to do, here?'

'Aaaaaaah....' The wrench rang under the car. 'I've been gettin' shitty oil pressure at the sender, and so I'm bettin' either the pickup tube is fucked-up, or just–' He ran the wrench again. 'Son of a bitch…. This is a pain in the ass.'

Bob stooped down to peer under the front bumper of the car and saw him on his back upon a low wheeled trolley with the pneumatic wrench above his head. 'Looks like a *lovely* job,' he said sarcastically.

Jon laughed a little, resting the wrench upon his chest for a moment. 'Yeah; it's a shitty job, but *somebody's* gotta do it.'

Bob bent lower and looked up at the finned underside of the aluminium oil pan. 'You said the oil pickup's bad? How do you know?'

Jon sighed. 'I *don't*, for sure. The oil pressure sucks, but there's plenty of oil; I know I ain't burnin' it, or leakin' it. And by now it's not so much of a new engine any more…. How it is now is as good as it's gonna *get*; and I'm just wonderin' if it's gonna be good *enough*.'

'It's not low on oil?' Bob asked, possessing less than a mechanic's knowledge of cars.

'Naah. It ain't that. Where the sender is is just not gettin' enough of it. Even if it was a quart or two low, like for the track, the pressure should still be all right. There's always enough oil, you know.' He winced, as though something were in his eye. 'Well; not now there ain't. It's all in the bucket.'

Bob turned and looked across the clean floor of the garage at the pail half-full of motor oil. 'Well; if you want help, dude, I ain't goin' anywhere.'

'Cool,' said Jon lifting the wrench up to the next bolt-head then. 'I may need a hand helpin' me take this off, lest it hit me in the face on the way down.'

The wrench ran again. 'So where's Holloway?'

Jon groaned. 'Aaah; hell if I know. Out with some chick, I think. Son-of-a-bitch's never around when I need him.'

'Girls'll do that,' Bob smiled, knowing that there were times when Jon did consider himself lucky to have no girlfriend. He took off his suede winter jacket, hanging it over Dave's usual coat-hook, and slid down on the clean cold concrete floor under the car.

Working as a team, they removed the oil pan together and inspected the oil pickup tube. Bob always made good help, making up for limited exposure to automotive problems by listening attentively and willingly lending muscle, saving the questions of inexperience for less crucial moments. Nothing seemed amiss; but Jon spent a few minutes tinkering with the oil pump before thoroughly cleaning the pickup tube. He installed in the pan the windage tray he had bought, intended to wipe excess oil off the crankshaft at higher engine speeds so more oil would stay in circulation. By four o'clock Jon had changed the oil filter and began filling the crankcase with new oil.

Bob helped by pouring the used oil into a can to be taken to the petrol depot for reprocessing. He was quietly amused by how fastidious Jon was with the Caprice. Everything was always wiped off and hoovered, and all the periodic maintenance was done according to a schedule Jon had drawn up and posted inside the car. Bob had never known him to be so painstaking with anything else; in fact Jon was notoriously sloppy with details in day-to-day routine. But rumour had been getting about that the silver Chevrolet would take anything in town from one traffic light to the next; and Jon was far too proud to let such a reputation escape him.

This was the car that Dave and Jon had spent all spring and summer rebuilding in this garage. The two had found a common passion, beyond the music of The Beatles, for high-performance automobiles and had undertaken the project as an educational endeavour. Even Jon's father, who had always had high expectations of all his children, had been impressed by what they were able to accomplish. When his son had taken up an active search for a car of his own, Mr Cavaliere took him to meet the widow of one of his clients, knowing she had little use for the full-size car her husband had specially ordered in November 1967 with almost every available option. Mr Cavaliere had thought the large, conservative Chevrolet a safe buy for a young man; and the widow was glad to offer it. Jon offered no argument, paid her a fair twelve hundred dollars and drove home in his first car, nearly broke.

He promptly signed on with his father's work crew as a labourer to earn side money to support his investment. His original idea was not to keep the car long. Either he would soon trade it for something a little more devilish or at least pull the factory-original big-block engine and repower the car with a milder 350 or 400 to sell it, saving the coveted 427 for a future project. But he found no affordable performance cars in the area. He and Dave considered all their options, talking often with Mr Cavaliere to gain objective opinion. Jon's father had in his youth a penchant for taking things apart out of sheer curiosity and was pleased to see them unafraid to learn from hands-on experience. But he did worry that the enthusiastic young lads might have had astronomical aspirations. Dave had envisioned a drag-racing Chevelle for the quarter-mile strip, and Jon had hoped for something like a Corvette for twisting country lanes; but by the time they had decided on a working budget there was but one realistic choice. The four-door Caprice and the project car would have to be one and the same.

They settled into the garage at Dave's Aunt Audrey's house and began by removing and inspecting nearly everything on the car that had bolts. The engine was torn down and rebuilt with balanced and blueprinted high-performance components, using high-compression pistons, ported cylinder heads, oversized valves, a racing camshaft, a dual-carburettor manifold and two four-barrel carburettors. The original automatic transmission was replaced with a Muncie wide-ratio four-speed gearbox with a twelve-inch clutch. Jon insisted on a relatively mild 3.43-to-one ratio in the positive-traction differential to keep the car long-legged for freeway driving.

Getting such a big car to handle well was Jon's concern from the start, so he spoke with a few mechanic friends who had worked on police cruisers for insight. The big Caprice received a full suspension rebuild, including an anti-sway bar set and lever-type traction bars; Jon even cut loops out of the coil springs, lowering the front of the car to aid weight transfer under acceleration. Sometimes Dave would work on the engine and Jon the body; but they traded tasks often and spent most of their time working together. It was a learning experience in teamwork and Jon was glad for the diary and photographs they maintained to record their progress. Dave had put up a calendar depicting lovely young women in various states of undress, not merely for its aesthetic value but to schedule the tasks to be completed each day; and they put in regular hours even whilst attending school and working other jobs.

The completed car was impressive beyond expectations. The padded white top, done after a long consultation with the upholstery specialist at a local Cadillac customising shop, gave the car a very rich, distinctive look. The silver colour, eight coats of lacquer base and three coats of clear metallic finish, gave off a shine like platinum in the sun. Dave brought a friend by to help with it but the two boys rigged a dust-free booth of cellophane plastic in the garage and sprayed most of the paint themselves over two days. Jon, with his delicate artist's touch, applied the maroon pinstripes by hand and, enthralled with the excitement of at last preparing his mechanical opus for the street, added the elegant script of 'Spellbinder' across the front edge of the bonnet one evening on a whim.

'So,' said Bob; 'I take you haven't been talking to her?'

'Who?' Jon asked, tossing the empty oil can away into the dustbin.

Bob watched him stick the funnel into the next can and then, without spilling a drop on his chromium-plated valve cover, turn it over and poke it into the engine's filler hole. '*Jeannie,*' said Bob, as though there should have been no question. 'That show was a good opportunity to talk to her, even afterwards, like in school. Man, at this point you could say *anything* to her; and she'd wanna listen. It's like you got somethin' to rap about now.'

'Aaah....' Jon rolled up the sleeves of his dark-blue mechanic's shirt, not taking his eyes from the cardboard can stuck on the funnel in the filler hole. It throbbed with a 'glub, glub' sound as the oil ran out, visibly jumping for air a few times. 'I don't know, man. I get the distinct impression—'

'Aaah, man; but you're just tryin' to avoid it. Just *say* somethin' to the babe. It ain't like she's gonna laugh in your face....'

'You never know,' Jon said quietly.

'And, yeah; I know how it is.   It's like by now, you got your expectations up so high, man, it'd like crush ya if it didn't turn out the right way....' They were both silent a moment, each considering that. 'Aaah,' Bob said at last; 'I don't know, man. I just don't wanna see ya pass up a good opportunity, and doo, when there is one.' He turned and wandered off into the other empty bays of the garage. That had been too much to say already. Jon would never respond to being pushed, no matter what the intentions of his friends.

'Aaah, yeah; but it's like I said, you know: what if she's *not* interested. Just... what if I'm really just makin' all this shit up, and I'd just be makin' an ass outa myself. Like, what if she'd be like, "Jon who?" You know?   Maybe she's like kinda pissed-off, that I'm like a snob, or somethin', that ignores her in the halls. You know? I mean that could really be the case, here.'

'So what's this Wolf's Head shit?' Bob picked up one of the emptied cans from the top of the dustbin. 'Is this stuff any good? My dad says use Quaker State, or Pennzoil. He says Quaker State's the best one.'

Jon shrugged. 'I buy the cheapest one that's any good,' he confessed. 'Any of those, they're all good. So long as it's the right viscosity.'

'Like Mobil, and all, that stuff's okay? Just with these *gas* prices goin' up, some of this shit gettin' pretty *expensive*. I'm just thinkin', I gotta get the oil changed in that car. I've been usin' it more than he has lately; I oughta at least do *somethin'* for him....'

Jon pulled the can on the funnel out of the valve cover and caught the drip with a rag. 'So bring it in,' he said simply. 'I got another six cans of this stuff. And being as that's a three-fifty, my oil filters should fit it....' He plucked the funnel out of the expired can and threw it to the dustbin.

'So; uh, not to be like naggin' you, but are you gonna talk to the babe, or what? Did somebody say she was in your English class?'

'I can't imagine who,' Jon said quietly, thinking instantly of Barry Hemphill, a mutual friend who worried like a mother about all the problems of his closest mates. 'And yeah; well; so what? I should write her a poem? Shit– that's not *even* corny....' Certainly he could not mention, even to Bob, that he actually had secretly composed a few odes and apostrophes over the last year or so expressly for that purpose.   'I'll bet you a hundred bucks the babe doesn't even remember. This is probably all just a waste of energy.'

'Yeah,' Bob teased; 'but only if you'd said that about this *car*.'

'Hey; shut up about the car. This thing's a goddamn *investment*.'

'Oh,' laughed Bob, 'that much; huh?   Seems to me people have bought *real estate* with what you and Dave have sunk into this thing.'

'Yeah; well; shut up. It'll still do the quarter in thirteen flat, and out-drive any police car in the fucking county…. I could deal *drugs* and get away with it. And you, you're drivin' your pop's *Chevelle*, which needs a tune-up so bad the damn thing won't even idle, and it needs the oil changed; so bring the fucking thing *in* here; will ya?'

Bob laughed at him. 'Look; so don't go tryin' to impress *me* with this happy hunk of horseshit; all right? Talk to Jeannie *Banfield*, for crying out loud, so I don't have to keep naggin' you about it; *Christ….*'

Jon laughed at him too. 'All right; let's assume for the time being that I'm workin' on it. The time being, damn near time for dinner. Go get the stupid car; and I'll see if I can get that two-barrel and them cold-ass plugs running with some semblance of power.'

'Yeah,' Bob scoffed, to tease; *'workin'* on it….' Jon got into the Caprice and fired up the engine, which settled down with its burly cam lope to idle at an even one thousand. He revved the throttle a few times, racking the stillness of the affluent neighbourhood with the vibrant blare of the exhaust; and Bob opened the door to the next bay for the Malibu. As he walked down to the street to the car, he thought, yeah; well; he's *workin'* on it…. It'll take him *years*. And so maybe some day, when we're all outa school, and he and the babe are old and grey…. And he'll probably *still* be a funny son-of-a-bitch.

* * *

The car and Jon had begun to earn equal notoriety about town. Neither seemed willing to be beaten in anything. Dave and Jon went to the Burkleigh drag-racing track in late October and turned in a very respectable time of 13.4 seconds at 108 miles per hour, surprisingly quick for a four-door car weighing over two tons. On the street the car stood its challenges well and Jon was able to out-accelerate anything under 350 cubic inches in a middleweight car. He met quite a few interesting people whilst racing late at night, typically Dave's friends from the upper years at school or those who had brought their cars into Aunt Audrey's garage for work. Many were intrigued by such a unique car driven so well by such a young mechanic. Side bets were often settled in beer or some other consumable commodity, and there was never much real animosity between competitors.

However such was not the result from Jon's temperament. He had never been one to incite violence, only quell it; but he was a warrior at heart and defending causes often meant enduring a fair share of verbal and physical abuse. Being slight his brother Andrew received plenty of undue bullying and it was not rare for Jon to find himself delivering a few well-deserved punches to his younger brother's more belligerent classmates. A strategic asset was to have loyal comrades like Chris

Santana and Mark Jenkins at hand when things got surly; and so, wherever teenagers gathered, the boys of Lake Drive were greeted with due courtesy and respect, despite the occasional bloodied lip or welt on the cheek.

Jeanne was one of the girls who noticed these reputations. The girls in school loved to carry any pertinent information about the more desirable boys round and round, embellishing it adoringly until it was nearly unbelievable. Debbie Blake was an avid storyteller and reported to Jeanne daily in composition class the latest and greatest news. After all, it was no small secret she had career plans in journalism.

Good-natured Mrs Hampton took all Debbie's chatting and Jon's antics as part of the high-school teaching experience. She was humoured along with everyone else when Jon would compare literary plots to recent television episodes or call characters 'dude' and 'babe' in oral dissertation. In writing he was deviously articulate and clever, deliberately using Malapropesque misspellings and misquoting classics as though to keep the teacher on her toes. Often she thought indeed he was giving her the lesson. His works were beautifully written when it counted, of collegiate quality and content, involving adult issues the other students might only ever have glimpsed on late-night television. Whenever she met his mother at a PTA social or school board meeting, Mrs Hampton had nothing but praise for the talented upstart with what his mother agreed was 'shamefully long' light-brown hair.

His mother had worried at first when Jon had begun to associate with Dave Holloway, the persuasive, self-reliant senior whose widowed father so relished the bachelor life on the West Coast. But rather than instigating unsupervised irresponsibility, Dave imparted a respectable maturity to all proceedings, even when the intent of those proceedings was merely to have fun. The quartet tentatively known as Dave's Disciples flourished over the winter, playing parties and dances about town for exposure value alone.

Dave seemed to know everyone who was anyone on the local rock-and-roll scene. Doug Davisson and Rob Alascan, two seniors who were the core of the band now known as Tobacco Road, were Dave's mates originally; in fact Dave had played bass guitar with them until Jimmy Kennedy joined and later rhythm guitar before the induction of a young Barry Hemphill. Worlds had collided over New Year's Eve 1971, as this informal association met the loose lineup of Bob, Jon and Mark Jenkins, with Chris Santana on electric piano, at the Santana house for a party and jam session. When all the amplifiers had fallen quiet and the drum kits were put away, two distinct music groups had emerged.

Tobacco Road had finally found their blues-rock drummer in heretofore frustrated Mark Jenkins; and Dave Holloway, a John

Lennon fan to the end, found fellow Beatles devotees in Bob and Jon. Melody Santana's classmate Ricky Denning, jazz-trained and yet pleasantly unsophisticated, would round out their quartet on drums. DJ Berryfield promised to be available as sit-in keyboard player to whichever group might call him and Chris resigned himself to the role of manager for both bands, as his talents were far more to the area of administration than performance. In so exchanging members the two groups became closer as friends; and a wealth of creativity would be the dividend.

Jon in particular developed great fondness and respect for his colleagues Tobacco Road. He never seemed to find much common ground with Doug, who was somewhat moody and aloof; but Mark, one of his oldest and dearest friends, Barry, a new friend with a gentle heart, and Rob, the tall, tan-skinned, daring and charming lead singer, considered him a welcome collaborator from the first. Jon and Dave often sat in on Tobacco Road's rehearsal sessions and sometimes even during their performances. As each group began to develop a characteristic style of arranging and songwriting, the friendly competition and exchange of ideas and influences proved invaluable. It was entertainment and education at the same time and, though they all thought the experience well worth the effort, the time spent on music began to intrude on too many prior commitments.

Patti, Jeanne, PJ and the rest of the cheerleading squad accompanied the junior-varsity teams to both home and away games. They travelled on the bus with the players, with whom they formed fast friendships. Football and basketball took up much of their time before spring; and they found little opportunity to follow Coach Weber's excellent swim team, much less to attend the meets at the township's indoor pool. However a faithful following of girls from school gladly braved the chill of winter afternoons and evenings to see their favourite bare-chested boys do their traditional finest for Wilshire High. The best of the juniors were Mark Jenkins and Jon Cavaliere, those two holding near-legendary status among the locals for their aquatic gallantry at the township lake behind the houses of Lake Drive and remarkably still able to beat the best of the competition in spite of their reduced time for practice. With a schedule so unsympathetic to that of the swim team, Jeanne, like the other girls on the squad and all the devoted basketball fans, had to catch the swimmers' results in Skip MacRae's column in the fortnightly *Wilshire High Record.*

Skip, senior-class president, covered the swimming and gymnastics events for the student newspaper. The journalistic staff were talented and industrious, whipping together an eight-page collage of school and local news, editorials, interviews, reviews, an advice column, community notices and paid commercial advertisements, distributing their editions every other Tuesday. With such a high profile about town the paper was besieged with dozens of unsolicited contributions from students every issue; and repeat publication was many an aspiring writer's pinnacle. Only two original comic-strip features would survive all eighteen issues of the 1973-74 school year; and one of them was the rib-tickling serial of *Wonderman*, created by none other than Jon Cavaliere.

When Jeanne had snatched up her first copy of the *Record*, *Wonderman* was an eye-opening surprise with its cleverly-drawn panels and suspenseful dialogue beautifully hand-lettered by her favourite junior. By the time of the third and fourth issues of the paper she, like everyone else, was eagerly anticipating the next cliffhanging adventure of 'Millville's mild-mannered motor mechanic'.

It was widely assumed that Jon had taken some advanced graphic-art lessons; but no-one could say where or when. Styled after classic superhero features of the 1940s, the lavishly-detailed four-panel serial chronicled the crusades of the character Howie Hudson, a sort of suburban Superman who helped right wrongdoing by way of a secret identity. Whether working on his 1953 Studebaker hot rod, attending high school with his beautiful but unknowing girlfriend, 'the delightful Darby Donovan', or garbed in his 'splendiferous silver suit' to battle the 'despicable, deadly dope dealers' for Mayor Wilton T Wipnoodle, Howie's saintly intentions and gallant gaffes delighted everyone, drawing admiration and envy from literature, art and journalism teachers as well as students.

Jon's prodigious creative output was a universal source of amazement. He was forever sketching or scrawling notes, conceiving and working out compositions of all kinds for ongoing projects; he was known to arrive late to class or appear inattentive during structured lessons due to his frantic mental pace. Mrs Hampton took the initiative among the faculty, grading his current writing against his own prior work rather than merely assimilating his superior academic potential into the class average. She encouraged and accepted his frequent extracurricular contributions, discussed his progress openly with his other teachers, and became determined to send him to the best university possible at any cost.

Jeanne loved perusing the school paper with her mother, who would be just as amused by the *Wonderman* episodes. During Christmas recess the Banfields from Maine were down, and Jeanne and her cousin Andria sat up in her room and shared news. When their talk came round to boys, Jeanne bravely got out her private scrapbook to display her clippings from the local publications and school announcements that concerned the one boy who had created the popular *Wonderman* stories, received a few draughtsmanship and design awards, and set a record or two with the school swim team. Andria was duly impressed with the idol of her childhood soulmate, although she admitted it seemed a bit extreme to hope for 'the most talented artist in school'. Jeanne did not mind the honest criticism. That Andria could scarcely guess the depth of her real sentiment was not important.

* * *

Jon spent a good deal of time at the bowling alley, although he never bowled. At the end of the long array of bowling lanes was the billiard room, with eight or ten tables that could be rented for a dollar an hour. Mike Jolson had introduced him to this place about two years ago and Jon and Mike had become regular players here. Now, despite his busy schedule of working with his father on construction drawings, keeping the Caprice in racing trim and playing in the band, Jon had found time to study under some fine pool masters.

One evening in late January, cold and brittle, he found himself shuffling out of the billiard room. Although he could appreciate watching a superior eight-ball player at work, losing control of a table had never been flattering for him. His father always said that there was no use doing anything if one were not prepared to give a full effort, and Jon liked to apply philosophies like that to rock music and pocket billiards, despite his mother's insistence that he excel at his schoolwork.

There were many who drank beer in the billiard room and often the age limits were blithely overlooked; but Jon was drinking soda tonight. He carried his Coca-Cola can and cigarette out to the bowling lanes and sat at the spectators' counter across the rear of the room. He was not a bowler and knew little of the scoring or strategy of the game. There were girls out tonight, though; and he watched them with a full understanding of what comprised good form. A familiar-looking blonde in lane twelve picked up her ball and studied the pins' arrangement before casting an impotent shot down the alley. Of eight pins three remained standing; and she shrugged in disappointment as the resetting machine did its work. Her two friends gave her some comforting words as she sat down.

She looked very cute tonight, despite the ugly bowling shoes that made her plaid wool trousers drag a little on the floor. Since the winter had begun he found he could accept her in heavier clothing; maybe it was those cheerleading sweaters that made all the girls on the squad look a little more voluptuous than they really were. He watched as she pulled the sides of her beige turtleneck down a little and sat stiffly, almost as though she were unwilling to be here. Jon had a thought about that. Perhaps there would be something he might do or say to make her want to leave with him.

He hated thinking like that. He despised boys who seemed preoccupied with picking up girls, though even Bob Prescott was not immune to gawking inordinately at the female scenery now and then. The boys he knew were forever talking about 'chicks' and 'babes' and 'broads' as though girls were some alien and inferior creature, necessary only for male pleasure and human procreation. Jon held all women in higher regard than that. He had an untimely notion that if the moment were right, all would pass as he desired it, not from any coercion or deception on his part, but because his feelings as a gentleman would be appropriately respectful and the young lady in question would be reciprocating the same sort of feelings for him as he held for her.

He took more than his share of teasing about it, but he had come to his own conclusions his way and would not be swayed by the influence of the general consensus. Surely there were very pleasant and decent girls out there; and he endeavoured to see from the outside those qualities that made for a suitable companion inside. Sometimes he found himself attaching those qualities to people who were simply not his type, merely because of some minor facet of their appearance or behaviour that had appealed to him. He found he stared at all blondes, especially those with long wavy hair. Rarely did he dismiss any girl who wore spectacles; if she were attractive otherwise, her glasses were no detriment to him. He loved the look of any girl in a short skirt or dress, not yet having accepted the 'midi' look in hemlines himself. Girls who laughed, not mindlessly but with heartfelt amusement, always attracted him.

Dave, not understanding, tried to interest him in some of his own acquaintances, girls who smoked and drank and swore to beat the devil; somehow an upward-aspiring gentleman like Dave seemed to attract such admirers. He would question Jon's tastes aloud in such company; and Jon would naïvely try to defend himself, which did nothing for anyone's good humour. Good-natured and forgiving though he was, Jon often felt burdened by such well-meaning criticism. It was good to get out from under the band's influence for a while anyway and spend an evening or two playing the billiards tables with old mates like Mike Jolson.

Jeanne Banfield picked up her ball again. Jon liked the way she cast, as though afraid to run too fast and seeming too willing to let go of the ball. She lost interest in the throw immediately and winced at a chipped fingernail. He smiled at that. Jeanne seemed perfectly feminine to him, unable to take a rather masculine activity like bowling too seriously; it was obviously not high on her list of priorities. In everything she exuded a woman's sensuality, sometimes not even knowing it herself; and he liked to think that was just like her. He knew that for every teenaged boy in town she was the ideal dream date, the one girl with whom they might live out all their fantasies. Jon hated that thought; for he could well imagine what their fantasies all were. His were far to the other extreme.

He stubbed out the cigarette in the plastic taproom ashtray on the counter even before it had burnt to the filter. He often daydreamed about what Jeanne Banfield would be like after graduation and after university, and about what kind of wife or mother she might make. It was very embarrassing, really; and he had never admitted it to anyone but Bob, and then only once, two years ago, in a discreet conversation about such matters. But Jeanne Banfield tended to elicit such thoughts in him. Sure, he knew, there would be some things, like sex, about which he might have wanted to fantasise straight away; but there were other more agreeable notions to contemplate. He imagined her buying produce at the market, getting her hair styled, driving the estate car and fixing soup and sandwiches for little children who come home from school in the rain. He thought about how beautiful she would be twenty years hence, not how she would appear physically, but with regard to the grace and charm she would exude then, in a perfectly feminine way, just as she did as a teenaged girl when he saw her at the bowling alley trying not to look too intimidated by the muscular nature of the game.

Anne Marlowe threw her two bowls, making eight pins. Debbie Blake, still talking away, threw a gutter-ball and then a perfect spare. Jon likened that to the inconsistency of her general nature: she was a contradiction in terms from the start. Jeanne got up to throw again; and right then Mike Jolson came and sat down beside him. 'So hey, dude; what happened to you?'

'Aaah; you know....' He watched Jeanne heft up the ball and sight down the alley. Go ahead, gorgeous, he wanted to tell her. Do your damnedest. 'You know, Scholes and all them, once they get a table from ya, they can hold it all night.'

Mike shrugged. 'Yeah; but they can still lose. You just gotta go at it, like it was a fight, and shit. Don't stop tryin', 'cause you'll get your ass kicked. Take a coupla hits; and–'

'Shit,' Jon said, shaking his head, not looking at him. 'That doesn't *even* sound like what I usually tell you, does it?'

Mike laughed. Jeanne threw. Four boys in the adjacent lane stood up and cheered her as the ball went straight down the lane, taking out all but one of the pins. Anne and Debbie applauded, and Jeanne spun about on her toes and gestured with a fist, imitating only slightly an athlete's enthusiasm. Jon smiled a little and slurped down the last of his Coca-Cola. All right, gorgeous, he wanted to say aloud. The lady done good.

Jeanne giggled, those braces on her teeth belying nothing of an irresistible smile, and for a moment looked right up at him. He kept

his eyes on her for as long as he dared, about a second and a half.
Mike spoke to him. 'So José's got a table now, dude. You could
probably take him, you know.'

'Yeah....' Jon looked at him then. 'Gimme a cigarette.'

'I thought you said you were quittin',' Mike teased, and reached into
the pocket of his olive-green M65 infantry coat. 'Shit– I'm like fresh
out now anyway. And I'm damn near outa moolah, too.'

'Shit....' Jon got up, tossing the empty soda can into a dustbin, and
went down the broad back aisle, crossing behind the lane where the
girls were playing. Jeanne realised he would probably see her throw
and cast the ball nervously down the gutter, almost intentionally.
Needless to say it missed the solitary pin entirely.

When she sat back down he was at the cigarette machine and she
was able to take a longer look at him. To her he seemed to radiate
masculinity, half fun-loving boy, half full-blooded man. At seventeen
he was what all the girls wanted in a mate, tough, strong and brave, yet
down-to-earth and believable, not like other boys who frequented the
same places. In fact Jeanne once wondered how he could associate
with so many different people of vastly varying tastes, preferences and
inclinations; it might have indicated a lack of integrity on his part. But
she knew better. It was they who sought his company, not the other
way round.

With change from the counter clerk he put the required coins into
the machine and she watched him light up a Marlboro before shuffling
back to his friend in the infantry coat. In that dark-brown leather
flier's jacket and the tight Levi's he was sexy in a romantic, heroic way,
as though that loping stroll was capitulating to some old battle injury.
But she was not so moved physically as emotionally. Some facet about
Jon Cavaliere evoked emotion; and for having studied him for so long
Jeanne knew she was as far from putting a finger on it as anyone else.
She, like all the others, could only attest that he was utterly fascinating.

It was her turn to bowl again. Jon lingered, to watch her. He tossed
Mike the packet of cigarettes and shuffled back to the row of vending
machines, buying another can of Coca-Cola with the thirty-five cents
left from his dollar. Jeanne's bowl was terrible, going into the gutter
with a wicked left hook just a few feet from the pins. Reluctantly he
started back towards the billiard room, but he expected to fare no
better than before with his mind so preoccupied. There would be little
chance of saying anything to her tonight and, anyway, he was certain
he would have nothing very meaningful to say.

Jon hated himself most of all for having no courage whatsoever
when it came to Jeanne Banfield. Something about her beauty, or her
reputation with the boys, or the way he had come to feel about her
stripped him of all his nerve. It had become something of a do-or-die
mission by now; for he knew failure in this would undermine his

confidence in all he would ever try again. He held faith that some day the right chance would come, and he would seize it; and then everything would be just as he had dreamt; but, for now, safely avoiding the risk of looking foolish seemed much more comfortable.

He took one last longing look at the pretty blonde in the beige sweater just now stomping back to her friends after a disappointing second bowl, and then turned to amble through the doors after Mike. The fact that he went home with just a dollar to his name came as no surprise indeed.

* * *

'Mom,' she called as she ran down the stairs, 'I'm going out now!'
'All right, sweetheart,' came the pleasant voice from the sitting room. 'When will you be back?'
'Not late, Mom,' said Jeanne, and opened the front door.
'Remember it is a school night, dear,' called Mrs Banfield; and the door closed.

A few blocks down curvy Old Mill Road, at the corner of Apple Way, the girls would gather in front of the 7-Eleven food market on the milder evenings to share girl talk and to watch the boys. The management rarely objected to their loitering; for it meant that the boys would invariably turn up and buy snacks and Slurpee drinks for the group. It was in all a good crowd of teenagers; and nothing negative ever reflected on the business. Indeed they were there not to find or cause trouble but to avoid it.

Debbie and Anne were already there, chatting amiably away with Marty Engel and some of his cohorts. Marty was always fun to have around; he was quite an entertaining young gentleman and so did not intimidate the girls, who were inclined to be wary of boys who seemed too forward. Often he would walk them home at night, never pressing for a date or expecting any preferential consideration in their social lives. Tonight he was all agog with the news that the band for which he sang had voted to change their name to Marty's Menagerie. They performed mostly old rock-and-roll standards from the 1950s and, though portly, Marty really looked the part on stage with his studded black leather motorcycle jacket and pompadour hairstyle. The girls enjoyed his jokes and storytelling; and they all giggled away most of the evening in front of the 7-Eleven.

Just before ten Marty and Debbie went into the store to procure a few drinks for the crowd. Jeanne stood outside with Anne and two of Marty's bandmates, and one of them, Charlie Palmer, asked her for a date to a film. 'Oh; that sounds nice,' Jeanne said sweetly. 'But I really should check first.' Thus put off by Jeanne's indecision, Charlie would not pursue the matter. He turned, a little disappointed, and gazed out at the street.

They all heard the sound long before the headlamps came up the road. A beautifully-polished red Dodge Charger swung in off Chester Pike, throbbing with the rich rumble of its exhaust headers. Close after the Charger came Jon Cavaliere's silver Chevrolet, still louder and deeper with that profound big-block growl that vibrated the glass of the building behind the girls. The cars stopped thirty feet apart at the kerb in front of the store and were shut down; and then, for a precious moment or two, all was calm.

A slender young man rose from the Charger, in an open denim jacket and white t-shirt; he must have been freezing. 'Yo Cav!' he called across the black vinyl roof of his car. 'This one on you?'

Jon Cavaliere alighted then, dressed in a black cotton jersey, jeans and those dark-brown high-heeled shoes that were like no-one else's around. He wore that much-admired military flying jacket, decorated with Army Air Corps patches, that was his signature. Even Marty envied it; something of a self-appointed expert on leather jackets, he had once said that though Jon's looked too new to have been his father's it was a perfectly authentic recreation. 'We'll see,' Jon called over to his acquaintance, jerking his head back to clear his eyes of that mop of hair. 'I just gotta get rid of these munchies, and shit.' He turned, saw Jeanne and Anne standing with the two boys then, and strode right past them towards the door of the store.

The other car door opened and Becky Barnett stood up, looking decidedly cute in a belted bronze-coloured leather jacket, dark-green pullover, snug jeans and black platform shoes, with her medium-brown hair recently styled into a loose, shoulder-length shag. For one who carried a reputation of being such a rebellious tomboy she could certainly look ladylike and appealing when so moved. Jeanne thought any girl would be, for a chance to ride in Jon Cavaliere's car.

It was a coveted place to be, that right front seat; she had heard more than a few girls talking about having designs on it since the start of the school year. She wondered about her own chances, especially now, seeing someone else there. But she could not have known about the special friendship between Becky and the boys of Lake Drive that dated back to the early days of elementary school, when they had all been scrimmage partners at football and members of the neighbourhood treehouse-construction league. Poor Becky probably dressed attractively these days merely to gain the boys' sentiments; for in the last dozen years she had never been specially treated like a girl by any of them. She shut the car door and bolted after Jon, calling, 'Yo; wait up! You're gettin' me a Tab; right? I'm flat busted—'

True to that tomboy reputation, Becky carried no handbag. Jon made a little noise like 'tsk!' and let the door close in front of her, just to tease.

'Yo,' Becky said, seeing the girls who were listening in on their tiff, 'Casanova!' She yanked the door open to follow him inside. 'Dag; some kinda *gentleman*, and doo!'

The door closed. Marty and Debbie emerged on its next swing, their arms laden with cups of soda and packets of potato crisps. 'Dag,' said Marty, seeing the two cars that had not been there minutes ago; 'what's the occasion?'

'Oooo,' smiled Debbie; 'looks like drag-race time.'

Suddenly it occurred to Jeanne that Debbie was probably right. In a minute Jon and Becky stepped out, each with a bottle of soda and a packet of snack cakes. 'Shit,' Jon called over to the young man with the Charger; 'you're still here? Guess I'll *have* to run ya.'

He and Becky both leaned against the left side of the Caprice. ''*Course* he's still here,' Becky proclaimed, as Robert Plant moaned through 'D'yer Make'r' over the Charger's loud stereo cartridge player. 'Dude's in the mood for losin' some bread tonight.'

The young man laughed, cupping his hand over the end of his cigarette to light it. The wisp of grey smoke ascended into the still night air. 'Broad's got balls,' he commented, as though disregarding the presence of his slight, skinny companion in her braided red hair, fringed suede jacket and moccasin boots, slouching sullenly against the right side of his car beside him. 'So what're *you* drivin' these days, Barbie-Doll?'

'Dag,' Becky told him; 'my grandpop's *Datsun* would outrun that piece of Dodge! Oh; I mean: piece of *shit*. Damn– I always get those two words mixed up.'

Jon laughed, and Jeanne felt her knees go weak at that irresistible dimpled smile. Marty and the others were laughing too. 'Now, now,' Jon said calmly to Becky then, over the music, 'let us *do* try to behave while we're out, shall we?'

'Oh,' she scoffed; 'let's just get back in the damn car so we can blow this jerk's doors off.' She downed a gulp of her diet soda.

The Charger driver made a wry face, although it was obvious he was just as humoured by her spunk. 'So where's it at, Cav?'

Jon shrugged, perfectly casual. 'Aaah; I don't care. Go down to the Ditch, I guess. So long as there's no ice....' He sighed, and then asked, quietly and more seriously, 'What kinda cash are you holdin'?'

The young man shrugged too, tossing the long brown hair off his forehead. 'I got beer,' he said quietly, and raised his eyebrows after a second.

Jon rolled his eyes towards the moonless sky. 'Aaaaaaah....'

'Come *on*, man,' Becky urged him; 'let's *go*! We could drink this jerk *silly*.'

'Yeah; if you even see me,' the other taunted.

'Yeah,' she came back; 'well; I don't have twenty-twenty *hindsight*.'

Marty and the other boys laughed at that. 'Yo Cav, do me a favour and find somethin' to occupy that broad's mouth; will ya? She's gettin' to be a pain in the ass.'

' 'Least *you* don't have to drive around with her,' Jon said, looking a little embarrassed by implied vulgarity in the presence of the nice girls from the Old Mill neighbourhood. 'Shit— she drinks at least half all the beer anyway.'

Becky belched aloud. 'I'm gettin' thirsty,' she said. 'Hope that beer's cold.'

'Why?' asked the long-haired Charger driver. '*You'll* never see any.'

'Right,' Jon said cockily, and the two parties turned to get into their respective cars then. Becky went round to the nearside as Jon watched his opposition get into the Charger. He tilted his head back and took a long gulp of Coca-Cola. 'So did you hear,' he said to Becky across the top of his car, just loud enough for Marty and the others to make out, 'that he *still* doesn't know anything about this motor? He thinks he's got me on weight advantage with a Torque-Flite and a three-eighteen.'

Becky's eyes went wide at that. 'No shit! Dag; I coulda sworn he had at least a three-*forty*!'

The two of them shared a sly little snicker and then quickly got into the car. The red Charger was fired up and backed round to go west on Apple Way. Jon put his clutch foot down and let his car roll back in silence, turning until he was parallel to the front of the store. The big 427 awoke with a lion's roar. He teased the throttle a few times and then gently slipped the clutch to pull away.

Jeanne and the others watched as those wide white-lettered tyres gained momentum and carried Jon and Becky off up the road. 'Jesus,' Charlie marvelled; 'what a *car*. Have you ever seen what he's got *in* that thing? He musta spent two grand on the motor alone.'

'Betcha he wins,' Debbie said secretively, and Jeanne looked at her.

They could still hear the thunder of the two engines, cruising out the west end of town to their clandestine racing rendezvous, far from the wondering eyes and ears of the township traffic patrol. There was a gritty kind of romance to it all; and Jeanne leaned back on the store window and fantasised about seeing Jon Cavaliere in action during a drag race. She would have jumped at the chance to witness that, even from the losing car, had she known anyone with a hot rod who might challenge him. That casual aloofness with which Jon seemed to dismiss all the hazards of life and limb and law seemed to make him even more attractive than ever.

Jeanne shivered excitedly just to imagine it. She had always been infatuated with anyone who defied the odds. The thought of accepting a dangerous dare for nothing more tangible than cold beer was somehow gallant and heroic to her. Indeed, despite her comfortable, sheltered life, that kind of risk-taking was at the root of all her daydreams about Jon Cavaliere. In her favourite fancies he was always sailing, climbing, racing, competing, doing something dashing, and not for any cash reward but for just the sheer thrill of it all; and it was seeing him looking so modest and so cute about actually doing such exciting things in real life that tingled her spine so.

Suddenly, including herself in the comfortable, university-bound crowd of aspiring young professionals began to taste as flat as the fountain soda. She yearned, at whatever risk to her reputation, for a taste of that other side of life, of hot rods and rock-and-roll bands and junk food and foul language and placing insignificant wagers on perilous stunts. She wanted desperately to fling herself after Jon Cavaliere and join him in his world and wear old jeans and drink beer and stand about in billiards halls for ever.   Steve and Marty and Bobby Crocker were all pleasant young men, and she was very fond of them; but they sought the safe routes through life, and in so doing they had become ordinary and predictable. Jeanne felt her skin light up with goosepimples just to consider a romantic relationship with someone who was boldly unpredictable. For the rest of the evening, she could concentrate on nothing but how exciting it would be to sit in that right front seat of Jon Cavaliere's powerful silver hot rod during a drag race for the mere thrill of it all.

* * *

By February the second semester had begun, and many of the class had elected to stay on through English Composition II. Mrs Hampton took each of her students aside at this time to consult about grades. Jon had never been eager to sit through these conferences and listened only politely whilst Mrs Hampton went on with a pitch about university, mentioning his parents and Mrs Donovan, his current guidance counsellor, and even Dr Cannon, the school superintendent. It amounted to only the same rhetorical song-and-dance he had been hearing from his other teachers; and he led them all on with promises to consider everything.

As the spring came on, Jeanne seemed to be taking on a glow, something that defied concise description. At first Jon took it for her growing familiarity with high-school life; but there was more to it than that. She had clearly gained something of a reputation with the boys, for one. He saw her with sophomores and juniors and sometimes even with seniors; and he could not help but feel a little intimidated by the newfound popularity she seemed to enjoy. When he had known her she had been a modest, innocent young girl, and he still appreciated modesty and innocence in females. Now, he was not sure that the change he perceived in her was entirely for the better. If she had not changed, perhaps she might still have welcomed the sight of him with a happy smile and a cheerful hello as she had so long ago.

She still looked much the same; and he was grateful for that. Jeanne Banfield possessed soft, gentle features, without the slightest despicable edge anywhere. Her jaw rose along the side of her face with a serene curve, and her straight, short nose was delicately rounded. She had beautiful naturally-long eyelashes and a doe-eyed decline to her eyelids that never failed to make Jon weak in the knee whenever she happened to look his way. The few times he was able to meet her gaze, coincidentally only, or at least always to look that way, her eyes, which he had first called *gorgeous*, sparkled like sapphires in the light, with a cool, sensual radiance that riddled his skin with goosepimples. He often fantasised about being alone with her, in some dark theatre, or maybe parked in his car, and then shuddered to think that upon gazing into those eyes, that irresistible sparkle would drive him into fits of passion. He would squeeze her as close as he could to his body and lower his lips onto hers; and, if he would only die like that, no man could wish for a richer fate.

Jon hated having those thoughts. He slouched in his seat at the back of Room 148, sharing snide comments with Barry about the subject matter at hand and snapping off accurate, articulate answers to the teacher's questions with what was meant to look like the hint of a drug-induced drawl. Barry was always amused by him and most of the others were too. Jon Cavaliere was, after all, the most entertaining individual in the class, if not of most of the student body.

But he had begun to realise that he was doing it all for the attention of only one person. During the autumn of his eighth-grade year a beautiful seventh-grade blonde had sat in front of him in his science class; and he had been captivated by the way she giggled at every silly joke he made. As a child he had always loved being funny; but it was then that he began to cultivate humour as in inseparable part of his personality. By the start of his junior year, boyish shyness had been replaced with a serious yen for the stage and an insatiable craving to entertain large groups of people. He still felt a little nervous when performing but had ample reason to be proud of himself, acknowledging that it was a remarkable metamorphosis for someone who had been too timid to appear in the sixth-grade play.

Jeanne ordinarily sat a little sideways in her seat, half facing him, though Jon attributed that to her sitting so far over towards the windows side. She would lean forwards with her elbow on the desk, looking either down at her notes or up at the teacher and quite often back at Debbie Blake. Debbie was an unusual character, shy in some ways and very outspoken in others. She would debate anything with anyone, whether or not she had all the facts, but apparently Jon had just what it took to put her in her place; for she would become stone quiet whenever he gave a dissenting opinion.

Jeanne, on the other hand, never seemed to volunteer anything. She responded intelligently when called upon, in a cheerful yet gentle voice laden with sultry overtones; Jon likened its timbre to raw silk, not rough, neither slick as glass. He absorbed everything she said, as though the assignment were to memorise her exact words, and found he could still recall her spoken contributions of Friday by Monday's class. When she was not in school, though it was rare, it was as though he had no further reason to continue the day. When she returned after an absence it was as if the sun had come up again after years of dismal darkness; and he yearned to tell her everything he had felt and thought and said since he had last seen her. But then, in the glow of those sparkling eyes, all his nerve would vanish in an instant; and he could only sit there like a fool and behold her.

* * *

In the first week of April, Mrs Hampton began announcing the objectives for the poetry unit. Jeanne slouched in her seat, thoroughly disinterested. After essays, written debates and the dialogues of events, it was all too probable that Jon Cavaliere would excel at verse as well.

'Poetry,' the teacher was saying, 'is really *not* just something that rhymes. Its beauty, and its real literary worth, lies in its *brevity*. A poem is intended to express the poet's thoughts as briefly as possible, using concise statements of imagery rather than paragraphs of information to describe his ideas. In fact, *imagery* is really the important thing to remember about poetry. For each assignment I want you to just convey your imagination. Don't worry about rhymes and meter and such, because as we get into them a little further you'll find that once your thoughts are down on paper, you can pretty much fit them into whatever form you like.'

Jeanne thought, this is boring. Poetry is really stupid. I want Jon Cavaliere to stand up and say this is all boring and stupid and give us some of his words of wisdom. Jon Cavaliere should be a teacher. He's too smart to be in this class. And then, if he *were* the teacher, at least *then* I'd be paying attention....

The door opened. No arrival was expected this late in the period and naturally all heads turned. The tall long-haired senior who was Dave Holloway strode assertively into the room, in old jeans and an untucked grey work shirt, carrying a cranberry-red Fender Stratocaster guitar in one hand and a single sheaf of notebook paper in the other. 'Jon?' he asked, looking about before locating him and starting down the aisle. 'Hey, man; I gotta tell ya, this is the *one*. The one I've been waitin' to show ya, dude. We're cookin' now.'

Jon sat up in interest and, with him, the entire class. 'So what's this? The fortieth draft of the same old thing?'

Dave sat on Jon's desktop, dropping the sheet of paper into Jon's lap. 'This'll only be a minute,' he said sideways at the teacher; and there were giggles of amusement as he set the guitar up on his leg and began playing from memory what he had written out in chord notation.

The teacher tried valiantly to stem her own disbelief. 'Uh, Jon–'

'No,' he was saying, waving her off as an untimely interruption; 'it's not bad.' He nodded along as Dave strummed a little too hard on the unamplified guitar, hacking through the quick, bouncing chord progression a second time.

'Let's see it,' said Barry. He leaned over the aisle towards Jon.

'See, we've been thrashin' this out for like two weeks, this same idea–' Jon looked up at Dave then. 'So what's this with just one word, here? You go all this way with only one word–?'

'*Yeah*,' Dave told him, and stopped playing. 'See, dude; it's like what I've been tellin' ya: it doesn't matter *what* the chords are.   *Or* the rhymes. You can't go writin' the music first, and then go tryin' to fit the words into what you already wrote. The song's about *words*, man, or, what they're tryin' to say, right; but like you, you always go and try to fit whole sentences into whatever sounds good. You gotta be more *succinct*, and doo; like, just dig on like the *imagery*. It's like what I've been tellin' ya, dude, the key to writin' good lyrics is the *brevity*.'

At that everyone in the room roared into great laughter, including the teacher. '*Dag*,' Barry cried aloud; '*déjá-vu!*'

Dave looked over at Mrs Hampton then. 'Oh, hey; did I wreck your class? Sorry, you know; but–'

'I think you just drove home a point,' she smiled; 'although–'

'*Good*,' said Jon, standing up abruptly; ''cause I gotta go down and work on this.' He went directly to where Mrs Hampton sat upon the corner of her desk, spying her pad of preprinted blue passes straight away. 'This'll be a really good assignment, Miz Hampton. A working example of brevity in poetry.'

Dave laughed, standing up with the guitar in the centre aisle of the classroom. 'Yeah; right. Like literally, a *working* example.'

Barry laughed, the only one in the room who knew how he had meant that. 'Jon,' the teacher asked calmly, trying to maintain her sense of humour as he filled out a pass in pencil, 'may I ask what you think you're doing?'

' "Pass, to piano, in auditorium",' he read as he wrote; and all the students laughed aloud.

'Now, Jon, just stop. You know I can't sign that pass.'

'No?' He looked at her, undaunted, and for a second they met eyes. 'Yeah,' he admitted; 'I guess you're right….' They all watched as he suddenly snatched a ball-point pen off Frank Genovese's front-row desk and, using his right hand, hastily scrawled a signature across the bottom line. 'No, Dave,' he said, peeling his facsimile off the pad; 'for once, I really think you may have something here....'

The two of them were to the door already. '*Jon!*' scolded Mrs Hampton.

He turned, giving the pen a perfectly accurate toss to Frank's waiting hands, and then looked at the teacher with a perfectly charming smile. '*Brevity,*' he assured her. 'Don't worry. I'll be back by the end of the period.' With a wink that left the girls in swoons he went out, and the heavy red door closed.

One by one, sighs of relief went up about the room, breaking the silence; another episode of Jon's deliberate delinquency had passed.

'Did he really sign your name?' wondered Cindy.

'He'd better not have,' Mrs Hampton said strongly. 'He'll get a suspension for forgery.'

'Oh; he's always like that,' someone said.

'Yeah,' agreed a girl in back. 'Nobody ever turns them in.'

'It's this business,' Barry explained, although doubtless none of them really knew what he meant. 'When you got a good idea, you gotta stop whatever you're doin' and write that stuff down, or you forget it. That's how come Holloway loses so many chicks.'

A few caught that implication. The teacher just stared back at them, embarrassed to have been so easily disarmed by an appealing, persuasive young man right in front of her students. She drew a breath and decided. 'Well; if he comes back with anything good, I'm going to consider it his homework assignment and grade it against whatever we've covered while he's not here. Otherwise, he's got himself a detention. There will be no more songwriting in the auditorium during *my* class.'

They must have been in the auditorium, where Dave had been scheduled for prep, for half an hour. To have two musicians composing a rock-and-roll love song at the piano was not a common occurrence; and other students gathered to witness their schoolmates at work. Jon ignored the distractions and soon felt satisfied with what he and Dave had achieved. Merely by coincidence, there were just three minutes left before the end of fourth period when he returned to Room 148 with another sheet of ruled notebook paper.

'All done,' he announced to the teacher, and went back to his seat beside Barry. 'Hey, man; you dudes are behind now. Dave's Disciples got another hit.'

'Let's see it,' said Barry, and took the sheet of paper from him to study it.

'Jon,' Mrs Hampton called cheerfully, 'may I see your pass?'

'Oh; sure,' he said blithely, and went up and handed the folded blue slip to the teacher, most of his attention on Barry's reaction.

There seemed to be none. 'I'm tellin' ya, dude, Holloway and Cavaliere are gettin' ahead of Alascan and Hemphill....' As he sat back down he realised that all in the room, including Debbie and Jeanne, were looking at him expectantly. 'Well, people,' he addressed them all; 'I actually extended myself here, lettin' Holloway go four whole chords with only one lousy syllable. It's a short song, and you play it quick, and even the title is only one word. I would say the operative word here today is definitely *brevity*.' Looking up at the teacher, he said, 'You know, Mrs Hampton, I think I just mighta learned a new poetic style here today.'

'Jon,' she asked, only now looking up at him, 'where did you learn to sign my name so well?'

He smiled. 'The bathroom.'

Several laughed. She looked at the pass again. 'Remind me to stop hand-writing lav passes.' There was more laughter.

'Let's see it,' Cindy said; but Mrs Hampton ripped it in half twice and dropped the bits into the dustbin.

'I've decided to grade your song, Jon, against what we've covered in class today. Whether or not I think it merits spending the entire period in the auditorium will directly affect the length of your detention.'

'Okay,' Jon said, pointing out something else to Barry on the sheet of music.

She was a little bothered by his cocky complacency; it seemed she was unable to concern him in the slightest. 'Well; if I can't come up with a grade for it, I want you to know you'll be carrying a handicap going into the poetry unit already, and it will be up to your extra-credit projects to bring your grade back up–'

'Okay,' he said again, and then looked up. 'Oh; you'll like it. Like I said: an exercise in brevity. Just a bit of iambic tetrameter, you know, a few Byronic similes, with a dash of Dante thrown in for good measure....'

'We'll see,' she told him, hiding the impression or fear that he actually knew what he was talking about or, still more frightening, that the song lyric composed in the auditorium by virtue of a forged blue pass actually contained such elements put to good literary effect. 'I'd like to see your work before you leave–'

'Yeah,' he said to Barry; 'gimme that. It wouldn't've taken so long, except that I wanted to get the bass part all written out in notation before I forgot it. That's on the other sheet, though. Holloway's got the masters.' He got up and handed her the sheet of paper; and just then the bell rang.

'Don't Holloway know how to write notation yet?' Barry asked aloud; and as Jeanne got up with Debbie she saw the teacher tuck Jon's song away in her briefcase. Wow, she thought; just think of having a copy of one of his songs.... Someday he's gonna be famous; and then that piece of paper will be worth millions of dollars....

That night, Jeanne dreamed of Jon and Dave Holloway marching in with guitars and performing the song they had written for the entire class. Jon had got an A-plus for the course and spent the rest of the period signing autographs. But the next day was only normal. A few people asked Mrs Hampton what had become of Jon's song and, during the hubbub of the free-composition session, she finally admitted she liked it, especially the lyric through the middle eight bars with its Romantic simile and metaphor. The song entitled simply 'You' was indeed written for the most part in iambic tetrameter; but she conceded she was not familiar enough with the works of Dante to tell if he had only been leading her on. Jon's spell of detention on Thursday consisted of a conference about what he planned to do with his writing talents after high school. Mrs Hampton wanted to know if he had ever considered an early graduation, although by now it was unfortunately too late in the year for that, and what universities he had contacted. Invariably, however, Jon would change the subject, like an unsavoury politician adroitly dodging incriminating queries from a nosy press; and though Mrs Hampton was left frustrated at not getting any straight answers from him she felt goosepimples all over to perceive the breadth of his intellect.

Mrs Hampton had begun to worry that this conspicuously gifted student had never received proper academic counselling, and she discussed the issue with some of Jon's past and present teachers. All concurred that someone of such extraordinary learning potential should be encouraged as ardently as possible. But despite their best efforts they had all been stymied by his indifference with regard to furthering his formal education. He seemed to take all his extraordinary talents for granted, as though he were willing only to grow up with normal people his age and with no special consideration. Mrs Donovan agreed fully with her that it seemed 'a crime not to grant him the opportunities to freely create in a more challenging environment.' The two agreed to put forth a concerted effort to cultivate Jon's interest in attending university and vowed to contact his parents whenever they encountered his resistance.

* * *

Ricky rode his bicycle to the Cavaliere house where he found Jon bent over the engine of his car in the back driveway. Over the engine's whooping he made his presence known, largely by waving. Jon was concentrating on adjusting the supercharger that he and Dave had installed on the Caprice during the week. The performance of the new induction system was not up to Jon's expectations and he was frustrated in trying to improve it. 'Man,' he complained; 'I don't know *shit* about this thing!'

'What's this, the new souper?'

Jon made a little laugh at the nickname. 'Yeah; the new souper all right. Holloway really put this turkey on; I don't know a thing about it. Just the theory, you know....' The idle was set high, at about two thousand. Jon laid his screwdriver to an adjustment screw in the carburettor casting and the exhaust note seemed to get a little heavier. 'Shit,' he said aloud; '*that* don't sound too bad!'

'Sounds good to me,' Ricky said, sipping from a cold can of Orange Crush without a clue either way.

'Man; I've been messin' with this thing for three days, and I *still* don't know how the hell it's supposed to be when it's right. Son-of-a-bitch Holloway's just like a girl; you know? Always breathin' down your neck when you're tryin' to get somethin' done; but where is he when you need him? Hell if *I* know.'

'Hellifino,' Ricky shrugged. 'Check there.'

Jon shook his head, lest the levity spoil his bad mood. It was typical of Ricky to intentionally belittle profound concepts, to crack a joke at just the moment when everything became too grave to bear. He was a born prankster, having had more than his share of corrective discipline for naughtiness in and out of school. But perhaps that hare-brained silliness was what most appealed to Jon; for he could admire anyone who gave the appearance, as opposed to the actual attitude, of refusing to take the gravity of life too seriously. That was something he might have liked to see in himself.

At first one might have thought that Dave Holloway and Ricky Denning would have made odd bandmates. Dave seemed far too serious about his artistic and organisational pursuits, and Ricky's infantile humour could at times try the patience of a saint. But that was exactly why the two needed each other. Since the beginning of their musical partnership Jon and Bob had come to see Ricky's true worth too, as both a dedicated musician and a reliable friend. His positive spirit and resilient nature were of great relief during those tedious moments; and they all respected his genuine respect for all of them. In many ways he was everyone's little brother; but when he was truly needed Ricky was more than able, and ever willing, to step in to guide the others like the natural leader he really was.

Jon readjusted the idle down to its usual rate, carefully aligning the linkage between the two carburettors every half-turn or so. The engine took on its familiar aggressive loping, due to the camshaft that was ground only for high-end horsepower. Jon let out a laugh. 'Hah! Son-of-a-bitch sounds like a joker! Nobody'd ever believe this bitch was *in* here!'

The faint ticking of the solid valve lifters sounded more prominent than the humming of the supercharger belts. 'Sounds like a piece of shit,' Ricky said dryly.

'*Right!*' They both laughed. 'So; do we go for a spin, and check it out?'

'We gotta be at Chris's, remember.'

The band did have a practice session scheduled for this afternoon. Jon acknowledged it with a nod. 'Shit– that's right. It's damn near three now. Well; let's go, so we can get back here and pick up my guitar.' He wiped off his hands on a rag and shut the bonnet.

Jeanne and her mother had taken the afternoon of fine spring weather to do some shopping together. At just three-thirty they were heading north on Route 9 towards Benton. 'So,' asked Mrs Banfield; 'who's the new guy Patti was telling me about?'

Jeanne looked at her. '*New* guy? But Patti's been seeing Brian since–'

'No, honey,' she smiled; '*your* new guy. Patti seems to think he's pretty special; but she says you never talk to him.'

'Oh,' Jeanne said, and blushed, embarrassed that her friends would report to her mother about such things. Still she recognised the catharsis in having to talk about it. 'Well; he's just a guy, you know.... We had a class together in junior high; and like now he has this really cool car, and he sings in a band... but like I don't think he even remembers me.' She thought to spare her any further detail. When she had last talked to her about him, it had been after that episode at the lake, almost two years ago; and surely now, after all her excited romantic raving at the time, she could not expect her mother to understand how that same young man still captivated her, even more so now than ever.

'Oh, dear,' her mother laughed; 'I can't believe that. And you remember him?'

'Well; yeah; but– He's really cute, you know.'

Mrs Banfield was well aware of her daughter's taste in young men; it was sufficiently sensible to give her no cause for worry. 'Well yes,' she said; 'and I know how these things can go on and on, and sometimes they just fade away and you forget them; but sometimes, they actually do grow into something wonderful, like when you find he feels the same way about you.'

'Yeah; I guess,' Jeanne said quietly, and thought how wonderful indeed that would be.

'You never know, child. It may happen, and it may not; but the best thing about these things is the way they make your day so exciting, and keep you in interesting daydreams.'

Jeanne smiled then, happy that her mother had always been able to recognise the very romantic notion she had been thinking. They were very much alike in that way and, having no sister, Jeanne had always felt very comfortable sharing her personal feelings in her mother's company. 'Yeah,' she said; 'that's very true.'

Mrs Banfield glanced down at the speedometer. 'Oh, no— I just realised why everyone's been whizzing by us. I'm only doing fifty.' She accelerated the big green Plymouth gently to fifty-five miles per hour, the legal limit.

Jeanne shifted a little sideways in her seat. All of a sudden the silver Caprice belonging to Jon Cavaliere, with Ricky Denning in the passenger seat, blew past in the offside lane. New supercharger wailing, that deep baritone exhaust note close behind, it was by them in an instant, doing at least eighty. Her head spun in a flash; the car was gone. She let out a little sigh and felt her stomach tingle.

'I suppose it's all well and good to keep up,' her mother said anxiously, somewhat flustered herself; 'but, you know, there are some people who take it too far. I always wonder what makes someone drive so fast, and risk getting tickets or causing accidents just to save a few minutes.... A driver like that can be very dangerous on the road.'

In light of this point Jeanne decided to not tell her mother that the driver of the speeding silver Chevrolet and the topic of their last conversation were one and the same and, instead, spent the rest of the afternoon browsing aimlessly about the Benton shopping arcade and daydreaming about what it would be like to cruise in Jon Cavaliere's beautiful silver car on Route Nine at eighty miles per hour.

* * *

Almost every day, Jeanne and Patti and Anne walked to school together, a routine they had kept since fourth grade. The spring mornings were especially the nicest, wet with dew that glimmered jewellike in the glowing sunshine. Jon Cavaliere's car had become a familiar sight to them, always parked in the same place in the yard out back, where Chris Santana and some of his student-council friends had mischievously stencilled *JCC* in bold yellow letters on the tarmac. Sometimes the car was reversed in and Jeanne would get a chill of excitement down her spine at seeing the pretty wine-red script of *Spellbinder* across the silver front edge of the bonnet. It was only when they were exceptionally early that the car was not there before them.

One morning when they were a few minutes later than usual, though not quite behind enough to be tardy to homeroom, they turned as always to walk up through the car park from the rear gate on Atlantic Parkway. Jon Cavaliere drove hard into the parking aisle at the opposite end and stopped the Caprice in his customary space amidst a great protest from his tyres. By the time Patti and Anne and Jeanne had come to the car he had already locked it up and run off towards the industrial-arts wing with his guitar case and schoolbooks. Jeanne sighed, looking over the car as they passed. The platinum-silver paint was perfectly clean, having been recently waxed, and the car looked just as it always did, except for one small thing.

Undoubtedly it had been Jon himself, with that delicate artistic flair, who had hand-painted a small black-freckled red strawberry on the lower right corner of his boot-lid. The little painting was no more than an inch-and-a-half across, yet full of detail, including thin black veins in its two little white leaves.

Jeanne smiled at this, seeing no significance to it at all except that it was adorably cute and a welcome delight to see. It only reinforced to her that Jon Cavaliere was an individual and different in positive, enriching ways. He was above everyone else, not merely unique. He was outstanding among high-school boys.

The strawberry brightened her whole day.

* * *

Chapter 3

Comin' down fast

The public-address system was trying hard to be heard above the bustling talk and motion of the students. Outside, low, dark storm clouds were just beginning to emit large drops of rain down into the courtyard. The week's weather for the most part had been little but grey skies and aggressive breezes, culminating in the thunderstorm now upon everyone at Wilshire High.

Jeanne sat sullenly and stared out the window. The voice of Chuck West, however appealing he may have been in person, only added to the dull buzz in her ears. In four of her six classes there had been major tests today. Biology had proved a godsend when Mr Reilly awarded almost thirty minutes of free study which was, in the unwritten tradition of all students before them, liberally interpreted to mean free conversation. And, in the unwritten tradition of all student-council presidents before him, Chuck West had taken the last five minutes of a Friday school session to augment his morning homeroom announcements.

–'And that shutout over the Hawks of Jefferson Township takes the Falcon booters to the regionals at East Dunham on Monday! Bus-trip tickets are still available from Student Council, but they are going fast! Good show, varsity soccer!'

How boring a free period is, thought Jeanne. Thank God it's Friday, but that's about all I can be glad for.... I wish Patti had something to say, because I really don't and I bet she's thinking I'm mad at her or something....

'Hey, Jeannie. Aren't you glad cheer practice is over?'

'Oh; yeah....'

'All we've got left is the soccer championship, and then the JV splash party....'

'Yeah....' That party I could look forward to.... Jeanne thought, her chin in her hand. I wish they'd just ring the bell. I mean: I don't care when the seniors have to pick up their caps and gowns; the girls' field-hockey tryouts don't interest me; I picked up my yearbook yesterday and my school ring last week; and however sexy Chuck West is, I'm tired of listening to him....

–'But before we wrap it up for this week there's just one more special message you should hear and so I'll turn it over to Skip MacRae! Skip?'

Oh; skip it, thought Jeanne; just ring the bell and let me go home.

—'Hey, all you rock-and-rollers out there in rock-and-roll land; Skip MacRae here with an invitation to the *whole* student body to come on out and experience Wilshire's *third* annual *Concert Contest*! That's right: *seven* of the township's best nonprofessional bands competing through their magnificent musical medium to pick up the title of Wilshire High's *best* rock-and-roll band! Come one, come all to dig the yesterday sounds of Marty's Menagerie, the disco-motion of Swat, and the dyn-o-mite power of Thunderbolt, plus a special return visit by the reigning champ, *Wipeout*, with Donny Pelose! Just one show only: tomorrow night, Saturday, May Eighteenth, in our own Wilshire High auditorium! Tickets go on sale at the door for two dollars; show starts at seven sharp for *four* solid hours of *rock and roll*! Get there early and cheer for your favourite group; that's tomorrow *night!*'

Chuck took the microphone again for his traditional sign-off. —'And that's all for this week, folks! Catch you up with all the latest news, *Monday!*'

Patti was tapping her shoulder. 'Hey, Jeannie!'

'What?'

'Are you going?'

'Going where?'

'Going to the concert contest.'

'Oh,' Jeanne sighed; 'I don't know….'

'You don't sound too excited,' Patti said.

'Well; I'm not really up to anything at all right now, and I don't think I'm gonna do anything this weekend, so….'

'What,' Patti smiled; 'didn't Bobby ask you?'

'Well; even if he did, I'd still….' Jeanne shrugged. '*You* know.'

'Yeah,' Patti said; 'we all go through days like that.' She laughed a little. 'I had thought to go with Debbie, you know, since she's such a rock-and-roll fan; and so if you feel better, why don't you come with us? It should be a lot of fun, with all that good music, and the excitement, and the great-looking guys….'

Jeanne smiled a bit; the event as Patti depicted it did sound inviting. The bell rang. The girls gathered up their books and handbags and started to the door. 'I don't know,' Jeanne said, following most of the other students out. 'Call me tomorrow and I'll let you know.'

Bobby Crocker waited for her in the corridor, with Debbie Blake who was still going on from an earlier conversation, saying, 'Yeah; but what *I* want to know is *why*. I mean it can't be a sudden *fad*, when nobody even *knows*….' She looked and saw Patti and Jeanne then. 'Hi, guys. Hey; maybe *you'd* know—'

'Know what?' wondered Patti.

Bobby smiled specially for Jeanne. 'Hi.'

'Hi, Bob,' she sighed wearily.

'Jeannie, what's the matter?' he asked her. 'You sound really out of it.'

'Oh; I don't know....'

'So hey; well how about tomorrow; huh? You wanna go to the show with us? Marty's gonna get us all in for free.'

'Oh, Bob, I don't know. I'm still trying to figure out how I'm gonna make it through tonight....'

He smiled and slipped an arm across her shoulders. 'So, hey; tonight, then. Me and you. We could maybe catch Smokey at the Jury Box....'

'Oh, really, Bob, I'd love to; but I'm just so worn out. I think I might just end up going to bed early....'

'Dag, Jeannie!' he teased, stepping back then; 'it's *Friday*! You can't be *that* out of it!' He laughed. 'Yo; you sure you're not pregnant?'

She managed to smile at his well-intentioned humour. 'Now *that* much I'm *sure* of,' she said, and they all laughed.

Two boys pushed their way past them, as they were all standing still in the crowded corridor, and Bobby excused himself and went off down the wing for his locker. The three girls started up towards the front gallery. 'So Jeannie,' Debbie asked, 'maybe *you'd* know. Who's sticking the strawberries all over the place?'

Jeanne felt her jaw drop open. For five full seconds she stood and gaped at Debbie like a fool. '*Strawberries?*'

'Jeannie?' Patti asked, looking at her curiously. 'You mean you actually know what she's *talking* about?'

'*Look*!' Debbie said suddenly, and rushed up the corridor ahead of them. 'You guys think I'm crazy; but here's one right *here*!'

Patti and Jeanne turned and looked where she pointed, to behold a small round paper sticker, adhered as if randomly to the face of a student's locker door. Patti regarded it for one second and turned to Debbie, saying, 'All right; it's cute. What makes it so significant?'

'Well; it's just that they're all over the place—'

But Jeanne knew. The small black-freckled red strawberry, no more than an inch and a half across and yet full of detail, with thin black veins in its two little white leaves, was a perfect copy of the original. Realising where she had already seen that hand-painted original, she quivered with the excitement.

There had been a mystery like this before. Even now her imagination still reeled. Chris Santana had proclaimed the event like a town crier beforehand; and it had ended up involving exactly whom she ha.d wished would be involved from the start. Everything about it had been like one of her fantastic daydreams come true; and now, at this one small hint, her mind was racing at full speed. If the same two guys could be involved, she thought— and then of course there's the *same car*....

Suddenly she looked up; and Debbie and Patti were staring at her as if she had flushed ghostly white. But the colour was returning many times over. 'What do you know that we don't?' Patti drilled her.

'PJ's not here,' Jeanne said abruptly. 'Is PJ going?'

'Going where?'

'Look!' exclaimed Debbie. 'There's another one! And *another* one! I told you they were all over the place!'

Jeanne turned and saw, affixed to some passing stranger's notebook, the same red-and-white strawberry. It was no longer of any consequence to her that the strawberry decals existed. She assumed they would be seen everywhere by now. 'Is PJ going to the concert contest?'

'You still haven't told us that you're going,' Patti said to her.

'Oh; I'm *going*,' Jeanne said, perfectly convincing. 'I wouldn't miss it for the *world*.' She turned and stepped off up the corridor, leaving Patti and Debbie thoroughly baffled.

* * *

Wow, she thought; is this place *wild*! I've never *seen* this place like this! They should go this crazy at the basketball games.... The last concert they had here was like a funeral; but this is *insane*! It's got to be even wilder than the time we saw Grand Funk up in Hartford, and at least as loud.... The girls up front are screaming their heads off. The boys in back are yelling and throwing things. The couple in the next row has been necking on the floor for an hour, and there's an awful lot of sneakers and t-shirts flying around. The air smells like dope or something; and, if the two kids fighting in the aisle ahead of us don't stop soon, they'll kill each other. And the music's so loud I think I'm losing my hearing.... If everyone sat down there would never be enough seats; but then no-one could see the group....

'Jeannie!' Patti said loudly over the din. 'Isn't this exciting?'

'It's wild!' replied Jeanne.

'What?!'

'I said it's *wild*! It's really far-out!'

The fourth band, Short Circuit, concluded their final number, 'Dinosaur', with an ear-shattering A-chord and bowed, a bit too early. The curtains closed and the crowd roared.

'This is outasite!' Debbie bounced excitedly. 'I wonder who's gonna be up next!'

As after the previous performances, a ten-minute interval was scheduled to allow the band to clear the stage behind the curtains and to let the next act set up. It was a full fifteen minutes this time, and then Skip MacRae, the master-of-ceremonies for the evening, stepped out in front of the audience. 'All right, rock-and-rollers! This next group has been in practice for over a year and is finally ready for their public stage debut! The group leader is Dave Holloway on guitar, with Bob Prescott doing lead guitar, Jon Cavaliere on bass, and Ricky Denning on drums. So; without further ado, I give you: *The Strawberries*!'

A sudden chill of excitement and ecstasy blazed down Jeanne's spine as the audience cheered ‚and screamed their welcome. 'Oh, *wow*!'

Debbie shrieked, and she and Jeanne screamed along with everyone else. *The Strawberries*! Jeanne's mind shouted. It's really *true*! The curtains parted, and before they were fully open there began that familiar introduction to The Beatles' 'Revolution'. The same song they played at the park! Jeanne remembered, knowing she did not always recognise such things. It is the same band! I wonder if PJ is here yet.... She'll never know what she missed!

As Dave Holloway screamed into his microphone and sang in his best John Lennon, her eyes ricocheted across the stage, trying to recognise the boys she had seen before. Dave, in black trousers and a white tuxedo shirt, had a gorgeous rare Rickenbacker electric guitar; he was known among the rock-and-roll musicians in the area to be the kind of Beatles fan devoted enough to insist upon the same kind of guitar Lennon played. Jeanne doubted many people here would be able to say they knew him from having interrupted her English Composition class with a guitar two months ago. At stage centre, in jeans and a half-open ruffled white tuxedo shirt, normally-neat brown hair almost into his eyes, Bob Prescott played that waxed and polished mahogany Gibson SG guitar. Behind them, encircled by a bright-red metalflake drum kit and half a dozen cymbals, sat mop-haired Ricky, wincing a bit from the smoke of a cigarette stuck between his teeth. He was dressed in black trousers and a white tanktop shirt from the Wilshire High gymnastics team and, sure enough, there on the kick drum head was that red-and-white strawberry design, a foot in diameter, with *The Strawberries* painted above it in sharp black letters. There could be no mistake about Jeanne's assumptions now. Feeling her body tingle all over, she turned her attention to the bass-guitar player at stage left.

It was hard not to pay attention to him; he was very appealing in the tight black stage trousers and a tuxedo shirt like Dave's, only open almost to his navel. His instrument, that violin-shaped left-handed Hofner, was beautifully lacquered in high-gloss black, so shiny it looked like a mirror. Leaning into the microphone to sing a harmony with his best friend Bob, swinging that mop of almost-blond hair about and grinning with that dimpled smile that could make the girls swoon, he was painfully cute to Jeanne who stood and stared at him wondering how many other girls round her would go home dreaming about that cute bass-guitar player in The Strawberries.

'Jeannie!'

'What?!' she called, not moving her eyes.

'He's fabulous; isn't he?'

'Who?' Jeanne glanced at her.

Patti leaned over and spoke right into her ear, for her to hear. 'Your beautiful, gorgeous Jon Cavaliere, silly. Whom else would you notice?'

'Oh,' said Jeanne, unheard by Patti and unseen as she blushed in the low light of the room. She was still thrilled that her hunch had been right about the strawberry stickers. That would be one more thing to look forward to telling him, some day.

'He's very talented,' Patti said nonchalantly, as though regarding a work of fine art. 'They all are.'

'*Oooo*!' Debbie squealed; and a few other girls echoed her emotion. 'They're *dynamite!*'

'He's also very sexy,' Patti said to Jeanne, in a serious tone despite the volume of her voice. 'Sometimes I wonder how it can be that they say he hasn't got *one* girlfriend.'

Jeanne had to consider that, not without staring up at Jon Cavaliere and his open shirt and his shiny black bass guitar from the eighteenth row. It was not often that Patti used a word like 'sexy' in a normal conversation. Jeanne sighed. Surely there were other girls here having thoughts like that for the first time tonight too.

'All *right*!' called Dave Holloway, either because the song had ended with the words or because his friend Rob Alascan of Tobacco Road would have greeted an audience in the same way. 'All *right*! Good evening, people; how you all *doin'*?' He paused enough to allow the rowdy fans their earsplitting response. 'All right!' he cheered back at them; and Jeanne saw Jon give someone a little wave as though greeting a small child. She giggled at that. He looked perfectly at-home on the stage; and she thought of how often she had seen him act up in class as though the other students were actually his audience.

The whining hum of guitar feedback rose up and the band began 'I Feel Fine'. Dave sang the lead to this one also, and Jon and Bob sang high harmonies together, letter-perfect as per The Beatles' original recording. The crowd enjoyed it tremendously. They went from 'I Feel Fine' directly into 'Day Tripper', a healthy dose of work for Jon who both sang the lead and played the bass part where it belonged, at the octave position, whilst Dave alternately handled the rhythm guitar and tambourine duties. By now even the noisemakers at the back of the room were satiated. For the first time all night they were not bawling out the names of competing groups during a performance. Instead they hollered out other Beatles titles as requests. The judges were impressed. Here was a band that could actually keep this tough crowd at bay after just three songs. All eyes were up front, towards the four teenaged boys who played everything quickly, spiritedly, and musically and technically correctly.

'All right!' Dave said into his microphone. 'Jon and I, well, kind of came up with a little number here, which we'd like to play for you now....' He broke off there, seeing Jon laughing at him from across the stage. Some of the audience laughed too, though at precisely what they had no notion. 'What?' asked Dave, a little away from the microphone, pretending that the people should not hear him. 'Did I say that right?'

Jon laughed aloud then, and the crowd with him. 'No,' he said, a little away from his own microphone; 'you say'd that just fine.' He leaned in then and told the people, 'Rock-and-roll history in the making, folks.'

No-one really knew what that meant; but they all laughed and cheered anyway. Jon Cavaliere tended to make people laugh; Jeanne could so attest from experience. The audience and the judges enjoyed the playful banter, all impressed to find what natural entertainers these boys were. But Jeanne had never expected any less of them. She thought what a wonderful show they might have put on, had they more of the evening to play.

Bob began with an upbeat solo introduction on his beautiful mahogany SG; and so Dave announced, over the playing, 'A little Cavaliere-and-Holloway ditty called "Try It Out".'

The drums and bass guitar picked up their cues and Dave came in with his rhythm chords a little late, giving the song the feeling of a loose, casual jam-session. But the judges would not be fooled. Given the calibre of the boys' presentation so far, they had every reason to assume it was all being played according to plan.

Dave sang:

'Well if you like what you see why don't you try it out;
You've got nothin' to lose....'

Jeanne kept her eyes on Jon, watching him enjoying his new popularity. He bobbed about, shared the microphone with Bob for the Beatlesque backing vocals of 'Oooo, la-la' through the bridge and teased the girls in the front row with his foot whilst they tried to grab him. It bothered her, because, as he grew more and more popular by the second, he seemed to grow farther and farther away from her. Gone forever was the shy young gentleman she had met in seventh grade. Since then dozens of boys had expressed their attraction to her, and Patti liked to tell her they developed crushes on her from the mere sight of her smile, but there was something about Jon Cavaliere that had always seemed pure to her, as though he could only love the one who loved him so perfectly. She did not want to harbour that out of jealousy, since she did not really have him at all; but still she had always piled hope upon hope that hers would be the love that would be perfect for him. After tonight, Jon would choose one from a hundred spellbound fans; and all her love would mean nothing then.

'All right,' Dave said; 'since y'all are feelin' so *good*....' He waited, and the crowd let go with a few seconds of high-volume uproar. 'This one here is another one Jon and I came up with; it's a nice song, a love song; it's called "Lovely".'

Bob Prescott opened with some pretty guitar picking on the SG. The stage lights went down and left him in the spotlight, and he played alone for about a minute, just broken chords and a few spare licks thrown in, but it was certainly not quiet and the sweet ringing of the guitar was an effective pacifier. Ricky and Jon came in on their instruments with a tender punch to the rhythm that carried the guitar-picking at a brisk but pleasant gait. Dave swung his guitar round behind himself, leaned into the microphone, and sang.

'Oooo; am I dreaming? This can't be real;
It's just the kind of thing that I know you feel....'

Girls let go in swoons. Jeanne felt a wave of emotion shower down through her whole body at the mere thought of hearing this song, the one written by Dave Holloway and Jon Cavaliere that could melt the coldest female hearts. She had never heard 'Lovely' before; no-one had. It had been carried by rumour until now; and now Debbie was tugging on her sleeve and saying excitedly, 'This is *it*! This is the one I was telling you about! This is the one that *he* wrote!'

Jeanne gazed up at the stage, enthralled. The second verse brought Dave in on rhythm guitar, and he sang:

'Oooo; do you feel it? This must be love;
It's just the kind of thing that you're dreaming of....'

The melody, all up and down and contorted over a gently-descending chord progression, was hypnotic. Bob played a proper guitar solo with a beautifully delicate touch to notes high and long and loud; it was a true rock-guitar hero's solution to a soft, sincere song. Dramatically the intensity mounted and the key modulated from A to C. For the third verse Jon was then required to sing his high harmony that much higher; but the arrangement was exquisite and the vocals unwavering. The judges were taking notes, unwilling to let the one performance of the evening worth remembering escape their memories any more than it would inevitably.

Jeanne had fallen completely now. Whether she would have him all to herself or share him with a dozen others was of no importance any more. She only knew that she would have to do something. Maybe it would mean complimenting him on 'Lovely' right out aloud in class; but surely she could no longer leave Jon Cavaliere to chance.

The three Wilshire High students on the judging panel had not been given any more prior information about the competing bands or their members than what had been circulating about the student body as a whole. To them, The Strawberries were a fresh new act with a familiar repertoire, covering Beatles songs faithfully through devout admiration. The three local music instructors were startled to hear such quality original material from such young boys; there were club acts in the area vying for studio recording time who had not the inherent sensitivity to write lyrics as touching as 'Lovely' nor the stage presence to make a soft song so appealing to such a tough crowd. The three Wilshire High teachers were impressed most of all; perhaps the four members' academic reputations were well-known to them. All had distinct personalities that belonged more to the limelight than to the classroom. Ricky Denning was notorious for flirting with the girls and drumming incessantly on the desktop, preferring activity to sedentary study in mundane topics. Bob Prescott was known for meticulous research and a knack for making his work stand out, which showed in his artistic approach to playing guitar. The brash, outspoken Dave Holloway and the vivacious Jon Cavaliere were stealing the show, not as they did in class, but entirely unrestrained. The stage was their true element; and it was all too obvious now that grading them low with the intention of imparting academic discipline would never hold them down.

The next song was announced as yet another Holloway-and-Cavaliere composition, 'from some time ago'. It was a favourite of Jon's, properly done as a breathless plea from a young man with the excitement of love in his veins and only one thing in mind. The crowd were driven straight back into their screaming frenzy, which was where they wanted to stay anyway, remarkably eager and enthusiastic after such a soothing rest. 'If You Need It, You'll Get It' was an extremely potent piece, lasting almost five minutes, full of tightly-wound guitar riffs and a thumping bass-and-drums drive. It was nothing like what the band had played, so far; but it was not far out of their character. They were already rising above the level of mere school-age rock-and-roll aficionados. In the eyes and ears of their fellow students, they were as good as gold-record superstars.

Dave had the honour of saying alone, in a false deep voice, the title line, with only Ricky's drum spill as accompaniment. Girls screamed and squirmed in every corner of the room, firecrackers went off from the back rows and The Strawberries cranked into the second verse at full throttle. The guitars never stopped; when one completed the riff, the other echoed it. Jon and Dave alternated lead vocals and did harmonies for each other when applicable; at all other times they were all over the stage. It was dizzying to watch even one of them.

Bob stepped up to the edge of the stage to strike off a guitar solo as though delivering a Shakespearean soliloquy.　　The barrage of screaming notes brought cheers of delight from the rowdy boys across the back of the room.　He soared up the neck for four full bars with nothing but Ricky's drums playing behind him; and then the song took off again, Jon and Dave singing the refrain and playing the riff whilst Bob's guitar ran on ferociously above them and the girls of the front row leaned out onto the stage to try to grasp their feet.　The judges, disturbed at the volume, were nonetheless thrilled with the band's innate dexterity at manipulating the mood of the crowd.　Surely these boys were setting their sights far beyond a high-school popularity contest.

'If You Need It, You'll Get It' ended on an A and might have crashed to a halt there, if not for Ricky beating on the cymbals and thumping on the kick drum.　Bob took off on a wildly screeching E-seventh, high up on the neck.　Jon smiled, letting him go a few extra measures to allow the crowd a chance to guess before he stepped up to his microphone and began the well-known, yet rarely-played, 'Helter Skelter'.

He and Dave bounced along on their lowest E notes, with Ricky thundering away behind them at a breathtaking rate.　As they raced into the chorus Jeanne's spine was stinging as if filled with ice.　After each of the three cries of 'Helter-skelter!' comprising the refrain, there came a beefy descent of bass and guitar notes even more furious than those in the previous number.　The boys were lightning-quick with the riff; they had to be, playing it so much faster than the original record. By now 'If You Need It, You'll Get It' seemed like a sing-along folk song from generations past.　The mob were drilled into mandatory attention.　There would be no escape.

Jon Cavaliere's once-docile voice tore vehemently into the smoky air. At the start of the second chorus he screamed; and he and Dave and Bob all sang along, the three boys' voices both blending perfectly and remaining distinct from each other.　Even in so spirited a song they would sing well.

The instrumental passage consisted of the throbbing rhythm section and Bob's SG guitar piercing virgin ears with bent-string exercises in chilling chirps and wicked whines.　It was pure hell to Jeanne.　Never in her admittedly sheltered life had she been subjected to such vile volume and intensity.　The room was full of the sound; she could barely move enough air to breathe.　Her ears throbbed painfully.　The murderous musical madness infiltrated everyone in one way or another; tears of pain and fear streamed down Patti's cheeks whilst Debbie danced the Bump with some strange boy to their right.　Jeanne sat in her seat, surrounded by the acrid odour of narcotic cigarettes and the liquid missiles of beer and soda overhead, tortured by the incredible excesses about her, no longer caring to see Jon Cavaliere's performance nor anything else.   None of this had been foreseen in even her weirdest nightmares.

A girl in the front attempted to charge up onto the stage and, thwarted by the security guards, she tossed her shoes up there and then began to take off her t-shirt, probably to have something else to throw. As soon as she was escorted away there were three or four more just like her, one of whom got past security and to within five feet of Dave's elbow before the stage crew wrestled her back.   A firecracker shot its sizzling remains over the crowd and disappeared in the far left corner.   A brassiere went up into the air to the right.   Two large boys had become involved in a brawl in the aisle two seats to Patti's left. Insanity, Jeanne cried to herself, just insanity....

Above the two whining guitars Jon sang another verse and the three of them, plus nearly all the audience, sang the next chorus.   There came a second instrumental; they were extending the familiar arrangement of the recording on the album.   Bob hung onto his guitar, bending the string at the twenty-second fret up to the highest note he could hold, and whilst his finger inched down, the amplifier on the stage began to feed back eerily.   As the resonant tones found grooves about the room, amplified through five thousand watts of public-address system, the wail took on heavier and lighter textures, shredding the stiff, noxious air into an agony no-one could block out.

To Jeanne it was unbearable.   Clouds of circus smoke billowed out from canisters at the base of the drum riser platform, making the room smell as though the carpet were on fire.   Dave and Jon kept up that thumping rhythm with Ricky; the crowd kept up their wild behaviour. Some poor girl's panties flew up and landed on the stage, two loose t-shirts were draped across the drum stands and, incredibly enough, Jon had a strawberry-red brassiere swinging from the headstock of his guitar.   Bob merely stood there, stonelike, as though under some strong tranquilliser, glistening with sweat as the feedback swelled and ricocheted off the walls.   An empty beer bottle rocketed over Jeanne's head.   Two of the judges had left the jury table.

Dave and Bob chanted 'Cha-cha-cha-cha-cha-cha-cha-cha' in harmony as Bob ran his plectrum down his guitar strings.   A flash-pot went off on the stage.   The final chorus was doubled in length; the crowd seemed perfectly happy to prolong the pleasure of screaming along with the band.

Dave played the riff on that hollow-bodied Rickenbacker guitar, its tame tones and natural resonance never intended for such wicked amplifier distortion.   Despite Ricky's furious back-beat, Jon and Bob struck only one E note at the start of every two bars.   Jon went off with a few cantilevered vocals: 'Oh; look out, now!'   Jeanne and Patti found themselves screaming right along with everyone else; the roar of the crowd was deafening.   Jon could still be heard above them all, the treble frequencies of the public-address system stabbing them all in the eardrums:

'Yes she is;
Yes she is;
Comin' down fast,
And I'm not gonna break her;
Oh yeah.'

Bob took to railing away on the guitar, with every two-string bend he could think of to draw out the chaotic discord. Inner-ear torture had never been done like this. Jon continued with a few double-meaning phrases. Ricky over-drummed deliberately, incredibly energetic after so long without a rest; yet he showed no signs of tiring, perhaps due to his diet of submarine sandwiches and chocolate bars. Dave winced at each repetition of the riff; he had blisters on his fingers. Jeanne wanted out. Through the smoke and the people she could no longer see a clear aisle that had once been three or four seats away. She tried screaming 'I hate you!' straight at Jon Cavaliere who swayed about the stage with an insanely calm smile on his face and his bass guitar pointing in the wrong direction. Patti caught her as her feet gave way, fearing that Jeanne had fainted. The two of them fell back into the seats behind them, holding their hands tightly over their ears for their very survival, crying real tears. Jeanne clamped her eyes shut and whimpered to herself, 'Oh; I hate you, I hate you, I hate you....'

The last ten seconds were an underworld of pounding bass and ungodly feedback. Dave's foot was flooring his wah-wah pedal and Bob was yanking up on his tremolo bar as though to remove it by force. The sound-system representatives worried about how much their speakers could take. It was a wonder Chris Santana could to control things so dramatically; but there he was, safe in the projection booth at the rear of the auditorium, under a set of tight-fitting headphones, having turned the echo and reverberation devices up for full effect. Beside him Andrew Cavaliere went mad with the lighting controls. The sight and sound of a thousand unleashed hellions was Dave's reward as his sly smile told of his satisfaction. The concertgoers were entirely at the band's mercy.

'Helter Skelter' was over. What the crowd heard now was only their own ears recoiling from the aural bombardment. A thousand excited teenagers had been treated to a massive overdose of music-induced hysteria. Jeanne lay weeping on Patti's shoulder, weeping just like hundreds of other girls, her wishes only for all the pain and all the noise and all the people to just go away and, for a brief moment, for Jon Cavaliere to come and take her off to someplace soft and quiet and just hold her in his arms. The little daydream brought on by the notion seemed so real to her that she wept just to realise it would not come true. 'I love you,' she breathed; and Patti looked at her as if she had actually heard.

When she looked up again the curtains were closed. A pair of guards restrained a few emotional desperadoes from clambering up onstage. The Strawberries' twenty-four-minute set was now history, culminating in over eight minutes of the loudest, wildest, most raucous rock-and-roll. Jeanne was everything she had under The Strawberries' control wished she had not been: alive, sane, in love and still with her hearing ability, although there was a fierce ringing in her ears above everything else. She had wanted to blame or hate everyone whom she loved, including Patti and Debbie and Jon Cavaliere. All that remained was the howl of the crowd, the only constant all evening. It had come as a vicious shock to everyone, first for the music to be so pleasant and appealing, then to become so unbearably strong, and then for all that sound to die away so suddenly. The noisemakers were getting hoarse and their pleas less intense. A few girls about the room began to chant, 'More, more, more, more!' although as a whole the mob were calming down.

Behind that closed curtain, The Strawberries cleared the stage of their material possessions. The 'road crew', consisting merely of DJ Berryfield, Andrew Cavaliere, one of Andrew's friends and a helpful Mark Jenkins, quickly disassembled the drum kit and wheeled away the amplifiers. Jon leaned absently off to the left, wiping the sweat off his face with a terry towel and trying to keep himself upright. Someone handed him some Gatorade of which he downed about half before lowering the bottle. Bob approached him, drinking from another bottle, and swiped the towel off Jon's shoulder. Jon seemed not to care, or notice, and then said in a rough whisper, 'Know what I think?'

'Yeah,' said Bob, and nodded as he mopped the sweat from his face.

Dave came over to the two of them with a towel wrapt about his shoulders like a mink stole. 'Whaddiyou think?'

'We blew it,' Bob said seriously.

'Yeah,' said Jon, a little louder; 'let's pull the jam and truck the hell on outa here. Yo Ricky!'

'Yo!' Ricky skipped down the steps from the side of the stage.

'Get your shit offstage.'

'It's off, dude. I'm ready when you are.'

Jon turned about. The drums and cymbals on the platform were those of the next band, already being set up. The whole backstage area was abuzz with musicians and equipment handlers; it seemed impossible that anyone could know where all anyone's gear was. 'Hey,' called a tall black-haired boy from the centre of the stage; 'let's try to keep this shit straight! I just picked up Holloway's guitar stand!'

Dave looked up at the mention of his name but made no comment. In a second DJ was there to retrieve the overlooked stand from the other crew. Ricky was up on the drum riser again helping the next drummer adjust his kit and sharing a few tips. 'Yo!' Bob yelled when he saw him. 'Let's *go*, RD; let's get *truckin'*!'

'Yeah, yeah,' Ricky said, and came down to rejoin his mates. 'Look, dude; just 'cause we fucked up *our* set–'

'Shut up,' Dave warned him.

Bob collared Ricky to pull him aside. 'Do you really think we fucked up?' he asked Ricky quietly.

'Well shit, man; I can see the crowd too–'

'All right; we're all in agreement here,' Dave said, sounding very weary. 'Let's just book.'

'Yeah,' Jon said quietly, after a moment's contemplation; 'we're fucked-up good. First, though, I think I'm gonna go puke.'

'*Don't*,' Dave told him, already feeling giddy over the inevitable smell of vomitus.

Out on the floor the scene had become much more civilised. The next band, Apollo, went on with a few Pink Floyd selections and a few older songs from Emerson, Lake & Palmer. The five-man outfit scored well with the judges simply because no-one became too excited over them. But Marty's Menagerie, formerly known as Dr Zoom And The Zingers, played all nostalgic hits which did not go over well at all. With their leather jackets and greased hair, the seven boys put on a wonderfully staged show, full of authentic details from the late-1950s era of early rock-and-roll. Unfortunately tonight they were in the wrong place at the wrong time. Poor Marty never should have been subjected to an audience yelling out requests such as 'If You Need It, You'll Get It'. The Menagerie closed with 'Melancholy Baby' and bowed out almost five minutes early; and their second bid for the annual concert-contest title perished in the wake of that new little band Dave Holloway had put together.

The jury were in a quandary. Last year's champion, Wipeout, had gone on at 7.05, with the idea of being a standard by which all the other bands would be graded. They had far more real stage experience than these newer, younger bands and were already playing small clubs about the area. But not one of the other acts had shown any similar promise, except maybe The Strawberries.

The Strawberries were not a top-notch band. Perhaps at one time they would be, maybe quite soon, as they seemed to have the right combination of talent and motivation, but for now they were not wholly professional in calibre. Still, they had put on the most exciting show of the night; and their obvious ability, sensitivity and sex appeal could not go unrewarded. It seemed to the jurors at once that no-one had seemed better polished than Wipeout and yet they had not intended for the semiprofessional Wipeout to go home with this year's prize. Skip MacRae tried to establish order out front whilst the panel postponed their decision.

Someone in the crowd took the initiative to call out 'Wipeout!' at the top of his lungs. Several others joined in, on all other sides. The security guards brought in for the event were not able to deter all physical contact.

Patti turned to Jeanne, who was just greeting Debbie's return from another corner of the room. 'So, Jeannie!'

'What?' Jeanne whirled about.

'Need I ask whom *you* want to win?'

'Strawberries,' Jeanne said seriously, and made a little smile as she stared up at the closed maroon curtains.

'Me too,' Patti smiled, sounding very calm and collected as always. 'They've got all the talent.'

'Oo; don'tcha just *love* em?' Debbie chirped, all aquiver with excitement. 'God; I hope they do make some records some day because I'm gonna buy every single *one!*'

Steve, Anne and PJ found them then, and PJ was surprised to see Jeanne had come to the show after all. 'So, Jeannie; you made it; huh?'

'Yeah,' Jeanne smiled; 'well; Patti kind of dragged me....'

As personally as possible in such an atmosphere PJ said, 'Hey; and so what do ya think of you-know-who; huh?'

'Huh? Oh; yeah; well....'

'I think he's fantastic.' She turned to Patti straight away. 'Hey; and so where's Bri? Have you seen him?'

'Oh; no,' Patti said, looking about; 'but I'm sure he's here; I mean he *is* a concert person....'

Steve got next to Jeanne and was able to look her in the eye. 'Are you okay?' he asked.

'Uh, yeah; well; yeah....' She brushed some sweaty strand of hair aside and tried to maintain something of her composure.

'Your eyes are all red, and everything.'

Jeanne knew she looked a fright. 'Oh; well; uh....'

'Been doing some screaming, I guess; huh?' He nudged her a little.

But Steve was only teasing her. 'Yeah,' she admitted; 'well; you know....'

The jury elected one student who nervously stepped out onto the stage to bring the news: 'The judging panel has decided to declare it a *tie,* and the two bands in question are to each do one number or forfeit. The tie is between Wipeout and The Strawberries.'

The crowd went wild. All kinds of comments were loudly aired, very few without some profane language contained within. Bottles and cans went flying as people vented their frustration. Fist-fights broke out almost instantaneously. With diplomatic severity Donny Pelose, the popular lead singer and group leader of Wipeout, met with Dave Holloway backstage. 'Oh; so Holloway, so what's gonna happen about the goddamn tie; huh? You wanna shoot for it?'

Jon stepped right in front of Pelose with his second bottle of Gatorade. Although half a foot shorter and thirty pounds lighter, he fixed his eyes squarely at the tall nineteen-year-old and said, 'Tell him he and his stupid head music can go on first, Dave.'

Dave smiled, content to lean back and watch the confrontation. 'You and your stupid head music can go on first, Pelose,' he said.

'*You* heard him,' Jon told Pelose.

'You didn't have to tell me, ya faggot,' Pelose came back.

Jon batted an eye at him. 'Only "faggot" in sight's you, sweetie.' The other three Strawberries laughed.

Pelose seemed a little disturbed at that. Jon saw him glance about to see if any of his comrades was within earshot. None was. 'Look, ya little prick; you just watch it, or I'll bust your ass open right here.'

'Oooo,' Jon groaned, feigning awe, or fear. 'Oo; I'd better watch it, or this faggot's gonna bust my ass open right here. Oooo; the great Donny *Osmond* is after me now!' He turned, stepped away and turned back to Pelose again. 'You know, Pelose, you're awful fuckin' deadly.'

Pelose smiled cockily. 'Yeah; ain't I, though?'

'Yeah, dude,' Bob drawled; 'you're pretty fuckin' deadly all right.'

Dave laughed then. Pelose turned from the others and said, 'So what the hell's happenin', Holloway? I'm goin' on first?'

'Yeah,' Dave said seriously, stepping away from the parked amplifier that was not his, with his arms still folded across his chest; 'you might as well. I don't care who goes on first. It's only a goddamn contest.'

'You better get going,' Bob told Pelose then. 'That captive audience out there is waiting to see your *last performance*.'

'Yeah,' laughed Pelose; 'at this cheap-ass piss-hole.'

'Oh; right!' scoffed Ricky.

'Yeah; like a bottom-of-the-barrel band like Wipeout could go pro!' Bob jeered.

Dave laughed at that. 'No; seriously,' Jon said calmly, as though sincerely coming to the defence, 'some desperate asshole'll pay 'em ten bucks a night to half-fill some sleazy Riverside bar.'

The other three laughed at that. Pelose only winced. 'Yeah,' he retorted; 'well; you assholes are gonna have a tough act to follow, here.'

'Yeah,' Ricky taunted; 'tough as in hard to *chew*, just like all the meat you bite!'

'Tough as in not well-done,' Bob added. 'You wait till you see what we put on. It'll be a song to remember, that's for *damn* sure.'

'Yeah,' Pelose told them; 'well; you assholes are all bubblegum anyway. This is a pretty stupid audience anyway.'

'Bubblegum!' Dave laughed. He had never thought of himself that way.

'Yeah; bubblegum,' Pelose told him. 'You can have your cute little pageant here anyway. Who gives a shit?'

'Wait,' Bob called after him; 'I got a shit for you–'

'Just wait,' Pelose smirked, and turned and went away.

'Just wait, just wait,' Jon mimicked him, like a child. Dave laughed again.

'My; what an asshole,' Ricky observed with mock gentility, when Pelose was out of range.

Pelose hopped back up on the stage where his band, behind the two sets of closed curtains, had already begun setting up again. Dave watched him a moment and turned to his own lead guitarist to ask, 'So all right there, stupid, just what is this number that'll be "a song to remember"?'

Bob only stared blankly back at him. 'Hell if *I* know.'

'Do I know that one?' Ricky wondered.

Jon whirled on them all. 'Oh; now that's just *great*!' he raved, and slung his towel off into the room somewhere. 'That's just fuckin' *great*! That asshole is gonna beat us! That asshole is actually gonna fuckin' *beat* us!'

'Calm down,' Dave told him quietly, 'and let me think.'

'Well,' sighed Bob; 'so much for the *tour de force* method.'

'Really,' Dave agreed, and made a little laugh.

Jon looked at the two of them and then at Ricky who had nothing else to offer. 'Yeah; well; you idiots can fuckin' joke all you want, then. I'm gonna go puke.'

'Yo, dude, cool it,' Dave tried; but Jon had turned and gone off towards the backstage toilets.

Chris Santana, cool and calm as always in his crisp white jeans, strode into their midst and said, 'All right, dudes; I was just rappin' with Barry, and he said– Hey. Where's Jon?'

'Bathroom,' said Ricky after a moment, as the others seemed unwilling to answer for him. 'So what's the plan, here, Manager?'

'All right,' said Chris, drawing a breath then; 'okay.' In a softer tone, he said, 'All right; remember the first slow number we rehearsed, years ago, the first *slow* number....'

'*Slow* number?' Ricky asked him. 'That ain't *even* a gamble, dude. This crowd–'

'No; *shhh*.' Chris ushered them all away from the light switches, which the stage crew were wanting to use. 'Look; I already sent Barry and Drew over to the garage for the acoustic guitars– the ones we didn't think we'd need. Should be back in a coupla minutes. Now; do you dudes know what I'm talkin' about? What do you think– uh,

Bob?'

'So much for the *tour de force* method,' Dave said; 'uh, Bob–'

They turned about for a reply; but Bob was no longer amongst them. Indeed their oft-acclaimed lead guitarist, ever so studious, had turned to his instrument in time of crisis. Already he was halfway across the room, sitting up on top of someone's unused speaker cabinet, gently finger-picking a chord progression on his unamplified SG.

'Yeah; all right,' Dave smiled, as they all had recognised the tune. 'Jon's favourite song; right?'

'And so that'll be why we're doin' it.' Chris suddenly turned to Mark and DJ and resumed his role as a man of action. 'All right! We need Ricky's drums, but not the floor toms, and say about a three-foot barstool from the music room....'

Jerry Fisher and Bobby Crocker found Steve and the five girls and crowded into the small space Patti and Jeanne had managed to hold all evening. Jeanne felt much more secure in the company of so many good friends but kept herself detached from any personal conversation. Bobby again asked her for a date; and she managed to comment on something PJ said then and thus put him off. Wipeout went on, hacking through a very choppy rendition of Roger Waters' 'Money', a piece they obviously did not do often. The players were unable to carry the seven-eight meter consistently, and Donny himself seemed a little lost. Doubtless half the crowd would not care. Wipeout had their following; and there were quite a few heated disagreements between the fans, even including hot-tempered Bobby Crocker and a Beatles-cum-Strawberries fan to their right; and as Jeanne clung to the edge of her seat anxiety set in about the next and last number of the night.

It was nearly 11.30 when, without introduction, the maroon curtains parted again. The four long-haired boys were back, Jon with his open tuxedo shirt and jet-black Hofner bass guitar to stage right, Ricky with an abbreviated trap on the platform and, all the way over to the left, a good five or six yards from the drum riser, Bob Prescott sitting with his foot up on the rung of the stool, holding his handmade Spanish flattop acoustic guitar in the proper classical position. Two microphones on low stands stood before him, and there was only one for the vocals, almost directly in front of Jon. No-one knew what to make of this arrangement; but just as it seemed the crowd would calm down and let them play, song titles and other comments went up in loud, hoarse voices about the hall. Nothing happened on the stage for what seemed like minutes on end.

Dave Holloway stepped out, laid his six-string acoustic guitar down on the carpeted drum platform, and stepped slowly over to Jon's microphone. At first he seemed almost statuesque, but then his face softened into a smile for someone special in the front row. The crowd began to quiet then. His heart hammering in his chest, he turned a little and looked at Jon. Jon made a slight nod and then stepped back and looked down. Jeanne saw Dave lower his head and take a breath, and she wondered what was really supposed to be going on up there.

'Uh; all right....' Dave's voice sounded weirdly ominous in the large room. 'All right; uh, people; just a minute....' But the crowd's abrupt tranquillity was frighteningly eerie. Dave drew another breath. 'All right; that's right.... Look; we don't know how it came around to this tie, but I guess we have one last number to play, so.... So; we just wanted to say that the noise, and the cheering and yelling and all; well; that's cool, you know, 'cause this is rock-and-roll. But like, the grass, and the booze, and all that; this ain't the place for that. I mean we're all here to have a good time, and all; but like people don't have to be fightin' and actin' stupid over something like this.... You came to cheer for your own favourite band, whether it's us or somebody else, and that's cool; but remember: it's still only just a contest; and we don't really care who wins or loses. We're only here so everybody has a good time. So; well; if anybody doesn't want to go along with that, just having a good time, and all; well; you know, you can leave and go home, right *now*. We'll wait.'

The four of them just looked back at the audience from where they were and waited. No-one moved, let alone got up to leave. The big auditorium, at nearly one-and-a-half times capacity, was deathly silent. Dave looked nervously about the half-lit room, suddenly terrified that he had committed the worst *faux pas* imaginable. In truth no-one there had expected a completely complacent reaction. The entire audience were just staring mutely back at him.

'Uh; all right,' Dave said carefully; 'if we can assume that those of you still here are interested in hearing it, then we'd like to perform this last song here, an older number, one of the first things we ever played as a band. Hopefully you'll be satisfied.'

He stepped back and walked casually back to his guitar, aware that they were all watching him in anticipation. The room and the stage lights went down. From Dave's guitar came the opening notes; and Jon and Ricky came in almost at once. There was a hint of feedback, probably from Dave's pickup, but it faded away as he found a comfortable position. Bob only sat on the stool, his hands folded over the upper curve of his guitar body, waiting for a cue that apparently was not due soon.

The rear of the stage grew darker, and slowly the stage came into a state of orange half-light, with the effect of an electric sunrise. Jon was only in shadow as there were no front lights yet. He waited eight measures instead of the record's four, just to feel more sure of himself. He had said often he thought it sounded better that way anyway and, fortunately, having had no opportunity to rehearse or even discuss the point beforehand, Dave and Ricky knew to expect this. Recognising the song at once, the audience were breathless in awe. Jon edged closer to the microphone, as a red light and a yellow one were brought up to land on his forehead. As clearly as he could, he opened his mouth and sang the memorable lyric to McCartney's 'And I Love Her.'

Bob came in for the second verse, playing arpeggio chords as one soft blue light lit him from above. The sheer delicacy of the arrangement and the precipitous risks inherent in a live performance had the audience on the edge of their seats. Everyone anticipated some dramatic catastrophe. Yet none came.

Dave and Ricky were still half in darkness, the steel-stringed acoustic guitar and the ride cymbal ringing together beautifully. The maroon curtain went pink in the light, as the bridge began on C-sharp-minor. Entirely alone Jon's dulcet voice seemed exquisite, sweet and sensitive despite having just rendered 'Helter Skelter' at full volume and full force a short while before. No-one complained at the dramatic change of musical mood. They were all just mesmerised in delight.

At the end of the chorus, all at once the light on Jon went down halfway, a spotlight came up on Bob, the key signature rose a halftone, and Bob began his instrumental solo in F. It was not the guitar's best key. Jon held his breath, resisting the urge to turn and watch him, conveying instead the impression that Bob could be trusted to play the dainty classical-guitar part without the slightest slip. In fact, there was not the slightest slip. Bob's fingering was perfect, even breathtaking; actual gasps went up about the room as the audience beheld the acoustic-guitar talent of the seventeen-year-old on the stage. As the red and yellow lights faded out, leaving the stage in a bluish twilight, Jon let out a sigh too. The home stretch, he thought, and took his breath.

But the song was now a halftone higher, and the notes required some extra stretching. Jon's voice may have seemed a little leaner; yet in that slight strain was every evidence of elevated sincerity, lending the song precisely what it needed as a panacea. The figures of the introduction were the finale also, with Ricky tapping one cymbal whole and Bob playing the broken chords he had taken up after his solo. For six measures the lights eased down to near-darkness, but came up again on the seventh, for that abrupt but welcome D-major which made every one of the judges smile in appreciation. With a proper bow together, The Strawberries submitted their bid for first place.

The audience were on their feet. Clapping and cheering like they had not done all night, they would give a five-minute ovation for a two-and-a-half-minute performance. The boys on the stage waved happily and hurried off; and the curtains slid closed as Skip MacRae bounded out with the instantaneous, unanimous decision from the jury.

'Ladies and gentlemen!' he yelled, barely audible, into his microphone. 'Ladies and gentlemen! Tonight's winner: *The Strawberries!*'

Pandemonium broke loose as the volume increased to a bone-chilling din. People rushed the stage and dodged the curtains to meet with the band. In from the front gallery poured more admirers, crowding down the backstage steps with loudly-proclaimed compliments. Dave, Bob, Jon and Ricky were mobbed by literally dozens of girls, all pleading for favours, from autographs and dates to well beyond. It was impossible to even acknowledge each individual, let alone grant any requests; yet they were tugging at their clothes and pushing hands through their hair like infatuated fanatics. Bob actually threw a five-hundred-dollar amplifier into the back of Dave's van, Andrew made off with his brother's bass guitar like a bandit and Ricky left tyre marks all over the rear courtyard with the van, in their vain efforts to escape the siege.

Jon was especially uncomfortable with such a sudden excess of praise. He considered that only minutes ago they were fighting for their very survival; for to lose in front of this crowd to an act like Wipeout could easily have spelt an end to the band with the catchy name which they had adopted only a month before. Now, the once-sceptical audience would enthrone them their sole idols. It seemed terribly fickle to Jon; and he wanted no part in their gratification beyond being polite for the sake of positive public relations.

He called for Chris above the heads in the tightly-packed front gallery, glad to be out from the tedious atmosphere of the backstage area. Half the people went right by him out here, not recognising him out of a performing element even in his stage clothes. Chris was calling for Jon too, and it was not until they were only ten feet apart that they could even make verbal contact with each other. Jon was about to make one desperate lunge towards his objective; but a strong hand tugged on the end of his arm from behind. He had no room even to turn round and look through the crowd, and so he was dragged backwards, tripping over a few feet, until he was cast free inside what was, incredibly enough, the girls' toilet.

The door bolt was snapped shut; and Jon turned at last. Barring his exit was a cute girl fetchingly dressed in short denim cutoff shorts, loose sandals and a taut red cotton tanktop shirt. Her sweaty light-brown hair was styled in sort of a wavy shag, dropping just to her shoulders. Those shoulders gave a very comely shrug; and it became all too apparent that those big blue eyes were very intent upon him.

With the shrug came a heated sigh; and Jon inferred all he wanted to infer. He put on a slight smile, feebled by his unfamiliarity with the situation, and tried to hold up a calm façade. 'Well, now, *Madame*; I do appreciate the offer, but, I really should be gettin' back to my colleagues—'

'It's not *"Madame"*,' she told him seriously, unfolding her arms and stepping away from the door; 'so don't get any stupid ideas. I just brought you in here to talk to you, about, well, what went on out *there*.' She turned then and extended a hand to him. 'I'm Cissie McKean.'

Jon sighed, relieved to find the girl already seemed much more than what he had expected, or feared. He took her hand and said, 'Well, Ms McKean; nice to meet somebody sane tonight.'

She smiled at him, and her handshake, so unbecomingly masculine, amused him. 'Well; I thought I should just tell you one-on-one what I thought of your show. I've been tryin' to keep up with you guys, you know; but Dave Holloway isn't exactly much for making his business known....'

'No; he's more fond of the *tour de force* method of PR,' Jon smiled.

'Yeah; well; at least now you dudes have a name.... Hey; I gotta tell you I really like that name. Who thought it up?'

Jon looked at her, impressed with such a direct question, although it had left him momentarily speechless. 'Uh; well; you know; we all voted on it, but I kinda made the motion.... It's not so original, you know; it's a takeoff on The Raspberries—'

'Yeah; I mighta guessed,' she said; 'but who cares? The Beatles was a takeoff on The Crickets. I think it's just fantastic. And you all can even *sing*. The whole show really impressed the hell outa me, I gotta tell you.'

'Good,' said Jon, feeling a little out of his element. 'I'm... glad you liked it.' The girl's undeniably appealing appearance and startlingly blunt manner made for a contradiction to which he was not accustomed. Still, she might yet have made a fun date. That thought made him nervous to be near her again. 'Well; uh; hey; you know; maybe I oughta get shakin'—'

'*Wait*,' she said quietly, as someone banged on the outside of the locked door. 'I just wanted to tell ya I was impressed, and doo.' He watched her pace over to the wall and turn back abruptly. 'What did you think of "Helter Skelter"?'

He looked right back at her, unblinking. 'What?'

'What did you think of "Helter Skelter"?'

'I don't think we ever shoulda done it,' he said seriously.

'Damn!' she laughed. 'I *knew* you would say that! Didn't I just know it! Don't you know what you did out there, man? You should be *proud* of it! *I'd* be.'

He tried to imagine her up on stage playing guitar to 'Helter Skelter'; somehow it was not a long stretch of the imagination. 'Well; we almost lost,' he said to her. 'It was a stupid move we made. "If You Need It" is a Tobacco Road song; it's more of what they do. Originally we were just gonna end with "Back In The USSR", goin' into "Get Back".'

She nodded. 'Yeah; well; that wasn't your fault, though. It was the mob's fault more than anybody else's. The people that normally come to this kinda thing are real dirtbags, man. They're all just heads, most of 'em, and most of 'em are higher than kites when they show up, you know, so they're just lookin' to grab a lotta ass and start fights with everybody in sight. Most of 'em didn't even notice you guys had the right stage setup and the right amount of mics and the right guitars. They're just assholes. And dammit; Dave had a *lotta* right to say what he said. It was somethin' that had to be said, you know, sooner or later, and it's just a shame somebody didn't say it sooner. I'm gonna tell ya, man, *you*, Jon, you and that band there, you dudes are gonna be the ones who put the *fun* back into rock-and-roll. Anything you *do* will do it. You just mark my words on that, man. You could really turn the whole goddamn thing around again.'

He only stared at her in amazement. Suddenly she felt very embarrassed and went off across the room again, leaning against the pink metal partition and folding her arms in front of herself. Jon had never seen her before or, if he had, he had never noticed her. She was just a healthy, normal, eleventh-grade girl who happened to have been blessed, or cursed, with above-average intelligence, confidence in her convictions and a fiery passion for speaking her mind. After a moment they looked at each other in the mirror. Indeed there was an earnest innocence in those wide blue eyes that he had already begun to like.

'Aaah; forget it,' she said, sounding regretfully disappointed in herself. 'I can't be all that sane if I'd lock a dude in the bathroom just to say it. This is all so stupid.... I mean: shit– we're even in the same grade in high school.'

'Are you kidding?' Jon smiled, suddenly realising that the slice of modesty lying just beneath her tough exterior was much of why she had become so attractive to him. 'You're all right. Besides,' he said, looking about, 'this is a whole new experience for me. I've never been in the girls' room before.'

She made a wry smile and stood up straight. 'Let's just get the hell out of here.'

'After you,' he said, stepping aside to allow her to exit first.

The front gallery was much less crowded now. Chris found him just as the toilet door closed behind them. 'Oh, look; so I get it– the superstar makes it with the babe, here; is that it?'

Jon went red. 'Hey; no, man; actually–'

'The *girls'* room, yet,' Chris said, pretending disbelief; and the girls with him giggled. 'Never knew you had it in ya, dude.'

'Oh, shit, man; you know I never–'

'Well; there's a first time for everything,' Chris teased, and then turned to speak with his companions. Across the emptying gallery, Jon spied Jeanne Banfield in her usual company and recognised her expression of shock and disappointment at seeing him emerge from the girls' toilets with a strange girl. He would have wanted her to think anything but so unsavoury a notion; but, for the moment, it was beyond his control.

'Hey, Chris,' he said weakly, trying to think of anything to change the subject; 'so what's up–'

But Chris and his new female acquaintances were wandering off up the gallery. 'Hey, dude,' Chris called back; 'so keep up the good work!'

Jon blushed. 'Shut up, Chris.'

Chris laughed. 'I won't tell if the rest of the school doesn't!'

Jon started away from the doorway, prodded gently by the girl called Cissie. Two girls went past them for the toilets, eying them both warily. 'Hey,' Cissie said personally; 'it's cool. They can think what they want. I'm not really like that.'

Jon slowed down and then smiled at her. 'Yeah; well; I had that pretty much figured out.'

'Don't you hate it, though?' she asked, holding his arm as though being escorted to the ball. 'People with only one thing on their minds, or two, if you count gettin' high. It's stupid, really. Sometimes I think the whole goddamn world is insane.'

'It is,' Jon said.

'I mean: can you believe how many kids got molested tonight? Shit– not that I was lookin', you know, but I musta seen about *ten*, at *least*. Grass and booze in every aisle, fights breakin' out everywhere, and dudes grabbin' at every girl in sight....'

'Assholes,' Jon said strongly, and then thought perhaps he should not use such vulgarity in the company of a young lady. 'It's all just stupid. This is why I wanted to start a band in the first place. Because I didn't wanna go to college, but I felt I gotta educate people; you know? And I know it sounds corny and all; but that's actually the kinda stuff that motivates me.'

Cissie made a smile; inside, she was tingling with delight. 'No, Jon; it's not corny at all. It's just that it's kind of a tough job; you know? But like I said, you're the ones to do it.'

Andrew Cavaliere met them inside the front doors, by the ticket booth. 'Hi,' he said deferentially to Cissie, and then reported to his brother. 'So; like the van's all packed up and outa here, and Billy rode over to Santana's with R D, so, I guess I gotta catch a ride back with you in the Pop-mobile.' Jon said nothing to the contrary; and Andrew wiped his hair out of his eyes and went on. 'And some of these paper dudes want you dudes.'

'Paper dudes? What paper dudes?'

Dave very literally bumped into them just then, carrying a bottle of cheap California champagne in a paper bag and accompanied by half a dozen giggling girls. Other people stared at him; he was not being very discreet about drinking in the school building. Dropping a hand heavily on Jon's shoulder he asked, 'Yo; where'd Santana go with my van?'

Offended by his behaviour in front of their public, Jon gave him barely a glance. 'Hellifino,' he told him.

'Where's that at?'

'Shut up, Dave.' Jon shook him off; and Dave took his admirers away up the gallery in search of someone who might answer him, or tolerate him. Melody Santana came up then and Jon turned to meet her a foot away. 'Uh; hi, Mel....'

'Jon,' she said as an introduction, even waving her hand, 'I'd like you to meet... some kid from the school paper.'

'That didn't take long,' Jon smiled, looking at Cissie.

Cissie smiled back at him, still leaning on his arm. 'Get used to it,' she told him.

'Uh, yeah,' said the short, slight reporter, poking his glasses up the bridge of his nose with his pencil eraser; 'so, I gotta get your opinion, like.... What was your reaction to the victory?'

'What was yours?' Jon came back. Cissie laughed.

The boy stared up at him for a long second and then looked down, adjusting his glasses again. 'Okay; uh, look, man; I kinda gotta get a coupla words down, you know, so I can stay on the staff; I mean: this is kind of a big event for me, and—'

'Hey, dude,' Jon said easily to him; 'it's cool. My reaction to the victory, in five hundred words or less, is, well.... Pride, relief, shock, and I guess conceit. Conceit 'cause it's great, you know, it feels great to win. Pride 'cause I'm satisfied, you know, as in I think we did damn good, actually; and we're all pretty happy. Relief because we put a lotta time into it, about a year actually, and I don't think everyone did; but, like, I ain't mentioning any names, but we were really sweatin' it out for a while. But most importantly, shock. Yes; shock was my reaction to the victory, because of all the stupid *ignoramusi*– that's plural of "ignoramus"– all the stupid idiots who show up lookin' for a party and don't know how to show some kinda decent appreciation for a band of sound. You gettin' all this down okay?' He leaned over to look where the boy scrawled hastily upon a clipboard, in some alien form of shorthand. 'What it comes down to is like what Dave said. The screaming, the yelling, the excitement, you know, that's cool, 'cause this is rock-and-roll. But the grass and the booze and the fighting, and girls getting molested, that's like a bunch of trash. I think I can say for the whole band that we're not gonna condone that kinda stuff; I mean: we're not into it, so why does the audience have to be? We're musicians, man; and all we want to do is play music for the audience that appreciates it, and for not a bunch of idiots who wanna throw some kinda orgy of violence. *That* is my reaction to the victory, man.   If you want a good story, you'll print all of it; 'cause it's somethin' that has to be said.'

Cissie was beaming with pride, ecstatic with finding Jon's real feelings were along the same lines as her own.   She hung onto his arm with both hands whilst others in the gallery looked on and the boy finished his notes. 'All right; cool, man,' he said, looking up; 'I'll see what I can do. Thanks a lot, uh, Jon.'

'Solid,' said Jon.

'Hey; so where can I find Dave Holloway?'

Jon shook his head. 'You'd better find Santana,' he said, calling him that even in the presence of his sister Melody. 'Holloway's smashed already.'

Bob Prescott and DJ Berryfield burst into the gallery then, sharing a bottle of the same cheap champagne with Chris's ninth-grade cousin Laurie Pepper and another girl whom Jon did not know.   Patti and Jeanne and Debbie all looked up as the crowd behind them got even larger and louder and heard Bob ask, like an angry inebriate, 'Where the hell's Holloway at?'

'You're smashed,' Cissie teased him, even though they had never been introduced.

'Not yet I ain't. So where's he at?'

'Hellifino,' said Jon.

'Where's that at?'

'Shut up,' Jon told him, 'and gimme that bottle.' He shook his head with a laugh. 'Dag; just *look* at these people. Ten minutes, and they're four sheets to the wind already. Come on there, *borracho.*'

Bob let him have the bottle without a care. 'So Holloway!' he called off up the gallery, wandering away through the thinning crowds. 'Yo, Holloway!'

Jon took a few gulps from the bottle straight away, catching Jeanne's eye in doing so. In a way it was amusing, although blatantly illegal; she wondered why none of the security or faculty on hand had noticed. Cissie took the bottle from him. Jon smiled at her prudish intentions; nevertheless he swiped it back from her for another swallow or two. Chris Santana returned without his ladyfriend and at first Jon ignored him, avidly discussing the film *The Sting* with his brother and Melody and Cissie.   Meanwhile Jeanne, still waiting with her friends, tried desperately to follow their conversation from twenty yards down the gallery. 'Yo, rock star,' Chris asked, a little loudly; 'what the hell were you tellin' the school paper?'

People's heads turned. 'The paper?' Jon shrugged as if it were of little consequence.   'Aaah; them dudes are all frickin' outa their gourds.'

'Jon, man, the *paper*! Our only *press* coverage?   I had a damn statement—'

'Oh; come on, man! —so where *were* ya?' Jon countered, sounding irate with the subject already. 'Some frickin' press agents we have! You and DJ, you're both drunk as a goddamn skunk!'

'Not *yet* I ain't,' Chris said seriously. 'Man, if you screwed this up, we'll be payin' for it till—'

'He told them the *truth*,' Cissie said strongly, whilst Chris wondered who this defensive stranger even was.

'Basically what Dave said at the show,' Jon said, calmer. 'We all knew what we wanted to say, man. At least it'll be recorded somewhere other than on *our tape*....'

Chris seemed to calm suddenly as well; Jeanne surmised that they were both much more in control of themselves than they appeared to be to others. 'Well,' Chris was saying; 'I had wanted to tone it down a bit with a little PR....'

'It'll be fine,' Jon assured him, sounding for all the world like a confident business manager. In that moment, Jeanne imagined that even her father might have been impressed.

'*Gimme* that bottle,' Chris said abruptly, and unhooked the champagne from stubborn Andrew's grasp. He appeared to keep the bottle down for a while but was later seen sharing a good deal of it with Bob and DJ up the gallery.

Cissie left for the toilet and Jon and his brother turned to go outside. The heat and humidity of the gallery had become very overpowering. Inadvertently they chose the same door as had Patti and PJ and Jeanne; so Jon allowed the ladies to exit first, none avoiding a blush at his polite attention. Jeanne shivered nervously, striving to think up some perfect way to acknowledge him. But before anything came to mind the moment had passed without either of them exchanging any words.

Jon and Andrew were halfway across the courtyard to the driveway when from the building Chris called out, 'Yo, *Jon*!'

The girls turned about, seeing the junior-class president hanging out the glass door and holding up a bottle. 'Yeah?' Jon called back to him. 'What about *mine*?'

'Here!' From a good ten yards away Chris gave the bottle a strong underhand toss towards Jon. His aim was a little off but Andrew took a mighty step and caught it just a foot from the ground.

It was chilled and unopened. 'Solid!' Andrew cheered in glee.

'*Gimme that bottle*!' Jon demanded playfully, whilst the girls by the door all giggled in amusement. They watched Jon peel off the hood and fire the cork into the air. Foaming champagne blew five feet out of the bottle.

Suddenly Patti lunged sideways, and Jeanne and PJ were amazed to see she had caught the flying plastic cork. They looked over at Jon who stood holding a lathering champagne bottle whilst his younger brother lapped idiotically at the drippings. 'Hey,' Jon called over to her; 'lucky you! Who's the lucky *guy?*'

Patti blushed at that; and Jeanne began to feel terribly embarrassed that her friend, and not herself, would receive such attention from him. However it was PJ, so customarily outgoing, who called back, 'How 'bout you?'

Jon pretended not to hear that and sucked on the bottle for a drink, even whilst Andrew kept a hand on it. 'Oh, *yecch!*' he complained aloud. 'Who the hell decided on this *domestic* shit, anyway?'

The girls all giggled again; they liked to think of him as a natural entertainer and had rarely seen this side of him. 'Gimme that bottle,' Andrew said, and took it for a gulp.

'I wanna know where the frickin' party is,' Jon was saying to him. 'Go in and find Prescott, or Santana, and if you see that girl Cissie, tell her I'll give her a ride.'

'It's cool,' Andrew said. He took one last swallow, handed him back the bottle and ran past the girls into the school building.

Jeanne turned and looked out again at Jon, in his snug stage trousers and open shirt and high black shoes, standing alone at the corner of the courtyard pavement whilst cars rolled out from the parking area. Concertgoers shuffled past, half the girls excitedly recognising him from the show; but he took several long drinks from the champagne bottle and paid no-one any mind. Jeanne yearned to tell him her impressions of the show; her muscles twitched in anticipation of taking her first step towards him. All right, she told herself; you have only to go up and say, Hi, Jon; how are you? You gonna be in class Monday? I just gotta tell you, 'Lovely' was beautiful. It's that easy– Of course she had always talked with other boys, but now she shivered to imagine herself actually initiating a conversation with Jon Cavaliere. It might have been only a second away. But no matter how weird you're feeling inside, Jeanne, she reminded herself, you can always talk. And then he'll say something back; and before you know it, he might even invite you to the party....

'Yo *Jon!*' came a call from the doors behind her.

Jeanne froze halfway through a first step towards him. '*What?*' Jon snapped, whirling about and muttering, 'you idiot–'

It was not Chris or Andrew but Bob Prescott, leaning out the door not eight feet from the girls. He glanced at them once, recognising them, and hid a smile to see how interested they seemed in what he and Jon might say. 'Party's gonna be at *Santana's!*' he called over to Jon.

'*Dag,*' Jon called back; 'it's *always* at Santana's!'

'So *what?* You know what a party engineer *Melody* is!'

Jon shook his head and then held up the bottle. 'Yo; and what's with this California grape-pickers' piss? Get Holloway to pick up some *real* junk; will ya?'

Bob laughed at that. 'Actually, *Alascan* bought it!'

Jon winced.   'Obviously acting from the wallet,' he mumbled. 'Yeah,' he called over; 'so, what *time* is it gonna be?'

'The *party*?'

'No, idiot; the plane to *Cuba*! Of *course* the party!'

Bob laughed at him.   They were still standing at least fifteen yards apart, holding what otherwise constituted a normal conversation in outdoor voices without regard for the people standing or passing between them. 'Like quarter *after*!' Bob yelled over.

'Well what time is it *now*?' Jon hollered back at him.

'*Now*?' Bob asked loudly. 'Like five *of*, ten *of*!'

'Oh,' said Jon, beginning to sound more tired than boisterous.

Bob Prescott disappeared into the building. 'It's two before twelve,' Patti called over to him, gently. Jeanne and PJ looked at her, both stunned that she would address him so casually.

He looked at Patti for a long second, deliberately avoiding eye contact with Jeanne. 'Oh,' he said, rather quietly, and turned away, raising the bottle for another gulp. Only then was it apparent how fully the show had drained him. The façade of wit and humour and mischief had been masking an intense exhaustion after such a dramatic performance. Jeanne likened him to a victorious warrior after a long, bloody siege for a noble cause and then blushed when she realised just how often she fancied such gallantry in him.   Still she yearned to be the one who might have nursed him through his recuperation.

She watched him shuffle slowly out to the fire lane, where his father's white estate car, the one she had seen about town with *J C Cavaliere* stencilled in the rear side windows, awaited. The car had been loaded with the band's guitars, including several spare ones they had brought for the show. Jon took another long drink, swallowing several times without lowering the bottle, and sat in the car to start the engine. Andrew Cavaliere came out of the building with the girl in the red tanktop and allowed her to slide into the front seat between his brother and himself. Jeanne sighed. She stared with longing as the laden car motored out of the schoolyard; and then PJ tapped her. Mrs Harper had come to drive them home.

There he goes, Jeanne thought. The one guy who's always been so cool and so cute, whom I've known all my life, since seventh grade anyway, and now, just about overnight, he's a star all of a sudden. Now his good looks and funny jokes and charm and talent and intelligence are going to take him where most of us will never even dream of, and I'll only ever be able to say I once knew him.

Suddenly she felt very sad. She thought back to when she had really known him, when he had been courteous and polite and very sweet to her in particular, mentioning that he liked her dress or thanking her for lending him a pencil for the entire school day. Even back then, as a twelve-year-old, a seventh-grader, a mere child, she had been touched by his sincerity and thoughtfulness and unfailing honesty. Whilst all the others were belching aloud and throwing food about the cafeteria and beating up on the younger boys, here had been one who remembered his manners and knew well how to be the gentleman in the company of a young lady. Jeanne had never forgot that he was indeed the first boy she had ever really dreamt of dating or loving or even marrying some day; and she knew she was only being stubbornly sentimental about it now; but it was why, after so long a time, Jon Cavaliere still captivated her like no-one else. All the relationships she had established with other boys had faded into polite, pleasant friendships, albeit pale ones.

And now, she thought, he's on his way to becoming famous. Someday, he'll find fame and fortune with his fabulous band, just like I always knew he would. And I'll still be stuck in this stupid lonely school, just thinking about how cute and nice he used to be to me. I'll have lost him for ever.

Oh, she pined; I just wish he would talk to *me*! He's even in my English class, every day but Friday, sitting three rows away for two semesters now, and he still won't talk to me. He probably hates me. He probably thinks I'm a jerk. Or a flirt. Well; maybe I do talk to everybody; but why can't I just talk to *him*? Why can't I be nice like Patti, or outgoing like PJ or funny like Debbie, and just step right up and say something to the guy? Oooh! she groaned, frustrated with her own frustration. What do I have to *do*?

* * *

Chuck West began the week with the concert-contest results: 'And sprouting right up from a deep-seeded past Wilshire High's own Strawberries were picked by the judging panel to tie with the favourite, Wipeout. After some deliberation the judges called for a tiebreaker and The Strawberries chose an old Beatles song, "And I Love Her", with the lead vocal done by Jon Cavaliere. This definitely upset the score in their favour. The group consists of Dave Holloway on guitar, Jon Cavaliere on bass guitar, Ricky Denning on drums, and Bob Prescott doing some fantastic lead guitar. Special mention should be given to sound man, I mean *light* man Andy Cavaliere and sound man Chris Santana; without them it wouldn't've been like it was for us Saturday night. And so for this year's reign as Wilshire's most popular rock-and-roll band we're all sure The Strawberries deserve it. Good show, Strawberries!'

Jeanne slumped into her seat in Room 148, expecting no more than boredom for the next fifty minutes. Sure enough, Jon Cavaliere was not in the room yet; and she suspected that now with all his new notoriety he would take the liberty of taking the day off. That's a shame, she thought. I would've liked to see how he handles being so popular all of a sudden. I mean: me being Prom Princess of Wilshire Township Junior High South doesn't even come *close* to what he's done. It would've been fun seeing him in here today. This class just isn't the same without his good looks and funny jokes.... God. I'm bored already.

But, just as the late bell was ringing and Mrs Hampton was opening the roll book, in through the open doorway strolled Barry Hemphill and Jon Cavaliere. Locked in discussion as they were it seemed to the whole class that if Room 148 had never presented itself to them, they might never have found their way to class at all. Jeanne hid a smile, silently thrilled with anticipation. She caught the gist of their talk, full of esoteric jargon though it was, and realised that on such an auspicious occasion she should not have expected them to be talking about anything other than music.

They came up the aisle, Barry ahead of Jon and still talking, Jon mimicking the descending notes to 'If You Need It, You'll Get It' and even pretending to play an imaginary guitar. 'Yeah, dude,' Barry was saying; 'but if you can dig what I'm sayin' except you went *up*, instead of runnin' down, you could make like the effect of–'

'I like it the way it is, man,' Jon said simply, and they sat in their seats. 'Don't go messin' with my tune, now. I spent a whole afternoon on that bitch to make it sound like that.'

'And like what I was sayin',' said Barry, even as Jon spoke, 'that other one, the way he plays it, is very much the same thing, even though it's a completely different song– What key did you dudes do it in the other night?'

Jon turned and looked at him. 'What?'

' "Lovely".'

'What about it?'

'What *key*?'

'A, man; what else? A, goes up to C.'

'I thought Holloway said it was in G.'

'It is,' Jon told him, 'on piano. It's just easier live in A, and Holloway can sing in any key, so–'

'Definition of a lousy vocalist,' Barry stated, with a laugh. 'Sings in any key.'

'Diggit,' Jon agreed. 'Or *all* of them, at *once*–'

'Hey,' Shari asked, tapping him; 'you guys were great the other night.'

'Hey; thanks,' Jon smiled sincerely.

'*See*?' she said to a friend on her right. 'I *told* you he'd be like all modest about it, and doo.'

Mrs Hampton looked up at them all, slapped closed the roll book and said, '*So*, Jon!'

'So, *what*?' he asked her aloud.

'So what exactly happened on Saturday night?'

'Blew away six lousy bands,' Kevin Moore laughed.

'Picked up a coupla chicks,' someone else said.

'Sure showed up Wipeout,' called a boy in the far corner.

'Dig *that*,' Jon said strongly. 'I hate that Pelose with mortal passion.'

'Hey,' Frank Genovese said to Jon from the front corner; 'I liked that, "Helter Skelter". You'll never see anyone else play that right. *Quite* cool. "Helter skelter; da na-na, na na na-na"....' He was recalling those guitar riffs which had driven the crowd into a frenzy.

Jeanne shuddered a little, even now. Her own memory was all too vivid. 'Hey dude,' Jon said; 'it mighta been a decent idea when it showed up in Holloway's head, but after we played it it was a nightmare, man, and we were all worried sick over it. We shoulda quit with "If You Need It", and everybody knew it.'

'Oh,' Cindy smiled; 'you know it was fantastic.'

'Yeah; well; it came off like we were tryin' to prove somethin', and we didn't have nothin' to prove. Really the only thing we did prove was that Gatorade doesn't stay in your stomach, because I puked up half a gallon of the green kind.'

The class moaned in distaste; but Jeanne could tell Jon had meant no humour. He's really serious, she thought. Jon Cavaliere was not happy with the reaction to 'Helter Skelter' the other night. It actually made him sick. Wow.... I wonder what he thought of the last one they did. I thought it was a very sweet song....

'Hey,' Cindy asked him, turning about in her seat; 'so how come you guys did that last one like that? I mean–'

'Yeah,' said Frank; 'I mean: that made me jump back. I was expectin' another rocker like–'

'Yes,' Jon said calmly; 'that did go over rather well; didn't it? That was Santana's idea; he had it figured that to keep from makin' any enemies we should at least attempt to reverse what we started.'

'You mean like for crowd control, and doo,' said a boy in the back.

'Diggit,' Jon said to him. 'That's all we really won for.'

'Yeah,' Frank said; 'but that's really the most important thing, though; isn't it? The band that can make the audience feel things, you know, make them feel what they want them to feel, that's the band people want to see. They go to a show to be moved.'

'That's an interesting point,' agreed Mrs Hampton.

'Yeah; but you guys have all the talent,' Cindy said. 'Well like some of the other guys were good, you know; I for one happen to *love* the Menagerie....'

Jeanne smiled at that. But she was surprised when Jon said, 'Yeah; I like them too.' It seemed a marvel to hear that someone so talented and newly influential would admit admiration for someone she knew so well; perhaps it might be something else about which she could speak with him, some day.

'And so like even if Wipeout *had* won,' Cindy went on, 'you guys would still be everybody's favourite band.'

'Really,' another girl agreed.

'Yeah; well,' said Jon, and he was getting red; 'just don't let Holloway hear you say that.'

'Modest, modest,' teased Shari; and others laughed.

'Yeah,' one boy said aloud; 'but some people are gettin' sick of bands like Wipeout. I mean: like *nobody* plays "And I Love Her" in concert.'

Jon turned about and looked at him. 'Yeah, dude; you know, I was hopin' somebody would say that. Even if that particular performance of it was botched up to the max. You can thank my idiotic brother for that, who spent so much time messing around with the lights that Santana had to go help him, and then no-one was minding the sound board and I came off soundin' way too weak.... I *hate* it when I sound like that. Sounds like it's comin' out of a three-inch speaker.'

'Yeah; but the record sounds just like that,' someone observed.

'And the lights did look fantastic,' a girl told him.

'Well; considering that I was scared to death, I guess it did come off pretty good,' Jon said; and the teacher smiled at his blushing. 'At least you guys weren't throwing rotten apples....'

'Yeah,' Kevin said; 'but I did notice a bunch of ladies' unmentionables flyin' around, though.'

A few laughed. Jeanne watched; Jon merely raised his eyebrows and said nothing. 'That changes key; don't it?' Barry asked him.

Jon looked at him then. 'Yeah; and it goes *up*, too, like everything else, and not down....' He laughed at him a second. 'But you talk about a hassle, man.... We start it in E; right? Well; C-sharp minor. And so right at the instrumental it goes up to D-minor, and we didn't even get a chance to practise it; so I'm there thinkin', man, if he forgets and muffs it up it'll ruin the whole effect.'

Barry scoffed. 'But Prescott *doesn't* muff it up.'

'Nope. Prescott never makes a mistake. Best guitar player any band could have. Dude studies the instrument like a freakin' religion, honest to God.'

Mrs Hampton was impressed with the pride these two young musicians had in their craft. It was encouraging to see them positively inspired towards creative expression. She smiled at them both and then asked, 'Well, Jon; just what kind of a future do you think you'll find in music?'

Barry laughed aloud. 'Anything to stay outa college!'

Jon laughed too. 'Dig that!' he agreed. 'More of *this?*' He waved his arms up in the air and his classmates all laughed with him.

'You're one of the best writers in this class,' Mrs Hampton said to him, diplomatically understating the truth; 'and it's just that I can't help thinking you may not be taking advantage of all your talents.'

'Aaah,' he said, hearing the moans go up about the room; 'I hate school, I really do. I mean like I hate studying, and all that doo, that supposedly makes you a better student. I know it's all supposed to be good for ya, and all; it's just— Hey, though; you think *we're* any good, you oughta hear *this* guy's band.' He jerked a thumb at Barry, who sat there shyly and gave a slight shrug. 'Santana'll have 'em full-time in a *year.*'

'But you're not interested in college,' wondered the teacher.

'Naah.' Aware that others might be taking an example he then said carefully, 'Nothing which higher education has to offer succeeds in stirring my interest, at this time in my life.'

A few of them were amused; he sounded like a politician. 'I just think you'd do really well, Jon. I hope you change your mind.'

'*I* don't,' he told her. He looked about the room, wary of appearing too disrespectful. 'All right; look. How many people in this class? Thirty? Okay; me and Barry ain't gonna be seen *near* any institutions of higher learning; so that's what, twenty-eight? If you all got an average IQ of a hundred like I hope you do, then there's twenty-eight hundred worth of IQ for the universities of the world to snatch up. You people are goin' to college to be what? Lawyers? —I can see Cindy here will make a great D A; and so maybe there's some accountants, or psychologists.... Oh; *there's* a good field, man, psychology. You don't know the suckers who go to college thinkin' they're gonna be the next Bob Hartley, man. That field is gettin' so saturated.... I know a guy with a Master's in psychology, and I got a cousin who's workin' on her Doctorate, and three paying gigs a week will net me a better salary in my field than both of them put together. College is no guarantee of anything, people. Least of all a good job. You know what my cousin does? She sells *shoes* in a *shoe* store. Six years in college, and she's sellin' shoes.' The class laughed. 'College is no more of a sure thing than anything else. So if I'm gonna be takin' chances, I'm gonna be doin' somethin' I like. Somethin' I enjoy.'

He saw Barry smiling smugly beside him. 'Well what are you gonna do?' a girl asked.

'Well,' he said; 'what I *ain't* gonna do is spend a lotta money and valuable time in college, get married when I'm twenty-three, have two kids with bowl haircuts, a nice big four-door station wagon with factory air and body side mouldings and a wife who wears pink hair curlers and cooks Hamburger Helper and makes Campbell's soup for the kiddies when they come in outa the rain, and come home on the five-forty-five LI local after a so-called hard day at the office with a tie on, to this nice Colonial house with an added-on rec room with flakeboard panelling and shag carpet and those fake Styrofoam beams like you buy at Woodbridge's, and kiss the little woman on the cheek and say "Hi hun; what's for dinner" after she's been out all day driving her Vega with an automatic and wood on the sides and spendin' all the so-called hard-earned pay at Macy's and the A-and-P with Mastercharge cards.... Not for *me*, people.'

By now the whole room was riotous with laughter, including the teacher. Jeanne could only think, *no*; Jon. I've never pictured you that way either.

'So what *are* you gonna do?' the girl asked him again.

'That ain't life, man,' Jon was saying. 'Not how I see it.'

No, Jeanne wanted to say to him. You're way above that.

'And so I can just see how alla you guys, and worse, your parents, are hating my guts and calling me a little immature scared-of-work draft-dodgin' little baby of a faery; but hey, look, people; I don't care. I don't have to follow any example. It just means that my concept of hard work and yours may be two different things. If I can create for myself a perfectly cool life, and make more money playin' rock-and-roll in ten years than you dudes'll make for the rest of your lives, then I'd say alla your comments are just about sewn-up. Let's see where we all are at the ten-year reunion, and doo.'

'Diggit,' Barry laughed; and Jeanne wanted to say, if you can do it, *do* it. God, wouldn't it be fantastic if it all really happened, just like that! 'Yeah,' Barry drawled, breaking the next silence; 'and I for one don't want no Colonial house with no Vega with wood on the sides, man. No *way*.'

The class laughed again. 'So what *are* you gonna do?' asked the girl in the front row once again. 'You can't just condemn it all without having an alternative—'

'All right; I'll tell ya what I'm gonna do,' Jon told her; and the others were attentive at once. 'I am gonna get a hot-plate and a coffeepot and a refrigerator full of *hors d'oeuvres* and *Möet*, and put my white grand piano and my guitars and an eight-track tape machine in a music studio on a beach somewhere, and *enjoy* life while I'm workin' hard for a living, man.'

'Diggit!' Barry laughed aloud, above the others' amused reactions. 'Takin' care of business!'

'What?' Mrs Hampton frowned.

'TCB,' Jon smiled at her. 'Takin' care of business.'

'What's "takin' care of business"?'

'Makin' music for a living.'

'And that's what you're gonna *do?*' asked Cindy, wide-eyed. 'With your *group?*'

'No,' Jon snapped; 'with my pet turtle.'

'Oh; real good!' she came back. 'What's he do? –splash in the key of C?'

The others roared with laughter, especially Debbie and Jeanne. 'One thing about that Chubs, boy,' Jon said wryly, 'she's got that *Mad* magazine *down.*' People laughed more then.

'Is that really what you're gonna do?' asked Donna, to his right.

'Yeah,' he said to her.

'For real?'

'Yeah.'

'You're crazy,' she told him.

'Yeah,' he said, and smiled.

'You weren't at the show,' said Barry, still slouching down in his seat, with his arms folded in front of himself and his eyes fixed straight ahead. 'I tell ya, them dudes are gonna make it, man. Them, and us. We got the *po's.*'

'You tell 'em, bro',' Jon smiled.

'Takin' care, bro'.'

With all eyes upon them the two sat in silence, each of them with their arms folded and their feet up on the book-baskets beneath the chairs before them, slouching in their seats with a pair of smug smiles staring straight up at the teacher.

Mrs Hampton took a breath and then said, 'Well, Jon; supposing for some reason you don't make it in rock music; and you must know there's a very good chance that you won't. Then what?'

His classmates were stone quiet. No-one had thought to burst his bubble of rosy optimism. Perhaps not one of them would have wanted to. Jon merely shrugged. 'Probably play pool for a living, or put my guitar case out on the street to bum money and eat Welfare potatoes.' He shrugged again, as though the possibility of such a prospect were of little consequence to him. 'So what?'

He and the teacher met eyes. The two of them shared a little smile. Only now Mrs Hampton realised that nothing she might suggest to dissuade him would be anything he had not already considered. What she was actually witnessing was a capacity for complex conjecture and creative speculation far beyond any other in the classroom and, in some ways, even her own. 'It's a gamble,' she said to him, and then realised he would have already considered that too.

He smiled at her; and the entire class awaited his response. Jeanne felt her spine tingling; she was seeing a side to him that in all those wild, fantastic daydreams she had never dared imagine he might possess. Just hearing him speak about his career plans made her feel as if she were glimpsing into the future and seeing what Fate would actually deal to Jon Cavaliere. 'Yeah,' Jon said seriously. 'Yeah; it's a gamble all right.' Abruptly eager, he sat up in his seat and looked about the classroom. 'Okay; look. Suppose we all go to Monte Carlo. Some real rich dude, he gives us each like five hundred dollars. A sure thing in Monte Carlo is a decent time with five hundred dollars; right?'

'No,' said Barry; 'make it 'Vegas. I *know* 'Vegas.'

'*I* know Monte Carlo.' Jon smiled at him. 'All right; we'll make it 'Vegas. Now me and Barry go into this place... let's say, the Sands, and play the tables. You other twenty-eight or twenty-nine people, you play a little, but let's say mostly you just go see all the shows, eat a lotta good food, buy a few souvenirs, or some nice clothes.... Me and Barry, we go in there with nothin' but the shirts on our backs, and drink Miller beer and eat soup crackers at the tables. The waitresses think we're nuts. You guys spend your five hundred dollars, have a real nice time, maybe save some of the money in case you need it in the future, and go home and show everybody your slides of the Hoover Dam; okay? But like me and Barry gamble with all our money. We don't drop a penny of it anywhere else. See we got some intelligence, and a little bit of talent and skill, and so we figure if we play our cards right, we got a good chance of *quadrupling* our money, so that we can give that eccentric old dude his five hundred back and cruise off down the street in a Cadillac, debt-free. 'Course we also got a fair chance of gettin' kicked out at six AM with nothin' to even stick in a slot machine. It's a gamble, man. You come into this world with nothin' but your own brains, you know; and it's up to you to use them as best you can. You can stand there and let it all hit you; and it's easy to just take what comes and be happy with that; and hey; anyone can survive rather nicely that way. But I just happen to think that what you're willing to take a few chances for is gonna be a whole lot better.'

There was a long silence. Finally Cindy said, 'Well hey; I may not be a gambler like you are, but I don't want some dumb Vega with wood on it.'

'So it's a Pinto. You know what I mean.'

'Yeah; so; so what makes you so different?' asked a girl from behind Debbie. 'Everybody wants to cruise off down the street in a Cadillac.'

He shrugged, looking past Debbie at the girl; Jeanne might have shrunk in her place. 'It's just how much you'll sacrifice to get it; that's all. You know, bad as it sounds to some people, it's not enough to just think you deserve it. Whoever's able to reward you for what you think is hard work may not think you've worked hard enough.' He shrugged again. 'Look; I'm not tryin' to say that I'm all that different from you, if you wanna suppose that there's a lotta people like me.' He scoffed at the notion. 'Yeah; I s'pose there's a lotta left-handed light-haired northern-Italian brats who play eight instruments and supposedly have IQ's of one-forty or whatever it's supposed to be, whose pops are supposedly engineering geniuses and whose moms are supposed to teach college-preparatory English literature.'

The class considered this; some were amused, and some were impressed. And are as fantastic as *you*, Jeanne wanted to add; but her lips stayed glued shut. Mrs Hampton smiled a little, aware that he had said more than he had intended, and then said, 'Jon, I didn't know your mother taught college-prep lit.'

'Yeah; and that's *another* one,' Jon said. 'My mom, there, always tryin' to tell me how great college is, and she's the one who went back to teachin' fourth grade. Where the *fun* is.' People laughed. Jon shrugged, unaffected. 'Naah; I really ain't so different. There's a million other punks just like me out there, who put down a lotta people and say "Down with the establishment" and "Make love, not war" and all sorts of other cute slogans. All I'm sayin' is that I might well be lucky to have a chance to do something I enjoy, somethin' that comes easy for me, somethin' people can appreciate; and now I'm gonna sound like a real "flower child", but it's somethin' that can like spread a little happiness around without really hurting anybody. And I just happen to think that if I spent my life listenin' to people like my mother, who starts to sound like a broken record with all that "go to college, get good grades and be a lawyer" rhetoric, then I just *might* end up in some damn Colonial house out in Nassau County and drivin' a stupid Vega with wood on the sides. And be bored outa my *gourd.*'

He folded his arms across his chest and slouched down in his seat again. The room was silent; no-one would offer a rebuttal. Observing this, Mrs Hampton said, 'Jon, you *should* be a lawyer. You can be very persuasive.'

Jon smiled, having an answer already prepared; apparently it was a comment to which he had to reply often. 'I thought about it, once. I don't admire their profession and I don't envy the stress.'

A girl in the far right row spoke up and said, 'Well; what's so wrong with a Colonial house? My parents worked all their lives for one.'

He turned about and looked at her. She was not one who normally spoke up and in fact he did not remember her name. She was pretty, though, if a bit upset. Jon smiled warmly at her; and it was obvious he meant no disrespect towards what she considered dear. 'Look; I'm sorry. I'm not trying to be some kinda preacher, here, or a lawyer. This isn't something I need to make you agree with, like somebody's on trial. If all that's what you want, I'm not going to put you down. It's easy to point fingers and say I'm right and somebody else is wrong. I'm not trying to do that.' He shrugged, made a conciliatory smile, and said to the girl, 'Look; I get this all the time. I only wanted to point out that if so many people think that what I want for myself is somehow wrong, then why can't it be considered that maybe *I* may be right and *they* may be wrong? Or maybe *nobody's* wrong, and it's a stupid argument. That's all I'm trying to say.'

He turned and looked at the teacher, who felt a little shiver to behold the workings of that exceptional intellect she had always hoped to find in a student. There might yet be a way to reach him; but the likeliest possibility was that it was already too late to alter him now. Jeanne felt her own little shiver. When Jon Cavaliere wanted to be serious and sincere, it was very becoming. She would have daydreamed about how sincere he might be in private; but he was speaking again.

'Look; I'm only saying that this is the way I am, and this is my goal in life. I'm not putting the rest of the world down. It's just that they don't understand.' With a perfectly innocent look in his eyes he said, 'In fact, it amuses me to see what other people think about this kinda stuff. They really think I'm completely off the deep end. I really get a kick– Aaah; I shouldn't really say that.'

Only Mrs Hampton saw that sly little smirk creep across his face and then vanish, hiding nothing of his intended comment from one who truly apprehended the depth of his intelligence. She smiled at him and then said, 'Well; all right, Jon; what plans are you making to get started in professional music?'

He shrugged; and they all watched him sit up a little in his seat, as eager to answer as they were to listen. 'Well; you know a lot of stupid little bands like us have no manager, or like maybe some moron who sits back and smokes a lotta dope and says "Play 'Lovely' again till you get it right" and keeps me and Holloway from killing each other, and like maybe keeps turning the bass down all the time. But we have Chris Santana. The dude is probably working for about twenty grand a year already, and nobody's even getting paid yet. He's trying to sell the band to anybody who'll listen, you know, dances, weddings, corny kind of stuff really; but it's work, and exposure, till we're worth a booking at a better place. He's just a real likeable guy; and no-one can turn him down. Like Saturday night, for that somebody just asked us, last year I guess it was, if we had ever heard of the concert contest. So Santana thought it was a good idea; so we put together a show, and worked out the lights, and practised the songs like eight million times; and I guess it was okay, because we won. Santana also handles Barry's band; and they're gettin' into some pretty good places now. The guy likes the work; and he wants the money that goes with it. Every successful business has to have a marketer who likes money. Leave the innovation to the guys that hate it.'

'And you're the innovative one?' Mrs Hampton smiled.

Jon shrugged again. 'Well; me and Holloway, I guess; yeah. And so Chris called Dave's dad out in San Francisco to get this friend of his to look at us; and as soon as we get a coupla tapes together, we're sendin' 'em out to him.'

'The Strawberries are good enough already,' Barry told his classmates. 'Holloway's dad has a tape of our jams now. After that it's just like a matter of time before we have to do a demo tape.'

'He'll wait for *ever* for *our* demos,' Jon half-laughed.

'Oo; you mean you guys are gonna make a record?' Debbie Blake asked aloud. 'I mean: like a real *record?*'

'Demo tape,' Barry told her, appreciating female interest even though he was not ordinarily one to speak so overtly to pretty or popular girls in class. 'There's a big difference.'

'Aaah; it's mostly just political hogwash,' Jon said to the whole class. 'We've got a long way to go before anybody ever takes us that seriously. We did three songs on Saturday night, and I'm not really crazy about them; they sound so juvenile. Writing material on a time schedule is only ever good for a coronary anyway.'

'And you said you didn't want stress,' teased the teacher.

Jon made a wry face at her. 'Those dudes are puttin' one of their tunes on our first album, and we're puttin' one of ours on theirs,' said Barry. 'That way both records will stand as advertisement of the songwriting abilities of Holloway-and-Cavaliere and Alascan-and-Hemphill.'

'Cool,' Frank admitted.

'Right,' smiled Jon; 'so if only one sells, the other band will at least get paid *something*. Now, if they both flop–'

'Hey,' Kevin called out to Barry; 'how come your group wasn't there Saturday?'

'They ain't really amateur,' Jon answered.

'Hey,' Frank asked; 'did Holloway graduate yet? Seems to me–'

'No,' said Barry; 'he gets set free this year. Same as Davisson and Alascan.'

'No,' added Jon; 'it's just that he's never in school. He's like a real worldly dude. Girls, if you're lookin' for a real worldly dude, I give you Dave Holloway. He knows something about everything. Ask him about hotels in San Francisco.'

'What's his phone number?' one girl called out. Everyone laughed at that.

Shari tapped him. 'Hey; so tell me, what's it like, singing by yourself in front of all those people? Do you ever get, like, real nervous?'

'Yeah,' someone else wanted to know. 'Like, what happens if you make a mistake?'

'You try *not* to.' Jon laughed a little. Others did too. 'But yeah,' he said honestly; 'it is pretty petrifying. The worst thing is having to sing lead *and* play the bass, because you can't screw up either one, because everyone will notice it right away. And you worry about the stupidest stuff, like stuff no-one will *ever* notice– The very fact that people ask what it's like when you make mistakes means that no-one ever really noticed them all; but like you're pretty petrified the whole time you're up there.'

'Well,' said Frank; 'that's what's so great about any live performance. The fact that, at any moment, it could all go haywire.'

'The human element,' the teacher concurred.

'Some audiences are real cool, though,' Barry said. 'The more you play, you know.'

'Oh; shut up,' Jon told him. 'You said you never even *look* at them.' People laughed. 'But yeah; like when you have to trust people like your brother, when you grew up with the guy and you know all his faults, and you're just waitin' for him to screw up and give you *black stage—*'

'Naah,' Barry said then; 'the kid was all right. Jenkins was there, you know, and he said we oughta get the kid to do *our* lights.'

'He ain't allowed to stay up that late,' Jon reminded him; and everyone laughed. 'The best part, though, is when everyone leaves but the true believers, you know, the music nuts. You get to meet all these really cool people.' He turned to the boy who had mentioned Wipeout and said, 'Well; not like Pelose; but—'

'Diggit,' the boy agreed. 'Is he like a strap, or what?'

'Diggit. But like you meet all these cool people. Guys in other bands, girls with bands, people who saw like The Rascals in concert, or like Traffic.... And so like Saturday night, this girl who says she's like a fan of our kinda music locks me in the bathroom and introduces herself. I mean it was cool, and all; she was a pretty cool chick.'

Jeanne stared, suddenly feeling like she had underestimated what she had observed that night. 'Some kinda fringe benefits,' Frank teased.

Jon smiled smugly. 'Takin' care.'

'So what instruments do you play, Jon?' asked the teacher.

He shrugged, perhaps embarrassed. 'Oh; well; a little on piano, you know, and a little on guitar; or like violin, I started learnin'....'

'You're *full* of it, man,' Barry told him firmly; and he looked up at Mrs Hampton. 'He's so full of it.... He plays everything, and he never had no lessons on none of them, 'cept piano. Let me tell you, this dude can *jam* on piano.'

'Aaah; come on, man,' Jon said, getting red, and his classmates all laughed to see such modesty in him.

'Yeah; well; you're full of it, dude. He's learnin' violin himself, with no lessons. His piano teacher kicked him out, 'cause she said she couldn't teach him no more.'

'Aaah; cut it out, man; she said I should try somethin' else.'

'That bad; huh?' Cindy teased.

'That *good*,' Barry said gravely. 'You should *hear* this guy play. I've been tryin' to learn off of him for years. I'm tellin' ya: this guy is *hell* on piano.'

'Everybody learns on piano,' Jon said simply, which, in light of his real accomplishments on musical instruments, was perhaps the grossest understatement he could have made.

'What kind of piano do you have?' Debbie asked; and Jeanne fairly whirled about in her seat, astonished that her own friend would address him so directly across half the room.

But the class was breaking up into smaller conversations by now. Perhaps it would not be so hard to speak to him after all. Mrs Hampton sat upon her desk up front, talking with Frank and some others about Beatles lyrics. Three girls ahead of Jeanne were discussing their experiences at Saturday's concert among themselves. Two boys in the back corner seemed to be asleep. Jon looked over at Debbie, for he could hardly ignore the question, and asked, 'Why? What kind do you have?'

'Oh,' she said, proud to be addressing him; 'the low kind, you know, the console kind.'

'Oh, *gross*,' Barry cringed. 'I can't *stand* them things!'

'No,' said Jon, perhaps wishing to not offend her; 'the consoles are usually okay. It's the spinet you should be afraid of.'

Debbie, characteristically, came straight back with an offensive. 'Why?' she asked Barry. 'What kind do *you* have?'

'Well; I got two, if you count the clunker. And my clunker's worse than Jon's!' He laughed.

'No, man,' laughed Jon; '*nothing's* worse than *my* clunker!'

'You have two pianos?' Debbie marvelled.

'Yeah,' Barry said; 'so what? Jon has three.'

Debbie looked right at Jon and said, 'You have *three* pianos?'

'Uh, yeah,' Jon said, turning back from someone else's question. 'So what? Santana has four.'

'*Four* pianos?!'

Barry and Jon laughed at that. Jeanne did too. 'So,' Jon said; 'my uncle has six.'

'Yeah; but they don't count,' Barry said to him. 'They're customers'.'

'No; the ones in the house are all his, not including the shop.'

'What do you *do* with them all?' wondered Debbie.

He smiled at her, and Jeanne thought she would fall out of her seat swooning at those dimples. 'Well; *play* them usually. The one in my room is usually covered with junk, though. That's the clunker.'

'You have a piano in your *room*?!'

'Yeah; but you should see their music room, man,' Barry said to the girls and a few others who were listening in. 'They got a real old Baldwin in there. I swear I'm gonna steal that thing some night, man. And what's the one in the living room?'

'Oh; that's a Steinway,' Jon said nonchalantly; 'but it's a real old one. My uncle sorta owed my dad a favour, so he redid it for us. Otherwise we never could've afforded it.' He smiled. 'That bitch must be worth, ten, twelve grand by now. I told my dad I'd kill him if he dies and doesn't leave it to me.'

'Yeah; I remember when that thing wasn't even up to pitch,' Barry said. 'But funny how all the music was invented on the clunker.'

'Except "Lovely",' Jon said to him, whilst the girls listened. 'That was on Dave's aunt's grand, in the summer parlour. Talk about a sweet instrument, dude. I swear I'm gonna use that thing for recording, some day.'

'Yeah; I can imagine how that tune would sound, in G, on that piano.'

Jeanne was enthralled with this rare opportunity to learn about Jon's opinions and his life but, whilst she quivered in her seat trying not to look more than casually interested, Debbie just sat and gazed adoringly at him. When he next looked over towards them it was Debbie who said, 'You know, "Lovely" was beautiful. I *loved* that song.'

Jeanne went white. She turned away, aghast that the one thing she had rehearsed to tell him had been unintentionally stolen *verbatim* by one of her closest friends. There would be no cheerful conversation with Jon Cavaliere today and no chance of riding home in his car and him asking her for a date and the two of them starting their lovely life together. She feared, now more than ever, that such would probably never come to be at all.

'Yeah,' Jon acknowledged, and looked at Cindy who turned about then; 'well; it probably ain't gonna get heard too much at any of these school shows any more, unless they start raisin' the ticket prices, or something.'

'Why do you say that?' asked Cindy.

'Well; I know it's like we just came out, you know, alt-hough to me it hardly feels like that. And it might sound cocky already; but like people have got to learn to appreciate a band that's playin' for them. They have to realise that the band is *good* at what they do, which is playing *music*. They wanna be known as *musicians*, and not just a bunch of background noise to smoke dope by. That's what we got out of that thing on Saturday night, man. The knowledge that most of the people that will come out to a show are just heads anyway.'

'I'm not a head,' Cindy said, 'and *I* was there.'

'Well; we like *you*, Cindy. You're the people we *want* to see there. It's just really discouraging after you put all this work and effort into it and see a bunch of dope addicts and drunks molesting all the girls, you know. It's the following that makes a band's image, and we've done exactly one gig at this school and already we're known as a band who appeals to a bunch of dope addicts and drunks.'

'So,' Frank called back, from his seat near the teacher's desk; 'what you're sayin' is: when people think of the concert contest now, and remember all the fights and stuff, they're gonna think of The Strawberries, and vice versa.'

'Yeah; *exactly*,' Jon said, and slouched down in his seat, as before. 'But, it's not all bad. We did get a lot more good out of it. At least people know who we are. We can play more often, and eventually define our own audience based on the kind of music we play, and how we go about playin' it. You can really influence a lotta people from a stage, and doo.'

The teacher was smiling at him. 'Maybe that's your real calling, Jon.'

He shrugged. 'Mm; maybe,' he said, with that knowing gleam in his eye.

Jeanne stared right at him now, something she rarely did with so many others nearby. It was an especially bold thing to do with her face still red from Debbie's assertive *faux pas*; but surely she was not in control of all her faculties now. Despite the intense, even painful pleasure she felt at just having a long look at him, she was profoundly impressed by how serious Jon seemed. Everything he had said all period was just like what she might have hoped to hear a successful rock musician say. He was far more dedicated to what he was doing and his reasons for doing it than anyone else she had ever known. Already it was conceivable that the band would be only a vehicle for him to rise to fame and fortune in other areas; she wanted to fantasise for hours about what those other areas might be.

'I mean,' Cindy was saying, 'I could listen to "Helter Skelter" all night.'

'Oh, yeah; I know,' said Jon. 'And I've *done* it.' He let out a little chuckle and then said in a sober tone, 'I mean: obviously; we're the only band I've ever known who actually does it right. And we even embellish on it, a little…. The point is that it's not the music of the devil, like some people's parents might say, or like Charles Manson would have you believe. It's how the event of experiencing the music is seen by everyone else, you know, the way people look at going to the show. I just think that maybe, the concert contest might have been exactly the *wrong* thing to get us started around here. Maybe my idea of the big free dance party would have been better.'

He paused for a moment and Jeanne tried to imagine what the big free dance party might have been like, seeing Jon Cavaliere and The Strawberries there for their public debut.

'I don't know,' he said. 'It's a little too late to be worrying about it now. I just hope there's enough people out there who will support a bunch of guys who are just tryin' to play *good*.' He shrugged. 'I don't know. Maybe that's a little too serious for some people.'

'No,' Cindy told him; 'not necessarily. It's just that you've got to find your audience, as you said. The heads will eventually figure out that

The Strawberries, and their *real* audience, don't approve of people brawling in the aisles, and that you're going for a higher class of people. Hey; I'm sure there were *plenty* of people at that show who got the real message, you know, who liked the show you put on for what it really was.'

'I suppose....' Jon looked at the clock.

Jeanne swallowed, although she felt fine. There was just a vicious nagging from within, insisting that she either say something now or forget it for ever. She blushed, realising that in the midst of a silence she was already blurting it. 'Well *I* liked it.'

Jon and Barry both cast their eyes at her, but Jon turned away almost at once. Barry made a smile at her, sufficiently pleasant, and did not notice her shyness as she grew redder and turned away just as Jon had done. But in the adrenaline euphoria from having conducted the entire period's discussion Jon would not pass up the opportunity to address any comment. He articulated the very first thought that entered his mind. 'Yeah; well; join the club, dearie.'

'Diggit!' Cindy laughed aloud. 'The Strawberries Fan Club!'

The bell rang. Jon bolted up out of his chair and made for the door. 'Damn– I need a drink,' he was heard to declare, and he disappeared down the corridor.

* * *

Chapter 4

There was love, all around

For the remaining few weeks of the school year, Jon seemed to change day by day. Jeanne saw how quickly he became accustomed to his newfound popularity, socialising with just about everyone except, it seemed, her. In the wake of The Strawberries' fabulous victory at the concert contest, Jon evolved from that entertaining yet modest young gentleman she had once known into something else entirely. In place of modesty seemed arrogance; he was even more outspoken, impervious to criticism and, apparently, incredibly cold towards the one and only Jeanne Banfield. It finally escalated to the point when, on that last Monday of the school season, she had gathered up all her nerve and made a nice comment about something he had said, in front of the whole class; and he shrugged without a reply and began a new conversation with Barry instead.

She had been crushed by that; but more to her distress was that Jon seemed to be taking an example from Barry Hemphill. Jeanne did not like Barry Hemphill. During the year of English Composition in Room 148 she had grown to dislike and mistrust him, shuddering at his mere presence as though he were an escaped mental convict. He looked to have no favourable influence on Jon Cavaliere. Perhaps it was that dirty-and-dishevelled look about Barry that made her feel so, but there were other boys who appeared the same and they were hardly so alarmingly cold and unsociable. Not yet seventeen, Barry had a thin little moustache that always looked like a dirt line on his face. His dark-brown hair hung in long unkempt strands and she imagined it laden with grease and grime. He only ever wore well-abused work shirts and ripped, faded jeans, except for the last day of school when he wore those ugly knee-length cutoff shorts; and Jeanne had been particularly concerned when Jon had begun arriving in his worst jeans and shirts too.

In truth, those who knew him well would readily attest that Barry, Tobacco Road's second guitarist and most prolific songwriter, was truly an artistic genius. He had a way with twisting a melodic passage or working out a romantic lyric that none his age could ever imitate. Whenever he put his heart into something it became a thing of beauty, and Jeanne had never heard Mrs Hampton make a fuss over him as with Jon only because Barry was far too sensitive about his real feelings to ever let them show in a class at school. This self-effacing, almost sociopathic young artist was seen by Jeanne and the others as a disinterested derelict.   Only real friends like Mark and Jon and the others of The Strawberries and of Tobacco Road knew him as he really was, all honoured that he considered them his truest peers.

Jon especially had great confidence in Barry's talents and was privileged to be one of the few able to see through his façades of insecurity.   He knew Barry had initiated the collective credit of 'Alascan-Hemphill' for his works to lend the impression of a true songwriting partnership; lead singer Rob Alascan willingly admitted that Barry composed most of the music and nearly all the lyrics. What Tobacco Road and their following heard was only what with great reluctance Barry was willing to release; for his most personal expressions of feeling were reserved for only himself. Jon knew of the hundreds of cassettes Barry had recorded alone with an acoustic guitar in his bedroom, dozens of beautiful songs, sentimental romantic ballads and patriotic folk tunes and hymns of faith that might never be heard by anyone else in his lifetime.   It was precious sensitivity like Barry's that they all came to value most; for they knew that, behind whatever guises they chose to wear for their public, they were human beings first and foremost and young businessmen with astronomical aspirations only second, and it was from that true humanity the real expression would have to come.   Otherwise, as Jon so often reminded them, they would only be selling off their souls.

* * *

Late in June, after the lifesavers had taken up station at the lake, Patti and Jeanne went swimming. It was here, two summers before, that Jon Cavaliere had been the first to identify Jeanne as the victim of a vicious muscle cramp and, defying the abilities and authorities of the guards on duty, had struck out to tow her safely ashore. The girls still believed she had fainted from the excitement and that Jon's quick thinking and mouth-to-mouth resuscitation had more than likely saved her life.   In her panic and unconsciousness Jeanne of course recalled nothing of what had really occurred, and since the incident she had only the storytelling of Debbie and Anne and PJ and Patti to fill the gap in her memory.

That was worst of all.   Doubting them, and so never knowing for certain what had gone on that day, had left her in blind confusion about Jon Cavaliere's interest in her.   She had never known how to approach him about it; and then the school season had begun, and he was off to high school and she had a year left to go in junior high; and she knew she could never have asked Steve or someone else to introduce him to her and thus make clear to her what had really happened in any believable way. It all seemed too paradoxical to her anyway, this shy, modest boy rushing into her life after a year's unexplained silence, like her very own knight in shining armour, bound by his life's mission to snatch her from Death's very grasp and then to vanish without thanks into self-imposed anonymity again. Even so she would lie awake at night in her bed with chills trickling through her entire body at the very notion of it all.

Now all that was an eon away. It bided uneasily in the back of her mind, haunting her like a skeleton in the wardrobe, forcing her to keep silent about her real feelings for him. She would have loved to just admit it all, in public, out loud, just to set the record straight for all and for all time so that everyone would know, so there would be no more secret feelings to hide and nothing of which she should be ashamed. She felt certain that from within that cold aloofness he displayed there just had to be something warm and wonderful, and that maybe he was struggling like she was to be rid of his skeletons too, to just get on with his life with her as a part of it. But there was nothing to make her sure. And now, with everyone still talking about The Strawberries and that concert contest, it was harder than ever to approach him about the past. Apparently he had passed the past and survived it; and Jeanne was frightened to think that it had been to live on without her.

Patti told her over and over she sounded like the tragic heroine in some silly romance novel. She liked to believe she was a sceptic herself and advised Jeanne to get over all that ancient history, the sooner, the better. She and Jeanne shopped at the arcade and. swam at the lake and went to the men's softball games and cheered the team with the best-looking male players, enjoying the attention they received from the opposite sex, boys and graduated seniors and men even older than that. They went to a party without being invited once and became so tipsy over the Southern Comfort liqueur in the punch that several of the university-bound footballers there sought to take advantage of them. In a fit of the giggles Patti pushed Jeanne into Bill Idle's lap; but Bill's gentlemanly reaction surprised them both. The handsome scholarship quarterback merely brushed away the spilt cocktail ice, made room for her to sit beside him in the chair and politely asked her for a proper date. Patti was incredulous; but Jeanne sobered herself quickly and accepted like the lady she really was. Patti giggled so hard she began to hiccup; and then she came down with a headache; and to avoid her mother she had to go home with Wendi Barrie for the night.

Although Patti worried about her, Jeanne did date several boys during the summer. Short, red-haired Jeremy Fisher tried so hard to impress her that she delighted in his efforts. He took her sailing on the knockabout his father, a local optometrist, had bought him for his sixteenth birthday in April; but the day of pleasant sunbathing and swimming in the Cove turned into a disaster. A sudden squall came up the river and Jeremy capsized the boat right off the yacht club quay.

Other than becoming wet and suffering dozens of subsequent jokes in the club lounge, Jeremy and his little boat were fine. Jeanne, however, lost the gold-plated necklace Joe Lorrimer had given her just two weeks before and considered that a substantial loss.   Actually Joe barely noticed. He had already begun seeing Anne Marlowe.

As a close family friend, Jeanne had sailed often with the Marlowes on their thirty-four-foot Tartan sloop, Papillon, but the time that most impressed her came on a weekend in early July. They had left Essex early that morning and were motoring out towards the Sound in anticipation of an eight-day sailing cruise, to take in Mystic Seaport and Block Island. Steve was well able to handle the boat himself and had the wheel when he pointed out a sleek blue yawl to Anne and Jeanne. It rode a mooring off a small marina just inside the inlet of the river, prancing nobly over the incoming swells. 'See that?' Steve asked over the drone of the inboard auxiliary. 'The Cavalieres' boat. Kinda weird seeing them all the way down here. Usually they're up the river at the little yard next to the Club.'

Jeanne squinted in the sun, studying it intently; for its owners alone made it of paramount importance to her. The boat was about forty-two feet long with a varnished mahogany trunk cabin, plenty of polished brightwork and absolutely immaculate navy-blue topsides, all superbly maintained.   Though its traditional design made it look perhaps forty years old, funnily enough the masts and booms were of jet-black anodised aluminium as on the latest race yachts, and the look was ominous and intimidating as though the boat commanded respect simply riding a mooring unattended. Jeanne caught a strong chill in the salty air; there was a sudden aura of something powerful yet undeniably benevolent. In spite of the warm summer sun, she felt herself shiver.

'La Cacciatrice,' Steve pronounced for her, reading the yacht's name as they closed from astern. 'Italian, for "The Huntress". Beautiful; isn't it?'

'Wow,' said Jeanne, unaware of how spellbound she looked. The stern of the yacht was adorned with a traditional nautical eagle and the name was spelt-out in gold leaf. The port, as on Papillon, was given as Essex. But the most awesome feature Jeanne noticed was the flag. Flying free in the breeze at the mizzenmast halliard, the banner of deep heraldic blue was fully five feet long, displaying its white knight's-head and double-edged sword entwined with a yellow olive-tree branch. For a second she could only point; and Steve knew her question.

'Their family flag,' he said, quietly as though in respect. 'From their family crest, you know, with the sword and all…. Pretty cool; isn't it? It's a one-of-a-kind. I thought about doing one for our boat once. In the old days all owners had their own flags on board. But their boat's been around for years.   One of the guys at the club says it's been around for something like ten years now; can you imagine? I'll tell you one thing: between that boat and that flag, everyone up and down the Sound knows them.'

Jeanne could say nothing. She sat turned about on the cockpit seat as they passed the boat abeam, sighing at the intricate gold-leaf on the trailboards and the elegant clipper bow and that long, rakish bowsprit, striving to keep the binoculars trained on it until it was lost in the haze astern.   To find Jon's family so exceptionally well-known and well-off was thrilling, even more than she had ever imagined or dreamt. The thought sent shivers down her spine and, for the rest of the week's cruise, she had no better fantasy than to envision a romantic evening sailing aboard such a yacht with the one whose company she desired more than anything else.

* * *

The Strawberries, under their new name, played a few local dances before Independence Day.   Dave was playing billiards that Saturday night at the Riverfront Pub, a favourite haunt of his since his eighteenth birthday last September, where without his bandmates he could enjoy more than one or two of the popular malt beverages.   It was quite by chance that Bell Howard, a local radio disc jockey, stopped in to observe the billiards players. When Dave recognised him the two struck up a conversation.   Dave was surprised to hear how much Bell had heard about the young band of teenagers making waves among the high-school set.   Talk came round to The Strawberries' future and, although Bell did beat him at eight-ball, Dave went home feeling quite confident he had actually found a real manager for the group.

He was surprised, too, after Jon and Bob had returned from the annual Cavaliere family cruise aboard La Cacciatrice and after the Dennings had come home from camping at Lake George, that the others were in complete agreement.   So Chris Santana set up a meeting at the garage. Bell was honoured to visit them in their own habitat, impressed with how serious they seemed and diverted by their natural ability to entertain. He gave a short lesson on his experiences in the music business and then shared with them his own opinions as to where they should play and how to proceed. These they debated for over an hour; and Bell was encouraged to find them so well-versed in the principles of public relations and marketing and running a small business.

It was agreed by all that Bell would assume responsibility for getting work for the bands and, in return, be paid with a percentage from the net income.   Chris, their advisor and director for over two years now, would remain in charge of scheduling practice sessions and recording financial transactions, rather like Bell's envoy within the group.   Bell was ecstatic with his new challenge.   A 1970 graduate of Berkeley, he was himself a former musician and rebel who had edited his school's underground newspaper, attended the Woodstock music festival and participated in enough rallies and sit-in demonstrations to have purged himself of the need to publicly display any social dissent.   So far his baccalaureate degree in communications had not served him to the fullest and he was stuck in a mild job with little further to go in the field.   But he had an expert way of expressing ideas and debating issues that really sparked Jon; and the two would often ring each other up at all hours just to discuss some new notion for getting more exposure for the band.   Jon thought it exquisitely noble that someone with so much to offer would devote any serious effort to such a relatively minor troupe of musicians.   He decided that, at the very least, no matter what happened to them in the future, they would owe Bell a 'thank you' on their first album jacket.   But, for now, no-one could be certain as to when that might be.

Jon was very busy all summer.   The band held practice three times per week; and all the boys held regular jobs for the season, even Ricky. Dave and Jon wrote a dozen new songs; at least half were so bad they were certain they would never want to perform them.   But they knew they were still in their embryonic stage.   All that had passed so far, since that fateful jam-session at Chris's birthday over two-and-a-half years ago, had been mere groundwork for what they would yet accomplish.

But Jon hated the interim.   He had always been rather impatient, despising phrases like 'strategic waiting', used by Dave and Bell, no matter how positive their intentions.   To bide time, or so he told himself, he worked with his father as a foreman's assistant, driving drawings and surveying gear and rented equipment to and from the blueprinters and the engineers and the borough clerks, collecting a great suntan with no shirt on.   This kept him in fuel money and bass-guitar strings and, since he was not needed every hour of every day, there was time for him to work on the boat and keep it in its ordinary Bristol-fashion.   Mr Cavaliere was grateful for the attention to his beloved La Cacciatrice; for one Thursday morning he took two prospective clients out sailing and, whilst his two sons sailed the boat handily, business talk could go on amidst the lovely summer greens of the upper Connecticut River.

But more than for his interest in the contracting business, or his upkeep of the family yacht, Jon would for ever be endeared to his father for taking up his oldest and fondest love: flying aeroplanes. Royal dynasties might have insisted that their heirs acquire fencing or equestrian talents; but the Cavaliere men all adored their sons who learned to fly. Since his formative years Jon had been seen by everyone in the family as the one who would most readily take after his father as an intuitive, accomplished flier; but all were surprised to see such innate aptitude and genuine passion about it. With Dave Holloway, himself a recently-licensed private pilot, Jon would run off to the county aerodrome on every free afternoon to hire the odd Beechcraft or Cessna; and the two would practise their own brand of aerial shenanigans, ducking the river bridges and inducing controlled stalls at altitude till nearly sunset. It was great fun for both of them and taught them sober responsibility into the bargain.

For young Jon it was far more an exercise in sentiment than anything else. He knew his father held regrets about having been unable, in the last twenty years or so, to maintain an aeroplane of his own and so felt a great surge of nostalgia whenever he soloed the same old Piper Cub in which his father had taken him flying as a child. Even before he had passed his final flight examination, the rental agency had begun allowing him their only Pitts Special, a feisty little biplane well capable of advanced aerobatic manoeuvres. Fortunately they would never learn of the time their model student had sought out his father's current site to buzz the cheering workers in inverted flight. Mr Cavaliere was far too lenient a disciplinarian to do more than feign worry. More often, in fact, out of his wife's earshot, he tended to encourage his son with tips on high-performance stunt flying. Recalling his own flight training in the wee months of the War, it was for him a haunting *déjá-vu* to witness his son with goggles in an open cockpit, his very own living reincarnation experiencing that singular thrill of earning his wings.

* * *

After the last of many unpleasant disagreements Jimmy Kennedy, bass guitarist and founding member of Tobacco Road, quit abruptly at the end of July. Barry took up Dave's old Fender Precision and covered the bass parts admirably but, even with Rob Alascan adequately handling some rhythm-guitar duties, their distinctive twin-guitar sound was sadly lacking. The search began straight away for a new member but there would be no time for auditions, arrangements and rehearsals before the first of three shows at an important local cabaret. Chris had been working for several months to get them into favour with more club managers who might pay them the higher figures; and Tobacco Road had been counting on the engagement. Now, with the scheduled dates just days away, it seemed that Jimmy Kennedy would have the last laugh after all.

But on 24 July, Dave flew out to California for a visit with his father, thus placing The Strawberries on hiatus till his return. Jon and Bob had planned a trip to Florida for this period, a holiday Jon postponed so as to lend his services to Tobacco Road immediately. After all he did know their original material; songs like 'In The Clubhouse', 'All Right', 'Oh Jane' and 'Momma Doin' It' were as familiar to him as his own compositions. It was Jon and Barry and Mark who met most often to arrange cover selections; in fact Jon's customary flair for dynamics had become something of an unsung hallmark of the Tobacco Road style.

And so for that Thursday, Friday and Saturday, Tobacco Road were a five-piece outfit once again, including an exuberant left-handed bass-guitar player with an impish grin and an impressively high vocal range. Jon was delighted with the opportunity to play things beyond the realm of the usual Strawberries repertoire; he was hardly a stranger to the works of bands like Aerosmith, The Who, Led Zeppelin and Deep Purple. The Alice Cooper Band's 'School's Out' had long been one of his favourites; and hardly anyone in the area knew the nuances of Rundgren's 'Open My Eyes' half as well. The other four indulged him the lead vocal to a rocked-up version of 'Day Tripper' whilst Rob handled the tambourine and back-up harmonies. For an encore, Foghat's famous arrangement of 'I Just Want To Make Love To You' led into a long, rousing rendition of 'If You Need It, You'll Get It' and the crowd were left cheering for more.

Chris diplomatically explained to his principals that a new bass-guitar player was on the way, though 'the definitive Tobacco Road sound' was just as it had been presented. But the club's management were well able to appreciate the potential before them. On Monday Chris went directly to the bank with the advance cheque, to open an account with which to conduct the band's financial business. At last he was on his way to real success as a promoter; and that very day, Jon, Andrew and Bob were on their way south along Interstate 95 for their holiday of fun in the sun.

* * *

'So hey, man; where you dudes playin' next?'

'Aaah; I don't know. That shit is always up to Santana, or Holloway....'

'So how was that show you just played, at the firehouse?'

'When? Last *month*? Aaah; I don't know, man, I think that after sittin' in with the 'Road, there, I can see how our stuff needs a lotta work. They've just got their shit together so much more than us. Well; you saw that show; didn't you? I told ya it was me who gave them that arrangement for "Day Tripper"; right?'

José nodded. 'Yeah; and that was a pretty cool version of it, too.'

'Well; *yeah.* Of *course.* Just so long as Barry stays off the bass; the guy's just too good a guitar player to be fartin' around with that shit. I *love* watchin' him play, man. He makes it look so easy…. Fuckin' *inspiring*, and whatnot.' Jon fired the three-ball into the farthest corner pocket. 'There you go, dude. Four down for me. You're down *now.*'

'Not for long, man.' José smiled as he lined up a shot. 'So would you rather just jam with the Tobacco Road, then?'

'Naah. The chicks *like* us, man. I'm in it for the chicks.'

A cry of 'Hey!' from the stairs made them both look up. Chris Santana entered through the narrow door and strode briskly into the broad, low room, in white jeans, a red paisley shirt and a white denim sportcoat. 'Say hey, dudes,' he smiled, and straightened his hair.

'Hey,' Jon said to him.

'Hey,' said José, and lined up his corner shot again.

'So where you goin', all duded-up?'

'Aaah,' Chris smiled; 'just around.'

'Right, bud. Ain't seen ya since we got back. You got a haircut.'

'No; I got 'em all cut,' Chris teased, and took out a comb from his back pocket.

Jon shook his unruly mop of hair, substantially lengthened and lightened by two weeks in the Florida sun. '*That* was a mistake, dude.'

Chris shrugged. 'Yeah; well; I got responsibilities now.' He laughed a little. 'So how about this weather, man? Anything like this down there?'

'*Nothing* like it,' Jon said. He turned to look out the slit-like window. Gusty winds kept the trees bending over and pedestrians blew down the street, struggling to stay afoot. 'Obviously, my mistake was comin' *back.* How long's it been like this?'

'Aaah; on and off, most of the week,' said Chris.

'Go, man,' José told him.

Jon looked at the table and took a shot, somewhat carelessly. The cue ball bounced off three banks and deposited itself in a corner pocket without disturbing a thing. 'Son of a bitch. And *another* shot well-missed!'

'Good job,' Chris said with a laugh. 'So; how was it down there?'

'It was pretty cool. Well; *hot.* Well; you know. The Lavenders have this dude workin' the shop with 'em now, named Kite, who's a real crier. That mug is such a riot, man…. I mean he kept me in stitches the whole time we were down, and whatnot. Apparently he just walked into town one day, and bumped into them, and the next thing he knew, he had a job and a place to stay. Dude's been with them all season. You know how Danny Lavender is, man; that's how he is.'

Chris knew.   He and his sister Melody had been acquainted with their neighbours, Jon's cousin Marjorie Bailey and her family, long enough to have met her mother's nephews, the three young Lavender brothers who ran a surf shop in Florida, on more than a few occasions. They were known as great humourists, but also generous and sincere.

'So where'd he come from, this dude?'

'New York. He said he used to be part of a gang; but he's like really cool, you know; like he's not a dope addict or anything. He said they spent most of their time gettin' chased by other guys, who were bigger. This is just how he talks about it; you know? It's no wonder everybody likes him, especially Danny. He's like part of the family already, you know; and he's learnin' to surf now, and everything.'

'So were the waves worthwhile; or what?'

Jon smiled. 'Ah, man; they were beautiful. Danny said it had to be a freak. We only had one front come over the whole time, and they were pumpin' before and afterwards.   Everybody kept tellin' us it would really suck this time of year; but I got some really hot rides. Drew and Lee even caught me on film a coupla times.'

'*Dag*. Woulda been nice to go with ya.'

'Yeah; well; you got responsibilities now, Chris.'

They both laughed. 'So did Margie come back up with ya?'

'Huh? Oh; no, man; no way. No; she's workin' with Danny in the shop for the rest of the season. And with all the luggage, and the guitars, and three sticks on the roof.... Hell; I wouldn't've wanted to have *her* in the car too, all the way back. Next summer, though, I told Danny I'm movin' down there for good. You know; like, he knows a lotta bar owners, and he said a lot of them might be interested in seein' us play. Well; I played him the tapes, you know....'

José had missed the shot for which he had taken out the mechanical bridge. 'Go, man.'

'What'd you do? –*miss*? You, *miss* a shot?'

José only smiled that row of pearl-white teeth at him. 'Looks that way,' Chris said.

Jon chuckled a little to himself. Sipping from his can of beer he took a long look at the table and then lined up a combination shot. Chris and José watched as he rammed the stick into the cue ball, which sent the fifteen into the side pocket and dropped the twelve into the near corner. 'Hey, man,' José laughed; 'can't you count?'

'Okay; okay....' Jon floored the butt of his stick. 'Five up, looks like.'

'Yeah; *now*,' Chris teased him. 'So; you think this'll be clear by the Twenty-fourth?'

'You tell me,' Jon said. 'I've only been back a day and a half. What's the Twenty-fourth?'

'It's for my sister's birthday. I told you about it. We're gonna have a big party and all, you know, out back, and doo.'

'Oh; yeah? Sounds fairly cool.'

'Well; it was my mom's idea.'

'What does your dad think? I know he generally hates those big parties....'

'Aaah; well; he's been out of town while we've been planning it. He's in Philadelphia this week, you know, sellin' more candy recipes....'

'To who?' Jon asked, curious.

'Oh; well; O'Brien's.'

'Outasite,' Jon said, as he was impressed. 'That pop of yours is really doin' good these days. I bet he's really happy; huh?' He looked at Chris.

'I guess,' said Chris, and he made a little smile. 'You know, that tan of yours is almost as dark as this Portuguese bandit over here.'

José laughed from the other end of the table. 'Yeah; but his isn't everlasting.'

'True,' Jon smiled. 'Still, it looks pretty tropical; don't it? I think I could get pretty well used to livin' down there in Florida, with Danny and all them.' He admired the colour of his arm under the low-hanging fluorescent fixture. 'So tell me about this party, dude.'

'Well,' said Chris; 'there'll be a whole mess of like banquet tables, and a lotta relatives, and a lotta friends, and doo. It's supposed to be pretty formal.'

'Sounds decent,' Jon said.

'Go, man.' José sipped some beer.

Jon saw a shot and lined up on the eleven. 'So; is there gonna be a band at this party; or are we it?'

'Hey,' Chris said with a smile; 'I didn't come to this dive to see *this* guy.'

José pretended to swing his cue at Chris; and Jon waved them away. 'Yo, *kids*; let's be cool. The *maestro* is at work.' He waited for them to step back; and they watched as he sent the cue ball towards his mark. However the eleven bounced squarely off the side bank half an inch to the right and ricocheted back to kiss the white ball, which took its leave of the playing surface via the opposite side pocket. 'Son of a *bitch*!' Jon hollered. 'Look what the hell you guys made me do!'

'I'd say that was you, man,' José laughed, with another white-toothed grin. 'I'd say my great-grandmother could make such shot.' He retrieved the white ball from the collector and set it down in line with his remaining two marks. The ten rammed the two and both balls rolled into the far corner pocket.

'Son of a bitch,' Jon mumbled.

'So were there any decent-lookin' chicks down there, besides Marjorie?' Chris asked him.

Jon smiled, realising how pretty his younger cousin had become. Still, to him she would forever remain his sister's childhood playmate and perhaps equally a nuisance. 'Yeah; well; sometimes I think the chicks down there are kinda snotty, you know. That's the impression I got, anyway. I met a few, though; mostly locals. The Lavenders know just about everybody in town. Well; it's not a big town. When you surf, you tend to meet a lotta girls. It's that kind of sport, you know; not like swimming....'

'Sure,' Chris said; 'and the way *you* probably show off....'

'Well; they won't watch *me*, Chris, 'cause I'm not any *good*. They watch Danny. I mean everybody on the whole damn *island* watches Danny. The guy is incredible out there. Wait till we get the pictures back.'

'Bring 'em to the party,' Chris suggested.

'So *tell* me about this party,' Jon said to him. 'Like, what kinda girls are gonna be there?'

'Oh, hell; well; there'll be *lotsa* girls. You guys are gonna be playin' up on the back porch, there, in white suits and doo, and they'll notice you like right away. You know, like, being the best band in Wilshire....'

'Diggit,' Jon smiled, and thought about it. 'That'll be damn nice.'

'Sure it will. My mom can't wait to have you guys play. She's been tellin' everybody about it.'

'Yeah; your mom does throw the best parties around, man. Just make sure that Holloway knows he has to get dressed-up. He'll never–'

'He knows; he knows,' Chris assured him. 'It's all been worked out. Even the set lists....'

'Cool,' said Jon, and looked up as the introduction of 'Band On The Run' came over the jukebox speakers. 'My *man*,' he said, and absently pretended to play an imaginary guitar, with the pool cue, to the music.

'Stuck inside these four walls,
Sent inside for ever;
Never seeing no-one nice again,
Like you....'

Chris watched José lining up the shot. 'Well; all sorts of people will be there. Deej, and Mark and Barry said they'd come.... My cousin Laurie, of course; and Becky and Cindy said they'd show up, and of course your brother, and my cousins Gina and Diana.... All kindsa folks.'

'Lotsa *girls*,' Jon said. He picked up his beer again.

'Dig that. But lotsa adults, you know. It's a class social.'

'Yeah,' said Jon, looking out the window again; 'it'll clear up by then.... And a lotta class, like you said. I like those kinda parties. I'm gettin' sick of these parties where the main objectives are to get everybody rolling-ass drunk, and then wait for some kinda wasted girl to fall into your lap. I hate them kinda–' The sound of billiard balls cracking together made him whirl about. Whatever dropped into the pocket nearest him escaped his sight.

It had been the eight-ball. 'Somethin' ails you, man,' José said with a laugh. 'Somethin' ails you, if you hate them kinda parties. You ought to be gettin' your head examined.'

'You ought to be gettin' your *arm* busted,' Jon told him. 'That's the last time I'm throwin' any more of my money away in this piss-hole with *you.* So when are ya comin' out to race me again?'

José laughed. 'You're gettin' the ol' Fury fixed right now,' he said, and held out his hand.

'Shit,' Jon moaned, and pulled out his wallet. He slapped his last two one-dollar notes indignantly into the open palm.

'Uh, José,' Chris said slyly, as José stood and stared at his latest winnings, 'don't you owe me about two bucks?'

'Huh?' José looked at him. 'No; wait– No way–'

'Sure you do,' Chris said. 'Last week, it was, for some beer....'

Slowly he lifted the two notes out of José's open hand and then slapped them against his own wrist. 'Yeah; two six-packs of Colt Forty-Five....'

'Say,' said Jon, an idea brewing in his head; 'uh, Chris, don't you think you could spare me, say, maybe about *two* dollars?'

Chris frowned. 'What for?'

'I really oughta be gettin' your dear sweet sister somethin' for her birthday.'

'Uh, no; but–'

But Jon had already removed the money from Chris's hand. 'Yo, dude, thanks a lot. I'm sure your *sister* will appreciate it.' He turned to go; and José met him with a congratulatory grin and an enthusiastic handshake. As they started towards the door Jon was saying to him, 'Lovely girl, that Melody. I'd feel so terrible coming without a present, you know; she'll be sixteen....'

Before Chris could reply the two were out the door.

* * *

Jon arrived at the party just before three, as per Mrs Santana's request. They had been over earlier to set up the equipment on the Santanas' rear verandah and now he needed only to plug in his bass guitar and begin playing. The Strawberries played a few Beatles tunes to warm up, including a rousing version of 'Taxman' during which Dave set down his guitar and stepped out onto the lawn to scrutinise the levels of the sound-reinforcement system leaving Bob to perform the lead vocal and guitar solo without him. Guests began to arrive;

and so the boys shut down to mingle and Ricky queued up a few tapes on Chris's cassette deck which had been set up to play through the big speakers. The recorded music might have been rather bland to the younger people's tastes; but Jon was able to appreciate the better selections of the big bands and especially some of the small jazz combos, and he was glad to hear Chris had mixed in quite a few bossanova tunes for his party playlist as well as the expected softer numbers from The Beatles, The Young Rascals and The Guess Who.

By four o'clock there were nearly two hundred people in the Santanas' back garden. The big blue three-storey Victorian house sat on a long waterfront section in the older country-club neighbourhood, with aged elms and oaks and ashes bordering a lumpy but well-groomed lawn along both sides. Far behind the house was a shaded stone terrace by the river, almost invisible from the upper grounds beyond a thick hedgerow and low-hanging foliage. The wide verandah across the back of the house made a perfect stage; and guests seemed to congregate at the steps in anticipation of a live performance.

Melody herself had an irrepressible spirit, greeting everyone with a hug and a kiss on the cheek. She was in her element as hostess; like her mother, she was beloved for her charm and gracious hospitality during a gathering. Mr Santana, the confection scientist, tended to shun the limelight, keeping to small groups of serious intellectuals and going on in long dissertations about chemical compounds before leading the interested few into his laboratory for more data or demonstrations. But such was nothing knew to his family, who were expert merrymakers and almost never ran out of enthusiasm.

Melody was indeed a lovely girl, having deep, dark eyes and a lush mane of wavy chestnut-brown hair, a striking beauty at just five days past the actual date of her sixteenth birthday. Those who knew her admired and envied her eclectic taste and distinctive style and, though she did not turn in the same circle as the cheerleaders and athletes, in spite of the Santana family's perpetually meagre financial situation Melody maintained a lead position in local fashion. There were dozens of her friends at the party, scarcely half as elegant or as charismatically appealing but willing to keep close by her, as though to bask in the radiance of her favour, whilst Melody sat like an empress enthroned in an ornate wicker fan chair beneath a big mimosa tree. When Jon presented his gift, she pulled him over eagerly and gave him a kiss squarely on the lips. 'Oh; *thank* you, dear sweet Jonathan,' she mushed, whilst the other girls giggled at the teasing. 'You are simply the sweetest one *here!*'

Naturally Jon blushed; Melody tended to enjoy embarrassing him. But it was difficult to accept her as a beautiful young lady with eye-catching legs in a short white chiffon dress; he had become too used to thinking of her as an eight-year-old tomboy in dungarees hanging from tree swings with her elder brother's friends. The contrast evident today was overwhelming. Uncomfortable with lingering in her company, he excused himself from the girls and sought refuge at the punchbowl.

Becky Barnett was helping herself to a glass and gladly served Jon in turn. 'So,' he asked her, more at ease with someone with whom he had more in common anyway; 'how are *you* makin' out?'

'Oh; well; wouldn't you like to know?' She laughed. 'No.... All right.' She turned at once, as though to leave him, and then asked over her shoulder, 'So *hey*. Who's the cute kid with the brown hair?'

'Well; since that narrows it down to about nine-tenths of the guys you've ever looked at....'

'Shut up,' she teased. 'You know I've always had a preference for blondes....' She reached up behind him to muss his hair, albeit only a little. Girls always seemed to enjoy toying with Jon's hair. 'See him, there? He's cute. Not quite as cute as you.... With the blue jacket.'

Jon scoffed. 'Looks like a chump. What makes you think I'd know some chump like that?'

'Shut up,' she told him again. 'Just because that jacket makes you look like Jay Gatsby....'

'Hah!' he laughed. 'Why, *Daisy*.... I've got a man in England who buys me clothes.'

Becky squealed. 'I've never *seen* such beautiful shirts!' She spun about in a small fit of the giggles and then came back at him with a fist raised as though to slug him. 'So; what's the plan, here? Are you gonna introduce me to him?'

'Hah! You're kidding; right?'

'No; really. Just go up and say, "Hi; this is Becky". You'd do that for me.'

'No; for *you*, I'd say, "Hi; this is *Rebecca*",' he teased, and laughed.

She did strike his arm then. 'Forget it. If you're gonna be like *that* about it, I'll introduce myself.'

He watched her stomp off, not in the direction of the brown-haired boy in the blue poplin jacket after all. A shy curly-haired girl came up to the table and Jon helped her to a glass of the cider punch and sat down to speak with her. He was proud of himself for that, because he had always been rather awkward about girls he did not know well. There were others, like Dave and Chris, who could comfortably embark on casual conversation with people they had just met; and normally Jon could too, except when the person at hand was a pretty girl. Then anything was likely to happen. Except, Jon thought, me getting a date with her. That *never* happens.

Melissa Knight's mother came over to see whom her daughter had met; and it turned out that she and Chris's mother had been university roommates. She had heard much about Jon from Mrs Santana, so she said, and complimented her daughter right in front of him for having met such a nice boy.   Jon, thoroughly embarrassed by the undue attention, made an opportunity to excuse himself, taking each of their hands just to be charming, and wandered off towards the house.

Mrs Santana caught him by the elbow once and asked how he was enjoying the party.   She did not keep him long; even talking she appeared to be preoccupied with someone else, although as she scanned the crowded lawn he saw no-one who reciprocated her attention.   He shrugged this off as the work of a busy party hostess and stepped up onto the porch.   Dave introduced him to a music teacher who was interested in meeting Bob Prescott and then Jon and Dave went off on the topic of The Beatles' music; anyone who knew them would have expected this discussion to go on for hours.   It was not until Jon was speaking with several women about the comparisons of music and art that Mrs Santana found him again.

'Jon,' she interrupted, 'come along. You've got to meet a friend of ours.'

'Oh; well; yeah; but—'

'We can return later,' she said, partly to him, and partly to her friends, who all laughed at Jon's blush. Mrs Santana was towing him half-sideways down the steps and out to the party on the lawn. Once he wriggled free but she caught him again; and he managed to snatch up a snowflake roll from a passing table. Two slices of bologna fell to hand next; and when at last she stopped directly in front of him, he was squeezing ketchup liberally onto the impromptu sandwich.

Mrs Santana spoke to someone ahead; and he forced a mouthful, chewing hungrily. It was the first he had eaten all day. Ketchup rolled out from the opposite side of the sandwich onto his hand and he switched the sandwich to his right, licking off his left. It was right then that she turned about.

'Jon,' she said, stepping back, 'I'd like you to meet a good friend of ours: Christine Polvere. Chrissy, this is Jon Cavaliere.'

Before him a silken voice responded, 'Hello, Jon. It's a pleasure to meet you.'

He looked up from licking the ketchup off his hand; and she unfolded before him: small feet in bone-coloured platform shoes, finely shaped legs in dark tan stockings, a short cream-white dress about a slender waist, long neck encircled in dainty gold, parted peach-pink lips, a gently-olive complexion with a sculptor's Roman nose, topped off with sun-streaked golden-brown hair. Two deep brown eyes were looking right back at him hypnotically.

Jon swallowed at the pinnacle of self-consciousness, and part of the sandwich stuck in his throat. More ketchup oozed out and he changed hands with the sandwich again, noticing only then that the girl had put out her hand to him. He gestured feebly to his full mouth whilst trying to force down what he was still chewing.

'Uh, hi; uh; sorry—' Still at a complete loss, he took her hand to acknowledge the introduction. For a second or two they just stood and examined each other's eyes. The girl's classic beauty was breathtaking; she might have been a goddess from antiquity. And there might even have been a moment between them; but they exchanged only sudden expressions of distress as they both felt the clammy cold ketchup between his hand and hers.

Reddening with embarrassment, Jon passed the dripping sandwich to Mrs Santana who took it only because he would have dropt it otherwise. He let go the girl's hand and pounced on the stack of serviettes on the table beside him. After spilling most of the serviettes all over the lawn and knocking over a jar of relish, he took her right hand again and nervously wiped off the ketchup.

He smiled weakly. 'I'm sorry,' he said, feeling his voice crack a bit. 'It's just that I'm so stupid at introductions half the time....' They both watched Chris's mother picking up the dropped serviettes and then together sought to right the upset relish jar. He took the sandwich back from Mrs Santana, noticing a few other guests as they turned away after having witnessed the episode. That did no-one's pride any good.

Mrs Santana worked her way round the table, in a guise of straightening the clutter and effectively slinking away from her matchmaking. Knowing her as he did, Jon recognised her attempt at subtlety; but he knew also that he was caught. For lack of anything else to do, he turned to the girl again.

She stood there uneasily before him, resting her fingertips as though casually on the table, looking right at him with what he had already surmised to be profound disdain. 'I'm uh, sorry, really, about this sandwich, and all— Well; sorry if I look like a jerk.'

'Oh,' she said. 'I didn't— Well; what I meant to say— You're a friend of Christopher's; aren't you?'

'Huh? Christopher? Oh; uh, yeah; well; I guess I am. Pretty good friend, I guess; you know, I mean: we've known each other a while.... Like eight years, or maybe nine.... No; I guess it's more like eight. Or eight-and-a-half years, you know; I guess about eight-and-a-half years, I've known Chris, uh, Christopher....' He looked down and tried to shake off his embarrassment without looking too obvious about it. He thought to curse Chris for insisting that he leave the mirrored sunglasses in the car. 'So; do you know, uh, Christopher, then?'

'Oh yes,' she said, nodding a little. 'I suppose we're what you might call friends of the family.'

'Oh; okay; cool.... So; uh, who else do you know who's here?'

'What?'

'Well; uh, like Holloway. Dave Holloway. *He's* here.'

'I don't, uh, know him—' She stopped, at a loss.

'Oh. Well how about like DJ, or maybe Becky— You must know Becky, Becky Barnett; she's like friends with Melody—'

'No…. I'm afraid we don't know many of the Santanas' friends here. We've only just moved to Wilshire from Greenwich.'

'Oh.' He turned about then and by chance happened to see Ricky standing by the punchbowl. 'Oh; uh, wait; there's Ricky—' He turned back to the girl. 'I gotta go see Ricky about something. We'll… talk later; okay?'

'Oh; okay—'

'Excuse me. It was nice meeting you—' He turned, stuffing half the remaining sandwich into his mouth just to be rid of it, and hurried over towards the punchbowl table. Not seeing him, Ricky walked off with a blond girl and Jon had to pursue him another twelve yards before he was able to tap him. His mouth still full of sandwich, he managed, 'Yo, man, what's up?'

'Hey, dude,' said Ricky.

Jon tried to clear his throat to speak; but it took some doing. 'I was like tryin' to catch you—'

'Hey, man; like this is Terri; and this, this is our bass player, Jon.'

The pretty blond girl beamed a giggly smile at Jon and chirped, 'Oh, wow; like I get to meet *two* musicians at one party; I mean: far *out*…. I mean: like I saw you guys play at school, you know; and I mean: like wow, it was *so* far-out….'

'Hey; cool….'

'So what's up?' Ricky asked him. 'You said you were tryin' to find me?'

'Oh; yeah; well; nothin' much….'

'What,' Ricky asked; 'is Dave itchin' to go back on again; or what?'

'Yeah; uh, *yeah*. Man, we gotta get this shit organised.'

Mrs Santana returned to find Christine standing alone beside the table where she had been before. She could not locate Jon anywhere in the crowd. 'Oh; where did he go? I was hoping you'd get a chance to talk with him. He's such an interesting person. Don't you think so?'

'Oh; um— Well; I suppose—'

'I'm sorry, Chrissy; I'm sure he's just nervous. Meeting pretty girls is never easy for young men.'

'Oh; well—'

'I'm sure you'll like him when you get to know him. He's very nice. Christopher and Melody think the world of him. As a matter of fact, the band will be going on again any minute. You just wait, and you'll see how talented he is. Let me go find that Christopher….' She hurried off into the crowd by the porch.

Chris, a born master-of-ceremonies, stepped up to the verandah with

a microphone.   He told a few well-rehearsed jokes and then gave an
introduction for his sister, who blushed and giggled at all the attention.
Surely her family and friends would recognise her apparent shyness as
just an act.   She thanked everyone for coming to the fête in her
honour, and then introduced the band, whose three-part *a capella*
harmony began The Beatles' 'There's A Place'.

The four shaggy-haired rock-and-roll musicians went over well, due
in no small part to the white tuxedo suits which Chris had insisted he
and the band don for the event.   But before such a large crowd of
diverse age groups, their talent was all too evident, even to those who
knew little about music.   Jon took the show to heart, and did the lead
vocals to three in a row, 'I'll Follow The Sun', 'PS I Love You' and
'And I Love Her', their concert-contest winner.   Dave did the lead to
'Nowhere Man' with Jon and Bob accompanying him at the other
microphone, and Bob did Harrison's 'I Need You', Liverpudlian lilt
and all.   Dave sang 'If I Fell' and 'No Reply' and then announced that
the next would be their last before a short recess.

Chris and Melody were sitting upon chairs on the lawn when their
mother approached and asked somewhat worriedly, 'Have either of
you seen Chrissy?'

'Aaah; not recently,' said Chris, and sipped some Michelob from a
can.

'She was down by the punch table,' Melody said.   'She couldn't've
gone too far....'

'Oh; good.' She turned and went off.

They both watched her go.   'All right,' Melody asked her brother;
'who is it *this* time?'°

'What?'

'She's trying to set Chrissy up with somebody.   I *know* you know
who.'

Chris laughed. 'Oh; come on. Take a *wild* guess.'

He was still watching the band, and Melody looked up just as Jon
sang:

> 'There was love, all around,
> But I never heard it singing;
> No; I never heard it at all,
> Till there was you.'

Christine watched from the punchbowl with Becky, who was chatting
amiably with her whilst the band played. 'So; have you met him?'

'Met who?' Christine wondered.

'*Jon.* Well; Jon, as in Jonathan. You know, the *cute* one.'

'Oh; yes; I did, earlier–'

'He's really pretty cool, you know. You'd probably like him.'

'Do you know him?' asked Christine.

'Oh *sure*,' she said, as though it were a needless question. 'I've known him since like elementary school. Then we were *both* little brats, and I guess I had like a crush on him, you know; but we've always been just really good friends. We used to go swimming in the lake together, and all, you know, like stuff like that.'

'Oh,' said Christine, and thought about it. She had noticed Becky seemed disinterested towards the band; she herself was quite intrigued by them. 'Have you seen them play often?'

'Oh; yeah….' Becky laughed a little. 'Oh; I guess I do look rude; huh? But I was kind of going out with Ricky, the drummer, so I've been dropping in on their practices a lot lately…. They're really very good, you know. Well; they're Wilshire High's favourite rock band. Everyone likes them.'

Mrs Santana found them and gave a sigh of exaggerated relief. 'Oh; *there* you are, Chrissy! I wanted you to see the band. Don't you think they're really talented?'

'Oh,' Christine said; 'yes; they seem to be….'

'I really love them,' admitted Mrs Santana. 'Christopher has them over three times a week. You could ask him what days they practise. Well; he's their manager. I'm sure he could even change the schedule, any time you wanted to come over.'

'Oh; well….'

The foursome on the verandah received polite and grateful applause, not at all what they had heard at the contest, of course, but appreciative enough. The partiers seemed happy just to compliment the boys and shake their hands; and Chris gave them each a pat on the back in thanks for their contribution to his sister's birthday celebration. As he explained to some of his guests, the band could easily have got two hundred dollars or more for playing at a similar function for anyone else. Becky took leave of Christine and Mrs Santana and met Jon as he came down the steps to the lawn. 'Hey, Jon. I gotta tell ya; I was just talkin' to that little Italian fox over there, you know; and, if it's any news to you, she's like pretty well hooked on ya.'

'Yeah? And who told you this?'

Becky smiled, walking slowly with him to the sandwich table. 'Well; *she* did. *Christine*. For whatever reason, she apparently thinks you're–'

'All right,' he told her, not wishing to entertain her teasing. He wandered off towards the barbecue grill for a hamburger and tried to think clearly about the whole situation. Well; he told himself; there seems to be some girl who's attracted to you. For whatever reason…. The poor girl. It can't be any better for her. I really hate it when all these people are tryin' so hard not to make it look obvious…. Too many people are involved already. I wouldn't be surprised if the whole damn party knows....

He was granted an audience with Melody who was back in her wicker chair, surrounded by an impressive stable of friends who looked for all the world like a bevy of Arthurian ladies-in-waiting. Graciously Jon fielded some of their questions about the band and about what songs they usually performed. Melody had him sit close beside her in the big chair and even lifted one leg over his knee, bragging to all her friends that The Strawberries were 'Wilshire High's favourite rock-and-roll band', using that moniker that had begun to stick to the band like bad barbecue sauce to the ribs. The popularity was fun for everyone, though; and Jon revelled in it, leading the girls on with amusing anecdotes about their performances at the park and at school and elsewhere, and the girls all thought him very charming and entertaining.

After a few minutes, with the other girls giggling and chatting amongst themselves, Melody was able to ask him her question personally. 'So,' she said, close to his ear; 'do you like her?'

'Who?' he asked, but his feigned innocence was far too transparent.

'Oh; come on,' she teased him, tapping him playfully on the knee; 'she's very nice. Our family has known her for years. They just moved to Wilshire this summer. We all like her, Jon. You should talk to her.'

'All right. So what happened to your brother?'

'Oh; he's around. Probably with Christine's sister. Promise me you'll talk to her.'

'Yeah, yeah,' he said, and got up from the chair. He went off into the crowd, acknowledging compliments and comments from the guests about the band, responding to more of the same questions and providing a bit of background and history on the principal characters. A piano teacher asked him about lessons; but Jon admitted he had little time for that now. He had in fact excused himself from working with his father this afternoon just to attend and play at the party. Dave came by and introduced him to a musical-equipment supplier who was interested in providing them with high-quality live-performance gear at a reduced rate, which perked Jon's ears immediately. The three stood and talked business for quite a while, oblivious to the rest of the party going on about them.

In fact Dave and Jon never took notice of the ceremony during which 'Happy Birthday' was sung to Chris's piano accompaniment and Melody made her silent wish and cut her birthday cake. Christine was on hand, however; and Mrs Santana took her aside and asked, 'So tell me, dear, have you been talking to Jon recently?'

'Oh; um, no. Not since—'

'Not since they played? Well; they're supposed to play again, soon. Honestly, I really don't know how long this evening is going to go on. They may even be playing till after dark.... If you like, Chrissy, I'll go speak to him.'

'Oh; um, *no*. No; it's quite all right–'

'Well; it's up to you, sweetheart. I just think it would be *marvellous* if the two of you got to know each other– Let me go find him; and I'll bring him over here; all right?'

'Oh; um, well….'

'All right,' said Mrs Santana definitely, and gave Christine a reassuring pat on the arm as she scurried off.

In a few minutes Chris sat down beside her, with a hog's share of white vanilla birthday cake, and said, 'Well; marvellous function; wouldn't you say?'

Christine crossed her legs in the chair, self-consciously drawing the dress down towards her knee. 'Oh; yes,' she smiled. 'It's very nice.'

'Yes,' he said indicating his mother, off a dozen yards engaging two more strangers in conversation; 'she does throw a pretty cool bash. It's just that she can be a little overbearing…. Especially when it comes to you, or Jon. She really loves Jon, you know. He's probably her favourite son.'

She giggled at that. 'Including *you*?'

'Oh; *especially* me. Jon doesn't tear up the house with the dog, at least, not all the time. He doesn't leave dirty socks in the parlour. He cleans up all his dishes and folds the hand towels in the bathroom. Yeah; she's really very fond of him. But that's cool, you know; I mean: he's that kinda guy. Everybody loves him.'

'He does seem very nice,' Christine admitted.

'Yeah; well; I was hoping you'd like him. He's not all that hard to know, really. It's just that he loves being on stage. He's a born entertainer, and he likes being funny and making people laugh, you know. Very rarely do girls get to see him like he really is.'

'And how's that?'

He looked at her, and then cut off a corner of the cake with his fork. 'Well; really he's a lot like you. He doesn't like to be too loud about himself, you know; he's really pretty modest. And I've known you for like ten years, at least; and you're like pretty modest too. He doesn't brag, and he doesn't lie about himself. You know, a lot of guys do; but Jon never has. I've known him since like third or fourth grade; and he's never lied to me. He's probably the most honest person I've ever met.'

Christine thought a moment and then said, 'That's very important. I mean: I think honesty is one thing too many people lack these days.'

'Yeah; really,' Chris chuckled. 'Well; if you can't trust the *President*….' He laughed at that; she did not. 'And I know it sounds corny; but Jon isn't really what you'd call a modern person. He comes from a family that's almost as weird as ours, or even more so; and yet he's very old-fashioned, and I mean really old-fashioned. Like, he still believes in honour, and virtue, and doo, stuff like that. He's really into all that stuff. I mean: this is like *really* old-fashioned; okay?' He shovelled another forkful of cake into his mouth.

Christine thought. 'That's not so bad,' she said after a moment.

Chris swallowed abruptly. 'No,' he agreed; 'it's not. And he really is a pretty good influence on all of us. He's the one you ask when you need to know what's right, you know, like with the band, or anything. I really do admire him, I gotta tell ya. There are not many people I'd say that about, you know; but, there are not many friends like him.'

Ricky found Jon and pretended to want to join the conversation, but the moment Dave and the equipment supplier went off on a tangent he tapped Jon on the shoulder. 'Yo, dude.'

'What?'

'Did you like talk to Chris?'

'About what? Hey; Dave's gonna get this guy to talk to Bell. We can tell—'

'No, man; about somethin' else. You know, about— that girl. What's her name?'

'The girl? Christine?'

'Yeah,' said Ricky. 'She's an old friend of his. He's kinda going out with her sister, you know. They just moved here, and, he wants you to ask her out.'

'Well; shit, man; cut me some *slack*. Jesus! —what's going *on* with all this shit?'

'What's the matter?' Dave asked, disturbed by the side conversation.

'He's not gonna ask her out,' Ricky told him.

'Shit— that's not what I said!' Jon complained. 'Just cut me some goddamn *slack*!'

'So you are gonna ask her,' Dave concluded.

'Says who?'

'Says me. I'm askin' ya. You're gonna ask the babe out; or what?'

'Yeah,' Jon said, embarrassed that a potential business partner was listening in on the entire conversation; 'and so what happens when she says "no"?'

'Well shit,' said Dave; 'why the hell should she say "no"? She doesn't even *know* you yet.'

'That's just the point,' Jon said seriously. 'Look, man: just cut me some slack; will ya? Jesus! —don'tcha think this is gettin' pretty stupid? I mean it's Chris, and his mom, and Melody and Becky, and now you two guys; shit— the whole damn *party* is after me. Just cut me some goddamn *slack*.'

'Listen to this, "cut me some slack"!' Dave laughed. 'Just go *talk* to the babe, so the rest of us don't have to keep hearin' the *shit* about it!'

'Really,' Ricky agreed. 'And I don't even *know* the babe.'

'Shit— you guys….' Jon shook his head, blushing.

The man from the equipment-supply company laughed. 'Girl problems are everywhere. I've got 'em too.'

Dave looked at him. 'We can handle the girl problems. What we need is a twelve-channel mixing board.'

Chris escorted Christine to the barbecue table where Christine fixed herself a hamburger sandwich. She had never been much for heavy food and it showed dramatically in her figure. 'So,' Chris said to her, still carving away at the enormous slab of cake on his paper plate; 'if you notice, there's a nice view of the water from here.'

She looked up at him and smiled. 'Christopher.... What do you mean by that?'

A tall man reached between them for a few serviettes. 'Excuse me; we've got a spill—'

'What did you mean by that?' Christine asked him again.

'Nothing,' said Chris. 'It was just a comment, that's all. It's a nice place to sit down and think. Down there there's this little porch, you know, with benches....'

'Christopher, I've been here before, you know.'

'Yeah; I know. Well we haven't really used it since the last time you were here; and I didn't really want anybody going down there for the party; but it is a nice place to go to like, watch the sunset.'

'The sunset,' she smiled, pointing back over the house, 'is *that* way.'

'Whatever. I might go down there in a little while and crack open a bottle of wine, or something. It's a nice place to go if you want to be alone.'

Christine blushed, thinking maybe that rather than Jon, maybe Chris himself wanted her company and not that of her sister Jenny with whom, both families knew, he had been associated for some years. 'Well,' she said, trying to remain diplomatic; 'I don't really feel like being alone—'

'Well; it's just that you don't seem to be in the mood for this party; and I thought that if you just wanted to get away by yourself, you could—'

'All right,' she said, stamping a foot in embarrassed frustration; 'if you insist, I'll go down there to look at the river with you.'

'With *me*?' He seemed a little surprised. 'Oh; I'm supposed to be over here talking to Jenny. I was thinking more about you.'

'About *me*?'

Chris turned without another word and left her. Christine watched him go, indeed feeling very lonely. Well; the way this day has been going, she thought, I'll go down there, and someone will jump out and throw me into the water.

He sat down on the old iron bench with his glass of wine and sighed. The small terrace on the bank of the Connecticut River was far removed from the party, accessible only by a narrow trail leading through ten or twelve yards of trees and undergrowth. The trees were hot and ridden with gnats during the summer; and the unpaved way was often muddy after a rain. For such an event as this, to have included the damp stone terrace as part of the party grounds would have led directly to guests soiling their clothing. Indeed it might have been a very lovely little retreat; but the busy Santanas had not been able to maintain it for a while anyway and undoubtedly the repair costs would have been astronomical. The low stone retaining wall along the river had begun to erode and often high tides would wash over the embankment and leave slippery deposits of moss and silt on the terrace. Even so the place had an unmistakably mystical, romantic aura about it, hauntingly reminiscent of a more elegant, civilised age.

Jon considered the afternoon so far; but it depressed him. Here I am, he thought, once again being expected to live up to everyone else's expectations.... I really hate it when people like my mom and Chris's mom and Melody and Marjorie and Beth are all tryin' to fix me up with some babe I've never met before.... The babe probably hates me anyway. I must've embarrassed the shit outa her back there; and now she figures I'm an idiot, which is probably true, and she doesn't want any part of me. Well; so what? I'm just gonna sit here till we play again, and then pack up my stupid guitar and go home.

He heard the sound of light footfalls in hard shoes on the stone steps and immediately stood up. In the grey pastels of the early evening she was even comelier than in the bright afternoon. The little shaft of light from the escaping sun touched the back of her head and made her hair look much lighter, an interesting contrast with that beautiful tanned skin. He watched her take a bite of a juicy hamburger with ketchup and mustard and relish and not even need to wipe her lips; it struck him as the epitome of ladylike manners and he wanted to compliment her. As she stood and stared out at the shaded river, he thought, yeah; but she thinks I'm some kinda idiot. I've already embarrassed her enough here today....

From under the low-hanging boughs he took a step; and Christine turned and gave a slight start. 'Oh–!' she sighed, clasping a hand over her heart in relief. 'I didn't see you there!'

'Sorry,' he said. He smiled a little at her, and for a long moment they just stood and stared at each other.

'I truly don't know why I've come down here,' she confessed. 'I suppose when I was talking with Christopher, he must have suggested it....' She turned from him then and looked out at the water. 'I haven't been down here in many years.'

'It's nice,' he said, stepping past her to look down into the water where it lapped against the retaining wall. 'We used to swim here when we were kids; and Chris's mom got really mad when we hung this tyre swing from one of these trees....' He looked up and pointed, not facing her. 'That one. We used to swing out over the water and let go....' He shook his head. 'Stupid, really. That water's only a coupla feet deep there.'

Christine smiled, thinking herself perhaps the only girl who actually enjoyed hearing other people reminisce. 'Christopher says the two of you are very good friends.'

'Yeah; me and Chris, we go way back.... Chris and I— He's a good friend.' He turned then and looked right at her.

She took another bite of the hamburger. He watched her; the sight of someone so perfectly beautiful as a goddess doing something so human as chewing food enthralled him. She might have been a little unnerved; but she smiled at him just the same. 'It would seem,' she said quietly, 'that I've forgotten my glass. I can't imagine how I could've misplaced that....'

'Here,' he said readily; 'have mine. 'It's red; so it should go with beef....'

She made a little laugh, then, and took the glass of wine from him.

'Thank you,' she said, and sipped. He watched as his glass touched her lips; not many teenaged girls he knew were so well accustomed to table wine as he was. They stood and stared into each other's eyes; and suddenly he wanted to reach out and touch her. The compulsion was so strong that he snapped his hand back with a shiver and abruptly looked away.

She turned from him too, just as suddenly, not even thinking that she still held his glass of wine. Jon felt his face go red as though with fever. 'Uh, hey; well; I, uh, think I might go up for a refill, there; so, uh, if you... want anything—'

She shook her head and closed her eyes, as if trying to throw off a frightening notion. 'No; uh, no. Thank you.'

'I'll be right back,' he assured her, and stopped mid-step. 'We... have to play again in a little while; but, uh, I'll be back here first. Okay?'

'Yes,' she said, and turned about only to see him go up the shrouded stone steps and disappear into the foliage.

Damn, he thought; what a jerk I am. I could have *kissed* her right then. Holy shit— what an idiot. It was a piece of cake, too. Yeah; there might be another chance, but never like that one, never again.... Oh; yes; I'm a *gentleman* all right. A perfect *idiot* of a gentleman....

Christine finished the hamburger and then downed her last bite with a hearty swallow of the Italian claret, staring fixedly out at the darkening waters of the Connecticut River. Perhaps, she thought, I could love this boy. Perhaps he could be the one to last for ever. But I may never know. It's too frightening to admit that I'm really feeling all these feelings. He does seem just as Christopher said, very honest and sincere, but I can't help worrying that he may only be trying to be polite....

Jon ran into Bob in a clump of people; and Bob took him by the shoulder to get him aside. 'Yo; I gotta ask you a personal question, man–'

'Does it have anything to do with Christine?' Jon asked immediately.

'Uh, yeah; why?'

'It's gettin' to be a sore subject,' Jon told him. 'Just cut me some slack about it; okay?'

'Look: I'm not gonna give you any shit, man,' Bob said sincerely; and Jon knew he could always trust his best friend. 'I just wanna say, I know everybody's on your case about it, but it's not up to them; it's up to you. Just ignore what everybody else says, and do what *you* think is right; all right? You're never wrong on this kinda stuff, not when it really matters. I just wanted to advise you that from what I understand, the girl will definitely go out with you, no matter where you'd want to go. You're not goin' out with anybody, and neither is she. If you don't mind my sayin' so, dude, you can't *possibly* screw this up.'

'Gee; thanks, Bob,' Jon said, with a smirk that meant he was not wholly sarcastic.

Dave came up to both of them then and asked, 'So; how are you two homos doing?'

'Shut up, Dave,' Jon told him.

'Hey; well; when there's this much female ass in one place, the smart man doesn't fart around with his buddies....'

'Shut up, Dave,' Bob said to him. 'Jon, man, just remember what I said, and take it in the spirit intended, and doo.'

'Yeah, yeah; I got it covered.'

'"Got it covered",' Bob smiled, as he liked the expression.

'So what's this? –Dear Abby?' Dave asked. 'Just *go* for it, dude. Grab a piece of ass while the grabbin' is good.'

Jon whirled on him. 'Oh; *right*, Dave; and I suppose you've been snatching butt all over this place, like the true ignoramus you are. Well look, dude; just eat *shit* with that. I don't have to be no ignoramus.'

Bob turned to Dave as Jon stomped away from them. 'Holy shit, dude; what *ails* you? Just let him the hell alone. All he wants is to make a decent impression. He's not *like* you with girls, and he doesn't have to be.'

'Well; shit– I know how he is. But *damn*– why does he always have to be so frickin' *fragile* about everything?'

'Dave, come on. Just let him be. He takes women very seriously. You've always known that.'

'Well....' Suddenly Dave felt a little ashamed. 'Shit. Then maybe I oughta go talk to him.'

'Naah. At least he's resilient, and doo. Let him be.'

Jon got away from the bar with not merely a full glass of claret but the half-emptied bottle as well. He made his way through the dense crowd, successfully avoiding Mrs Santana and Melody and Becky and Chris and Ricky and Dave and Bob, and ducked through the narrow gap in the hedgerow to walk carefully through the trees to the stone steps. She was still there, holding the empty wine glass, standing alone in the centre of the terrace, still staring out at the water. By now it had indeed become quite dark. 'Hi,' he said, trying not to appear nervous. 'I brought you a refill anyway, even though you said you didn't want one....'

'Thank you,' she said, and exchanged the empty glass for the one he handed to her.

He filled the other glass for himself. 'Bottoms up,' he said with a smile. 'To Melody's birthday.'

'All right,' said Christine, returning the smile. 'To Melody.' They touched the rims of the plastic glasses together and drank.

'You know, I still can't think of her as being sixteen years old,' he said, just to have something to say. 'She still seems like a little kid to me.'

'No,' said Christine; 'she is. She and I will be in the same class.'

'You're in *eleventh*?' he asked; and she nodded. 'Dag. When's your birthday?'

'March Sixteenth,' she said to him. 'Melody is about five months younger than I am.'

'Dag,' he said. 'I mean– I'm sorry. You just struck me as being older than that. For a minute I thought you were older than me.' He got a little red; that had been a silly comment to make.

'Why?' she asked, somewhat amused. 'How old are you?'

'Seventeen,' said Jon, a little shy about responding to her. 'Till November, anyway....'

'Oh,' she said. 'You'll be a senior.'

'Yeah....'

'What college will you attend? Have you decided?'

'Naah....' He shrugged. 'If the band ever pans out, I'll do that. Make a heck of a lot more money, that's for sure.'

Christine smiled. 'I've often thought that would make an exciting life,' she said, 'being a professional entertainer.'

'Yeah; I think I could stand it.'

'It would be very busy. I'm not really a busy kind of person.'

He shrugged again and walked round her to stand at the low stone wall by the river. 'Look; uh, about what's been going on at this party.... Just so you don't get the wrong idea, I didn't know any more about it than you did. It was all Chris's mom's idea, you know; she started it, and then Chris and Melody got everyone else into it.... The more people got involved, the more I hated it, you know; but, believe me, it has nothing to do with whether I was, well, whether I wanted to meet you or not; okay?'

'Okay,' she said carefully, and drank some wine.

'I just thought maybe we could talk, like this, you know?'

'Yes,' she said, and stepped a little closer to him.

Jon looked at her then. 'Would you like to sit down then, over there?'

Christine looked over at the little roofed belvedere built upon the stone terrace to the right of the steps. Despite its age it was sturdy enough; and the wooden benches were cleaner and drier than the masonry ones on the terrace. 'All right,' she said, and followed him over to the low wooden step.

He allowed her to step up to the deck first, with a polite gesture of the hand; and she seated herself demurely, without even disturbing her wine, and crossed her ankles. 'I'm sorry if I embarrassed you, before,' he said, still standing under the roof, across from her. 'I guess I didn't make too good of an impression on you back there.'

'It's all right,' she said.

'Well; let's just say I wasn't exactly expecting to meet anyone here. Not someone who would make such an impression, anyway....' He looked at her; but she took a sip of wine and gazed over at the water beyond the rail. Her quiet, modest femininity was intoxicating; he was thinking and saying things he had only ever known from romantic film stories. 'Anyway,' he said quietly, 'I'm sorry if I look like a jerk. I'm just not really used to being introduced to lovely young ladies.'

She looked up at him then, and her eyes sparkled like distant stars in the dim light. In a very hushed voice she said right to him, 'That's very nice of you to say, Jon.'

He blushed and turned to look out at the river. 'Uh, yeah; well....'

'I only wanted to say, that, well, I'm not used to hearing such nice things about me. No-one ever says anything nice about me, because no-one ever says anything about me at all. And you're very genuine about it. I've just been worried that I was embarrassing you.'

'No,' he said. 'I was embarrassing myself.'

She smiled a little, sincerely. 'Christopher says you're a born entertainer,' she said.

He shrugged, with a little smile that belied his attempt at modesty. 'That may or may not be true,' he said frankly. 'We'll have to leave that to the critics some day.'

She looked up at him with a pretty smile. In the white tuxedo suit he seemed surprisingly gallant; only the slightly-mussed hair and the shyly dimpled smile belied the image of a prince at a royal ball. 'Well; I'd like to think that I had met a famous entertainer, back when he was just a nice young gentleman.'

He stared at her then, feeling his face go beet-red. 'Uh, yeah; well....' No other girl had ever complimented him so directly before. For a minute he had no immediate reply; and then he realised that he had best say or do something, before she thought him a complete cretin. 'Well,' he said, trying a brighter tone; 'I don't know about you, you know, but I haven't had a piece of that cake yet. Would you like to go get some with me?'

Suddenly she was thrilled to have met him; her smile was indelible. 'I'm not much for cake,' she admitted, standing up beside him; 'but, if you'd like to have some, I certainly wouldn't mind accompanying you.'

He smiled and gestured to escort her back up to the lawn.

Perhaps it was only Jon's perception; but the party seemed to have changed. He was no longer seeking to avoid people, as before, and no longer embarrassed when the mere subject of Christine Polvere surfaced in conversation. Christine seemed buoyant and in good spirits and impressed him with her willingness to be introduced and her ability to converse intelligently with his acquaintances, so long as she held his arm. The Strawberries went up to play on the verandah again at eight o'clock. Christine stood with Melody and Becky in the fore of the crowd as Jon sang one of his personal favourites, McCartney's 'World Without Love', and Dave did the lead to Lennon's 'No Reply'. Together they sang their latest opus, 'You', for which they had already become the stuff of legend after Jon excused himself from composition class to complete its arrangement with Dave in the school auditorium. They performed a very passable 'My Love', featuring Dave playing his own bass guitar and Jon at Chris's old electric piano singing straight at Christine. She blushed; but at the sight of his impish smile she began to realise the truth in what Chris had told her. Jon Cavaliere loved performing. It was what he did best; and that probably included everything else. She thought that maybe it was the clue to his charm as a gentleman but, even so, she believed in his sincerity as if it were one of the few reliable constants in the whole world.

The evening was over too soon; and The Strawberries went off by nine-fifteen to spare the neighbours. Jon and Christine found themselves outside the open rear door to the Polveres' dark-blue Lincoln, trying to arrive at what they wanted to say. He had picked a long-stemmed lilac from Mrs Santana's garden and given it to her; and she felt as though she would cry. Before making a scene she hurried to get in beside her sister. 'I had a nice time,' Jon said quietly, close to her through the car window. 'It was fun; huh?'

'Yes,' Christine said sadly. 'It was.'

'I'll see you again,' he said, and smiled at her. 'Next party; huh?'

'Yes,' she said, and brought the flower to her nose again.

'Well; uh, so see you later, I guess....'

'Good night,' she said, and met eyes with him for a few long seconds. Mr Polvere put the gear lever in *Drive*, and Jon stepped back from the car. In a moment she was gone round the tree-lined curve in the street; and he stood there on the kerb, guitar case in hand, as though he could still see her in the window holding the lilac up to her nose and wishing the night had hours left to go.

* * *

'And once again, the original Some-Dunce Kid is late,' said Ricky, adjusting his cymbal stands.

Chris was just coming back from the house. 'He's not here yet? I thought I heard him come in.'

'How's your hearing, Chris?' Ricky teased, without looking up from the drum kit. 'You oughta get that stuff adjusted.'

'Really,' Bob agreed, with a laughed. 'And you call yourself a band manager? I bet you can't even *hear* this shit we're crankin' out.'

Chris made a wry smile, hoping to display an unruffled façade. 'Just watch the gutter language, boys,' he said calmly. 'Don't forget we have ladies present.'

'Ladies?' Ricky queried, pretending to have not noticed the two pretty Polvere sisters sitting on the old picnic table in the front corner of the garage, swinging their legs almost perfectly together. 'Ladies? Where?'

Chris Santana laughed aloud. Dave came round the corner from the house and stepped in, picking up his guitar without a word yet to anyone. 'Well?' Chris asked him. 'So what'd he say?'

'Oh,' Dave said, as he put the strap over his head; 'well; he says it looks pretty good; but we'll know more after the weekend. You wouldn't believe it, but those kinda people are kinda hard to get a hold of on the weekend.' He looked about at the others. 'I guess we're still waiting for the idiot; huh?'

'Yep,' Ricky replied, and sighed as he sat down on his drummer's throne; 'as soon as the *idiot* gets here....'

As if on cue, they all heard the deep rumble of a hot rod cruising slowly up the street. 'There he is,' Chris said wryly. 'I'd know that hole in the muffler anywhere.'

'Muffler?' Ricky asked, to no-one. 'Muffler? The word's not even on his spelling list.'

The girls laughed, as everyone knew they would. Ricky was always making girls laugh. 'Does he have headers on that car?' asked Jenny Polvere.

The boys all looked at her curiously. 'Uh, yeah,' said Dave, and had to ask; 'why?'

'Oh; I don't know; I just sort of found out what headers were, so....'

The platinum-silver Caprice rolled into view, gleaming like a diamond in the summer sun, and turned to enter the driveway. The driver gunned the throttle a few times and then shut down the thundering engine, allowing the car to glide up towards the crest of the driveway. Just as it came to a stop, he dropped in the clutch and the car took a firm stance on the gravel. Stillness reigned again in the quiet neighbourhood.

'Hell of an entrance, Jon,' Bob said with a sigh; and they all heard the parking-brake engage.

Christine Polvere was surprised by the car; since moving to the township she had seen it a few times, but even at the party she had not thought to connect the unique car to its possible owner. 'That's his car?' she asked her sister.

'That's his car,' Jenny assured her.

'I didn't know that.'

'You didn't know *him*, either.'

Christine smiled; in any case she was pleased with the developments. 'True....'

Jon Cavaliere got out of the cockpit of his famous silver Caprice and gave a yell. 'Yo! Somebody give me a hand with this shit!'

'*Must* be high,' Ricky commented, not moving from his seat as Bob and Chris went out to assist him.

Bob came back up the driveway carrying Jon's heavy amplifier head. 'This is what you get,' he complained, 'for insistin' on bringin' your amp home all the time.'

'Aaah, man; just ease up with the same old horseshit; will ya? Jeez....' He squinted in the sun and then noticed the two girls on the table just inside the garage door. Recovering some composure, he carried his guitar case past them both and smiled casually, saying to Christine, 'Well; haven't seen *you* here in some time.'

She smiled, a very appealing gleam in her eye just for him. 'Nor I you,' she said in a soft, personal tone.

'So,' he said, more to Jenny then; 'what brings you ladies out here anyway? Don't you know rehearsals are always a drag? Or are you more interested in seein' how we like to torment your dear sweet Christopher, over here? Man of a few words, that Christopher— except during rehearsals. We run outa tape; and he's still givin' directions. Yeah; he's some slavedriver, that Christopher....'

Chris had wheeled the big bass speaker cabinet up from the car. 'Hey, motor-mouth. Where do you want this hunk of junk?'

'Same place it always goes, Chris,' Jon said with a smile, and set down his guitar case. The cabinet was parked beside the electric piano; and Bob heaved the heavy amplifier head up on top of it with a sigh. Chris went back to sit down adjacent to Jenny in his director's chair, the red one with *SANTANA* stencilled in bold letters across the back.

Bob connected the speaker cable and plugged the power cord into the wall receptacle whilst Jon began to tune his instrument. 'This is the shit you get for takin' your stuff home every night,' Bob was saying. 'What the hell's gonna happen to it here, that won't happen anywhere else?'

'Yeah, dude,' said Dave. 'We were ready to start without ya. You gotta try harder to be on time, man. This lateness shit is a real pain in the ass for everybody.'

'Yo; like a little slack here; huh?' Jon responded, apparently not taking them seriously. 'You guys couldn't live without me and you know it.'

Ricky laughed cynically at that. 'Yeah,' Dave told him; 'but the night I have to pick up the bass because you're late for a gig, you're gonna catch some bad doo, let me tell ya.'

'Oh, hell, man; it's only a practice—'

'Yeah,' Dave said, quite adamant about his point; 'it's only a practice; but the moment we can all show up on time, and treat every practice like it was just as important as a gig, then we'll be in the groove. And until we do, this grungy boilerhouse of a garage will be the only venue you'll ever see our name over.'

The two girls looked up at the wall again, admiring the big banner Jon and his sister Eve had painted, proudly proclaiming *The Strawberries* in bold black letters, embellished with four little red strawberries in the image of the stickers Chris had passed out during the week of the concert contest.

'All right,' Jon said, satisfied that his guitar was in tune; 'let's cut the lecture and just go for it.'

' "Loving Is Hard Now",' Chris told them, 'because Bell wants to hear it at that place next week. Oh; and damn— we really oughta be taping this shit.' He reached over to the retired bedside table next to his chair, where the PA mixing console and the stereo cassette recorder were set up, and happened to meet eyes with Jenny then. 'Sorry,' he said sheepishly; 'I seem to have shifted into work mode, here.' She only smiled and looked away. He set the controls on record and then said, 'All right; "Loving Is Hard Now". *Go.*'

'Take thirty-six,' Ricky called from behind the drums; and the girls smiled at his whimsy.

Dave sat at the piano and began the introduction. 'Loving Is Hard Now' had been mostly his composition, inspired by a girl he had known whilst spending a summer holiday in California. The chord progression had been conceived at a party at Rob Alascan's house in May; and Dave had been so enthralled with what he had been playing that three verses of lyrics came to him in twenty minutes. Jon contributed a few dramatic changes and the lyrics and chords for the middle eight bars; and even before its public stage debut the song seemed a born hit. Chris admitted it was one of his favourites and Bell had been impressed as well.

Dave stayed at the piano for 'Which Way To Turn', something he had composed with Jon only this month. Jenny and Christine enjoyed watching him play. At eighteen he seemed exceptionally grown-up to them, a tall man with the cherubic facial features of a wide-eyed innocent. His hands were strong and calloused, his shoulders broad, his hair thick, wavy and quite unruly. Yet when Dave Holloway, mountaineer, private pilot and hotrod mechanic, sat at the keyboard, the resulting dainty arpeggios and trills were like something from the surrealistic illusions of some Romantic poet.

Jon and Bob did the carefully-constructed harmony to Dave's lead, and they ended on a very pretty major-seventh. But, no sooner than the chord had been struck, Dave let go the keys and whirled about in the chair. '*Damn*, man! –why do you keep *singin'* it like that?'

Jon spun away from him, just as riled. 'I can't hear what you're *tellin'* me, man; it just doesn't *fit!*'

'The *hell* it doesn't; it's a major sixth! Sorry, Bell,' he called round towards the tape recorder, still rolling; 'we got some wicked harmonic dissonance goin' on here....' The girls were amused at that, suppressing their giggles as Chris had asked them to remain quiet during the session. 'Look, dude; it's too simple for somebody like you to not get it. You just gotta think of it as a major sixth. It's not a dominant seventh at all. In fact there are no C-sevenths in the entire song.'

'I know, man, I know; it's just that it's an awful hard thing to hit, because you're expectin' somethin' else....'

'I know, man; that's why it's like that. Look. Play it again.' He turned to the keyboard to play, and when Ricky and Jon came in with their instruments, he told them, 'No; you guys shut up with that. Just listen.' He played the last line of the song as a series of three-note chords, to illustrate the three vocal lines. Even the girls thought they could hear what he meant. 'Look, dude. This is you.' He played, singing Jon's part, 'Da-da-da-da, da-da, da.... See? Hear that? Now *you* sing it.'

He played, and Jon sang alone, 'Da-da-da-da, da-da, da....'

'*Right!*' Dave expounded. 'That's it! *Now*. You and me and him. *Sing.*'

He played; and he, Bob and Jon sang together. The difference was startlingly dramatic; the effect of the chord progression was a change from anxious anticipation to a soothing surprise. Both the girls were able to discern it immediately. 'That's it,' said Chris.

'But you can tell; right?' Dave was asking Jon. 'I mean: you can hear that?'

'Yeah; but–'

'*No* buts. Play it again.'

The girls smiled at Dave's serious persistence; he might have made a great teacher. 'I just keep thinkin' it's supposed to be B-flat and not A,' Jon said.

'Yeah; and so does everyone else; but it'd be wrong. If you're gonna be a good singer, you have to be able to pick that out.'

'I can hear it,' said Bob. 'Want us to switch parts?'

'*No*,' Dave insisted; 'he has to get it. *Everybody*. Play from the second-to-last line; two, three... and I don't know which way....'

They all played, Bob merely strumming simple chords on the guitar instead of the more formal arpeggio figures of the whole arrangement, and they sang, 'Da-da-da-da, da-da, da....'

When they were done Ricky collapsed on the drums, with the accompanying crashes and bangs. '*Finally*, at *last*....'

'Get out,' Bob teased him; '*you* didn't hear that.'

'Did *so*,' Ricky came back, like a child.

Bob shook his head and then turned back to Jon. 'Look, man; it's a sixth. Just remember "The Shadow Of Your Smile", and "East Of The Sun", stuff like that. All those great old tunes liked to use a major-sixth for a transient instead of a dominant-seventh. It's got that gentler, mushier sound to it.'

'*Right*,' said Dave; 'and that's just what I was thinkin' of. How soft and mushy it would sound, like all those old tunes you and your dad like to play.'

'Rock music, 'Forties style,' Jon smiled.

Dave accepted the notion seriously. 'Exactly.'

'So; all right,' Chris called from his director's chair; 'are we satisfied with that?'

'*No*,' Dave told him; 'it has to be right. We're doin' it again.'

They began before Chris had a chance to change to a fresh cassette; and for Bell's benefit, and their own, they performed 'Which Way To Turn' all the way through again. Jon got his final harmony part exactly right; and the girls clapped and cheered along with Chris, despite the serious intentions of the recording.

'This place is hot as hell, man,' Bob said. 'Whaddiya say we take a break, and get somethin' to drink?'

'Not yet,' Chris told them. 'Do something else that needs work. "Do You", or something. We'll break in about twenty minutes.'

'See?' Jon said to the girls. 'Slavedriver, I tell you.'

Chris ignored that. 'How 'bout you play "Lovely" again, and then....'

'"Lovely", "Lovely", "Lovely",' Ricky moaned. 'I'm gettin to *hate* that song....'

'Just do it,' Jon said, 'and get it over with. Look; we could do the *piano* version. *That's* something that needs work.'

Thus they played the older arrangement of Dave and Jon's 'Lovely', with Dave at the electric piano, the way it had originally been written, in the key of G. At first, in the spring, Dave and Jon had planned for the song to be performed as a solo number, just Dave singing and accompanying himself on piano, or perhaps to Jon's accompaniment, or even the other way round. But at one rehearsal Bob had started playing along on guitar, and Ricky, impatient as ever, came in also; and suddenly their contributions had turned a very sincere, sensitive ballad into a straight-from-the-heart rock-and-roll love song, the kind a whole band could perform with great dynamic impact. Since the concert contest it had become one of their most popular stage numbers.

'Do You' was something else entirely, a shivering impatience over a sharp, danceable rhythm. Dave and Jon had developed this one also; and Melody had bragged to all her friends that it was already one of her favourite party songs. There was an exceptionally exciting edge to Jon's voice that made him seem even sexier to Jenny and Christine; although whenever he sang girls were practically swooning over him anyway.

By now it was two o'clock. 'Christ,' Dave complained; 'this place is like *hell*.'

'Cool it,' Chris told him.

'"*Cool* it"? Bob cried. 'Cool *what*? Cool is the *last* thing this place is! I mean: shit, dude; the *least* you could do is provide some refreshment—' He looked at the girls. 'Look, uh, Jenny. Run down to the 7-Eleven and pick up a coupla eight-packs of soda, from the cooler window. I'm sure we can't count on any ice around *here*....'

'Yeah,' Jon said, and put down his guitar. 'Doctor Pepper. Pick up a coupla eight-packs, and some chips and stuff.' He reached into his pocket and withdrew his wallet. 'And damn, man— I'm all outa bread.' He shook his head. 'All right; donations now being taken for a worthy cause. Four famous musicians held hostage during the hell of August in their manager's *un*-airconditioned garage.'

'Cool it about the heat,' Chris said then. 'I can't help it.'

'At least you could un-board-up this *window* back here,' Ricky suggested, turning about on his swivelling stool to look at it. 'Get some air moving....'

'Diggit,' agreed Bob, the other one of the band who ordinarily occupied a space towards the back amid the clutter of the garage.

'Just ignore it,' Chris told them, whilst he and Dave sorted out a shopping list.

Dave was handing Jenny a ten-dollar note; he always had money. 'Look; just get a whole bunch of stuff. Chips, and soda, and some Gatorade—'

'*Gatorade!*' Jon laughed. 'You with that frickin' Gatorade! Like we're a frickin' *football* team!'

'Well; I happen to be sweating,' Dave countered; 'and Gatorade is good for—'

'Aaah,' Ricky teased; 'you think *you're* sweating? I got this boarded-up *window* back here—'

'Cool it about the heat,' Chris said.

'Take my car,' Bob said to the girls, of his recent acquisition, a bright-blue LeMans coupé. 'Keys are in it.'

'Okay,' Jenny said; 'but…. It is an automatic; right?'

Bob laughed. 'Oh; no. Don't tell me—'

'Oh, jeez,' Dave teased her; 'you can't drive a clutch…. How 'bout Chrissy?'

'Chrissy doesn't drive yet—'

Jon looked at her; Christine was shaking her head with a helpless expression. He made a wry smile, to tease her, and said, 'Jeez…. And *my* car's a clutch, and *Bob's* car's a clutch, and the van's a clutch— Hey, Chris. Your *mom's* car. *That* ain't a clutch!'

'Jeez,' Ricky said aloud; 'what a brilliant *deduction*, man! You and that Sherlock Holmes, man, you oughta—'

'The heat's gettin' to his brain,' Bob sided to Ricky. 'Slowin' it down.'

'Shut up about the heat!' Chris told them all. It was arranged, then, that Dave would drive the two girls to the store in his van, since he had parked behind Mrs Santana's Impala. Ever eager to play, Bob and Ricky went off on a few musical tangents, just drums and guitar, playing loud and fast for the complete disruption of the entire neighbourhood. Though he could tell ever-enthusiastic Jon wanted to join them and play, Chris managed to get him aside without a guitar. 'Yo; I gotta like talk to you, dude.'

'Yeah? What's up?'

'Well; it's about Christine.'

'Yeah?' Jon shrugged. 'What about her?'

'Well; she kind of wanted to come over today because of you.'

Jon smiled a little, hearing Bob and Ricky go through The Cream's 'White Room'. He leaned against the tree next to his car and watched them. ''Cause of me; huh? Sounds serious.'

Chris knew he had meant that without the least seriousness. 'Yeah; well; I guess you've heard that she likes you.'

'Oh, *jeez*, man; now don't start with that shit again; all right? We talked at the party; okay; and we have some kinda understanding.'

'Like what?' Chris asked him. 'Like some kinda noncommittal Platonic garbage? Shit, dude; I *know* you better than that. The lady's really very hooked on you, you know. Don't tell me you're content for her to be another Becky Barnett, now….'

'Becky Barnett?' Jon laughed. 'Come on, dude; Becky and I are just—'

'Just friends,' Chris said; 'I know. It's no big deal, dude; but I know how you are with shit like this. All I'm sayin' is that if you want to go out with her, just ask her. She's the kind of person who'd love to go out with ya. Really. It's just that I happen to know her pretty good, you know; and I do know that much about her.'

'Yeah; well; okay; but like maybe I'm not so willing to go out with her, then.'

Chris looked at him; that was something he had not considered. 'Why not?'

Jon stood up away from the tree. 'Damn, man– I gotta get somewhere where there's a breeze. This heat is *intense*.' He walked farther out to lean on the boot-lid of his car.

Chris followed him, two feet behind. 'And you're the one who wants to move to Florida,' he teased.

'Yeah; well; where Danny lives, the town's right the hell on the beach. There's always a breeze, with no damn hills to break it up–'

'So what's wrong with Christine?' Chris asked him. 'How could you not like her?'

'Well; it's not that I don't *like* her, man; but, well; you can see how she is; right? She's like totally different than me. Like, she just said she doesn't even drive, and she's sixteen-and-a-half. Shit– I was drivin' my dad's trucks when I was *fifteen*, man. Like, she doesn't curse, she doesn't belch out loud–'

'Shit,' Chris laughed; 'you're talkin' about Becky there.'

Jon looked at him. 'Well; at least Becky *drives*. She runs guys with her mom's Cutlass. You should see how good she is, man, even shiftin' with an automatic–'

'Jon, man, *I* know you. That's not the kind of girl you want. You're more of a gentleman, and doo; and what you really want is a lady. And that's what Christine is, man: a *lady*. And I know it sounds corny, you know; but, I wouldn't be shittin' ya about somethin' like this.'

'Shit, man; don't you *get* it?' Jon winced and turned away from him, as though to be rid of the subject. 'Jesus Christ! –it's still all as stupid as it was last *week*.'

'Jon....' Chris stepped round to look at him again. 'I'm sorry, man; I'm not tryin' to force ya into anything. I just thought it was something you'd want, you know. Jeez, man; I'm just tryin' to help you out.'

Jon looked down. 'Aaah....'

'And she's not really like some fragile sweet young innocent, you know. She's a lot more intellectual, and versatile, than you think she is. A coupla curse words might do her good. And you might end up gettin' somethin' out of it, too, for some day when it really matters.'

Jon looked at him then; but his stomach jumped and he had to look down at once. Is he thinking the same thing I'm thinking? he wondered, and almost asked out loud. But the two of them had been through too much together for either of them to think a little

mindreading between soulmates was not inevitable.   Perhaps Chris's
proposal was in his best interests, after all.   And maybe, Jon thought, I
have nothing to lose in this.   It might just not be important enough
that I should even care.

'It's just that I am thinking about *her*, too,' Chris said sincerely.
'Someday she's gonna find out the awful truth about guys, you know;
and I just thought that if she knew what to look for in a *real*
gentleman, then she'd be able to handle it all right when they all start
hittin' on her.   'Cause you *know* they're *goin'* to.   She's a beautiful girl,
Jon; and I keep thinkin' that you're the one guy who'd appreciate her,
or, who *wouldn't* take advantage of her.'

Jon turned away then, feeling himself blushing bright-red.   He
leaned in to the car for his sunglasses and put them on, hoping to use
up time whilst his face cooled down.

It did not; but Chris made no mention of it.   They both looked up as
the red-primered van turned in the driveway.   Dave pulled up to the
right of the Caprice and shut down his engine.   'You're on your own,
Jon,' Chris said quietly to him.   'Do whatever you think is right.   Just
do *something* about it; okay?'

'All right!' came a cheer from the garage; and Bob and Ricky ceased
'School's Out' and switched off the amplifiers and the PA.   They all
gathered about the picnic table at the front end of the garage and
delved into their refreshments.   Dave had been overly generous,
bringing back two eight-bottle cartons of Coca-Cola in addition to one
of the requested Dr Pepper, plus two quarts of Gatorade and two large
bags of potato crisps.

The afternoon progressed through a few Beatles songs, most notably
'And Your Bird Can Sing' featuring Dave and Bob on twin lead
guitars.   Jenny and Christine were enjoying the opportunity to watch
four young men who were most certainly destined for stardom in the
early chapters of their success story.   Despite constantly teasing and
gybing each other, they all seemed to have great admiration and
respect for each other; and Christine could sense no strife amongst
them.   They were amusing and entertaining, making jokes about the
tape recording, complimenting each other on their performances, and
adding intelligent criticism and artistic suggestions liberally.   She had
heard from Mrs Santana several times about her son's participation
with this band; but until seeing them play at Melody's party she had
never imagined how well he might have succeeded.   Only seventeen,
sensible, conservative Chris was already sighting far down the road,
not at all in keeping with the short-term goals and unrealistic
aspirations of many of his peers.   He had explained to her that to
manage a group of talented boys who were also unforgettably good-
looking posed a number of special marketing problems.   'I'm not
trying to make a bubblegum band,' he had said to the Polvere girls

earlier. 'I can get them exposure today on their appearance; but then no-one will pay attention to their music tomorrow. I want people to *think* about this band, not just look at them as a bunch of pretty boys, or whatever.'

The seriousness of them all impressed Christine, as she sat there on the old picnic table swinging her legs back and forth and watching Jon sing as he played. He still had on the sunglasses, though Chris generally forbade him to wear them onstage. He sang 'I Saw Her Standing There' and a few others, slowly realising he was staring at Christine as though hypnotised by her legs swinging in front of him. But she was beautiful; only a fool would have been able to look away, and Jon would be no fool.

Whilst Jon and the others cleaned up after the snacks and put away the instruments, she sat there, watching him as though spellbound herself. 'All right,' Chris said; 'I promised Bell I'd run this tape out to the station today, so…. Jenny, you're comin' with me; right?'

'Yes,' said Jenny straight away. 'If we won't be all day….'

Chris stepped past her and looked at Jon. 'Hey, dude; I promised Jenny I'd take her to the mall afterwards, you know; so could you–'

Jon looked at him, feeling more than a little nervous as he anticipated the request. 'Well; I was gonna take my amp home–'

'Oh; come *on*,' Bob told him; 'you don't need to take that thing home, man. Shit– it sure as hell ain't goin' anywhere here. I suppose you'll tell me you practise with it every night; right?'

'Well; sometimes–'

'His brother uses it,' Ricky said.

'Sometimes–'

'Get out,' Bob said, and carried his two electric guitars in their cases out to the immaculately-polished LeMans. Ricky carried Bob's acoustic guitar out after him, rolling his eyes in exaggerated sarcasm.

Jon turned and watched them go and then met eyes with Chris. Only then did he realise that they had indeed set up the entire afternoon the way it had happened, just to ensure that he would have to drive Christine home. He made a little smile at their collective slyness. Right or wrong, they could never be faulted for putting forth less than a full effort when it really mattered. Because of them, Jon knew, he was that way himself. 'So,' he said to her then, with a silent prayer that his composure would hold up; 'how are *you* gettin' home?'

Christine shrugged, still sitting on the old picnic table and swinging her legs, as though fully confident that all her dilemmas would solve themselves. In the short white cotton shorts and a dainty yellow camisole, she looked about as far as could be imagined from the elegant young lady in the beautiful party dress whom he had last seen just a week ago. But that irresistibly feminine demeanour had not changed. 'I don't know,' she said, looking right at him. 'I suppose I could call my mother....'

'Oh; get out,' Jon said. 'Don't call.' They both turned to watch Dave lift the Rickenbacker guitar case over the driver's seat and set it inside the van. 'Everything unplugged?' Jon asked aloud, and went about the garage checking that the power leads were all free of the sockets, lest the building be shocked by lightning and ruin all the equipment. 'Looks cool to me.' He leaned on the table beside Christine. Together they surveyed the place, full of tools, ladders, old furniture and the wealth of the band's black cabinets of electric sound gear. 'What a hole,' he said, merely for something to say.

'I like it,' Christine admitted, smiling at what she saw. 'It has... *character*.'

'Yeah; right,' he said wryly, and then looked at her. She was a foot away, looking right back at him. 'You don't have to, like, see Chris's mom, or anything; do you?'

She shrugged. Dressed as she was, she was attractive anyway; but the little lift she gave to her shoulders to indicate a carefree attitude was more than appealing. 'No,' she said, with a slight shake of her head. 'Why would I?'

'I don't know.' He stood up straight. 'So; well; feel like goin' for a ride?'

She smiled and stood down to the lumpy concrete floor in front of him. She was not so statuesque after all; at the party he had been fairly intimidated by how mature she had seemed and now, here, she was merely a girl, gentle, vulnerable and perfectly harmless. Perhaps to her, in his faded, worn Levi's and dull red t-shirt, he appeared as much a contrast to the charming, unpretentious young gentleman in an elegant white tuxedo last week. For a second they both stood and looked into each other's eyes and were reminded of their interlude on the little terrace behind the Santanas' house. But this time neither of them would dwell on such awkwardness; that was over now. 'Sounds fine,' she said cheerfully, and picked up her little cloth handbag.

Jon left the garage for Chris to close up and carried his bass-guitar case out to lay it in the boot. He hid a smile to see Christine stop and stand by the car door for him to open it for her; it was the epitome of ladylike decorum that she would expect such proper consideration from a gentleman and he was immensely impressed that she would flatter him so. The engine fired up with a '*vroom!*' which took her by surprise; and a chill went down her spine at the inherent sexiness of an attractive young man driving a fast, powerful car. Out on the street Jon shifted into first and held down the clutch pedal. 'I hope you don't mind,' he said, looking at her in the car; 'but there's somewhere I'd like to go.... Something I'd like to show you.'

'Wherever you'd like to go,' she said pleasantly. 'I'm in no rush to go anywhere.'

'Cool,' he said, and dropped the clutch, producing a chirp from the rear tyres, and proceeded straight for the marina. He had always been proud of La Cacciatrice, designed by his Uncle Rick, built by his father and uncles and cousins in 1964 of white cedar over mahogany frames, strong, light and nimble. From a young age Jon had regarded the boat as a priceless work of art, a paragon of timelessly elegant design. It was an honour to be able to share it with a new friend.

They sat in the middle of the main cabin, surrounded by the beautiful joinery to which Jon himself had applied the most recent topcoat of satin varnish just this spring. He located a half-gone bottle of claret in the wine locker and poured two glasses; and, with the water lapping quietly at the hull and the river breeze floating in through the open hatches, it was not at all uncomfortable below.

Christine leaned back in the settee, listening as Jon told her of some cruise the Cavaliere family had taken on the yacht. She felt completely at ease being alone with him. He was very interesting and informative, well familiar with a vocabulary most high-school boys could not even pronounce. She was interested, not just in what he had to say, but in why he had chosen to relate these experiences to her. They were a source of pride to him; yet they impressed her not because he had intended to impress her but just because he wanted to share with her something of his life, that she might know what he had done and from where he had come. For today, that satisfied her perfectly.

That night in his bed, Jon looked back on the afternoon and considered it well-spent. It had been quite an experience for him, listening to Christine tell of her family's two excursions to Italy, including one during the same two weeks of July, 1971, that the Cavalieres had been there. Possibly they had even been flying on the same airliner; they both found that ironic and amusing.

The two of them had found much in common, actually; and Jon was thrilled with the new relationship he had established. He would be going off to the cinema with her next weekend, his very first real date with a most lovely young lady. The picture she wanted to see, Streisand's latest, *For Pete's Sake*, was reported to be a great comedy; and he was encouraged that they might even have the same taste in films; but he knew that seeing it would be only a brief distraction. It was really just the experience of being with her that he wanted to have; and all through the week he would be looking forward to Friday evening.

* * *

Chapter 5

With a thousand voices talking perfectly loud

DJ Berryfield, of the old guard from Lake Drive, was one of the many who looked up to Jon as a mentor. DJ had always been an overachiever at school, much more akin to how all the teachers had hoped to find Jon, and when the opportunity came to advance to senior year and to graduate early he had sought Jon for advice straight away. Although Jon had not taken advantage of the same chance himself, he was quick to recognise DJ's potential and became determined to keep an impressionable boy from being misled by the overzealous guidance counsellors at school. He insisted DJ quit his job as lot attendant at the local Ford automobile agency and secured him a nominal but steady rate with The Strawberries' road crew, so that they might share time for the intense cramming necessary to bypass four whole yearlong classes of school curriculum. Jon had a serious head for academia his teachers never saw and was an invaluable tutor. The two boys seized moments of study even during intervals during a show; and the chances increased that DJ would indeed be able to graduate with the class of 1975 in June. DJ knew that once in business college he would be forever indebted to his childhood friend, lending credence to his own theory that success was one-third talent, one-third perseverance and one-third luck, through knowing the right people.

By the time school began The Strawberries had already begun to reap the benefits of a producer who knew the right people. The first week of September was a turmoil of conflicting schedule demands for Jon, car repairs with Dave and work with his father, new faces and new subjects in the classrooms, two practice sessions and four well-paying jobs in the River Valley area. At the garage Bell sat down with them together and asked each of their ideas for a homogeneous band sound, adding his opinions only when he felt they were warranted. Not one of the four was far off his own idea of what might make a competent music group commercially successful. Concentration would remain on the influence they had gained from emulating The Beatles; but to use that alone would have shown them to the public as a mere copy group and Bell had already declared they had far more promise than that. His own suggestion was to lean heavily on the acoustic guitar as rhythm and even principal instrument, because it would enhance their vocal prowess and because, as he put it, '*no-one* uses acoustics on stage any more!'

Bob was a true lover of classical guitar who had first learnt jazz from Jon's father's original recordings of the bossanova masterpieces by

Getz and Gilberto. Jon favoured what he called 'electrified R&B', the old soul and pop tunes of the 1960s done over in a slightly more modern, energetic vein. He was openly fond of artistes such as The Miracles and The Temptations and The Young Rascals. Ricky agreed with that influence and said the same type of revamping could be done to an even heavier repertoire, including works by Aerosmith, The Who and Deep Purple. Dave leaned towards the other side of Jon's pet sounds, admitting blues greats like Joe Cocker, Joe Brown and even Fats Waller as his inspirations.

Bell took all these diverse sources very seriously and at last proclaimed, 'All right; so use them *all*! And *that* will be the collective sound.'

It was probably after Jon began to see that this blend of sounds could indeed be melded together that he finally began to trust Bell with the reins of their future. If Bell had discounted even one of their ideas, it might have made him much less a prophet and more a self-centred opportunist or frustrated ex-performer. But Bell knew they would have to feel passionate about what they were doing. He conceded that it would be his job to promote the band no matter what they felt they had to play; and if that repertoire seemed a little unorthodox it only made his job that much more interesting and challenging. Jon was determined to keep from getting stuck performing some middleaged has-been's idea of what rock-and-roll should be. If Jon Cavaliere was to play it, then it would be what Jon Cavaliere would believe in, and Jon Cavaliere would have it no other way.

But the conglomerate of styles and the harrowing agenda began to pay off almost from the start. The Strawberries as a working musical outfit seemed poised at the top of a very long gold mine. Even as stage hand, DJ now earned half again what he had at the Ford agency for far more exciting work; in comparison to his high-school peers Jon himself was earning a dizzying wage just doing what he loved most. Bell had already advised him that in the spring he would have to file income-tax for the first time.

Jon did well with a hundred and twenty dollars weekly, banking over half of it unless there were work to be done on the car or a new tool or piece of equipment he needed. He had little in the way of debts; the Caprice had been built on what Dave termed 'pocket money', a little at a time, without borrowing. His father had put off collecting an outstanding loan of two hundred dollars 'for now', which Jon really knew meant for ever. But mere money had never been an issue in his relationship with his father, for whom he had worked so long and so hard for scarcely more than an adolescent's allowance; once, overhearing his parents' distress about a client's cheque that had not cleared, he quietly left five twenty-dollar notes on the desk and thought nothing more about having made the family's mortgage payment for that month. In fact he shared little information about finances with his mother or Beth, as they were both after him unceasingly about saving for university, and Jon had already decided he would have no part of that. Instead he sought the solace of his father's company; and the two kept late hours together on the off nights, pouring over some new design or an old jazz standard, using the topic at hand only as an excuse to share philosophies and advice.

* * *

The first big fête of the new school term was held at Carole Martin's house. Just about anyone who was anyone was usually welcome at Carole Martin's parties. But, though Carole was always gracious and indubitably sincere, Jon tended to shun the party crowd, fraught with varsity athletes and cheerleaders, people with whom he was not ordinarily wont to socialise and who scarcely knew of him beyond the band's reputation. Now, with The Strawberries' schedule coinciding with most of the party evenings, Jon had a welcome excuse to avoid such shallow gatherings. After playing to lorry drivers and labourers in roadside taverns all week, it seemed rather silly anyway, to think of mingling with immature people who considered high school the apex of culture and who thought sneaking a few sips of some ill-gotten alcohol might make them that much more astute.

Chris Santana coerced him into going. Wednesday had been the band's regular off-day for a few weeks now; but the two Polvere sisters were away at a family gathering in Greenwich and so the silver supercharged Chevrolet found itself parked in front of Derrick Martin's spacious split-level house in the Millside section just west of the high school. As the newly-elected student-council president Chris was well received here; he got on well with all the prominent members of high-school society. Jon felt out of place, but he secretly enjoyed making a dissenting fashion statement in a black t-shirt, old jeans and his prized leather flier's jacket. All were surprised to see him; and whilst besieged with questions about the band and his car and his participation in the upcoming swimming season, he would maintain a courtly façade and tried not to look bored. He found an uncorked bottle of zinfandel in the refrigerator and helped himself to a glass; and that charming smile put off Carole's scolding. But there did not seem to be much to drink at the party at all. He had begun to wonder just what the attraction really was when Joe Lorrimer and Dusty Watkins burst in with a few six-packs of beer. Seeing them, the partiers whooped and cheered like idiots. Jon could only look at Chris and roll his eyes.

Chris knew Jon was having a dull time and sat at the piano to play a few sing-along songs. Jon had joined his draughtsmanship classmate

Jimmy Burke, who was impressing a few girls with his knowledge of architectural design; they were perhaps the only two people at the function who might have made such a topic interesting, even amusing. But Jon could not resist criticising Chris's playing and, as he neared the piano, it was Jimmy who coaxed him, saying aloud, 'C'mon, JC, tickle those ivories for us!'

'Aaah, shit....' But the roomful of people were all in agreement. Jon sat as though banished, not even removing his jacket to play. Debbie Lehigh came by and set a can of Miller on the lid as enticement for him. 'Oh; well,' he said wryly, as it was hardly his favourite beer, and began Taupin-and-John's 'Crocodile Rock' just the same.

Jimmy began singing at the verse and the partiers all danced or sang along. Then Arlen Bishop volunteered to do a vocal solo, so Jon indulged him with the arpeggio progression to 'Colour My World'.

Around nine Jeanne Banfield arrived with a few other girls, escorted by a few rowdy boys from the teams. She was quite lovely in a soft beige turtleneck sweater and tight jeans, her headful of wavy blond hair spilling all over the shoulders of a rich brown suede jacket. There was an enchanting grace about those sparkling eyes and glowing smile that sent tingles up and down Jon's spine. He found that even whilst playing he could single out her voice in the crowd; he heard her greet many of the same people he had. When she realised who was playing the piano, she seemed to linger near the opening to the sitting room, intrigued by the extraordinary guest and the uncommon spectacle. But the emotion had grown too strong after all these years. There was no way he would let himself be coerced into performing solo in front of her again. He allowed Arlen to finish Terry Kath's lyric and apologetically bowed out. Chris was the loudest of the disappointed; but Jon was quick to fade into the party again. Not long after midnight, when Jon was sure Chris would have an alternate way home, he slipped out and drove home alone.

* * *

'Chrissy, look– Well; I really can't tell you a thing now, because I've still gotta talk to Chris or Mark, so.... Hey; I gotta shake it.'

–'It will be nice.... Don't you think so?'

'Yeah; it will.'

–'And I do appreciate it.'

'All right. Look; I gotta shake it here. It's no big deal. Chris'll get us some tickets.'

–'I'm sorry if it seems like a big deal to me, Jon; but I've never been to a rock concert before.'

Jon smiled. Christine really did enjoy having someone make a fuss over her. 'Well; for a lady, any time. Really. Look; I really gotta shake it here.'

Ten minutes after ringing off, Jon had parked right at the kerb and been admitted backstage, using the pass Bell had printed up for the members of his two bands for them to gain admission to restricted areas during each other's shows. That individual was on hand to greet him with his own unique brand of cordiality.   'Thought you were s'posed to be here earlier.'

'Yeah; yeah…. What'd I miss?'

'Not a thing, dammit. We're late in settin' up; these fuckin' school shows….'

Jon smiled at the irony. Not three months ago, Tobacco Road's best-paying jobs were at high schools, particularly this one. 'Yo, man, look; what I need's a pair of tickets to this upcoming gig of theirs….'

'Yeah; we got that mess to straighten out too…. *Hey!*' He yelled off to a pair of student stage hands mounting some lighting gear above the stage. 'The blue ones are too close together! Christ! –do I have to do *everything?*'

Jon followed him across the stage to the far corner. 'Well look, man; if I gotta sneak in and stand backstage–'

'Hey,' Chris said, tapping him on the shoulder; 'thought you'd be out with your ladyfriend tonight.'

'Oh,' Jon said with a little smile, thinking how respectable that sounded; 'they're havin' some family thing over there…. Wanted me to come over with a guitar.'

'Hah!' Chris laughed, as Jon might have. 'I *told* ya she was hooked on ya. So how come you didn't go?'

'Well; I thought I could get us some seats for the 'Road gig next week but like I can't get no tickets–'

'Here, Bell,' Chris called up; 'do you need a hand with that?' Jon looked up and saw Bell at the top of a tall folding ladder rearranging the light cans. Someone activated the switch for the inside curtains and they closed inside the outer ones, brushing Bell in the arm as they passed.

'Jesus Christ!' he swore; and it was fortunate that the outside curtains and the gathering crowd's own noise masked the backstage sounds. 'What the hell *ails* this place?'

Jon laughed; to him it was a comedy of errors. 'So,' Chris asked him; 'so you're gonna take Chrissy, then; huh?'

'Yeah,' Jon told him; 'but like you gotta get me *tickets*. I had no idea I was gonna have to *buy them myself*–'

'Yeah, yeah; I'll get 'em.'

'You *better*. I sorta already promised her.'

Chris smiled. 'She's hooked on ya, dude.'

'So you've said.'

Bell came down and the ladder was carried offstage. '*Who* the hell is the light man around here; fuck if *I* know....'

'Paulie's sick,' Chris sided to Jon.

'Well *shit*, Bell,' Jon said, following him back across the stage again; 'do you need *me* for anything? Hell; just *ask* me, man.'

Bell spun about as though to seize him and barked, '*Yeah. You* go over there, take that kid by the hand, and make sure he and Kevin get the snake straight on those two gels I just changed.' He turned and stomped off for another swallow of Pepto-Bismol.

The opening act, a brother and sister from Benton, went on at 8.15. They played a number of Joni Mitchell folk songs and a few more popular things from The Eagles and Linda Ronstadt, both as an acoustic-guitar duo and before their four-man backing group. Chris and Bell had invited them to open for the evening as the group had been considering engaging their management assistance. Jon actually liked them, although the audience were not as grateful. This was after all a Tobacco Road crowd.

'Dammit; I *hate* these school shows!' growled Bell, beleaguered by some new irritant. 'Where the hell is Davisson *now*?'

'Back in the bathroom,' a student assistant called.

'Natural habitat for Davisson,' Jon commented; for they all knew Doug's constitutional anxiety wreaked havoc on his digestive tract before a show.

'That's it; crack jokes! *You* try to get all these idiots straight! Go back and make sure Vinnie off-loads that tape and puts a new one on! I want a good long leader on it! And make sure the goddamn *house* lights get brought down on time; will ya?'

'Jeez,' Jon sighed, waving over his head as he bounded up the steps to the backstage door.

Tall, tanned Rob Alascan bumped into him in the front gallery. 'Hey,' said Rob in that easy tone he had; 'what's up, my man?'

Jon grinned at the sight of the popular singer in his silver eye make-up and styled hair. '*You*, man,' he said, and ran off up the gallery. He forged his way through the crowd of ticket-holders at the doors and got into the sound booth by presenting his pass-card again. 'Hey,' he said to Vinnie, Tobacco Road's salaried sound technician; 'I don't know *what* the fuck I'm doing here, except that Bell wants you to change tapes....'

'That's no problem,' Vinnie said, and switched his Teac quarter-track machine to rewind. 'Get me one of those Ampex reels there.'

Jon turned about in the dark little room and located Vinnie's cache of blank tape in an old plastic milk crate. 'Bell's the problem, man; he's goin' fuckin' *bananas* back there.'

Vinnie off-loaded the tape when it had stopped and handed it to Jon. 'He's just an old grouch,' he said without a care. 'Just because *Paulie's* sick, it turns into a catastrophe. Mark that "Anna Goodhart", and put the date on it, whatever the hell day this is.'

Jon found a marking pen and lettered neatly with the big tip on both the tape's little label and the end of the case whilst Vinnie loaded the new reel. 'Yeah,' he said, setting the tape into Vinnie's other milk crate; 'and he wants me to handle the house lights till he gets up here. Since *Paulie's* sick.... What else?'

Vinnie sat back, lit a cigarette and pressed a small button on the audio console as he exhaled. 'Nothing else, if Bell would only answer his goddamn page....' He tapped his headset then. 'Bell? Ready when you are.'

'He wants a long leader on it,' Jon remembered.

'Yeah,' Vinnie exhaled; 'as if I'm so frickin' stupid to forget *that*....' Jon watched as he set the tape machine on record that moment. 'There. Long enough?'

Jon laughed a little and pulled up in the other chair to the lights console. He eased the fader control for the auditorium room lights down slowly, and as the room grew darker the crowd's reaction increased to an ear-piercing din. The spotlight operator, just outside the booth, waved his beam about a few times and brought it down to the closed curtains at stage centre. Marty Engel, the junior-class president, stepped out in front in his pale blue crushed-denim suit and` shiny black shoes. 'Ladies and gentlemen!' he shouted into his microphone; and Vinnie had to reduce the attenuation. 'On behalf of the Wilshire High School Class of 'Seventy-Six, it gives me great pleasure to introduce to you tonight: *Tobacco Road*!'

'What a goddamn cornball,' Jon said disdainfully, as the crowd wailed in welcome, and Engel departed with a short bow and a wave.

Vinnie laughed; and then Jon got up to allow Bell the chair at the lights deck. The crowd's roar went up even more. In a second the curtains parted, and a quick drum spat opened the first song.

Alascan-and-Davisson's 'In The Clubhouse', about the maturation of a childhood romance, was their oldest and most popular stage number. The guitars crunched out the first few bars and then Rob was prancing out in his white jumpsuit to sing the verse. The tape was rolling; and Bell Howard was into his first promising demonstration recording with which to tempt the record companies. Jon knew Bell would soon be doing the same for The Strawberries. He had met the short, well-dressed producer from Hollywood who had just launched a new label in Florida. The man had been some past California associate of Bell's; and Dave's father knew him as well. The connexions so close to home were to keep Jon awake long into the night, dizzy with all the possible manifestations.

He had to envy Doug Davisson's superb guitar work. Barry, always so reliable, cranked out solid rhythm parts to stage right. Occasionally he did a few lead solos and also provided most of the acoustic-guitar work when required.   Two-thirds through the third number, Mark Jenkins' autobiographical 'Oh Jane', Mark was spotlighted for a sixty-second high-energy drum solo, neither tedious nor excessive.   Kirk Mahoney was the band's youngest and newest member, having replaced Jimmy Kennedy two months ago; but already he had integrated his style into the band's sound.   Jon had given him some coaching and Barry, having done bass guitar for a few shows after Jimmy's hasty departure, had been an invaluable help.   In fact Jon and Barry met often to discuss their respective futures at length.   They liked to talk about the day when their two bands might actually be competing with each other for record sales, and what profitable fun it would be, each holding interest in both outfits.

There was no telling yet how far they would go; but throughout the River Valley area The Strawberries were regarded as the best new band to come about since Tobacco Road had begun playing regularly in public over a year ago.   Cover acts like Wipeout and Power Play were being forgotten in the wake of new original hits like 'All Right' and 'Lovin' You', both of which Tobacco Road hammered out tonight at a volume to shake the foundations.   It was just one more mighty fix for the rock-and-roll addicts of Wilshire who thundered in gratitude. From his place behind Vinnie in the auditorium control booth Jon surveyed the performance with a calm, contented smile.   The excitement of a live show was invigorating; the smoky air, hellish volume and rickety table to serve as a chair did nothing to lessen his enjoyment and as he and Mark shuffled out to the Caprice it was still the only thing in his mind.   'Man; it's lookin' damn good these days,' he said, smiling and shaking his head.   'What do you think?'

'Real nice,' said Mark.

'Yeah; pretty damn sweet.'

'Waxed it lately?'

'Huh?   Oh; the car.   No; uh, not really.   I think I still owe it one before winter.'

Mark sniffled.   'Yeah; well; get it the hell done, or it'll stop lookin' so good in no time.'   He sniffled again.

'What; you got one too?'

'One what?'

'A cold.   Shit– it's good you don't sing much.   That'd really show up on tape.'

Mark laughed.   'Aaah; I had my share of chokes up there.... And *then* some.'

Jon sniffled loudly.   'Aaah; shit– I just remembered I gotta give Marlowe a ride.   God damn it; and I got a party to attend....'

'Where's this at?'

They stepped down off the kerb.   'Well; it's at Christine's house, you know; some family birthday or somethin'....'

Mark walked round to the other side of the car. 'How's the team?'

'Aaaaaaah....' Jon unlocked his door and opened it. 'Got a meet next Tuesday.' He put his finger on the electric lock switch. 'You should come see us.'

'Aaah; I never have the time, man....' Mark opened the door and they sat down together in the front bucket seats. 'Whatcha workin'?'

'Aaah; two hundred free and four-by-two relay.'

'That's *all*?'

The engine caught; and Jon let it run up. 'This car needs a tune-up so bad....'

'How come you're only working two things?'

Jon sniffled. 'Well; he says the sophomore kids need a break, and it's an easy meet, so....'

'Who is it? –Benton?'

'Burbury East. They're easy as shit.' Jon shook his head. 'Shame you quit, dude; now it gets fun. Senior year, undefeated; all you do is mouth off for the rest of the season....' He pushed the *Abbey Road* cassette into the tape player; and the second track, 'Because', was nearly over. With the door still open, Jon could hear the front gallery doors closing again over the rumbling idle and the quiet vocal music. He looked up.

'Yeah,' Mark was saying; 'but you know this music business takes up alla your time, and the swim team was gettin' overly rah-rah for me.... Next thing you know, they'd have the cheerleaders–'

Steve Marlowe, the star all-round gymnast, was walking slowly out towards Jon's silver Caprice. In his maroon-and-gold school jacket he was the picture of the all-American high-school letterman. But despite his impressive upper-body muscle Steve never appeared very intimidating, due mostly to pleasant facial features and a cheerful, outgoing disposition which made him very easy to address as a friend, even for those who barely knew him. He and Jon had been associates since kindergarten, in school, at church and at the marina; but it had not been since their junior-high years that the two had held a real conversation about anything of substance. Still neither would ever have denied the other a favour for old times' sake. Jon nodded in acknowledgement as Steve took one hand out of his pocket and waved.

The girl followed him. She was short, slender and well-proportioned, though bulked-up by the hooded school jacket, the one with her name embroidered in the cheerleading patch on the shoulder. Younger than Steve by nearly two years, the blonde with the long wavy hair was one of the prettiest and most popular girls in school. Her gold-rimmed glasses caught a glimmer of moonlight as she looked up; and Jon turned away. He could only stare straight at the tachometer, unwilling to face those sparkling, spellbinding eyes.

He reached down and let the choke slip in a little; and the idle dropped to one thousand. 'Just play it cool,' Mark said, in a very private voice.

'Right, bud,' said Jon, with no expression.

'Hey, Jon; glad you waited.' Steve tapped the car roof over Jon's open door, leaning in to him. 'Could you do me a big favour and drop off Jeannie too? Promised her a ride; but, you know….'

'Aaah….' Jon tapped his foot on the throttle. 'Because' was over.

'Get in, Jeannie,' Steve smiled, and opened the door behind Jon.

Nervously Jeanne dropped herself into the left rear seat, only to find that the console extended back through the rear seats as well. The big Caprice about which everyone like to talk was really only a four-seater. She put both feet over the console, rather awkwardly, and after kicking the back of Mark's seat with her block-heeled shoes she was able to slide her bottom into the right rear seat. Warm air wafted out through vents in the side of the console and she rubbed her bare hands on her denim thighs. Steve got in behind Jon and shut the door.

Jon took his foot down off the door and reached out to close it. 'Okay, people; everybody buckle up.'

As the inside lights went out Jeanne groped about the sides of her seat for the belts. She found a fixed ring of sorts down near the door, and there was a wide strap with a heavy aircraft-type clip beside the console. Steve finally reached over and showed her how he had latched his own. From ahead there came a click as Mark buckled in. She put her head back in the tall seat, and the rumble of the engine and the pounding of her heart made her whole body shiver. This car in which she would now be taken home was entirely new to her. The oiled rosewood trim, the power-window switches and the glasslike door pulls all seemed out-of-place in the town's most notorious hot rod. She tried to relax, hoping the soft piano music would not distract her from thinking up something intelligent to say to the young man at the wheel. It seemed too much to hope just to initiate a pleasant conversation with him.

The boys were quiet until Wilshire Pike. 'So Steve,' the driver said. 'What'd you think of that show, man?'

'It was fantastic,' Steve smiled. 'Really. Mark, that drum solo was outasite.'

'Yeah,' Mark smiled, remembering how cathartic it had been for him; 'it came off pretty good.'

'Mark and Barry wrote "If You Need It",' Jon said.

'*And* you,' Mark added.

'*And* me, *and* Dave,' Jon said quietly, and listened to the middle passage of 'You Never Give Me Your Money'.

Jeanne thought of something to say and heard herself ask in a nervous voice, 'Is that The, uh, Beatles?'

Jon smiled a little; she did not see. 'Well; it sure isn't David Cassidy,' he said wryly.

Slighted by this, she would not go on to say she recalled her elder brother playing the same album when he was home. She had to kick herself for that. It might have made a great opening for further conversation; both Steve and Jon had shared classes with Curt in their tenth-grade year. 'All he's got are Fab tapes,' Mark informed her. 'Nineteen thousand of 'em. All Fab tapes. Every Fab tape there is, and some that nobody has.'

'And,' Jon teased him, 'none of *your* favourite: Andy Williams.'

'Right,' said Mark sarcastically.

Jon slowed and stopped for the traffic light at Atlantic Parkway. He meant to turn right, towards the Old Mill section where Steve and Jeanne both lived; but before he had signalled a red Vega with a bold white stripe down each side pulled up in the left lane and captured his attention. 'Uh-oh,' Jon announced, with the expected derogatory sarcasm. 'Check *this* junk out.'

'Really,' Mark agreed, as he had seen it too. The subcompact Vega coupé had been modified with a raised rear end, pneumatic dampers and oversized tyres. Jon and Mark heard the gears mesh as the driver shifted into first. 'Uh-oh,' Mark laughed. 'Chump's even got a four-speed.'

Jon surveyed it for another second and then made up his mind. 'All right,' he said; 'little car, big motor. Bigger car, even bigger motor. This is kinda like sleeper versus sleeper.' He and Mark chuckled a little at that. 'Everybody buckled in?'

The light for Atlantic Parkway turned yellow. Jeanne held her breath.

Four fat tyres screamed as the Wilshire Pike light went green. Slightly underestimating the reaction of the Vega's driver, and perhaps in deference to his passengers, Jon ran first gear only to four thousand and the little red car put its tail to them with a naughty snarl from its twin pipes. '*Damn!*' Mark cursed. 'Son-of-a-bitch is a small-block!'

'No *shit*,' Jon snapped, and downed the throttle. Wilshire Pike narrowed to just one wide lane each side beyond the Parkway intersection which made it the ideal dare for drag racers leaving the school. Charging up the mild incline Jon was gaining on the Vega, disregarding the kerb closing in on his right.

Steve saw it coming. 'Uh; easy, Jon,' he tried; but the tachometer was up to five thousand and the clutch went in for another gear change. The needle teased the red zone for a second. 'It's not so–'

'*Listen* to this hunk of shit!' Jon said angrily, slamming the throttle to the floor again. The acceleration pressed them all back into their seats; Jeanne thought she felt her heart skip with the chirp from the rear tyres. The roar of the engine was a pounding in her ears. 'It sounds like *horseshit*! It's like I'm losin' compression.'

'The way you shift, maybe you oughta torque up the head bolts some,' Mark said wryly.

The supercharger wailed to deafen the devil. Jon swung over to the left, by now sufficiently ahead of the little Vega, with its transplanted V8 engine, to claim the lead. Only at eighty-five, his opponent well behind, did he even pull the stick back into fourth. The tachometer resumed a saner reading.

'Now, Steve Marlowe, if you'd like to discuss transmissions....'

Steve smiled a bit, accepting only then that they were indeed in safe hands. Jeanne let out a breath in silence. 'Just keep it clean, boys,' he said gently. 'You forget we have a lady present.'

'And we all know how Jon loves the ladies,' Mark teased, whilst Jon tried not to look embarrassed and Jeanne felt her neck and cheeks growing warm.

At Pacific Parkway Jon changed down to third and steered into the off-ramp at well over fifty. The big Caprice took the curve like a champion race car; but soon they were cruising comfortably within ten percent of the legal limit. Jeanne watched him as he drove. He slouched down in his seat with one elbow sinking into the armrest and two fingers hooked loosely round the lower corner of the wheel as though aloof to the rigours of performance driving. Jeanne felt a shiver in her spine to realise she was seeing him in his own element at last. This is so *fantastic*, she thought. He really is all casual about it and everything. Just like I knew he would be.... But it's obvious he's got nothing to worry about; I mean: everybody says he did build this car himself.... And it's like the fastest car around, and he's like the best driver around; so I guess it must be something like a well-trained horse and the knight who rides it–

That notion was too romantic not to embarrass her; and Jeanne blushed in the dark. But his posture looks terrible! she thought. I can't believe he looks so short; it must be that he slouches so much. I could never slouch like that. And even so, he's like the best swimmer on the team. A guy can't be out of shape and still be competitive; that's what Steve always says. And like Jon was the one who carried me out of the water; and for that he's got to be stronger than *anybody*! She blushed more at that thought in particular.

Jeanne had always wanted to know everything she could about him, so if by chance they should meet somewhere, like tonight, she would at least be able to keep up a conversation. But for all her attention to gossip and rumour there were several things about him that she could not have known. Most of what circulated about The Strawberries, and about Jon Cavaliere in particular, was only well-seeded propaganda for the promotion of the band. Chris Santana had been the first to suggest that they let the public think whatever they wanted to think, so long as they still paid attention; and the strategy had resulted in the most talked-about rock-and-roll band in the county.

This philosophy offended Jon personally; but he accepted the nature of public relations as a necessary evil and its monetary compensation was enough to rest his conscience for the moment.   The band's followers portrayed him as a reckless drag racer, a notorious Casanova, a hopeless alcoholic, and a brawling street-gang member.   In truth the general public knew nearly nothing about the four mannerly young gentlemen who took their careers and their future so seriously.   They were actually incredibly particular about the character of all their associates, and all four of them were very adamant against the overuse of alcohol or the mere tolerance of illegal narcotics.   Jon was in fact often avoided by teenagers of the area who were involved with drugs simply because they found it so disappointing that the lifestyle of a popular rock-and-roll musician should be devoid of such controversial or rebellious influences.

However, all else meant nothing to Jeanne when she found herself even in the same school corridor as he.   She was known to lose her place in conversation, drop her books or bump right into people in the flurry of nervous emotion that came upon her when she realised he was nearby.   The world and Jon Cavaliere were of equal importance; yet in her awe she could only remain silent.   She knew no resources with which to communicate with him and struggled in her mind with ideas to attract his attention in just the right way.   Like now, she thought, when I asked him if that was The Beatles, he was like sarcastic about it.   Not to be rude, or anything; but it's just that, to him, the fact that this tape is The Beatles is like common knowledge, and I was just asking a stupid question.

That is my problem, Jeanne thought as they rode the long way round towards Old Mill Road and Jon and Mark sang in harmony with John Lennon and The Beatles through 'Mean Mr Mustard'. Jeanne did not know the song.   She sat quietly in the back seat and thought. Actually, he and I are very much *un*-alike.   I'm like a flirt, like Patti's always saying; but Jon is a star.   He doesn't have to flirt.   I have to work at getting people to like me; but they all just fall in love with him from a distance.   I try so hard to be outgoing and friendly and easy to get along with; and like he says something sarcastic and they all still think he's the greatest guy in the world.   He can do whatever he wants and they'll always be crazy about him.   He doesn't have to worry about what they think.   If I changed into a totally different person tomorrow, they'd all think I was crazy; but, if he were to change like that overnight, they'd all just think it was just like him, and no-one would mind at all.   Except maybe me....

'Hey, man,' Jon said to Mark; 'so what did Santana tell you about this party?   Where is it?'

'Oh; uh, at Rob's. Just boozies and floozies. Sounds like a drag.'

'Who's goin'? Are you goin'?'

'It's like I said, man. Just boozies and floozies. You know the kind of people he has. I thought you were goin' over Chrissy's.'

'Yeah; well; it's just some family function, you know, her grandmother's birthday, or something.... You know that means Santana'll be there too.'

'Because of– Oh yeah.'

'And I was supposed to go home and get my guitar.... Man, I'll *never* get there.' He looked up in the inside mirror. 'Steve. So where do I go? –your house?'

'Well; first, if you could drop Jeannie off–'

'Right,' he said seriously, and spoke to Mark straight away. 'Which reminds me, man; I'm gonna need two decent seats for Saturday. Third, fourth row, centre aisle.'

'Oh; what's *this*? A little picky-picky, this late–'

'That's right. And you just won the task of gettin' 'em for me. You can't believe the hassles I get from Bell, and *Santana*–'

'Oh; Jon likes Chrissy, Jon likes Chrissy,' Mark sang; and the two in the back seats laughed.

But Jon knew the teasing was not meant to embarrass him. Mark had other, more supportive motives. 'Yeah,' Jon told him, as though ignoring it; 'well; just remember all the crap I *do* for you guys, without getting paid, even; and to think such a strong supporter like *me* has to actually *stand in line* and *buy* tickets like everybody else....'

'Hey Jon,' Steve asked; 'you guys are playing the Starlight, when, uh, Saturday?'

'Yeah; the Twenty-third,' Jon replied; 'day before my birthday....'

'Really?' Steve smiled; and Jeanne made a mental note of that.

'Where is that place, exactly?'

'It's kind of outside Carleton,' said Mark, 'on Wallis Road.... It's a regular hall, like.'

'Oh,' said Steve; 'yeah; think I know where that is....'

'They have plays there a lot,' Jon said; 'but they also have a lotta local bands, too. People like Whirligig, and Skyrocket, they play there a lot. I saw Abbey Road, that Beatle band, there once.'

'The big names,' smiled Steve. 'What time's the show?'

'*Dark*,' Jon told him, whilst Jeanne listened intently. 'There's an opening act, this guy me and Holloway know from Essex; he's pretty good. Writes a lot of his own material, so.... He's goin' on at like eight.' He turned, looked at Mark and laughed. 'So did you dig that shit Bell was spewin' out tonight, man? About the money, and the "we'll make bucks" speech?'

'No,' laughed Mark. 'I was kinda like steering clear of him. He was in a rare mood tonight, boy.'

'Well; it was because *Paulie* was sick,' Jon said. They both laughed.

'Yeah,' said Mark; 'and that ain't exactly a rare mood for him any more. When it's cool, it's cool; but as soon as you need a cymbal stand or a new vocal mic, it's like everybody's in the poorhouse, and doo.'

'Really,' Jon agreed. 'Guy'll never be happy with what he's makin' now.'

Mark shrugged and said offhandedly, 'Yeah, man; but, actually, neither will I.'

'Diggit,' Jon said then; and they both laughed.

'Jon,' Steve said, 'pardon me for asking; but, with all the shows you guys have now, you do pretty well; don't you? I mean: money-wise—'

'Ah; would it were so,' Jon said with a smile. 'Tell you what, Steve. Make it a date, and contribute to the cause. Three bucks a ticket. Good cause.'

'Right,' said Mark, heavy on the sarcasm.

'Yeah,' Jon laughed; 'namely, my next coupla meals.'

Mark laughed, and Steve and Jeanne smiled at their joking. 'No,' Steve said; 'but, seriously. Always wondered how that works. You get like, what? Fifteen, twenty percent?'

'*Twenty percent?*' Jon laughed aloud. 'That's damn near a *joke*. Good joke, Steve. Hah, hah….' Mark was laughing with him. 'No, Steve. More like eight percent. Eight percent of the profit, is my share.'

Steve was surprised. Jeanne looked at him. '*Eight* percent? Where does it all go?'

Mark laughed aloud. 'Shit! —that's not even my *exact* question, every payday; is it?'

Jon smiled. 'Well,' he said; 'there really isn't that much profit, like that. We have roadies, you know, and a light guy and a sound guy…. You have to pay for gas and insurance and for any rentals of stage gear; and there's stuff like all Chris's posters and stuff, like those little stickers we gave away in the spring…. And then half the profit right away goes into the Strawberries Profit Fund.'

'The *what?*' Jeanne and Steve asked together.

Jon and Mark looked at each other and laughed. 'The Strawberries Profit Fund,' Jon told them. 'It's just a big bank account. Santana came up with the idea. I guess, if you wanted to get technical, it's really the cash assets of the company. All of us have shares, including Bell and Santana. The eight percent we get is kind of like a stock dividend.'

'What's it's really for,' Mark said, 'is like if we needed new equipment, or a loan, or like some day if we wanted to invest in a studio of our own….'

'Right,' smiled Jon, as though that had been his idea too. 'Which would again be considered the assets of the company. And both bands have one. Theirs is called the Tobacco Road Profit Fund.'

Steve and Jeanne were both visibly impressed, although Jon had not really expected them to be. To him, this was all part of his everyday life. Actually he had no real idea how uncommon it would seem to other people his age. 'So,' said Steve; 'just to be curious–'

'How much are we worth?' But Jon would not be offended by the inquisition. He knew Steve was planning a career in business; such things would interest him. With a shrug he said, 'Steve, honest, I have no idea. Melody Santana keeps the books. It goes up a hundred and a quarter or so every show.'

That was impressive to the point of sending shivers down Jeanne's spine. She tried to think of how often she had heard of The Strawberries playing somewhere, and then to multiply that by a hundred dollars or more; it was staggering. And Jon was still not yet eighteen.

'You think we could drop in on Barnett?' Mark asked.

Jon looked at him. 'Who? *Becky?* Oh, hell; I don't know. What for?'

'I don't know. I just feel like goin' somewhere and gettin' a drink.'

'Aaah; her old man don't keep no booze,' Jon said, turning off Laurence Drive onto Apple Way.

'Dewar's-and-water,' Mark stated, as though ordering in a bar.

Jon steered round a car that had stopped to pick up two hitchhiking teenagers. 'Aaah, hah; shoulda let 'em walk!' he laughed, marvellously for his own amusement. In the next second he turned to Mark looking perfectly grave. 'Yeah; well; I can see we're gonna end up at Rob's party.'

'Yeah; but he'll have Scotch,' Mark sighed.

'Remind me to get you a bottle, for Christmas,' Jon said to him, and then slowed for the right turn onto Old Mill Road. Jeanne was stunned; she had suddenly realised no-one had given him directions to her house. Four years ago she had mentioned her address to Jon and then only in friendly conversation. If he knew today just where she lived, he would either have to have a very good memory or a more recent interest. She began to hope mightily that the latter would be the case, although upon second thought the former might prove just as positive.

'Up on the left, about half a block,' Steve told him; and at that Jeanne's heart sank. Even so, she could not tell if Jon had not begun slowing before Steve spoke; he did not change up to third gear in any case.

'Right,' Jon acknowledged, and thought, shame it's 'She Came In Through The Bathroom Window' playing here; it should be 'On The Street Where You Live'. And my *My Fair Lady* tape is at home....

'Where that green Plymouth is,' Steve told him; and Jeanne was sorry to have lost the chance to see how much Jon really knew of her. 'See it?'

'Ah yes.' There was in fact a streetlamp right in front of the Banfield house across from where Cherry Lane intersected the street. He put in the clutch pedal and swung over to the left kerb. Jeanne looked out, past Steve, at the red front door of her house and the *119* illuminated by the porch lamp.

'So,' Steve said to her; 'do you want me to call you, or–'

She looked at him. Suddenly it felt very strange to be talking about a date, with Jon Cavaliere listening at arm's-length. 'Well; I should really check first, you know; but…. Suppose I call you, just in case?'

'All right, Jeannie,' Steve smiled.

'All right.' She unbuckled the seatbelt and opened the door. With one foot out on the street she hesitated and then drew a deep breath to address the boys. 'Well, Steve; I'll see you, then; and Mark– I really enjoyed your show. And, thanks a lot for the ride– *Jon.*'

Bravely she smiled at him in the mirror, feeling her hand shake on the door. He made a little salute to her, like maybe an airline pilot might have done. 'Right,' he said to the mirror, not turning about. There was just enough feeling in his voice to keep her from thinking he meant to be cold towards her; and despite the nervous little shivers that had infected her entire body she began to feel warm inside. Good things were yet to happen, she knew. It would just be a matter of time.

Jon was surprised that Steve did not get out to walk her to the house; he began to form an opinion about it, or about Steve, and then put it out of his mind. Still he would not drive off and leave a lady in the street and so pretended to adjust the inside mirror for a moment until Jeanne had stepped up onto her front porch. He slipped the clutch, but the whole car shuddered; the gearbox was still in second. Blushing bright-red he jammed the stick up into first and accelerated away a little too heavily, only narrowly avoiding a tangle with a car coming up the hill from behind. 'So, uh, Steve. Where the hell's your street? Second one; or–'

'Uh, Linden; yeah,' said Steve, as though coming out of some deep reflection. The three boys were silent as Jon flung the car round the corner and dashed down the block to the Marlowe house. 'Well,' Steve said, as they stopped at the base of the driveway; 'enjoy your party, guys.'

'Really,' said Jon, as it made a suitable topic for minor conversation.

'Boozies and floozies,' Mark added.

Steve made a little laugh at that. 'All right….' He opened the door. 'Hey, Jon; really appreciate the bus service. Thanks a lot.'

'Leave the driving to us,' Jon said, with that same little salute; and they laughed. 'Really, dude, it's no problem.'

That was too honest; but Steve could never have understood. 'Owe ya one,' he said to Jon.

'Good. Come to the show.' And be sure Jeanne comes, he would not add.

'Will do,' Steve promised. 'Take it easy, guys.' He closed the door and left them with a thumb's-up.

Jon went round the block and drove up Maple, going left on Old Mill Road and passing Jeanne's house on his way out to Apple Way. Mark would not question the choice of routes; they both observed that the front porch lamp had been put out. Out on Atlantic Parkway he turned and said to Jon, 'Well? That wasn't too bad; was it?'

'What wasn't so bad?'

'Jon, knock it off. She's not goin' steady with him. They're just good friends.'

'Yeah; but–'

'Look, man. Anybody else can see she's just as nervous around you.'

'Nervous? She ain't nervous. She don't even know the meaning of the–'

'Look, man,' Mark said, shaking his head; 'the very fact that you say that means you ain't lookin' at it sensibly. Just take it easy. She's gotta be nervous around you for some reason; right? I mean: she's still human.'

Jon sighed, exasperated and embarrassed. 'Right, bud.'

'She is, dude. In biology class all she does is sit up front and *talk* with everybody. And these dudes are so obviously pantin' all over her, and doo; but she ain't nervous around *them*, man…. It's only *you* that makes her nervous.'

'Fuck–'

'It's like I've been sayin'–'

'Shit–'

'You can see she's just–'

'Damn–'

'Look, man; will you cut it out? You know I'm right. I'm just tellin' ya, I think you should go for it.'

'"*Go* for it"! *Listen* to him; like it's all so easy–'

'It *is*, man; don't be an asshole! Shit– it's so *obvious*, man; she'd probably listen to anything you could say!' He shook his head with a rueful sigh. 'It's just like Santana says; there's a hundred babes, damn foxy ones too, but he never says anything to them, never calls them, never *looks* at them, *nothing*. Come on, man; look how fascinated they were about the stupid bank accounts. You could tell her about the demo we cut tonight, or the recording Bell's makin' at the Starlight next week…. Or the *contracts* we're both gonna get, when it's all good and ready…. It'd impress the hell outa her, man. She'd be–'

'Right, bud,' said Jon sarcastically. 'And then Bell comes after my ass, since all that shit is supposed to be top-secret for now. Remember him telling us about the on-stage side and the off-stage side—'

'Yeah,' Mark told him; 'but that don't mean you gotta be like cold to her. Maybe you could tell her you could like *confide* in her, and shit. It couldn't really hurt. Or even make *up* some shit; who cares? I'm tellin' ya, man, just *talk* to the babe.'

'Aaah; you know how it is, man. I never know what to say. I'm such a clod at introductions—'

'Look, man; I swear you're just makin' it into a bigger thing than it is. All you gotta do to start is say "Hi". Try that, next time you see her. It ain't such a big deal.'

'Aaah....' By now he was feeling terribly embarrassed. In his head he could picture himself going out of his way to say 'Hi' to Jeanne Banfield in the corridor, and then in his awkwardness bumping into half a dozen cute girls or, worse, half a dozen football players. He winced at the thought.

'Look, man; it's just that me and everybody else are gettin' tired of coachin' you through this one goddamn thing. Either talk to the babe or don't, but quit tryin' to pick up the sympathy.'

'I ain't tryin' to pick up no sympathy—'

'The *hell* you ain't, man. Why else would you be draggin' this thing out so long? Jesus Christ! —I don't have to tell you how long ago it was that I got pissed-off at that asshole lifeguard at the lake—'

'No; you don't; so shut up.'

'All right; and maybe you'll just say "Hi" to her tomorrow, and get it over with.'

'Yeah; right, bud,' Jon said sarcastically. 'Maybe *you* should say "Hi" to her.'

'Maybe; but then *I* don't have the crush on her.'

'Get out; I ain't got no crush on her.'

'No; you just live every day in hopes she says "Hi" to you first.' Mark slouched in his seat and stared out the side window. Only now did he realise that half of what he had said was futile. 'Look,' he said, in a gentler tone; 'all I'm sayin', which is for your own damn good, is that you gotta assert yourself in times like these, and get it the hell done. So what if you look like an idiot then; because right now all you're doin' is buggin' the shit outa everybody else. 'Cause where you are now, you ain't got nothin' to lose.'

'Shit....' Jon shivered, to be rid of the topic. 'So where are we goin', man; home?'

'Naah.... Might as well go over Rob's.' Mark sighed, accepting the shift in conversation. Jon would never feel too comfortable being pushed, even by a close and caring friend. 'Yeah,' he said; 'those boozies and floozies....'

* * *

On Monday, Jon drove Christine to school. Her mother was on hand to pick her up afterwards and take her to an appointment with her doctor straight away. Jon stood in the drizzle, leaning outside the driver's window of the big blue Lincoln and talking with Mrs Polvere when Steve came up and tapped him. 'Jon, man, hate to ask; but I was wondering....'

Jon looked at him. 'What, another ride?' He smiled at once. 'No problem, dude. Go ahead; I'm parked over there behind the shops.'

He turned back to Christine. 'These kids.... We'll see. So I'll call you, then; all right?'

'All right,' agreed Christine from the other end of the wide front seat. 'See you soon.'

'Bye, Jon,' Mrs Polvere said impassively, and pulled away. Jon turned, slowly, and shared a few words with a few others on his way back to his car.

He found Steve Marlowe in the front passenger seat and Jeanne Banfield in the right rear seat behind him. 'Oh,' he said, suppressing his surprise, and leaned in the open door to effect an easygoing façade. 'So I guess this is my bus; right?'

The two inside laughed. It was hard for him to not smile at Jeanne, looking right back up at him, giggling with her teeth tightly together and those cute little dimples in her cheeks. 'Yeah,' said Steve. 'The Old Mill local.'

Jon laughed a little, bravely keeping his eyes on Jeanne for more than a second or two. She did not look away. Her smile delighted him to where it was nearly impossible to swing down into his seat; but then, should he need to check traffic to the rear, he knew the inside mirror was set for him to see her back there. The engine roared into life. 'All right,' he said to either of them; 'so who's got Morris for history?'

'Nobody,' Steve said. 'I have Howell; and I think Jeannie has–'

'I gotta find somebody with the stupid take-home test for tomorrow. P's me O'. I was out all night last night; and I'll be out again tonight....' He cranked the wheel hard round to the left and cut into the line of cars leaving school in the driveway. Jeanne looked out the window; he had just barged in ahead of Lisa Hardy's mother's brown Volkswagen.

'What's this? –a party?' asked Steve.

'No; just practices. All kinds of practices. Yesterday was the band, and tonight's the team. This business is for maniacs, man. Just ask Weber how much I've put into the team this year. It's pathetic. And now I can see why Jenkins finally quit. Going TCB is taking up alla my time, to the point where I can either sleep, or do homework, but not both. It's a real drag.'

Jeanne smiled at hearing such disparity between Jon's opinions now and what he had said about the music business in composition class this past spring. It amused her; yet she could hardly believe it was all as disappointing to him as he made it sound.

They were out to the street in a minute. 'Actually,' Jon said, as though mostly to Steve, 'it's really because of the damn team; he wants me to be at the meet tomorrow night. But the place we're playing Saturday should be pretty cool, though. Our first show with all solid seating, you know; not general admission, and no dance floor. Like, the press is gonna be there, and everything. Bell and Santana have all these ideas; Santana's really stoked. He wants us to– Aaah; you better just come and see.'

Jeanne and Steve smiled. 'So who's Bell?' Steve asked him. Jeanne had wondered the same thing.

'Oh; he's a DJ over at the jazz station outside Chester. Bell Howard. He's Tobacco Road's producer; well; he's ours too. Dave met him at the bowling alley this summer. He's one of these old overgrown hippies from southern California; drove a van to Woodstock.... But he's cool, you know; he's been really good to us.'

'*Woodstock*? How *old* is he?'

'Oh; I guess like twenty-four, twenty-five; I just know his birthday was last month.'

'Oh,' said Steve.

Jeanne sat back in the seat, trying to relax and to appear casual when, inside, her excitement was racing at full speed. Wow! she kept thinking, over and over. *Wow*! Here I am, riding in Jon Cavaliere's car! For the second time! Oh, Steve, I'm *glad* we got stuck in the rain last week! And *Patti*! –poor Patti, she's been home sick, and I haven't *called* her! I've just *got* to tell her....

–'Yes, Jeannie; it's me. How have you been?'

'You sound terrible, Patti. What did they say it was?'

–'Well; the doctor thinks it may only be a virus, but he says that if it's the same tomorrow I'll have to go in. Mother's worried that it may be pneumonia; but I'm sure it's not that bad.... So how have *you* been?'

'Oh, Patti; Patti, I am *so* sorry I haven't called you; we were down to visit Curt– it was his homecoming weekend– and then I've been *so* busy....'

–'Doing *what*, that's so exciting?'

'Oh; you couldn't guess! I got a ride home from Jon Cavaliere!'

–'*God*! Are you *serious*? When was *this*?'

'Well; actually twice; once on Friday and once today. I *did* try to call you....'

–'*Twice*! God! I *knew* I should've called you back!'

'I *know*!' Jeanne giggled excitedly. 'Patti, I just couldn't *believe* it! Of course Steve was there. He and I went to the concert Friday night, and like of course I saw *him* there, but I knew that wasn't anything; I mean: he probably knows every rock group in the *world*. So anyway

Steve's mom drove us over because Steve's little car was in the shop, and he didn't want to call her so late; I mean: it was like almost eleven; and so before I knew it we were getting into Jon Cavaliere's car!'

–'Wow!' Patti emitted.

'It is *so* cool inside, Patti; it has like power windows and power seats and power everything, and the seats are so comfortable, you could fall asleep; but of course I *couldn't* fall asleep, not even that *night*; because oh, like we had this drag race Friday night and of course he *won*; I mean: you know, he wouldn't be beaten in *anything*.'

–'I would imagine not. And so why were you there again today?'

'Well; Steve's car is still in the shop; I think it's like the linkage or something; and so Steve asked him if he could give us a ride and then got me into *that car*. And Jon Cavaliere was over talking to somebody else and so when he turned around there we were. I mean: like he wasn't going to throw us out; so....'

–'Wow; Jeannie, that's just fantastic. So what did he *say* to you? You've *got* to tell me....'

'Well; he really didn't say that much to me.... I asked him what tape it was–' She was embarrassed by that thought and did not finish. 'It wasn't like what he was saying to me as what he was saying to *everybody*. I mean: like the first time, Mark Jenkins was there, you know; he's the drummer in Tobacco Road; and like Steve told him how good the drum solo was.... And like Mark Jenkins and Jon Cavaliere were talking about the music business; and Steve kind of asked them how much money they make, not in a rude way, you know– and my God! –Patti, Jon Cavaliere said they make like a hundred and fifty dollars every *show*! Can you *imagine*? And like he said he doesn't even know how much money they *have*! And I was thinking, what is it they say, that rich people never know how rich they are; I mean: like they've got to be *very rich*!' She stopped, only to catch her breath. 'He said his birthday was the day after they play, which is Saturday; so, Sunday is his birthday. The twenty-fourth. I think he's going to be eighteen.'

–'Oh; well; yes, Jeannie; that would follow....'

'God! –Patti, do you think he'll be a millionaire before he's twenty-one?'

–'*Jeannie!*' Patti laughed weakly. –'*Listen* to you!' She coughed then. 'Now do tell me what you said to him.'

'Well; not that much.... But, oh, Patti? You know what? I think he knows where I *live*. I mean: like when Steve was telling him where to go, I realised even before that he was going the right way anyway. I mean: I think maybe he's known where I live for a *while*.'

–'That's significant.' Patti seemed to think about that.

'That's what I thought too,' said Jeannie.

–'But you say he really didn't talk to you?'

'No,' Jeanne lamented; 'and I really wanted him to....'

—'Well; it might have a lot to do with Steve being there. I mean: they do say he's a flirt; but even a flirt wouldn't flirt with somebody who's with someone else, at least not one you'd want to flirt with you.... You did thank him for the ride?'

'Oh; of course, Patti! And he was like really cute about it–'

—'Well; good. All I can say is, keep hanging round with Steve. He's nice and he would understand, if– Well; you know, if anything fantastic happened. And just hope his car stays in the shop!'

'Oh; I know!' They both giggled.

* * *

Steve phoned on Wednesday afternoon and told Jeanne what he deemed good news: that his car was repaired and out of the shop. Jeanne would not let on that she was slightly disappointed. Besides, Steve had been wanting to take her to see the major Tobacco Road show on Thursday evening. The most popular rock-and-roll band in the area were vigorously supported by the students of Wilshire High, who purchased their t-shirts and bumper-stickers and badges in quantity, proud to consider the band as having come from their own. The band provided impressive and familiar entertainment, and their original songs, which had begun to to come out with increasing frequency, were like million-selling hit records to fans' ears. Any Tobacco Road show became a major event; and one's social stature was dramatically enhanced merely by being seen there.

Steve was a good boy, so her mother had said; and not all her male friends met her father's approval as well. Steve and Jeanne had achieved a closeness over the years that few of her other friendships with boys might ever rival. He was polite and intelligent and considerate, and she could look forward to any gathering where she would be seen entering on Steve's arm. But there were other reasons why she simply had to attend the concert, to the point where she might have accepted a date with an escaped convict just for a glimpse of Jon Cavaliere in the audience. She remembered Jon requesting from Mark two tickets, after which Mark had teased him about an obviously female person called Chrissy. It had been somewhat surprising to her; and she dwelt upon the thought for a full week afterwards. She had never witnessed him holding hands or sharing any romantic moments with anyone; and most of the people she knew might kiss their steady dates quite blatantly in public. Though she had in fact dated many different boys, it still seemed unimaginable to her that Jon Cavaliere might have been so human to have taken a mere mortal girl.

I wonder what she's like, Jeanne thought, all through the afternoon and early evening. Maybe she's as far-out as he is. Yeah; I bet Jon Cavaliere's got a real foxy girlfriend. They probably do all sorts of fantastic far-out rock-star things, like go to parties in New York and take vacations in the mountains and fly off to the Riviera.... The kind of people that magazines like to do picture stories on and put on the cover and all sorts of other great fantastic far-out things; and I bet if they're not on any magazine covers right now, they sure will be *next* year.

But I'll keep wishing he really wanted a plain old nice girl like me, she thought. I hope he's somebody who can love her for her personality and not for what her body feels like, in bed.... *No*, Jeanne thought then, repulsed by the thought. *No*-one as far-out as Jon Cavaliere could want a girl only for sex. He's got to be the kind of guy who can love you for what's deep down inside. He's just *got* to be. The type of guy who would save you from drowning in the lake, no matter what you looked like.... If he's not, she knew, there's just no reason to try any more.

Steve was there to pick her up at 7.20; and by a quarter to eight they were seated about halfway back in the left-side section, a few seats in from the aisle. The Lion's Den was a small theatre not far out of Wilshire that was normally the host for chamber music and local drama groups. Tonight it was packed with excited rock-and-roll fans.

The lights had gone down at five minutes till eight. A few late arrivals were ushered to their seats. Jeanne turned to Steve, in conversation, and saw the couple passing by in the aisle beyond him. Jon Cavaliere in his jeans and pilot's leather and his friend in the short dress and rabbit fur were following an usher down front. Jeanne blushed a little and forgot, in her envy, what she had meant to say to Steve. The seats Jon had received were third row, dead centre. Mark had got him excellent seats.

Dave Holloway, funnily enough without a date tonight, sat sullenly beside Bell Howard, immediately to Jon's left. Just to Christine's right sat Becky Barnett in a new black leather jacket, and her escort for the evening, Bob Prescott, slumping in his seat like an insolent child. 'Oh,' said Becky, when Christine had seated herself; 'and as usual, *you* look disgustingly fantastic.'

Christine smiled graciously, having grown accustomed to Becky's often acerbic humour over the last few weeks. 'And you're looking nice tonight. Especially with the man who brought you.'

Becky laughed. 'Oh; he wouldn't've brought me. I had to drag him.' From her other side, Bob rapped her in the shoulder.

There was an opening act, a local quintet known as Hot Flash, with whose producers Bell Howard was well acquainted. The guitar player's fast solo licks and the pretty female singer in tight red dance trousers went over well with the crowd; and with six fresh high-energy numbers in their forty-minute set, Hot Flash were off to a good start with the rock-and-roll lovers of the River Valley area.

Tobacco Road went on to a roaring audience at 9.05, shooting off half a dozen entirely new songs in their first hour alone. These six and the five from last week's show at the school were what Bell hoped might comprise a second LP already. 'It's like I told you,' he told Jon. 'You want to avoid what they call the sophomore jinx. You might put out one album and have it sell like wildfire; but it's all stuff you've been playin' for years, when you weren't concentratin' on makin' records. Then when the record company signs you, you've got no new material.'

'You gotta be able to keep writing tunes,' Jon understood.

'Right,' said Bell, loudly, close to Jon's ear to be heard. 'This is why I keep nagging at you and Dave. If you wanna be in it for the long haul, you gotta keep workin' at it.'

Jon nodded seriously and watched the band.

'I sent their tapes off,' said Bell to him.

'So Dave told me.'

'Yeah; well; you can't blame the record companies if they're afraid to invest in somebody new. They're just as afraid of what I've been tellin' you. No-one can seem to put out more than two albums— one to introduce them and one to flop.'

'I hear ya,' Jon told him. 'I've noticed that lately.'

'Keep writing tunes,' Bell said, and turned to box him in the arm with a jovial smile. 'You may well be the ones to break that trend!'

Steve and Jeanne were impressed by the performance. They were unaware that Bell Howard had any plans for any demonstration tapes. They could not have known why last week's show before the home crowd had seemed stiff and tight nor why tonight's performance, for a broader audience, was spirited and free, with the band jumping about dressed in wild colours and seeming to enjoy themselves much more.

Barry sang the lead vocal to 'Touch And Go,' one of his latest. In the second's break before his guitar solo Jon leaped up enthusiastically to yell, 'Do it, Barry!' right at the stage. There were many who heard and saw him above the crowd, including Jeanne. She thought it impressive that half the people in the room recognised and cheered him as a celebrity in his own right. This was, after all, that kind of crowd. 'Touch And Go' was new to her, but there was a familiarity about it that made her feel as though she had heard it often before. What she was really getting used to was the sound of Tobacco Road.

An extended version of the Alascan-and-Hemphill 'Where I Stand' brought a formal end to the show; but naturally the audience screamed for more and got seven minutes of 'If You Need It, You'll Get It', followed by a rousing rendition of The Beatles' 'Day Tripper', done as Jon had helped them arrange it over the summer to be more in keeping with the Tobacco Road style. The guitars rang in the ears with that last sustaining E chord, and the flash-pots competed with Mark's fabulous drumming whilst the curtains closed and the crowd thundered in gratitude.

Jeanne and Steve separated for their respective toilets; and Steve returned to the lobby first. Quite accidentally he bumped into Jon and Christine. 'Hey,' Jon said politely, 'Steve. I don't believe you know Christine.'

'Hello,' Christine said modestly, with a lovely smile, and extended her hand.

'Nice to meet you,' said Steve; and they met eyes for a long moment. She looked down first; and only then Steve released her hand and turned to Jon. 'So; quite a show; huh?'

'*Yeah,* man,' Jon said wholeheartedly. 'They can really kick out the jam when they want to.'

'And this from one who's seen them all,' Steve smiled.

'Well; not *all,* but, you know....'

Bob and Becky joined them by the doors; and Bob asked, 'So; where's the party?'

'Oh,' Jon sighed; 'that little greasy-spoon, in town.... What's it called? Pablo's.'

'*Pablo's,*' Becky mused, disdainfully. 'I *hate* that place. It's so *dull.*'

'Well; it was Rob's idea,' Jon told her, 'on account of so many youngbloods....'

Becky boxed him. 'Who *you* callin' "youngblood"?'

Jon shrugged her off. 'Well *I'm* game,' Christine said to him. 'I could sure go for a late-night salad.'

'God!' Becky teased her. 'Like you *need* to diet!'

Steve smiled at that, as Christine's figure was certainly pleasant enough to his eyes. He looked up and saw Jeanne searching for him in the crowd. 'Jeannie!' he called across the lobby. 'Over here!'

Jeanne waved and made her way towards him. Steve took her by the hand and turned about to introduce her; but Jon and Bob and the girls had gone. When Jeanne realised she had just missed meeting that girl face-to-face, her heart sank. Jon Cavaliere as an obsession would not leave her mind.

* * *

'Hey, Chrissy?'

—'Hello, Jon. How are you?'

'All right. So look; there's this party at Mark's place, that I kind of have to go to, and I'm wondering if you'd like to come along.'

—'I'd be happy to, Jon. When is it?'

'Oh; well; Wednesday. It's kind of a meeting, you know; but everyone always brings their girlfriends, so....' He knew she would enjoy being considered his girlfriend. She was, as Chris had said, quite enthralled with him.

—'It sounds nice. No practice this week?'

'Oh,' he smiled; 'no; not this week. No time for it. It's just gonna be the two bands, you know, and Chris.... I'm hopin' Bell might have some news about the demos. Look; if you want, I'll get us a bottle of wine. What's your preference?'

—'Oh; any wine is fine with me, Jon.'

'All right then; the traditional Dago red.' They both laughed.

—'Will there be food there, or just drinks?'

'Oh; I don't know; I imagine there'll be something.'

—'It does sound like fun. Will that be the next time I see you?'

'I don't know; but I'll call you if I get the chance....'

—'Remember I have my photo appointment Friday.'

'Oh; right.... I think I can still drive you to that. Hey; I gotta eat something here, 'cause I'm on my way over Santana's now.'

—'What time shall I be ready on Wednesday?'

He smiled to think how proper she always was. It was indeed very pleasant dating someone so traditional and ladylike; he felt like a true gentleman. 'Oh; I don't know; around eight, I guess....'

—'All right. I'll be looking forward to it, Jon.'

'Okay,' he said; 'me too. See you then, you know, if not before.'

—'Good night,' she said sweetly; and they rang off.

His sister Eve met him at the refrigerator. 'So; you goin' to a party?'

'When?'

'Whenever you just said it was. Wednesday. Are you like goin' steady with Chrissy now?'

He got out the milk. 'Her name is Christine, and *no*; I'm not goin' steady with her.'

'Well; it's like you're always goin' out with her....'

'Right, bud,' he said, and poked her in the stomach on his way across the kitchen.

Eve brushed her unruly wavy brown hair off her forehead and watched him take down a box of Quisp cereal from the cupboard. 'If you're in such a hurry, how come you're eatin' cereal?'

'What are you, like *Beth*, or somethin', with all these questions?'

'I should *kill* you for that,' she said through clenched teeth, and made a fist.

He reached round with his right hand and took a hold on that fist, squeezing her hand until she pleaded for him to stop. 'Right,' he said, as though she had provided the correct response to a behavioural test, and let go of her. 'No, little Miss Radar Ears; it's just that I ain't got any money to buy a real meal at the diner when I get hungry at ten o'clock, and Chris's basement ain't exactly stocked full of ready-made food.... Shit– that reminds me; I gotta get some money off of him too; dammit....'

'So; would you go out with Valerie?'

He stopped pouring the cereal to look at her. '*Your* Valerie? *Short* little Valerie? Valerie, who's fourteen years *old?*'

'Well; not yet she isn't– Look; Jon, you gotta do this for me.'

'Oh; I gotta; huh? For you? Hah! Like *hell*.' He poured more cereal into the bowl and then added some milk.

'Come on, Jon; she's my friend, and I gotta help her.'

'All right; *you* go out with her.'

She watched him get out a spoon and carry his bowl of Quisp and milk over to the kitchen table. 'Jon, I really gotta talk to you about this; it's like real important–'

'Talk fast. I gotta split in like ten minutes.'

She sighed and sat down across from him. 'Well; Valerie– She's my best friend, and I don't know what to do....' She sighed again, folding her hands upon the table. 'Jon, she's turning into a pothead.'

'Who isn't?' he said, and forced a large spoonful of cereal.

'Jon, please.... Did anybody ever tell you you eat like a slob?'

'Many times.' He spooned up more cereal but paused a moment to sigh, closing his eyes reverently for a moment as The Raspberries' 'Overnight Sensation' came over the radio. 'Go turn that up; will ya?'

Eve merely shot a glance at the radio in the corner and remained seated. 'Jon.... I just thought you could maybe like talk to her, if you could.... She really likes you, you know; she has a picture of you up in her room, and everything–'

He looked up at her. 'Whoever gave her a picture of *me?*'

'It's just that she's getting into all this kind of stuff; she's always talking about all this drug stuff I can't even pronounce.... And I just know she would listen to you, Jon; she's–'

'No she wouldn't. That's the thing about potheads. Potheads do not listen to older people who tell them what they're doing is wrong. That's the first sign, you know. You can't talk to 'em about it. I'd look like a loony.'

'Jon....' Eve sighed again.

'Look; even *you* think I'm some kinda loony. *You* never listen to me.'

'You're not a loony,' she said quietly. 'You're my brother.'

'Look; forget it. You can't change potheads. They're that way for life. It's like your most favourite car, and you see one in the junkyard, and it looks like it's completely rotted-out with cancer. And you could take it home, and spend every penny you have on it, and go completely broke; and as soon as you get it all painted and lookin' good, it's gonna be rottin' out somewhere else. It's all because of that one thing you can't fix. You just have to give up on it, and just leave it rot where it sits, 'cause it's beyond hope.' He sighed, with a forlorn tone. 'All Miss Valerie there needs is to inflict my little sister with the goddamn Colombian disease, there, and I swear I'm gonna do somethin' drastic, I'm tellin' ya. You can't change Valerie, Eve. She's like a 'fifty-seven Chevy convertible rotting away in the junkyard. My advice is to dump *her*, before she changes *you*.'

'Jon, I *can't*. She's my *friend*.'

'You said she's a pothead. It's like I've been tellin' you for two years, Eve. Never the two shall mix.'

'Jon, I can't just *dump* her.'

'The *hell* with her.'

'Shhh, quiet; or Daddy'll hear you—'

'Daddy oughta hear *you*,' he said, pointing right at her. 'Daddy oughta hear *you*. You oughta listen to yourself. You're clingin' to some old friend you met in kindergarten, who's workin' on gettin' you messed-up in drugs. And you wanna know *why*? Because potheads don't like to smoke pot alone. They gotta do it *with* somebody, as if doin' it *with* somebody makes it all right. That's how they are. I'll tell ya, Eve, you wanna start gettin' messed-up in her problems, you might as well sit down and smoke pot with her then, 'cause it'll be a damn sight easier on ya then spendin' your life tryin' to deal with it.'

'You know what kinda stuff she's been through, Jon,' she said; but he was still going on.

'It just pisses me off, all this horseshit about drugs, man; it just pisses me off. Just what the hell is the point? Did you ever try to *talk* to somebody on dope? Huh? You feel like an absolute *idiot*. They're not *like* you and me, Eve; they're like of a different consciousness, like they're a different *animal*. It rips up their brain, physically, even; and it gets so pretty soon they're like never the same. It's like they're just as stupid when they're not high as when they are. They're like permanently stupid. You start watchin' little Valerie, there, and pretty soon she'll get stupid. You won't be able to tell when she's high, and when she isn't. I know lots of girls just like that; and I'll tell ya, man, I for one can't stand no stupid-ass pothead girls.'

'I'll tell her that, Jon,' she said to him.

'That's what they call *burned-out*,' he was saying. 'You hear me? *Burned-out*. Like, *worthless*. Good for *nothing*. And you know, they all think it'll happen to somebody else, and not them. Well; it happens to them *all*. They're just too stupid to tell.' He looked right at her and said, 'You start smokin' grass with Valerie, you'll get stupid too. You'll turn into a burnout, and you won't even know it. I swear to God you'll be damned to hell as far as *I'm* concerned.'

'Jon; but don't ever say that,' she said gravely. 'That's a *sin*.'

'Oh; so it's a sin; huh? So you tell me where in the Bible Moses said it's cool to walk around with your head on a different *planet*. Don't fall into that kinda defensive bullshit, Eve. I ain't no stupid worthless burnout, and I don't have to argue this crap with you or anybody.' He rushed through the rest of the cereal whilst she watched him without a word. 'Shit,' he said; 'now I'll have indigestion the whole goddamn night.' He got up to carry the dish to the sink.

The radio announcer was talking over the end of 'Overnight Sensation'. Eve turned in her chair. 'Jon?'

'Look,' he said with a sigh; '*you* go talk to her first. She's *your* friend. I don't know what you could say to her....' He thought; and before she could speak he said, 'Well; *you* have to call it like you see it. If she's not too far gone, you could remind her that it's not any kinda way to rise above her problems, no matter *how* bad they seem. It'll only make her more of a loser. But if she gives you any crap about it then just walk way from her, Eve; and I mean it, just walk *away* from her. And yeah; it'll break your heart; but if she doesn't think she's doing anything wrong, then you've lost her already.'

'Jon, I couldn't—'

'Trust me, Eve: it's all you can do.' He turned round, looking about the room whilst he talked. 'It's like what they teach you in lifeguard class. If it comes down to you or the drowning guy, then you have to save yourself. The world has no room for dead heroes.' He found his leather jacket on the bench by the fireplace and drew it on. They met eyes; and he asked, in a gentler tone, 'Do you know if her father still beats her?'

Eve looked squarely back at him for a long second. 'She doesn't talk about it. But I know he's not home so much any more.'

'That may be good or bad,' Jon said gravely. After another moment of deep contemplation, he said, 'Well; look. Talk to her about it, and see how she is. Then, let me know. If she seems cognizant, you know, then maybe you could invite her over here for dinner; and then we could talk.... Maybe we'll go to a movie; I don't know.'

'That'd be nice,' Eve said happily. 'She really likes you, you know.'

'Christ,' he sighed, pulling his car keys out of his jacket pocket; 'how I get mixed-up in this junk, *I'll* never know....'

Mrs Polvere looked up from her knitting to call Christine over when she had rung off with Jon. 'What is it, Mama?'

'Are you going to Jon's party, then?'

Christine sat on the arm of a side chair. 'Well; it's at Jon's friend Mark's house. It's a kind of a meeting; just the two bands. Everyone's girlfriends are invited. I believe Chris will be taking Jenny too.'

'Tomorrow night,' said her mother.

'No, Mama; it will be Wednesday.'

'I just don't want you out late on a school night.'

'Oh, Mama....' Christine made a pretty smile.

'If they're all going to be smoking and drinking....'

'Oh; I don't imagine so. I'm sure it will just be a regular party—'

'What kind of wine do *you* drink?'

Christine looked at her mother a long moment. 'Mama, I really don't drink at *all*, and I would never drink any more than I do here at dinner....'

'Under the law, you know, you're not allowed to drink outside your parents' home.'

'Oh, *Mama*,' she said with a smile, 'I'm certainly not irresponsible. And neither is Jon. You've already said what a nice boy—'

'Jon isn't perfect.'

Christine had to shake her head. 'What?'

'I just don't think,' said her mother, still not looking up from the knitting, 'that you should have to smoke or drink or God-knows-what to impress a boy like Jon.'

'But I don't have to impress *anyone*, Mama.'

'I hope not.'

'I don't. Besides, Jon wouldn't want me to be anything but what I *am*. That's how he is.'

'I hope so,' said Mrs Polvere, effectively ending the conversation.

But her mother's worrying had begun to worry Christine. Christine was ordinarily very serious about worrying, and she lay awake much of that night and turned in early on Tuesday evening as well. Sometime after two in the morning, she tiptoed down stairs to her father's study in the white satin bikini lingerie she wore to bed and helped herself to a short glass of cognac from the cabinet. Her parents had always been proud of their daughters' responsibility and maturity; she and Jenny had been raised very openly and had been carefully instructed within their family and the Church about subjects like drinking and sex long before their classmates had even thought to wonder. Though she seemed outwardly shy, Christine demonstrated a fearlessness about adult issues that few teenagers could mention without blushing. Both girls had been toasted with champagne for their sixteenth birthdays and had been served wine at dinner for years before that. Their father liked to say it was a family and cultural tradition and knew the girls were no more inclined to abuse the privilege than any full-fledged adult, no matter what the pressure from their peers.

Christine dropped into the soft leather chair and draped her feet over the corner of the desk, drawing several thoughtful sips from the glass. But what could be so bad about Jon? she kept worrying. Mama so loved him when we first met. Mrs Santana has nothing but good to say about him. Christopher loves him like a true brother. And he is such a gentleman, so well-mannered, so good-natured, so... *tame....*

She drew another sip and put back her head, cradling the glass in both hands upon her bare stomach. Despite her scant experience in actual romance, she liked to think her preconceived notions about the subject had always been on target. *No*, she thought. He's not a bad boy. I would know a bad boy if I met one, or held one, or *kissed* one…. She closed her eyes; and her chest swelled with excitement at the notion.

And Jon is definitely *not* a bad boy! I just cannot imagine what has begun to make Mama worry like this….

At Mark's house on Wednesday night there occurred much cigarette smoking and considerable drinking, even among those under legal age, but nothing for which anyone could be hopelessly condemned. It all made her wonder why the members of Tobacco Road had such a raunchy reputation about town and why anyone could ever have said anything bad about The Strawberries, or about Jon Cavaliere. The conversation was interesting, even stimulating; and the guests seemed articulate and intelligent. The entire affair had much more the mood of some adult colleagues gathered together after work than a mob of rowdy teenaged delinquents. Her mother's puzzling apprehension had certainly given Christine just cause for worry.

Bell Howard stood up to make a few statements, mostly about the upcoming show schedules for both bands, and announced that The Strawberries show at the Starlight Theatre was already sold out of reserved seating. This brought up a cheer from everyone. He reported on the status of the demonstration tapes sent off to New York and it was, as expected, too early for any predictions. Chris Santana gave a financial report; the gathered shareholders were happy to know that both bands' projected operating costs for the balance of the season would leave them solidly in the black. Both accounts together totalled over four thousand dollars. At this everyone cheered again; and some of the girls kissed their boys. Chris raised a toast to 'the best damn job I ever had.'

'And the *only* one,' Jon reminded him; and everyone laughed and drank. Later just about everyone, including Bell, had a go at the piano, playing and singing all kinds of popular music, old jazz standards, recent rock hits, and spontaneous original creations. The talent for performing seemed inherent in them all; and Christine had to think, as she rode home in Jon's car, that the evening had been most enjoyable all round.

Her mother was sitting up in the parlour. Jon saw Christine inside, bid a polite good night to Mrs Polvere and left his date with a little kiss on the cheek in front of her mother. It was just ten past midnight.

'How was the party?' her mother asked seriously, from her armchair.

'It was very nice, Mama.' Christine took a casual-looking hold on the edge of the desk by the doorway, hoping to not appear too lightheaded.

'Did Jenny and Christopher leave when you did?'

'Uh, yes, Mama; I think so; but, I think they were driving someone else home, you know, so—'

'What did you have to drink?'

She stifled a yawn. 'Oh; well.... Well Jon brought a bottle of red, you know, Bolla I think, so—'

'How much did you have?'

Christine had begun to feel red; it was not the wine. Never had she been interrogated like this, especially by her mother; but then neither had she ever come home from an unchaperoned date at midnight. 'Well, Mama; I think about a glass or two, you know, or—'

'Or a little more?'

Her mother was not smiling. Christine felt a tremor in her stomach; more from worry than from wine. 'Well,' she said sheepishly; 'maybe just a *little* more—'

'What did Jon have to drink?'

'Oh; well; I did watch him, Mama, and I think he only had about... two drinks, or maybe three, you know....' She shivered as her mother rose from the chair. 'He mostly just played the piano for us, Mama. You know, he plays really well; he played—'

'You have to get up for school tomorrow,' said her mother; and the parlour lights went out.

* * *

Beth covered the phone. 'It's Steve Marlowe. Why's *he* callin' you?'

He snatched the receiver from her without a word and paced round into the kitchen. 'Yeah, Steve? What's up?'

—'Look, Jon; hate to hassle you about this, but, it seems you're the only one I can get a hold of tonight....'

'You need a ride,' Jon supposed.

—'Well; sort of.... See, my car had a relapse. You know how the transmission goes up against the engine?'

'Yeah....'

—'Well; it seems they didn't put it back together right; and—'

'Is that an automatic?' Jon asked him.

—'Yeah. See, it was in for a checkup, you know, the bands and linkage.... They had to replace some rod in there. It wore out, or—'

'What year is that car?'

—''Sixty-eight.'

'Mmmm,' Jon thought. 'Them older automatics are nothin' buÎt a pain in the ass. The Japs never did learn how to make a good automatic.'

—'Well; so anyway they apparently didn't hook it up right and I lost all the fluid. Coming home from the movies last night it slipped into neutral. Now it's like in permanent neutral. So they said they'll have to do it all over.'

'Sounds like they didn't change the seals. On any take-apart like that they should always change the gasket. You gotta watch those tranny shops, man…. They need your business. I suppose the new rod's broke too; huh?'

–'Uh, yeah; think the guy told me it would need a new one….'

'I'll bet he did. Got your receipt?'

–'Right here in my wallet.'

'Good. They may charge ya for a new rod, and they'll *definitely* charge ya for the gasket; but I wouldn't pay 'em for nothin' 'cause it sounds to me like it was their fault. Next time, take it to Holloway's, and me and him'll tackle it.'

Steve laughed. –'Yeah; may just take you up on that.'

'Well; sure. I can help you out, like if you need a ride home or somethin', except for tomorrow, 'cause I have to take Christine to the photographer.'

–'Tomorrow?' Steve asked. 'When?'

'Well; I'm leavin' right after school, 'cause I gotta get her out to Benton by like quarter of….'

–'Benton? Benton *mall*? That's where *I* gotta go.'

'Yeah?'

–'Yeah. I mean: if it's no trouble…. Gotta see this guy about gettin' my camera fixed before the ski trip–'

'Yeah,' said Jon; 'well; Christine missed the yearbook pictures and they scheduled her out at the mall; so….'

–'Jon, if you could, man, could I catch a ride with you, then? Hate to intrude, and all; but, can give you money for gas–'

'Oh; forget it, man; it's no problem. I gotta go there myself; right?'

–'Hey, Jon; that'd be great, man.'

'Cool,' said Jon, as he liked feeling so appreciated. 'We're gonna leave right from school. You can catch me like over where I was before, behind the shops.'

–'Hey; great. Have to owe you another one. It'll just be Jeannie and me–'

'Right,' said Jon; and it was not until they had rung off that he realised how awkward a situation he would have to face tomorrow. *Great*, he thought. I gotta give *her* another ride. I don't know how this all started but it seems I end up givin' about four rides to a girl I'm supposed to be scared to death of. I wouldn't turn Steve down; I've known the guy for about a dozen years, and at least he's nice enough to ask; but then so why do I have to give *her* all these rides too?

But *wait*, Jon thought, a little calmer. Man; all this embarrassment could really work to my favour, here. Maybe having Christine around won't be so bad at all. We're not going steady. Really just as friends.

Christine will be there, all dolled-up for her picture, and then Jeanne Banfield will get to see what taste I have in women. I do have exquisite taste. And Christine is an exquisite lady. And so if I even matter to Jeanne Banfield, even a little bit, she might even get jealous....

Jon hoped that would not be too much to anticipate. Yeah, he thought; but I'll know if she gets a little jealous. She'll feel just like I do, when I find out things like Steve Marlowe, a guy I met in kindergarten, and used to hang out at the boatyard with, is a good friend of her family. And maybe, if what they say about a jealous woman is true, that she does things she normally wouldn't even dream of doing, then maybe this might just begin to get interesting. We'll just have to wait and see....

* * *

The rain seemed to chase him inside; and as soon as he shut the door the windows began to fog up. The engine caught and he let it run up, switching the demister to its highest setting. At the first gap in traffic he drove straight over the low rounded kerb and turned left, heading back towards the shop wing against the flow of cars on their way out of the schoolyard.

Illuminated by the light of the classroom beyond, the open doorway sheltered Mr Collins, his draughtsmanship instructor, and Christine as they looked sullenly out at the downpour. The sky had gone very dark and it was more like a midsummer thunderstorm than the prelude to a late-autumn sleet. In a crisp off-white dress Christine was perfectly lovely; and Jon had remarked that she seemed as pretty to him today as on the day they had met. Now, bundled up in her pale tan macintosh, she still had that film-star look, half noble heiress, half peasant farm girl, that had always appealed to him.

From the midst of the departing traffic came the silver Caprice, emerging from the grey deluge and stopping just two yards from the building. Christine would liken it to a royal chariot come to whisk her away; but unfortunately her chauffeur merely leaned over to lift up the door-handle rather than gallantly coming out in the rain to let her in. It was Mr Collins who stepped out under the overhanging roof to hold open the car door for her; and she looked quite flattered by the courtesy nonetheless.

'Thank you,' she said nicely to him.

'Thanks,' called Jon, from inside the car. 'I owe ya one!'

Mr Collins gave a laugh. 'I'll remember that, Jon,' he said with a casual wave.

'Yeah; I'll behave myself in class tomorrow,' Jon teased.

'You won't *be* in class tomorrow,' Mr Collins told him, and closed the door for Christine.

'Tomorrow is Saturday, dear,' Christine reminded him, and then blushed to realise she had called him 'dear' for the first time.

Apparently Jon did not notice, or did not mind. 'Don'tcha love *rain*,' he said rhetorically, sarcastically, as he tried to look ahead through the rain-spattered windscreen whilst the wipers sawed back and forth at full speed. Cautiously he eased in the clutch and rolled off towards the literature wing.

'And my hair,' she sighed, pushing back her hood; 'now it's all ruined....'

'Don't worry,' he said, as though it were of no consequence. 'They'll have stuff there. They always do.'

Steve and Jeanne saw him from the gallery behind the cafeteria and ran out past the students smoking on the loading dock and hurtled down the steps to the yard, splashing through the puddles in their platform soles. Steve ran right into the side of the car behind Christine, and she twisted about and tried to reach the lock button behind the tall seatback, whilst Jon simply pressed the electric lock switch. Steve flung open the door and Jeanne clambered in, kicking the backs of both seats this time, and got into the seat behind Jon. Steve plopped down behind Jeanne and brought the door closed.

'Don'tcha love *rain*,' Jon said, in the same manner as before. He searched as though in vain for an opportunity to cut into the line of cars.

'Oh, yeah,' Steve smiled.

'*Oooh*!' moaned Jeanne, pushing the wet hair off her forehead with both hands. Her varsity jacket's hood was of little help in this type of weather.

But already the airconditioning was dehumidifying the car's cabin. Jon saw a chance and took it, turning tightly to the left. He had to go into reverse as the big Caprice ran out of room and, in turning about in his seat, shared eyes with Jeanne for a moment. Before he had changed to first gear again a short, hunched figure, devoid of all distinguishing features, suddenly rapped on Jon's window. This startled everyone, especially Jon. He lowered the glass. The short person stuck a head of dripping wet hair through the opening and said, 'Comin' to my party?'

Only then had Jeanne recognised Carole Martin bundled up in a chequered CPO coat and shivering like an old woman in the rain. She smiled. 'When?' asked Jon.

'Tomorrow,' said Carole, spying Christine, 'right after your show. Bring a friend.' She looked into the back of the car. 'Steve? Jeannie? Comin' to my party?'

Jeanne shrugged. 'I guess.'

'Do you want a ride?' Jon asked, putting a hand on her sleeve in a sincere wish that she should not have to conduct her invitations in the rain.

'I've got one,' said Carole.

'You look like you'll die of exposure.'

'I always look like I'll die of exposure. So who's comin'?'

'I don't know—' He turned to Christine. 'Want to go to a rah-rah party?'

Carole punched him in the arm for that, not lightly. 'If you like,' Christine said coyly. 'Tonight, was it?'

'Did I say tonight?' wondered Carole. 'Shit— I meant tomorrow.'

Jon turned again and looked at her. 'Carole, our *show* is tomorrow.'

'So? Come right after. It won't be jumpin' till eleven or so anyway. It's the weekend. Steve? Bring Jeannie.'

'All right,' said Steve; 'but it'll be after the show, so….'

'All right,' she said; 'so I'll see you guys then. I gotta split.'

'Are you sure you don't want a ride?' Jon called after her.

'I'm not sure of *anything*!' she called back, running backwards against the rain.

Jon put up the window. They all saw Carole duck into an open door a few cars ahead. 'Kid oughta be in pictures,' Jon said, sounding quite serious, and Jeanne thought it a very interesting insight. She yearned to hear more of Jon Cavaliere's opinions on other subjects or other people. He seemed to have a sage-like wisdom, or clarity of vision, that saw right through deliberate deceptions and flimsy façades.

There was a silence. Jeanne thought that no-one had introduced her to the girl in the front seat. She hated herself for staring; but she could not help but be intrigued by the new girl in town who was getting known as Jon Cavaliere's girlfriend and about whom no-one seemed to know much more than that. Steve was about to speak when Jon interrupted him on his first breath.

'Okay, uh; well; you remember Christine; and so, that's Christine, and that's Steve, and that's Jeanne, and this is me, Mister Common Denominator; and well— so much for that.' He shrugged. 'I've always hated introductions anyway….'

Jeanne shivered; she had not heard Jon say her name in nearly four years. Not only was it obvious that he remembered who she was and felt he was the one among them who knew everyone present, including her, but it touched her immeasurably that he would refer to her by her true given name and not 'Jeannie' as she was popularly known now. It was as though he remembered her best not as the ninth-grade prom princess nor as the social star she had become in high school but as the skinny, sweetnatured seventh-grader sitting in front of him in his physical-science class. That was hardly so terrible. Jeanne wondered just how much he actually had noticed her over the last four years. She felt a jump inside then.

'Hello,' said Christine, sitting half-sideways, her legs together off to one side, smiling round the seatback at Jeanne.

'Hi,' Jeanne acknowledged quietly, and then blushed to think she would have loved to add, I'm in love with your boyfriend and have been for years; so there! 'And I remember you,' Christine said to Steve. 'We were introduced at the Tobacco Road concert, last week.'

'Right,' said Steve, and smiled at her. He did have a very pleasant smile. Jeanne was nervous. Somehow the girl was nothing at all like what she had expected and yet, in some ways, she seemed exactly right for Jon Cavaliere. In any case, her eyes fixed demurely upon Jon with a gaze of admiration and affection, the lovely young lady in that right front seat was fast becoming the greatest worry Jeanne had ever known.

If only it wasn't raining, Jeanne thought. How come her hair isn't all wet and destroyed like mine? Oh; it doesn't matter, because the girl's just a fox. I just knew Jon Cavaliere would have a real foxy girlfriend; and here she is. The way she looks, and speaks, and just sits there.... And I bet she's probably Italian. Sure she is: the dark hair, the dark eyes, and her nose and lips and complexion.... It just figures that Jon Cavaliere would end up having some foxy Italian girlfriend who looks just like an actress.... Or a goddess. She looks exactly like some Roman goddess. If only it wasn't raining; and then maybe I wouldn't look so much like a drowned rat.... Oh; *forget* it, Jeanne decided right then. I can't compete with her. She's got way too much class. She looks for all the world like some rich European countess....

Jeanne thought hard about it all. There was no way she would ever give up hoping for Jon Cavaliere. He was the first boy she had ever really loved; and maybe it was only because she had never told him so that she would insist on seeing this dream of hers through to fruition. She would just have to come up with a way to get his attention, keep it and thus win him over. It did occur to her that she had indeed had many boyfriends, with almost all of whom she was still friendly, and almost any of them she might easily date again. Steve Marlowe was the first who came to mind; they had always been more friends than anything else and as such they were free to enjoy themselves more in shared activities and on their own.

But whilst she had been flitting about playing the social butterfly, Jon Cavaliere had apparently been seeking something a little more substantial in a relationship. This notion, coupled with the girl's classic beauty, had utterly ruined Jeanne's day. If Jon Cavaliere really were the type to love someone for her true character, then perhaps she had been going about it all wrong; and perhaps he and his girlfriend here, since there would be only the one, really might just be taking off for holidays to the mountains and vacations on the Riviera. They really might be even going to bed together because they truly loved each other; and there might be very little else Jeanne might be able to do about it now.

'So Steve,' Jon said, out on Atlantic Parkway, 'you say you're comin' tomorrow night?'

'Oh yeah. Got my tickets on Monday.'

'Good. Student council; right?'

'Uh; yeah,' said Steve, frowning a little. 'How did–'

'Santana held about two hundred for 'em. Show sold out Saturday, otherwise. We done damn good.'

Jeanne smiled; he was still fun to listen to, even if his affections were momentarily unavailable. 'So what songs are you gonna play?' Steve asked him.

Jon laughed. 'What, Steve? –are you afraid we might not have enough material?'

'Oh; no; but–'

'We'll be doing all the usual stuff, you know; probably concentrate the Beatle stuff into one set– that's not official yet. Plus all the original tunes everybody's already heard, and a bunch of new ones no-one's heard yet. The finale should be good; Dave wants to do "Johnny B Goode", with him on piano…. Should be a blast. Just remember, alla you dudes gotta call for an encore.'

Jeanne laughed a little, thinking she would be among the loudest in cheering them on all night. 'Must be great,' Steve said, 'being able to play that good.'

Jon smiled. 'That *well*,' he said, raising one finger like a teacher.

'Yes.' Christine smiled at Jon. 'We must always remember our grammar….'

'By all means,' Jon smiled back. Christine giggled at that.

Jeanne was still nervous, or envious. She had something to ask him, and then she decided she had nothing to lose any more. 'So; uh, Jon?'

'So,' he replied, in the same tone; 'uh, what?'

She saw him glance at her in the inside mirror. The teasing was only meant in a friendly way; but the girl Christine's damp glare was far more unsettling. Jeanne had never been stared-down by anyone before, least of all so sceptically. 'Well…. Are you gonna play "If You Need It, You'll Get It"?'

He shrugged, with a passable semblance of nonchalance. 'Hm. Good question. I don't know. Maybe as an encore…. It was not discussed.' He looked up at her in the mirror again. 'You'll have to make sure you remind me, by yelling for an encore. If the audience thinks we're good enough to stay, we could use up a lot of material. Then, just about anything could happen.'

She felt herself getting red, not accustomed to speaking so openly to him. Still, after so long, it was quite exhilarating. 'Uh; well; I just thought you would think it was more of a Tobacco Road song.'

'Naah,' he said, by now feeling much braver in speaking to her himself. 'Not really. It does have four of our names on it. Dave started it, but he thought it was a little heady for us. He's really fond of that double-entendre type of thing, you know; but that lyric is still really unlike him, no matter how dirty you think his mind is. Mark was the one who resurrected it out of the trash can, and he changed some of the words, just a little; and then it was me who came up with the riff, actually; and then me and Barry rearranged the whole tune, and put in the middle bars. So; if you and your friend there in class last year wanted to keep score, on the record it would say "Holloway-Jenkins-Hemphill-Cavaliere".'

Steve laughed. Jeanne was fully blushing; but the embarrassment was only from hearing just how much Jon really seemed to know of her after all. She recalled how, back when they had been first associating with each other, in spite of everyone else calling her 'Jeannie' he had only ever used her proper name; and it was obvious that even now he felt as he did then, that to do so showed proper respect for her as a lady. Her stomach quivered at that. She had told him where she lived, once, dizzy with infatuation in the hope that he might call on her some day, or choose to walk her home, or help her with her homework; and, though he never had, he had actually considered the information important enough to have retained it for three-and-a-half years. She felt the goosepimples rise up at that. She had sat with Debbie in composition class last year; and, though Debbie had done so much talking in class and she had never really said anything to him herself, he had remembered that she had been there; and perhaps that one sentence she had felt so forced to say after the concert contest had been enough for him to keep her alive in his memory. Jeanne shivered all over at that. She considered that there might be much more of their meagre past he still remembered, and fondly too; and she silently prayed that they might yet have a chance to share memories together. Perhaps she would find him very sweet and sentimental after all. There were far worse traits in young gentlemen.

'Yeah,' said Jon; 'speaking of records, I suppose I could let you all in on a little secret, just between–' he gestured, making a circle in the air with his hand– 'just us here; okay? I mean, Chrissy already knows; but since we've all been riding around in the same car recently.... The truth is: Bell has already sent demo tapes of Tobacco Road off to some record companies. That show at school, that I gave you guys a ride home from, that show was taped and sent off as part of the demo. You weren't supposed to know, but the record companies in New York will be hearin' your applause on their first example of Tobacco Road. But Bell also has his eye on this guy from California, who's starting a brand-new production company. Once it's open, you know, we may be able to cut a few demos too.'

Wow, Jeanne thought. So they *are* going to make a record. Wow....
I wonder if I could tell Debbie....

'Well,' Steve asked; 'are they going to take tomorrow's show as a
demo for your band?'

'God!' Jon laughed. 'I hope not! That'd be just the thing to get me
to kill Santana.'

Christine laughed at that. 'Well,' said Steve; 'it's just that a lot of
people think you guys are pretty good, you know; and so maybe Bell
might want to tape your shows for demos too; right?'

'No, Steve; I don't think so, because Tobacco Road is pretty much of
a live band; and Bell's already said he thinks we would be much better
in a studio. Like, we all play more instruments than they do, and we
have a broader range of ideas. And of course all the shows are put on
cassette, you know, just for our purposes; but I probably won't know if
he wants to use one for a demo till Vinnie shows up with the quarter-
track.'

Steve was taking all this in with a grave expression. 'So do you think
there's a chance you could have a record out by next year?'

Jon looked up in the mirror at him. 'Are you by chance with the
school paper, Steve?' he asked. Jeanne and Christine both laughed.
Steve did too. 'It's just that you're askin' the same questions....
Honestly, I'd say yeah; I think there's a chance, the way *I* see it. But it's
not up to how I see it. It's the way Bell, and, worse yet, the record
companies see it, that really matters.'

'Why?'

'Well,' said Jeanne; 'if you record a demo, doesn't it mean—'

'Mean that we're gonna release a record?' Jon shook his head.
'Naah. Not even close. See; just because somebody like Bell might
think we're worth the three or four grand to put us in the studio
doesn't mean the record companies will think we're worth the thirty or
forty it'll take to cut the whole album.'

'Oh,' said Jeanne, and thought about it.

'Look,' Jon said, drawing a breath; 'I didn't say anything about
making an actual record, you know, that you or anybody else can
actually buy. We're a very long way from there. All I said was that
we'll be recording a few of our tunes in the foreseeable future, to send
out to some people, to see what they say. Now this is kind of like a
company secret and I don't want the whole galaxy to know about it. I
only mentioned it because you guys seemed pretty curious, you know,
and because you've been riding around in my car a lot lately....'

'All right,' Steve smiled, with a secret-keeping smile. Jeanne looked at
him and then vowed that instant that she would keep it to herself for
as long as she could. She could do far worse than to have Jon
Cavaliere think of her as a friend worthy of his trust and respect.

'See,' Jon went on, looking at Christine for a moment; 'like I was tellin' you, there's a lot more to it than just being good, and having your whole school like the band, and all.   There's a million other stupid little bands in garages all across the country who are just like we are.   The fact remains that nine out of ten tapes the record companies get are sent back unopened.   It's all a game of convincing everyone you'll make them a fortune.   You have to be marketable, like you're a new brand of shoe polish, or something.'   Steve chuckled at that; but Jon shrugged and said seriously, 'So there really isn't a whole lot of romance to this junk.   It's business; and the bands are usually viewed as expendable resources used to make the more important people rich. That's what it's really all about.   And so, in order to make them think we're worth their investment, Bell wants to go to them with this whole package of these guys and their guitars and their image and logo and everything.   Like he's startin' to think about album covers already.'

'Really?' Steve asked, intrigued.

'Yeah, well....   See; he's really concerned, because this is really a lousy time to be new.   If you're gonna come out with somethin' different, you gotta be ready to go all the way with it, and not die on the second album, like Bell was sayin' so many good new bands do these days.   You gotta be able to stay alive in the marketplace, and doo. That's why I've been sayin' the only people who are really gonna make it during Nineteen-Seventy-Five are the big old established acts like Pink Floyd and Elton John, and Led Zeppelin, guys like that.   Nobody who comes out actin' just so-so next year is gonna be around in 'Seventy-Six.   You can bet on that.   You heard me last year, if you were awake in class.'   He had meant that for Jeanne.   'It's a gamble.   You can either win big or lose big.'

'I remember that,' Jeanne said to him, thrilled with an opportunity to show that she had noticed him, too, even if a little too late.   *Awake?* she wondered.   As if I could have missed a *second* of it....

'So I for one am gonna be cautious about investin' a lotta money and time into some album, when it's only gonna be up to some idiot record producer on coke whether it sells or not.   So me and Dave are gonna start a speed shop somewhere.   So in case we don't make it playin' music, we'll be buildin' race cars instead.'

'Hah!' Steve laughed.   'I can just see that now!'

Jeanne smiled, recalling the day he had told the class how willingly he would gamble everything on his high aspirations.   It was amusing now, or even a little ironic, that he would admit to having planned a safer alternative; suddenly the thought of him sounding so practical and serious about it impressed Jeanne all the more.   She felt herself shiver.   No, she decided; he won't fail.   He *can't* fail.   He's already a success.

'Yeah; so anyway, like Bell says, we gotta keep workin' on the tunes. Bob just put this tune together, and he's gonna sing it tomorrow night.

It's called "Lovers' Lane". Really a good piece.'

'Really?' Steve asked, interested.

'Really. I mean it when I say the guy's written some pretty good stuff, you know; but this one's my favourite of all the things he's come up with. Tune's pretty primo.'

'Primo!' said Christine with a smile.

'Like that, do you?' He smiled back at her. 'That's Holloway's word, "primo". Apparently it's like the big expression out in California.'

'That's Italian,' she said.

'Ah,' he said, without a second's hesitation; *'e le parla Italiano?'*

'Oh,' she replied; *'no; non bene.'*

'*"Non bene",'* he teased her. *'Quanti anni le parla?'*

'What?' She looked at him, not recognising the accent. Steve laughed. Jeanne was trying to listen; she had never heard Italian spoken before her.

'You heard me,' Jon said, and signalled for the turn into the ring road of the shopping centre. *'Quanti anni, le parla Italiano?'*

'Oh; *cinque anni, mi amico, cinque anni.'*

'Bene, bene….' As they started up towards the building he turned and smiled at her. 'So…. *C'e una concerto serata. Posso prenderia alle… oh, sette, mi ami?'*

'Oh; *SI,'* she smiled, with a ladylike blush; *'mia fortuna.'* She smiled sweetly at him.

'Cool,' Jon said, and the two in the rear laughed, though they knew not precisely why. Christine just sat there gazing at him lovingly. Jeanne shivered. Jon stopped the car at an intersection and looked up in the mirror. 'Steve. Where do you have to go?'

'Gimbel's,' he said. 'Straight ahead. It's cool; if you just want to drop us off anywhere….'

'Naah; it's cool.' He let in the clutch in first gear. 'So,' he said to Christine; 'what time is it, that you have to be there?'

'Quarto pre una,' she said, with that smile. 'We've got about fifteen minutes.'

'*"Non bene",'* he said, to tease. 'You can't tell me you never learned Italian at home, when you were a kid.'

'No; not really; not much. Only Papa–'

'That's not what *I* heard,' he said, still teasing. '*"Cinque anni"*….'

Christine laughed then, with the bare hint of a blush; and to Jeanne they sounded just like lovers engaged in those play arguments bantered just for fun. She went red at the thought of feeling so envious; this girl was exactly where she had always wanted to be herself. Beside her Steve seemed somewhat uncomfortable at seeing them tease each other too; he was not much for affectionate little games himself and definitely not with Jeanne who was too valuable a friend to risk offending. 'Uh, right about here is cool, Jon.'

'Right,' said Jon, and slowed the car. 'Uh, wait; I'll save you another cold shower.' To the complete surprise of everyone, including a few shoppers waiting by the doors, Jon steered over to the kerb and, teasing the clutch, prodded the two offside tyres to climb up onto the pavement. Thus he was able to stop the car, albeit tilted, with the entire left side under the overhanging roof of the portico, out of the rain. 'There you go,' he smiled; and right then Jeanne was certain he had performed the trick before. She and Christine both giggled.

Steve laughed his usual laugh. 'Hey, Jon; really do appreciate all the rides, man, really. Can't thank you enough.'

'Then don't worry about it,' Jon said casually. 'You'll pay me back some day.'

Jeanne felt a jump in her stomach as she thought up a few implications of Steve Marlowe being indebted to Jon Cavaliere. Another, stronger jump came at the thought that maybe Jon might have been having the same notions. Such would enhance her situation dramatically; it was titillating. 'Will do,' Steve said sincerely, unaware that some devious romantic plotting might have been taking place right before his eyes.

'And you do have a lift home—?'

'My mom,' Steve assured him. 'She'll be here getting her hair done around three.'

'Cool,' said Jon.

'All right,' said Steve; 'see you.'

Jeanne opened the rear door; sure enough, no rain would fall in the opening. 'Bye-bye,' she said. 'Thank you for the ride, Jon.' She realised she rather liked calling him by name.

'It was nice to have met you,' called Christine.

'*Ciao*,' said Jon; and Steve shut the door after himself.

Once inside Gimbel's they shook off the rain; and Steve shed his wet jacket straight away. 'Those two are a real pair,' he said with a smile. 'Good to see Jon has a nice girl; isn't it? She seems like the perfect person for him.'

'Is she?' Jeanne wondered.

'Well; sure. They have a lot in common. They're both Italian, they're both good-looking, you know, and they seem like they have a lot of fun together. And they both have a lot of class…. You're always watching who goes off with whom. Would've thought you'd think they'd be a pretty good match.'

'Well,' Jeanne said seriously, beginning to take off her jacket as they walked; 'except for one thing.'

Steve assisted her in pulling one sleeve down. 'And what's that?'

'Well; he's just—' Suddenly she realised she had never given her honest, objective opinion of Jon Cavaliere to anyone, not even to Patti or P.J. She wondered if by now she might ever be able to remain objective where Jon Cavaliere was concerned. 'Well… in some ways, she looks like she's way above him. Not that I would ever say anything bad about him–' she blushed at that understatement– 'I mean: he's a great guy and all that; but, well…. Well; he's like down-to-earth, and believable, you know, and like… *real*. You can see what he's really like, you know, and you can believe that that's the way he really is. And she's like some movie star, you know, like… like– Like Sophia Loren. I mean: like you would never see Sophia Loren and somebody like Robert Redford in the same movie.'

Steve laughed. 'Just because you like Robert Redford….'

'No,' Jeanne told him, embarrassed that she had let that comparison slip out; 'but he's a lot like Robert Redford. He's glamourous, and all that, but not like in the same way she is. He's like real, and believable. And she looks like she'd break like glass if you touched her.'

Steve was silent a moment. Then he said, 'Guess maybe I never thought of it like that. Maybe I just didn't know you knew him like that.'

'I don't.' That hurt to admit. 'I mean: not so much any more. You know, like, I used to; but–'

'Turn here,' Steve directed, and steered her off towards the left at the cross aisle. 'Let's see if Jeff's in yet….'

* * *

The Strawberries Profit Fund from which Jon and Mark derived so much humour was in fact a large and growing savings account into which a set minimum percentage of the band's revenue was regularly deposited. Bell was interested to see how well they would operate under the constraints of a business budget; but he was surprised to find how well they understood the importance of providing for major capital investments. Within twenty-four hours of the formal decision to purchase some more state-of-the-art sound-reinforcement gear, the four Strawberries and Chris were at the music store, negotiating prices and credit terms with their new friend there and producing all the necessary cash from the group savings account. Whilst Bell worried himself into insomnia over the prospect of borrowing against his own personal accounts, the boys were unloading the new power amplifiers, mixing board, loudspeakers and all the necessary connecting cables into the garage behind the Santana house. Bell dropped by the following afternoon; and they all put up a ruse that the three microphones were the only new items. When he at last realised what they had bought on their own and learned how they had arranged it, he put Chris in charge of all the financial matters for both bands.

Dave's pet concern was for the design and layout of the stage.

Ricky's suggestions were well warranted, incubated by months of playing his drums atop makeshift platforms made up of school tables, cinderblocks, or sawhorses. They spent a full weekend at the Cavalieres' home workshop, designing and building a system of compact modular drum risers. Bolted together, using wing-nuts, these formed a beautiful two-tiered stage arrangement, all painted high-gloss white, which added a dimension of professional appearance unknown to any other teenaged rock-and-roll outfit of the area.

Perhaps the most popular visual effect The Strawberries ever used was the three-colour costumes. Ricky's drums, bright metallic red, and the guitars of Dave and Jon, both black with white trim, dictated that those three colours would have to be accommodated. Bob's suggestion was for tuxedo shirts and flared-leg dance trousers in each of the three colours, black, white and deep red, for each of the four members. Each of them would select two of the colours on his own for each show; and the resulting random combination on stage would be the relief from an otherwise contrived look. They all loved the idea from the start; and the four of them and Chris took a day trip into New York to visit the professional theatrical-costume houses. Three weeks later their routine deposits into the bank account had replenished their capital; and The Strawberries as a now well-dressed and well-equipped performing act were again well into the black.

From their inception the wardrobe and stage design impressed their fans immensely. The boys sat and smiled for photography sessions and had a few hundred group portraits and posters printed; and plenty of local establishments were eager to advertise The Strawberries' up-to-date performance schedules. Chris Santana was quick to see the merchandising potential in selling the posters to fans; girls craved them, and he had sold out of his first three hundred before the first week of November. He responded to the demand with more posters, autographed collectible photographs, bumper-stickers and a reissue of the little adhesive paper strawberries that had so successfully heralded the concert contest in May. All over town people were collecting Strawberries paraphernalia, including Dave's idea of the imprinted guitar picks and miniature drumsticks that could be given away with album purchases. Soon the retailers were besieged with the inevitable enquiry: when the first Strawberries record would be available for sale.

Jon stuck to what he knew best: the original music. He fancied himself a creator at heart, not a businessman. At his insistence he and Bob sat up till late at night rearranging 'Do You' and 'Lovers' Lane' and 'Which Way To Turn', using tape-recordings of Dave strumming simple chord inversions and singing the most basic lead line. They dissected every last nuance of each guitar solo and bass-guitar line and went over the vocal harmonies until they were thoroughly satisfied with what they both hoped would stand as world-class rock-and-roll standards.   By the engagement of 23 November their instrument playing had become almost second-nature to them; and they were able to concentrate on their singing, astounding the audiences with the tightest harmonies, eerily reminiscent of The Four Freshmen and The Beach Boys.   Even Jon's father, the eternal critic, was impressed.

Mr Cavaliere sat out in the crowd, somewhere in the middle of the Starlight Theater concert hall, with his wife and two daughters.   There was a surprising number of adults in the audience tonight, parents and teachers intrigued after hearing of The Strawberries' legendary debut at the concert contest.   Tonight would be their first show with full seating, as opposed to a dance floor, since then.   Girls bounced excitedly, awaiting any glimpse of the band, and the boys lauded a reputation for such a vast repertoire and unforgettable playing style. All were here to witness a real rock show, performed by four engaging young men who sang and played with the deepest conviction.   In every corner of the room the air was thick with anticipation.

Jeanne took her seat, two-thirds back from the stage, with Steve beside her.   Half of those whom she knew wanted to come had been unable to get seats.   What the local media had begun to call 'Strawberrymania' had become an undeniable phenomenon; at three dollars tickets had gone fast.   Like everyone else Jeanne was literally on the edge of her seat wondering what she would experience, the exhibition which Chris Santana's posters were calling 'the definitive live Strawberries concert'.   She had seen them play a half-dozen times before, but never for a promised ninety minutes before a full seated audience.   Surely no-one would stay calmly seated for long.   Whatever they do, she thought, I know it'll be *fantastic*.   How could anyone be disappointed by The Strawberries....

'All right,' called Bell, over the backstage commotion; and they all quieted and assembled together to give him attention.   'I'm not gonna say any more about it; but this really is our biggest gig yet.   It's liable to be a lot bigger crowd than you expected; like DJ said they were still waitin' out front for SRO tickets.'

'Dag,' breathed Frannie, their now-regular sound technician.

'Hey,' Ricky smirked; 'who do you think you're *dealing* with, here?'

The others laughed.   'Yeah,' said Bell; 'well; including the local press, and the radio-station people and the record-store people, it's a packed house.   I would say it's definitely our biggest gig yet.'

'Really knows how to relieve the stress; don't he?' Jon sided to Bob.

'Yeah, Bell,' Ricky said, standing up straight; 'well; just go and take your three glasses of Pepto-Bismol now and sit down in the corner. I'm ready to rock and roll.'

'Diggit,' Bob smiled.   'You're just worryin' too much, dude.'

'Diggit,' Jon agreed, although he could feel the pangs of nervous apprehension deep in his own innards as well.

'All right,' Dave was saying; 'well; the lights are all straight now; right? And the sound-check settings are still okay on the board; like those idiots didn't—'

'Never mind, Holloway,' Chris teased him. 'Not your job any more.'

'The hell it *ain't*,' Dave said sternly; but the others laughed at him.

The teasing was only a thinly-disguised attempt to recode the feelings of anxiety into amusement or anything else less than gravely serious. Jon looked about the gathering and saw the others all looking about too. The youth of the whole organisation was daunting now, in light of what they had been able to accomplish. Bell Howard, lately twenty-five, was the eldest by far, saddled with the livelihood and future of a group of close friends that might have followed him blindly into Armageddon. Chris Santana was still only seventeen but had already earned a name for himself as a shrewd negotiator, financier and promoter. Frannie Fitzpatrick was the student master of Wilshire High's audio-video systems and had since worked his way into the band's permanent staff; at seventeen he was an experienced and respected sound-reinforcement technician in the area. Senior stage hand and instrument technician DJ Berryfield, sixteen, had begun as a sit-in pianist and substitute drummer for the band and had been with them in a variety of capacities for over two-and-a-half years. Andrew Cavaliere, fifteen, the second stage hand and lighting technician, had been losing sleep due to many late nights on the road but gaining notoriety ever since his deft handling of the concert-contest finale. Richard Anthony Denning, the band's drummer and additional stage hand, since he usually set up all his own drums, was sixteen-and-a-half now but, a legal driver for only three months, he had adopted the responsibility of driving the van full of valuable equipment to and from the shows. Nineteen-year-old junior-college freshman Dave Holloway usually rode in to a show by some girls or in Jon's car, in concession to his dream of becoming a real star some day. But Dave was not beguiled by the purported glamour of life in the spotlight. He gazed about at the others too, those gentle eyes looking greatly pained by the ardour of the road they had chosen to follow.

The prodigy of the Wilshire High School music department, Robert Prescott, sat quietly with his unplugged Gibson SG in the corner, practising a few lead lines. He was still ten weeks from eighteen yet as well-studied as many of the music teachers. Major universities were constantly calling on him to grace their music programmes, even promising him one-on-one instruction throughout his curricula. He never missed a note and never lost his composure. That youthful face that belied even a teenager's maturity became a wrinkled frown under pressure; he could look like the gravest little boy in the world sometimes.

Bob looked up at Jon, his blood-brother for ten years now, who gave him a wee smile. Jon was to all of them their greatest source of pride. This bona-fide academic genius and accomplished pianist and composer, to be eighteen tomorrow, was such a stunning performer and so brilliant a debater that both musicians and educators in the River Valley area were speculating on whether he would attend Juilliard or Yale next September. Perhaps not one of them dared seriously consider that he would as likely select neither option. Now, this small band of long-haired young men to which he had pledged all his efforts was poised to begin their foray into the vicious, volatile world of professional performing; for, once the press had begun writing about them, their journey could only be conducted along strict, almost predetermined lines. For the near term their choices would be limited: they had merely to follow the road before them or fail.

Jon downed another gulp of Pepto-Bismol and handed the bottle back to Dave, who took his second swallow in as many minutes. 'All right,' Jon said; and that characteristic exuberance was sorely lacking tonight. 'Let's just go *do* it.'

Ricky pulled the drumsticks out of his back pocket. None of them had yet become used to his reedy frame in tight-fitting spandex trousers. 'Yeah, man,' he said, effecting that ever-impish grin. 'If you can do it, *do* it.'

Jon made a wry face at him; once again Ricky's humour would serve to momentarily abate the unbearable tension. Dave stood up and put the guitar strap over his head. 'All right,' he said nervously, picking out his three comrades with eye contact; 'so where is it we're going?'

Ricky and Bob and Jon all smiled, cheering together, 'To the top!'

'And what top is that?'

They responded together as they always had, mock Liverpudlian accents and all, 'To the *very* top!'

Dave turned to look over at the dark stage, from which the opening act's equipment had been cleared over ten minutes ago. The new white drum risers gleamed in the cold blue light behind the curtains; and the amplifiers warmed silently, their little red eyes ominous in the greyness. The crowd obscured by those curtains seemed even more formidable, evident only as a carnivorous rumble lacking any human feeling. Ordinarily their mood was casual, even jovial, before a show; for they all loved to play; but now the importance of this particular performance to their mission was weighty upon them all.

The three awaited Dave's response, the last line to the cheer, which they had always used just before stepping out to greet their public. When it came, after too long a pause, it was hardly climactic. Everyone there realised it would probably be the last time they would say the cheer together; it seemed devoid of enthusiasm now. They had a job to do; and, whether or not it was fun any more, it would still have to be done.

Dave wiped his nose; his hand felt cold. He clenched it into a fist to regain sensation. Then he took a breath and said, too seriously, 'Let's rock.'

Andrew turned and cued the house lighting technician, a man perhaps twice his age, to dim the lights outside the curtains. The white noise of the audience intensified to a deafening wail; and Jon, Bob and Dave used the din to mask the sharp clicks as they plugged the amplifier cords into their guitars. Ricky located all his spare sticks and adjusted himself upon his new white-padded drummer's throne. Bell tucked the bottle of Pepto-Bismol into his jacket pocket and ran back to the sound board to supervise Frannie and Chris. Andrew played a few lights about the curtains as they began to rise. The 'definitive live Strawberries show' was under way.

With three quick taps on the high-hat, they launched into that unmistakable opening to The Beatles' 'I Want To Hold Your Hand', with that marvellous bounce to the introductory chords and the boisterous cymbal ringing that captivated an audience all over again. Dave and Jon stepped up to their microphones to sing together; and the crowd was unanimously on its feet. The real world was upon them; and it might yet be benevolent after all.

They played a quick quartet of Beatles songs and went eagerly into their original material, the bubbly brevity exercise 'You' and then 'Since You've Been Gone', a great new rock number of theirs featuring Dave at the electric piano and Bob with a very punchy rhythm guitar part. Dave did look the star in his open-necked black shirt and tight red trousers. The girls all shrieked in ecstasy to hear him sing 'I can't go on without you', and Jon turned to Bob and made a little smile. The two shared a microphone, their two parallel guitar necks pointing out towards the audience together whilst they sang into each other's face and tried not to laugh in joy during a serious love song. It was not so bad at all tonight, no worse than was any other show. It was just another performance; and they could only do their best and hope for mercy. That was all they had ever done before.

But their best was exceptional and, in some ways, beyond exceptional. Ricky's drumming was solid and superb as always. His natural flair for dynamics led him to over-drum just a touch, even during some of the softer songs, but always in the right places and never to exceed the boundaries of good taste, lending not excess but excitement to each piece. He twirled sticks and grinned out at the girls, and with his long hair, tight red trousers, little boy's face and burgeoning muscle evident beneath and beyond his sleeveless white Wilshire High gymnast's shirt, he was undeniably cute.

Bob Prescott, solemn as always, won his share of hearts. In a ruffled white tuxedo shirt buttoned almost to the neck and his black stage trousers, wavy dark hair now dropping to his shoulders and occasionally into his eyes, he looked more like a Romantic poet at a recital than a popular rock-guitar player.   Yet his solos drew loud cheering from the musicians in the crowd, and the girls were titillated to hear him sing.   'Lover's Lane' came off perfectly, its soft middle section, for which he had planned an acoustic-guitar passage, losing nothing when translated by Dave to piano; and then of course that *tour de force* electric-guitar solo immediately thereafter, on his gleaming mahogany Gibson SG guitar, was dazzling.

To the left of the stage, with his strawberry-red shirt and tight white trousers and jet-black Hofner bass guitar, Jon attracted all of Jeanne's attention once again.   Even through Bob's solos and Dave's vocal numbers she stared at him as though hypnotised whilst Steve made enthusiastic comments she could not have heard anyway.   That almost-blond hair, the longest of the group, fell in waves and curls down the sides of his face and occasionally hid his eyes.   But when she saw that dimpled smile, her heart melted; and she shivered to imagine him smiling just for her.

'Day Tripper', its octave-fret bass figures spirited enough, was by now merely a staple for Jon; and he sang and played it effortlessly, going off with just enough vocal and fretboard *ad lib* to stun those anticipating silly mistakes.   After Carmen's 'I Want To Be With You' and Jon's 'Do You', Dave picked up his own black-on-white Fender bass guitar and Jon sat at the piano, singing and playing McCartney's sad 'For No One', its French horn solo no trouble at all for his right hand on the keyboard.   'Sleep With Me' was something new, a gentle ballad of ostensibly tender, nursery-rhyme lyrics conveying hot, sanguine desire, that double-entendre for which Holloway and Cavaliere had already become notorious as songwriters.   Dave sang Lennon's 'In My Life,' whilst Bob provided the delicate guitar figures and Jon was there for that infamous keyboard solo, recorded deliberately slow on The Beatles' album in order to lend a Baroque harpsichord effect when returned to real time.   Jon had learnt it only the way it was heard, both hands alternating complex phrases at tempo; he even added a little downpour of notes at the close of the solo, drawing its own share of spontaneous applause.

He bounded back up to the bass guitar to kick in the bottom of 'And Your Bird Can Sing,' featuring Bob and Dave on twin lead guitars, and Harrison's ever-raucous 'Taxman', which they had always played much faster and wilder than the original recording.   Dave sang at the piano again for their own 'Since You've Been Gone' and then 'Lovely', its sensitivity no worse for wear; and in under two hours they went through all of thirty songs leaving the audience breathless and on their feet after Jon's searing vocals on a rousing rendition of the Credence Clearwater Revival hit 'Playing In A Traveling Band' and an even more rollicking 'Back In The USSR'.

The audience did cheer long and loud for an encore; Andrew would not raise the house lights, alternating red and blue overhead lamps at opposite corners of the stage. The shrill shrieking was deafening to people like Mr Cavaliere who was otherwise impressed with the calibre of the show. The boys had done well; and he considered that his son, so eager to entertain, had probably been right all along about his choice of careers. But there was, as he and young Jon had agreed, only one way to do it, and that was to soldier on, to do it right, to give a full effort, to never give up. Up on that wide stage, Jon showed no signs of surrender. He was a warrior at heart; and to wrest a dream away from him would mean a struggle to the death. Such serious dedication seemed the rarity for teenaged boys in this age; and his father was silently thrilled to think of his namesake going on to be famous and wealthy and successful in his own chosen field. The greatest worry now seemed to be keeping those university recruiters and guidance counsellors off the phone.

'All right,' Jon said to the crowd, still on their feet, and waved a like a child. He could scarcely see past the first few rows due to the wall of stage light and could hear even less over the foldback speaker at his feet broadcasting his own voice straight back at him at nearly a hundred decibels. 'All right; just one or two more, and then we gotta go. You guys are gettin' more than your money's worth, here.' They cheered loudly at that. 'All right. Another silly little Holloway-and-Cavaliere number here, something to go home with. This one's called–' he smiled happily at them all– ' "Run… Like… A Rabbit".'

The song burst into life with a crunchy rhythm that was utterly infectious; the crowd were dancing from the second note. Dave sang this one. Jeanne tried to think of the words, trying to memorise them; there was something about a chase and the 'hot breath of the dog', but then on that final crashing A chord they went straight into 'Revolution' and the crowd were on their feet, their wail up to peak volume. Fast and furious, their playing was electrifying; and Jeanne jumped up and down and sang along with everyone else: 'All right! All right! All right! All right! *All RIGHT!*'

All were disappointed to see the curtains close. For Jeanne it had been a one-man show, and she was full of the experience; and with the ringing in her ears, the excitement remained alive and tingling in her nerves for two days and two nights afterwards.

* * *

Chapter 6

No sign of love behind the tears

It was still dark when Jon pulled up in front of Bob's house. The clock in the car indicated 5.25. Bob hurried out, slipping a little on last night's ice, and slid sideways into the passenger door with a cold thud. 'Hey,' Jon said as a joke, albeit with a voice laden with the gravity of the morning; 'fine time to bust your ass.'

'Diggit,' Bob said seriously, with the same hoarseness. He sniffled aloud as Jon eased in the clutch.

Mark was already at the school when they arrived. Worrisome as always Mrs Jenkins had driven him over herself, in spite of the rude hour, wanting to wait with him at least until the coaches had come. Mark had sent her home, embarrassed in front of his peers to have his mother doting so obviously. The coaches had come up the school driveway as she was driving off; and now all the students were milling about on the broad pavement in front of the building, surrounded by their skis and luggage.

Jon was preoccupied. Thoughts of three girls were running through his mind; it was an unprecedented dilemma for him. He was concerned about Eve's friend Valerie, now more than ever. He had always been fond of the pert little brunette, having seen her grow up from a child of kindergarten into quite an attractive teenager; and he wondered if he, like Eve, was allowing the sentiment to dilute his objectivity. True, Valerie was in dire need of a positive male influence; for her father would be of no help and the older boys with whom she had been associating too often were, at best, less than gentlemen. Jon was well aware of how enamoured she had always been with him, but now he was not sure whether it was for his casual yet daring and rational demeanour or his fancy car and his status as a successful local musician. He knew only that he could hardly refuse to see someone who so desperately needed a good example; and if that meant staining his own reputation by being seen a few times with an eighth-grade girl it was of little consequence.

However, haunted by her mother's boundless fears and groundless suppositions, Christine had been shockingly blunt with her ultimatum on the telephone. Jon was left speechless. Needless to say the evening's swim meet at Carleton Township had not gone well for him; for the first time he failed to place among the top three finishers in a high-school two-hundred-yard freestyle event. He had never dreamt she might actually feel jealous over his purely Platonic attention to a not-yet-fourteen-year-old crony of his little sister, especially when Christine had only to ring up her family friend, Chris Santana, for a character reference to ease her mind. Jon had pleaded his case calmly and firmly, reminding her that, in carrying a high profile in local teenaged society, he was saddled with certain inherent responsibilities, paramount among them the presentation of a good example to those who might admire him. 'It's a matter of principle,' he had told her; 'and I can't compromise what I believe; can I?'

But to his surprise Christine had not been impressed by such noble intentions. Suddenly he realised her own self-centred motives and her inherited insecurity; and he saw the true price of his own high moral principles of which he had always been so proud. Disappointed, he spent Wednesday evening alone, playing the piano quietly in his darkened room. But between gulps of inconsistently-mixed vodka-and-tonics, he came to recognise that in the long weekend ahead there existed the perfect opportunity to improve his situation. After all Christine would not attend the ski trip; and at last he could be grateful for how overprotective the Polveres were with their daughters. Her decision of Tuesday night had put his destiny right back into his own hands; and his thoughts came back, as they always seemed to, to the one girl who had been a tenant of his mind for over four years.

I just hope, he kept wondering, that she won't be hanging around a whole mess of other dudes. If there's other dudes, then…. Then this whole thing'll be a waste. I don't wanna think that I blew a whole free weekend just to watch her hang around other dudes….

In his preoccupied state he did not heed the teacher chaperon waving him off and brought the Caprice right in behind the second parked coach, stopping with all four wheels up on the pavement. This drew dissatisfied grumbling from the chaperons and some cheers from the assembled students. Even the two coach drivers had a laugh, relieved from the tedious boredom of filling in their passenger manifests.

Barry and Vinnie arrived at about 5.40, in Vinnie's battered Mustang coupé; the engine shut down only after a few pitiful gags and backfires. Jon went right over to them and said aloud, 'So when the hell *are* you gonna bring it over to Holloway's and let me fix the damn thing? Jesus Christ! –it sounds like *shit.*'

Others nearby laughed at that. As chaperon Mr Haney came by and asked Jon and Barry and Vinnie to separate themselves from the group, since they were not on the trip roster. Nevertheless Jon got aboard the first coach by carrying Bob's acoustic-guitar case. Mark and Bob took a pair of seats on the right side and Jon conversed with Becky and Cissie and a few others. The chaperons soon urged him to leave the vehicle as he held no ticket for the trip. 'Yeah, right,' he laughed; 'like, "Ticket To Ride", and doo.'

Those aware he was not part of the trip had a laugh at that; and Bob, the consummate rock-guitar player, actually began to mimic the opening guitar figures to the Lennon-McCartney hit from ten years before. At once Bob recognised a weird irony in the mention of that particular song. He had noticed where Debbie Blake, PJ Carson, Patti Harper and Jeanne Banfield were all seated across one row of the coach, five or six rows ahead of him and about four rows from the front, and he laughed a little at how perfectly tailored those lyrics seemed to the situation of Jon being expelled from the coach.

But Bob knew nothing of Jon's disagreements with Christine and could not have known then how doubly, even trebly, ironic it was. Jon had actually awakened to the song on the radio this morning and, typically inspired by the first piece of music of the day, considered it fitting that he should be singing it to himself on his way forwards in the aisle.

Like others Jeanne looked up and heard him as he passed; but then he was stepping down and out the door of the coach and another of the teacher chaperons was chastising him for having been aboard at all. 'How many times must we remind you you're not a part of this trip?' Mrs Battaglia pleaded irately. Jon ignored her, going down along the side of the coach to wave cheerfully and to exchange thumb's-up gestures with his friends behind the windows. Jeanne watched him go and gave a sad sigh. Surely, she thought, this trip might've been more exciting if Jon Cavaliere were coming along. But that's just how it's been going for me recently....

At first, like Barry and Vinnie, Jon had mixed emotions about participating in the annual skiing trip to Vermont. He knew precious little about skiing, only what Mark had shown him last winter at a local slope, and, although it was an intriguing sport for him, he hated cold weather and all its pursuits. It was only after a close inspection of the trip roster that he had coerced the others into joining him for a concurrent extended weekend at Snow Lodge.

Originally Dave was to have gone with them. The idea had come to Jon that the journey up to Vermont should be taken as a road rally, with wagers placed as to each vehicle's estimated arrival at the lodge. Vinnie and Barry were game, and Mark and Bob even put down a bet as to the coaches' time, thus making the coach drivers viable if unwitting contestants in the rally. On very short notice, however, Dave changed his plans and sought an early Thursday flight to the west coast for a visit with an old girlfriend and his father in Palo Alto. Jon was disappointed in him but, sportsman to the end, he promised to uphold the challenge with no driving partner.

The coaches were under way at five past six. The students due in for the morning school session at 7.45 were not even out of bed yet. Jon stood alone, watching the two corrugated aluminium vehicles roll off towards the street, and then looked across the quiet, empty courtyard at Vinnie's battered green Mustang running at a high but uneven idle in the fire lane behind the Caprice. Vinnie slipped his clattering clutch and pulled up beside him, leaning out the window into the cold. 'Hey, man. You okay?'

Jon turned then and looked at him, as the coaches were steered out onto Wilshire Pike, towards Route Nine. 'Yeah,' he said, reflecting on the moment. 'Yeah; it's cool. I'm just still asleep, you know.'

'Oh,' said Vinnie; and the Mustang rolled forwards a few feet. He caught it with the brakes then. 'Well; look, man; you don't have to drive up by yourself. I mean: it was only supposed to be a gentlemen's wager; right? Get your stuff and come with us.'

Jon looked at him for a second and then let out a laugh. 'Hah! In *that* piece of junk?'

Vinnie and Barry both laughed at that and pulled away, hesitating near the Pike to be sure that Jon had started his engine to follow them. 'Dude's makin' a mistake,' Barry said, and drew a breath on his cigarette. It was no secret that he worried about all his friends, even though he would rarely admit it aloud.

'Yeah,' said Vinnie, cranking the wheel against the balky power-steering pump at the light. 'He does tend to push himself pretty hard.'

Acknowledgement of that by someone else did nothing to soothe Barry's apprehension.

Jon did seem uncharacteristically overconfident. He had predicted a time of three hours at most; and with snow in the forecast and an unfamiliar route ahead it was an imposing mission. Even the coach drivers, who knew the route well, would be reduced to a mere crawl at the first hint of a snowfall. They were not expecting to arrive at the lodge before 9.45. But by himself Jon could take far greater liberties manoeuvring at speed even in poor driving conditions. He did like to think he could thrive on such risks.

At twenty past six, on the northbound highway, the coaches had settled into the middle lane in a two-vehicle convoy. Mark leaned against the glass, almost asleep, when from just below the window came a flashing of bright-white light in the predawn greyness. All the nearside passengers looked up.

'It's Jon,' said Bob, and shook him. 'Open the window.'

Jon sounded his horn. Mark sat up with a groan and slid the window forwards. The sudden blast of cold air was a sure cure for drowsiness; everyone aboard protested vocally. 'Hey; move over!' Mark yelled down at Jon's open window. 'I'll jump!'

Jon took his eyes from the road for half a second to call up, 'Tell Bob I'm lookin' forward to blowin' his money!'

A chaperon asked then if Mark would close the window.

Mark paid no mind. 'Hah!' he scoffed, and turned to Bob. 'He thinks he's frickin' winning already.'

Bob laughed aloud. 'He's a fool. Tell him we'll see when we all get there.'

'Hey!' Mark called out over the frigid rush of air. 'He says don't get cocky!'

'Hey; close the window!' someone in the coach called.

Having had to stop for fuel, Jon was curious. He took another second to look away from the road and asked, 'When did Vinnie pass you guys?'

'Will you *please* close the window!' came a demand from inside the coach.

'Wait– About five minutes ago!' Mark told him.

Jon nodded and then called up, '*Adiós*, dude!'

'See you at the lodge!' Mark watched as Jon pushed the stick up into third gear. The silver Caprice dropped back for a second and suddenly shot off like a bullet, roaring out of sight ahead in an instant.

Mark slid the window closed and latched it again. The girl in the seat directly behind him muttered something nasty; but Mark turned to Bob and said, in the sudden quiet inside the coach, 'Damn– what a car, man. Downshifts at sixty miles an hour!'

'If you can do it,' shrugged Bob, and slouched in his seat.

By the second window, Jeanne had seen the silver blur go by and sighed as the taillamps disappeared ahead into the slate-grey morning. Unaware of Jon's plans she assumed he was merely heading to turn round and go back to report to school. Patti had leaned over her to catch a glimpse and then asked, 'So; that was him, then?'

'Who?' Jeanne asked.

Patti smiled knowingly. 'You know, Jeannie. Your… *paramour*?'

'My *what*?' Jeanne got very red then and said, 'Oh, Patti, come on…. He's not– He's not my anything.'

'All right,' Patti said with a smile, and leaned forwards to share a few words with Holly on the aisle one seat ahead. They both giggled, and then Patti turned back to Jeanne and said with a sly smile, 'Well; just let me warn you, if you really don't want him, I'll be glad to take him off your hands!'

Danny Harris, the handsome senior who had begun dating Jeanne only last week, leaned over the seat from behind them and asked, 'All right, Patti; come on. Who do you have a crush on *this* week?'

Holly and Patti laughed again; and Jeanne thought Patti should have been royally embarrassed. She felt quite red herself. But Patti only smiled sweetly up at Danny and said, with scarcely the hint of a blush, 'Oh; well Jeannie and I were just thinking about which one of us will be running off with Jon Cavaliere first. It seems we'll just be slugging it out.'

'Cavaliere?' Bobby Crocker asked aloud, turning about in his seat ahead of Jeanne. 'God! —that's *sick*!' Danny and several others got a hearty laugh out of that; but Patti just turned her head, smiling smugly to herself.

Snow did begin to fall, but not until the Vermont frontier. Jon was over eighty percent of the way there and the navigation had just begun to get tedious, with only broad highway maps and no clue as to how he would identify the village when he came upon it. On top of his concern was the fact that he had not seen Vinnie and Barry at all; it seemed inconceivable that they could have stayed ahead of him at seventy and eighty miles per hour and in any case they had been betting on a slower time. Now, the snow had cut his speed almost in half. After fifteen minutes of frustration creeping up a mild incline behind a line of cautious drivers, he heard himself say aloud, 'The hell with *this*!' The Caprice swung out to pass almost by itself. Charging up the hill in the opposite lane, he attracted the attention of a local traffic officer in a conventional patrol car which, due to the snow, could not give effective chase. With that positive-traction differential and his rear wheels changed to steel rims mounted with new snow-tyres, Jon was up to fifty again within seconds; and his silver-and-white car vanished in the snowfall.

It was tough going, on winding mountain roads slippery with new snow and old ice, under a sky darkened by the lowering weather front, with guardrails too decorative to restrain an errant vehicle from plummeting dozens of yards down some wooded slope. He almost overlooked the miniature sign pointing up the lane towards Snow Lodge and had to slide to a stop from forty-five in the wet snow and reverse ten yards in the shoulder to the corner itself. With the throttle down, the twelve-inch-wide snow-tyres churned through half a foot of unplowed snow and clawed up the bumpy road.

Patti and Jeanne were awake when the coaches rolled into the Snow Lodge car park at 9.55, having spent the last half-hour trundling along at under thirty-five miles per hour. The two drivers had not risked the safety of their passengers by rushing; and no-one in the coach besides Bob and Mark was aware that any money had been wagered as to their time of arrival. When Patti sat up and noticed they had reached their destination she did not know then that it was the rally winner she saw standing there in the snow. 'Look,' she said to Jeanne; 'there he is.'

Jeanne had seen him too. He leaned nonchalantly on the boot-lid of his supercharged Chevrolet, parked near the very entrance to the lodge building; and the car and the building were now coated in a substantial layer of new snow. His leather jacket hung open and the white flier's scarf draped loosely from his neck upon a lightweight fleece jersey inside it, making him look scarcely affected by the temperature and precipitation. His hair was dusted with white snowflakes which melted a little as they settled. In tight Levi's and leather hiking boots he had a hardy, outdoor look that appealed to quite a few girls on the coach, especially Jeanne. That serious expression was belied only slightly by the casual pose and the ever-present gleam of amusement in his eyes.

Patti had a thought about that, even though she had never considered the sophisticated sex symbol called Jon Cavaliere to be much the rugged type. His composure seemed almost in disregard of the weather, in defiance or disinterest, as though it were not winter at all; he might have had the same look in his eyes had this been a gentle drizzle in June or July. Some summery kind of warmth emanated from him; and she suspected, with her usual emphasis on romance, that he was probably beautifully warm to hug, inside his jacket where no sane girl could deny wanting to be.

So she uttered the first thing about it that came into her mind then, not thinking how silly it would seem at first, nor how it might be taken by anyone else later. With a little smile she whispered, almost to herself, 'The Summer Man.'

Jeanne turned. 'The what?'

'What?' Patti shook her head, not realising she had been heard. 'Oh; well; I was just thinking about you-know-who out there. Your secret admirer, or whatever you want to call him. The Summer Man.'

'The Summer Man?' Jeanne wondered.

'Well; you know what I mean. Look at him. It's as though none of this weather even affects him. As though it's still summer to him, in his own world, somewhere....'

Jeanne thought about the notion and had to acknowledge it was very romantic to think of Jon Cavaliere keeping her warm in his radiance. She was certainly surprised, delighted and even impressed to see that he had actually come up here in his own car to join the trip after all; and she thrilled to the possibility of meeting up with him this weekend. Surely she would not stay committed to Danny every moment of her time here; he had already told her he planned on doing many things on his own. The opportunities might prove perfect for her.

But Patti's romantic assessment, however in-character it seemed, had begun to appear very threatening. Jeanne had never thought of herself as being very demonstrative when it came to love. She ordinarily preferred a gentleman who knew just what to do and say to attract and keep her interest; and as much as she welcomed male attention she would refrain from excessively forward gestures and statements herself. Assertiveness was not her style. It was not ordinarily Patti's style either; and yet suddenly Patti seemed like just the person to give her a good run for Jon Cavaliere's affections. Except that Patti, thought Jeanne, may have a much better chance.

Bob and Mark both alighted from the coach with their bags; and Jon smiled to see them plod through an hour's worth of virgin snow to greet him. 'I got a porter here who says I got in at ten of nine,' he told them.

'I'm sure you do,' Bob said wryly to him, and set his bag down in the snow to pull out his wallet. The tyre-tracks behind the Caprice had quite obviously been filling with snow for some time. 'What happened to Vinnie and Barry?'

'I don't know,' Jon said in a serious tone. 'I never saw them, man. The guy at the desk says there ain't been no accidents, so…. They all listen to the cops' radio up here. I figure they just got lost. Man; I damn near missed the turn myself.'

Lugging their luggage, Patti and Jeanne passed them on their way into the building and saw Bob handing Jon a twenty-dollar note. 'Take this now,' Bob was heard to say, 'so I don't end up losin' it to ya at the pool table, or something. At least this time it was good odds.'

Jon laughed, with those cute dimples in his cheeks; and Jeanne turned to watch as he folded the note round his finger and wedged it into the pocket of his jeans. 'Aaah; it's always good odds, dude. You just gotta know how to play 'em.'

The girls went into the building with the rest of the students, dropping their bags on the wet tile floor with tired sighs. Jeanne knew no details of the bet, but she assumed correctly that Jon had won it. She had become fond of thinking of Jon Cavaliere as one who liked to take chances. There was something daring and dauntless about him; and she yearned to tell him some day just how much she admired him for what he was and what he believed; but, aside from attending every Strawberries performance she could and blushing bright-red at the mere sight of him, all she had been able to do for the last three years was to adore him from afar. Perhaps Patti's strange new interest in the same popular senior would spur her into action.

Vinnie and Barry did arrive at the lodge at about 10.30, joining Jon in the four-bed room he had reserved in advance. They reported having seen his car and then the coaches pass them at a fuel depot just before Hartford, where they had been delayed in replacing a broken sparking-plug and ignition wire on the Mustang. They had stayed off the major limited-access highways for the rest of the way up for fear that the car would need oil replenishment or further repairs en route. Jon promised to give the car a once-over for Vinnie when they got home; but nevertheless he collected his second twenty dollars of the day, mainly in point to teach Vinnie a lesson about routine automotive maintenance. He promptly fell asleep in the room alone whilst Vinnie and Barry went off in search of the breakfast they had forsaken in their fruitless efforts at expediency.

Bobby Crocker looked the part of the seasoned Alpine skier, dressed in a dark-blue down jacket, tight ski trousers and black gloves and hat. But Steve, ever conservative, had the experience Bobby could only look to have. In his orange-and-yellow anorak he seemed far less the showoff and far more the authority on the sport. Novice Jeanne placed all her trust in him straight away. She and Steve knew each other too well and their families had been close for too long for her to ever think he would not take all her best interests to heart.

The snow was falling still; and despite everyone's enthusiasm Steve knew a persistent snowfall could bring as much bad as good. He kept the girls on the easier slopes all afternoon and understood their fondness for riding the ski-lift chairs, especially after their wind had been knocked out a few times. The rides were good to rest weary arms and legs. But Bobby grew bored with the beginners' slopes and urged them all towards the intermediate trails; and soon they were carrying their skis up the first gentle incline. 'Don't worry,' Steve assured Patti and Jeanne, though he knew that both of them had tried skiing before. 'Remember what I told you. Just *think* in that direction. You barely have to turn at all, once you get going. My dad always used to say to just think in that direction and keep your feet down, and it always worked for me.'

'Sure,' Jeanne said, able to joke even whilst worrying. 'So why do I always feel like my life passes before my eyes?'

Steve laughed. 'Just so long as you don't remember when my car broke down coming home from Benton, last month. And walking home in the rain....'

'Yeah,' Jeanne smiled, recalling instead her first rides in Jon Cavaliere's car; 'it rained that whole week.'

They were out about two hours according to Steve, the only one among them who had worn a watch. He noticed with some distress that the sky was growing more ominous. The sun was going down but the clouds that almost obscured its light began to look like the biggest worry. Besides, though he had been to Snow Lodge before, he was unsure of exactly where they were now. 'Hey,' he said seriously, unwilling to spoil anyone's fun; 'it might be a good time for us to start heading back. This looks like a decent-sized snowstorm coming up.'

'Aaah,' said Bobby; 'let's just go down this trail here.'

'Look!' Patti exclaimed. 'Isn't that the ski lift?' They all looked off where she pointed, far off to their right.

Jeanne sighed. 'God! –if it is.... I'm getting exhausted.'

Visibility had gone down in the whitening air; but Bobby gave the scene barely a glance and said, 'Yeah. See? We're almost back to the lodge.'

Steve studied the view of the two pairs of cables until the next chair went by and then said, 'No; that's not the one we came up on. That's the expert lift.'

'Expert lift?' Bobby asked, disbelieving his own error. 'How can you tell? They all look the same to–'

'The cars on that lift are red,' Steve said in that calm tone. 'The beginner lift is yellow.'

'Ours were red,' Bobby said blithely.

'Ours were *yellow*,' Patti corrected him firmly, 'which means we're lost.'

'Naah,' Bobby said then, turning away. 'We can't be lost.'

'Look,' said Steve; 'there's no use arguing about it. There's people, down there. Let's just follow them home.'

Under the lift cables, a man and his female companion danced nimbly on their skis, obviously well experienced on these trails. Jeanne squinted to see them, but inside the goggles her eyeglasses were fogging up. 'Well,' said Bobby; 'let's go.' With that he shoved off.

Steve allowed the girls to go ahead of him, knowing he could easily catch them if they encountered any trouble. He was glad for the opportunity to do some real skiing today in any case. Patti and Jeanne stayed together, manoeuvred as best they could and silently prayed they would make it alive to the bottom of a hill that was well beyond their skill level. Actually Patti kept S-turning all the way down and managed to look quite graceful. Jeanne felt the terror creeping up as the speed increased and finally had to sit right down in the soft snow to stop herself, sliding on her bottom to where Bobby had stopped. She stepped out of the skis straight away, not even attempting to pole herself over to him, and took the goggles up off her face to clear her glasses.

Steve skied in and stopped beside Bobby, and the two boys stood and were staring off to the right of the slope. 'Hey you guys!' came a boy's chipper shout; and Jeanne put her glasses back on and turned to see who it was. 'Check it out!'

The voice was not directed at their party. Sixty yards off, a boy in a maroon ski coat and bright-orange hat stood on his skis at the top of a five-yard-high ramp that swooped up abruptly, ending in the air above a thick drift of snow. Three other skiers stood to watch him, just about forty or fifty yards from where Jeanne and her friends were standing.

'Check it out!' called the boy again, to his three friends below.

'I hope you break your ass!' one of them yelled back up at him.

'This'll be for the 'Seventy-Six Olympics!' With a mighty shove he started down. Patti and Jeanne both held their breath. The ramp was neither fast nor long; but obviously the boy felt uncomfortable with it, going down on one hip and sliding helplessly over the end of the ramp, to land ingloriously in the soft snow three feet below.

The light-haired boy with large goggles but no hat, in a white down jacket and tight grey ski trousers, broke up in hysterical laughter. 'Aaah-*hah*!' he laughed hoarsely. 'You call that *Olympic*? Jesus Christ! The agony of defeat!'

In fact he could scarcely remain standing in hysteria; the others, though laughing too, went to extricate the skier from his demise. It seemed amazing that his only injury was to his dignity. 'Christ,' sighed Bobby Crocker; 'talk about your idiots....'

'All right,' announced the one in the white jacket; 'ten bucks says I'll at least get *off* the damn thing.'

'Oh; listen to *this*!' one of his friends yelled at him.

'Any takers?'

'No bet; but I'll *dare* you,' the other said, and the two of them ran, skis in hand, for the steps at the rear of the slide.

Jeanne and the party were happy to watch this, as it represented a momentary respite from the apprehension of being lost. The snow in fact had become no more serious in the last fifteen minutes, and these people did not appear to be too concerned about it. The light-haired boy reached the top of the ramp; but his companion was already in the bindings and ready to go. In a dark-blue anorak like the one Bobby Crocker wore, with a ridiculously long stocking-cap, the skier gave a mighty shove and took off down the slope. The light-haired boy called out in protest to no avail.

The jump was beautifully done. Blue-and-white striped stocking-cap trailing behind, the one in the blue jacket made a very neat landing about ten yards from the end of the ramp and skied up to within a few steps of where Steve and Bobby were standing. A gloved hand came up to pull back the stocking-cap then; the skier was clearly a girl.

'Hey,' she said to the boys, with a cute little dimpled smile. 'So what's up?'

But she poled off again before either of them could reply. Jeanne thought she should have recognised the girl, as though she were someone she had seen about school; but this place was not exclusively Wilshire High students and anyone could have been here on holiday, even well-known celebrities. 'Yeah,' Bobby said, moved by the girl's apparent interest; 'I think we'll just hang out here and rest a while, and maybe when these guys leave, we can ski down with them.'

Steve and Jeanne silently concurred; but Patti boxed him on the arm. 'Sure, Bob,' she teased. 'Anything to avoid admitting you're lost.'

'Diggit,' Bobby said quietly, and then made a little smile.

'Yo Cissie!' yelled the one with no hat, from on top of the slope. '*This* is how it's done; okay?'

The other three in the jumper's party all laughed at this and watched him. The run he made was straight and fast; perhaps the speed was exaggerated for the length of the ramp. On takeoff he whipped his head back with an audible grunt, executing a beautiful laid-out back somersault, landing with his skis rather wide apart but otherwise very impressively. He swung round to his left as the girl had done and slid sideways to a stop beside her, a little less neatly; only then was it apparent just how inexperienced he really was. 'And I see you again,' he sang to her; 'yeah yeah yeah-eh....'

She batted him on the arm with the pompon of the stocking-cap. The other boy, who had not yet jumped, went down the slide as the girl had done and landed quite well, stopping just ten feet from where Bobby Crocker stood. By now Bobby had given up on his pride. 'Hey,' he said casually; 'so which way *is* the lodge?'

Wilshire High's charismatic student-council president lifted his yellow goggles and looked at him. There was a sudden moment of awkwardness as the two parties all began to recognise each other, and yet not one would draw attention to the fact. Chris Santana made a little smile and then stifled it, turning to point down the hill to their left. 'The lodge?' he asked, trying to sound like a seasonal regular at the resort. 'The lodge is right down there. See, man; look. There's the lift up there.'

They all turned about again and Jeanne and her party were stunned to see the lift with the pale-yellow chairs just visible through the trees in the snowfall, not a hundred yards up the hill beyond the upper end of the ski ramp. Having been so close and yet so disoriented was indeed embarrassing.

The others in Chris's party started away from him; and he turned, calling, 'Yo! So what the hell's the plan, here? Are we going back, or what?'

The boy in the maroon coat took off the orange bobble hat and shook out the snow. The long, well-coiffed hair was unmistakable as that of Wilshire High's favourite guitar player. 'Yeah,' said Bob Prescott, feeling a little stupid after having jumped so poorly; 'might as well. I'm still half-asleep from this morning.'

'Humiliated, no doubt,' teased Chris. The others, including Steve and the girls, all laughed. Giving his head of almost-blond hair a toss to shake out the snow, Jon Cavaliere poled off and was the first to leave the gathering, followed closely and with a giggle by his friend Cissie, whom he had met in the girls' toilet on the night of the concert contest in May, and then Bob and Chris.

As their schoolmates left them Steve came up to prod Jeanne along. After just one turn of the slope in the woods they were able to see the lodge building. Jeanne saw the two silver coaches in the car park, slowly being covered in snow, and thought she could even make out Jon Cavaliere's car in the valley as well.

So, she thought; he's got another girlfriend now. I wonder what happened to that Italian girl, the one with the disgusting good looks.... I just can't believe that Jon Cavaliere has *two* girlfriends already, when I can't even get used to him having *one*. Oh, she thought; I know I'm getting jealous, but I still wish he'd pay attention to *me*....

Cissie McKean, an accomplished skier, had talked novice Jon into going up on the lift to the main slope and skiing down into the valley in front of the lodge building. In fact the predominant view from the second-level lounge area was of the broad hillside, which began to look even bigger and steeper from where Jon and Cissie stood in the queue at the top.   Having spent the afternoon exploring a few of the backwoods ski trails and then discovering the practice ski-jump ramp behind the lodge, they planned to ski once down the big slope and to retire to the lounge where they would toast themselves on a very full day.

Jon hated to admit, even to himself, his reservations about the whole idea. Something about the chance of taking a spill on the slope before countless spectators caused a stew in his stomach. Even for an avid risk-taker this opportunity for a new experience seemed overpriced. Whilst driving hard on a tight schedule along snow-covered roads was something he had studied and practised considerably, skiing was an alien skill to him, and he was not willing to hazard a try when so much was still left to real chance. Despite the image he liked to perpetuate he preferred to accept high risk only when he felt he could retain reasonable control over the situation. Snow, skis, the people in the queue, pressure from Cissie and the unseen faces of a hundred of his schoolmates watching from the windows of the lodge building added up to what looked like a no-win situation for him; and, suspended between accepting a dare and bowing out to rational fear, he stepped stiffly off the lift chair and carried his skis over after Cissie towards the crest of the hill.

Only six skiers were allowed to go every minute, to reduce the risk of accidents. Someone in the queue remarked that his probably had something to do with the holiday tour of 'schoolchildren'; and Jon wanted to take offence to that but was unsure about his chances debating it in this crowd of people.

'Hey,' he said, close to Cissie; 'tell you what. How about if we, you know, kinda skip this for today; huh?'

'Why?' she asked him, turning about to look pointedly at him. 'Turkeying out?'

'I ain't turkeyin' out; it's just that with this line—'

'You're turkeying out.' She giggled a little at him.

Jon sighed. 'Yeah; all right; I'm turkeyin' out. Now let's get the hell outa here.' He turned, as though to leave the line.

'Come on,' she insisted, tugging on his jacket sleeve. 'It'll be fun. You might just beat me down there, you know.'

'I might just break my neck, too.'

'It'll be an adventure.'

'Sure. I've never been in the intensive-care ward before.'

She laughed. 'All right then; tell you what. You can ride the lift back down on the turkey side, and I'll pick up a drink at the bar while I'm waitin' for you.'

'Yeah; but *you* can't get served in there.'

'Oh; well; you know, I'm sure there'll be one or two *older guys* who wouldn't mind buying a lady a drink, or two….' She turned from him, hiding her smile. 'I could really go for a Black Russian….'

'How 'bout a little white Italian?' he said, effectively ending his indecision.

Cissie laughed, still staring down the hill. 'Are you always gonna give in like this when we're married?'

He thought a second and pretended to take the question seriously. 'Well; it's just that I don't think it's a subject for discussion here.'

At that she turned, eyebrows raised, and looked up at him, catching the zipper of his jacket in two gloved fingers. 'Well,' she asked in her sweetest tone; 'would back at your room be a better locale?'

He shrugged, avoiding her adoring wide-eyed gaze, and would not take that so seriously either. 'Well; if I chase out those other idiots, maybe I could mix us up a couple of Black Russians myself….'

'With what?' she scoffed. 'Cold coffee and soda?'

'Oh,' he said, with a sly smile; 'didn't I tell you? I've got a whole car trunk full of Dewar's and Bacardi and Smirnoff and Kahlua.'

Cissie's eyes went still wider. 'You *do*?!'

'Oh; hell yeah, dearie; you better believe it. I don't like snow *that* much.'

The man and the woman behind them both laughed at that; and Jon realised he had best not go straight to the car when they got down. A mob of thirsty people might follow him.

It was still snowing, although not quite as hard as it had been in the middle of the afternoon. The girls had changed and showered; and whilst Patti took half an hour to refashion her hair Jeanne sought the opportunity to enjoy a cup of hot cocoa by herself. Now, she thought, if Jon Cavaliere's seeing that girl from the concert contest, then where does that leave that Italian girl? Someone had said he had been seeing the Italian girl since the summer. I bet she looks great in a bikini…. Jeanne shook her head at the idea. It would only be one more thing to worry her. But, she thought, if that was only a few weeks ago, and now he's seeing someone else, he really can't be too serious about this girl; can he? I've got to know how serious he is about all these people. I'm not too serious with Danny right now; it could be the perfect time to do something…. But Jeanne had to admit to herself that she had not decided exactly what it was that had to be done.

Even as she stared out at the hill, a sudden spectacular mist of snow went flying. A skier had gone down, almost to the bottom; and the entire lounge area was aflurry in excitement. Jeanne squinted as another skier in a white jacket sailed in gracefully and stopped beside the less-fortunate companion with such good form that the witnesses in the lounge voiced their impressions. The second stepped out of the skis to assist the first.

By now Jeanne was feeling that nervous tingling way down in her stomach that she always felt when Jon Cavaliere came round the corner in school; in fact, she had come to blame that anxiety for the cramp at the lake when, in her new yellow bikini, with Jon and his friends so close at hand, she had understandably become quite jittery. After half a minute the skier in the white jacket, who wore no hat, took his fallen friend by the arm. At that very moment Jeanne recognised the girl's long striped stocking-cap. It was indeed Jon Cavaliere helping his friend who had taken a fall.

Obviously she was quite all right; but a small orange lorry pulled up at the foot of the slope and the girl in the stocking-cap was helped into a seat and driven off. Jeanne watched Jon, in that beautiful Italian ski jacket, pole himself off and ski slowly and smoothly down to level ground. A medical aide met him as he stepped out of his bindings, and they were seen talking calmly on the way in. From the evidence it was plain that the girl was not seriously hurt and conversation in the lounge resumed as before.

Jeanne was jealous. She had just witnessed Jon's exquisite gallantry bene fitting someone else. For most girls, to be saved once from the very jaws of catastrophe by an appealing and modest young gentleman might have been enough for a lifetime. Perhaps it was all too far in the past for her now. She should have begged her father to require her to marry Jon that very day; and then Jon would have really saved the rest of her life too; for she would have had her white knight with whom to live happily ever after.

But this was not the twelfth century. Jon was by now an entertainer of renown in their own home town, and his charm and appeal were for a broader audience now. A solitary girl with a genuine attraction to the young man who impressed her made little impact in the 1970s, with so many other things going on in the world. Perhaps it was an age when a girl could at last step in and plead her case to the man she loved; but still it was very romantic to fantasise about some glorious knight astride a beautiful grey steed sweeping in to save her from wicked crosscurrents and dangerous avalanches and evil sorcerers, and until Danny came to escort her to the group dinner it was all she could think about.

Cissie, in fact, had only sprained a wrist. It was expertly wrapt by the Snow Lodge emergency staff, and she and Jon returned to their respective rooms to wash and change. They met half an hour early for dinner and caught a quick meal instead from the vending machines in the snack bar. Becky and Leslie were planning a party in the room afterwards but Cissie wanted no part of that. At Jon's suggestion they rode one of the lifts up into the woods and back down again, talking quietly and holding hands. Jon put his arm about Cissie to keep her warm. He had realised her fondness for him some time ago; but he knew he was only casually attracted to her. She was witty and amusing and loved to laugh at his jokes but she had little elegance; and elegance was something he expected and required in a lady. Cissie was more like one of the boys.

Of late he had begun to think that perhaps he did not deserve a real lady. He had often dreamt of becoming famous some day and finding for himself a real countess or heiress; but with Christine, who had at first impressed him with that type of maturity and grace, the formality had been stifling. He enjoyed having fun with the crowd, loudly and unabashedly; and Christine was one who insisted, nonverbally, that she be entertained on her own terms, which usually dictated a quiet *tête-à-tête*. Jon was a very open person who liked to discuss and compare wishes and dreams and desires; but Christine was very closed about what she truly wanted. He had always been in the position of having to guess at her mood for the moment; and his guessing had been usually wrong. It was not an area in which he could expect to have reasonable control.

Leslie met them in the hallway, reminding them of the party in the girls' room. Cissie politely declined and, when she had gone, turned to Jon. 'So, Mr Casanova; any more bright ideas?'

'Listen to you,' Jon said to her, and thought.

'Hey,' she said; 'how 'bout those little Black Russians? What's happenin' with those?'

'What little Black Russians?' he asked, and turned to go off down the gallery. 'Whatever do you mean?'

She hurried along, close by his side. 'Why Daisy,' she laughed, 'whatever do you mean?'

'Why, *Jordan*....' He laughed and opened the stairwell door. 'What the hell are you talking about?'

'You owe me some *cocktails*, man! Your trunk full of booze?'

'Shut up,' he told her, using a hushed tone, although the upstairs door had closed. 'Where do you think I'm going?'

'Oh,' she said quietly, as Jon opened the outside door; 'good. Goody.'

'Goody,' Jon sighed, with pretended exasperation. They tromped out across an inch of the evening's unmolested snow to the car park. Jon located his car and drew his keys from the pocket of his leather jacket. 'Yeah,' he was saying; 'but like where do we take this shit? Your room, my room....'

'So what? We'll find a place. Shit– a broom closet....' She stopped to wipe off the window and peered into the car; but Jon was going round for the boot. 'All right,' she said; 'give me some bottles, here. I'll put them in my jacket. We can say I'm pregnant.'

'God forbid,' said Jon, under his breath.

'Diggit,' she agreed.

He pushed away some snow and opened the boot-lid. Inside, under three military-surplus wool blankets, two cardboard liquor cartons and two cases of bottled beer were pushed up against the front wall of the padded, carpeted compartment. 'My winter-weather traction,' Jon said proudly, and looked at her with a smile.

'Jesus!' Cissie sighed. 'You could *live* in here!' She began to open her jacket. 'Here! I can carry half in here!'

Jon laughed at her. 'Get the hell out. You think I'm gonna waste alla this right now, on *you*? Shit– there's gonna be a major *festival* here, before I go home.'

'Oh; listen to you,' she countered, and suddenly looked up. 'Shit!' she said in a hushed voice. 'It's Mr Dreyfus! Don't let him see–'

'He won't see–'

Suddenly she rolled headfirst into the spacious boot compartment. 'Come *on*!' she urged in a whisper but, with Mr Dreyfus, one of the faculty trip chaperons, and two other adults walking towards him from the main hall doors, Jon had only one choice.

He reached in and snatched up one of the blankets, tucked it under his arm and said quietly to Cissie, 'Bundle up, kid.'

She saw him reach up to shut the boot-lid. 'Shit–' But he could no longer hear her.

The Wilshire High science teacher and his companions, who had seen only Jon closing his boot, passed him on the walk. 'Nice night; huh?' Jon said to them, and they replied with equally polite niceties and continued past his car. He watched from the stair hall as they drove off in an older Volvo saloon towards town and then smiled at his slyness before strolling back.

'You dope addict!' Cissie scolded as he opened the boot-lid again. 'You idiot! What the hell do you call *that*?'

'Shut up,' he told her, and sat down on the edge of the opening, above the bumper. 'You hardly gave me any chance to play it cool, you know. I couldn't very well jump in with you after they saw me, now could I?'

'Hey; so what the hell was I *supposed* to do?' She sat up under the open boot-lid. 'And so you walk *away*!'

'So what? You can get out. Look.' He showed her the lever he had made, for opening and closing the lid from inside the boot. 'You always think you know more than me,' he smiled; 'but I'm older than you are, and at least that much smarter.'

'Big deal,' she said. 'Four months.'

He sighed. 'Still, it becomes readily apparent at times.'

She clenched her teeth. 'Just watch it, big-mouth.'

Jon laughed. He turned to look out across the car park at the trees being gently showered with wide, warm snowflakes. The main slope was brightly lit by huge floodlights; but of course no-one was actually out this late. The moon was just a pale-grey glow beyond the snow-clouds, and a very soft, intimate mood had settled upon the evening.

'Hey,' said Cissie; 'so much for sitting out here in the snow. Are we gonna get drunk; or what?'

'Yeah, right,' he said; 'like there's so many places that aren't full of people, and that means a party, and that means–'

'How about right *here*,' she said then, and grabbed him about the waist. His eyes grew wide with surprise as he tumbled down onto his back upon the compartment's padded, carpeted floor, almost on top of her. She managed to keep her hold on him; and when they found each other their noses were just inches apart. 'Now tell me,' she smiled, those dimples looking cute as ever, 'that you made this trunk so comfy just for *luggage*.'

He smiled back. Surely there could be far less pleasant experiences elsewhere. He brought his feet and legs inside, and Cissie reached up to close the lid. 'Here; you have to latch it,' he said, taking the inside handle. 'You can't slam it from here.' He leaned over in the dim shaft of moonlight from the narrow opening and pulled the lid down gently to latch it with the lever.

It was completely dark inside; no light invaded from any corner. There would be plenty of air, however; Jon had made the carpeted bulkhead behind the rear seats to open into the boot and he knew it did not fit precisely. Such a small space would grow comfortably warm in very little time, and he began to worry that the snow would melt off the outside of the boot-lid and look terribly obvious. They arranged themselves on their sides, facing each other, and Jon drew the woollen blanket over them both.

The chilled vodka was evil at first, without a mixer; but Cissie giggled and said, 'What the hell; right? I mean: this is how those Russkies keep warm; ain't it?'

They both laughed at that and drank several more gulps each. Once, they met each other nose-to-nose in the dark; and Cissie pressed her warm lips upon his. Chills went through both of them; and Jon returned the offer straight away. He had never dreamt that being cooped-up in a boot could be so comfortable, even exciting.

* * *

After breakfast the boys came by to meet them; and Jeanne, Patti and PJ happily accepted their invitation of a cross-country skiing excursion along the backwoods trails. Steve met them out on the slope and took up with them without ever soliciting their permission. He was concerned about the girls; certainly they might have had more experienced and gentlemanly skiing companions in Marty Engel or Dave Cartwright.   In fact, though he was sure he was not jealous, Steve had come to wonder what Jeanne had ever seen in Danny Harris in the first instance.   Jeanne had always had far too much integrity to fall for a boy on looks alone; and yet Danny seemed to have the good looks and precious little else.   He was known for his vanity and short temper; and more than once or twice other girls reported that his insensitive attitude with regard to their feelings had brought an end to a relationship.

Steve worried about that.   The girls all liked him, and Bobby greeted him enthusiastically as ever; but Danny took grumbling exception to Steve's very company.   Steve had realised his presence would undermine Danny's pride. Wary of what measures Danny might take to further gain the girls' approbation, he would not challenge Danny's overt efforts to keep him as far away from the girls, especially Jeanne, as possible.   Civilly he tolerated the chiding, even about his second-place finish in the gymnastics all-around championship last week. But Steve was worried when Danny would challenge Bobby to best him in silly stunts such as racing down a trail or skiing backwards. Danny was hardly proficient enough to take incalculable risks but Steve, who never took unnecessary chances and had been skiing for years without serious incident, saw such excessive indulgence in reckless behaviour as grave disregard for common sense.   Passing up the opportunity to do some advanced skiing by himself today, Steve went along purely for the girls' benefit, whether they would acknowledge him or not, reminding himself that it was a responsibility willingly accepted and without any expectation of tangible reward.   Hopefully tomorrow Jeanne and the others would have better-qualified companions, or perhaps join a guided hike or a skills class; and then Steve would worry far less about them.

Bobby and Danny, swapping trite little dares to compare their prowess and impress the girls, wanted to try the expert trails.   Steve was relieved to hear the girls all agree that as a group they were not sufficiently experienced for them.   They stayed on the beginner slopes all morning and went in to take lunch at about twelve-thirty. Afterwards Steve saw that the girls were going off again in the same company and so went with them as before.   By this time Patti had his motives rather well sorted out.   She was impressed that he was deliberately acting not out of petty jealousy over Jeanne, but in the interests of all their well-being and in the hope that he might yet prove his own suspicions wrong.   Patti too had been harbouring some reservations about Jeanne's recent selection of young men and wanted to discuss it with Steve, if only for a moment; but there had not yet been an opportune time.

Jeanne asked to rest; and just to the right they all sat down on a few fallen logs leaving their skis right where they had stepped out of them. Danny remained standing coldly in front of the girls, like a sentry. 'Come on,' Bobby kept saying; 'enough rest.'

'Come on yourself,' Patti countered. 'What do we have to do, that's so important? We're supposed to be on vacation, here.'

Bobby could not argue with that. Patti had such a sweet, ladylike demeanour that no red-blooded male could refuse her. The other girls all envied the way she seemed irresistible, especially to older men.

Danny Harris smoked a cigarette, unwilling to speak to anyone. Steve sensed his resentment, but he was glad that the pride which kept Danny so stoic would also prevent him from making a scene in front of the others. 'I was just looking at that tree,' Jeanne said; and she pointed across the clearing. 'See it? There's an owl's nest in it.'

The others all looked to see the black opening in the tree, thirty yards away. 'Are you sure that's an owl's hole?' Steve wondered. 'Looks too small for an owl.'

'Well,' said Jeanne fancifully; 'an owl isn't that big. Besides, birds like a hole that no-one else can get in.'

'We're all a little like that,' Danny said; and they all looked at him. He tromped over, discarding the cigarette in the snow, and prodded Jeanne to her feet. They continued on in the same direction; and the way grew steeper and the skiing became easier. The woods which bordered the trail on both sides were eerily silent; their voices carried crisply and quietly over the stark white snow. Once a rabbit darted out of the undergrowth to their right and froze in the presence of potential danger. Bobby snatched up a handful of snow as he passed and flung it sidearm over his pole at the rabbit, who sprang back into the trees disgusted with the blatant invasion of his homeland.

Steve advised that they begin making their way back. But the others vetoed him. Soon they turned down a narrow trail, and Bobby and Danny skied on ahead down through the woods, ducking branches and undergrowth whilst Steve tried to keep up and still stay close to the girls. PJ tripped upon a snow-laden stump once and received a mild welt on her shin from the fall. Good sport that she was, she would not complain and continued eagerly without ado. Steve merely shook his head. So far, they were still lucky.

They arrived on a broad slope where skied a number of skilled people. 'Ah!' sighed Bobby Crocker. 'Some real snow! These back trails are boring as all hell.'

Steve lifted his goggles and took a long look at the scene before them. He had been to Snow Lodge only once before, two seasons ago; and, though he could not be expected to remember every detail of the surrounding countryside, this place was no more familiar to him than to the others. 'Yeah,' he said, after a minute; 'real snow, but not Snow Valley.'

Danny looked at him. 'What are you talking about? The *hell* it ain't Snow Valley! Where *else* would we be?'

'No,' said Steve, using a calm tone to avoid raising too much concern; 'I mean it's not part of the same lodge. This is some other resort.'

'Holy cow,' PJ said quietly; and they all looked over the scene before them. A green-and-white ski lift carried people towards the top of the hill, considerably above where they were all standing now. This was a broad slope, steeper and wider than the rise at the lodge; but, even if it might have been mistaken for the hill they knew, there was no lodge building where it should have been. There were only more of the rolling hills of Vermont, going far down into an even deeper valley beyond.

'All right,' said Patti, as a wave of apprehension swept over them all; 'we can figure this out. How far do you think we've come?'

'It was that turn we took in the woods,' Bobby said with certainty. 'Whose idea *was* that, anyway?'

'The lodge is that way,' Danny said then, and pointed.

'Hard to say,' Steve answered Patti; and Jeanne and PJ looked at him too. No-one had regarded Danny's indication. 'Could've come, oh, maybe two miles, in about two hours…. That is, if we've been moving directly away from the lodge the whole time, which I'm sure we haven't.' He looked up at the soft grey of the sky. 'These clouds make it hard to see the sun.'

'Aaah; sun, bullshit,' Danny said disdainfully. 'We sure ain't been out anything like two hours, that's for sure.'

'Well; my watch says twenty after three,' Steve said gently, checking it again; 'and we left the building after lunch at one-thirty.'

'There. You see? An hour and fifty minutes.'

Steve sighed, exasperated. 'Well,' Patti suggested; 'why can't we just reverse our steps? It might take us another two hours, but at least we'd be sure of the right direction….'

The girls all looked at Steve, who nodded and stared at Danny's turned back with renewed disrespect. With no further words PJ, Patti and Bobby all turned to follow Steve. Jeanne turned to Danny and patted him on the shoulder. 'Danny? Come on. Steve knows this place. We can't be that lost.'

Danny grumbled a little, dissatisfied with the shift in leadership; and the six of them carried their skis off up the hill again. It was very tiring and discouraging to trudge up a long, lonely slope instead of skiing down into a populated valley furnished with ski lifts. Worse, in going back up through the woods, none of them recognised anything they might have seen coming down. The girls were shivering more with worry than with cold, each whimpering regrets quietly to herself.

Steve bore it all like the gentleman he was, never letting on that he felt responsible for all of them. He carried PJ's skis when she became tired and helped the girls into their bindings whenever they came upon a downhill run, however slight. The other boys followed at a distance or skied on ahead. Danny voiced contrived doubt in Steve's judgement at every turn and fork in the woods, since all three girls had without a spoken vote invested all the rest of the day's confidence in Steve's mature guidance. For Steve it became very tedious to merely bite his lip and allow the dissenter his opinion.

The girls grew weary of the pride feud and tired of the hiking. By now it had become evident to Steve that the flurries of snow floating down through the trees were not windborne drifts but increasing precipitation. The light had gone low in the shade of the forest and Steve had taken to consulting his watch on a minute-by-minute basis in uneasiness. The girls pleaded for rest and he judiciously allowed them a brief siesta on a group of fallen logs in a clearing to the left of the trail. Danny went on a few yards and then turned back, but Steve only stood in the centre of the trail and gazed up at the sky anxiously.

'Damn,' he said quietly. Jeanne looked up at him. Never before had she heard him swear. 'This doesn't look good.'

'All right, Marlowe,' Danny asked him; 'what's your plan now? We're all putting our trust in *you*, man. What's the plan here?'

Steve looked at him; and they met eyes. There was no respect intended in Danny's leer and no more in Steve's wince. But Steve had already surmised that the line would have to be drawn. If it had been no-one but Danny and himself, lost and disoriented in a strange forest, it might have been far easier to choose to care about him or not. But there were others here who needed his leadership and were willing to accept it. 'Okay,' Steve said, gathering his wits; 'all right. Maybe you all should just wait here. I'll go out the way we came in, as best as I remember it, and when I get back to the lodge I'll come back out with a snowmobile or something and lead everybody back in. If I know you'll be waiting right here, I can find you again.'

Danny scoffed. 'That's a hell of a plan, man.'

Jeanne looked at him. 'Danny, please.... I don't think it's a good plan, because I don't think anyone should go off alone. If anything happened–'

'Nothing will happen,' Steve said seriously, more for the girls' sake than for his own. He stepped into his bindings. 'As soon as I get to a familiar place, I'll be fine.'

'You'll be fine,' Danny repeated sardonically.

Jeanne scowled at him. The other girls shared her concern. Bobby Crocker stood up and said then, 'Well; look, Marlowe; let me go with you. We could split up, or–'

'No,' Steve smiled at him gratefully; 'it'll be better if you stay here. If the girls needed you–' He resisted the urge to look at Danny, instead sighting up the gently-inclined trail. His cross-country skills were not far out of practice. Surely it would not be long before he regained his bearings for good. 'I'll find something I remember, and then I'll be fine.'

They all watched as he poled off with strong, swift, smooth strokes. He went over the crest and disappeared into the grey-white air; and Jeanne felt her heart sink. If anyone can find his way out of here, she thought, it's Steve; but I just hope nothing terrible happens to him, or to us…. Danny came to her and put an arm about her, rubbing her shoulders to keep her warm. With the fading light the woods had become quite chilly. PJ paced about, nervously, shivering and rubbing her gloved hands on her arms. They all saw her suddenly freeze, staring straight off across the clearing. 'Oh my God!'

'What *is* it?' Patti gasped. 'A *bear?*'

Mouth open, PJ slowly raised one arm to point shakily across at the trees. All of them shivered to follow her finger. 'It's Jeannie's owl-hole!'

'Dear God!' Patti exhaled, more relieved than surprised.

'My *what?*' Jeanne sat up.

'Your *owl*-hole!' PJ exclaimed. '*Look!*'

Twenty yards away, in one of the trees by the edge of the woods, was a small black aperture, the same one Jeanne had noticed nearly two hours before. 'And these are the same rocks, and the same log,' Patti said, realising their situation; 'so that *must* be it.'

'You mean we made a complete circle?' Bobby asked her.

'Yes,' Patti said seriously; 'well of course I mean that. Or– half a circle. The last time we were going that way.' She looked down the trail and then up the way Steve had gone. 'And now we're heading this way….' Her voice trailed off into the snowfall as the worry took over. 'I just hope he figures that out,' she said quietly; and Jeanne and PJ shivered in worry.

'So where's our tracks?' asked Danny. 'And which is the way back? We should have left tracks here.' He stomped about looking for evidence.

'Well; it's been snowing, man,' Bobby told him. 'It's been at least an hour since then. They'd be covered up by now.'

'Has it really been an hour?' PJ worried.

'Well,' Danny said with a wince; 'I just don't believe it can be that simple. Or that Simpleton up there didn't figure it out first.'

'He's only trying to help, Danny,' PJ told him.

'Really,' said Bobby. 'Come on, Harris; be fair. He's a real good skier and he's been here before. At least he's trying to help somehow.'

'Now, now,' said Jeanne, whilst Danny glared at him.

'So the lodge is that way, then,' Bobby said to Patti. 'We can be sure of that now.'

'I just hope he's all right,' Jeanne said, of Steve.

'You know,' Danny said, turning to her, 'you worry a hell of a lot about a guy you supposedly broke up with. I'd hate to think that when you're out with somebody else some day you'll worry half as much about *me*.'

Jeanne made a face of distaste. 'Danny, that is not fair. I've known Steve's family since I was about eight. He's a very good friend.'

'Yes,' PJ said, hoping to talk about something far less volatile; 'well; let's just hope he gets back to the lodge, anyway. Better to be lost than to have a broken leg, you know.'

'Better to have a broken leg back there than out here,' Bobby reminded her, pointing at her injured shin; and the thought sobered them all.

They sat there, scarcely talking, half an hour more. The snow continued to fall. Restless, the girls thought of making a snowman; but the two boys dissuaded them, as neither would be party to something so lighthearted now. The girls reverted to worrying about Steve and Danny smoked about three cigarettes in a row, lighting the next from the last. Finally he stood up.

'Where are you going?' Bobby asked him.

He picked up his skis, brushing off an inch of new snow. As he stepped into the bindings the clicking sound was lost in the insulation of the snowfall. 'Well,' he told Bobby; 'since you're such the great follower of idiotic plans, maybe you can just stay here. I'm not dwelling on that cretin's condition any more.'

'Danny!' Jeanne complained.

'Hey, dude,' Bobby was saying; 'I happen to think he'll be back here any minute, with somebody to help us. Like he said. And somebody's gotta stay with the girls. If you can't follow a simple plan like that—'

'That's right; it's *simple*! It's the most simple goddamn thing I've ever heard of! He's only after the frickin' *glory*, man; don't you see that? He's so pissed-off at me, and about Jeannie, and about everything else all day that he's takin' it upon himself to play Joe Hero and *rescue* us! Well I don't *need* to be frickin' rescued, man! I don't *need* that asshole's help!'

'Danny,' Jeanne tried, 'please—'

'*You're* the asshole, man!' Bobby shouted back at him. '*You're* the one who's been actin' so proud and so damn conceited you're turnin' into a complete pain in the ass! I'm just tryin' to help keep everybody's vacation from turnin' into a total catastrophe! I happen to *trust* the dude, man!'

'Guys,' Patti asked them, 'if you—'

'Yeah,' Danny told Bobby; 'well; that's *your* problem then. You can deal with that asshole's stupid ego.'

'Yeah; well; I think your problem is that you're beginnin' to get on my nerves.' He started towards Danny; and all three girls became alarmed that they would fight. 'I'm sick and tired of caterin' to *your* stupid ego, when you've done nothing to add to this whole frickin' *day.*'

Danny turned about and stepped out of his skis. He lifted the goggles off his eyes and said, 'So; you think there's something you wanna *do* about it, then?'

'Guys, *guys*,' PJ said, stepping between them as they approached each other. 'Guys, really, come on. This is still our vacation, now, and we should get along with each other. Everybody's scared, and everybody's cold and tired and upset. It's okay, really; you know? Steve's a good guy, we all know that; and he'll do his best to come back for us; okay?'

'Shhh!' Jeanne urged them. '*Listen*! Do you *hear* that?'

They all listened. Far off in the woods, from the general direction in which Steve had gone, came a weird humming noise. Like a growing horde of locusts the eerie whine grew louder and stronger, until Danny and Bobby actually ran halfway up the clearing to see what was approaching. The girls got up also, spooked by the sound, and then they saw the four round headlamps coming towards them through the dim light of the late-afternoon snowfall. One steered over towards them as though knowing precisely where to go and the other three took up the course a little behind.

'It's *Steve*!' Patti exclaimed; and the girls all cheered for joy.

Steve took the snowmobile out of gear and eased to a stop, a few yards out from the logs upon which they had stopped to rest three-quarters of an hour before. He lifted up the yellow goggles and dismounted the idling vehicle. Patti ran up and hugged him.

Jeanne looked out at the other three who had stopped in the centre of the clearing. She could not be completely sure at first, but the skinny lad in the short black jacket and dark-blue woollen watch cap looked just like Ricky Denning, who had sat in her health-science class last year. The one in the maroon anorak, sitting up on the blue machine, was most certainly Bob Prescott; though in the suede drover's hat he appeared unexpectedly rakish. And there, astride the white one, looking exactly as he should have, in that beautiful white Italian ski jacket with no hat, sat the one young man who had captivated her for what felt like a lifetime.

'Well,' Steve said, smiling honestly at Danny; 'I'm sure you'll all believe me when I say it wasn't my doing at all. It was they who found me, not the other way around.'

Danny would offer nothing. 'I don't care, dude,' Bobby Crocker said happily to Steve. 'I'm just glad you made it back here alive.'

'All right, people,' came the easily-recognised voice of Jon Cavaliere; and they all knew they had heard him say those exact words from a performing stage more than once. 'So what's the plan, here?'

The girls all giggled at that, happy at last to hear that question without any anxiety or frustration.   'It's okay, man,' Steve called cheerfully out to him; 'unless any of you Mounties out there feel like driving these young ladies home!'

Jon Cavaliere laughed and hauled back on his throttle.   The mechanical steed squatted down at the rear and kicked up snow; and he charged off, only to spin about a hundred yards down the trail and roar back to the others at full speed.   It was Bob Prescott and Ricky, then, who were on hand to load skis into their racks and to drive Patti and PJ back to the lodge.   Jon locked up his brakes and crunched to a halt in the snow, realising only then that he might have had the honour of having Jeanne straddle the seat close behind him.   Only that instant she had seated herself behind Steve.   'Well,' Jon said, with characteristic nonchalance, as he lifted his goggles to clear them of mist; 'I guess she's all yours, dude.'

Jeanne blushed.   Suddenly the words she longed to say froze solid inside her.   'All right,' Steve smiled, and awkwardly gave him an uncharacteristic thumb's-up gesture.

Patti beamed, astride the blue snowmobile behind Bob Prescott. 'Well,' she said, happy to put her arms about him; 'I suppose this is a little like The Strawberries to the rescue; isn't it?'

He laughed, thinking of something else entirely as he watched Bobby Crocker and Danny Harris step into their bindings.   'Yeah,' he said quietly; 'the start of a new TV cartoon….'

Jeanne sat and stared longingly over at Jon Cavaliere, twenty yards away; but before she had found the right words Steve put the vehicle in gear and started off.   Jon flung his wrist round without regard for his fuel supply and the white snowmobile bolted off like a majestic stallion.   Jeanne swallowed.   Behind her glasses, her eyes flooded at the price of her indecision.   It might have been so easy just to leap off, away from Steve and Danny and really that whole phase of her life, and to jump on behind Jon Cavaliere and throw her arms about him and never let go again.   She might have done it without a word to any of them; and no-one could have stopped her.   She would have whispered sweet little love secrets into his ear all the way back to the lodge, holding on tightly and loving every second of being so close to him.   They could have gone off in his car with a bottle of Southern Comfort and a nice warm blanket for two, hiding from the world in the back seat all night whilst kissing and saying 'I love you' over and over.   If the temperature had dipped well below zero, she might never have felt the cold in his arms.

Steve, of course, would drive slowly to keep in sight of the boys on skis.   Bobby Prescott stayed back too and, holding him securely, Patti waved over at Jeanne and giggled happily.   They both heard PJ shrieking with delight as Ricky raced off far ahead with Jon; and the whining of those straining little engines was sharp and cutting, even above the one right below her. Jeanne was satisfied to see Jon so adept at driving the snowmobile.   He appeared perfectly at-home on the thing, as though he had been riding one all his life.   She thought about that; it seemed like something she should have always expected of him.

When they came to the hill the boys skied off under the lights and yellow lift chairs, at last free to do some satisfying skiing, albeit in inclement weather and on short novice slopes.   The lodge staff were out in full, trying to escort guests in before the snowfall became any worse, and Bobby and Danny were waved right through.   They soon disappeared down the hill and Steve and Bob Prescott were directed in towards the snowmobile garages.

Jeanne saw Jon Cavaliere slowing down to greet a pair of girls in taut ski tights near the lift-chair line.   She had come closer than ever to having him next to her; and the opportunity had come and gone in an eyeblink.   Such a chance might never come again.   She thought that in his own way he had actually extended to her an invitation, and she had in effect turned him down and selected the safer option, the familiar and comfortable instead of an exciting new unknown.   Jeanne felt a tear roll onto her cheek and eke out from under the goggles at the thought of what she might have found.   It would be very hard to dance with Danny tomorrow night at the mixer.

Later in the evening she excused herself from Holly and PJ at the table and wandered off round the bar in the great hall, sitting by herself on the wide cushion of the window seat and gazing out the glass.   The slope was lit as it had been last night, although the weather had become quite fierce and the sky was brilliant with floodlit snow. Just inside and to her right was the billiard room.   She could see some of the players through the door.   Hearty laughter and quieter curses could be heard above the jukebox music.   After such an uneventful day, it was soothing just to be alone for a few moments and to immerse herself in her thoughts.   She put back her head against the insulated glass and let the clicking of the billiard balls and the rumble of conversation lull her into a relaxing trance.

Ordinarily she liked to think herself quite brave with speaking to boys, and often she had astounded herself with her own bold, even provocative behaviour.   But it had only ever been false bravado; for, when it counted most, for the one boy she wanted most of all, she went to gelatine inside and found herself with no courage and nothing to say.   Jeanne knew she would have to regain that courage she once knew; for Jon would never know her true feelings if she would not make them known to him.   After all, she thought, this is Nineteen-Seventy-Four, almost Nineteen-Seventy-Five.   Women are permitted to approach men, and even ask them for dates these days. It's not so bad. Debbie and PJ do it all the time....

But I'm not *like* that, Jeanne kept thinking. And I can't help thinking that Jon Cavaliere would never approve of some girl throwing herself at him. God! –he probably gets that all the time.... Jeanne sighed. It's just not what he's like, she thought, or at least it's not what he's *supposed* to be like. He's supposed to be nice and thoughtful and considerate, and not like–

Like Danny, she thought, and swallowed a big gulp of Coca-Cola. That's what I'm really trying to admit to myself. Danny can be nice and everything, but he's like so bossy sometimes. And so thoughtless.... Even Bobby was being thoughtful and sensible today; and Danny was just being obstinate. Men can be such jerks when they're like that....

God! –I just wish Jon would come up to me and say something this weekend. About getting lost in the woods, maybe even like as a joke.... I don't care. I just want to have a nice conversation with him. She thought about that. It could be about almost anything, she decided. So long as we don't talk about *music*....

She smiled a little now, recalling that horrible awkwardness she had felt in the car when Jon Cavaliere had driven them home from the Tobacco Road show. But she had to know to expect some awkward moments. Most of the boys whom she had dated had interests similar to her own; but Jon Cavaliere would be very different. He was highly intelligent and well-read on a variety of esoteric subjects. There were girls who said it was nearly impossible to hold his attention, that he became too involved in the conversation, that polite banter usually became very formidable and technical. He was said to be too clever for high school, too clever even for university, too clever for ordinary people.

Jeanne was intrigued by the thought of getting to know someone who was so different from those whom she had come to consider her peers. It was a challenge she was eager to accept, if only she could have the correct preparation. Just one subject, she thought; that's all I'd need. One thing I could talk about that he wouldn't expect. Something he knows about; and then I could surprise him by knowing something about it too. It would really impress him.

She looked into the billiard room and saw two or three young men leaning against the wall, holding pool cues. Laughter went up from the room and occasionally she saw a player pass by on the way to lining up a shot somewhere else. Like pool, she thought. Like I could say, Jon, I hear you're a really good pool player. Do you know any of those fancy shots, like on TV? I could ask him that. It wouldn't be so terrible....

Suddenly she brightened with an idea. I'm going to learn something about pool, she decided.   It was a quick decision for her; but its rashness only made it more of an exciting challenge and she knew straight away she would have to accept it. She need not tell anyone of her ulterior motives.   She would stroll right into that billiard room, pick up a pool cue and flirt coyly with the young men just as she had always done before. None of it would really matter after this weekend. It would only be practice, a dress rehearsal for the real thing. At worst she might actually learn something about the game and have a pleasant evening.

Intoxicated with her own pluck, then, Jeanne rose and carried her half-gone glass of Coca-Cola through the archway and into the midst of over a dozen males gathered about the billiard table. They all took immediate notice of the youngest one in the room, a pretty young blonde in snug jeans and a soft white woollen sweater.   She sipped demurely from the glass, gazing at the table itself, trying to avoid eye contact with anyone in particular until she was sure she would have their complete attention; it would be no different than any other occasion on which she wanted to make a memorable appearance. But she had blithely overlooked the possibility of encountering a spanner in the works.

'All right, people,' said that familiar voice, as though addressing a crowd of fans; 'what's the plan, here? Holy shit– what the hell *time* is it? I gotta go to bed soon.'

There was laughter, like that she had heard earlier. 'Yeah,' someone else said; 'but's it's who you're goin' to bed *with*. *That* is the question.'

'Yeah; right. To bed, or not to bed; that is the question.... Whether 'tis nobler in the mind, when we have shuffled off this mortal coil- spring mattress....' Others laughed again, though this hardly seemed the crowd for Shakespeare jokes. She caught a glimpse of him in the group then.   Sleeves rolled-up, cue in hand, he seemed all-business, taking a few grateful swallows of a light-coloured drink from the narrow shelf along the wall. 'So; what's the plan, here? Harold; right? Is that your name? I think you're up, dude.'

'Hey, asshole,' one spoke up; 'you're a cocky son-of-a-bitch. Why don't you just shut the hell up and play; huh?'

Talking stopped abruptly. Everyone turned to behold the newcomer, a tall, dark-haired man of about twenty-five in a black leather sport- jacket, with a long-haired girl holding his arm. Jon seemed not to flinch at the inhospitable greeting. 'Hey, dude,' he told him; 'cocky is as cocky does. The game's got rules. Your money will do fine in that corner.'

Jeanne gasped, stunned to hear such unmitigated arrogance from someone she had believed to be so genuinely modest. More surprising was that the others in the room would defend such an attitude. 'Yeah,' said one with a moustache.   He sipped from a bottle of beer and stepped past someone next to Jeanne to address the new arrival. 'My man's been goin' like hellfire all night. Put your money where your mouth is, and shit.'

'Yeah,' someone else agreed.

'Fuckin' A',' said a third.

Jeanne took a nervous sip of her Coca-Cola and shrank back against the far wall, cowering from the vulgarity even as her heart began to flutter anxiously. The man in the black leather sport-jacket winced in hesitation and reached up to slowly withdraw his cigarette, drawling, 'All right, then. Twenty bucks says the kid's not so hot.'

Jeanne recognised the corner of Jon's sly little smile, just like the smirks he made in class; he quickly covered it with the cocktail glass. 'Get you another one,' one man said, taking the glass from him and shuffling out to the lounge.

'Make it fifty,' someone said. 'Dude's been waitin' for a real sucker all night.'

Most of them laughed. A few others wandered in from the gallery. The man peeled off his leather coat and his girlfriend took it over her arm. 'Whatever you're comfortable with losin'; huh kid?'

'We've just been playin' for five bucks a rack,' Jon confessed, in a strangely feeble tone; 'well; most of the night....'

There was no-one to corroborate that. The man looked about for a moment and then pulled out a startling wad of cash. 'I ain't gonna hustle ya, kid,' he said disdainfully. 'But I got a fifty here that says I'll clean your ass.'

Jon looked at the man's hand; and Jeanne might have seen a genuine look of distress. God, she thought, holding her glass in front of her face with two hands; how I'd love to see him beat this jerk.... Jon's drink came and he took a stiff swallow. Setting the glass on the shelf along the wall he turned back to his opponent, who had already begun racking the balls. The room was silent but for The Rolling Stones and 'Tumbling Dice'. With the eight-ball sequestered in the centre of the rack, the man looked up at him. 'All right,' Jon said, suddenly sounding terribly uneasy. 'I'll stand you one game.'

Jeanne was silently thrilled with this opportunity to see him in what might have been his true element. Somewhere between the onlookers' rowdy greed and the distasteful put-on cockiness, there was a beautiful gallantry about Jon now, as though he were able to survive and even thrive in a hostile environment if the prize were right. And Jeanne had already ascertained that the prize was in the vicinity of fifty dollars, tax-free.

From the first impact of Jon's powerful break the game was tense and heated. Neck-and-neck the two players went, making the first, sometimes the second, never the third. With one left to go Jon sank the eight-ball instead; and the the onlookers groaned in disappointment at such a catastrophic blunder.

'What'd I say?' laughed the man, and turned to share his victory with his girlfriend. 'Hope ya got it on ya, kid.'

The man met his gaze but Jon immediately looked down, looking disgusted with himself; he looked about a second from shoving something through the wall in frustration. Jeanne thought it would have been disappointing, having expected him to show more dignity, even in defeat. 'Shit,' Jon said under his breath, and withdrew three folded tens and a twenty. 'Tell you what, dude,' he offered, in that feeble, boyish voice. 'I'll play ya again. Gimme a chance to win it back.'

'The game was fifty bucks, kid,' said the man. 'I ain't wastin' the time again unless the stakes go up. Say, a C-note this time?' He laughed, a cruel snicker shared by his girlfriend.

Looking terribly worried, Jon dug in his right hip pocket and produced what seemed to be a thin sheaf of wrinkled tens and fives. One note even fell to the floor, and he ducked to scoop it up at once. The others in the room were silent as he said, 'All right, dude. One more; and then that's it.'

Seeing Jon's money, the man laughed. 'Hey; if you got it to lose, I don't mind stickin' around, little man.' He laughed again and his girlfriend with him.

Jon turned to rechalk his tip and then grudgingly poked the crumpled notes into the dry beer mug at the end of the table. Jeanne had never dreamt she would actually see such amounts of money being wagered in real life; it was like a scene from the Paul Newman film. She watched Jon rack up the balls for the next game. Her favourite entertainer had suddenly become gravely serious, almost frightened, and she shuddered to think she would be witness to the night he fell from grace.

The two men beside her shared a joke in whispers; but when one of them saw her there they both turned and moved a little away. It sounded as though they were placing a side bet as to how many turns the game would take; and she frowned a little, not grasping what their predictions meant. But it was obvious that neither bettor meant to be heard too well.

The champion was awarded the rack. Nothing found a pocket. Jon sunk two low numbers straight away and then sought a difficult corner shot that drew rousing cheers from his audience. '*Adiós,*' one man pronounced, giggling like a small boy at his joke.

'Diggit,' said someone else, seeing Jon smile then; 'a hundred bucks is *plenty* of money for kids these days!'

Jon made a little laugh at that, passing his opponent on his way round the table. 'Hey, there, uh, Sal,' he said to a new friend in the room; 'bring our guest something to sit on; would ya?' The others all laughed. He pocketed the seven and then reached across the table with the end of the stick to tap a nest of notes at the far corner where two men sorted out a side bet. 'Table gets twenty percent, dudes. What's good for the geese, and shit....'

'Diggit!' someone agreed; and everyone laughed heartily.

Jon turned then, lined up a split shot and fired the white ball into the five, which went into the three. Both balls found separate pockets. 'Way to go, dude,' someone complimented him.

'Make it happen, dude,' said another; the enthusiasm was catching.

Wide-eyed now, Jeanne stepped away from the wall and watched Jon make the next shot as though he had never even aimed it. She was glowing with increasing glee to see him so capable and confident after all. One or two of the men stood in front of her; but when they realised they had blocked the view of a lady they stepped aside at once. Jeanne felt richly flattered by the strangers' attention; the billiard-hall types were not so rude at all. A rather attractive man of about twenty-five stepped closer, attempting to start a friendly conversation. He seemed pleasant enough; but Jeanne had already lost all interest in flirting for the rest of the night. She merely smiled and nodded, to look agreeable, and kept her eyes glued to the game.

Jon spanned the stick over an unwanted mark, not using the mechanical bridge. The shot was slow and neat; and the one-ball landed in its pocket. There was just one mark left: the eight-ball.

'All right, wise-ass,' said the man who had not shot at all since the break. 'Since you're so sure you're the heavy hustler around here.... Another C-note says you don't put it in clean.'

The crowd hushed. Even Clapton's rendition of 'I Shot The Sheriff' sounded quieter over the jukebox speakers. Jon eyed his opponent for one second and returned his attention to the table. It was not a difficult shot. The safest goal was the near corner pocket, though the table seemed littered with all seven of the striped balls. The game and the two hundred dollars would be his if he would merely carom the ball off the bank and dodge the ten and the fifteen. There was naturally some risk of failure; but the odds were the shot would be easily made. It was up to him; and Jon knew that. It was a situation over which he could expect to have reasonable control.

But the years spent in the billiard room at the bowling alley with mates like Mike Jolson and José Morales had not been for naught. Jon knew neither of them would have wanted him to resist the opportunity for teaching a lesson in humility to an impudent opponent such as he had now. He made a little smile and made a slow lap of the table before bending forwards and taking an aim. 'All right,' he said carefully; 'that side there.'

Everyone was surprised by the selection; any of the other five pockets might have given a much easier shot. Jon's next stroke would be the last one of the game; if he missed, or pocketed any but the eight-ball alone, all would be lost. Side bets went down in haste about the room. Surely the odds were against him, or so it looked on the surface. But Jon was sighting a bit higher than that.

Jeanne held her breath, staring straight at the table from the front of the crowd and completely disbelieving what she saw. Jon fired the stick into the cue ball, which leaped over the twelve-ball directly ahead, whirled round to dodge the fourteen and danced over to lightly brush the eight, which took a gentle lean to the right and disappeared quietly down the side pocket as promised. The whole roomful were breathless in suspense as the white ball inched dreadfully closer to the pocket. But Jon, beaming with confidence, simply ignored it and looked up with a smug grin at his opponent.

'Believe you owe me two bills, dude,' he said; and there was some laughter.

The man pointed but, sure enough, behind Jon's back, the white ball had come to its final rest not an inch from the rim of the side pocket.

Below, the eight-ball clattered home into the ball pit. The game was over. 'Holy shit!' someone emitted; and everyone expressed relief and amazement at once. Jeanne exhaled, last of all, and quickly drank some Coca-Cola.

Indignant, the man flung two fifty-dollar notes down on the table and hurried out with his girlfriend and his black leather coat. Jon watched them go, inadvertently meeting eyes with Jeanne. After a second he turned away embarrassed, realising only now she had seen the entire game. She watched him pick the money out of the beer mug and scoop up that left on the table, giving it all a mere glance before stuffing his winnings into his pocket. People slapped his back; loud voices filled the room; the episode had passed. Danny Harris came in, quite distraught to see Jeanne looking so outnumbered and vulnerable as the lone female in a room full of rowdy older males. 'What are you doing here?' he worried.

She shrugged sheepishly and put on a smile. 'Don't worry, dude,' one man told Danny. 'She ain't gettin' into any trouble.'

'Yeah; it's cool,' said another; and Jeanne was flattered that they actually liked having her among them.

'*Jeannie*,' Danny said nervously, close to her ear, 'maybe we'd better go.'

'Why don't you play?' she asked him, smiling so sweetly that several others nearby were moved to agree.

'Yeah, dude,' someone said to him; 'I think the table's open.'

'Jeannie,' he tried, ignoring their earnest invitations; but she took a hold on his arm and turned to see the young man called Harry racking up the balls for a game with the next challenger. Jon had abdicated his reign over the table and stood off to the side sharing a few jokes with two other men. Someone had brought him a fresh drink of which he downed about half in one gulp. Danny watched as two ten-dollar notes were laid out on the table. 'Too rich for my blood,' he said, and started to usher Jeanne out.

'Hey,' one of the onlookers called across the room; 'where you goin' with the babe, dude? She's all there is to look at in here.'

Jeanne saw Jon look up at that and they met eyes again. 'Hey, honey,' someone said to her; 'stick around. I'll getcha a drink, if you want.'

This seemed to be the general consensus for the room; but Danny would have none of it. Jeanne went red, ashamed of her escort's overt jealousy, and as he towed her out she looked down at her empty soda glass and felt Jon's eyes drilling into her. She could well understand if he thought less of her than ever now.

It was two o'clock when Jon left the billiard room, considerably wealthier for his efforts of the evening. Some switching of roommates had been done and it was rather like Tobacco Road, Barry and Mark and their sound man, Vinnie, in one room and The Strawberries, Bob, Ricky and Chris with Jon in the room he had reserved exclusive of the school-sponsored trip. Jon was glad for the quiet place to sleep, no matter who his companions might have been.

Being the star of the party was never easy work and his head spun from a few too many vodka-and-tonic drinks with the players down stairs. But this was why he had come to the ski lodge, not as much to ski as to enjoy a little recreation in friendly company with no schedule to keep. The peace of mind was soothing; and he clambered into the upper bunk with a profound sigh.

'Ricky!' came an urgent whisper below him.

'Who's that?' Jon asked.

There was a pause; and then it came again. 'Ricky! You still awake?'

'Aaah,' came the groaning reply, as Ricky rolled over in the top bunk across the aisle.

'What, you guys been fakin' sleep on me?' Jon asked.

'Surprise,' Bob whispered below him, his weary voice devoid of enthusiasm.

'Damn,' said Jon. 'Had me fooled.'

'So tell him,' Ricky said in a whisper.

'Tell who what?' asked Jon.

'I thought you were gonna tell him,' Bob said.

'Well hell,' Ricky told him; 'it's your news, and doo.'

'What news?' Jon wanted to know. 'What's going on?'

'Is Chris still awake? Yo, Chris?' Ricky leaned out to look down on Chris, sound asleep in the bunk below him.

'Chris,' said Bob, 'you can stop faking now....'

No answer came.

'Shit,' said Ricky, in a whisper. 'That dude's asleep in two minutes.'

'Shit. So who's gonna tell him?'

'Tell me what?' Jon asked, almost aloud.

'Shhh! The teachers check in on ya.' Ricky rolled over again.

'Not in here they don't,' Jon said, as his room was not part of the school trip. 'So tell me, God damn it!'

'Shit— I guess I'll tell him. You want me to tell him?'

'Tell him,' Ricky said into his pillow.

Bob sighed, and then leaned out of the lower bunk. 'So Jon.'

'So *what*?' Jon asked, frustrated by their secrecy.

'Did Chris say anything to you tonight?'

'About what?' he asked, and then thought not to press for too much detail. 'No; he didn't. Nobody told me nothin'.'

'Well; it kinda concerns somebody you kinda know.'

'Who?! A *girl*? Who?'

'How'd you know it was a girl?' Bob asked him.

Jon looked down at him as though gazing upon a total cretin. 'Bob, I had a fifty-fifty chance. What the hell is going on?'

'Well; okay…. See; it's kind of about Patti Harper.'

Jon frowned. That was surprising. Of all girls in the world he had never imagined he would have anything to do with Patti Harper, much less the other way round. 'Okay….'

'He *knows* her?' Ricky rolled over. 'I didn't know he *knew* her.'

'Well; he does know who she *is*,' Bob said up to him.

'Shit,' Ricky said; 'this is stupid then. He probably already knows.'

'Knows *what*?' Jon demanded, almost breaking out of the whisper. 'Assume that I don't know nothin'.'

'Well,' Bob teased; 'we've all assumed that for years.'

'Shut up, Bob, and give me the bullshit about Patti Harper.'

'Well; basically, if I can be blunt—'

'*Be* blunt, for Christ's sake!'

Bob sighed. 'The babe's hooked on ya.'

Ricky stifled a giggle. 'Broad's hot for your pants,' he said, and rolled over face-first into his pillow.

'Shut up,' Jon said, and leaned out to look down at Bob. 'So how did you come across this piece of debatable bullshit?'

Bob laughed a little, and then said in a whisper, 'It ain't bullshit, Jon. That's why it's so unbelievable. Well; not that it's not— Well; you know what I mean. The chick is absolutely dynamite over you. Shit— she damn near told me outright, in those same words.'

'*Told* you?' Jon scoffed. 'I doubt that very much, dude.'

'Well; shit— I did happen to drive her back on the damn snowmobile, you know. You deciding to do a doughnut in the snow with the damn thing sure did your reputation with girls a hell of a lotta good. Just try to remember who rode back with who.'

Jon felt himself getting a little red; he knew he had been shortsighted there. 'Yeah; all right; so what did the babe say?'

'Well; I kinda ran into her in the lounge tonight. Somebody said you were in there playin' pool.'

'Yeah; to the tune of like two hundred and seventy *bucks*,' Jon told him. 'Some of us are downright *productive* on our vacations, and doo.'

'Yeah; well; I wanted to come in and watch ya, but this other shit was goin' on.'

'Yeah? You mean this bullshit?'

'Well; like the usual club of rah-rahs was all in the lounge, you know, Harper and Carson and Curtis and I think Barrie, but I don't know where Jeannie Banfield was.'

'Yeah,' said Jon, volunteering nothing of his evening; 'so–?'

'So; Harper,' Bob said, 'Patti Harper, she comes up to me and R D just to thank us for gettin' them home in one piece, like they were totally helpless out there, or somethin'. Like Marlowe didn't exactly tell you *who* was out there; right? I mean: we just went; right?'

'Yeah,' Jon said; and that was true. 'He didn't tell us who. I think we were really just the first people he found.'

'Well; yeah. So she's like all appreciative and doo about it. I was pretty well taken aback, you know.'

'Yeah....' Jon thought.

'So anyway, what she said was– Ricky. What was it the chick said exactly?'

'Huh?' Ricky lifted his head and turned over.

'What was it that Harper said about this chump here?'

Ricky let out a long groaning sigh. 'Oh, shit.... "Summer Man".'

'"Summer Man"; that's it!'

'"Summer Man"?' Jon said aloud. 'What the hell's that?'

Ricky chuckled. 'Cavaliere's solo album,' he said, and lay back down.

'Shut up,' Bob was telling Jon; 'or you'll wake up that jerk over there.'

Below Ricky, Chris sighed in his sleep. 'Dude could sleep through an earthquake,' Ricky mumbled.

'So what the hell does "Summer Man" mean?' Jon asked, quieter.

'It means you,' Bob told him. 'It *is* you.'

Jon was silent a moment. Summer Man, he thought. Summer Man.... 'What's the significance of it?'

'It's you,' said Bob. 'It's what Harper– It's what Patti Harper said about you. She said you were a summer man, who hates the winter and likes the summer.'

'I do hate winter,' Jon said. 'Just tonight, I was sayin'–'

'She said you were the Summer Man,' Bob said.

Jon thought and then shook his head. 'You dudes are makin' this up. This is all bullshit; ain't it?'

Bob laughed, having expected the reaction. 'No, man; I swear it.'

Ricky was laughing too. 'Aaah; you guys....' Jon shifted in his bunk. 'I swear, man, this is all bullshit.'

Ricky leaned over and looked down at Bob. 'I told you not to tell him. I knew he wouldn't believe it.'

'It's because it's bullshit,' Jon said simply, folding his hands over his chest and staring up at the ceiling.

'Look, man,' Bob said; 'I ain't makin' anything up. If I was gonna invent some bullshit story, I woulda said the chick wanted to— I don't know, maybe move to Hawaii with ya. I wouldn't make up something like this.'

'"Summer Man"?' Jon laughed. 'Like, Superman, but— Shit— that's not even *good* enough to be bullshit.'

'Yeah, maybe, man; but I swear it's just what she said.'

'She was drunk,' Jon supposed.

'Man; I'd like to *see* her drunk,' Ricky contributed.

'No, man; they ain't been servin' everybody,' Bob said. 'You know that.'

'Bullshit, man— *I* got served. *Cissie* got served. This is all so much bullshit....'

'No, man; no way. Look. Harper and Curtis and I guess it was Barrie were all in the lounge, and like we walk in and Patti Harper comes up to the bar, gets a Coke, or somethin', and starts talkin' to us, like she knows us. This was like eleven o'clock, I guess. It wasn't long before they all went off to their rooms. She just came up and thanked us for the snowmobile rides, you know, and it kinda started a conversation, and doo.'

'Just you and R D, and Patti Harper, were standin' there.'

'Yeah,' Bob told him.

'This smells like bullshit,' Jon said.

'No; this is true. She asked us about the band, and doo, and then she asked where you were, and finally said when she saw you when the buses first pulled in, and you were waitin' for us to get there, how you reminded her of summer.'

'Man, it was *snowing* when the buses came in. It's been snowing up here for two goddamn *days*. I'm gettin' so sick of *snow*—'

'Yeah; well; it was some feeling the chick got, then. How should *I* know? I'm not in her head. All she did was ask questions about you, dude. She asked me why you didn't offer Jeannie Banfield a ride, because she thought you were goin' to.'

Jon thought about that. Suddenly there was a point which he had never bothered to consider. 'Well; like Marlowe was there,' he excused. 'Shit— she's been goin' out with—'

'Yeah; that's what I told her. That you naturally thought she was goin' out with Marlowe, and that Marlowe is like your friend, and doo. But dig this, dude– she's not goin' out with him at all. Actually, I think Patti Harper said Jeannie Banfield's not really goin' out with anybody right now. And then, like I told her how you said Marlowe should take Cissie's snowmobile and lead us, so Cissie could run back and tell them what we were doing, just in case–'

'Bob, that was *your* idea.'

'Well; whoever it was….' They were both silent a moment. Jon thought about it and decided he had to believe at least half the story. It would be like Bob to give Jon credit for an idea just to help him make an important impression; he had done so before. They were, after all, blood brothers. 'So what's the plan, dude?' Bob asked him. 'You muff this one up and I'll never forgive ya.'

'Shit….' Jon stared at the planking of the ceiling. 'I don't know. Guess I'll have to do *something*.'

'Shit yeah,' Bob said.

'Broad's got a sweet ass, too,' Ricky said. 'I was checkin' her out, before.'

'She's too old for ya,' Jon smiled.

Ricky scoffed. 'I doubt that, dude. My birthday's before hers.'

'She's also a very nice girl, too,' Bob said sincerely. 'I was talkin' to her for a while, you know, and she's very pleasant to be around. Damn good catch.'

At that Ricky made a noise like a fishing reel singing out; and Jon and Bob laughed aloud. They all heard Chris moan in his sleep again.

'Girl's definitely a fox,' Bob stated. 'I say we get some zees, and let this idiot contemplate his situation, and doo. But in the morning, dude, you'd better be workin' on it, 'cause I never wanna speak to ya again if you're not.'

'Yeah,' Ricky said; 'a bird in the hand, and doo. I don't have to tell ya where your hand should be.'

'Shut up,' Jon told him, and rolled over. It would be hard to sleep, now. There were just too many new developments occurring for him to consider even during the waking hours.

* * *

Bob had awakened before nine and soon found Jon down stairs, pounding out laps in the indoor swimming pool. The warmth of the water produced a heavy mist on the big windows, masking the view of the snowy hillside, and it was a soothing place in which to spend an early morning, especially when suffering from a hangover.

Despite his headache Jon had accomplished twenty-two laps of the pool by the time Bob had come down, and Bob sat in a chair by the deep end and timed him over his last twelve. Jon climbed out of the far end of the pool and collected his towel from two doting young women who seemed pleased to appreciate the sight of an attractive young man in a bright-blue bikini swimsuit. He had a few words with his two admirers and then greeted Bob on his way in to the showers.

They took breakfast in the lower lounge, feeling very pampered with pretty waitresses bringing them muffins and tea and hotcakes, and Jon paid the bill from his wad of tens and twenties as though it were *carte blanche.* Living on permanent holiday would certainly be an enviable way of life. Jon and Bob had always enjoyed fancying themselves as famous, successful rock-and-roll stars some day; but now, with the band beginning what seemed certain to be a long, hard crawl to the top, such fantasies took on a whole new significance for them. There at the table they made a pact about their future lifestyle. Never would they immerse themselves in reckless excess as did so many other popular performers but rather, in the manner of prestigious young royalty or wealthy old noblemen, they would conduct themselves with grace and dignity and, as Jon put it, 'with a social conscience tuned to the impressionable public.'

Bob had always been aware of Jon's desire to project a good image. Only last night had he learned of the abyss that had developed between Jon and Christine; though Chris had made Bob promise never to tell from whom he had heard. It was unfortunate; for Bob hated to think of his soulmate enduring any emotional turmoil. But he knew too that Jon would be steeling himself against the disappointment with the knowledge and satisfaction that, in spite of the cost to himself, he had done what he believed was right for someone who needed him and would do it again. That was admirable. But Bob had always known Jon to be exquisitely noble. He was an inspiration to all of them and was certainly becoming even more so to young Valerie, whose self-esteem and outward behaviour had already begun to show the effects of having been favourably influenced by the courtly deference of a true gentleman. That was impressive. And so Bob was not at all surprised that Jon would be so serious about the pact they had just made. It was all too easy to imagine him as a world-famous composer and performer and producer, leading the industry with cutting-edge creativity, social responsibility and uncanny clairvoyance about artistic trends, yet wearing the finest suits, in the conservative styles, being chauffeured about in a pedestrian but dignified Bentley or Daimler and living in one of those big old Edwardian mansion houses with seven servants and a dozen pedigreed hunting dogs.

The daydream amused him; and so Bob paid little attention to Jon's antics on the snowmobile that morning. Chris, Mark, Jon and Cissie all drove off together, their flasks of liquor hidden under their coats, to terrorise any neophytes they found who had strayed from the regular slopes. Jon was only enjoying himself on holiday, perhaps the last long weekend he would be able to take for quite some time. But it was the price paid for The Strawberries' financial security; amongst rock-and-roll outfits their gross income was phenomenal, second in the Wilshire area to only their Howard-and-Santana stablemates Tobacco Road.

Steve Marlowe left PJ, Patti, Jeanne and Debbie when they promised not to venture into any distant forest trails; and he joined Bob, Mark and Jon on the sun deck for a hot drink. He had seen them rioting about on the snowmobiles earlier but silently acknowledged that, whilst with someone like Danny Harris such misbehaving might have seemed irresponsible, with Jon Cavaliere it was only humourous, just another proportionate part of his personality. Danny was far too proud a person to capitulate to levelheaded restraint and sanity, especially when requested or imposed by someone else; but Jon seemed a world away from such pettiness. He was refreshingly open and unsophisticated, with no room or need for pretentious façades. In fact he hid nothing, wasting no mental energy in disguising the reality of his own character. Steve admired him for such self-confidence; it was something he liked to think he had cultivated in himself. By the end of the afternoon he and Jon, once academic peers in elementary school, were at last renewing their former friendship; and this time it would have a firm foundation of mutual respect and admiration.

That evening Jon met Bob and Mark in the lounge. All three of them had been drinking at a good rate all day; in fact the table maid recognised them from the outdoor deck. Seeing as they appeared none the worse for wear, she went off with an order for another round for the boys. 'Shit,' sighed Mark; '*that* was easy.'

'Aaah,' said Bob; 'they don't care who gets served. Shit– I haven't seen one of the teachers say somethin' yet.'

Jon only shrugged. 'Just keep actin' like you're not part of the trip,' he said simply; 'and they won't even think you might be.'

Mark and Bob could scarcely disagree with what he had proved a successful tactic. 'So hey, man,' Mark said to him; 'where's your better half, and doo?'

Jon smiled, assuming rightly he meant Cissie as they had all observed he had been spending quite a lot of time with her over the weekend. 'Aaah; she's off with Leslie and all them; I don't know. Those girls she knows are all a bunch of rowdies, man, always lookin' for a party…. They're not exactly my kinda people, you know.'

Bob nodded at that. Perhaps he knew better what girl might have been his kind of people. 'So what's with the vodka, man?' Mark asked. 'Thought you were a gin man, and doo.'

Jon shrugged. 'Aaah; well…. It grows on ya. Vodka's cheaper than gin anyway.'

Mark laughed. 'Since when does money ever make up your mind?' he teased; and Bob laughed at that too.

Jon turned then. Two cute ninth-graders from some other school's skiing trip were attempting a three-handed arrangement of 'Heart And Soul' on the big black grand piano in the corner. Hampered by glasses of soda and a shared fit of the giggles, they were getting nowhere. One of them would invariably make a mistake and they would both give in to loony laughter; and it was certainly beginning to wear on everyone else. But Jon was quite entertained by them. Bob watched him intently, recognising Jon's compulsion to fairly leap out of his chair. In a way it was funny; for he knew that once Jon joined the girls at the keyboard the evening would never be the same.

Bob knew Jon's innate inclination was to avoid the worries of typical teenaged boys like impressing the opposite sex and showing up his peers. It was perhaps because of this and not in spite of it that Jon Cavaliere was so popular; for his resistance to peer pressure and refusal to be self-indulgent made him a sort of role model for everyone else. But he knew too that Jon immersed himself in music to mask his fears of emotional rejection and social inadequacy. A performing stage was just like a swimming pool for him, a place where he might perform at his peak, hone his skills, meet his own standards, and still be sufficiently distanced from the more significant strangers. Never able to appreciate anything phoney, he nonetheless revelled in his newfound notoriety as an entertainer, if only because the public would never believe that someone so universally admired could actually be terrified of meeting pretty girls.

Bob turned !to say something but then, sure enough, up bounded Jon, carrying his glass of vodka-and-tonic. There he goes, Bob thought, hiding behind the piano again. As usual.... He hid a smile. But they sure do love him, he thought. Everyone loves a clown....

Twisted about in their chairs, Mark and Bob watched as Jon leaned over to greet the duetting pianists with that unforgettable smile. The ninth-grade girls, of course, were thoroughly charmed and soon moved apart for him to sit between them on the bench. Steve Marlowe came up to the table just as Jon was demonstrating his two-handed arrangement of 'Heart And Soul' for the girls, in which his left hand played both bass notes and chords alternately. 'Uh-oh,' Steve smiled, setting a glass of soda down on the table beside Mark. 'What's this?'

Bob turned round. 'Hey, dude,' he said. 'Oh; this is just the entertainment coming on.'

Steve laughed and sat down across from them at the table with his back to the doorway. He did not notice, then, as PJ, Holly and Jeanne came in, with Patti Harper a second behind. Patti was lovely as always, in a soft pink-and-grey Shetland sweater and a short plaid wool skirt. She wiggled her fingers at Bob in greeting; and Bob made a quick little smile and lifted one hand off the table in return.

Mark spun his head from one to the other, shocked by the apparent change in protocol, and leaned over to whisper to Bob. 'So what the hell is *that* all about?'

Bob moved his hand in a horizontal motion above his cocktail. 'Shhh. Tell ya later.'

Steve, still watching Jon, had perceived nothing. Bob kept his eyes on the four girls. They all turned their heads as they crossed the room, passing the piano where Jon sat with two strange girls and performed a flawless yet well-embellished 'Heart And Soul' for the whole lounge. The patrons seemed quite satisfied; maybe half of them had turned in their seats to pay attention. Jeanne Banfield, eyes fixed on Jon as she walked, actually stubbed her toe on the corner of someone's chair. Patti, far bolder, stopped still in the centre of the room for half a minute as he played, gazing wide-eyed as though hypnotised.

Bob smiled at that. Dag, he thought. She really *is* tuned into him then. If this doesn't work, maybe nothing will....

The girls sat down across the room at a table held by Marty Engel and Bobby Crocker and a few of that crowd; Bob nodded a little to himself as he had expected as much. One of the boys got up straight away to push two tables together and a waitress came by to take their bar order. Jon ceased with the hackneyed 'Heart And Soul' and went on to a few other tunes, notably 'Sleigh Ride', not one of his favourites though it delighted everyone else in the room. The lounge was near capacity already, with a large proportion of single people in their twenties and some adults even older, and the two separate high-school groups were not very well represented here tonight. Jon played on; and soon a varied crowd of admirers gathered about the piano to clap and sing along.

Bob ordered a drink for him from the bartender, who offered to take Jon's drinks out of his own tip cup if the crowd continued to be so well-entertained. Bob smiled and gave a little nod. That might have been expected too, he thought, and headed over towards the piano.

Jon looked up, having completed 'Moonlight In Vermont', which seemed a natural for the season and the locale. 'That for me, bro'? Thanks a lot.'

'It's cool, dude,' Bob told him, as Jon took a gulp. 'Just wanted to tell you, though, if you keep it up, yours and probably mine will be on the house.'

'Sol,' Jon replied calmly, and drank again.

'Do you know any Elton John?' someone asked him; and Jon looked up to find a pretty dark-haired girl of about twenty staring straight at him on his left, and then, across the top of the closed lid of the piano, three total strangers as well as Marty Engel, Debbie Blake, Patti Harper and Jeanne Banfield.

'Yeah,' said Patti, setting her glass atop the lid too. 'Play some Elton John.'

A few others agreed. Jon shrugged, and took another sip of his cocktail. 'Oh; I don't know…. You don't wanna hear any Elton John.'

To his right, Mark made a little laugh; he was standing right next to Bob. ' "Great Balls of Fire",' he said quietly, and drank more Michelob.

'No,' Jon told him with a sly smile as he set down his glass; '*I* know.' With no further words he suddenly assaulted the piano with a honky-tonk introduction, the left hand bouncing up and down for fifths or octaves and the right splashing down on a rapid sequence of chords.

Bob and Mark recognised it at once, debating playfully with each other as to who would take the vocal lead; and Mark took to drumming on the piano lid. So Bob began with the words to Bobby Darin's 'Splish Splash, I was Takin' a Bath'. Shrieks of glee went up from the audience; for that was what they had truly become. Clapping, whooping, laughing in unrestrained glee, the entire roomful chimed in loudly on every chorus.

'*Take* one!' Bob cheered, even whilst Jon went into a rollicking instrumental verse. This was welcomed by even more shouts and cheers from the lounge patrons, who until now might have had mixed emotions about the long-haired teenagers mingling and drinking with the adults. But there could be no mistaking the professional calibre of the performance, regardless of the informal setting.

Bob sang and Jon played, and Mark wandered off to get himself another beer. He would have to pay actual cash for further refreshments; the two cases of Michelob from Jon's boot were nearly gone already. One of the ninth-grade girls from the other school slid an arm about Jon's middle as though adoringly possessive. Two inebriated men hooked elbows and danced a circle about the floor. A woman, surely closer to the teens' parents' age, sassed herself from table to table flirtatiously. Someone spilled a soda drink on the piano lid. Patti Harper smiled straight at Jon, cheering 'All right!' at him once. Jeanne had begun to feel mightily jealous; but she could hardly deny the sheer joy of being so close at hand whilst Jon Cavaliere excelled in yet another of his many areas of expertise. The crowd, made up of so many diverse generations and interests, was completely his, just as was each and every Strawberries audience.

Danny located her there and escorted Jeanne back to the table like a shepherd losing his patience with the errant lamb. Patti would linger amongst the strangers gathered about the piano; and Jeanne lost sight of her across the floor. '*Someone's* in love,' Holly sided to her, meaning to taunt Patti about her obvious infatuation; but it was Jeanne who felt the brunt of the gibe.

So what is *this*? she worried. Everybody knows it's *me* who's crazy about him, and with good reason.... So why is Patti over there acting so weird about everything?

Barry and Vinnie wandered in, having finished off a fifth of Jon's Bacardi, and found Ricky and Mark table-drumming on the piano lid and Chris and Bob swapping verses to Taupin-and-John's 'Saturday Night's Alright For Fighting'. The front row included Marty Engel, Cissie and Leslie, Steve, Wendi Barrie, Debbie Blake and Patti Harper, with their schoolmate, Jon Cavaliere, the modest second singer and co-arranger of The Strawberries, Wilshire, Connecticut's favourite rock-and-roll band, at the keyboard as the centre of attention. The teacher chaperons from both high schools were hardly the quietest of the crowd; having so much fun themselves they agreed to extend their charges' curfew till one AM. Mr Crowley, Wilshire High's perennial ski-trip organiser, openly congratulated Jon for having provided such delightful entertainment and then proposed a toast to the success of the trip. Sunday turned out to be the most enjoyable evening so far; and all retired to their rooms wishing the party had gone on another hour, or even two.

* * *

On Monday evening the room was already crowded when they came in. After a full day of swimming, snowmobiling, cross-country skiing and archery Jon was certainly not the only one to think the presence of a professional disc jockey for the Wilshire High buffet dinner and dance less than welcome. The black piano was rolled off to one corner and covered with a dropcloth. Well, he thought; so much for this evening....

Bob found them an empty table in the far corner, where Jeanne Banfield and her circle of friends had been last night. 'So; you want a drink, man?'

'Yeah,' sighed Jon, and slouched in the chair. 'I can't think of any other reason you'd expect me to come down here.'

Bob made a wry smile and left for the bar. The disc jockey put on Helen Reddy's 'Angie Baby' just as he returned. Seeing Jon's childlike wince at the song Bob laughed. 'What the hell's *your* problem?' he teased, nonetheless irritated that Jon would be so resolutely bored with the proceedings already.

'Aaah....' Jon took his glass and swallowed heartily. Still it had not yet occurred to him how casual the bar staff were about serving alcoholic beverages to the high-school students. To him it seemed perfectly natural; he had come to take his own ability to hold his liquor for granted and there had never been a time when he had not known his limits. Bob knew how he was. They could all enjoy a good time without feeling a need to drink to excess; indeed, though he had been a legal drinker for only two weeks, it was usually Jon who ended up soberly driving inebriated younger friends safely home. The boys in both bands looked up to him for that; and perhaps his mature attitude about things like drinking alcohol had begun to rub off on them after all. Despite all their antics this weekend they had impressed others to where not one of them had been asked to provide proof of adult status at the bar.

And the antics were not always of adult calibre. Mark and Ricky and Chris stomped into the lounge, with Cissie and Leslie in tow, all singing 'Yellow Submarine' in boisterous outdoor voices; still, everyone took them for enthusiastic natural entertainers and not rowdy underaged drunks. Jon winced with a hand over his forehead; at least they were singing the harmonies adequately. 'Hey,' Mark bellowed; 'should we have reservations?'

Jon sighed. 'Oh; I've got reservations.'

Cissie giggled at that, with a shrill 'Hee-hee-hee-hee' that was terrifically annoying. 'Hi, honey; I'm home,' she announced to Jon, and slid a chair over to sit not six inches from him.

The beer on her breath was unmistakable. 'You guys are through the last case; aren't you?' Jon asked them all in a quiet voice.

'Yo, dude,' Chris said calmly to him, 'cool out. That's what it's there for; right?'

'Yeah,' Jon said with resignation, and seemed not to agree in any case.

They all nibbled on *hors d'oeuvres* until dinner was brought out; and people queued up at the buffet, the disc jockey began with a few dance numbers and the party got itself into swing. For Jon, it was a senseless, silly gathering with no redeeming social value, too much like those few parties he had attended amongst the high-school set where the conversation was shallow and those conversing even more so. He welcomed the opportunity to sit and chat with his closest friends, though, and he and Bob and Mark went on for quite a while suggesting solutions for Tobacco Road's lack of sincere, passionate ballads. Jon suggested they write something in other than straight four-four rock time. At once Mark began tapping in twelve-eight on the table. Only Cissie cared to listen in; Leslie and Marianne looked about with expressions of pained boredom and finally got up and left them.

The boys seemed not to mind, nor even notice. Despite having worn a black velour suit-coat with his jeans instead of his usual leather pilot's jacket, Jon was in his element here, amidst good company, a drink in one hand and creative matters to discuss. Cissie sat and gazed at him, wide-eyed in sincere admiration. Bob wondered if perhaps he had been wrong all along; perhaps Jon might really be happy with her. Perhaps happiness was all one could ask for a best friend. Perhaps the destiny everyone had assumed would happen was not destined to happen at all.

But destiny was known for its quirks. People rose to dance or to wander the crowd; and finally only Chris was left with Jon and Cissie. He looked across the table at the two of them, sitting a foot apart, and said, 'Yes; well; I... gotta go. I have, uh, an engagement, uh, somewhere....'

They both turned their heads to watch him meander aimlessly into the crowd. 'I love his subtlety,' Jon said wryly. Cissie giggled and snuggled closer.

Bob danced with a few girls; he was no great dancer, but the girls thought him gallant enough. Once he happened to see Patti Harper sitting alone at a table by the window and suddenly blushed bright-red, as though he had made a grave mistake. Uh-oh, he thought. There seems to be some unfinished business I neglected to consider....

When Preston's 'Nothing From Nothing' concluded the disc jockey put on Manilow's 'Mandy' for a slow dance. Consequently the floor thinned out. Bob excused himself from Rosemarie and made his way back to the table where Jon and Barry sat talking by themselves. 'Where's your better half, dude?' Bob asked, and took his seat.

Jon shook his head, still not used to hearing his friends consider Cissie his girlfriend. 'Oh, shit; I don't know; she and Leslie had to go up to the room for something.... Leslie's got a bug up her ass about some shit or another.'

'It's that time,' Barry smiled.

Jon nodded towards him in agreement. 'Diggit.'

Bob watched him take a strong gulp of vodka-and-tonic. 'So?' he asked brightly. 'Find somebody else.'

Jon scoffed. 'Yeah; right, bud.'

Barry laughed. 'Diggit,' he agreed. 'Any port in a storm, and doo.'

Ignoring Barry's inelegant attempt at double-entendre Bob leaned a little closer to Jon. 'No; seriously, dude. What was it we were talkin' about the other night? I don't think I have to tell you who's been sittin' by herself half the evening.'

Jon got a little red and stared into his drink. Barry turned in his seat and gazed off across the room. 'Yeah, dude,' he drawled, having recognised a certain blonde; 'and she's like all by herself right *now.*'

Bob craned his neck; he could not see the table in question from here. Jon turned round too and, though no names had been mentioned, he felt sure he knew whom they had meant. He got a little redder but assembled his composure in a second. Pushing his chair back from the table he took a brief glance at his two friends' anticipation and stood up. 'I'm just goin' for a refill,' he said uneasily, and went off into the crowd.

'Damn,' said Bob, and began to worry about him.

'Naah; he'll be all right,' said Barry. 'Gotta happen sooner or later, dude. It's been too many years, and doo.'

Bob looked at him and suddenly frowned. 'Wait a minute. Who did *you* see sittin' over there?'

Barry made a silly laugh. 'Shit…. Who do you think?'

Bob blanched and spun about again to try to see. '*Damn*,' he said again, and worried even more.

Danny Harris returned to the table and handed Jeanne her soda. He took a long gulp from his bottle of Miller and then sat down beside her. 'Hi,' she said to him then; and the others all sighed to behold what they believed to be sincere mush. Patti smiled respectfully and turned away, feeling a little out-of-place with no escort for the evening. Debbie so far had made herself newly friendly with three Wilshire boys already; that was how she was. Darryl, not known as an avid slow-dancer, excused himself to speak with some friends at another table. Holly said a few words to Patti and then lit a cigarette, staring off into the dancing crowd as though heavy-headed from too much beer.

Jon tried not to look over that way, feeling his heart hammering in his chest. Asking a dance of a girl with whom he was not on regular speaking terms was nothing he had ever known. The thought occurred to him that she might not even know who he was. Oh; that's bullshit, he told himself. She sure as hell does know who you are. Babe's probably crazier about you than you think.

He stopped at the bar and slid his glass across the counter, admiring the dark-varnished walnut planks. 'Smirnoff-and-tonic,' he stated, recognising the bartender who had served him half a dozen last night.

'How ya doing?' the bar man asked him.

Jon sighed and leaned heavily on the bar with one arm. 'Aaah; I don't know. By now I think I'll just be glad when this whole damn vacation's over. Get my ass back to work where I belong.'

The bar man laughed. 'Must be nice to have that kind of job,' he said, and dropped a swizzle stick into the glass, giving the mixture one quick spin. 'What is it you do, anyway?'

Jon smiled at him and peeled two dollars off his pocket wad for the drink. 'I play in a band,' he said smugly, and left. He was always instilled with great pride upon boasting of that, and he inhaled the confidence like some aromatic elixir as he pranced away from the bar. Two couples were seated right before him, and at the table just beyond he had seen Jeanne Banfield, Patti Harper and the rest of that group. The disc jockey announced a duet of Elton John numbers. At the start of 'Goodbye Yellow Brick Road', Jon lifted the drink for a swallow, to look unaffected, allowing the glass to obscure his sight for just a second. When he had lowered it, he saw that nearly everyone at the girls' table had abruptly risen to dance.

He stood there feeling stupid as Jeanne skipped off across the dance floor to the far side, towing her tall, well-built, well-dressed escort by the hand. In fact everyone at the table except Holly and Patti had got up with their escorts. Patti turned about in her chair and saw him just a yard behind her; and when he looked down he felt his whole face go red. She smiled and said in a cool, quiet voice, 'Hullo, Jon.'

He composed whatever scrap of self-possession he had left and bent his knees to squat beside her chair. 'Hi,' he said, and put on a calm smile. 'So; do I hear that you're the one spreading the rumour around, then?'

She smiled back, happy to be conversing with him, and asked sweetly, 'Which rumour is that?'

That was not expected. Jon could not tell if Patti were teasing him or merely asking for clarification. The situation was not up to his standards at all; he was spinning out of control here. A thought whirled by and he snatched a hold on it, recalling, in flying class, they teach you to concentrate on regaining control of the spinning aeroplane or prepare to die. There are only the two options. And I've got to choose one of the above, right now…. 'Oh,' he said, jingling the ice in the glass to disguise his shaking hand; 'the one about how I hate winter so much.'

She giggled, in a soft, lovely tone that sent shivers down his spine. Simply looking at her was breathtaking. 'Oh,' she agreed; *that*…. Well; I guess it's just something that's hard not to notice, you know, with the way you seem to be….'

He tried not to look up at the dance floor to see if Jeanne would look this way. Half of him wanted her to become raging jealous, and half of him wanted to run and hide and bury all of this exchange from her for ever. 'Well,' he said; 'it was kind of an interesting concept you came up with, there.'

Patti giggled again, in the same way. It was hard for him to listen to her gentle Welsh accent and not shiver; he felt like he was addressing some countess and wondered if she would even think him worthy of her. 'Yes,' she said to him; 'well; pity is I don't know you well enough to be sure.'

For a second, he did not realise how much that sounded like a proposition. Before he could blush he heard himself say, 'Well; let's just say for now that you're right.'

'All right.' They smiled at each other for a full five seconds, whilst Holly sat sideways in her chair pretending to pay absolutely no attention. 'So,' said Patti cheerfully; 'shame there's no piano tonight.'

'Yeah…. And I would play, you know. I really had a fun time last night.'

'We all did,' she smiled. 'Everyone's been talking about it.'

Jon shrugged and listened to the opening strains of 'Don't Let The Sun Go Down On Me,' a passionate, sensitive ballad he had loved since he had first heard it on the radio. Suddenly he felt a surge of inner strength. Certainly she would not turn him down now. 'So,' he said to her then, slowly reaching up to rest his drink beside her on the table; 'would you care to dance?'

Patti shivered and took a firm hold on the side of the chair, lest she tumble off into his arms before the dream subsided. A wonderful dizziness came over her; and she heard herself coo, 'Oh; I'd *love* to.'

Her cool peppermint breath tingled upon his face. Carefully he pushed his glass in from the edge of the table and stood up; and she laid her hand in his as she rose beside him. In the pale-grey skirt and soft cashmere sweater she was perfectly feminine, the kind of girl his mother would adore and his father would enjoy seeing popping through the house on a regular basis. Those thoughts were embarrassing, and he hated them and dismissed them at once; but they were unwilling to leave. As he and Patti each took a gentle hold on the other and began to dance, fantasies chased themselves round in his head. For once, there was no notion of Jeanne Banfield amongst them, only this girl, a wonderfully new, exciting prospect that he had neither expected nor even dreamt before.

She was not so short after all; in her high-heeled grey shoes her forehead came just to the top of his nose. He took her right hand in his left, to lead her, the reverse of how he would have held a guitar, which felt awkward for him. Patti seemed not to care. Before the song was half over she had slipped both hands up his shoulders and leaned closer towards his neck; and then he was holding her snugly about her trim little waist, turning her slowly as they danced and inadvertently seeing Bob and Leslie dancing together somewhere else on the floor. 'You're a very nice dancer, Jon,' Patti whispered softly on his cheek.

He shivered. True, they were swaying together beautifully, as if they had always been dance partners. 'Yeah; well…. I don't like fast dancing. I can't boogie to save my life.'

She smiled, letting out a cool sigh. 'No; nor can I,' she admitted. 'I'd much rather dance like this, all night….' At that moment she caught a glimpse of Jeanne with Danny Harris and suddenly went white. Oh, God, she thought. Oh, God, *what* am I doing….

Jon blushed as they passed by Chris Santana dancing with Pam Donovan. He was not really so embarrassed that everyone's eyes were soaking up the sight of him dancing with Patti Harper. It should not have seemed odd at all that someone as popular among the rock-and-roll enthusiasts should be able to cross the boundaries of high-school cliques and dance with one of the cheerleaders. Perhaps he should always have expected people to expect such things from him.

'Don't Let The Sun Go Down On Me' ended and at the start of Wonder's 'Boogie On Reggae Woman', he let go of her self-consciously. Now what? he wondered to himself. Now that you've got her, *now* what? 'That was nice,' Patti said, as she led him back to the table. 'It was so sweet of you to ask me.'

'Hey,' he smiled, trying to appear nonchalant; 'well; you're the one who wanted to.'

Yes I did, thought Patti then. I always seem to say 'yes' first and worry about the consequences later.... Jon pulled out the chair for her and she sat, crossing her ankles demurely under the table. She looked up, starry-eyed, as he picked up his glass and took a wee sip from it. Only then did she realise she had best try to salvage at least something of her noble intentions. 'Well, Jon; would you like to sit down for a while?'

'Oh; uh; well; I really shouldn't.... There are people who— Well; I kinda feel like a host deserting his party, you know.'

She did notice he seemed careful not to ask her to join him. But perhaps they both knew the reasons why that would have been unwise. 'Oh,' she said sadly, and then saw Danny and Jeanne coming back through the crowd on the floor. 'Well; I do thank you for the dance, Jon,' she said sincerely. 'I had a very nice time.'

Those grey-green eyes were quite an invitation, even if he could not accept. 'Yeah; it was nice,' he agreed, and laid one hand gently on her shoulder. 'I'm sorry; but I do gotta shake it. I'll see you around, I'm sure.'

'I hope so—' But he was already turning to go. 'See you,' she sang.

Jon smiled a little at her before raising his glass and downing the entire drink. With a slight step back to keep his balance, he let out a sigh and went off.

Holly turned then and leaned over to tease her, 'Oooo. Just look at you. I'd say *someone's* in love.'

Indeed Patti was staring after Jon. So was Danny Harris. 'Dag,' he said, as he stopped at Jeanne's chair; 'some kinda serious alkie. Who the hell was that?'

Patti spun round with an embarrassed frown. But her mouth dropped open upon meeting Jeanne's eyes. Before either of them could say a word, Jeanne turned and bolted off like a terrified rabbit. 'Hey, Jeannie—?' Danny worried; but she was gone.

Patti was up in a second. '*I'll* get her!' she insisted, and scurried off.

'Dag; what's the matter with her?' wondered Bobby Crocker, indicating Patti as he and Debbie sat down. 'Is she gettin' sick too?'

'Oooo; I hope not,' Debbie said; ''cause they're really watchin' the juniors.'

'No,' said Holly calmly, and turned away to puff on her cigarette. 'I think it's a little more serious than that.'

Patti assisted the self-closing door behind her. 'Jeannie?' she asked gingerly. 'Are you all right?'

Jeanne was sitting on the padded bench in the ladies' lounge, wiping her eyes with a tissue. 'I'm fine,' she lied, and sniffled aloud.

'Jeannie….' Patti sat down beside her. 'Oh, Jeannie, I am so sorry….'

Jeanne sniffled. 'It doesn't matter,' she said.

'I feel really terrible about it, Jeannie. I want you to know that. I should have been thinking about you.'

'It doesn't matter,' Jeanne said again. 'Why should you feel terrible?'

'He just came up and asked me; you know? I mean: I didn't want to say *no*….'

'I *know*,' Jeanne said, and blew her nose. 'I mean: like you always say, he's irresistible.'

Patti put an arm across Jeanne's back and patted her shoulder. 'Well; I guess that's an appropriate word. I'll admit I just lost my head. But I want you to know I did mean to do something for you.'

'Oh, Patti….' Jeanne blew her nose again. 'You don't have to say things like that to keep me from getting upset. I'm not a little kid. I mean: well; it's not like I own the guy or anything. I hardly think you're the first girl he's danced with.'

Patti patted her again. 'Oh, Jeannie…. I know how you feel. But I really was thinking about how much you would *love* to go out with him. And I knew it wouldn't feel right, if you wanted so much to go out with him and I let him ask me out, or whatever. So it's just as well that we only had one dance, as we did. Really, Jeannie, there was nothing more. Just a dance. I promise it doesn't mean any more than that.'

'It means he likes you,' Jeanne said, mopping up new tears. 'And he probably doesn't even know I'm alive.'

'I'm not so sure about that,' Patti smiled. 'I had thought that it would be good for one of us to get to know him, just so we'd have a chance to see him more often, and see what he's really like. How would you feel, when after all this time he was really a jerk? Then you'd be even more upset.'

'But he's *not* a jerk,' Jeanne said firmly. 'I'm sure you're gonna tell me he's just perfect.'

Patti smiled again and closed her eyes for a second to purge herself of her own thoughts on the subject. 'He *is*,' she said softly. 'A perfect gentleman. And, if only–'

'*See?*' bawled Jeanne, and sprang up at once to go to the mirror. 'You said it yourself, Patti,' she cried; 'he's *perfect*. And you're perfect too. You're probably in *love* with each other by now.'

Patti got up then and stood behind her at the mirror as Jeanne blotted away the runny makeup. 'Oh; *no*; Jeannie…. If I really wanted to fall in love with the guy you've been dreaming of, do you think I'd be in here trying to make you feel better about it?'

'I don't know,' Jeanne said, and ran water in the basin. 'I don't know anything. I'm probably just being stupid about the whole thing, and you're in here worrying about me when you should be out there having a good time.' She sniffled. 'Maybe I should just try to forget it all, and be happy for you.'

'Oh, Jeannie; but you don't really want it to turn out like that; do you?'

'I don't know. About all I know is that this whole weekend's been a big waste of mascara….' She sniffled again and then opened her handbag. 'I'm just very mixed-up right now; that's all. This whole place is so mixed-up…. Danny wants me to go steady already. I just know he's gonna ask me. But I don't know if I'm ready to go steady with him, or with anybody. And I'm afraid to tell him anything, because I'm so totally mixed-up….'

'Well; maybe I can help un-mix you.' Patti smiled. 'Look; going out with some guy, even if it's somebody like Jon Cavaliere, is not important enough to me if your feelings are going to be hurt over it. I've always thought our friendship goes beyond things like that.'

Jeanne thought about that. It was true; she had never known Patti to have ever hurt her feelings, and yet it could hardly be said that Patti lived her life in deference to anyone else's wishes. Honest and principled, she was perhaps the best influence Jeanne had; and Jeanne knew it. It was just that she had never expected to be rivalled by her own friends when it came to who would date Jon Cavaliere first, or at all. The thought was too disturbing to consider.

'We've shared too much,' Patti was saying, 'to let things like this get in the way. Like your going out with Danny. Whether I like him or not shouldn't matter. I won't judge you, Jeannie. I just want you to be happy. If you're really my friend, I have to care about you.'

'Oh, Patti; I know….'

'I just have to keep thinking that everything always turns out for the best in the end.'

Jeanne put back her head, sniffling up her tears. 'I know,' she said; 'because you're a believer in Fate.'

Patti smiled. 'Well; sometimes it seems like the one thing worth believing in, especially when everything else seems so mixed-up. What will be will be, you know.'

Jeanne wiped her face dry with a paper towel and looked at their combined reflection in the mirror. 'You really do want to go out with him; don't you?'

Patti smiled, refusing to remain maudlin. 'Maybe half of me does….' She giggled. 'I'm sure I won't tell you which half!'

'*Patti!*' Jeanne whirled on her.

Patti shrugged. 'Oh; really, Jeannie, I don't really. I swear I haven't even considered it. He's a nice guy, and all; but to be perfectly honest, I think you'd appreciate him more. He's more your type.'

Jeanne frowned and looked up to the mirror again. 'Oh; my "type".... What makes you say that?'

Patti smiled, eager to see Jeanne's spirit return. She could be very strong-willed when sufficiently encouraged. 'Oh; you know. He's a gentleman. He seats girls at table and opens the doors, you know....'

The notion gave no encouragement. '*So?*' Jeanne sniffled again. 'You like gentlemen *too.*'

'Yes, Jeannie; but there's something else about him. It's not something that's so easy to describe, you know. But the feeling I got was—'

'Patti....' Jeanne made a face. 'I thought you said you had only one dance with him.'

'Yes; I know; but.... You can tell so many things about a guy just from dancing with him. And the feeling I got was that, in a way, he doesn't need someone like me.'

'Oh; come on.... Why do you say that? It sounds to me like he's *exactly* your type.'

'I don't know,' Patti said, and wondered herself how she really knew for sure. But that feeling that this was all Fate's handiwork was still haunting her, reminding her that, no matter what would ever happen, she and Jon Cavaliere would never be more than just friends. And yet, there was the unmistakable and encouraging impression that they would most definitely become close friends at that. 'There's just something about him, Jeannie. There's an aura about him, you know, in the way that everyone has an aura about them, but his aura seems more like your aura.'

Jeanne could only respond to that with sarcasm. 'That's not an aura; it's just my period coming on.' She shrugged, as though no longer willing to discuss the subject. 'He's probably starting his period, too.'

Patti made a wry face. 'Jeannie.... It's not like that. It's not something that's physical. It's more like.... Something passionate. Something emotional. He needs someone who needs him, Jeannie. It's why he doesn't pick just any girl at all; he's too deep for that.' She drew a breath. 'I think he's lonely, Jeannie.'

'Lonely?' Jeanne asked; and they met eyes in the mirror. 'How could Jon Cavaliere be lonely?'

But then the whole significance of what Patti had said occurred to both of them at once; they even shivered together. 'He's emotionally alone, Jeannie,' Patti said softly, barely breathing the words. 'He needs someone who needs him back. Someone like you.'

Halfway back to the table he was collared by Bob Prescott who ushered him towards the gallery doors. 'Damn, man– was that *you* out there? What were you doin' dancin' with Patti Harper?'

Jon smiled, sucking on a piece of ice from his despatched drink. 'Man; I don't know. Musta been some zombie. The evening's a total fog.'

Bob laughed. His intentions were not going completely awry. 'Yeah, man; well; all I can say is– So… did you ask her out?'

Jon laughed at him. 'Ask her out? Shit– this whole damn vacation is over tomorrow, at about nine o'clock….'

'So?' Bob asked impatiently. 'You could take her out when we get back! Ever think of *that*?'

Jon shrugged. 'I don't know…. And so what about Cissie?'

'Cissie? Shit– you're not goin' out with *her*!'

Jon looked down, twirling the ice about in the glass with his finger. 'Well,' he said, lifting the glass; 'I was thinkin' about askin' her, you know….'

Bob felt his stomach jump then. *No*, he thought. That won't do at *all*…. 'Why do you wanna do somethin' like that?'

Jon shrugged and poured a bit of ice into his mouth from the glass, breaking it with his teeth. 'I don't know. It was just an idea, that I had.'

Bob thought for a second. Here was Jon avoiding a challenge, settling for an easier way out and for less than what he deserved. That could never be encouraged. But Bob would not trample on his best friend's feelings yet. 'Yeah; well; you shoulda seen the look on Patti Harper's face, man. I'm tellin' ya, dude, the babe is in *love*.'

Jon smiled then, pleased with the notion himself. 'Yeah; she did seem pretty cool about it, didn't she?'

Bob shook his head, brushing his hair back with one hand, and sighed in exasperation. 'Shit, man…. Don't you *get* it? Why the hell did you dance with somebody then, if you were only goin' to–'

'Shit, man; because you *told* me to! You've been on my case about this shit for the whole goddamn weekend! Just cut me some goddamn slack; will ya?'

'All right, man….'

'And by the way,' Jon told him, 'your "Summer Man" bullshit almost didn't cut it. As a matter of fact, I still seriously doubt that you didn't just make up the whole damn thing. So do me a favour, dude, and stop tryin' to fix me up with all these chicks; okay?'

The wound to Jon's pride had gone deeper than expected. 'Jon, man, I'm sorry; really. I was just tryin' to help–'

Jon sighed, calming himself. 'Yeah; I know, dude.' He reached out and boxed Bob's arm, very lightly. 'I'm sorry too. But I don't think that rushin' this stuff is ever good.'

Bob thought. So Jon was right, after all. All his friends knew he preferred to take his time when getting to know young ladies and, just maybe, there was nothing wrong about being prudent. Half the boys they knew were already concerning themselves with intense physical relationships and the preeminent birth-control concerns and subsequent anxieties, and they tended to judge people too hastily, using sexual prowess as the only standard worth measuring. Jon was only being characteristically sensible and old-fashioned. He was a gentleman above all else; and none could compare to his integrity. Right then Bob realised that any sensible, old-fashioned girl would be a fool to refuse him. And yet any other type of girl would never merit his attention.

They were both silent a long moment, standing there alone at the end of the gallery, looking not at each other but about at the panelling of the walls or down at the patterned carpet. Neither needed to speak to confirm that they were both thinking the same thing. Jon crunched on another piece of ice from the glass and then said abruptly, 'I'm goin' out for some air.'

Bob nodded. 'All right,' he said quietly; and Jon went up the gallery towards the stairwell.

Jon was hardly suffering from the drink; he was far too used to it by now. The concentration on his love life had embarrassed him. *Damn*, thought Bob; I shoulda known better. He's too sensitive about this kinda stuff; you can't force him. Now he's gonna be pissed at me; dammit…. He shook his head and brushed back his normally tidy hair, sadly regretting all the weekend's well-meant but misguided efforts. Damn, he thought. I should've known better.

After a minute Bob took his drink up the lobby to the windows and looked out at the floodlit main slope. Jon emerged from the doors a storey below, flinging the last bits of melting cocktail ice from his glass into a thin layer of evening snowfall. Bob sighed and watched him tromp out across the courtyard. A door opened in the lobby and he heard the footfalls of someone trotting away up the corridor towards the suites. Only unconsciously he turned and saw Patti Harper in her lovely cream-coloured sweater starting towards him. She stopped, awkwardly, gazing up the corridor in genuine devastation at having lost someone dear to her. For a moment he was too preoccupied over his own friend's situation to do anything but stand there stupidly and stare at her. Finally he took a sip of his drink. She heard the ice tinkling in the glass and looked over at him, a lost lamb utterly abandoned by hope. To Bob the sight of those green eyes gleaming with tears was utter torture. 'Hey… what is it?'

'Oh, Bob,' she whined, and spun about on her heels then, as though she should not have been seen weeping.

'Jeez—' The grave reaction had caught him completely unprepared and he rushed to her, putting an arm across her shoulders to escort her out of the centre of the lobby. 'Hey, hey; don't be so upset.... What *is* it?'

She sniffled and turned from him again, staring out the window at the snow. 'Oh, Bob, I just did something really stupid....'

'Hey,' he said, trying a little smile. 'It couldn't've been that stupid. You're not exactly a stupid girl.'

'No,' she acknowledged with a melancholy sigh; 'but, nevertheless, it was very stupid.'

He patted her shoulder and they sat on the wide cushioned bench of the window-seat, about eighteen inches apart. 'Come on.... Don't be upset. I'm sure it's not something that can't be mended, you know.'

She shook her head. That luscious strawberry-blond mane gave a buoyant bounce. 'No,' she said in a firm voice. 'I'm afraid it's exactly the opposite.'

Bob looked down then and took another sip of his cocktail. By now it was mostly ice. 'Well,' he said after a moment; 'if you want to talk about it....'

She turned half away from him, patting him softly on the shoulder. 'Oh, Bob....' With a sad sigh she stared out the window again. 'You are a good friend.... This may sound really strange to you; but you're just the person I needed to talk to tonight.'

Oh, thought Bob, and felt a little jump. Is it me, he worried; or is this babe moving a little fast, here?

'I did a really dumb thing,' she said bravely, 'and I think I might've hurt two people who didn't mean to be involved at all. The whole thing is really my fault.'

'What is?' he asked.

She shook her head. 'I danced with Jon, Bob. He came right up to me and asked me to dance. And I wanted to, you know; I really did want to....' She suppressed a shiver at that thought. 'He's a marvellous dancer; you can tell him that for me. I just don't think I should talk to him for a while now.'

Bob frowned. 'Why not?'

Patti held her chin high. 'Because,' she said in the same brave tone, 'for one brief moment there, I forgot all about *Jeannie*. She's such a dear, sweet girl, my best friend in all the world; and I'd never want to hurt her, you know; but I'm sure I just did.'

Bob shook his head, only half understanding. 'How did you hurt *her*?'

Only then did she acknowledge the tears, blotting her eyes with one finger, neither smudging the mascara nor getting much on her fingertip, and then turned to face him eye-to-eye. 'Because she thinks I want to go out with him.'

That did not answer his question. 'And you *don't*?'

'*No,*' said Patti, as though it should have been clear to anyone. 'Well;

whether I do or not isn't important. I *can't*. It'd be like I was taking him away from her.' She sniffled a little and made a bittersweet smile. 'She's got such a *crush* on him....'

A sudden shiver went down Bob's spine, something he did not expect and could not control. In the wink of an eye the entire situation had changed. '*Jeannie* has a crush on *Jon*–?'

'Why yes,' Patti said to him. 'Didn't you know that?'

He blinked, unable to believe what he was hearing. 'Patti... did you know Jon has a crush on *her?*'

She blinked too; it was exactly the same gesture right back at him. 'Are you *serious?*'

Bob made a smile then, as though they were teasing each other like small children who had known each other all their lives. Abruptly he got up, strode three paces away from her, turned and strode back to sit down again. 'Patti,' he said, 'I thought you girls all *knew* that.'

She shook her head. 'And you *didn't* know she was crazy about *him?*'

He laughed and then, suddenly, she did too. In that moment a great weight had been lifted off their shoulders; and the release of the laughter was wonderfully therapeutic. 'God,' Bob said aloud, to the ceiling; 'this is so bizarre....'

'*I'll* say.' Patti wiped her eyes again with her finger and gave a heartfelt sigh. 'I just can't believe that all they've ever had to do is–' She shook her head. 'How long has Jon–?'

'Like... all his life,' Bob told her with a sigh. 'Well; you know why he dove in to save her, that time at the lake?'

Patti smiled, remembering the incident of two-and-a-half years ago. 'Because she had a new bikini and got nervous worrying if he was looking at her.'

Bob smiled too. 'Well; yes; and because he saw her in trouble before the lifeguards did. He'd been looking at her for two years then.'

'In her new bikini,' Patti half-giggled.

'In her new bikini.' Bob laughed. 'Patti, I could tell you stories; stories no-one knows.... I *won't*– but I could. All I can say is... he's pretty much in love with her. That's why he doesn't date anyone else.'

'God,' Patti breathed; 'then it *is* true....' A chill shot down her back just then; her skin sprouted with goosepimples. She shivered visibly. 'Bob, you don't know how much that explains to me.'

'Well; it still doesn't explain much to me,' Bob said seriously. 'Like, who's that guy she's goin' out with?'

'Oh; that's nothing to worry about.' Patti shook her head and looked down at the carpet to hide the blush brought on by the fib. 'Well; she does date a lot, you know; she thinks people expect it of her. But I can tell you for sure her heart's not in it. Nothing ever really happens, you know. It's all just wicked rumour.'

'I know,' Bob smiled. 'Jon's the same way. He's very old-fashioned, and very moral. Whatever you've heard about him is probably not true.'

'Jeannie's very old-fashioned too!' Patti said, delighted to be hearing such news. 'My God! –it is so weird, to think of how much they might have in common....'

'Really,' Bob agreed; and they sat there and just looked at each other for a few long seconds. Suddenly Patti reached over and caught him round the back of the neck, pulling him closer and kissing him on the cheek. Bob let out a laugh. 'What was that?'

She blushed, only a little, and then giggled happily. 'I don't know. All at once, I feel very close to you.'

He smiled at her. 'We are a pair of really good friends, aren't we?'

'Yes,' she said; 'we certainly are.'

The stroll was good for both of them. Freed at last of the senseless stiffness they had known for so long, they chatted away about all manner of things and soon found they had much in common themselves. Patti was first to suggest a friendly partnership, two couples of close friends double-dating together; and though Bob flinched at the idea at first he had to admit he had already considered such an arrangement. He was, after all, a gentleman himself, and he appreciated Patti's ladylike reserve and maturity. Patti had taken a liking to him too, recognising his gallantry from the moment he had arrived on the snowmobile to rescue them in the woods; and this she told him, sipping decorously from a glass of iced claret and looking every inch the lady she really was. They talked about Jon saving Jeanne in the lake, and about The Strawberries' debut at the concert contest, and about cheerleading and Jon's car and Christine Polvere and Steve Marlowe. A great barrier between them had been lifted away for ever.

'I guess we could get them together,' Bob proposed. 'Drag them into the same room at the same time, go out and lock the door.' Patti giggled girlishly at that. 'Yeah; but really,' Bob smiled. 'Come back in a week, see if they're... expecting.'

Patti broke up into wonderful, gay laughter. 'Oh no they wouldn't be! Jeannie's just starting her period.'

'Oh,' said Bob, and got a little red. 'Well... you know what I mean.'

'Yes I do,' she said seriously; 'and I can't say I've never thought of it myself. Only I know how Jeannie would feel if she knew I was trying to force her into anything, even if it's what she really wants. She won't let anyone push her at all.'

'Jon said the same thing to me, just now. He hates it when people try to set him up. And they always do....'

'It is so weird,' Patti said excitedly, 'to see how alike they really are.... I'm a believer in Fate, you know. If it's made to happen, then it will, and there won't be a thing to stop it. But Jeannie's very stubborn. She has to think it's her own idea, or she simply won't do it.'

'Yeah; that's Jon too,' Bob mused.   He looked at her, as they
ascended the soft carpeted stairs to the skylight lounge. 'Do you really
think it's made to happen?'

Patti shrugged and took a wee sip of her wine.   'It has all the
hallmarks,' she said confidently.

Jon dove into the warm chlorinated water and let his body drift
slowly down to the bottom as he exhaled all his air. A swimming pool
was like a piano or billiard table to him; he could never avoid one for
too long. The swim was soothing to the soul as he cranked out stroke
over stroke with a musician's rhythm, keeping his eyes closed as much
as he could to block out what few lights he had switched on for himself.
He contemplated what the weekend at Snow Lodge had wrought: it
had been at least a partial success and more than a little disappointing.
But the financial costs had been covered, and the promise of work
would drown his other anxieties. In the next two weeks there would be
five club shows, two concerts at the Lion's Den and three private
Christmas parties to play, his gift shopping to finish and then at least
two holiday gatherings at which his presence would be expected. On
the 27th he and Dave would fly out to California for a visit with Mr
Holloway; and so whatever energy he had left would be sorely
depleted by the time school reconvened in January. Patient though he
was, Jon knew that only time would reveal to him what he wanted to
know; and he was growing weary of the wait.

* * *

Chapter 7

The minute you let her under your skin

The first weekend of January was productive, with the gathering at Dave's aunt's house and the conception of a new song. Dave had cautioned against moving too quickly into what they both termed the 'Sergeant Pepper' phase of songwriting, in which they would become quickly bored with the sound of just two guitars, bass and drums and start itching to get on with more complex passages and more involved arrangements that belonged more to the recording studio than to the stage. Jon agreed; he rather enjoyed writing within the confines of a simple four-piece outfit. It was after all their performing forte. 'This Dance' was a good one, though, something Jon knew his mother would love but relevant enough for that stereotyped 'fourteen-year-old girl' Bell kept reminding them was the core of the record-buying public. Jon liked songs like that, able to transcend boundaries and stand merely as music, and not Black music or feminist music or teenagers' music or whatever. Someday he would be paid well for writing music for the masses and retire into his nineties with the royalty cheques still coming in. That was his goal: a lifelong career writing music.

Writing music had taken a back seat to more political issues during the week at Palo Alto. Dave's father entertained them and fed them and showed them about the area; but whenever they thought they were getting close to the right people he was always reminding them to 'look good for this guy', and soon it became obvious to both of them that the road to meeting the right producer was a long and arduous one. Mr Holloway's friend John Corelli took them to a dance club where one of his acts was performing, and Dave and Jon saw a first-rate rock-and-roll band do all the progressive standards; but when it came to asking where The Strawberries, with their veritable reams of original material, would fit in, Corelli the producer seemed to put them off. Jon feared even Dave would fall in with the line of thinking that The Strawberries would need to endure half a decade or more on the club circuit before their own producer saw them fit to apply for a recording contract.

But on the flight home Dave had set those fears to rest. 'Well; it's obvious that's not our type of guy,' he told Jon; and they discussed the reasons why for two hours. Bell Howard would remain their manager; and they resolved to seek a contract through him for recording, and not merely performing, directly. 'It's only smart to exhaust the possibilities we have first,' Dave proposed. 'That way we'll never look back and regret not trying something with what we've had all along.'

'Right,' said Jon. 'And Corelli's only in it for his commissions. If we took a guy with that attitude now, we'd be six years in those stupid clubs waiting for *him* to make enough money to let us do a demo for somebody else. And *I* think we're ready to do one *now*, or, at least, damn near.'

'Well; so do I. We've got plenty of decent material that guy's never heard. I'm just sayin' that now's the primo time to start lookin' around.'

'Right,' Jon smiled.

* * *

He wandered through the empty galleries of the building with those notions battling themselves in his head. What if you *aren't* really that good, he kept asking himself. What if you really do have just this silly little band, full of guys who think they're hot shit, and all they are is—

Naah, he argued with that; that's all bullshit. This band *is* good. We haven't been working this hard all this time for nothing. And just like we've planned, everything's been coming together, all along, the right people, the right attitudes, the right material.... The concert contest, the promo stuff, the shows, the *fans*.... Yeah; we've got good fans, Jon thought gratefully. If not for the fans....

Yes; the fans, he thought. And one fan in particular.... So much for getting the new year off to a great start. This is the second day I've been back, killing time in this stupid building, hoping she'll need a ride home or something.... Frantically dreaming up some kinda casual greetings, and doo, like I'll even have the guts if I *do* see her. So much for resolutions....

He found himself outside the empty auditorium and shuffled inside, strolling without a care down the carpeted aisle towards the stage. No-one was about; but Jon knew somewhere inside that he had not come here to be sociable. He was not in a sociable mood at all. The old black grand piano beckoned him and he smiled as though greeting a childhood pet again after many years. He had played this piano hundreds of times, even composed tunes on it; but somehow the feeling he got now was not that anxiety or loneliness he had known on other occasions. For the first time in his life Jon thought he might truly know that rush of sentiment when a veteran performer returns to the stage of his first success.

He raised the lid silently and dropped himself on the bench. I should play a little something, he thought. All these good people who braved the snow should not be disappointed.... He smirked to himself and looked out at the eleven hundred empty seats in the still, darkened hall. Well; those of you who are still here....

He hit a few octaves. It was always surprising to find the oft-abused Baldwin grand was kept in such good playing condition. Almost at random, his hands fell upon a pretty E-flat-ninth. This of course resolved to an A-flat-major-sixth; and as he tried to think of something to play the stage lights came on with a resolute 'clack!'.

He blinked a little in the new light. Through the triangle under the open piano lid he saw Bob Prescott standing offstage, one hand still on the switches. The lights were adjusted a bit; Bob brought up only three spots to light up the whole centre-stage and then sat down on a chair just inside the tall maroon stage curtains. He crossed his legs, folded his arms and, still without a word, gestured for Jon to play.

Jon smiled, saying nothing either. Nonverbal communication had become more the norm than the exception between them anyway. He thought a second; and his hands came down on an F-major. All right, bro', he thought, playing a little introduction in that key; let's see what we've got for you today....

There was a song which had been running through his head since he had stepped off the aeroplane at LaGuardia; and in spite of that he had not played the record nor heard it on the radio once during the last several days. It was not something he ever usually played and sang, really; but the words were all there in his head, just as Paul McCartney had written them six or seven years ago. He took a good stage breath and began.

Recognising 'Hey Jude', Bob smiled, satisfied. He thought of all the times he and Jon had played all The Beatles' songs, with guitars up in someone's bedroom, from a book that would not stay open in the lap, to make sure they learned all the chords and all the words correctly or to create new guitar solos and vocal harmonies. After hundreds of hours of study time he and Jon had become the premier Beatles musical experts in the area, to the point of knowing in which key everything had been played, and who sang and played what on the records or on stage, and how the songs were written and by whom and for whom and under what circumstances and from whose inspiration. They were Beatles scholars of the highest calibre; and Bob had always enjoyed it immensely.

Jeanne closed her locker and started down the stairs. 'Hi, Jeannie!' Lynn Murray greeted her; and Jeanne replied with a wave and a pretty smile before Lynn disappeared into the upper corridor. She pushed open the main-level door, mostly by leaning on it, and looked out the corridor windows at the snow falling in the rear courtyard. And it's coming down *harder*, she complained, to no-one. And there's no-one left here to drive me home....

She sighed wearily and muscled the burden of books higher up on her arm.   Well, she thought; it serves me right for dilly-dallying around.   Maybe if I'd hurried, and not kept talking with Miss Douglass in the art room, I'd've caught Wayne or Dave or one of the boys on the team....   Maybe if Danny didn't have wrestling practice again....   Maybe if it wasn't snowing– Who can look forward to a one-mile walk in the snow? In the central lobby she shuffled past the first set of auditorium doors, hearing what sounded like a boy singing to piano accompaniment.   She had almost passed the centre-aisle doors also when curiosity made her stop just for a moment to peer in.

There was almost always something happening in the auditorium, especially during the break between 12.15, when the morning session ended, and the start of the afternoon session's homeroom period at 12.45.   Often the drama group would hold a dress rehearsal or the orchestra might go through a few pieces; but most of the time it was just some mildly-competent student who had found the piano free to poke out a melody full of mistakes.

But, thought Jeanne, this is not just some lame loser banging out mistakes.   She had learnt enough from her own childhood piano lessons to tell what did or did not sound pleasant. Most likely it was a pair of students practising for the February talent show. Curious as to who would attempt a too-iconic Beatles song, she stopped and stared into the darkened room to see.

He sat slightly hunched forwards on the bench, singing out clearly despite the empty house; she imagined he would rather have had a full audience.   However fallible his voice seemed now was due to an acoustically imperfect room, or maybe the lack of an amplified sound system; but she fancied it as his modesty, that trait of his which she had come to think was his most appealing one. With her gasp of surprise resolved into a sigh of satisfaction, she leaned a shoulder against the door frame to watch.

The lights changed, so subtly going from a green-blue to a pale blue-pink that at first Jeanne did not notice.   Apparently others were watching too, and she thought that maybe he was indeed practising for the talent competition. The notion was exciting, because she would have loved to see him play there; but this performance, as though for her and her alone, was beyond ecstasy for her. With each second that white spotlight looked more and more like his halo.

He had realised the presence of someone standing in the doorway, but he could hardly stop or disappoint his audience whether one or one thousand. Come on, he told himself; you're a professional now. One more high-school kid won't make a bit of difference. Where you're going, they'll never be able to put you down.

He changed to the F-seventh, diverting his attention back to his favourite part of the song, the second bridge, about the impetus one needs resting right on one's own shoulder. It was a comforting notion.

Perhaps he really did have what he needed after all.

The shadowed figure in the doorway was definitely that of a girl of average stature, holding what seemed like a large heavy coat before her. Light from the bright hallway beyond lit up her blond hair and, in a moment or two, reflected off her gold earrings and gold wire-framed glasses. His heart skipped then. All right, Jon told himself; calm down. Lots of blond chicks in this school wear gold-rimmed glasses.... It could be somebody totally new.

He swallowed and almost rushed through the last verse but pushed down the final F-major and looked up at Bob, feeling clever at having truncated the song down to its lyrical verses. But, instead of walking out onto the stage with a comment or two, Bob did a curious thing. He stood up, made a little bow, and waved a hand towards the centre aisle doors. Before the blonde in the doorway had even considered his presence, he had turned to leave.

Jon rose; his foot slid off the sustain pedal. He wanted desperately for Bob to stay just to relieve the pit growing in the bottom of his stomach. But, at the finality of the backstage door banging shut, his heart sank. In leaving Bob had made a statement louder than any words could have done. Jon would have to face his admirer alone.

Slowly he turned, raising his line of sight off the stage and up the carpet of the aisle, past the heavy lump of winter coat, and into her eyes.

She was staring straight back at him.

At once he looked down, realising it was his move, as though she were only waiting for him. It took intense concentration just to step off the stage but, even in his heavy shoes, he took the four-foot drop with barely a sound. Twenty yards was too long a walk, yet he would rather it had been twenty miles; at once he wished he were already there and that he would never arrive. His heart pounded. He took a few breaths, trying to make them sound like sighs of nonchalance. To feign a casual attitude he looked about, at the empty seats, at the stains in the carpet, at the scuff-marks on his shoes, all the while leaning on his hands in the back pockets of his jeans in that habitual slouch that no-one else could take too gravely.

As he neared, she straightened, forcing her neck back and her spine erect, hoping at least to look presentable with such an unflattering and cumbersome load before her. Ten feet from her he stopped. He seemed unwilling to be here, as though he had been put up to it; and she wanted to worry that maybe his heart was not in it at all and that she would be made the victim of some horrid joke. But trying in self-defence to keep her hopes from soaring would have been harder than stopping a locomotive from running her down. She was nearly bursting with the urge to say hello.

With the bare tinge of a smile he said, 'Well; uh, some performance;

huh?'

She was still much in shadow to him; but her smile was radiant. 'It was nice,' she said.

He stepped up the one last riser and they met eye-to-eye. She was more in the light now and he could see her better. She wore a very pretty light-blue woollen sweater and a thin gold necklace with a little cross charm on it. Her lips, done in very pale pink lip gloss, gleamed alluringly. Her spectacles had always looked like soft ovals to him because he never got to study her up close; but now he could see that the lenses were actually octagonal, with all those facets of the gold-coloured frames reflecting light. Behind them her long lashes were done in a soft dark-brown, after a whole session of school still separate and distinct. He remembered the last time he had seen her this near to him and recognised that same magical sparkle in her eyes now. That same word came back to him; and he felt a little shiver of awe come over him to consider it. *Gorgeous*, he thought. She's still gorgeous.

'You're very good,' she said to him.

He thought she seemed much more sure of herself than he felt. 'Aaah; well; I don't sing any better than anyone else. It'.s mostly just the echo loop, and the reverb, and the PA bein' so loud....'

She shrugged; it was painfully appealing to watch. 'Well; just now, it sounded just fine to *me*.'

He shifted his weight to one foot and looked past her, out to the central lobby. Some teacher walked by then. 'Well; that's one,' he said quietly.

'What?'

'I said that's one. Now I know of at least *one* person who thinks I may be talented, at least somewhat....'

'Oh,' she said, with an engaging lilt in her voice; 'come on.... You *know* everyone thinks you're a good singer. You and that band of yours brought down the house last spring.'

'Okay,' he said, with a little smile, not facing her; 'you're right. I *know* I'm the greatest. *Now* do you see why all us rock stars are humble?'

At that he looked her in the eye. She did not look away. His light sarcasm was amusing, as it always was; and she laughed a cute little laugh, right in front of him. There was some sensual sweetness about being so close to her, hearing her speak, seeing her eyes light up, that made him want to fall apart in laughter, giggling happily away for hours at the thrill of it all. Just being with her, alone, and talking like old friends was something that had been long overdue. There was so much he wanted to tell her about having looked forward to it for so long a time.

'You're not going to be in the talent show; are you?'

He looked at her again. 'Oh; uh, no; uh, *no*. No. With that?' He turned and looked back down at the piano on the stage as though he could see himself still playing down there. 'That wasn't very good. That wasn't nearly as smooth as it should have been.'

'Well *I* thought it sounded pretty good,' she said with a smile, and looked right at him.

He looked at her too but got a little nervous and lowered his eyes to the floor. 'Well; like I said, you're *one*.' He made a little laugh, very casually, as though he were thinking of an inside joke. 'And it's very nice of you to say so, and all; but I've come to be very critical. Like, well, as a piano player, I've come to accept the fact that I'm really just all show and no go. I jazz everything up, and slush over all the hard parts, and– well; like I can't play classical for– for *anything*. Only the stuff I've memorised, you know.... I guess I never shoulda stopped takin' lessons.'

'Yes,' said Jeanne; 'but you'd *win* that talent show; I just *know* you would. You could play it just like you did just now.'

'Well,' he said, praying almost aloud that he might avoid blushing; 'I don't think they'd let me in, you know. I'm not exactly amateur any more.'

'Oh....' She considered the point; it impressed her. 'Oh; yeah; wow....'

Jon shrugged. 'I'm gonna go anyway, you know, just to get a grip on the other people. I always get a kick outa those shows.' It was on the tip of his tongue to ask, 'you wanna go with me,' but it seemed ridiculous, with the event fully five weeks away. Too much could happen in five weeks.

An uncomfortable moment of silence followed. 'Well,' she said abruptly, unintentionally sounding quite confident; 'what *I* always liked was that song you did at the concert contest. The one to break the tie. I can never remember the name of it....'

Jon smiled at the thought, relishing the memory. ' "And I Love Her",' he said slowly.

Jeanne looked at him then but suddenly turned away. '*That's* the one. You don't really play it any more.'

'Yeah; well; it's not exactly a concert song, you know. We mostly did it as a goof, like, to trick the judges again. They musta all thought we were pretty raunchy, after....' He shrugged, as though without an opinion either way. 'I guess people like to have their ears destroyed. Soft songs rarely cut it, except to relieve the volume, you know.'

'Well,' she said, shifting her weight; 'not everybody wants their ears destroyed. Some of us– Well; somebody, I think Debbie, said it was her favourite song. That, and "Lovely".'

Jon smiled. 'Yeah; I think I remember hearing that more than once....'

'Everyone liked you at that contest,' she said, of the band. 'I guess–
well; I guess that's why you won.' She giggled a little.

'I guess....' Somehow he did not feel so nervous now. 'Well; like I
said in class that time, it was all just a big trick to sway the judges onto
our side. We don't play that way any more just because we don't have
to, you know.   It's like the whole game is to just manipulate the
audience....'

'Yeah,' Jeanne agreed, and thought, *Spellbinder*. He binds them into
a spell– 'Well; I guess it worked....'

They both stood there, restraining their joy, trying not to look as
though they were looking at each other. He was still hunched forwards
at the shoulders with his hands in his back pockets, kicking at the
carpet with his heel, whilst she held her coat and books at arms'-length
down in front of her, watching his heel strike the carpet over and over.
She was not put-off by his habit of looking down or looking a little
past her even as he spoke to her. In his shyness he seemed to regard
speaking to her face-to-face as a rare honour to be known by only a
fortunate few. Perhaps, in his own way, he had more respect for her
than all the boys at the basketball games put together.

In fact he was intimidated by the way she seemed perfectly at-ease
with him, as though talking with boys who were crazy about her were
an everyday occurrence. He thought then that maybe it was; everyone
was crazy about her.   Her little half-giggles and the moist crispness
with which she pronounced certain consonants and that magical
sparkle in her blue-grey eyes, since he had not seen her this close in so
long he had forgotten their actual colour, were all hypnotic to him, and
not in the way that they would have been attractive to anyone else.
They were beautiful to him just because they were hers.

'Well,' he said, looking about; 'you're not waiting for anybody, are
you?'

The question surprised her as much as it pleased her. 'Uh– *No*,' she
said, hoping to sound definite without sounding too much so.

'All right,' he said, as though unconcerned. 'So; uh....   Oh; hey;
wait; I gotta go catch these lights. It'll just take a minute–' He turned
at once and shuffled down towards the stage again, taking the first
pairs of steps in short skips, still with his hands wedged into his back
pockets.

Jeanne shrugged herself away from the wall and followed him down,
a bit stiffly. Wow, she thought; this is really unbelievable! It's just as if
he's known me for years! And I'm just so nervous....   Well; it really
shouldn't be so strange; should it? He *has* known me for years. And
maybe he's nervous too.   And maybe there's nothing to be nervous
about.

He vaulted nimbly up onto the stage, noticing almost immediately
that only the white lamp directed at the piano keyboard itself was still

lit. The blue and red ones were now out. He mumbled to himself, sarcastically, assuming no other likelihood than that the lamps or their circuits had expired; they were, after all, not meant to be left on for more than a few minutes at a time. 'Jeez; the junk in this place....'

She stopped below the foot of the stage, staring up at him. 'I'm sorry; what did you say?'

Looking down he met her eyes for half a second, and a sudden shiver went down his spine. There was another possibility for why the lights were out, and as he realised it he felt his face go bright-red. 'I... don't know,' he said quietly; for he had truly forgotten.

She made a cute little laugh. 'So; play something for me.'

'Yeah; right,' he replied glibly, because it was his first reaction; but then slid himself over onto the piano bench. Surely this would be a much more comfortable venue for a conversation with her anyway. 'So okay,' he said; 'what would you like to hear?'

She gave a shrug, a delightfully coy gesture for her. Inside she was thrilled that he would actually consider playing piano for her alone, even in jest, and then realised that it was her rare streak of boldness reaping its due. 'I don't care,' she said happily. 'Something you like. What's your favourite song?'

'*My* favourite song?' He made a half-laugh at the notion. 'All right; my favourite song of all time. You can play like "Name That Tune".'

'Okay,' Jeanne agreed, with an elated giggle.

'Okay,' he said, mostly to himself, and was playing, accenting the melody with his right fingers when it was not contained within powerful, even anthemic chords, slowly, forcefully, as though building momentum for an epic emotional journey.

The song sounded only vaguely familiar to Jeanne. She looked about the empty hall and felt very pampered that the school's favourite entertainer would perform only for her, even on demand. The thought excited her still more. 'Does your band play this song?' she asked.

'This song? Naah. It's an orchestra song.'

'I'm afraid I can't guess,' she confessed, although she knew she had not really tried.

'Aaah,' he moaned, and stopped. 'My favourite song; and she cannot even guess. Now I *know* I need lessons.... Naah; that was *supposed* to be "The Long And Winding Road"; you know, McCartney, 'Sixty-Eight. His ode to Jane Asher, after they broke up. Not intended for an album till 'Sixty-Nine, which was "Get Back", which of course wasn't released till 'Seventy, as "Let It Be". Actually the album was never formally finished. The Beatles went into lawsuits and Phil Spector ended up finishing it, including his "wall-of-sound" strings on "Long And Winding Road" which McCartney said he personally hated. Personally I happen to like them.'

She smiled. 'You sound like you know a lot about The Beatles,' she observed.

'Oh, yeah; well; music does that to ya.' He smiled at her, playing on at something else. 'Actually, I've been reading a really good book about all that stuff, so….'

She could well imagine him speed-reading through volumes on subjects that interested him. 'What song is that, that you're playing now? Does your group play this one?'

'Naah,' he said, 'well; we did do it a few times….' With his right hand he played the horn solo to "For No One". 'I'll tell ya, though, we never really play enough of what *I* like to play….' He stopped with the solo. 'Stuff like "In My Life", and "I'm Only Sleeping", that's what I like to do. I like doing material no-one thinks we'd have the guts to do, that we don't have enough instruments for, so it kind of challenges you to arrange it in some new way. That's the real fun in this kinda stuff.'

She smiled to consider that. It would be like him to accept more of a challenge than would other people. She thought of all the times she had seen him playing billiards or skiing or riding snowmobiles or driving his car or swimming in competition; and always there was some kind of prize involved, or some risk to life and limb; and always he was winning and coming out alive and ahead. He was not one to play by the rules of the common man and, although most of the people Jeanne knew were, it excited her to think of knowing someone like Jon, because he was not. She had never known anyone like him before.

'So why do you play so many Beatles songs? Or, why do The Strawberries play them?'

Jon smiled; he liked the question. 'Well; you know, in everything there is a kind of growing-up process. In music, it pretty much starts with The Beatles. Everyone starts with The Beatles, except that in the three years we've been together, we've never left them.'

'Your band has been together three years?' she asked in amazement.

'Oh; yeah.' He was playing something else now, in the key of E. 'We got together on New Year's Eve, Nineteen-Seventy-One. It was all Chris Santana's idea.' He laughed at the memory. 'Before midnight me and Bob and Ricky and Dave had formed a band; and so at twelve o'clock we played "Birthday" for Chris. His birthday is New Year's Day, you know.'

'I never knew that,' she said, relishing the opportunity to hear the history of the township's most beloved rock band from her favourite member, who at the same time was still serenading her with instrumental Beatles songs on the piano.

'Yeah; "Birthday" is the first song we ever rehearsed and played together as a band.'

'Wow....' Jeanne smiled, pleased and grateful to have that piece of trivia. 'How many songs have you written? You've written quite a few....'

'Oh; not many, or, you know, not many good ones.... Me and Dave, though, we actually do write together. Unlike the majority of tunes from that other infamous duo, John and Paul.' He smiled; and she did too. Gone now was that horribly forbidding feeling of awkwardness and anxiety. They were just there together talking. Suddenly the last four years seemed very silly to both of them.

He made a mistake in "She's Leaving Home" and stopped. 'Aaah....' He turned on the bench and looked down at her, where she leaned on her stack of books at the edge of the stage. She would not take her eyes from him. 'So; well; do you have like a ride home?'

She lifted her chin off her hands. 'Oh; well... *no*. I was going to call–'

'Naah,' he said offhandedly; 'please don't call.' He struck an E-flat chord and began the easily-recognisable introduction to Taupin-and-John's 'Your Song'. Once he glanced down and saw her eyes, staring straight up at him with her chin on her hands, and immediately blushed to recall that he had only ever learnt 'Your Song', back in eighth grade, because it reminded him of her. The lyric about forgetting whether her eyes were green or blue seemed a bit too real now; considering he might never again forget her eyes' colour made him make an unconsciously deliberate mistake in the fingering and he stopped. 'Aaah; Elton John I *ain't*. This must be getting boring.'

'It's not boring!' she insisted, raising her head as he stood up. 'I like listening to you play. And, if you can do it, *do* it.'

He scoffed at that and turned from her to draw closed the keyboard lid, blushing again to realise that what she had just said to him had been first told to her on a bright spring day almost four years ago, upon the banana-seat saddle of a chopper bicycle at the shopping arcade, and that it had been his own philosophy. She had never forgotten; and he was both touched and embarrassed by her memory and sentimentality. 'Uh, yeah; well; let me go get these lights.'

'Okay,' she said, disappointed that they would be separated even for a minute. He strode round the piano and crossed the stage, his high-heeled footfalls resounding in the stillness of the auditorium even after he had passed the curtains into the wings. Only the switch for the single white lamp needed to be put over; the others were, without exception, safely in their *off* positions. He shrugged, more excited by the dizzyingly realistic prospect of driving Jeanne Banfield home than concerned with how the lights might have been put out whilst they were talking up the aisle, and thought only to hurry back lest she disappear.

But she was still there, waiting in the dark. Just as he emerged from between the curtains she had a thought for what he might be like alone with a girl in a dimly-lit room. Light from the open lobby doors did not carry well down front; and Jon tripped his foot on a stray fibreglass chair standing by the edge of the stage. The chair tumbled four feet to the carpet, and Jon lost a bit of composure; but right then Jeanne was able to see him for what he was. Jon Cavaliere, precocious pupil, hot-rod racer and rock-and-roll singer, was only as human as the next earnest yet humble young gentleman in the company of a popular girl.

'Stupid chair,' he cursed it, and hopped casually off the stage, landing unruffled before her. 'So; did you say you could use a ride home? I could drive you, you know, if there's no-one else—'

'Oh; well; *yes*, um…. That's very nice of you to offer.'

He suppressed a shiver that he had actually secured an opportunity to be alone with her. 'Yeah; well; while I'm wastin' gas….'

They walked up the centre aisle, Jon deferentially keeping half a step behind her shoulder, and blinked in the bright light of the central gallery. 'Well,' Jeanne said with a little smile, looking back at him; 'thank you for the private concert….'

'Aaah….' He waved his hand to dismiss that. 'Some concert….'

She enjoyed seeing him so sincerely modest and shy. Until now she might never have known such qualities were possessed by popular young men. 'So… can I ask you a silly question?'

'What's that?'

'Well— How do I put this…. Well; how come you were in there, you know, after school, when it's snowing, and no-one's around…. I mean: I would've thought you hated this place.'

He shrugged, trying to appear cool when he knew inside he could never tell her the real reason. 'Oh; I don't know…. I guess it does seem a little stupid—'

'No; not *stupid*, but—'

'—but when there's me and a piano in a room, the two are just drawn together, by this odd magnetic force…. It's a law of physics.'

As he said this, inadvertently, they both remembered their first meeting in that physical-science class, when she had been a cute little seventh-grader, new to junior-high school, and he had been a bright eighth-grader who could convince everyone he knew it all. All either of them had gained by the end of the semester was a deeply-rooted attraction for each other, one with the power to direct all their dreams and even commandeer their courage; for it had lasted almost four full years in a state of unrequited remission. The silence their remembering left was uncomfortable; and they were haunted by those terrible silences when they had passed in the galleries, even yesterday or a week ago. Now, they both felt sure that, at the very least, that much awkwardness would remain in the past.

'Hey,' Jon said brightly, rapping the stack of books in her arm with the back of his hand; 'so how come you're takin' so many books home? All these girls, man; they carry half the Metropolitan Library around with 'em all the time.'

She smiled, with a little blush. 'Well; I have a lot of homework and stuff to do, you know—'

'Man; I don't have *any*— that I'm gonna *do*. Here; let me take this.' He stopped in the centre of the gallery and lifted the heavy pile of textbooks from her arm. 'You shouldn't have to....'

Jeanne's face went beet-red. If anyone had told her yesterday that Jon Cavaliere would be carrying her books and seeing her home from school this week, she would have dismissed the poor clairvoyant as a worthless cretin. But he seemed to think nothing much of it, as though there were never question of his allowing any girl to carry her own books. She was touched by that. At the glass doors by the boys' gymnasium she hefted up her varsity coat and began to put it on. Jon was even able to assist her with his free hand. 'Well,' she teased, shifting her handbag to her other shoulder; 'how you're able to go through school without doing homework *I'll* never know.'

'Yes,' he said with a sly smile; 'but I've been working on it since about eighth or ninth grade. See the thing is: you just bluff it. I either do it right before class, or sometimes I just get out of having to do it altogether. Prescott says I probably put more effort into avoiding the homework than the homework actually requires; but I've been doing it like this for too long to change now, especially with only five months left. And so much of it is irrelevant anyway. It's like what I tell the teachers, "There are more things in heaven and earth than are dreamt of in your trigonometry, Mr Kantarski".'

Jeanne laughed. He opened the door for her and they stepped out into the light snow. It was landing on the pavement like mere rain but would soon freeze there. 'Well,' she asked him; 'so what *do* you do, when you're not in school?' But even as she said this, she thought it a terribly bold question; for she knew what she hoped to gain from it. Over the last six weeks, since those rides in Jon's car with Steve, or maybe since Patti's declarations during the ski trip, something had been making her very uncharacteristically bold. She was doing and saying things that made her red in the face as soon as she did them; but afterwards she had been quite pleased with the results.

'Practise, man,' drawled Jon, as though to convey that stereotype of the haggard jazz performer, 'practise.' He smiled. 'Every waking hour I have right now, I'm either singing or playing or writing or sitting at meetings with people.... I barely have time to sleep, usually. The band is really taking up all of my time.'

Jeanne thought that if he were not exaggerating it did answer the question she had been pondering since the ski trip, when she had noticed that the girl Christine had not attended. But she realised that it might also mean he would have no time for anyone else, either. Already she felt certain there could be nothing ordinary about his life, or what he might be able to share of it, after all. Any of his attention would be something of an honour, then. He really would have time for only one special someone. And the rumour mill had been saying that, for now, he had no-one special at all. The possibilities in her imagination gave her shivers.

She sighed, to appear calm, but upon stopping beside the right side of that magnificent silver car she was fully trembling with excitement. He unlocked the door for her and she seated herself, taking pains to appear extra ladylike. Gently he lowered the books into her lap and she took them with a demure smile. 'Thank you,' she said in a soft tone.

'Good,' he said. 'I guess that was kinda stupid.'

'Stupid? What was—?'

'Naah; it was stupid.' He closed the door for her and went round to the other side.

She watched him put the key into the ignition switch. 'What was stupid?'

The starter ground coldly. He adjusted the choke knob. 'Oh; you know. Carryin' the stupid books.'

She smiled, flattered and even amused. 'Why do you think it was stupid?'

'Because it *was*.' The engine caught and he ran it up to idle at about fifteen hundred. 'Come on; it's embarrassing. I'm sorry.'

Jeanne felt her face going red. For the moment, his eyes were fixed on the tachometer. 'Well; it shouldn't be embarrassing. It happened to be a very nice thing to do. I do get tired of lugging these heavy things around, you know; and it was very thoughtful of you to offer to help. I was going to tell you I appreciate it.'

Jon blushed a little, turning from her to wipe condensation from the side window. It was hard to accept how comfortable Jeanne seemed here whilst he still felt like a twelve-year-old on a first date. The thought was more than a little disconcerting.

The snow was still only light; and the windscreen was clear with a pass or two of the wipers. Jon looked out his side window for traffic and reversed out of the parking slot. 'Dag; there's still a mob out here,' he said, just for something to say. 'Way too many cars at this school.'

'Don't blame me,' she smiled. 'I walk here.'

'That's right; *you're* sixteen. Got your licence yet?'

'Yes,' she said proudly; 'I got it last month.'

'Fun, fun, fun,' he teased.

'Oh,' she said; 'and already I've been stopped by a *cop*. Right before Christmas, this was. Can you *believe* it? He said I ran a "Stop" sign.

The stupid thing was hidden behind a *tree*. How do they expect you to *see* it?'

'I bet I know the corner,' Jon said. 'Over your way, there; Tyrol Street, at Slowham. Prescott just jacked up his car over there, day after Christmas.'

'*Wow*,' said Jeanne; '*that's* the one, yeah....'

'Yeah; and so the day me and Holloway come back from Palo Alto, he comes over the garage, sayin' we gotta fix it for him. Said he never saw the sign, and went to go right there, like you go up towards Bucky's Tavern; and some guy came up from behind and sideswiped him. Everybody thinks you just pull out and merge into your own lane, like, but you don't. And so they hide the "Stop" sign behind a pine tree. Brilliant, when you come to think of it.'

'I think it's pretty *dumb*, if you ask me,' said Jeanne.

'Yeah; well; only if the guy who put up the sign *doesn't* run a body shop.'

Jeanne laughed. 'Oh; wow, yeah; *that* would be weird....'

They had come to the gate at the end of the driveway and the uniformed traffic warden held up her hand for Jon to stop. '*Here's* your traffic problem,' he said seriously. 'This dumb woman here, holdin' everybody up so some dope addict can stagger across the Parkway in the middle of the block....' He thought then that he could easily go on for hours about his pet peeves and decided to best spare Jeanne the boredom. 'And so here *I* go, complaining to the nice young lady about traffic....'

She giggled a little. 'So? Talk about something else?'

He thought a moment and then drew a breath. 'All right. We'll talk about you.'

She felt a sudden nervous shiver then. '*Me?*'

'Yes; well; so much for cars, and me, and The Beatles.... You might like The Beatles; huh?'

She shrugged. 'I might? I guess. Why?'

'Well....' He swallowed. 'There's a special showing of some Beatles movies at the Stage Door; and if you'd like to, you know, I was gonna go, so...'

Suddenly her heart was pounding in her chest at the thought that he would actually suggest a date to her. 'When?' she asked, at the verge of losing her composure.

'Well,' he said carefully, with every effort to appear nonchalant; 'only this week.' Already he was expecting to hear her turn him down. 'I thought, maybe Thursday.... Well; if you're not busy, you know, well... we could go. I mean I have to go anyway; but....'

She made a smile then and stared straight ahead at the dashboard. As though from someone much more decisive she heard her own voice articulate the greatest understatement she had ever conceived. 'Well;

sure, Jon. I would love to.'

He smiled then too; and at that moment they were both aware that they had made each other happy. 'Cool,' he said casually, though he felt charged with adrenaline as though flying an aeroplane for the first time all over again. 'Well; if you want, you know, I know of this little place, just up the street; and well, if you wanted to go out a little earlier, you know, maybe we could get something to eat, like, sort of for dinner…. It's just a little place, you know, not that great, or anything; nobody really goes there.'

'Oh,' she said sweetly; 'that'd be nice.'

Nice, thought Jon. She says it'd be *nice*. Wouldn't it be nice….

'So,' she asked brightly, as though eager to change the subject; 'is your whole family as musical as you? Like, your brother is, sort of; isn't he? I mean: I know your sister is in choir….'

He looked at her for a second and smiled a little in relief. Indeed he would definitely feel more comfortable answering questions about his own life than attempting to engage her for a date to a film, especially when it was now no longer an issue. 'Well,' he said with a shrug; 'yeah; I guess he is, in a way. Like, he's been takin' up guitar, you know, some of the stuff me and Bob have shown him, and then my little sister plays drums, and my mom and Beth both play piano, a little…. My *dad*, though, he's pretty good. I play jazz like real rigid, like it was clockwork; I guess 'cause I had lessons on stuff like Bach, you know, but he plays really loose, like, really… *Black*. Like Errol Garner, Teddy Wilson, all those kinda guys. I've listened to them too, to try and learn that style; but, as far as jazz goes, I'll never be as good as my dad. I'll only ever be able to imitate him, or *look* like I'm imitatin' him. Like, that time at the lodge, you know, that night, well, that was really just me imitating the old man.'

'That was so much fun,' Jeanne said, smiling to recall it. 'Everyone loved having you play that night. And like the way Mark sang? People talked about it all weekend.'

Jon smiled a little. It had been a memorable evening for him as well. 'Yeah; well; you should hear my dad play some time.'

She smiled, considering that, in light of recent developments, such coveted opportunities might yet come to pass. 'Did you ever think of going to college for music?' she asked. 'I bet you could do really well—'

'No way,' he told her, and then smiled. 'I'm not that good, really; and anyway I have other plans.'

She did remember what he had said in Composition last spring and how much he was said to despise structured education, most especially that which was compulsory under the law. She had even heard teachers refer to him as 'an exception to the rule' when it came to normal high-school learning ability. 'Well,' she said, firmly inclined to agree; '*I* think you're a good musician. Everyone says The

Strawberries are very talented. Like, they say Bob Prescott is the best guitar player in school.'

'Oh; because he *is*,' Jon said seriously, and was silent a moment as he calculated Bob's contribution to his present situation. 'He's the best guitar player I've ever known. Far better than Barry or Doug…. He's the one who got me to learn bass. He's very dedicated, you know.'

'How long has he been taking lessons?' Jeanne asked, as she might normally have been impressed by such statistics.

'Oh; I don't know…. I think he quit the summer before we played at the Hill, so that's, uh…. I guess he was takin' lessons about five years then.'

'And he doesn't take them any more?' She was mildly surprised.

'Oh; no. No; they conflicted with the schedule. Also, you know, for people like him, regular lessons are a pain in the neck. All you do is pay the teacher to sit with you, while you play some inane passage over and over again…. The best way to learn anything is just to *do* it, and not worry so much about the damn theory all the time. The problem with too many guys is that they constantly try to apply everything to theory, and they haven't *played* enough to really know what they're talkin' about. The theory comes naturally, man; as you learn to play you figure it out. It might be frustrating at first; but really anybody with half a brain could figure out the stuff. If you're gonna give up before you even try, you weren't gonna last very long at it anyway.' He realised he had gone off on a tangent and his face went red. 'Sorry,' he apologised, in a softer tone. 'I was beginning to preach.'

But Jeanne was just sitting there staring at him, thrilled to behold the mental processes of a largely self-taught hyperintelligent intellect. He was so thoroughly unlike anyone she had ever known that, attractive or not, she might have listened to him go on for hours. 'No,' she said; 'don't be sorry. It's a very interesting point.'

'It's boring,' he said.

Maybe to anyone else, she thought, who didn't appreciate you, it might be…. 'It *isn't* boring,' she said sincerely. 'It's just so different from what most people think. But I know what you mean: there are lots of guys who just try to impress you with trivial stuff that really doesn't matter. And it's like all academic. It's just refreshing to hear when someone's actually… earned his abilities, you know.'

'Yeah; well….' He tried not to blush, but thought, *damn–* the babe is actually paying attention…. 'I guess I'm not like most guys, you know. I come from a weird family.'

She laughed, having no doubt of at least the first part of that. 'Like how weird?'

'Pretty weird,' he smiled.

'Well,' she said, still willing to compliment him; 'I just think that you and The Strawberries will go really far some day.'

He smiled at her optimism. 'Yeah; well; when we do, you and your friend Debbie there can have the first copies of the record.'

'Hey; now I'll hold you to that.' Jeanne laughed, and he did too. It felt wonderful being together and, though they were both still worried about saying the wrong thing, there was a very welcome warmth about being in each other's company. The last ten minutes of their lives had been all they had anticipated for a seemingly endless time. Now, all that nervous shyness would be gone for ever.

Jon steered right at Apple Way and they started up into the Old Mill neighbourhood. Both were quiet as they neared her house. Jeanne was just about to point it out to him, as she had always done for new dates, but she remembered Jon had already driven her home several times. It was just one more thing about this new experience that had thrown her off-guard. In Old Mill Road he changed down early and swung the car round in the intersection of Cherry Lane to draw up with the near side to the kerb in front of 119. 'So,' he said then; 'you really think it would be okay, then, on Thursday?'

'Oh; yes,' she said to him; 'well; I don't see why not. I really ought to check, you know, but like I'm pretty sure.'

'Well; you know, it could be like something to eat first, too, so…. If you like.'

'Okay,' she said happily. 'That'd be nice.' She was glad that it meant so much to him; he was very charming when he was sincere, especially since in his slightly-unpolished way he was only revealing his earnest intention to merit her interest. She loved to see such gracious, gentlemanly aspirations in a young man.

'Good,' he said, and smiled at her for a brave second. 'Oh; uh, wait.' And he got out of the car. Before she had realised what he would do he had come round to open the door for her. 'There you go.'

She beamed, ecstatic to behold such chivalry, and lifted the books off her lap. He took her hand to help her rise; and as she tried to avoid the puddle of slush at the kerb the feeling of his fingers folded round hers made her knees go weak. At that she blushed bright-red and had to look down. 'Oh; thank you,' she said feebly; and their hands separated.

'Okay,' he said, as though it should have gone without mention. Perhaps he did not realise how rare such courtly gestures were these days. 'Oh; and so if you want, on Thursday, I could give you a ride home, you know; so…. If you like.'

'Oh,' she said, and looked him right in the eye then; 'that's so nice…. I mean: I had meant to tell you it was very nice of you; it does get hard relying on friends with cars, especially in this weather….' She made a little giggle then.

'Yeah,' he said, looking up and about at the sky; 'well; it sure isn't what I'd choose for winter….' Actually the snow had become no heavier and it was not at all unpleasant to be standing outside amidst the mild flurrying. Given the present company he might not have gone cold for hours. 'Okay; so, if you want a ride, you know, on Thursday, just meet me by those doors there, by the gym.... I always go out that way, you know; well; most of the time....'

'All right. I appreciate it, really.' She smiled at him.

'Okay,' he said, right to her, though more to himself out of delight that she had in fact accepted the date with him. 'So; well; then; I'll see you on Thursday.'

'Yes,' she said, lightheaded to realise she was actually telling him that.

'And you'll know, for sure, about the movie, and all?'

'Oh, yes; sure. And dinner, too....' She made another little giggle, sounding much more confident than she really felt. 'Sure. I'll be looking forward to it.'

'Cool,' he said, and smiled a little. 'I'll uh, see you later, then.'

'Okay,' Jeanne smiled, and started with her books up the front walk carpeted with almost an inch of fresh snow. In open-toed shoes it was no joy; but fortunately the platform soles kept her stockinged feet dry. 'Bye-bye,' she said, looking over her shoulder at him.

'Bye,' said Jon, and watched her walk away. Get the hell out of here, he told himself; you're making yourself into a jerk. He went round to the other side of the idling Caprice then, stopping with the door open to see that she had made it to her porch. At the bright-red front door she turned, and he smiled and returned the wave as she went inside.

When he had shut himself inside the car, he could not resist rubbing his hands together in adolescent glee. 'Hot *damn*!' he cheered, under his breath, as if to reveal his joy aloud would spoil everything.

Jeanne called hello to her mother in the kitchen, dropped her books on the chair by the foyer and bounded straight up stairs to the phone in her parents' room. Patti answered her bedroom line.

–'Hello?'

'Hi, Patti,' she said calmly; 'it's me. Well– I take it you got home okay?'

–'Oh; Marty gave us all a ride. There were like six of us in his car, and you know it's not that big....' She giggled. 'So you didn't have to *walk*; did you?'

'Oh; *no*–'

–'Well; good. I'm sorry; but Marty didn't even want to wait for us. He hates driving in the snow. He kept saying, "oh, Harris will get her", but I know he felt guilty....'

'Patti,' Jeanne sang happily, 'Danny wasn't even *in* school today. And he *didn't* drive me home.'

–'What? Somebody new? Jeannie, how many times must we tell you! You're–'

'Oh, Patti, you have to *guess*. Without Steve, without anybody else....'

–'Oh my God! –Jeannie, you can't *mean*–'

'Oooo, Patti,' she squealed; 'you wouldn't *believe* it....'

–'Eeek!' Patti shrieked. 'You've got to *tell* me!'

Jeanne shivered all over and fell back on her mother's bed. 'Oh, Patti, when I tell you it was just like a dream, you just couldn't *believe* it! I saw him in the auditorium, and he was playing the piano, all by himself, like; and then he just came up to me, and like we talked.... I told him how nice his playing was; and it just kept *going*. And so then, he takes me down to the stage, and like starts playing the piano for me, just for me, just a little; and you know, he's so talented; and then he just comes right out and asks me if I needed a ride *home*. Oh; and so Patti, you'll never guess what *happened*!'

Patti held her breath.

'He asked me *out*, Patti! Can you believe it? We're going to dinner and then the movies!'

–'Oh, Jeannie, how *fantastic*! The grand prize!'

'Oh, Patti....' Jeanne closed her eyes and sighed dreamily. 'I can't even believe it myself. It's just like a dream, that I can't believe is true....'

–'Oh, Jeannie, I'm really excited for you. You just wait and see. Wonderful things are going to happen. I just know they are.'

'Oh; I hope so,' Jeanne sighed. 'But I did tell him I would check first, you know, and let him know for sure on Thursday....'

–'Jeannie, what do you have to *check* for? Just *go*! Get it while the getting is good!'

'Oh, Patti; but what I was thinking was– Well; like what about Danny?'

–'Danny? Danny Harris? You're not seeing him every *night*, Jeannie.'

'No; I know; but I thought–'

–'Jeannie, after all that's happened, I would call that foxy guy up right now and tell him you can't *wait* to see him. Like I said: grab him while you've got the chance. I don't think he'll like you playing hard-to-get.'

Jeanne laughed. 'Get it while the getting is good; huh?'

–'Hey; you're the luckiest kid I know right now!'

She smiled; and then an excited chill ran down her spine and tingled her all over. 'Oooo; and Patti, you wouldn't believe how *sweet* he is. He carries my books– can you *believe* it? –and opens all the doors, and takes my hand to help me out of the car....'

–'All right, Jeannie; but just don't rub it in; okay?'

They both laughed.

* * *

Jon did not attend school on Wednesday. Past the age of eighteen and thus permitted to write his own absence excuses for school, he went along with Dave and Bell for a series of meetings, first with their solicitor in Chester and then to New York with a collection of recorded Strawberries shows in the hope of enlisting a few agents' interest. In all it was only tedious, putting on smiles, enduring disappointing responses and trying, as Bell had urged them, to look 'artsy' and not too sensible though he knew that ran counter to their real nature. Supposedly the artiste-and-repertoire people were intimidated by too businesslike an approach; and the two young men both tended to be very conservative and cautious when their own fortunes and that of their band hung in the balance. Jon had never been comfortable playing the part of a dizzy 'creative genius', as some local journalists had begun to call him. The day went long, including the debriefing session with Chris Santana in the pub up the road; and Jon was reduced to falling asleep in Aunt Audrey's parlour with Dave, a half-gone vodka martini still in his hand.

He was tardy to school on Thursday. Only the thought of driving Jeanne after school made him rush home and confront his worried father, shower, change and race off in the Caprice just in time for second period. By 12.15 he had begun to regain some semblance of alertness and managed to get down towards the gymnasium before Jeanne gave up on him.

She was there, in a grey pullover, flared black slacks and her usual varsity coat, with Holly and Patti, waiting as promised just inside the glass doors in the gallery leading to the boys' cabana. The three girls looked up as he strolled towards them accompanied by Kevin Lane, one of the lead actors in the school drama guild. Patti immediately recognised Kevin, as she had been wishing for a chance to meet him for some time; and, since Jeanne and Jon were now on speaking terms and Jon seemed to know Kevin well, her hopes leaped for the sky. However that meeting would not be today. Kevin went straight for the cabana, passing the girls at a distance of not less than five yards. 'So,' he was saying with that charismatic smile; 'looks like your bus is full.'

Jon laughed, not for the girls' sake but at Kevin's teasing. Still he was charming to them. 'Yeah,' he said, as Kevin pulled open the door. 'Break a leg, dude.'

Kevin smiled; he even lingered a moment upon meeting Patti's absorbed gaze. 'Uh; yeah,' he said, turning to Jon after another second; 'and keep on TCB.'

'Right on,' Jon said, smiling again. The heavy red door closed; and he turned to the girls. 'So; is this the bus, then?'

Jeanne smiled right at him, genuinely thrilled to see him. 'If it's okay,' she said, and then felt a little silly to have so imposed on him.

He sighed, feigning exasperation, to hide a smile. 'Oh; I *suppose*....'

He turned to the glass doors and stopped to look round at the three girls. They all just looked back at him like lost lambs. 'All right; all aboard for the Old Mill local.'

The girls giggled sheepishly and filed out as Jon opened the door for them. Jeanne lagged after the others and looked him in the eye. 'I hope you don't mind,' she said sweetly, stepping down the walk just half a stride ahead of him, 'giving them a ride too…. But then, I didn't think a gentleman would.'

'Aaah….' He shrugged, as though it were nothing, and tried not to blush. As a consequence he never saw how she had shocked herself by saying such a thing. 'So; well; uh, haven't seen you in a while; huh?'

'No,' she smiled, thinking how in fact she had missed him. 'You weren't in school yesterday, someone said.'

It was strange but heartwarming to think Jeanne Banfield would enquire into his attendance. 'No…. Business first; you know how it is.'

Jeanne made a little laugh, certainly not knowing what he really meant. She saw how hesitantly Patti and Holly were walking now, unaccustomed to going straight for Jon Cavaliere's car. Something about the whole situation made her swell with pride. Jon got out his keys and led the way past them, with Jeanne trotting a bit with her armload of books, clearly enamoured with staying close by him. She wished he had offered to carry the books for her again, just so the girls could have swooned to witness his chivalry with their own eyes.

He opened the right front door and unlocked the others with the lock switch. Holly bounced in and got herself over the console, and Patti sat in the seat behind Jeanne. 'My God; I *love* this car!' Holly whispered, toying with the acrylic door-pull as Jon shut the doors for them and went round to the other side. Patti tapped Jeanne's shoulder as though to congratulate her on her fortune. Jeanne felt wonderful to be suddenly so highly regarded and so openly envied. Everything about the possibility of associating with Jon Cavaliere on a regular basis made her head spin.

Jon shut his door. 'Okay, kids; everybody buckle up.' He started the engine, which came alive with a roar and idled with a deep throbbing that they all felt through the floor. The girls pulled the seatbelts across themselves and successfully latched them, and Jon adjusted the choke and put the gearchange into reverse.

The parking-lot was full of the usual traffic. Jon drew even with Jimmy Burke's seven-year-old beige Electra convertible, stopped beside a small knot of students at the side of the lane. Two electric windows went down at once. 'Hey, Jon-boy!'

The girls in the Caprice all laughed at that. Jon got a little red and called back, 'Yo! I *told* you never to call me that! You want me to put my *boys* on you; or what?'

Jimmy shook his head, not hearing him so well with Bowie's

'Diamond Dogs' blaring out of his stereo speakers. 'You're goin' to Cindy's function this week; aren'tcha?'

'No, dude. We gotta practise. I guess I could stop by later, though....'

'Hey, Jeannie!' Jimmy called over, just now recognising her in the front seat. 'How'd you end up stuck with *this* guy?'

'I don't know,' she called out past Jon. 'I guess it's a long story!'

Jimmy laughed; and a driver behind him hooted. 'So, Jon, man; do ya think you could do a tune-up on the old girl? She's not her usual self.'

'Yeah,' Jon told him; 'call me on the weekend and I'll let you know. I gotta paint Holloway's car Saturday, so....'

'Solid,' Jimmy acknowledged, and pulled out. He guided his car into the queue ahead of Jon, and Jon slipped his clutch and followed him. Thirty feet later traffic stopped again. Jeanne was rather proud of her answer to Jimmy's teasing. She was not yet ready to fully confess her true feelings for Jon; but a what she had said had fully satisfied Jimmy for the moment, and that was all she needed to say for now.

Mike Jolson came up to Jon's window with a few words about an upcoming billiards match at the bowling alley; Jeanne gathered from their talk that they shared a draughtsmanship class. Kirk Mahoney and a girlfriend waved from across the lane; and Jon made a little laugh to himself. 'Dude's got a different girl every week,' he commented wryly, and then thought better of expressing ungentlemanly notions in the company of such nice young ladies.

Melody Santana, all bundled up in a new wool coat against the cold, ran over from a group of friends and hopped up to sit on the bonnet. 'Yo!' he yelled out at her, and poked the throttle once, holding the clutch. 'What ails you?'

For a second his passengers might not have been sure he even knew her. Melody bounced about on her bottom for a moment and then jumped down to her feet to come back to put her head in the window. 'Hey there, lover,' she teased him.

Jon laughed at her. 'Right. And now I s'pose you'll tell me you're in the market for a ride.'

'Gee, hun; what kinda ride didja have in mind?'

Jon seemed not the least embarrassed by this in front of the girls. 'Right, bud,' he said. 'So go catch Prescott. Last I saw he had one last lesson with that kid in the guitar room. This bus is full, dearie.'

'Ohhh, come on,' she whined, as though crestfallen. 'I could sit on your lap....' A giggle in the next second gave away her bad acting.

'I'm gonna *kill* you, Mel,' Jon told her, and let the clutch in abruptly. The tyres chirped as the Caprice leaped away.

As he steered round Melody and her companions Jeanne noticed he had indeed become a little red. But she suspected only that Melody, the sister of Jon's close friend and a close friend herself of Jon's sister, was more like a sibling than a suitor for his romantic attention; and in any case she was amused by the girlish teasing.

His tenth-grade brother Andrew came up to him with a female friend and demanded, 'Yo, dude. I need a ride home, man.'

'Yo, dude,' Jon came back, 'I can't. This bus is full.'

'Aw, man; Charlie's got a detention.'

'Yeah; well; you'll have to wait for him, or wait for Prescott. You could thumb it. *She* could thumb it.' He looked over the girl in her taut jeans and imagined they would not wait long for a ride at all.

'Aw, shit, man…. It's damn cold out here, you know.'

Jon sighed. Ahead, Melody was getting herself into her family's old turquoise Impala. 'Yo, dude, there's Santana. *He's* got room.'

Andrew and his friend both turned, recognised the car and ran round in front of the silver Caprice to beg their ride home. The window went up at last, and Jon adjusted the heater and pushed in a cassette.

Jeanne and the others were left reeling from such brusque exchanges. Well, Jeanne thought; at least his life isn't *dull*….

Once they were out the gate and past the overeager traffic director on the Parkway she leaned back in her seat and listened to Jon's tape of the *Rubber Soul* album. It was important to her that she absorb as much of The Beatles as possible to avoid feeling too uneducated about things that interested him. As though in deference to her new status as a female associate of Jon Cavaliere, Holly and Patti were uncharacteristically quiet. Jeanne thought about that. She had always been popular, among teachers and students alike, and especially amongst the boys. In seventh grade she had met Jon but also many others, like Marty and Bobby Crocker and Lee and Jerry and eighth-graders like Frank and Jimmy Burke, all of whom she still knew well. It had always seemed strange to her that, of all the boys she had met in junior high, the majority were still good friends, but the first one to whom she had ever taken a particular liking, in any romantic context, had actually eluded her. Because of his elusiveness he had become to her even more alluring; there had never been any chance for her to grow used to having him as a mere friend. Since that very first day of junior-high school she had been completely spellbound by him. Her grades had stayed high; and she had become popular among the others because she was naturally pleasant and polite. And though her reputation as something of a flirt seemed to have been built on being only friendly, it was not so bad; for having the boys all chase after her had indeed been quite flattering. But the one male who did not take after her at all had been the only one she wanted.

Paul McCartney sang 'Michelle', those innocent French lyrics sounding so sexy even a decade later. Jeanne pondered some of her old daydreams, realising how none of them had ever been as exciting as the real-life bliss of Tuesday afternoon. All the stirring fantasies she had invented were no match for the elation she felt at merely riding in the front seat of Jon Cavaliere's elegant, powerful car at just forty-five miles per hour. It was then that she decided she would never be able to let him get away again.

Bob Prescott had been right in predicting that girls would change Jon's life. Jon had always been polite and mannerly when it really mattered but now, at eighteen, the old junior-high-school concept of 'cool' had gone. Forever forsaken were the cigarettes, the lewd jokes, the vulgar language and the blatant lack of respect for even appropriate authority. The notoriety of the band, too, had caused his appeal to broaden. Now, his admirers would see a charming young gentleman who could impress anyone with uncommon intelligence and undisputed moral integrity. The girls in the car this afternoon were seeing him at his very best, nothing at all like the awkward lad who had met Christine Polvere in August.

Chris Santana had thought it a shame that his two longtime friends had not proved so right for each other. Christine had been a shy, sheltered young lady, and Jon had been far too naïve and roughhewn to leave any lasting impression on the female of his choice. Chris had never imagined her so jealous; he knew why Jon had felt so strongly about wanting to see Eve's friend Valerie on one of his rare nights off and admired him for the profound positive influence he could have on all young people, especially those in dire need of it. Christine's stunningly self-centred, even spiteful reaction had demonstrated that she had already learnt all she wanted from the relationship; she responded by accepting dates with more males than she had ever even known before. Jon, gracious to the last, took pains to stay on amicable terms with her. He accepted her disdain with disappointment but felt grateful to her; for he acknowledged she had helped refine him into a true gentleman.

Danny Harris had called on Jeanne last night. They drove over to Sandal Lane, the local lovers' rendezvous, but she had to put him off. He had be en hoping they might get more serious and, even though she knew on romantic matters he was never much for discussion, she felt too bewildered by recent events and feelings to be very receptive to any intimacy. Still she had never been happy to disappoint anyone, especially a desirable young man like Danny. Any of the girls in school would have loved to be dating him. He was handsome and well-built, and everyone said they made a very good-looking couple; her father even said so. Jeanne had always felt proud to be with him, and he had been more than accommodating in accepting her apologetic refusal on Wednesday night.

But this was Thursday afternoon, and things came to light that were not evident in the dark of Sandal Lane. Jeanne recalled clearly her conversation with Steve Marlowe over the Christmas recess, when he and Anne had both cautioned her about Danny's reputation for being domineering, possessive and inconstant. Steve made no secret of his mistrust of Danny Harris, retaining his principles even at the risk of upsetting a longtime friend like Jeanne. Since the episodes at Snow Lodge he had come to see Danny's shortcomings well, the faults of one who tended to put pride before a fall. At first Jeanne wanted to dismiss such notions as Steve's jealousy; but she knew she knew him better than that. Steve really did care for her best happiness. It just doesn't make any sense, she argued the point with herself. Why would he push me away from Danny, when he knows how everyone else was telling me what a nice match we were....

She glanced at Jon for a second as he drove. In an instant the position to which she had to turn her head reminded her of Danny's car last night, when he had been asking for a more intimate or more public sign of their commitment. And suddenly she saw why Steve had been subtly trying to dissuade her from dating Danny steadily. Steve had alluded to the week in November when Jon had kindly chauffeured them about, admitted to Jeanne he was glad Jon Cavaliere was not two-faced or insincere, and then added in the same breath that he could hardly have said the same thing about Danny Harris.

Jeanne could recognise Steve's noble intentions, however likely they were influenced by his all-seeing sister Anne. But Danny had assured her he was not the type to flirt with her and trade her in on next week's definition of a dream date, no matter what the rumours reported. He had said even last night that he had always strived to deserve and keep a steady girlfriend. Jeanne shivered. It was exactly the ploy of one bent on possessing her, upon her at the worst possible moment. She knew Danny was far too proud to have asked her without fully expecting she would assent. Even if, prior to Tuesday, she might have readily accepted, she could hardly go steady with him now. At the moment she had no desire to date him even once again. But the last thing she wanted was for Danny to think she had refused him in order to see someone else; for, upon her refusal, however polite, he would only be spurred on to further efforts.

Uh-oh, Jeanne thought. I may have really done it this time.... I can't let Danny find out I'm interested in anyone else. He'll feel like a fool. He probably already does now, after last night.... And how can I do any of this to Jon? Her face began to feel red. Dating Jon now might well be the worst thing she could do for all concerned. The situation had become a powder-keg about to go up in her face.

'Hey, Jeannie,' Holly, in the back seat, said to her; 'you okay? You look—'

'Oh; um— It's nothing.'

'Is it too hot?' Jon asked her, in a calm, gentle tone. 'I can turn this down–' He leaned over and moved the heater control.

Suddenly Jeanne felt very ashamed. Surely Jon was too decent to be party to her real thoughts of the moment. 'No, Jon; really, uh–'

'It's just that I hate bein' cold....'

'You know what you looked like, Jeannie?' Holly laughed. 'Like you just realised you left the bathtub water running. I saw this movie on TV where–'

'I think I did,' Jeanne whispered to herself, and turned to look out the window.

Jon glanced at her for a second and then looked up in the mirror at Patti. 'Hey. So where do I go?'

Holly tapped him and pointed over his shoulder. 'Right here. The first one off Sycamore.'

Prudently wary of the melting snow, Jon steered slowly round onto winding Sycamore Drive and then turned left up onto Oak Lane. At the bottom of the steep incline was Number Six. 'Bye, Holly,' Patti said, as Holly opened the door.

'Bye,' Holly smiled. 'Thanks for the ride, Jon. Oh; and Jeannie, make sure ya hang onto this one. He is real cute!'

The door closed. Patti smiled a bit and said, 'I get off at Maple, Jon.'

'Which is, uh, where?' He let in the clutch, trying to hide his blush at Holly's comment by wincing as the tyres slipped on some soft ice.

'The very next street, to your right.'

'Ah yes.' Jon turned in the snow onto the side street without signalling or even applying brakes. The road went up an incline and levelled off.

'My house is the last one on the right,' Patti told him.

'Ah yes,' Jon said again, and eased the car to a halt in front of the well-kept grey-blue split-level on the corner with the new blue Oldsmobile parked in the driveway.

'Well,' Patti said with a smile; 'I do appreciate the ride, Jon.' They looked at each other in the mirror. She paid his blushing no mind. 'It was very nice of you. Hey, Jeannie; I'll talk to you; okay?'

'Okay,' Jeanne said absently.

'Well okay, kids; have a nice time tonight,' she bade them cheerfully, and the car door closed.

Jon shifted into first and steered round onto Old Mill Road. 'What's the matter?' he asked gently, feeling the anxiety coming up inside him like a volcano in his stomach.

'Nothing....' She sat up straight in her seat and looked at him for a second. 'Well; it's something. I know you're gonna hate me for this–'

'You checked, and you can't make it tonight.'

They stopped in front of her house. She turned and looked out the window at her front door. 'Jon,' she said, 'I'm really sorry.... It's like one of those things that are so hard to get out of, you know—'

'Oh; I know. It's okay. It's no big deal, really.'

'Jon, I'm really sorry…. It's not like I don't want to go, really; but just—'

'Hey,' he said; 'you're a popular kid. You always have stuff going on. I know how it is.'

She knew he was hurt; this was sarcasm. For Jon Cavaliere to find an evening free to spend alone with someone must have been a scheduling feat of monumental proportions; surely it should have been taken as the height of flattery. 'No, Jon; it's just that there's this old friend I have to talk to, and—'

'It's all right,' he said. 'It's none of my business. I only wish you coulda told me on Tuesday.'

'Well; actually, Jon, I—'

'Tuesday, it woulda been better. You shoulda told me on Tuesday.'

She looked at him, but he sat there, staring at the dashboard. 'Jon, really, I'm very sorry, you know; really I am. I had no idea this whole thing would be so big, even to me. It's just—'

'Well; even if it was anything to you on Tuesday, you coulda told me.'

'Tuesday this whole thing was easier…. It all kind of came up last night. I'm really sorry, Jon; I don't mean to upset you—'

'Oh; I'm not upset,' he said blithely.

Jeanne would not believe him. 'Well; could we go another night? Saturday, maybe? I'll make sure I can go on Saturday—'

Jon shrugged. 'Saturday we play the civic centre in Hoakum. Tomorrow we have a meeting and a practice. You know, like with school and all, I only ever have like one or two days off a week. Yesterday I was in New York most of the day and tonight we were supposed to have a meeting, that got cancelled till tomorrow just so I could get to see the rest of the Beatle movies.'

Hearing that only made her feel worse. 'Jon, I'm so sorry; I just don't know what to say. I just know that I really didn't want to hurt your feelings….'

'Don't worry about it,' he said.

'Really, Jon. I am sorry.'

He shifted into first and held down the clutch pedal. 'It's all right. It wasn't that bright of an idea I had anyway.'

'It was so, Jon. And I'm very flattered that you asked. I was really looking forward to it, you know…. Oh; this whole thing is so *stupid*; I just wish—' But she caught herself there. In order to free herself of Danny's web of jealousy and keep Jon out of harm's way, she knew she would have to settle things with Danny first. It was only fair. 'Jon, really, I'm just really sorry—'

'Yeah; well; just forget it. It was a dumb idea I had anyway, being as no-one in their right mind would ever want to see a Beatle movie with me. I talk through the whole picture, you know.'

'Jon, it *wasn't* a dumb idea and I do wish you wouldn't say that. It's my fault, and it's definitely me who loses out on a nice evening. Will I see you again tomorrow?'

'Sure,' he said. 'Tomorrow.'

'You won't be mad at me; will you?'

He looked at her, at last, and then made a casual shrug as he turned forwards again. 'Mad? Me? Naah....' He worked the stick up into first gear again.

Jeanne realised he would make no effort to open the door for her now. 'I'm sorry, Jon,' she said sadly, and then pulled the door handle. With great reluctance, she stepped out of the car; as it was, she put her foot down into a puddle of slush at the kerb. 'Oook.... Well; I'll see you tomorrow, and I'll let you know then how it goes; okay? And then we can talk; well; you know, we can work it out. All right?'

'Right,' Jon said seriously, as though with a new positive outlook on the situation. 'Okay.'

She wanted to see him smile; but he would not. She swung the car door closed, taking special effort not to look as though she were slamming it, and stepped up out of the street. Suddenly the Caprice was growling rabidly, shredding the quiet of the snow-covered neighbourhood with engine noise and ripping up chunks of ice and snow with both spinning rear tyres. It was gone over the hill and round the bend; and Jeanne was left wiping her eyes, not wholly sure it was from the exhaust.

The doorbell rang at about one o'clock, and Patti answered the door to find Jeanne standing alone at the doorstep. She was still dressed as she had been for school. 'Oh; hi,' Patti said brightly. 'I'm glad you're here, Jeannie; I wanted to ask you–'

'Patti, I've got a problem.' Jeanne stepped right by her and marched in towards the stairs.

'Jeannie, what's wrong? Is everything all right?'

'No,' Jeanne said boldly. '*Nothing's* all right. Everything's *wrong*.' She stomped up the steps to Patti's room, in her squeaking wet shoes. 'Wrong, wrong, wrong, wrong, *wrong*.'

'Jeannie....' Patti followed her. Jeanne sat down on Patti's bed and fell back on the ruffled pillows. 'What is it?'

'*Danny*,' said Jeanne. '*That's* what's wrong.' She turned her head and looked at Patti. 'I'll tell you, you know, sometimes I just don't understand that guy. I really don't. I mean: like I'm easy to get along with; right? I mean I *try* to be. But the moment I want to be myself, you know, like maybe talk to somebody I know, even Steve, you know, he gets cold and like so *aggressive*....'

'He's jealous,' Patti said simply.

'He's *more* than jealous. He's *unreasonable*. I mean it's like I can't have any freedom. It's not that I want to hurt him, you know. I just want to be able to like say "hi" to people I like.'

'Like Jon,' Patti smiled.

'Oh; poor Jon....' Jeanne stared up at the ceiling.

'Poor Jon?' Patti giggled. 'Not even. He's got himself a date with the nicest girl in school. And if Danny thinks–'

'He doesn't now,' Jeanne said quietly.

Patti looked at her. 'Doesn't what?'

'Oh....' Jeanne put her hands over her face and began to weep. 'Oh,' she said aloud; 'I could *kill* myself!'

'Jeannie, *why*? What's the matter?'

Jeanne lifted her hands off her face for one second to look at her and then cried, 'I broke it!'

Patti nearly jumped off the floor. 'You *what*?!'

Jeanne sniffled loudly and sobbed. 'I broke the date, Patti. Oh; I could just kill myself!'

'Hey....' Patti sat beside her on the pink beaded bedspread. 'Why?'

Jeanne wiped her eyes with her hands and got up to look about the room for a tissue. 'Oh, Patti.... You don't even know. I tell you everything; but you don't know. God! –*I* don't even know.... You know how Danny is; he's like so jealous and all.... He's just being possessive, you know; but last night....'

'What?' Patti asked worriedly. 'What happened last night?'

Jeanne blew her nose into the tissue. 'He wants to... *you* know. He wants me to go steady with him. He says he *loves* me.'

'He said that?'

'Oh; you know how he is. He doesn't actually say it. But he means it.'

Patti thought about that. 'Do you love him?' she asked, very seriously.

'Patti, I'm like *afraid* of him. Especially after last night.... And I'm getting so scared to tell him anything he might not want to hear, that like I don't even know what to do now....'

Patti shook her head. 'Well; it's obviously come to the point where you've got to tell him. I mean: if you can't even tell him no... then you've *got* to tell him no. And you *do* want to go out with Jon Cavaliere....'

'Oh, God,' Jeanne sighed. 'More than probably anything. I've just been so afraid to hurt anybody's feelings....'

'Jeannie,' said Patti, 'don't you think you just did?'

Jeanne looked at her and her eyes filled with tears. 'Oh, Patti, I *know* I just did. Of all people in the world, who I'd never want to hurt– That's why I could *kill* myself!' She groaned. '*Oooh!* Just once, you know, just *once*, I'd like to do what my heart says, and not try to make so much *sense* out of everything! I've only been crazy about the guy for like four years; I mean: it's not even funny.... How dumb could I *be*? It has to be the dumbest thing I've ever done in my entire life! How *juvenile*!' she cried at the ceiling. 'How *stupid*!'

'All right,' Patti said calmly; 'there's no use getting all upset.' She stood up and paced to the window.

'But what can I *do*, Patti? He'll never go out with me *now*. I bet he never even *talks* to me again. The whole thing is *over*, Patti, and I might as well go kill myself. Do you have a razor? I'll slash my wrists.'

'Oh; *stop*,' Patti told her.

'I mean: like he's only the coolest guy in the whole world, you know; and I have to wreck the only possible chance I'll ever have of going out with him over some jealous conceited over-possessive jerk like Danny Harris!'

'Maybe you could call him up and talk to him,' Patti suggested.

'Who; Danny? He won't talk on the phone. He's such a jerk about things like this—'

'No, no, silly; I meant *Jon*. Call Jon up, and apologise.'

'*Jon*?!' Jeanne nearly shrieked. 'Call up *Jon Cavaliere*?!'

Patti laughed at her. 'Oh, Jeannie, of *course*; can't you see? Just call him up and tell him you've made up your mind, and that you're sorry to have hurt his feelings.'

'Oh, *Patti*,' Jeanne said, embarrassed. 'I can't do that. What would I look like?'

Patti smiled at her. 'You'd look like a nice girl,' she said sincerely. 'Someone who cares about him.'

'I *do* care about him,' Jeanne admitted, and wiped her nose with another tissue.

'Of course you do.' Patti started out to the gallery. 'Come on.'

'Where?'

'Down here. Do you know his number?'

'*Patti*! I'm not gonna call him.' Jeanne would not move.

'Sure you are,' Patti insisted; 'don't you see? Come on; you'll feel really great afterwards.'

'Yeah; but– I'd feel silly. It's all wrong.'

'What's so wrong? You've called guys before.'

'But not *Jon Cavaliere*, Patti!'

Patti laughed at her. 'Jeannie, you are making this into some terrible *thing*. If he really likes you, he'll *love* to hear from you. You wouldn't happen to know his number, would you?'

'*No*,' Jeanne fibbed.

'Yes you do; you've probably got it memorised. Hence my going down stairs for the phone book.'

She stopped at the door, and Jeanne would not look at her. 'Three five four five,' Jeanne blurted, and then clamped her mouth shut.

Patti smiled, having known all along Jeanne would acquiesce, and went to the pink Princess phone by her bed. 'Now just ask for Jon, in that nice way you have,' she said whilst dialling. 'Okay? Here you go.'

Jeanne took the handset from her and sat down on the edge of the bed. The line was ringing the other end. She forced a swallow and wet her lips. The Cavaliere phone was picked up by a strange boy.

–'Yo?'

She stared straight at the wall, deriving no confidence from such a curt greeting. Her voice sounded as though coming from someone else.

'Uh, hello; can I talk to Jon, please?'

–'Uh, wait; uh, sorry–' The receiver was dropt, not gently. In the distance Jeanne could hear voices, barely audible over the sound of an electric guitar. –'Yo, man! Where's your brother at?'

–'Is that Charlie?' The guitar stopped.

–'No, man; some babe. It's for Jon; so....'

–'He ain't home, say.'

–'But *is* he, though. *That* is the question.'

–'I don't know. Tell 'em he ain't back from school yet.' A chord was struck on the guitar. 'I don't know what the hell happened to him; he didn't drive *me* home.'

The first boy returned to the phone and picked it up. –'Naah, sorry; he's not here. Probably still at school.'

'Still at *school?*' Jeanne asked worriedly, and Patti looked at her in surprise.

–'Yeah; looks that way. He ain't here, anyways. Who's this?'

'Uh; well; this is Jeanne. Could you tell him that I called, please?'

–'Yeah; okay. Is that it?'

'Yes; please–'

–'Okay, cool. Later.'

'Thank you–' There was a click as the boy rang off. Jeanne looked up in a panic. 'Still at *school?*'

Patti took the handset from her and replaced it in the cradle on her night-table. 'Who was it; his mother?'

'No.... I don't know.' Jeanne spun about on the bed and looked up at her. 'Patti, that means he didn't go *home*. He was so mad at me when he drove off; you didn't see– He was really upset, Patti; and it's all my fault!'

'All right; calm down. I'm sure there's a simple explanation–'

'But you didn't see how he drove *off*, Patti! You didn't see how *upset* he was! He just kept saying, "You coulda told me on Tuesday", over and over....'

'Well; maybe he had somewhere to go. Like maybe to *band* practice....'

'No,' Jeanne remembered; 'they practise tomorrow– God! –what if he went to some *bar*? Here I am, sixteen years old, and already I'm driving men to drink....'

Patti shook her head. 'Jeannie, you're being overly dramatic. Sometimes I think you're a born worrier.'

'But Patti, what if he got into an *accident* or something?'

'Well what do you propose we *do*? Go out and *look* for him?'

'Oh, Patti....' Jeanne stood up and paced to the window, staring out at the snow on the Harpers' rear lawn. 'I don't know *what* to do. I'm just so totally mixed-up right now....'

Patti sat on her bed, crossed her legs and looked up at Jeanne for a long moment with an expression of sane serenity. 'Well,' she said finally; 'it certainly looks to *me* like you've made up your mind.'

Jeanne turned round. 'What do you mean?'

'I mean that obviously you've made up your mind.' Patti smiled at her. 'I mean: Jeannie, look. You've been going out with Danny for a month now, or, a little more than a month. He wants to get serious, and so he asks you to go steady, and then actually gives you a little time to think about it, which is nice. Now then you've got this other guy, a really nice guy, whom we don't have to say any more about. Right?' She waited for Jeanne to look up and smiled a little. 'Right?'

Jeanne nodded, looking down at the carpet, and managed a wee smile. 'Right,' she conceded.

'All right. And it's obvious he likes you, I mean: he *did* ask you for a date, dinner and all; and he's nervous as can be around you, Jeannie, and of course you're nervous as can be around him.... Personally I don't like Danny, Jeannie. I know it's not my place to judge your boyfriends, you know, but I don't think he's really your type. I mean: look at all Jon Cavaliere means to you. It's so obvious he's really attracted to you, even now; I mean: he's so incredibly sweet and gentle with you, it's just like out of a faery-tale.... If he ever asked *me* out to dinner and a movie, like the way he asked me to dance that time, I swear I'd drop everything and *go*. Which of course I did, that time, and got you so upset.... I was really mad at myself for that.'

'Oh, Patti, just forget about that. You had a really nice dance with a really nice guy. Why be mad at yourself over that?'

'Well; actually I had been hoping he'd want to dance with *you*.'

'Well; so was I,' said Jeanne; 'but forget it.'

'So what would you like to do about this now?' Patti asked her.

'I don't *know*,' said Jeanne, in a forlorn tone, as she sat down on the arm of the chair. 'I mean yes; I *do* want to go out with him, and if he ever speaks to me again, I *swear* I'll beg him to forgive me, you know; but I'm still afraid of what Danny will do when he finds out....'

'Yes; and find out he most surely *will*. You and Jon Cavaliere are about the most noticed people in school these days....'

'Oh, Patti,' Jeanne said, blushing to hear herself mentioned in the same breath as Jon Cavaliere; it sounded like they belonged together.

'And Danny,' Patti said boldly, 'is a ladies' man; and he's bound to pick up a new girl just as quickly as he picked up you.'

'Patti!' Jeanne whirled about.

'Oh, Jeannie, I'm sorry; I certainly didn't mean for it to sound that way, but– Well; you know what I mean. It's the way Danny is. He'll only turn it around to make you look like a creep and then pick up someone else at the very next party.'

'God…. I can picture him doing that,' Jeanne admitted. 'And so then what will *I* look like?'

Patti smiled. 'You'll look like Jon Cavaliere's girlfriend.'

Jeanne closed her eyes and sucked in a long breath through her teeth, imagining how that would actually feel; at once it seemed inconceivable and yet only a daydream away.

'It's Fate, if you ask me,' Patti said, in a softer voice. 'You were meant to have someone like him, and sooner or later, you will. It's just a matter of time till it actually happens.'

* * *

Friday, Jon thought, dropping into his usual homeroom seat in Room 219. Ordinarily my favourite day. But what an ace blue meanie of a day this is. I shouldn't've gone drinkin' over Doug's last night…. I never should've even got up. What a waste…. Round about him, students filed in and took their seats like mindless zombies, only to rise again for the Pledge of Allegiance. Homeroom roll was taken; and Judi Catalano was the only one absent. So what, Jon thought; Judi Catalano is a frickin' junkie anyway….

Out in the corridor, where the diverse smells of wet hair, cigarette smoke and a hundred different perfumes blended into a mind-altering stench that could permeate the very walls, one thought echoed about the hollows of his consciousness: I hate school. I really hate school. In fact, I've always hated school….

Bob came into room 120 and sat in the seat to Jon's right. 'So; hey, man,' he said cheerfully; 'tell me how it went last night.'

'It *didn't*,' Jon said coldly, wishing more to avoid the subject than to even convey his disdain for it.

'Didn't what?' asked Bob.

'Didn't *happen*.'

'Shit,' said Bob, genuinely disappointed. 'Why not?'

'I don't know.'

'Shit, man; that's lame.'

'Yeah; it is.' Jon slouched lower in his seat.

Mark strolled into the room then, sitting in his usual place behind Jon. 'So hey, man; how did the big number go last night?'

'It didn't,' Jon said.

'Shit…. Why not?'

'We're tryin' to figure that out,' Bob said.

'No reason,' Jon said, irritated by the attention to his lack of success. 'I suppose she just had other plans.'

'Shit,' said Bob. 'That's lame.'

'Well; who the fuck cares?' Jon sighed, adjusting himself still lower in the chair. 'Maybe the chick just decided it wasn't for her.'

Bob laughed. 'Shit…. Not *even*. I happen to have it from very reliable sources that she's quite anxious to see you.'

'Yeah; you're just pickin' up sympathy,' Mark told him.

'Oh; eat shit with that,' Jon said, bothered still more by their incessant pursuit of the topic. 'She's obviously got some other dude she's not willing to give up on. Why not just let it die?'

'Yeah,' Mark said then; 'well; rumour has it he's not so willing to give up on *her*, either.'

At that Jon whirled about. 'All right, man; so *you* tell me. Who the hell is this "old friend" of hers?'

'Well, man,' said Mark, shaking his head; 'let me just say you don't wanna mess with him.'

'Let *me* tell *you* who I wanna mess with. What's his name?'

Mark was still hesitant. 'Look, Jon; you don't—'

'Mark,' Jon said, snatching a hold on his friend's arm, '*tell* me. What's his name?'

'Harris,' Mark sighed, and shook his arm free. 'Dan— well; Danny. Danny Harris.'

'Harris,' Jon thought. 'Do I know this guy?'

Mark shook his head. 'Not unless you're a rah-rah.'

'A rah-rah,' he mused. 'Figures. What kinda car's he got?'

Mark smiled. 'A Goat,' he said. ''Sixty-Nine. Nice car, too, with mags, and all…. Son of a bitch would probably haul ass; but he never seems to run anybody.'

Jon thought a second. 'Is it a four-hundred?'

'I don't know. Might be…. All I know is it's an automatic. It's pretty stock.'

'I can take that,' Jon said, mostly to himself, and then looked up at Mark. 'Where's he live?'

'I don't know—'

'What's he look like?'

'Oh; tall, I guess, not too raunchy-lookin', you know, kinda short hair, wears this felt coat a lot—'

'What can he bench?'

'Bench? Oh; I don't know; maybe two-thirty, two-forty?'

'Shit,' laughed Bob; 'forget *that!*' This news was as good as any to dissuade him.

But Jon would not be dissuaded. 'Forget it? What the hell!' Jon looked hard at him and then at Mark. 'The lady got me all pissed-off, because of that dude. I'm gonna dent his skull a little.'

'Good luck,' Bob said sarcastically, and turned forwards.

'So how do I find this chump today?' Jon asked Mark.

'Uh, Jon,' Bob said, turning back, 'I don't think–'

The bell rang to begin the class; and Bob barely heard Mark whispering to Jon, 'He's got my study hall. Always comes in late.'

Bob glared at him. 'Mark, what the hell!'

Mr Able passed them on his way to the front of the room. Jon turned to Mark again. 'Meet me outside the auditorium,' he whispered; and the teacher began the lesson.

Jon had nothing with him but the leather jacket on his back when he met up with Mark at the auditorium. Anyone else might have wondered how Jon could get away with skipping his physical-education class; but Mark knew better. Of the old clique who had gone through grade school together, Jon was still the craftiest of them all. He had always taken pride in his ability to leave one class at the bell, drop off his books at his locker and then simply not attend for the next period, as if by luck or magic avoiding everyone associated with that class for the rest of the day. Now, maintaining such a prominent profile about town, it had become something of a challenge to remain anonymous for an entire school session. But anyone who knew him would expect Jon to accept that challenge just to stay in practice.

Overcrowded as the school had become over the last few years, nearly no classrooms were regularly free and so student prep sessions were most often held in the auditorium, a venue far more conducive to casual conversation than to serious study. Jon and Mark sat together in the very back, the usual domain of those who craved a cigarette in secret or who had just missed too much sleep. Several sought to sit in the row and Jon waved them all away without a word. He was taking charge of the situation, as he usually did, and Mark began to worry about the intensity of his tactics. Jon could be very single-minded when a dream had been close to his heart for a long time; and more than once the consequences had proved very sobering. But it was not the job of a good friend to deny him the chance to realise such a dream. They all knew that his life was full of important dreams; there would be no deterring him anyway.

In a few minutes Mark tapped his shoulder. 'He just came in,' he whispered by Jon's ear.

'Where? Jon looked up.

'Right here.' Mark leaned closer. 'With the jacket.'

Jon turned and looked over the young man who had just stepped into the room not five yards to his right. His dark-brown hair, not quite past his collar, was very fastidiously kept. He wore a pair of black trousers and a dark-blue shirt with the collar out over the lapels of a maroon velvet sports coat. Jon watched as the boy stood there with his hands in his back pockets, talking amiably with a few girls in the centre back row. They all seemed quite smitten with his impish smile and eager laugh. After a moment he moved down the aisle to chat with another group of girls farther along, never turning to see who else might have taken notice of his arrival.

What a showman, Jon thought. Struts in here, so sure everybody's been awaiting his appearance all day. What a cocky son-of-a-bitch. Man; would I love to tear this bastard apart.... 'So this *chump* is who I'm s'posed to fight?'

'Don't call him out, Jon. He may be a rah-rah, but he *can* reason.'

'I'll handle it,' Jon said, and got up.

'Right,' Mark sighed, and moved his legs to let him pass. He watched Jon go down the left aisle and cross the section down front, starting up the left centre aisle towards Danny Harris. Harris was just stepping away from a few more female friends when Jon bumped him with a shoulder. Mark tried to hide a laugh at such an audacious gesture and put his head down as though suffering from a hangover. He did not see Harris start to turn just as Jon took him by the elbow and, without breaking stride, escorted him out the open doors into the central lobby.

'Like a few words with you, dude,' Jon said, turning and letting go of him.

Harris spun away on his black heels and scowled at him. 'What the hell's *your* problem, faggot?'

Jon sighed, as though unaffected. 'Well; I'd kinda like to talk to you about–' he looked up at him then– 'Jeanne Banfield.'

'Yeah? And so *what* about her?'

Jon looked him squarely in the eye, thinking, well; at least Mark was right about him knowing her.... 'It would appear that you're goin' out with her, then?'

'Yeah; and so what of it?'

'Well; I'd kinda like to know how much.'

Harris began to laugh at him. 'Shit.... And who are *you*, for me to tell you?'

'She was mine before you ever knew her,' Jon said gravely.

Harris looked hard at the young man who had dragged him out here to boast of such a thing. He was not used to being confronted with such bold self-assurance in someone so much slighter than he. But he would not take the claim lightly in any case. 'Oh; yeah? Well she isn't *now*. Look; I'm goin' steady with that chick; and if you don't like it you can go play with yourself. That's what *I* think, little man.' Satisfied with his response he turned and started back into the auditorium.

Casually Jon leaned back on the brick wall of the lobby beside the doors. 'Harris,' he sighed, 'get back here.' Harris did indeed step back out; and Jon, as though thoroughly unconcerned, merely rolled his head round to look at him. 'Suppose I was to tell you that *I* was goin' out with her also?'

Harris made a little laugh, perhaps not wholly believing him. 'I'd say you were full of shit.'

'Yeah,' Jon said wearily; 'well; we were talkin' about it yesterday, on the way home in fact, and she said she had to talk to you about it. And that kinda pissed me off, you know, 'cause we've known each other for like *years*; so I figured I'd better let you know that *you* don't cut no horseshit with *me*.'

'Oh; *yeah*?' Harris countered, his loud voice revealing more than a little faith in what he had heard. After all there were two days in this week alone on which he had not seen Jeanne home from school. 'Well *look*, faggot, lookit *here*. I don't know you, and I don't *want* to; but you're out to get your *ass* busted. I don't care if you watched Jeannie bein' *born*. You just stay *away* from her; you hear me?'

'Oh,' snapped Jon; 'and on your words I'm s'posed to; is that it?'

'Hey; I'm not up for this kinda bullshit from faggots like you, so just take a hike.' He waved as though Jon were a pesky fly and turned to go back into the auditorium.

His boldness at its peak, Jon actually reached after him and caught his coattails, yanking him back out into the lobby. In a flash Harris whirled on him and shoved him back into the brick wall. He gave Jon a good punch in the middle; but Jon was not unprepared and recoiled with a solid left to the jaw. Somewhere a teacher shouted.

Harris stood up straight and had almost got off another punch when a strong male PE instructor grabbed him from behind. Jon would have seized the opportunity to take another swing at Harris but he was taken from behind also; and the prep-period students crowded in the doorway to watch the action whilst both boys wriggled about puffing like caged bulls.

The PE instructor apparently knew Harris; for he was let go first. Cockily Harris made to strut back into the auditorium and then was compelled to tag Jon with a quick jab to the cheek. The crowd in the doorway cheered approval; and as Harris gloated in the applause Jon, still held from behind, kicked up both feet and landed the heavy heels of both shoes into the small of Harris's back. Again there was response from the crowd.

'*Hey!*' shouted the second man, stumbling backwards but still able to keep an impressively strong grip on Jon. 'Who do you think you *are*?'

'A big fan of Danny Harris,' Jon growled, his eyes still fixed on his adversary.

'Danny,' said the first one, 'get going to where you're supposed to be.'

'I *was* in here,' Harris quipped, and turned.

'Oh; cute, Harris,' Jon called after him, 'you limp faggot!'

Harris spun about to respond to the crowd's encouragement but the PE instructor intercepted him and diverted him back into the auditorium. Finally, Jon was able to writhe free. He turned at once to the two teachers and gave them both a displeased frown, and one of them caught him by the arm and said in a rash tone, 'What do you need? —a trip to Mr Anderson's office?'

'*No*,' said Jon, straightening his leather jacket; 'I do not *need* a trip to Mr Anderson's office.' He turned and stalked off whilst they called disciplinary threats after him. In the doorway, Mark only rolled his eyes and returned to his back-row seat.

Jon and the others of The Strawberries had become so well-known by the school music instructors that, though they were too conspicuous to be seen cutting other classes, they could pop in at any time and use the music department's facilities. In return for the privilege the teachers, knowing the four boys were not much for the rigours of academia, exacted a certain amount of free teaching assistance from them. Well-organised and businesslike Dave was often called upon to administer and even help grade classroom tests; he had graduated already and had little incentive for inciting cheating among the rank and file. Ricky tutored drum students quite well; but he was only a junior and had less expendable time to skip classes than had Bob or Jon. Bob was most talented at teaching slower students guitar, having exceptional patience and disciplined manner with lessons; and they all benefitted from his organisation and methodical practice regimen. Jon was usually expected to help out with the piano students, most of whom were girls looking forward to having his charming personality to themselves for the period, though often he would wind up the session playing some classical piece or even arranging some new composition whilst the enchanted student gazed on at his adroit fingering upon the keyboard.

Today he was in no mood to share anything and inconspicuously closed himself in one of the little rooms, playing a few old standards on piano for only himself till the end of the period. At the bell he strolled empty-handed out of the music wing, crossed the central lobby and bought a single-serving carton of orange drink from the vending machine just inside the cafeteria.

Mike Jolson was sitting at one of the long tables, uncharacteristically studious amidst a mass of papers and textbooks. 'Yo,' Jon said, shuffling over to him; 'what's shakin', Professor?'

'Huh? Oh; hey, dude; what's happenin'?'

Jon sat on the end of the table beside Mike's books whilst students began noisily passing through the dining area en route to their fourth-period classes. 'You goin' to next period?'

'Why,' Mike asked, looking up; 'you leavin'?'

'No; but like you gotta get that last test over with. This is the end of the marking period, you know. You're gonna be late.'

'Yeah; and I gotta finish my house....'

'Yeah; and finish that house.... Serves you right for drawin' somethin' so damn complex.' Jon took a sip of orange drink, recognising Jeanne as she entered the cafeteria from the opposite corner. 'So, Professor; what's this here? –actual *homework?*'

'Yeah....' He looked about at the empty tables. 'I gotta get this shit done. Some other class was in here, you know. I kinda crashed on them.'

Jon shook his head with a wry smile, as Mike resumed his academic exercises. 'Typical,' he said, and drank.

Jeanne, somewhat surprised to see Jon there as he usually came from the gymnasium, stepped out of the flow of traffic and came right up to him. 'Hi,' she said, nervous yet dizzyingly excited to think of addressing him as a regular acquaintance, particularly in view of so many passing schoolmates.

'Hi,' he replied, and, as a second thought, stepped down to the floor. 'What's up?'

'Oh; um, nothing....' Grateful for what seemed like a positive greeting from him, after what had transpired, she suppressed a shiver, hefted her books on her arm and tried to muster the courage for what had to be said. 'Well; uh, Jon; about yesterday, I, um–'

'I talked to him, last period,' Jon said to her.

She shook her head. 'Who?'

'Harris.' He drained the carton.

'Oh,' she said, and considered it a second. 'I didn't know you, uh, well, knew him.' Blushing sheepishly she shifted uneasily from one foot to the other.

Jon folded the top of the juice carton into itself and, with no dustbin nearby, slid it five feet down the table to Mike. 'There you are, Michael. Present from me for studying so hard.' He turned and looked at Jeanne again, but only for a second as he had begun to feel anxious himself. 'That movie is still playing tonight, you know; but, it's the last chance I have off. So; well; if you still want to go....'

She beamed then, not realising how she was blushing. 'I'd *love* to.'

'Cool,' he said, looking down as he felt himself growing red as well. The thought that she might actually be very eager to date him, even in spite of the potential problems with Danny Harris, had not yet manifested itself in his confidence. Harris came in at the far corner, from the side gallery and not from the direction of the auditorium as Jon had expected. 'Uh-oh,' he said brightly, as though there were good news; 'it's the executioner himself. Look; I'll, uh, call you tonight. Mike, come to class and *I'll* finish your house. You owe me another orange, dude.'

Mike waved over his head at him, still absorbed in his maths exercises. Jeanne turned and watched Jon slip into the moving crowd of the passage; Danny Harris came right up to her and went several paces beyond, trying to get a look out the door to the gallery. He only caught a glimpse of Jon skipping down the stairs to the vocational-studies wing. 'You *know* that dude?' he said to Jeanne.

'Uh, yeah,' she said warily; 'you know, sort of–'

'Who is he?'

'Danny, he's just an old friend–'

'So I heard. Look, Jeannie; just stay away from him; okay? He's an asshole, and I don't like his attitude.' He put a hand on her back to escort her off, towards the girls' gymnasium. Behind them, Mike shrugged.

He was nervous, which he had expected to be, and deathly afraid of saying the wrong thing. This was certainly nothing like ringing up one of the guys to take in a film or check on who might attend which concert. He and Christine had usually scheduled a time for him to phone; and of course Cissie or Becky often rang no matter what the hour just to speak about anything at all; he accepted them both as just part of the gang. It occurred him as he picked up the handset that he had never rung up a girl merely to ask her for a date, much less the one girl whose number he now dialled, having memorised it long ago despite never wholly expecting to ever actually use it. It was just 6.45. The phone was answered with a female 'Hello?'

He recited his practised line. 'Hello; may I speak to Jeanne, please?'

–'This *is* Jeanne.'

Perhaps he had rehearsed too long or too well; for a second he felt stupid. 'Oh; uh, hi. This is Jon; uh, Jon Cavaliere.'

–'Oh; hi; *hi*.... How are you?'

'Okay; well....' He felt his face go red and thought, just be cool; she can't see you right now, which is a plus.... 'That, uh, Beatle movie is still at the Stage Door; and I thought, well, since this is the last night they have it.... Well; it's at nine-thirty tonight; and I thought–'

–'Oh; okay....'

'Well,' he said, as she did not seem to be volunteering; 'so, if you're not really busy, you know, and you'd still like to go....'

–'Oh, sure, Jon. I would.'

Suddenly he felt very relieved. 'You're sure?'

–'Sure. Tonight, at nine-thirty?'

'Uh, yeah.' His face went still redder. He had to admit to himself he had given the whole idea much less than a fifty-fifty chance. Asking girls for dates had never been something over which he expected to have reasonable control.

—'That would be nice.'

Nice, he thought. She says it'd be— 'Okay,' he said, for the moment unable to think of anything else to say to her. 'Well; uh, I guess we'll go then, uh, then.'

—'All right.'

A smile came over his face; nothing could have made him erase it. 'Okay, cool,' he said, and spun round with the telephone cord in the kitchen. 'I'll, uh, pick you up around nine; okay? Is that all right?'

—'It's fine.' She actually sounded happy. —'I'm looking forward to it.'

'Oh; okay; well; okay. See you then, uh, then.'

—'All right. Bye-bye, Jon.'

'Bye,' he said, and rang off with a big grin. That wasn't so tough, he thought. Wasn't so tough at all.

She showered and dried her hair and made up in front of the mirror, primping and preening with a quivering in the bottom of her stomach. All the make-up was applied by rote, as on every night before; but slowly the realisation of why and for whom she was doing it tonight swept over her like a tidal wave. The mascara brush quivered in her hand. God, she thought; how will I ever keep him interested? He's going to compare me to people like that Italian girl; and there's no way I'll have what it takes to look like an actress, or a countess, or whatever it is that she looks like....

In her underwear she stood shivering in the cool air of her room, staring into the open wardrobe for ten minutes to no avail. A dress for a date in January would seem terribly out-of-place. But perhaps he would see it as demure, feminine, romantic. On the other hand she should dress sensibly, so that she should not seem silly and impractical; he was, after all, exceptionally intelligent and would probably not settle for a stupid girl lacking common sense. In a dress or a skirt she could look vulnerable to the cold and thus perhaps garner herself a cuddle or a kiss; the notion warmed her to the point of excited shivers. She reached in for her new wool skirt and stopped short before lifting the hanger off the bar. It might have worked on any other date; but this was no ordinary date. She was not vulnerable here; she was an equal. In slacks, she would look more mature and perhaps a bit more confident; and if that would make a more favourable impression to be compatible with her personality it just might be worth a lifetime of kisses and cuddles.

Beth was not in her room; she had been unusually scarce all day. Jon swiped her handheld blowdryer and hurried round to the little bathroom over the kitchen to fix his hair. He had always had beautiful hair for a boy, light and wavy; and his sister delighted in toying with it, never passing up an opportunity to help him set and dry it when The Strawberries were to play somewhere. Actually her help was usually a godsend. But he knew Beth was aware there was no show tonight and surely she would be curious as to why he was going out at 8.45; she would want to know with whom, and where and for how long, and he was not in the mood even to put off her inquisition. Fortunately he had little trouble juggling the comb and brush and dryer and at last achieved something satisfactory. Making a good first impression was important; but he had never been one to fuss over his appearance. He had a natural luck with the way his wardrobe fit and a preference for clothes that kept in-step without looking overly fad-conscious.

He worried that perhaps with such an understated style he would not look worthy of her. She was after all the crown princess of the junior-class girls, replete with a court of eager, admiring consorts and a bevy of ladies-in-waiting who mimicked her hair and makeup and sensible, smart clothes. Jon knew that when it came to social or romantic prowess he was no-one special. For the last four years, though she had held his interest from afar, he had been concentrating on playing music and developing his other talents, establishing himself as his own man regardless of what others his age were doing. In his own casual way, then, he liked to think he evinced an image of personal integrity. If ever a girl were to appreciate him for what he really was, then he would go to no great lengths to appear to be anything else.

She had descended to the sitting room and noticed it was just a minute after nine. Her father looked up from the paper; funnily enough he was not watching television as he normally did in midevening. 'Going out?' he asked her, scarcely looking up.

'Yes, Daddy,' she said, feeling awkward and shy, and perched herself on the edge of a side chair by the door. 'To a movie, um… you know.'

'Danny not working late; huh?' he commented, behind the newspaper.

Jeanne brushed a speck of lint away from the slacks. 'Oh; well; it's not Danny, Daddy,' she said, and saw him put the paper aside to look at her. 'Someone– Someone else.'

'A new one?' he marvelled, with the hint of a smile; and she made a wee smile back at him, a little embarrassed. 'Anybody we know?'

'Uh; no.' She looked down, feeling herself blush on top of a shiver. Her frugal father did like to keep the house somewhat cool.

'Hmmm,' he said, and returned some of his attention to the newspaper.

Her mother came out and sat down on the sofa, remarking, 'Well, sweetheart; you look very nice! Who's the lucky guy?'

'Oh, Mom….' Jeanne got even redder. 'He's just a guy from school– What time is it?'

Her mother looked at the clock on the mantel. 'It's nine-oh-six,' she replied.

The doorbell rang.

'God,' Jeanne sighed, mostly to herself; 'now just stay cool….'

Slowly she stood up and patted down a few minor wrinkles, drawing deep breaths to slow her heart rate. Her hand dropped firmly upon the doorknob. Carefully she turned it and opened the door.

He made a little smile at her, standing there on her front porch for the first time, with his weight on one foot. Hands wedged in his back pockets, he uncrossed his ankles as though she had caught him loafing and said blithely, 'Hi.'

'Hi,' she said in return, smiling nonchalantly as though he had been here a hundred times before; it was a pleasant supposition. Something passed between them then that defied articulation. For a moment they just stood there, each feeling a tingle race down the spine, he with his hands in his back pockets, she leaning casually on the edge of the door, each taking in the sight of the other. Rarely had she seen him in school in other than denim jeans; he looked very handsome in cuffed and pleated black wool trousers and a maroon-and-grey shirt open at the neck, with those dark-brown heeled shoes and that famous leather pilot's jacket, embellished with military patches, that bore his surname across the left chest. She was a lovely picture to him, in the snug dark-grey slacks and a soft pink cashmere sweater. Her hair was her signature, naturally blond, lusciously full and wavy all over, past her shoulders and cut in layers, tapering back along the sides. The bangs in front were long and curved up and out past the ends of her eyeglasses. Others had copied it, most notably PJ and Patti and Wendi Barrie; but everyone seemed to acknowledge it as Jeanne Banfield's own style. He let a little smile escape at the joy of being so close to her, willingly meeting her eyes and wishing the sight before him would never change.

But there were plans for the evening. 'So; uh, fancy meeting you here,' he said, hoping that levity might help him through the moment.

She smiled right at him and, still leaning on the edge of the door, took a step back to open it further. 'Can you come in for a minute, please?'

He made a little shrug and stepped in, having to squeeze by her rather closely as she would not open the door too far. 'Uh; sorry if I'm a little late; but I kinda didn't get out on time.... It'll be cool, though; there's not too many cops out on Friday nights....'

Jeanne shut the door quietly. 'It's all right,' she said in a personal tone, and stepped into the sitting room to introduce her date. 'Mom, Daddy,' she said carefully, though she had never imagined she would actually speak the words of which she had so long dreamt, 'this is Jon Cavaliere.'

Jon took one hand out of his pocket and waved, a little shyly. 'Hi, there,' he said with a self-conscious smile, and then turned to take Mrs Banfield's hand in polite greeting. Pretty in the same way as her daughter, she seemed dizzily charmed by the gesture, her gentle face and bright-blue eyes suddenly aglow. Seeing this, her husband rose from the chair; and Jon crossed half the room to meet him. 'Mr Banfield,' he said seriously, as though meeting a business associate. 'Good to know you.'

They shook, leaning towards each other with their feet planted two paces apart. 'Jon,' the tall, sandy-haired man replied in the same manner, to press the name into memory. Already he had sensed a no-nonsense directness about the young man. As an engineer he appreciated such a lack of frivolity; so many of his daughter's dates had gingery handshakes and put up obvious façades of being respectable and artless; but in spite of the overly-long almost-blond hair this one gave the discernible impression of being the sort to whom the reins of the company, or even one's daughter, could be trusted without qualm. 'Going to a movie; hmmm?'

'Yes; that's the plan,' said Jon, and looked at Jeanne then.

She smiled at her mother and then said, 'Jon's a professional musician, Mom. He has the most popular group in town.'

'Well; it keeps one in gas money,' Jon said, with another shrug.

At the glaring understatement Jeanne gave him a wry look, half in surprise, half in amusement. Mrs Banfield delighted in his modesty, suspecting there was more to it than what was stated. 'I'm sure you've got quite a few admirers,' she said, 'to have earned a title like that.'

'Yeah; well; we've got something of a following, I suppose...' He smiled a little and looked again at Jeanne, by far his favourite fan, who smiled right back at him. Perhaps she would soon think him her favourite, as well. 'So; well; are we off, or.... I'm sorry; we are almost late.'

'Let me get my coat,' she said happily, and led him out to the foyer.

Both her parents watched him hold the rabbit jacket whilst she put her arms through the sleeves. 'Oh; thank you,' Jeanne said with a coy blush, and as they met eyes again she went wobbly all over with a terrific shiver, perhaps never realising how her parents would recognise her infatuation.

'Jeanne,' her mother called carefully, 'may I ask what time you'll be home?'

'Oh, Mom, I don't know....' She looked to Jon for an answer.

'The movie should be over at like eleven,' Jon told them; 'so, I guess not too late....'

'Well; we'll probably be up, dear. Have a nice time, now.'

'Okay, Mom,' she said, as Jon opened the front door. ''Night, Daddy.'

''Night,' Jon said to them both. 'Nice meeting you, now.'

The door closed. Jeanne zipped her jacket then and walked down the walk just a step ahead of Jon. 'Oh; you could've parked up here,' she said offhandedly.

The Caprice rested at the kerb, across the foot of the driveway. 'Yeah; well; it is kinda late, you know; I didn't want to disturb anybody.... To tell you the truth I sort of glided in. I think I shut it down a block back.'

He stepped in to open the door and she got in daintily, trying hard to look unruffled by the uniqueness of the evening. She sat stiffly in the cold vinyl seat while he walked round the rear of the car, like a chauffeur. There had been too many awkward moments already, though he seemed not to have noticed. Just be cool, she tried to tell herself. He doesn't have to know you're petrified....

He got in beside her. 'Seat belts,' he said bluntly, almost forgetting who she was. 'Always in this car.' He started the engine which lit with the usual roar. 'Oh; sorry. It's just– the last thing I want is for somebody other than me to go through the window.'

She reached down and found the belt. These slacks *are* too tight, she thought. I just knew it. He probably thinks I look like a hooker. Now he'll be ashamed to be seen with me....

'You look nice tonight,' he said softly, thinking that no man had ever understated anything so pointedly, and revved the engine a little.

She smiled, reluctant to appear as nervous as she felt. 'So do you,' she said lightly.

'Right,' he said, with that sardonic slant for which he was well known. 'Well; it's not really fair; of course it doesn't really do the clothes justice, seeing as you'd look good in *canvas*....' He shrugged. 'The jacket especially becomes you. I like the look of a lady in a fur coat.'

She thought about that. It was a nice enough comment for him to make; but then a shiver trickled down her spine. Perhaps Jon Cavaliere might insist that his girlfriend have things like fur coats. Of all the senior boys in school he and Bob Prescott were considered most able to afford such gifts with their own finances. Indeed the notion boggled the mind. 'I usually don't wear it to school,' she told him. 'I usually wear my school jacket, you know.'

'I know,' he said, smiling, and the car began rolling. 'I've seen you.'

She smiled too; and they were off.

The paper rustled. 'I don't like her going out so late,' he said; and his wife looked at him.

'Ralph, she goes on dates all the time. I've never worried about her.'

'You don't know this kid,' he said.

'Jeanne knows him. I understand he's very special to her.'

'Special!' he scoffed. 'She's never been out with him before.'

'She's known him for a long time,' Mrs Banfield said, and smiled to think about it. 'Really I can't imagine how you could say anything bad about him already.'

'He's a rock musician,' said Mr Banfield, 'for starters. Probably into drugs and God knows *what* else.'

'Oh, Ralph!' she laughed. 'Why think of things to worry about?'

'She's sixteen years old, going out at nine-thirty at night with a long-haired rock musician in a loud hot rod who worries about getting caught by the cops on Friday nights. Why *worry?*'

Mrs Banfield shook her head. 'Do you really think Jeanne would go out with anyone like you make him out to be?' She smiled. 'I have perfect confidence in her choice of young men. I don't think there's been one yet who hasn't been a gentleman to her. I know that she happens to be particularly fond of this one.'

'How do you know that?'

'Oh; she's told me a thing or two about him. He happens to be the same boy who saved her at the lake a few years back.'

He put down the paper and looked at her. 'That's the kid?' he asked, his interest piqued.

His wife nodded cheerfully. 'He's the one. She's quite infatuated with him, you know. Lord knows how hopelessly romantic she is; it's a very big thing for her to be asked out on a date by someone who may actually have saved her life. And he seems very charming; and anyone who helps her with her coat like that—'

'Steve Marlowe helped her with her coat,' he said tersely, and looked into the paper again.

'Yes; but she thinks Jon is much more romantic. He's a hero to her. All the girls love him; they think he's wonderful. Patti says they're all envious of Jeanne by now....' She smiled with maternal pride then.

'She's too young to be romantic,' said Jeanne's father. 'She's sixteen years old, Tina.'

'And very well able to choose a boyfriend for herself. She's been raised well. Try to see it the way she does. All she wants is to feel happy inside. She wants someone romantic, who brings her flowers and makes her dream about things like happy endings. That's all any girl wants. She wants to be able to lose her head in the stars.' She was quite pleased with the thought herself.

'You can't live your life with your head in the stars,' he said seriously. 'I don't know where these kids get these fantasies....'

'They get them from *us*, Ralph,' she smiled; and they met eyes then.

From the first exotic yet amusing scene, Jon was thrilled to see his favourite Beatles movie on the wide screen. The Stage Door was noted for playing art films and foreign pictures; and tonight the house was packed with devout fans of the four famous musicians from Liverpool. Jon whispered to Jeanne, just as he had warned her he would, pointing out the classic comedy sequences and occasionally explaining the esoteric humour for her. Far ahead of its time, *Help!* had been a flagship for the British film invasion, a milestone to be copied for years to come; yet, in its day, it was panned as a blatant commercial vehicle for fan-worship with inexcusable James Bond mimicry. Jeanne cared little for movie reviews or cinematic history. She was seeing a film for the first time with the dream date of a lifetime, elated with seeing him so happy and with how he wanted to entertain her. It was barely in her mind that every girl in school would be livid with envy on Monday morning when they learned she had attended a Beatles film with Jon Cavaliere of The Strawberries.

'*Dag*,' he kept saying, as they crossed the car park to his car; 'I *love* that movie, man. I've never seen that in a real movie theatre before. The sound was *great*.'

'So you're happy you came,' she teased; for she certainly knew the answer.

'Yeah, man,' he said, and then thought to tone down his impolitic enthusiasm. 'I just... hope you didn't think it was stupid. Lots of people do.'

'No,' she said; 'not really. It's just that with English people, you know, I don't always understand what they're saying.'

'Yeah; I know; and lots of people don't get the jokes. But that kinda thing broadens you, you know, in a cultural sense. That's what I like to think. All foreign film is great like that. I've watched French movies and Italian movies where you barely understand a thing and you can still follow the story if you want to.'

'Like some of those operas people go to see,' Jeanne said. 'Do they really understand everything?'

'No; not always. You have to figure it out, from what you're given. You just have to think a little. Sometimes I think a lot of people are too lazy; you know? The average Joe Public just doesn't want to have to exercise for his entertainment. Consequently you see the quality of the average person's entertainment in this country.'

'That's a very good point,' she observed.

He opened the car door for her. 'I'm sorry. I was beginning to preach; wasn't I?' He looked at her seriously.

She shrugged, still standing up inside the open door. 'No. Not really. I happen to agree with you. I just wish I had, you know, more opportunities to see different things.'

He smiled at her. 'Get out. With all the places you've lived in?'

She was touched to see he had not forgotten what she had told him of her life, so long ago. 'Well; I was very young then, you know.'

He shrugged. 'My mom does have a subscription to a theatre group in the city,' he said offhandedly; and she was left to assume he meant Manhattan. 'I'll have to steal a coupla tickets to something good from her, sometime.'

'Wow; I think I'd really like that,' she told him honestly, with a genuine smile, and sat in the car.

He went round to the offside, slid the key into the ignition switch and turned to look at her. She looked right back at him in the dark, scarcely two feet away; and the courage with which he had been able to look her in the eye all evening still astounded him. Then again she always had been his favourite sight. 'I really am glad I got to see that movie,' he said quietly. 'It was kinda something I've been looking forward to, you know.'

She smiled at him, though her heart was pounding. For a second she could not reply; they only sat and stared at each other in the darkness. At last, in a strangely soft voice, she managed to say, 'I'm glad I got to see it with you.'

He smiled at that and made a little shrug before turning to start the engine. 'Well; I might've gone by myself, or with one of the guys; but, well, it was nice to get to see it with you, you know, so…. Hah! —now you get to see what I'm made of.'

Jeanne made a little giggle then. The engine caught and he ran it up whilst his face blushed red. Well, he thought; I just blew a good opportunity, there. I actually think I could've *kissed* her right then. It probably would've actually worked, but no; me, the idiot, has to blow the one and only chance he'll probably ever have to kiss the one and only Jeanne Banfield; and now, I just look like the one and only jerk. Well; all jerks get what they deserve; right? Nothing left to do but try to salvage what's left of the evening….

He let in the clutch and steered the car out onto the highway. 'I was just thinking,' he said carefully, 'if you like, you know, if it's not too late, we could maybe go out and get something, you know; like I was thinkin' maybe hot cocoa…. It's up to you.'

She smiled, feeling herself growing warmer already. 'Oh; that'd be nice.'

'Cool.' He smiled a little and thought, *nice*. She says it'd be *nice*….

Jeanne noticed how smoothly and conservatively he drove, never racing the engine nor even winding gears out very far, patiently enduring the camshaft's boisterous idle at the traffic signals and easing in the clutch gently when it was time to go. In a way, she would have loved for him to just stomp on the accelerator and give her the ride of her life, as the speed was exhilarating and this car in particular carried the distinction of being the fastest in town. But she was thrilled to witness this other side of him, the earnest gentleman who wanted so much to make a good impression for a lady. The evening had certainly been a date to remember, the stuff of dreams that no daydream had ever been able to predict for her. Her stomach was atremble with butterflies; she could barely contain the yearning desire to shriek aloud in sheer joy.

At Annie's Ice Cream Heaven in Wilshire, they sat in a booth along the back wall and had jelly doughnuts and hot cocoa with marshmallows. For a while they were both uncomfortably silent and then, merely for conversation, Jeanne said, 'So; did I hear your brother made the varsity swim team for next fall?'

'Yeah,' Jon said; 'lucky him…. He's got good endurance, though. He'll be Weber's top distance man.'

'You sound pretty confident,' she smiled.

'Yeah; well; you get to tell, you know. And from lookin' at everybody's little brothers and from the juniors there now, Drew could beat them all. He has the stamina that I don't have. All I can do is sprint well. I really never put in enough practice time.'

'I bet everybody in your family swims well,' she supposed.

'Well; yeah; it's a natural thing, you know; and we were raised around boats, and like my dad always wanted to have a pool; so…. He grew up on the Sound; and they had always been able to swim. Anybody can swim.'

She laughed a little at that. 'Well,' she said; 'that time you fished me out of the lake, I wasn't doing too well.'

Jon said nothing at that. That memory was only a source of profound embarrassment for him now. He had hoped they would discuss nothing more than four days old.

Jeanne sat and stared into her cocoa, appalled at her own boldness. She had never dreamt of saying that to him; at once she regretted it. His silence made it still worse; and she realised she would have to say something or face that all she had gained over the entire evening might dissipate into thin air. 'Jon,' she said, 'can I, uh, ask you something?'

'Sure,' he said, more to be polite than to willingly field the question he feared she would ask.

Feeling herself go red she stared down at her half-finished doughnut. 'Well; I'm not really sure how to put this; but, uh, well; I was just kind of wondering, you know, how since— Well; it might seem like a stupid question; and I don't want to— Well; since that class, you know, in physical-science—'

She looked up and stopped; he was shaking his head mournfully. 'I was pretty stupid, wasn't I?'

'*Stupid?*' She shrugged. 'No, Jon; I wouldn't say stupid—'

'Yeah,' he said, with a nervous little chuckle; '*stupid*. Stupid's the best word for it. I was just being scared of you, you know; and being that scared of somebody so much is really pretty stupid.'

She stared at him, quite surprised to hear such a thing. 'Jon, I would never want you to be *scared*…. Why would you be afraid of me?'

'Well….' He shook his head, making a little smile; but she could see she had struck a sensitive nerve within him. Somewhere there was a side to all this that she had never imagined. 'I used to kind of… think about you a lot, in those days. Well; I was a lot younger then, I guess; but the point is like I never grew out of it. The more I thought about you, the less important everything else began to get; and pretty soon, well, I guess I thought I had you pretty much figured-out the way I expected you should be. And then I started thinking that maybe you wouldn't really be like that at all. So I became afraid that you wouldn't be; and then I just stopped being able to face the real person any more. I know this all sounds pretty stupid–'

'Jon, it's not *stupid*,' she tried to tell him.

'Naah; basically inside I'm pretty stupid,' he said.

'No you're not,' she said in a soft voice. 'You're just a real person, that's all. Everybody has feelings like that; but, the thing is, nobody ever wants to admit them. I guess I used to– Well; I know I used to think about you, too, you know, pretty much in the same way.... I mean: like all the time, I thought about you, and what you'd be like, if I really did know you again.... But like when I first saw *The Strawberries*....' She smiled a little and, when he gave a little laugh at that, she knew she had come in with the right approach. 'I mean: you couldn't know what that felt like.'

He smiled at her and then quickly looked down at his cup of cocoa. 'Yeah; it felt like sitting down front at basketball games in junior high just to watch the cheerleaders,' he said. 'And I even hate basketball.'

At that they both laughed. 'You know,' she said openly, 'when I first saw you playing at that concert contest, the first thing I thought was how fantastic it was for you, that you were gonna be so successful, and have so much fun.... And the next thing I thought was that it was sad, because I'd probably never get to know you again.'

He smiled. 'Yeah; but why not? Because I'm some unreachable superstar?' Scoffing a little he laughed at the notion. 'Hah. Get out. I could never be like that. Like, I always used to wanna be this big famous recording star, like on TV and doo, and still attending public high school. That might've been really cool, maybe. But I've always wanted to be a performer of some kind. It's not like I'm some kinda showoff, you know; I'm not really that outgoing, really, and it has nothing to do with my ego. It's just that it's... so much *fun*.'

'Mmmm,' she mused. 'I can imagine.'

'I mean: here I am, doing something I honest-to-God enjoy, and I get paid for it. Man; I'll take *all* the bad with the good for that chance. Do you know how many people can honestly say they'd keep doing their job tomorrow if they stopped getting paid? I'll bet you the number's not very substantial. I just know that I'll play music, all kinds of music, for the rest of my life. I know it sounds corny; but... it's like a part of me.'

'Mmmm,' she smiled, impressed with how satisfied he seemed with his own life. She could only hope to have something to add to it, to make it all even better for him. 'I guess I must look like a real groupie, then; huh?' she said, smiling right at him.

'Naah. You just look like a nice girl who happens to like watching a bunch of guys who formed a band play every once in a while, that's all.'

She was still looking straight at him, as though incredibly self-confident or just utterly mesmerised. 'Especially one of the guys in particular.'

Jon looked down, feeling himself blush like never before. To relieve himself of the embarrassment he would just have to admit his inadequacy. 'Well,' he said after a moment; in a purposely bright tone of voice, 'I'm not going to top that, so I won't even try. We'll talk about something else.'

Jeanne began to laugh, and suddenly she felt so at-ease with him that she wanted to giggle on for ever. Jon laughed a little too; and the two of them sat there and smiled at each other for a long minute without a word. The joy of merely being together at last was thrilling; at last they had something that could truly be called a friendship.

He glanced up at the clock on the far wall and then said, 'I hope the car wasn't gonna turn into a pumpkin at midnight. It's ten after *now*.'

'Yeah,' she giggled, loving the analogy he had just made.

He smiled at her with a beautiful white-toothed grin that made her heart skip. 'Well,' he said, raising his mug of cocoa; 'I would say a toast is in order.'

'By all means,' she agreed readily, supremely struggling to resist exploding in an uncontrolled outburst of giggles as she picked up her mug.

They touched cups over the table. 'To a pleasant evening,' he said; 'or, something like that. What shall we say?'

'To getting to know each other again,' she proposed sincerely, 'after too long.'

Jon was touched by her sentiment and chose his words with care. 'All right, then; to two old friends chatting away in the ice-cream parlour. May they both chat away till they're old and grey.'

'*Perfect*,' Jeanne said happily; and they could barely contain their delight, both exhilarated to know that what they had shared this evening would never belong to anyone else.

He opened the car door for her in front of 119 Old Mill Road. Wearily she stepped out onto the slippery kerb, stifling a yawn. 'Sorry,' Jon said; 'but I guess I do have that effect on some people.'

'No,' she apologised; 'it's not you.' She stood up straight then. 'I just didn't really expect to be going out tonight, till you called....'

'A polite enough excuse,' he smiled. 'I'll buy that.'

'Oh!' she sighed, and tapped him on the shoulder to tease. He shut the car door and allowed her to lean on him as they walked up the path to the front porch. 'I'm just so worn-out!'

'And, amazingly, she does not look it.'

'Oh; but I *feel* it!' They stepped up to the door. Lights were still on in the sitting room. Jeanne turned to Jon and said, in a forlorn tone, 'Oh; and you won't be at the party tomorrow night; will you?'

'No,' he said with a smile.

'I was hoping maybe you'd go, and maybe I'd see you there.... I mean I've never been to one of Cindy's parties, at least, not since junior high. I usually go to PJ's, or Carole Martin's or Debbie Lehigh's.... Do you know Debbie Lehigh?'

'I know *her*,' he said. 'Ask her if she knows *me*.'

'Oh; she must know *you*. Everyone seems to know you–'

'And *you*,' he smiled.

She sighed. 'And you have a show tomorrow....' She stood up straight on her high shoes, and her forehead came just to the bridge of his nose. Right to him she said, 'I really wish I could see it.'

Her sensuality was irresistible. No girl had ever been more alluring in dropping so blunt a hint. 'Oh,' he said, feigning nonchalance; 'it's all the way up on the other side of Hartford. It'd just be a long boring ride. Wait till we start playing around here again, after the end of the month. Lotta good shows then, like the Den, and the Pub.... I could get you in to see some of those gigs.'

'Oh; *could* you? I mean it is exciting, you know, seeing someone you *know* up there, being famous....' She laughed, lightly; and he was captivated by her radiance. 'Oh; but really, Jon, thank you *so* much for such a *really* nice evening....'

'It was nice for me too,' he said sincerely. 'You made it all worthwhile.'

Jeanne smiled a little, and suddenly she seemed very shy, even vulnerable. 'Well; it was your favourite movie, and your money.... I just want you to know it was very special.'

Jon watched her turn and rest her hand upon the doorknob. She hesitated; he was not sure if she intended to, but something told him he could not let the evening end just yet. Something about it all, the film and the doughnut shop and what they had discussed, would never leave him, no matter how long he lived. This is it, he thought; and the notion raced wildly about in his head. This is it. There will never be another night like this. It may be the only chance I'll ever get. There's only ever *one* first time. It *has* to be that way. It's Fate....

She turned, spontaneously, and found him just a foot away. As she looked up into his eyes, he reached to her, gently, laying one hand to her side and touching her very softly on the cheek. Her hands went to his chest as if by instinct, and she took in one last shaking breath and closed her eyes. His eyes closed too; and their lips found each other. Terrific tingles rocketed through them both, and the goosepimples arose up all over. For three very long seconds there was only ecstasy on the doorstep.

Jeanne let out a faint whimpering sigh and opened her eyes only halfway, unwilling to awaken from her trance. Jon shivered, realising he was just standing there looking into her eyes, and then shyly turned away. She knew what he felt; it was what she felt too. Her eyes went down, seeing the olive-green Army patch on the breast of his jacket imprinted with his surname. She slid a hand up and touched it with her fingertips; something made her want to gaze at it for hours. 'I, uh, have to go in,' she whispered, regretting that her parents had waited up for her. Her eyes went misty; she might have felt safe and warm on the doorstep all night.

'Uh, yeah,' he said, looking about a bit before turning back to her. 'Well; uh, I'll see you in school, I guess….'

'Yes,' she said in a hushed tone. 'I had a nice time.'

He looked straight into her eyes then and whispered, 'Good night.'

'Good night,' she whispered too, still softer. He took a step back, hating to leave, and she released him only at arm's-length, very reluctantly. Her hand lifted to him in farewell; and he smiled, made a trite little wave and stepped down off the porch, walking back the way he had come, with his hands in his back pockets. When he turned at the car she had gone; and the bright-red door had just swung closed.

He sat in the car and laid his hand on the key he had left in the ignition, staring for a few long seconds at the other seat where she had been. Over the past few days she had become more than a dream to him; she had really been there, giggling at his jokes with that cute, enchanting laugh, talking to him with that melodic, silky voice, and smiling with that unforgettably gorgeous smile he had not seen so close in four years. Now, he had nothing to prove that it had all actually happened, nothing but the two ticket stubs in his billfold and the paper receipt from the ice cream parlour and the feeling on his lips that tingled even still; but he knew in his heart that it had all been real and that he would savour the memory for ever. A more perfect dream-come-true he had never imagined.

She gave the door a gentle push to close it, watching through the linen curtains as the silver-and-white car coasted away under the crisp winter moonlight. Sad to see the evening close, she turned towards the staircase. *Wow*, her mind reeled; he *kissed* me…. I actually went out with Jon Cavaliere, and then he kissed me…. Wow…. Slowly the realisation came to her; and still she could only think, *Wow*….

'Did you have a nice time, dear?' called her mother; and when there was no immediate answer she got up to find her daughter leaning dizzily against the banister. 'Is everything all right?'

'*Wow*,' she breathed, unable even to see clearly through tears of euphoria. 'He *kissed* me….'

Mrs Banfield smiled, knowing well her daughter's love of romance. It had never been cause for worry; for she knew well that Jeanne only sought the noblest intentions in young men. If she was happy she must have found someone worthy of her. Carefully Jeanne negotiated the stairs, taking each step with great deliberation, though she barely saw them. As her mother watched she tiptoed into her own room and silently closed the door.

Eve was sitting up at the kitchen table, halfway through a trite teenaged romance novel and a dish of chopped apricots in whipped cream. 'Hey,' she said cheerfully as her elder brother came through the door; 'what's up? How was the movie?'

'Oh,' Jon sighed, draping his leather jacket over the doorknob; 'it was *okay*.' And without any more words he tromped quietly up the back steps.

* * *

Chapter 8

Danny boy, this is a showdown

Jon spent a very long Saturday, first helping Dave with the detail painting of his Monte Carlo coupé in the garage behind Aunt Audrey's house. Dave was proud of his recent acquisition, a rare one indeed with its factory-installed four-speed gearbox and positive-traction rear differential. They had rebuilt the original 454 engine to blueprint specifications over the autumn and sprayed the metallic black colour just last week. Jon did a beautiful job with the gold-enamelled pinstripes.

After that evening's successful show at the Hoakum Civic Center, The Strawberries held a practice on Sunday during which Chris addressed the subject of the Beatles films which had played at the Stage Door in the week. They all agreed that the band would have to produce a few similarly clever video recordings to present and promote their material since, as Dave pointed out, the visual presentation of popular music would soon become as important as the sound.

Jon had no chance to consider his new social stature until after supper on Sunday evening. He retired to his room in the attic over the kitchen and sat back with a glass of dinner wine to contemplate his situation. Not only had he secured a date with Jeanne Banfield, although after some doing, but he had actually kissed her and it had obviously been to her great satisfaction. The idea of keeping such a popular and desirable girl happy merely by being himself had always been something of an unreachable star with him; he had never really expected to have any success in the area despite all his wishes to the contrary. Now the mere notion of Jeanne Banfield actually remaining interested in him made his insides quiver. In the dark of his room he closed his eyes and revelled in the thrill of it all.

But Danny Harris loomed up as a nearly insurmountable hurdle before him. Certainly Harris was very possessive; and Jon considered that with Jeanne Banfield in the offing perhaps no-one in his right mind could be expected to be otherwise. The situation was now that he had in effect gone out with another's girlfriend, something he had promised himself long ago that he would never do if only for his own profound respect for the sanctity of a lady's reputation. But though he knew in his own mind that, no matter what the consequences of the inevitable power struggle, the ends would certainly justify the means, he did worry as to how far Harris might want to draw out the issue.

Jon had no plans for surrender. In fact he had the memory of an exquisite evening with a lovely young lady to cherish for ever and nothing to lose beyond the potential for many happy returns. Harris stood to lose the most popular girl in school, one he considered exclusively his own. Armed with only the bold determination to make his dream come true, Jon steeled himself for a siege that might be quite long, even bloody.

Monday marked the start of the second semester; and for Jon that meant all but his physical-education and draughtsmanship classes changed over to new rooms and new teachers and, of course, new classmates. He had been nervously wary all day of discovering Danny Harris in one of his new classes, most of which were college-preparatory or senior-level, and was relieved when last period came round and he found an old junior-high schoolmate and fellow class clown beside him in Room 152. 'Hey, dude; what's up?'

'Hey, Jon,' Paul Orwell said, with that indelible grin. 'So what brings *you* here?'

'Dude, I don't know,' Jon sighed, leaning back in the seat. 'British Literature, man. I can tell *this* class'll be a thrill.'

'Diggit,' Paul laughed; and the two of them shared trivial chatter whilst the room filled. The seat to the left of Jon had been reserved with someone's notebook and textbook since he had come in; and soon a blonde in black passed him and sat down there. The late bell rang, still with no sign of any teacher, and only then Jon happened to turn forwards.

'Jon,' she said to him, 'you must be blind.'

He saw her out the corner of his eye and spun round to face her pretty smile. In the soft black pullover she had an irresistibly sultry look; for a moment he wished they were alone somewhere and then dismissed the thought with embarrassment that she might have read his mind. '*Hey*,' he said offhandedly, as he might have addressed anyone else. 'Didn't expect to see *you* here.'

Jeanne made a little giggle, her voice making that very alluring musical tone. Perhaps they had shared the same thoughts after all. '*I* did,' she confessed. 'I happened to see in the schedule this morning that we would both be in this class.'

'How underhanded of you,' he teased, 'to find out and not let me know.'

Paul laughed, somewhat surprised or impressed that Jon was apparently more than a passing acquaintance of Jeanne Banfield. The same could not be said for the overwhelming majority of high-school boys, no matter what the rumours reported. 'Who did you have last semester?' she asked, leaning on her hand with her elbow out on the desktop, quietly overjoyed with the opportunity to make friendly conversation with him.

'For what, English?' He chuckled, aware others were paying

attention. 'I had Mrs Cool. And she was cool, too.'

'Diggit,' agreed Paul, and Jon looked round at Jeanne again.

She was still leaning on her hand, looking straight at him with a cute smile. 'I don't know her,' she said.

The teacher came in, a tall, slender brunette of about twenty-five called Miss Simpson. She admitted she had no long-term goals but to have a good time introducing the literature curriculum to cooperative students. 'It can be very interesting if you let it be,' she said. 'It's always neat to see how writers have progressed over the years, and yet there's so much that remains the same....'

'Oh, *yes*,' Paul Orwell said aloud; 'we all know how much fun literature always is.'

The class moaned and grumbled sarcastically with agreeing dissent. 'Hey; speak for yourself,' Jon said. 'I prefer to look upon the study of literature from western civilisation as an intellectual challenge.'

People laughed; none of them took him seriously. 'Funny,' mused John Artis; 'I look at *Playboy* the same way.'

Miss Simpson laughed along with her students. 'Well; I'm glad to see this is an outgoing class.'

''Long as I pass,' Jon said blandly.

'Diggit,' someone else agreed.

'Well,' asked the teacher; 'so what's everyone interested in?'

'The *chicks*!' someone called out.

'A lot of good sleep,' came a comment from the far corner.

'Yo,' Jon spoke up; 'is this gonna be one of them classes where we gotta sit in alphabetical seats?'

'No way!' Terri Milgram complained.

'Well,' Miss Simpson tried; 'I *had* thought, since it's easier to take roll–'

'Hey; I'm just sick of sitting in the same seat in every class,' Jon told her. 'You'll recognise us.'

'How could anyone not recognise *you*?' came a familiar voice.

'Oh *jeez*,' Jon complained; 'now I gotta deal with Chubs in this class too....'

Cindy took it all in stride. 'Yeah,' she came back; 'well; just remember the rest of us gotta deal with *you*, too.'

The class laughed; and Jon allowed himself to bear the gibe. He was after all most interested in being entertaining, whether the joke be on himself or someone else. 'We could take roll ourselves,' suggested Sylvia Monteone. 'You know, like call out our names, and–'

'No thanks,' Jeanne spoke up; and the majority of them laughed in agreement.

'Too *corny*,' Paul said. 'It'd be like "The Dating Game", and doo.'

'Diggit,' said Jon. 'Our next eligible bachelor is a handsome young senior from East End Drive who likes speedboats and fishing; let's welcome: Paul Orwell.'

'Diggit!' someone seconded; and the class howled in laughter.

'So hey,' Jon called up to the teacher; 'can we do without the alphabetical seats, here; or what?'

Miss Simpson smiled at him, having identified that amusing and intelligent student of the class who would be the catalyst for her casual teaching style. 'The first amendment shall be: there are no alphabetical seats.'

'Dig *that!*' cheered Paul; and they all applauded.

The literature class in Room 152 began to look like a lot of fun for everyone, especially for Jon and Jeanne. By Tuesday the students had settled into what would remain their permanent seating arrangement. Jon sat fourth back in the third row, almost exactly in the centre of the room, with Paul Orwell just to his right, Jeanne just to his left and his old fifth-grade classmate, Cindy Bell, ahead of Jeanne. He was overjoyed that Jeanne seemed so willing to accept him after all. Such had only ever been a dream of his before. But now, after the date and the kiss and the achievement of a real speaking relationship that could be adequately exhibited in public, the reality of it all had transcended his wildest daydreams. Just to consider it all was dizzying.

On Tuesday afternoon Jon happened by the gymnasium, where he knew the cheer squad held their regular practice. He strolled across the varnished floor of the boys' side in his high-heeled shoes and leaned in the open doorway of the folding divider wall, gazing off into the opposite side as the girls went through their routines. Of the thirteen girls on the varsity squad only four were not seniors: Wendi Barrie, Patti Harper, Paula Jean Carson and Jeanne Banfield. In their short maroon-and-amber skirts and soft white woollen sweaters they were all cute to him, and he was proud of himself for having dated the prettiest one of them all. Once, as a part of one of the routines, she turned round, saw him there and gave him a little wave, happily surprised that he would stay after school to watch her.

Across the girls' gymnasium Danny Harris saw Jeanne wiggle her fingers at the long-haired boy in the leather jacket who leaned in the little doorway. It had upset him that she had met his proposal to go steady with nothing more than absolute indecision; but he had thought at first how it was just like her to take her time in making up her mind. Since that ludicrous scuffle on Friday morning, however, he had begun to see things in a different light. Jeanne had been unusually out of contact with him all weekend; and upon the start of the week the rumour mill's headline was that she had gone out with Jon Cavaliere. Danny looked up and suddenly remembered the dashing young man from the ski trip, the one riding the snowmobile in the woods, winning bets in the billiard room, entertaining everyone at the piano and dancing with Patti at the mixer.   He felt his face growing red at the embarrassment this slight little babyfaced musician had caused him. Something would certainly have to be done about it.

Jeanne did not see Danny get up but, once, she saw he was no longer seated on the bottom row of the bleachers with Miss Robb's bag and PJ's new fur coat.   Out the corner of her eye she saw him walking round the end of the line of girls; but they were in the middle of a cheer and she could not turn about to watch him.   She wanted to look at Jon, too, but there were a few frog-leaps to do in the routine and she needed to concentrate.   Anticipation was making a giant pit in her stomach.

Harris walked right up to Jon and took the open door in his hand to close it. 'We have something to discuss, I think.'

'Oh?' Jon asked, feigning nonchalance. 'I'm open to discussions.'

Harris stepped in past him and pulled the door closed so that they were both in the boys' side of the gymnasium, out of sight and earshot from the girls.   'I don't like your attitude, man,' Harris said to him, stalking towards him from two feet away. 'You're out to get your pretty little face busted.'

Jon scoffed. 'Oh; and so *I'm* the one with the attitude, then? Hell; I thought *you* were the one with the attitude. All I ever said was—'

Harris shoved him with both hands.   Without a second's hesitation Jon shoved him right back. 'Look, pretty boy; don't *push* me,' Harris said angrily, and shoved him again. 'You've got a *hell* of an attitude problem, man.'

The cheer ended and a new one began. Jeanne wanted desperately to take any excuse to see what had become of the two boys.   She stood and stared at the closed door until Miss Robb yelled 'Cut!' and they had to begin the whole cheer over again. She thought she heard what might have been a fight but with the girls all stamping their feet at once and clapping and cheering it was impossible to hear anything too well. God, she prayed, maybe they'll just talk it out. Jon's a rational person. Maybe they'll just argue a while, and get it all settled....

When the cheer ended there was no sound at all from the other side of the wall. Jeanne went white with worry, putting no stock in her optimistic suppositions of even a few moments ago. The other girls all stood and watched as she whirled about and marched straight over to the little door.   'Hey Jeannie!' Michelle called; but Patti was already going after her.

Jeanne dropped her pompons and got the door open, after some trouble as the latch did tend to stick.   They all saw her stare openmouthed off into the boys' side and then suddenly run off, disappearing beyond the wall. Patti flung herself round the corner of the door straight after her, and the other girls all bolted for the door too.

He was on his hands and knees on the floor about ten yards from the door, close to the wall. Jeanne rushed over and slid to a stop, landing on her knees right next to him. Bending to look at his face she saw the gruesome pool of blood on the floor. Still more ran out of his nose. At once she felt faint, wishing she could turn her head; but there was a more urgent need to care for the one who cared so much for her.

The cheerleading girls, as well as a dozen boys from the cabana and several people from either gallery, had all come in to see what had gone on. Jeanne bent over, close to his cheek, and said softly, 'Jonny? Are you all right?'

Jon nodded, unwilling to speak, ashamed to have her see him inglorious in defeat. He sniffled, pinching his nose closed with his fingers. Blood ran down the back of his hand. 'This sucks,' he said in a quiet voice.

'All right, Jon,' Patti said, calm through any storm. 'Can you stand up?'

'Oh my God,' PJ said, feeling ill at ease; 'his nose is broken. Oh my God....'

'It ain't broken,' he said, impatient with all the attention. 'This always happens.'

'This is all my fault,' Jeanne said, and started to weep. 'I'm sorry, Jon; it was all my fault....'

'It ain't your fault,' he said, and put one foot down to stand up. 'This always happens. Dude's gonna think he can take me just 'cause a little blood starts flyin'. It's a little hard to finish a fight when the other guy leaves at the sight of blood....'

Patti and Cheryl helped him stand up as Jeanne held onto his elbow and wept guiltily. He put back his head but the rush of blood was dizzying. Immediately he put out a hand and went into the wall; Patti kept a hold on him and would not let him go down. The wall felt good to lean on; and he stood there with his head back for a few minutes, breathing through his mouth whilst his nose filled with blood and trying to ignore all the attention. One of the PE instructors came out of the boys' cabana and called over, 'So what's this? —another fight victim?' The girls all turned and glared at him, repulsed by his cynical lack of compassion; the man actually shrank away from them in humility.

Jeanne stood in front of Jon, trying to look up into his eyes under the hair. She put a hand on his shoulder and would have hugged him had it not been for the blood that ran down the sides of his cheeks and stained his neck and chin. 'I'm sorry,' she said, in a very quiet tone of sadness. 'I'm so sorry. I just had no idea, really; and I just wish I had been able to talk—'

'Forget it,' he said, sounding stronger, or bolder. 'It was just a dumb thing that happened. I always get nosebleeds. Best thing to do is let it run. Just let me get to a bathroom; huh?'

'Are you sure you're all right?'

'I'm sure that I'd like to go puke, if you'll excuse me,' he said, exasperated, and got away from all of them. Patti asked two boys in PE attire to escort him to the cabana, and they did, somewhat intimidated by the pool of blood and all the pretty cheerleaders and the evidence of the fight, of which they had only caught the aftermath.

Jeanne watched him go through the doors at the far end of the gymnasium and then turned to sidestep the puddle of blood, so horribly broad for a mere nosebleed. PJ met her eyes first and went to put an arm about her good friend. 'God,' Jeanne sobbed; 'I just don't know what to *do*. I just wish that everything would go away, and let me start over....'

'Oh, no, no, *no*,' whispered PJ, patting her on the back; 'don't say that. You don't really mean that, Jeannie. The good stuff has been too good. It'll all be all right.'

After ten minutes the girls had all given up on today's cheer practice. Miss Robb, considering the circumstances, requested a conference with Jeanne for the next opportunity and dismissed them all. Actually only Donna and Heidi left.

The 12.45 bell rang, beginning homeroom for the afternoon session; and finally Jeanne decided she would have to go in to the boys' cabana to bring Jon out. PJ and Patti were trying to dissuade her from this when he came out alone, holding a clump of toilet tissue up to his nose. 'Dag; you guys are still here?' he asked, attempting to appear unaffected by the episode in front of two or three disinterested boys and eleven pretty, popular girls who were obviously interested in his condition. 'Yes; well; the zombie walks, and doo, just as all the dead shall rise from the grave....'

A few of them did laugh, understanding his need to be entertaining rather than an object for female pity. They had all come to expect it of him anyway. 'You look like you feel better,' said PJ, as Jeanne hurried up to take his arm.

'Oh; yeah. I'm going skydiving right after this. So who's got any tissues? Come on; don't be holdin' out on the tissues, now....'

'I've got some!' Wendi said; and she and Patti ran back round to the girls' side of the gymnasium, slipping hurriedly through the little doorway.

'I'm glad you feel better,' Jeanne said to him.

'Oh; yeah.... This stupid school toilet paper rots; let me tell you.'

Patti and Wendi slid back up to the door and came up to him, both with their handbags and handfuls of tissues. 'I guess it pays to have a cold,' PJ teased.

'Really,' said Wendi, saving a few for herself.

'You have a cold?' Jon asked, as PJ handed him a wad of clean, perfumed tissues. 'Forget it then. All I need now is *more* junk from up my nose.' Some of the others giggled at his earnest attempts at humour in spite of the circumstances. He took the tissues anyway.

Jeanne got him to put an arm about her which made her look as though she were helping him stand, an appearance she felt she had to make for all involved. 'Are you gonna be all right?' she asked.

'Oh; I'm fine, I tell you. Skydiving; was that it?' Now it was only sarcasm, sharp and cutting, and she felt terribly belittled by it.

He met eyes with Patti, who looked none too amused. 'Jeannie,' she said sensibly, 'make sure he gets home okay; all right? And you know a trip to the doctor wouldn't hurt.'

'Aaah,' Jon winced; 'I don't need no doctor....'

Jeanne turned to escort Jon out to the rear doors, in front of the boys' locker-room entrance where they had met last week for their ride home. 'Patti,' she said, 'could you–?'

Patti nodded. 'Yes, of course; I'll bring your stuff home.'

'Oh; let me get you a coat!' PJ said suddenly, and ran back to the girls' side again.

'So hey, kids,' Jon said over his shoulder to them all; 'thanks for all the nursing service....'

'Take care,' Wendi called after him, her cheerful tone at odds with Patti's worried wince.

Jon waved absently at them all and got away from Jeanne's arm. The profuse bleeding bothered him; for when he had been about eight a lesser artery inside his nose had ruptured and had to be surgically mended. Since then he had frequently suffered minor nosebleeds; though this one had been going for fifteen minutes straight.

PJ scuffled up with her own dark-brown rabbit-pelt jacket and helped her friend into it whilst Jeanne tried to keep up with Jon. He kicked the panic bar on the gallery door, which banged into its stops and recoiled to bump his shoulder as he passed. Jeanne pulled PJ's coat up her shoulders and hurried after him. He opened the exit door in the gallery the same way and stomped out into the cold. Jeanne caught up with him and took his left arm in both hands. 'Look,' he said; 'you don't have to do this. I'm fine, really.'

'I just want to make sure you're all right,' she told him.

'I'm fine.'

'I can't believe he would *do* this; I just *can't*....'

'Yeah; that's some boyfriend you've got there,' he said sarcastically. 'Really a mature little *gentleman*, that one.'

Perhaps neither of them recalled her complimenting him for being the gentleman in driving her friends home. 'Well; just wait till *I* get a hold of him,' Jeanne said strongly. 'I just might beat him up *myself.*'

'Right,' Jon said with no expression. 'Next time *I* see him, the chump may well have a switchblade to deal with.'

She shook her head, watching the pavement. 'You're not a fighter, Jon.'

'Pity you didn't know me when I was,' he said under his breath.

She looked up at him then and might have shivered. 'Well; I'm just sorry you had to be involved,' she said. 'You're not the kind of guy who gets messed up in stupid situations like this.'

'Oh; I'm not; huh? Well you know I *was* stupid enough to go out with somebody else's girlfriend.'

'I'm *not* Danny's girlfriend,' she said emphatically. 'I'll be anyone's girlfriend I *want* to be. And if I want to go to a movie with you, then I *will*; and Danny's not going to beat up people because of it. If he's mad at me, then he can take it up with *me*. I'm just sorry *you* had to get wrapt-up in all this, Jon. It's too far beneath you.'

He wanted to think about that, because he had never considered what kind of battles she might be willing to fight for him. He unlocked the nearside door for her, merely flinging it open and stomping round to the other side. 'I don't know where *you're* going,' he told her; ''cause *I'm* going *home*.'

'I'm going *with* you,' she said across the roof of the car; and they both got in together. 'I want to make sure you take care of that nose.'

'Yeah; well; you could wash the blood outa this shirt,' he said, as though to make her feel responsible, or guilty, and slid his key into the ignition switch.

'Do you want me to drive?' she asked cautiously.

'No.' He started the engine and shifted into reverse straight away.

'Are you sure you'll be all right, shifting gears, and—'

'Better than you'd be. Your seatbelt's not on.'

She reached down to fasten it; and he let out the clutch pedal at once. The car jolted back and he shifted into first, yanking the wheel round with the same hand and releasing the clutch pedal again. The tyres threw up chunks of melting snow and scattered it about the car park. Jeanne gasped at the speed at which he drove out the snowy lane, in second gear with the rear of the car fishtailing about at every turn. 'Jon, do you have *your* belt on?' she asked, and looked up with the inside half of his seatbelt in her hand to see the open gate of the Atlantic Parkway entrance directly ahead. '*Ee!*' she squeaked.

But Jon only flung the wheel about with his right hand and nailed the throttle. The rear of the car slipped to the left in the snow and he lifted his right foot for only a second, ending the slide on course to head west down the Parkway. Down went the throttle again and, with that positive-traction differential, they accelerated away in precisely a straight line.

'Jon,' she worried, 'maybe you should let me drive—'

'Forget it,' he said, letting go the wheel to shift up to third. They were doing forty in the snow already. His angry impatience frightened Jeanne; he drove with only one hand, still holding the bloody clump of tissues up to his nose with his left elbow propped on the top edge of the door. Least of all for the moment was the worry that the nose was in fact still bleeding. They slid round to the left to make the U-turn towards the east end of town, speeding out in second gear with a great squall of snow-slinging tyre-spinning. The engine took on its usual snarl as the supercharger crept up to pressure; and they were by the schoolyard and doing sixty on the packed snow of the Parkway within seconds.

Jeanne held her breath as they swept past a few traffic lights barely before the yellow had turned to red. Her heart rose to her mouth each time he let go the wheel to shift; neither the snow nor the nosebleed seemed to make any effect on his driving style and he changed gears as often as ever. They entered the end of Lake Drive with another deliberate, controlled slide in the slush. Winding down the street to 159, Jon left the gearbox in first and simply let the engine wail; such did nothing for Jeanne's emotional discomfort.

This was hardly her neighbourhood but, in junior-high school, when she had learnt where her classmate Jon lived, she had often gone by the Cavaliere house on Lake Drive, riding her bicycle to and from the shopping arcade or even walking entirely across central Wilshire Township just to spend the time alone here with her thoughts and daydreams. It was her favourite sight of the town; for she had something of a fancy for elegant old houses and favoured in particular this brick Colonial-Revival two-and-a-half-storey hall, pleasantly proportioned and so stately with its tall chimneys and slate-tiled roof, flanked by old shade trees on a sloping wooden section with a brick walk bordered by shrubbery extending to the street. As Jon turned in the driveway he put in the clutch and let it out again, bucking the car to more slowly descend the curving downhill grade to the back yard. Only now did Jeanne realise that at last she would be visiting the house of her fancies firsthand. Suddenly everything she saw impressed her, and she was stunned by the apparent affluence of the family. The driveway curved down between the trees and round behind the house where two small sailboats sat on trailers beside the in-ground swimming pool, their covers all laden with leaves and snow. There were two separate garages under the house plus a detached shed out back. Several fenced-in gardens took up much of the remaining yard and a wide sun-deck extended across the back of the house itself.

Jon stopped the car at the foot of the outside steps. He pulled his keys from the switch and got out, leaving Jeanne to follow or not as to her own wishes, and pounded up to the deck. She went after him straight away, not so much revelling in her first visit to his home as worrying about helping him with his bleeding nose.

He went in the back door to the kitchen and marched directly to the sink. Jeanne brought the door closed quietly, self-conscious about intruding without a proper invitation. Her classmate Elisabeth Cavaliere, in an aquamarine sweater and a tan plaid skirt, sat with her back to them, facing across the long narrow refectory table at a small smouldering fire in the wide brick fireplace, too absorbed in a textbook and a bowl of tossed salad to look up. 'Hello, Jon,' she said cheerfully, confident that the engine sound below and the spirited entrance she had perceived behind her could only have been that of her elder brother. 'You know Kathleen was asking about you again today....'

Jon ignored her, laying his face under the running water and letting the blood drip into the sink. Jeanne winced at this treatment and went to help him tear off some paper towels from the dispenser.

'So how was your day?' asked Beth, still not looking up from her book.

'It *sucked*,' he told her fiercely, and spat into the sink.

'Here,' Jeanne said softly; 'please, let me—'

Astonished at the sound of a female voice, Beth whirled about. In PJ's short brown fur coat and the brief cheerleader's uniform the unannounced guest was attempting to help Jon wash his face under the water. 'No; *wait*,' he was saying to her. 'Let *me* do it, please—'

Beth hastened to have a look. 'Here, Jeanne; let me.' Jeanne only stepped back, pleasantly speechless that Jon's sister would acknowledge her by name on the spot. Though they were of the same year they had never shared a class and had never been introduced, having turned in vastly different social circles. 'So whaddiya call this?' Beth asked her brother.

'Whadda *you* call it?' he snapped.

She put one hand to his forehead and tilted his head back whilst he resisted. 'I'm just trying to determine if this was a fight, or if you were just being fresh.'

'Just lay off,' he told her, and started to turn away.

'*Freeze*, cowboy,' she told him, forcibly holding him in one position. 'You're not getting out of here without me taking a look at it.'

'Sure; for your damn diary, no doubt.'

Beth bent over, genuinely concerned despite the appearances. 'Jeanne,' she said, not moving her eyes, 'the ice is in the bottom part of the refrigerator, there.'

Jeanne bent to open the lower freezer compartment and brought out the plastic bin of ice cubes. 'Do you think it's broken?' she asked worriedly.

'No,' said Beth, taking a cube out of the bin Jeanne held and laying it to the side of Jon's nose; 'I don't think we'll be that lucky. I'm just thinking about that blood vessel in there....' For the moment the blood flow had stopped. She bent to look up into his nose. 'No....

He'll live.'

Jeanne hid a smile at the way Beth had to hold up her brother as if he were a frightened house pet. Actually he had found a comfortable position in which to stand with his head back and, for the moment, seemed at bay. 'Is it stopping?' Jeanne asked.

'It will.... So when did all this happen?'

'*Hours* ago,' Jon said, irritated by her questions. 'You *missed* it all.'

'It wasn't quite an hour ago,' Jeanne said, wanting to have medical facts straight but amused by his impatience with his sister.

'Look, Jeanne,' said Beth; 'if you want anything, help yourself.'

'Oh; no,' said Jeanne; 'thank you.'

'I'm just having salad; it's my diet–'

'*Diet*!' Jon scoffed, and turned from them both to spit blood into the sink. 'Like you *need* one so bad!'

'Well; it does keep me from looking like all you boozers.... I take it this was a fight, by all these other bruises.'

'No; I fell down on the ice,' Jon snapped.

'Shut up,' said Beth, like a domineering nurse; 'or I'll add a few more. Your lip is cut. Anbesol will do that. Jeanne–?'

'Where is it?' Jeanne asked.

'Right behind you.' Beth nodded towards the cupboard beside the refrigerator as Jon fidgeted like a small child. 'I'd get it myself, if this bird could stand upright–'

Jeanne opened the cupboard and found the bottle of antiseptic in a shoebox of other medicines, only because it was the way her own mother kept them at home. 'Oh, *no*,' Jon said, shrinking away from them both when he saw the bottle. 'Not *that* stuff, man. No *way*.'

'Stop squirming,' Beth ordered him. 'Just one shot; and I'll–'

'No *way*,' Jon insisted. 'I'd rather bleed to death.'

Jeanne stifled a laugh. Beth took the bottle from her with a free hand. 'One squirt; and I'll leave you alone.'

'Don't be a sadist, Ears,' he said, turning to spit blood into the sink again.

Jeanne smiled to see how Beth seemed to mother her elder brother. Beth was known in school to be modest and polite, if a bit reserved, and a model student consistently on the honour rolls; but at home she now seemed like the one personality to humble Jon's fiery spirit. Jeanne could well imagine that at times he might understandably resent such attention. 'Come on,' Beth was telling him; 'be brave, in front of the lady, here.'

'Brave, *shit*,' he said. '*Stupid*, more like.'

Jeanne wanted to laugh at that but held her tongue. Beth was not amused. 'Just remember; if I have to, I'll beat the crap outa you.'

'Outa *me*?' He turned to scoff at her. 'Hah! You wanna see blood flyin', it won't be Type A, let me tell ya.'

'You don't even *have* Type A,' Beth told him, and shot at his lip with the spray bottle of antiseptic. Jon emitted a whine like a wounded animal and spun about, cringing from the sting and spitting into the sink. 'Don't you *dare* rinse that off,' she ordered. 'That has to be kept clean, and that *doesn't* mean city water.' She capped the bottle and sat it on the counter. 'Let me see it now,' she said in a softer tone.

'More ice,' Jeanne suggested.

'More ice,' Beth agreed. She took the two cubes Jeanne handed to her, wrapping them in a dishcloth and holding it to the side of Jon's nose. 'Hold this on it,' she told him. 'We can't let it start to swell up. You have a show to do tomorrow; and I won't have you going on looking like a gang leader.'

He stepped back to get away from her, almost bumping into Jeanne. 'Oh, jeez; knock it off,' he told her. 'I mean *really*. Cut me some damn *slack.*'

They both watched him turn and stomp out past the back stairs towards the dining room. The two girls looked at each other for a moment, realising that, though they had never even been acquainted before, they now shared a wonderful community. 'Thanks,' Jeanne said openly to her, handing over the ice bin and starting after Jon.

'He'll be going for the parlour,' Beth told her. 'Don't let him drip blood all over the place.' She tossed a roll of paper towels.

Jeanne caught it handily. They exchanged little smiles; and then she turned and followed Jon off into the house.

He went out to the dining room, with its long, regal mahogany table, and through the archway to the central hall, past the large sitting room dominated by a polished black grand piano and tall windows in sheer white curtains giving a marvellous view of the deck and rear garden. However Jon gave her no time to inspect the place, striding up the hall and round the foot of the stairs. He opened the door to a cosy parlour and, when they were both inside, shut the door at once, turned the lock and tossed the key to the middle of the soft Oriental carpet.

Jeanne wandered about the room in a flutter; whether due to anxiety or joy at being alone with him, she could not tell. Despite the wine-red fabric on the walls the decor of the parlour was subdued, with no single underlying theme; it was just a collection of comfortable old furniture and treasured accessories, some genuine antiques, and whatever colours or patterns seemed to compliment most of them. There were several original oil paintings in heavy frames on the walls, their dark hues contrasting against the brilliant ivory of the intricate ceiling mouldings and other woodwork. Opposite a Victorian sofa in gold-and-olive striped chintz, two tall windows with sheer white curtains overlooked the snow-covered front lawn; another was on the end opposite the door. An old oil of a yacht sailing the river hung above an Italian-marble mantle and the green tile and ivory joinery of the fireplace in the corner.

'This is a nice room,' Jeanne said sincerely. 'In fact, the whole house is nice. I like it.'

Jon dropped himself on the sofa, kicking off his shoes and draping his feet over the arm. 'You can have it,' he said with disdain. 'The roof leaks, the windows are jammed, the floors creak, it's always cold, it needs paint everywhere—'

'Oh,' Jeanne smiled, typically romantic in overlooking such practicality; 'but it's such a pretty house. And like all old houses creak, and need paint—'

'What, "old"? This house ain't twenty-five years old.'

'I thought it was old,' she apologised.

'No; it's just inhabited by people who don't care to fix it up,' he said, and hung his head off the edge of the sofa. 'See? It fooled even you.'

'I think ours is about fifteen,' she said. 'The houses in our neighbourhood were all built about the same time, like around Nineteen-Sixty....'

'Where you are was a Rudderow development,' Jon said. 'They were out of there by mid-'Sixty-One.' He sniffled. 'Do me a favour?'

She turned about. 'What?'

'Paper towels? –please?'

'Oh–' She ripped a few sheets off the roll and handed them to him. 'Here,' she said, and watched as he dabbed at his nose. 'Is it still bleeding?'

'I'll live.'

'The ice will help,' said Jeanne softly. 'Please, just keep this on there.' She crouched in front of him and held the ice cubes wrapt in the dishcloth whilst he wiped the blood from his nose. 'The ice really will keep the swelling down. I wonder if you should see a doctor.'

'Naah. I'm saying, this always happens.' He took the ice back from her, but she kept her hand on it to see that he laid it gently to the swollen place. For a moment their hands were in contact. Both blushed and shrank away then. 'I was going to ask you something,' he said, laboured by the blockage in his nose; 'but... I don't know if I will now.'

They met eyes. 'What is it?'

'Well....' He looked up at the ceiling. 'Well I don't know; but I just don't think it was all that cool that this guy seems to think that he owns you. And not just 'cause it's me, you know; but like anybody who would wanna kill somebody.... Well; it's not like it was any big deal; right? It was just like two people going to a movie. And like you said, you're not exactly his girlfriend, or whatever.... It's just that I don't feel like having some guy wanna bash my brains in on account of drivin' you home from school once or twice, or out to a movie....'

A lump rose and stuck in her throat; and for a second she could only stare at him. The hot wave of embarrassment that came over her had nothing at all to do with squatting on bent knees in a short cheerleader's skirt just two feet from him. He had brought the subject out into the open, as she had always dreamt he would; and she could hardly avoid it now. She only hoped to have the strength to speak up and tell him how she really felt.

'Well I don't know,' he said after half a minute, and rolled a little away from her on the sofa. 'I guess it's really up to you. I just don't want you to get the wrong idea, you know. It's just that I had thought maybe this guy wasn't really, well, I guess *good* enough for you.' He made a wince then. 'That sounds corny; doesn't it?'

She swallowed. 'No....'

'I shouldn't've said that,' he said. He chuckled a little at his own lack of tact. 'I sound like a TV show; don't I?'

'No,' she said, and managed a little smile at him.

'Well; it's up to you,' he said, and stared up at the ceiling.

Jeanne lowered her eyes. Self-consciously she rose to her feet and stepped over to the window to gaze out at the snow on the front lawn, feeling her heart hammering hard in her chest. She hated herself; the very moment for which she had longed and prayed had come and she could not bring herself to articulate her true feelings. All her desire and resolve could scarcely rally a dram of courage. She worried if it was too early in whatever relationship they had begun, too grave a set of circumstances at the moment or too late to salvage her own reputation in the face of Danny's disappointment for her to state what she really felt and really wanted. Making an error here, now, would be catastrophic. But she was here with Jon, now; and she would have to say something.

Boldly she turned about, only to freeze in place upon recognising the pair of statuettes occupying the corners of the mantelpiece: David the modest but valiant giant-slayer, looking protectively over his shoulder at the beautiful but defenceless Venus DiMilo. Her cheeks went beet-red at the metaphor; and her half-dram of nerve vanished like a fainthearted ally. Still she drew a shaky breath and, despite being fairly terrified of his reply, turned to him and said, 'Jon, are you asking me to go steady?'

Only at that moment he too realised what he had said or, at least, how she would have interpreted it. It occurred to him that perhaps, unconsciously, he had meant to say it, although he had always hoped that such a conversation and question would take place at a far more amenable place and time. He felt a blush of embarrassment come over him, exactly the reaction he had never wanted to have. 'No,' he said quickly; 'just forget it.'

She went red in a panic. 'No; that's not what I meant, but–'

'Forget it. I take it back.'

Jeanne turned to the window again, suddenly feeling very foolish. She was hardly encouraged; but neither would she be convinced all had been lost. Too much potential benefit lay in the balance. 'I'm sorry,' she said carefully, taking pains to form her words as the blood pounded in her veins. 'I never thought any of this would happen. But it is my problem; and I know that I'm the one who's going to have to deal with it. If only he didn't want so much to go steady—'

'With *you?*'

Jeanne looked round at him again. 'Well; he did mention it, you know. The night after; well; after you asked me out. And I knew he was going to say it, and he did; and I didn't know what to do. I didn't think I was ready for that. But now I'm sure he thinks you were the one who like, well, changed my mind.'

'Wonderful,' Jon said sarcastically, though he rather liked being considered the pivotal factor.

'I can only say I'm sorry,' she said sadly; and she sounded much more sincere than he expected. The accepted sentiment among Jon's associates was that the cheerleaders were generally insincere towards other people. It was somewhat like the commoners being dispirited emotionally by the nobility. Jon had always remembered Jeanne as more sensitive than that, a softer soul than the rest of her society, and it was gratifying to perceive that she probably had not changed so much after all. Now she sat gently and strangely at-ease in his mother's antique armchair, crossing her bare legs at the ankles and folding her hands primly in her lap, partly to hold down the heavy but too-short maroon-and-amber pleated skirt. 'I mean: I had really wanted to tell you all this before, but—'

Jon held up his hand to silence her. Voices came from the hall; the front door had opened. 'What are *you* doin' here?' a boy asked amidst the stomping of snowy feet.

—'Oh; nothing.' It was Beth's voice, clear and close to the other side of the door.

—'Waiting for Prince Charming, no doubt.' There were at least two others who laughed.

—'Hi, Billy; hi, Tony.'

—'Hey.'

—'What's up.'

—'I'm makin' some cocoa,' came the voice of Jon's brother Andrew, from farther back in the house. 'You dudes want any?'

—'All right,' said one; and there were heavy footfalls going back towards the kitchen.

Jeanne opened her mouth to say something but saw Jon reach over and pick up one of his shoes from the carpet. From his awkward position he gave it a deliberately hard, accurate toss straight at the closed parlour door. The heavy heel struck squarely on the wood above the doorknob with a great bang, and they both heard a surprised chirp from the other side.

'*Beat* it!' Jon hollered at the door. 'Get lost, *now!*'

Jeanne sat up, alarmed. 'Who is—'

'It's *Beth*, it is, sitting right the hell outside the door! I'm talking to *you*, Radar Ears!'

—'Are you bleeding all over that good couch?' came the voice from the hall. She tried the door and found it bolted. 'Why is this door locked?'

'So *you* don't come in!' Jon shouted back. 'Now get lost!'

—'If you get blood on that good couch Mommy'll kill you!'

'If you don't *leave*, I'll kill *you!*' He waited; and they heard her stomp off in a huff. 'I apologise,' Jon said calmly to his guest, in a much softer tone. 'She can't be helped. Now where were we?'

Jeanne was rather flustered from the curious exchange. 'I, uh…. I don't remember.'

'I guess since your brother's out you don't have this problem. Although I'm sure you never did. Who could? Anyway…. Oh yeah. You had meant to tell me something.'

'Oh; well….' She recollected her wits. 'Well; it was nothing. I just hope that you know, well, how sorry I am that all of this happened. I can't help thinking it's all my fault….'

'It's not your fault,' Jon said seriously. 'Well; like if it was me, and I was goin' out with somebody who wanted to go out with somebody else, I'd wanna kill *her*.' He realised how that sounded. 'Well; you know what I mean. It's just not really a relationship any more if the two people don't get along; right?'

'Right,' she smiled, happy to hear him say such a thing.

'And I ain't just sayin' this because it was me, you know. I would hope I'm a little bigger than that. It's just something I happen to believe.'

'I know,' she said; and she believed him.

'But don't go thinkin' it was *your* fault. Maybe the guy shoulda talked to you about it. Maybe he should, I don't know, be a little nicer, and doo, like, a little more understanding. Maybe then you could get along. I don't know. I'm not very good at relationships either.'

She smiled, thinking the truth certainly had to be to the contrary. 'Why do you say that?'

'Aaah; I don't know.' He sniffled; and she realised he was swallowing the blood. 'In a way, I'm like too honest; you know? I say whatever's on my mind at the time. A girl would have to be pretty strong to deal with me. I say the wrong thing at the wrong time and forget to say the right thing at the right time. I can be pretty forgetful sometimes.'

'That's no sin,' she said honestly. 'It's when you really don't *care* that the misunderstandings start to become important.'

'Yeah; I guess….' He shrugged. 'I don't know.' Jeanne watched him lift the tissues away from his nose and look at them for a second. 'Dag; this has become a really stupid conversation; huh?'

She smiled at that; he was being modest, or embarrassed. 'Why do you say that?'

'Because it is.' He sat up and looked over at her; the blood seemed to have stopped. 'We don't know each other well enough to be talkin' about this kinda stuff.'

They met eyes. She felt confidence now she had never known she had. 'Well,' she said readily; 'maybe it's how we *do* get to know each other.'

'Maybe,' he said seriously, and looked away. 'I just feel a little dumb. You know, interrupting your relationship with the guy, and all. It wasn't fair.'

'Jon, you said yourself it isn't a relationship at all if two people don't get along; right?'

'Well,' he told her; 'what I really said once is that it's not a relationship without trust. A relationship without trust is just two people lying with each other, figuratively and literally. *That* was the original comment, that I had.'

The thought warmed her immeasurably. This opportunity to see him in his own environment had become priceless to her for the insights to gain and the memory to cherish. She was nearly bursting with glee at hearing him say the same kinds of things she had always dreamt she would hear him say. 'And sometimes,' she said, barely containing her happiness in a glowing smile, 'not even that.'

He was mightily relieved to hear that from her. But he could never let her know the fears that had just been on his mind. 'Right,' he said then, and stood up. 'So anyway, I'm sorry I made you feel a little stupid. Some other time, maybe, we'll have a nicer talk, without any stupid interruptions, and, like you said, find out a little more about each other. Well; it's up to you.'

Jeanne sat there and smiled up at him, thinking him stunningly appealing even with a badly bruised nose. She thought, God! –how I would *love* to know him better:…. And yet, he's already everything I've always wanted him to be. It would be so easy just to say, well; actually, Jon, there isn't a guy in the world I'd ever want, or need, or trust, or love, or even look at, but *you*….

'Well,' he said, stepping into his shoes where they were; 'suppose we get in on some of this nationally-advertised cocoa; huh?'

She fairly melted at the offer. '*Love* to,' she mushed, and rose from the chair. Jon picked up the key from the carpet and opened the door, leaving the key on the stand in the hall. Back in the kitchen Beth, Andrew and Andrew's two longhaired friends had sat down to table for cups of hot cocoa and biscuits from the box. They all looked up and became quiet as Jeanne came in behind Jon; and she got the impression that she had been their subject of discussion. The attention was quite unnerving. That dreaded blushing came over her once again.

Jon got two mugs down from the cupboard. '*Damn*,' he swore, staring at the empty canister of instant cocoa mix. 'So what the hell happened to all the cocoa?'

'Ain't none left, dude,' drawled Andrew. 'Gotta fix more.'

'Son of a *bitch*,' Jon swore, and slammed the can down angrily on the counter. 'Holy shit– it's not enough I gotta put up with Nurse Hitler over here, in the Nazi Secret Service, but then the rest of you guys all *indulge* her, like it's some major bullshit story outa the *New York Post*, so when I come out, and *jeez*, you didn't *even* know I'd come out here, since you all heard me chase Miss Radar Ears outa my face, there, you can't even leave enough for two lousy mugs of Swiss Piss. Jeez; if that ain't petty, I don't know what *is*.' Whilst going on with the tirade he had opened the new can, poured an approximated amount into each of the two mugs and filled the mugs with hot water from the kettle on the cooker. He stirred the two servings and then abruptly brightened as he recognised an appropriate *coup de grace*. 'Well,' he said then, looking up at the four assembled at the table; 'what comes around goes around. *We* happen to get little marshmallows in ours.'

He turned on his heel and went out. Jeanne picked up the second mug, peered into it and had to hold back a giggle. Boldly she looked up at the others, who were all just sitting there staring at her, and made her best attempt at a smug smile, though certainly she looked more cute than anything else. 'Marshmallows,' she taunted childishly, and flounced off after Jon.

At the end of the hall stood a little round table and two chairs by the French windows between the dining room and the piano, surrounded by tall potted plants, with a pretty view of the rear deck and garden and woods beyond. Jon set down his mug and pulled out a chair for Jeanne, and they sat down together. 'Now,' he said through his injured smile; 'so how was *that* for throwing a temper tantrum over something really dumb and insignificant?'

She looked up, stunned to behold that whilst she had been standing there feeling infinitely awkward the act had only been to amuse her. 'Really!' she said, smiling right back at him. 'I'd say you've got the part, Jon.'

'*Really*, have I,' he smiled, not at all taking her too gravely, and took a cautious sip from his mug.

She realised only then how that had sounded, certainly not the way she would have wanted to say it. 'Well; you know what I mean,' she said, and hoped he did. 'I just think that I should talk to Danny about it. After today, I think he owes me an apology. And I'm going to make sure you get one, too.'

'Not that it makes any difference to me,' he said with a sniffle.

She looked down a little. 'Well; I happen to believe what you said, like about trust, and relationships. I mean: if something were wrong, I would hope he would want to *talk* to me about it, instead of like taking it out on someone who's really not involved....'

'I'm not totally uninvolved,' Jon confessed. 'I did attempt to talk to him about it myself, you know.'

'Yes; I know,' she said, and he wondered how much she really knew; 'but it's not fair. He and I don't have any commitments to each other. We're just dating, you know.'

'I know,' he said. 'Like, kind of, you and I.'

She smiled at him; it was something she liked to do, and the subject at hand was very pleasant. 'Yes,' she agreed, deciding for certain that very instant. 'Like you and I.'

He smiled then and raised his mug of cocoa. 'All right, then; to trust in relationships, and to just dating.'

Jeanne lifted her mug to touch his over the table. 'I'll drink to that,' she said happily; and they sipped. Only then she happened to glance across through the archway to the big sitting room and see the flag. Spread upon the wall above the fireplace, it was a larger and much older copy of the banner she had seen flying aboard La Cacciatrice last summer. She felt a long, slow chill creep down her spine to regard the symbolic significance of the ancient family crest, a white knight's-head with a sword entwined with a gold-coloured olive branch upon a field of deep heraldic blue. As she realised the true essence of the young gentleman at the table with her, she shivered in the chair right in front of him.

'What's the matter?' he asked her.

She shivered again. Her mug rattled on the table, her cheeks went beet-red; she could not face him. Only now was the eerie notion apparent that perhaps all her intense daydreams and wishful thinking had still managed to underestimate him, that he was probably even nobler and more honourable than she had ever imagined. Perhaps all this really was her fault, after all. Surely it was not his. He was only being himself; this was his nature. At that she shivered again, even more than before.

'It's this house; isn't it? I'm sorry; my mom's too cheap to turn up the heat.'

'No,' she said softly; 'it's just—' She shook her head, to be rid of the thought, but something inside told her she would never be able to forget it. Still she could not bring herself to look again upon the flag on the wall across the room. 'Is it... still bleeding?' she asked him.

He shrugged, as though without a care. 'Aaah.... A little.' He sniffled then.

'It's just not fair,' she said then, and the sadness nearly overwhelmed her. 'I can only hope that it all heals up again all right.'

He smiled a little, humbly pleased to think of her being so genuinely concerned about him. 'Don't worry about it,' he said offhandedly. 'I'll live.'

* * *

Again Jon did not attend school on Wednesday. His mother had him visit the doctor that afternoon; but the blood vessel in his nose was fine, and he was assured his nose was not broken. He was inoculated for tetanus, and his cuts and sores were properly treated against infection. Beth dressed his bruises with facial cream and some rouge for the show, and the performance at The Patriot went well in spite of his aches.

That afternoon Danny Harris had called on Jeanne at her house. 'Hello, Danny,' Jeanne greeted him, with the usual smile. 'This is a surprise.'

'I, well; kinda wanted to talk to you,' he said uneasily, stepping inside. 'If you're not busy....'

She gestured for him to come in, leaning on the door as she opened it further. 'That's good, because I kinda wanted to talk to you, too, about–' she closed the door– 'about Jon Cavaliere.'

'Oh.' He turned to her. 'What of him?'

She leaned on the doorknob. 'I really want to know what exactly gives you the right to beat somebody up who drives me home because you were nowhere to be found, and– Oooh, Danny; the whole thing just makes me so *mad*! Since *when* do you have the right–'

'Hey; hold it, Jeannie; *hold* it. The guy's a jerk. Whaddiyou care?'

'*I* happen to *like* him,' Jeanne told him, her eyes flooding at once at the understatement. 'I happen to like him, and admire him, a lot. And I always wanted to go out with him. Whadda *you* care?'

Harris shook his head and leaned on the wall by the sitting room. Jeanne was becoming upset; and he did not like thinking he had been the one to upset her. Never one to raise her voice, she was fairly yelling in the quiet house.

'Look, Danny; I don't *care* what you think of him, all right? I happen to care for him a *lot*! As a matter of fact, *he* doesn't like you, either! He says the next time he sees you, he'll have a *knife*! He's that mad at you! And *I* don't blame him one bit!' She turned from him, tears streaming down her cheeks, and put her head against the bannister. 'I'm just glad my mother isn't home to hear me,' she wept.

Danny stood silently for a moment. Finally he said, 'Look, Jeannie;

what do you *want* from me? You think I *like* the idea of you going out with that guy? *Huh?*'

'I want you to leave Jon alone,' she told him, not looking up. 'I want you to apologise to him for hurting him like you did. If you're mad at all, it's because of me. Jon isn't even involved in it.'

'Jeannie—' He shook his head. 'A week ago I asked you to go steady. Two days later you were going out with that Cavaliere chump. I mean: like what kinda answer is *that?* I just don't want to lose you, you know, to him or anybody. I really *care* about you, Jeannie.'

'No,' Jeanne said; 'no you don't, Danny. You only care about your precious *ego.*'

'No, Jeannie…. I do really care about you.'

Jeanne sniffled and tried to contain herself for what she had to say. 'His nose was almost broken, Danny. You really hurt him. It might be okay now; but it was bleeding for hours.'

'He's a *wimp*, Jeannie; I don't know why—'

'Danny!' she cried. 'Just *stop* it!'

Danny sighed and leaned on the banister beside her. 'So he's this "old friend" of yours; huh? How long is it you've known him?'

Jeanne wiped her eyes. 'Since before I was twelve,' she told him.

He scoffed. 'And I'll bet it took him till now to ask you out!'

She turned about and looked right at him, no longer fearing the tears. 'Danny, there are some very sensitive reasons why that is; and I don't *ever* want to hear of you putting him down for it. I don't expect you to understand it. It took me until now to speak to him. But I know I'll never lose him as a friend now.'

'Friend, *bull*,' he said. 'You're in love with him. That's what they all say.'

'Oh, Danny, that sounds so childish. I never thought you would listen to all those little rumours—'

'*Rumours?* I didn't think you'd be ashamed to admit it, Jeannie. I mean I thought all you girls thought he was *"gorrr-geous".*'

'He *is*,' Jeanne sobbed under her breath; and some residual trembling came over her then. She closed her eyes, savouring a second's recollection of the hot cocoa with Jon yesterday. The thought of that flag on the wall still haunted her. A sigh eked past her quivering lips. All her doubts were settled now. Summoning her nerve she paced to the door, wiped the tears from her face and turned to yell straight at him. 'Well all right, Danny; maybe he *is!* What would *you* know about being such a nice guy? Sometimes I don't think you even know what a nice guy *is!* Oh, sure; so I'm such a nice girl; right? So why on earth should I have to settle for anything but a nice *guy?* Huh? Why should I have to deserve *you?*' She rotated away from him, shocked to hear herself shouting so angrily yet unable to care a whit for the tears streaming down her cheeks. 'Then so *what* if it took me four-and-a-half years to go out with him! So *what?* All right, Danny, all right; so maybe I *am* in love with Jon Cavaliere! There; I *admitted* it! Is that what you wanted to hear? So beat *me* up then! But just leave *him alone!*'

Harris looked about himself in indecision for half a minute and edged himself towards the door. 'Hey,' he said quietly; 'I, uh, gotta go. I'll talk to you tomorrow about this; okay?'

Jeanne waved absently at him. The door closed, and she was alone in the quiet house. Oh, she fretted; I just wish I'd've told Jon when I had the chance! He *is* such a nice guy, and he does make me feel so special.... Oh, God! –I *know* I'm in love with him! He's just so nice and sweet to me.... And like Danny can be such a rat sometimes. Oh; I know Danny is furious. I can tell he's mad, at me *and* at Jon. He wants to be mad at me, but he doesn't want to lose me. He still wants me for his girlfriend. His steady girlfriend.... In a way, it's very sweet. And, in a way, it's all very nasty. This whole thing is getting so weird; I just don't know what to *do* any more....

* * *

It infuriated Jon that news of his fight with Danny Harris had been carried like a press-stopping story all over school. Throughout Thursday morning he was approached by people, many of whom he barely knew, with questions about the bruises or about the fight itself or about Harris. At least half of them were less than civil about it, with caustic comments and scornful teasing that became increasingly difficult to tolerate even for the noblest of peacemakers.

The doctor had asked him to sit out from PE because the nose was still healing and so, still dressed in his pilot's jacket and jeans, Jon took a seat where the bottom row of the folding bleachers had been pulled out in the gymnasium. Just before roll was taken, Jerry Fisher, his grade-school classmate, marched over in the company of some bigger and less-intellectual friends. 'Hey, Cavaliere,' he chirped in his nasal tone; 'so I heard Harris got the best of you on Tuesday.'

'Naah,' Jon said, trying to contain his wrath; 'if he'd've gotten the best of me, he'd be in a pine box somewhere.'

'Yeah; but from what I hear, he wasn't the one bleeding all over the floor, over there.' The folding partition had been opened to the girls' gymnasium today, perhaps in anticipation of tonight's basketball game; and Fisher pointed to where the cheerleaders had found him that afternoon as though he had actually been there with them.

Jon cast a glance out at the place on the floor where the blood had been. No trace remained. This was probably fortunate for the girls in their maroon shorts and amber t-shirts who mingled with a few boys in the centre of the big room waiting for class to begin. 'Yeah; well; what's a little blood; huh?' Jon said. 'Dude turned and bolted like he was gonna faint when he saw it.'

Fisher sat down on the lower row of bleachers, immediately to the left of Jon, and his henchmen closed in a semicircle about them. 'And I hear it was all over Jeannie Banfield,' he pretended to marvel. 'Imagine, the foxiest piece of ass in the school; and the rock star here thinks he's good enough for her.'

'Apparently *you* weren't,' Jon told him; and a few boys nearby agreed.

'Or *she* wasn't good enough for *me*,' Fisher sniffled.

Jon rapped him in the chest so quickly that no-one could have interceded. In the next second he had bounded to his feet, deliberately bumping into some of Fisher's disciples. Fisher began to rise but Jon snatched him up and shoved him back against the bleachers. 'All right, asshole; you just dropped your last load of horseshit on *me*.'

The boys round about them were full of comments, as they all loved to watch a good scuffle. 'Aaah,' Fisher squeaked, dancing a little away from him; 'you already got taken by Harris this week....'

'Yeah; like his *snot* couldn't take you without even tryin',' Jon came back.

'Like Cavaliere couldn't even kick your ass right here,' someone said.

'Diggit,' agreed another.

'So come on, Fish,' one of his bullies called out; '*hit* the faggot!'

Jon turned to see who had said that; and Fisher leaped in with a trite jab to his cheek. Jon spun about and ran at the little ginger-haired gremlin with several good punches. 'Hey!' shouted one of the instructors; and the whole room was alerted to the excitement of a live conflict. Mr Heyges caught Jon from behind and held him. 'What's the problem with you today?'

'*Him.*' Jon glared hard at Fisher, who was only now straightening.

'This is not to be done in school; do you hear me?'

'I hear; I just couldn't resist. I've been waitin' for that since third grade.'

Cheers and applause supported the remark. 'Cavaliere; isn't it? I oughta run you and your smart mouth on down to Mr Anderson's office; huh?'

'Hey; what the hell? I could use a vacation from this joint.'

This was popular as well; but Mr Heyges saw little humour. 'I can see by these cuts and bruises you've been pickin' a lot of fights lately; huh?'

'Hey, man; listen– I don't hit first, just *last*.'

'*Diggit!*' someone cheered; and a dozen more added their opinions.

Mr Heyges looked about at all the others and realised he was getting nowhere. 'All right; everybody shut up and get into your squads. Let's start class.'

Jon squirmed away from the man and returned to his place on the bleachers, and Fisher shuffled back across the floor to the eleventh-grade class to sit out the rest of the period in humility.

By last period Jon was growing weary of all the verbal and psychological abuse and was only interested in concluding the day at 12.15. At the start of literature class Cindy turned to him and said quietly, 'So, Jon; what's the lowdown on this fight action?'

'Wasn't no fight,' Jon said, having expected more compassion from an old friend. But perhaps no-one else really knew how serious it all seemed to him. 'I got slaughtered; okay?'

'I heard it was about some g–'

She stopped; Jeanne had passed her seat and was sitting down behind her. 'Hi, Jon,' said Jeanne cheerfully. 'How are you today?'

'Just lovely; thank you,' Jon sighed; and with that Cindy had no further questions.

Paul Orwell came down the aisle to the right and, hearing him, leaned over Jon's seat. 'Hey, man,' he said quietly; 'are you still pissed at everybody about Harris? I thought you got all that shit outa your system in gym.'

Jon looked up at him, in no mood for criticism. 'Do you have a seat?' he asked him insolently.

'Look, man; I'm just suggesting that you calm down. Sounds to me like you're makin' it into a bigger deal than it is.'

'Hey, dude; I'm gettin' real sick of people tellin' me what to do; all right? Sit the hell down and shut up.'

'I'm sorry,' Paul said, and sat in the seat beside Jon as the bell rang. 'I'd be pissed too, you know, but not enough to be actin' like an asshole to everybody else.'

Miss Simpson strode in then. Jon called out to her, 'Yo; you're early. Do you have an excuse?'

She looked at him and laughed, and so did a few others. 'Very funny, Jon,' she teased, and sat down with her roll book to take attendance.

For the duration of the period Jeanne sat and contemplated the whole situation, scarcely able to pay any attention to the lesson on Shakespeare's sonnets. *He's really angry,* she thought, *at everyone and everything. And it's still my fault.... Somebody said he picked a fight with Jerry Fisher in gym. I* know *it's all because of me; and Jon just doesn't seem like the kind of guy who would make such a big deal over it all. I mean: like he's so nice all the time. It's like there's no contest; but then there's Danny.... I only wish there were some way I could just like sit down with both of them so we could talk about it, and like everyone would finally understand....*

Cheer practice was held that afternoon in the girls' side of the gymnasium. The folding partition was closed again as the team went through manoeuvres next door; even so the thunder of two or three bouncing balls and ten pairs of basketball shoes from the other side of the wall was horrendous. Danny Harris stopped by and got Jeanne aside just long enough to suggest that they meet after the game and hold a rational discussion 'in some quiet place.' She was touched by his more gentlemanly approach to resolving the misunderstanding, and so she tentatively accepted.

Performing the routines with the other girls, she thought, well; the most important thing is to keep everyone from being mad. I can't go around losing friends left and right just because I change my mind once in a while. Danny seems very genuine about it; and I can't hold anything against him for that. It's obvious he really does care for me; and he is basically a nice guy....

Boldly Jon strode down the front gallery towards the girls' gymnasium with such dreadful severity that small knots of conversation were silenced as he passed. He yanked open the door and saw Harris sitting at the lower corner of the bleachers watching the cheerleaders. 'All right, dude,' he said gruffly, stepping up next to him; 'let's go.'

Harris looked about and let out a sigh of feigned exasperation. 'Oh, *Christ*,' he moaned, and made a little laugh.

'You and me, dude,' Jon told him. 'Let's go. Little– *discussion*.'

Jeanne had seen them from the far end of the line and immediately stopped with the cheer to hurry towards them. 'I ain't messin' with chickenshit like you again, Cavaliere,' Harris said wearily, and turned to share a laugh with two girls sitting beside him.

'Well *I'm* messing with *you*, asshole,' Jon announced aloud, and snatched him up by the collar and thrust him bodily towards the gallery. Jeanne shrieked and broke into a run. Jon was alarmingly quick; before Harris could gain his footing, he had given him another mighty shove into the gallery doors. The doors exploded open and out tumbled Danny Harris, in his elegant maroon velvet sports coat, sliding backwards across the polished terrazzo on his bottom.

Some girls just outside in the gallery went white with shock. They watched as Jon swiped up an odd fibreglass classroom chair by the doors, inadvertently bumping one of them in the leg with it, and swung it round in front of himself as a defensive weapon. '*Jon!*' Jeanne cried out, and slid to a stop on the floor in her slick-soled cheerleading shoes. 'Now just stop it,' she said, panicky; '*please!* What are you doing?'

'I'm sorry,' Jon said seriously, not taking his eyes from Harris as he rose; 'but this isn't to concern you. This is just between me and the idiot, here. Cheer for either side you like.'

The girls from the gymnasium had all assembled for the episode, all keeping a wary distance, some staying inside the doors that had closed themselves and some cowering behind a few tables in the gallery, none willing to be caught in the midst of what would certainly develop into a major conflagration. 'Now Jon,' Jeanne said fearfully, her voice quavering; 'I promised to talk to him, and–'

'That's not what this is about,' he said in a stern tone. 'This is about when somebody attempts to humiliate you, and then doesn't stick around to finish the job.' He glared right at Harris, who stood straightening his coat and his hair, and lifted his hands to present himself. 'So here I am, dude. Here's your chance. We can hold your little "discussion" right here.'

'Jon; please; *no*,' Jeanne said to him. 'This isn't the way; it's just not *right*.'

'She's not impressed, Cavaliere,' said Harris, with a cruelly smug smile. 'You're not impressing her with being such a nice guy now, you know. Looks like all you've done today is make yourself into more of a fool.'

Jon shrugged. 'Maybe. Maybe there's nothing to prove here.' He turned to take in the crowd of perhaps two dozen and then looked back at Harris. Surely he could not back down now. 'Well,' he said then; 'maybe I'll just have to kick your worthless ass for *sport*.'

Jeanne turned to look at him; but he lunged fiercely at Harris, driving him back-first into the water fountain on the wall. The girls all shrieked at once. Harris winced, shrinking just a little from the pain, and then shot a knee up into Jon's hip, shoving him back. 'Little faggot!' he growled; and the two of them stood there recuperating for half a second.

'Now, *stop* it!' Jeanne cried, and made to step between them. Jon suddenly seized the chair and, when she had turned towards Harris, he slid it right into the backs of her legs, causing her to quite naturally sit down on it. Harris saw his chance and charged at Jon. The two of them collided in a savage body hold, slinging each other sideways to the floor. The students from up the gallery all yelped as the two combatants crashed into one of the tables, tossing each other about with a ferocious swinging of fists.

Unable to appreciate such violence, several of the braver cheerleaders dove at the two boys to prise them apart. Somehow they were able to get them separated just as Jon was raising a fist over Danny's face. 'Come *on*!' he complained from behind Holly and Patti. 'I had a good shot there!'

'You have to *stop* this!' Jeanne wailed, stamping her feet and looking from one of them to the other and back again. 'Just stop it, stop it, *stop* it!' She whirled about dizzily and cast herself into a corner in tears.

'All right,' Harris said; 'you wanna step outside, we'll see who kicks *whose* ass.'

'No,' said Jon breathlessly; 'I know.' Still held by Holly and Patti he stepped closer to Harris, who was just noticing a rip in his shirt, and said quietly, 'You just meet me out back of this place around eleven-thirty. We'll settle it then.'

'What,' Harris taunted him; 'you gonna bring a whole army of wimps; or what?'

'No,' said Jon seriously; 'just you and me. Nobody else is involved. But if you want you can bring *her*, 'cause you might just need the inspiration.'

'And you might need a nurse,' Harris laughed.

'You two can't be serious,' Patti told them both. 'This is getting ridiculous; two mature young men fighting like children—'

'Just you, Harris,' Jon told him; 'and you can bring your girlfriend there if you want. And make sure you've got gas. We're not gonna be followed by any cheering sections.'

'*Why?*' Jeanne demanded of him, whirling about to march back into the fray. 'What's gonna happen? *Huh?* Where are you gonna go?'

'You'll see,' Jon said, with a special smile for her that under any other circumstances would have made her weak in the knee. As it was she had obvious difficulty concentrating on the gravity of the argument at hand. 'Nothing so bad at all, if this jerk will only act his age....' He turned and said right to Harris, 'Your mistake was not finishing me off, asshole; but don't worry. I promise I'll bring ya flowers.'

Harris made to lunge at him; but Cheryl and Donna held him about a foot short of arm's length. Jon merely shrugged and gave him a trite little smirk before turning and going out the front door. 'Like *hell*,' Harris said when they had all seen him go round the corner of the building, and then saw to brushing himself off.

Jeanne looked about the gallery, breathless with the shock of it all. Michelle Reni stood holding Danny Harris by the lapel, and the other girls and the people who had come to watch were all standing in what Jeanne felt was a big circle about her. 'God,' Jeanne sighed; 'I'm a nervous wreck!' She stepped over the back of the chair where it had fallen and went to the water fountain to rinse her eyes. Patti paced halfway to her, turned about with a hand up in her hair, and winced at the entire episode.

Miss Robb came out of her office and put everyone back where they belonged, giving her cheerleaders some chastisement for allowing these things to happen whenever she was not right with them. The other girls all seemed to avoid all unnecessary words with Patti or PJ or Jeanne, as they did not want to become involved in this sort of thing. Patti, roundly stunned by how the whole affair had amplified and feeling partly at-fault for having convinced Jeanne to date Jon Cavaliere, made sure she called on Jeanne that afternoon. 'Are you all right?' she asked in a worried tone.

Jeanne had not changed from the grey fleece training breeches and her cheerleading uniform sweater in which she had walked home from school. She sat down on the sofa and put back her head. 'Yes; I'm fine.'

Patti sat in Mr Banfield's chair, crossing her ankles in ladylike fashion. 'Jeannie, I just can't help feeling responsible. I mean: *I* was the one—'

'Oh, Patti,' Jeanne smiled, modest as ever. 'You always try to be responsible. Believe me: nobody forced me to go out with him, you know.'

'But I just can't help thinking that it may not all be worth it.'

'Oh; Danny's always been short-tempered. You know how he is.' She brushed her hair aside with one hand.

'And Jon?'

The hand dropped to her lap; the hair fell into her face. 'Patti, surely you can't be suggesting that I forget about *Jon Cavaliere*.'

'Oh Jeannie, I know what you must be thinking; but it just seems so— Well, I just can't see you as that type of girl who gets tangled-up in anything so unsavoury…. Do you know what I mean? It's like after everything's all said and done, maybe you're just not—'

'Not made for each other?' Jeanne asked, aghast even to hear such a notion aloud. 'My *God!* –Patti, you've never been *kissed* by him.' She looked right at her. Patti stared straight back. 'I would fight Danny Harris myself for another minute of looking into his eyes. God! –he's worth *anything* to me.'

Patti swallowed, feeling a strange chill go down her spine. 'Like, including… the big "anything"?'

'*Anything*,' Jeanne stated definitely. 'My pride, my reputation, my *virginity*…. God *knows* I'd make love with him, tonight even, if he wanted to….' It would hardly be the first time she had entertained that fantasy; but now, her insides aflutter with emotion, the prospect had a particularly stirring effect on her. She put back her head and closed her eyes and sucked in a quivering breath through her teeth. 'Oooo; even my *life*, Patti; he's worth that much to me.'

Patti shook her head. 'Yes, Jeannie; you say that now; but from how he acted—'

'Oh, Patti, he's just being old-fashioned.' She smiled at the thought. 'I mean: he looks like the coolest guy on earth, you know, but really he's just a sweet old-fashioned guy. He's exactly like the kind of guy we all dreamed about when we were ten years old. Like, he told me he dreams about me, just like I dream about him. You don't think we could be made for each other; but, *God!* –how could we *not* be? He's so *like* me, you just couldn't *believe* it. And so I'm beginning to think that I could never live without him. Two weeks ago, or like before you danced with him, but never again.'

'You *must* be in love with him,' Patti smiled.

Jeanne ran her hands up into her hair and put her head back on the sofa. 'Oh, God,' she sighed; 'I *must* be. If I really get to thinking seriously about him, I actually scare myself. I mean: like if he asked me to go to California or someplace with him, it's like you couldn't *stop* me. You said it yourself, Patti; he's like *different* somehow. It's like he's from another time, like way back in the past....' She lifted her head and looked over at her. 'I mean: I actually *think* about this stuff. Isn't it stupid? It's like everything, everything about him, is like part of some legend out of the Middle Ages, like the time at the lake and him rescuing us in the woods and now this thing with Danny.... I mean I honestly think it's like a duel to him, Patti. He thinks he has to fight for me to win me.'

Patti shook her head with a wry face. 'A *duel*? Come on, Jeannie. Guys just aren't like that any more, and you know it.'

Jeanne smiled, closing her eyes and putting her head back again. 'You *see*?' she giggled. 'I said he's *different*, Patti. He's not *like* other guys. Danny couldn't hold a candle to him. I don't think *Steve* could hold a candle to him. He's like one of those knights, in shining armour, like on a beautiful white horse, with a mighty sword....' She sighed. 'Mmmm.... Just like the flag. Oh; and Patti, the *flag*–'

'Oh, Jeannie; you're just being sappy. As usual....'

Jeanne only giggled. 'No,' she said happily, shaking her hair about with her hands; 'I'm in *love*.' She looked over at Patti again and said, 'You've known me to go out with other guys; right? Have I ever been this silly over anyone else?'

'No,' Patti conceded, smiling warmly at her. 'But I do think that a lot of this is just because you've liked him for so long, and he's so cool and everything, and now you have a chance to actually go out with him, and it's all going to your head. He may not *be* that perfect, you know.'

'I know,' Jeanne said, a little more seriously; 'but it doesn't matter. If this really were the Middle Ages, my father would've made me *marry* him after he saved my life in the lake, and like all this time I would've been *married* to him, and I'd have to live with him no matter what; so there you are. Whatever he turns out to be like, I'd still love him. He's not somebody who could ever change very much from what he is now anyway.'

Her friend smiled at such romantic reasoning; it was typical of Jeanne to come up with a far-fetched rationale for something she was going to do anyway. But Patti was not immune to casting levelheaded reason aside in the face of strong and particularly exciting emotion herself. 'Well all right,' she said, considering the point in the spirit intended; 'so if you really do love him like you say you do, then you know you've got to *do* something.'

Jeanne laid her head back and stared up at the ceiling. The elation fell from her face in the time it took her hands to fall to her lap. 'Oh, God! –I *know*; but it's like I just don't know what to *do*....'

'Well; you have to *tell* him, Jeannie. Tell *him* all this crazy stuff, and not me. You've got to let him know how you feel.'

'God,' Jeanne said seriously. 'I never have the nerve. It's so scary, you know? I just don't want to mess it up.'

'Yes, I know; but who *knows* what he's going to do? It's so obvious he's half insane over you, with everything he's done.... Who knows? If he's as old-fashioned as you say he is, then he might *just* duel for you, and get himself killed. Eight hundred years ago it was a pretty honourable way to go, you know.'

'I *know*,' Jeanne said gravely; for she had already considered the point. 'But like what am I going to say to Danny, about all this? He wants to talk to me about it, tonight, after the game. He's really being so nice to me about the whole thing; I really hate to–'

'Danny will find himself a new girl,' Patti told her, sure of the fact. 'It's the way he is, Jeannie. I'd even volunteer to go out with him, if you had to get rid of him. At least maybe *I* don't have another boyfriend to deal with; well; not unless–'

'Oh, Patti....' They all knew Patti was still having difficulty adjusting to her irrevocable separation in November from Brian Court after three months of going steady. 'I wouldn't do that to you. You're too good a friend.'

Patti laughed a little at that. 'Well; all I can say is that if you really love this guy, and you can't live without him, then you've got to *tell* him. It's not fair to anyone, least of all you. I mean I've noticed it too, you know; and he does seem really sweet; and it's obvious he's crazy about you; and so if he is so old-fashioned and thinks he's got to win you, then you can't let him *lose*. A guy who would fight for you like that might be one in a million. One in *ten* million. You'd *never* find a guy who was so serious about whether you lived or breathed. I mean you must be like a *goddess* to the guy, Jeannie.'

'I *know*,' Jeanne mushed. 'God knows I *feel* like one, when I'm with him.'

Patti could feel the emotion radiating out of her friend. She had never seen Jeanne so enraptured with the thought of someone before, it was true; and yet it was strangely comforting to behold, as though Jeanne, incurably romantic, were at last in her own element. 'I was just thinking,' she said softly, 'that if you both really feel that way, he might just turn out to be the last one ever.'

'Oo, Patti....' Jeanne closed her eyes and drew in another of those long, shivering breaths. Almost afraid to break the spell should she admit it too loudly, she said in a tense whisper, 'I really believe he *might* be.'

Patti shivered. She wondered if all her proclamations about Fate had been true after all and then shivered again to think that the things which had not yet happened might yet come to pass. That would prove her a clairvoyant; the concept was too staggering for her. 'I hope he is,' she confessed. 'I love you and just really want it all to work out for you.'

Jeanne smiled at her. 'I knew *you'd* understand, Patti.'

'Well of course I would, Jeannie. You're my best friend.'

Bob would not sit still. 'Man, it's *insane*; that's what it is! The dude'll *kill* you!'

'Aaah; what the hell, man? I'll survive.'

'Yeah; but, knowing you, what gets killed worse is your *ego*; and for you, that's a fate worse than death!' He made his way across the room again and sat against the edge of the cluttered desk. 'Tries to beat up Danny Harris three times in one week! Man; that's sheer insanity!'

Draped over the armchair, Jon lifted the wad of tissues away from his nose with a weary arm and inspected it by holding it far over his forehead. 'Shit,' he said, squinting at it. 'Crimson as all hell.'

Bob turned, giving him less than two seconds' glance. 'Yeah, yeah; it's still bleedin'.' He looked out the dormer window at the silver Caprice down in the driveway. 'I'm tellin' you, man; you're out to get yourself killed. So what are you gonna do? –run him?'

'I don't know,' Jon lied. Then he added, 'Maybe… if he doesn't back down.'

'Yeah; right. Like, run him right off the road?'

'Maybe,' said Jon.

'*Sure*. Yeah; that's the way, man.' Bob stood up straight and paced the room again, carefully avoiding the magazines and books and musical instruments that were integral to Jon's domestic life. 'Yeah, man; that's what *I'd* do. Just run him off the road with that car of yours. Off of Dead Man's Curve; right? Ad-ee-*yose*, Danny Harris! Off you go, dude; you're dead as a fuckin' doornail, now. Yes, sir, man. That would be your best bet. Run him right off the road with the Caprice, down there. Of course you'll have to paint it over, so no-one suspects–'

'Will you cut it out?' Jon pleaded.

'I just can't get over it, that's all. I mean the dude benches close to twice your weight, knows all the decent fighters for twenty miles, and goes steady–'

'*Not* steady,' Jon corrected.

'–with the foxiest piece of ass– sorry; *girl*– in the whole damn school! Now no way is no dude with them qualifications gonna get taken at *anything* by some hundred-pound punk who mighta met the babe a decade ago–'

'First,' Jon interrupted, 'you got my weight wrong twice; second, he *ain't* goin' steady with her 'cause she told me herself; and third, I met her four years ago, not ten.   And fourth, I got as much reason to wanna kick his ass without the babe at all, because he's such an asshole.'

'Mark introduced you to that dude; I gotta talk to Mark about this.'

'Man; so do I.'   Waving a fist at the ceiling he said, 'Yo Mark, man; I owe ya one, bro'.'

Bob groaned in distaste.   'God *damn*, man! —you're like *sick*, or somethin'!   The dude could *kill* you, or worse yet, put you in the *hospital*!   I just don't understand it, man; I mean I've heard of living dangerously, but like you top 'em *all*!'   He was quiet for scarcely a second.   'And you know you're lucky you're not suspended yet.   Or detained. Or expelled. Or, while you're at it, why not just pull the old switchblade on him, and get thrown in *jail*.   Assault.   Assault with a deadly weapon.   Assault with intent to kill— *that's* you.   Possession of an *illegal* weapon.   And how about smuggling that thing into the country?   Sneaking past customs.   Smuggling illegal contraband. Yeah, man; what you really oughta do is pull the old switchblade on him.'

'I can't find it,' Jon admitted, hanging his head over the arm of the chair, and pointed to the desk. 'Check that top drawer.'

Bob sighed.   'At least a hundred and sixty years, the way I figure it. Twenty for assault.   Fifty for assault with a deadly weapon.   Fifty for intent to kill.   Twenty for possession of an *illegal* weapon.   Ten for smuggling.   A thousand dollars or ten years for illegal contraband. Man, you know that with good behaviour they might just let you out with a hundred and twenty.   Just think, when you're a hundred and thirty-eight you'll be a free man again.   My best friend, the hundred-and-thirty-eight-year-old ex-con!'

'Uh, Bob?'

'What?'

'Shut up.'

Bob turned and paced the length of the room twice. 'I don't know, man; I guess I used to think I understood you.'

'Will you please sit down, man; you're makin' me sick!'

Bob sat on the edge of the bed.   'I got this nervousness shit off of you, you know.'   He tapped his foot impatiently.

'I feel consoled.   Now will you please calm the hell down?'

'You never did tell me how you got this one,' Bob said of the nosebleed.

'Bumped it again,' Jon told him. 'Actually goddamn Beth pushed me.   Man; I'd like to run *her* off of Dead Man's Curve.'   He lifted the tissues to look at them again.

Bob glanced over and recognised more wet blood.   'Keep it on there, still.'

'*Damn*,' Jon swore.

Bob got up and handed him the box of fresh tissues and then took to pacing the room again. 'So seriously, then; I take it the babe means that much to ya.'

'In a word,' said Jon, '*yes*.'

'Yeah... in a way, I have to admire you for your guts,' Bob told him rather solemnly. 'And, in a way, it's got to be the *stupidest* thing you've ever done! Man, what the hell *ails* you, that you have to pull this stupid stuff all the time, while me and Mark and Chris are here tryin' to bail you out of it all! Christ! —man; cut us a break!'

'Hey, man; cut *me* a break! I gotta challenge the dude to get him off my back! Besides,' he said, a bit calmer, 'I happen to believe she's actually crazy about me.'

'You "happen to believe" that?' Bob asked, as his voice rose. 'You "*happen to believe*" that? Holy *shit*, man; people have been tellin' you that for *years*! And all of a sudden you "happen to believe" that she might even *like* you? Jesus Christ!'

'Yeah,' Jon said, enjoying the thought of such things; 'I think there's a pretty strong indication...'

'Holy shit....' Bob shook his head, his patience waning. 'So then why the big *scene*, man? I mean it's not like before, you know; at least now you can *talk* to the babe....'

Jon sighed, as if having explained this a hundred times before. 'Because she's too nice a person to just dump the guy. And he'll just keep buggin' her for ever, till he gets the message. I have my own reasons. Besides, it'll look incredibly good for me to challenge him to somethin' he knows he'll have to back out of.'

Bob looked at him. 'Suppose he doesn't back out?' he asked. 'And you know there's a pretty strong indication that he's just too stupid to give up, you know.'

'Then I'll run him,' Jon said simply.

'With that bucket of bolts down there? Are you out of your gourd?'

'Bob, man, get real; you know I can take him. I've been runnin' honest twelves, last I checked. He's only got a stock Goat; it's a four-hundred.'

'A four-*hundred*?' Bob shrieked. 'I thought it was a three-*fifty*! Man, you'll never even *see* him!'

Jon laughed. 'Get outa here, man; it'll be no contest. With equal cars I'd out-*drive* the son-of-a-bitch. Besides, he's only good at these chickenshit little fist-fights anyway, and he knows it. I figure since he picked the advantage the first time, I get to pick it second.'

Such gallant confidence was eerie; Bob had never seen Jon so motivated, yet it should always have been expected of him. He shook his head again and resigned himself to the inevitable. After all, it was a decision for Jon alone to make. 'Shit.... I just hope you *do* get the guy off your back, so I don't have to keep hearin' the shit about it.'

'So do I, or you'll be tellin' me "I told you so" till frickin' *dooms*-day.'

Bob stood and gazed out the window. 'No I won't, man. You just gotta do what you believe in, you know, what your heart says, and doo.' He thought about that. 'Just as long as you think it's right.'

Jon smiled then. The bleeding had nearly stopped now, and he raised one hand in a thumb's-up gesture. Bob saw him, pretended to ignore it and then finally returned it with a wry wave for levity. But their friendship had never been treated lightly by either of them. Their loyalty to each other was unwavering. They loved each other; and no words were necessary to communicate that.

Jeanne was shaking like a leaf; but, she thought, it's from the cold. This has got to be all one big joke. It's just *got* to be. I'm going to wake up any minute and find that the last six days were nothing but a bad dream, and it's the day after Jon kissed me, and everything will be all right. And maybe he'll call me again tonight, and we can go out to some other movie, and he can kiss me again. And again, and again, and *again*....

She began to feel sad, because it was only another fantasy. What had happened had been real; and now she really was sitting in Danny's red GTO coupé behind the school building at a quarter to midnight, freezing cold, waiting for something to happen. The building and grounds had been vacant for over an hour, and since the team had lost there were no late-night parties anywhere and no-one hanging about reminiscing over how well it had gone. Jon had said he would meet them here; but he was already fifteen minutes late. He had been acting strangely since the fight with Danny in school, first with the odd episode at his house, with Beth and the cocoa, though there had been that wonderful talk; and then he was absent for a day and trying to beat up Danny Harris in the gallery on the next; and it had all become silly to her; but still she knew it had all been frighteningly real.

I'm going to have to tell them my decision tonight, Jeanne thought, though she hated the whole idea. She had always disliked being forced to choose between two options, worrying that there might yet be some factor she had not considered, and then maybe her decision would be imperfect, and someone might be hurt, or she would lose something precious, or a friend might lose respect for her. Now, there seemed like nothing left but to decide and to announce the terms of her decision. I just don't want it to be *wrong*, she worried. But I can't bear to think of these two guys going on killing each other....

Funny how guys are! she laughed to herself. Their ego and their pride are so important to them that they'll do anything to keep from looking silly. And what they do usually ends up making them look even sillier.... Women are lucky in that way. No-one ever insults a woman; and, even if somebody does, it's usually like rude, or maybe funny....

This isn't funny any more, Jeanne decided. When Jon gets here, I'm just going to stand up and say I've had enough of this nonsense. That's all it is: *nonsense*. There's just no sense *to* it. If Jon wants me, he's just going to have to come out and ask me, instead of thinking he has to beat up Danny over it. And if Danny wants to keep a girlfriend, he's going to have to think about *her*, instead of worrying about how it would look, or like how other people are going to think of him for it. I just wish he wasn't so immature. I want a guy who's more concerned with making me happy than in worrying about what other people think about him. Someone who really cares about me, and what I'm really like, and not because of how I make *him* look. God! –Danny can be like so *vain* sometimes....

And Jon, poor Jon; he's been like the victim in all of this. She wanted to dwell on the nobility of Jon's intentions; it was something she considered often. I would love to just sit down over some cocoa and talk with him, she thought, and we could get to know each other better, and then we could be good friends. And like even if we had nothing else, we could at least always be friends–

How *dare* they subject me to this stupid ego war! Jeanne thought, her ire on the rise again. How can they let it go this far, fighting and fighting over something so stupid, like their pride, or their reputation; and not one of them has asked *me*! I should get up and walk home. When Jon gets here, I'll–

But Jon *would've* asked me, she thought. He wanted to; I could tell he did; but he was trying to be too nice. He's such a gentleman, the way he kept apologising for comparing himself to Danny; it was so sweet.... And I should have *answered* him! *Oooh*!

Jeanne wanted to kick herself, now, when the situation was so much clearer to her. Instead she could only recall the conversation with Danny tonight at his house and how he had seemed resolutely unwilling to let her go. She felt locked in a power struggle between her feelings for the two boyls and their feelings for her. To think of discussing it all rationally with both of them was terribly daunting, and yet, it seemed like the only way to avoid the confrontation that otherwise seemed inevitable.

'Danny?' she asked, leaning over a bit. 'It's five of twelve. Let's go home.'

Danny said nothing, still standing outside with his cigarette, leaning against the driver's door of his car.

'Danny? Could you put up the window, please? It's freezing cold.'

Still he said nothing. Jeanne leaned over to roll up the window; but he stopped her.

'No. Leave it down.'

She pulled her varsity coat a little more tightly about herself and shivered.   Under jeans, a pullover and a heavy sweater, she was still cold.   In her stomach, the piece of apple pie she had eaten at Danny's house began to swirl about ominously.   Well, she thought; I guess this is it.   Jon is not coming.   He's just going to make us sit out here all night, freezing to death, and then when it's all over he'll be spreading rotten rumours about us in school tomorrow.   Hah, hah, she laughed sarcastically.   You win, Jon.   The joke's on us.   Now let us go home.

But it was nearly midnight; and the joke was wearing thin.   Maybe he'll just come out here, she thought, and like ask Danny if he can take me home.   I don't care if he doesn't want to fight; he'll never be a coward to me.   I mean I do hate it when guys think they have to fight....   She found herself wishing that Jon would arrive and ask her to prove her love for him by doing anything at all.   Maybe he'll want to seduce me, Jeanne thought; and after one second she could see nothing terrible about it.   She found herself wishing he would come and demand that she go home with him at once, and then of course she would, with no further discussion.   A huge part of her was telling her inside that, despite any outward appearances, Jon Cavaliere was incapable of doing her any harm.   She realised she had put her complete trust in him already and, in some ways, she barely even knew him.

Light flickered in the side mirror.   Jeanne whirled about in the seat. Even Danny give a start.   The silver car gleamed eerily in the dim moonlight, its white roof glowing as if luminescent.   The headlamps were dark.   As it came round the bend in the driveway behind the shops, the sound of that powerful engine rumbling at a mere idle sent a chill down Jeanne's spine.   This is it, she thought.

Danny cast aside the cigarette and stood up straight to greet his adversary.   He watched intently as the car crept slowly towards the upper end of the rear car park.   Jeanne felt a lump rise in her throat. The suspense kept her shivering.   Now she was not as bold as she had fancied herself even three minutes ago.   The car turned right, entering the main aisle, and stopped there.   Danny leaned back against the car again and sighed, folding his arms across his chest and effecting a bored expression.

Suddenly all four headlamps came on and the engine ran up.   Tyres screamed; smoke rose; the ferocious roar of the supercharger was deafening.   They were both blinded by the wall of yellow-and-white light charging straight at them.

Jeanne held her breath.

Danny forced a yawn.   The silver Caprice shot right up and screeched to a halt within three feet of his toes.   The engine returned to its loping idle; and with a soft electric hum the front passenger window glided down.

'Good evening,' said the quiet, boyish voice from inside the car.

Danny bent over, still with his arms folded before himself, and looked in the open window at the occupant of the dark cockpit. 'So do we have another discussion now?'

'We'll see. It's just you two–?'

'The TV crews went home,' Danny told him.

'Their loss. Follow me.'

'Gonna tell me where to?'

'We'll see,' he said, and the window glided up again.

Danny opened his door and got into the GTO beside Jeanne. 'Where are we going?' she wanted to know.

'We'll see,' he said flatly, and started his engine. He shifted into drive and followed the Caprice out past the athletic field to the back gate. Jeanne watched the car ahead, with its six round red taillamps in the rear bumper, as they turned right on the Parkway and made the U-turn to head down towards Chester Pike. As though in a funeral procession they never exceeded thirty miles per hour.

Her stomach began to feel light; she worried that the anxiety might actually make her sick. 'Danny,' she asked, 'what's going on here?'

'Don't get in the habit of asking me questions,' he said sternly to her. 'Don't bug me with bullshit right now.'

'*Danny*,' she said, not at all approving of how he sounded, 'just remember I'm here too. And *I* have to *know*–'

'I won't kill this guy,' Danny said with a cruel chuckle. 'He's good for a laugh.'

The silver Caprice stopped at the intersection of Chester Pike. The signal was actually showing green, though there was no traffic at all on either road. Jon got out quickly and strode briskly back to the GTO. He looked to be in a chipper mood, as though there were nothing more at hand than a friendly chat. Jeanne looked about at the desolation of the corner on such a chilly January night and shivered, wishing she were home in her bed. Danny got out and Jon, in his leather flier's jacket, tight jeans and long white pilot's scarf, came right up to him.

'All right,' he said brightly; 'this'll be the start; you can take the right side so you can swing wide at the corner. Slowham runs all the way out to Foxglove, you know; the finish is the light at Milburne Road, the very next one you come to. I think it's like four or five miles. You don't have to stop if it's red unless you have to. I'm generally very fair about these things; so....'

Danny was gaping at him. 'Oh, shit; dude– Are you *serious*?'

'Hey; if you got a three-fifty, and it's runnin' good, this oughta be pretty good comp. This car of mine's pretty damn heavy, you know.'

'Hey, man; wait a second–'

'You got radials?' He stepped over to Danny's front wing and kicked the tyre lightly with his striped leather running shoe.

'Listen, man; just *listen* to me?'

'Oh, yeah; right.' Jon looked up and smiled at him. 'The winner gets the prize.'

Danny blanched. 'Uh; what's the prize?'

Jon smiled, with those irresistible dimples. 'Uh; why are we here?'

Jeanne felt an icy shiver trickle down her spine. Her hand froze on the door-handle. 'Oh; come *on!*' Danny yelled at him. 'You're *crazy*, man!'

'Oh; come *on*, dude,' Jon said disdainfully to him; 'don't give me that shit! Look; if you think you can take me because I strut around with a hell of an attitude and nothin' to back it up, well, then maybe I think I can take you because you put mag wheels on a car that really ain't worth shit. I didn't back outa your stupid ego war. Are you gonna tell me you're backin' outa mine?'

'Man, that's a little different—'

'The *hell* it is, dude. The *hell* it is.' Jon kicked the pavement with his heel, looking back at his idling Caprice, a dozen feet away. 'Look, man; at least it's good odds. I ain't gonna kill you, and you ain't gonna kill me. The winner wins, and the loser loses. The girl's worth a little more than goin' through life with two assholes fightin' over her.'

Jeanne shivered again and, for a second, her muscles relaxed. It was a perfect opportunity to open the door and stand up. 'All right,' she said to the two of them across the roof of the GTO; 'this has all gone too far. Danny, you know what we talked about, tonight even, and I don't think this is the way to settle anything. And Jon, well, I think you know what I feel for you, and I want you to know, well, that I did think it over, and like I thought—'

'All *right*,' Danny said suddenly, and paced back to his car. 'So; Cavaliere, it's Slowham out to the next light.'

'You're *on!*' Jon grinned, and darted back to the Caprice.

'*Jon!*' Jeanne cried out, but Danny grabbed her from inside the car and pulled her down into the seat. 'But Danny, *wait!*'

'Get in and shut up,' he told her. 'Put on your seatbelt and your shoulder-belt and any other belt you can find.' He put his shifter into drive and steered round the Caprice to stop beside it in the right lane.

The traffic signal for the Parkway had gone yellow.

Jeanne reclosed her door just as Danny stopped the car. 'Danny, we have to talk. This is *not* the way—'

'Are your belts on? If they're not, then tough. You're gonna see this Prince Charming of yours get his ass creamed.'

The Parkway signal had gone red. She stared at him in total shock for a long second before something masquerading as sense sent her scurrying about for the safety belts. Her stomach turned over a few times. Her throat felt dry and sore. Her heart pounded in her chest.

The light for the empty Chester Pike turned yellow.

Beside Danny, Jon's big 427 ran up a bit. Danny clicked his console gear lever into drive.

Jon shifted into first.

The Parkway light turned green.

Four tyres screamed as they left the light. The GTO's wheels spun wildly; and the powerful Caprice leaped into the lead straight away. Right in front of them the fat tyres shrieked again as Jon dropped in the clutch for second gear. The roar of the engines was murderous.

It was a short block to Slowham Road; Jon was there in five seconds. Jeanne watched with her heart in her mouth as his car leaned into a slide fifteen yards from the actual gap in the Parkway median. The big Caprice slid sideways to align itself perfectly on course for the side street, diving artfully through the opening and charging off, tyres spinning, up Slowham Road.

Danny wrenched the wheel to the left; but his tyres broke traction and the car swung far over to the right. The rear wheels jumped sideways up the low kerb of the far section of median, and he had to brake hard to regain control. The lesson had been costly; already Jon was ten car-lengths ahead and pulling away. Frustrated, Danny flattened the accelerator.

Jon was cruising along at a mild speed of sixty-five, supercharger humming, exhaust snarling through the cutout valves behind the header collectors, when Harris closed in doing at least eighty. In an instant the red GTO was beside him and then ahead by two dozen yards. Jon smirked, seeing how well Danny's pride had been snared by the challenge. The residential district fell away behind them; and the road narrowed.

Beyond the sharp right bend up ahead the road left town, where it would make a small series of smooth hills and valleys that could be taken easily at high speed. Danny straddled both lanes at about seventy. Jon changed down in preparation for the fast section of road and pulled even with the GTO on the right, not four feet from Jeanne's shoulder.

Harris would not let him by. Wary of turning this into a contact contest with Jeanne at stake, Jon steered away from him but found no tarmac beneath his wheels. The Caprice ran up a four-foot-high incline of dirt and into a fair-sized cabbage patch. Ploughing two fat furrows in the dormant soil, Jon mowed down a few shrubs, dodged a clothesline and coincidentally bypassed the sharp bend in the road.

Danny was just wondering what had happened to his opponent when, seemingly out of nowhere, the Caprice pounced down on the pavement just ahead. Stunned, he jabbed needlessly at the brake pedal and lost valuable distance on Jon. With vehemence he slammed down his right foot again.

Jeanne removed one hand from the dashboard just long enough to feel her chest for a heartbeat. In his anger Harris dropped the lever back into middle gear and let the engine run up for the acceleration. Changing up at last at eighty, he was able to stay with Jon through the smoother section of rural road.

Fast approaching was the most dangerous stretch of the course, where the roadway would narrow still further, take a fast plunge down to water level and then bend sharply to the left, going straight for only a hundred yards before crossing Mill Creek. The bridge was old and narrow, having an ill-maintained surface and no lights. The only houses in the area were as old as the Revolution, clustered closely about the far end of the bridge, where a flotilla of confusing yellow signs heralded a tight right turn.

Well into that sharp left Jon was still doing over sixty. The tyres whined a bit and he braked hard, feeling the Caprice's rear end loosen a little on a bit of night ice. He changed down to third and came out of the turn nearly sideways at about fifty but, having expected this, calmly corrected with the wheel to avoid running off into the creek. The steel deck of the old bridge was under him in a second; he felt dizzily weightless as the car flew over it. He put down the clutch for an upshift but then dared to release it again in third. The Caprice twitched its tail with the renewed torque and bolted away.

Jeanne gripped the dashboard, her knuckles white with fear, as Danny's six-year-old GTO hurtled over the bridge. The steel framework blurred in her side window. An old stone wall straight ahead demanded that all drivers steer right, and painted yellow arrows on the wall, amidst the graffiti, supposedly warned night travellers of its dangers. With Harris so close behind, Jon just steered hard and kept his foot down. He cleared the wall easily but his left flank was snagged on the trunk of a stubborn old oak tree standing too close by the side of the tarmac. Nimbly the Caprice bounced away from it and charged ahead, losing two of its offside taillamps and all the beauty of that hand-painted monogram.

Jon shoved the stick back into second and downed the accelerator, inhaling deeply with the new expanse of wide, flat country road. Danny geared down again also, running the GTO into the eighties before changing up. The Caprice was far ahead; Jon had run second to sixty-five and third to almost a hundred. With the coming of three digits on the speedometer Jeanne's nausea increased with a vengeance. The electric-line poles outside Danny's window blended into a long black picket-fence. The grey-brown skeletons of hibernating trees were but ghosts in the cloudy winter moonlight. The white lines on the roadway blurred into a solid ribbon; and the tyres' eerie whine became louder than the engine's straining moan. Every bump, so shockingly harsh, sounded and felt as if it would hurl them off the road. Jeanne's stomach heaved with every motion of the car; and the heat of her face and neck were ill at odds with the rude chill of the night.

The speedometer pointer teased 120; and they closed on the lopsided arrangement of Jon's four remaining taillamps. Perhaps the Caprice was not so fast in the long run after all. Jon led them straight through two isolated 'Stop' signs and under a railway trestle before sweeping through a wide left curve at well over ninety.

Danny Harris, silently fuming, clung tightly to the wheel of his strangely temperamental car, desperately endeavouring to keep it on the road. It had never been driven like this before and he was not a fast driver at any rate. Jon was performing as though there were some kind of art to it all, smooth and slick as a professional; even the collision with the tree had looked calculated, or at least inconsequential to him. Danny was frightened now more than ever, but he tried to remind himself that the end might all be worth it. The race had become much more than a contest for a young lady's affections or even a challenge to a gentleman's pride. In his very real hatred of Jon Cavaliere, he had begun to recognise the excellent opportunity to see him dead.

Jeanne only wanted the entire evening to come to a calm, safe, happy ending. She prayed in whispers, afraid that maybe the Devil himself might hear her and conduct this nightmare even more to his wishes. They flew over an unused railway spur and she watched Jon make a four-wheel landing very close to the gravel shoulder. Lord, she prayed, save us all in this hour of need! Don't let a thing happen to any of us, God; just let us all slow down and go home....

Jon went up an incline in fourth gear; and Danny drew nearly even with him. Both cars rocketed off the crest and dove down the other side together. The GTO hit hard, vaulting them both up against their seatbelts; and Jeanne caught a glimpse of the well-sprung Caprice's catlike landing just a length-and-a-half ahead. They were coming into Foxglove; the Milburne Road traffic signal was less than a mile away. Jeanne stared longingly at Jon's battle-scarred car, its rear quarter now even with Danny's right front. The left rear wing panel was dented well in from where it should have been and the chromium bumper had been peeled away from the corner. A lamp bulb, still lit, dangled in the free air from the cornering-light opening now void of all lens material. Her heart sank to see the chipping remainder of the proud owner's monogram; and she remembered the excitement and optimism she had felt on the balmy September morning she had first seen it. Now it was like a battle flag trampled in the muddy ground of no-man's land that only waits for the honourable of the future to come and resurrect it for victory. Tears flooded her eyes at the worry that she might never again know the thrill of seeing Jon in all his glory. So much was already irrevocable now. And at any second it could all be over for ever.

Jon never did relinquish the lead. He kept two or three car-lengths on the red-and-black GTO, as though he could read every jab of Danny's right foot behind him. He favoured the left lane as they came into town; Jeanne could only ever think that he had done so in premonition, to keep her safely on the legal side of the road. Yet with all her inexperience in driving, she was actually the first to realise the coming hazard. She opened her eyes and immediately recognised a pair of headlamps snaking lazily down the road from just beyond the intersection ahead. For a full second they disappeared behind what in the next second was revealed as a tree.

'Oh, God,' she squeaked, her throat tight with terror. 'God! –it's… a *drunk!*'

Danny lifted his foot; he had seen the white car too. Warily his left toe hovered over the brake pedal.

Two lengths ahead the 427 whooped up as Jon opened the clutch to change down.

The white Ford saloon had run the red light at Milburne Road and aimed inadvertently between the two cars. Danny was legally in the proper lane; for whatever reason he would not acknowledge. *'Hah!'* he laughed, yelling at the silver Chevrolet through his closed side window. 'Stupid son-of-a-bitch! You *lose*, asshole!'

He had pulled almost even with Jon's car; there seemed nothing for Jon to do but to duck behind him.

'Danny!' Jeanne cried. 'There isn't–'

'Lose, son-of-a-bitch!' hollered Danny. 'You're gonna *lose!'*

'But there's no way he can–'

'He's gonna *lose!'*

The white Ford drifted into its proper lane and presumed to take a straighter course. With two pairs of headlamps ahead, perhaps the driver thought he was seeing double; perhaps he thought nothing at all.

'Lose, dammit!' Danny shrieked frantically. 'You have to *lose!* Stupid son-of-a-bitch!'

'Danny!'

Jon was as far to the left as he could go; but it was only a two-lane road. The white Ford meant to run right between the two speeding cars. Not one hundred yards away, that car forced Jon to choose only one of two options. He made up his mind in less than half a second.

The Caprice ricocheted off the Ford's right front wing panel with a loud metallic bang and drove off into the unpaved shoulder, bouncing down on its springs and recoiling off the ground. Jon's car was airborne at seventy-five.

Jeanne screamed.

Moonlight glinted off the edges of the Caprice as it rose into the still night air. Beautifully poised, the front left corner took only a slight dip as the car slammed into an aluminium lamppost at over four feet above the roadway.

Danny and Jeanne swept through the green light at Milburne Road, victorious. From behind them came a horrifying series of bangs and crashes, a terrific screaming of tyres and then nothing. In a cold sweat, Danny floored the accelerator.

'*DANNY!*' she screamed at the very top of her lungs, out of control in panic. 'We have to go *back!* Go *back*, Danny, *go BACK! WE HAVE TO GO BACK!*' She hung over the back of her seat, twisted about within her safety belts, the tears streaming out of her eyes as she wailed. '*Danny!* We have to go *back*; oh, *GOD!* Oh, God! –please, *please*–!'

'Shut *up!*' he shouted at her. 'Just shut up; will you?'

She never noticed the panic in his voice too. 'Oh, God! –Danny, please, *please*, oh, *PLEASE!* He could be–' At that she let out a long, loud, bloodcurdling scream of horror, letting the blood rise in her throat and her forehead pound with the pressure. Her stomach gave up its futile battle and she coughed in convulsions. Danny understood at once. He came down hard on the brakes, reaching over to open the door for her. 'Oh, God,' she cried, and leaned out to bring up her dinner and the apple pie she had at Danny's house. 'God, this can't be happening; it just isn't real....'

'The hell it *isn't*,' he said, his voice shaking with anxious nausea and abject terror.

All the way back to Wilshire, down the west side of Mill Creek to avoid Slowham Road, Jeanne wept in her hands. There was no hope. There would be no tomorrow at all.

She tore herself out of the car and ran straight up stairs without a word to her parents in the sitting room. On her pillow she cried and cried with tears that would never stop. Only sheer exhaustion put her to sleep.

* * *

Chapter 9

Bright are the stars that shine

The sun was very bright. Acres upon acres of tall yellow tulips swayed back and forth in the breeze. Out into the meadow she ran, wearing the pretty white dress Aunt Liesl had bought her for Easter. She sat down amidst the tulips and smelled them. Yellow was her favourite colour. Her father appeared, with his skinny tie and round glasses, and his voice echoed across the open meadow: 'You must not marry the knight!'

'But Daddy,' she cried, 'I *love* the knight!'

'*No!*' he bellowed. 'You will *never* marry the knight!' He disappeared.

The tower loomed up against the darkening sky; and she saw Danny Harris, in his black robe, pacing outside and mumbling to himself, 'All of the sheep must die. All of the sheep will die. All of the sheep are dying....'

She was afraid, and she ran from him; but he chased her into the tower. She ran down the steps and it became colder, and soon it was snowing. Chris Santana bumped into her from behind, calling over and over, 'Avalanche, at the park! Avalanche, at the park!'

Just then Danny Harris caught her and said in a deep voice, 'The sheep are dying. The sheep are gonna *die!*'

Suddenly, one metric ton of snow fell on top of her, and she could not breathe. She was pulled down underwater and got caught in a riptide. There was nowhere to go. All about were bubbles. She kept falling deeper and deeper. She lost the white dress and had only her white woollen sweater and cheerleading socks. It was very cold. She tried to breathe. There was no air.

'You may not marry the White Knight!' boomed her father's voice.

'The sheep are dead, the sheep are dead,' chanted Danny Harris.

She gasped for breath. Bob Prescott rode off on a motorcycle with Patti Harper, doing fifty miles per hour; she saw the speedometer pointer. Steve Marlowe got caught in the mud, with no trousers on. The White Knight rode in on his beautiful grey stallion and said to Danny Harris, 'There's no more doughnuts at Annie's.'

Danny Harris gave him directions to the 7-Eleven and then turned about as the White Knight rode away. 'I ain't messin' with chickenshit any more,' he said, and then he laughed.

There was no air left.

* * *

'*No!*' came the muffled cry from up stairs. '*No, NO!*'

Mrs Banfield looked up from the cooker and ran out to the foyer and up the steps. 'Child,' she called, 'dear child, what *is* it?' Worriedly she opened the door.

The room was stuffy and dense. In the midst of it all Jeanne writhed about in the centre of her bed, twisted-up inside the blankets and sheets. '*No,*' she was crying; 'don't go! Come back, come back.... No, no; you have to come back, please....'

Mrs Banfield sat on the edge of the bed and reached over to pat her daughter's shoulder. 'There, there,' she soothed her; 'it was just a bad dream....' She put a hand to Jeanne's head and brushed back some damp hair. 'Dear child, you're sweating. Do you feel sick?'

Jeanne rolled over and looked up. She was still in her clothes from last night. Her throat felt hot and dry and raw. Her skin was drenched with sweat; and she imagined she had not bathed in days. 'Mom?' she called, frightened by her own condition. When she found her mother she fell over and hugged her. 'Oh, *God*! –Mom,' she whined, and began to sob on her shoulder.

'Oh; there, there, Jeanne; it was all a bad dream. It's all right now....'

The hug was comforting; and Jeanne held on like a small child. 'Oh, God! –Mom, I feel so *hot*....'

'You *do* feel warm, sweetheart....' She slid a hand up to lay it against Jeanne's forehead. 'I'd say you had a fever.'

'Oh, Mom....'

'Well; I don't think you should go in, if you feel that warm....' She rose and started to the door. 'Can I just take your temperature, just to make sure?'

'No, Mom.... It doesn't matter, because I'm not going in anyway.' Jeanne sat up and wiped the wet hair off her face. 'I'm *sick*, Mom.'

'Were you sick last night?'

'I threw up.'

'Well, sweetheart; it could be the flu. Maybe you should see Dr Moretti. You haven't been over there in quite a while.'

'I don't want to go over there.'

Her mother smiled; since childhood Jeanne had always hated going to the doctor. 'Nevertheless, child, maybe you should.'

Jeanne shook her head, as if disoriented, and looked about the room for a second. 'God.... What time is it?'

'Your clock says almost seven-thirty, dear. Your alarm never went off.'

Jeanne slumped down into the bed and pulled the bedclothes up to her neck. 'I don't care. I'm just gonna stay here and sleep, till I feel like getting up.'

Mrs Banfield nodded. 'All right, dear. I'll keep this door closed so you can rest.'

'Okay,' Jeanne said, as though sulking, and her mother swung shut the door.

Jeanne did not sleep. She lay wide awake under the blankets, staring straight up at the ceiling. Thoughts chased themselves about in her head, and they were all about as bad as the dream she had just had. She did not want to think about anything at all; but still those thoughts persisted, as if to haunt her against her wishes, and they terrified her.

Jon is dead, she felt something telling her from inside. It was impossible to conceive and yet painfully apparent. Jon is dead now, she concurred. He was killed last night by a drunk driver who ran him off the road and killed him. He was killed last night in a drag race that he started in order to win me away from Danny Harris whom I don't even *like* any more. He could've had me anyway, whether he won or lost or didn't even race at all. He died in that crash because he loved me; and he didn't even have to, because I would've loved him no matter what happened.

That thought, of how senseless and pointless the whole thing had been, was the one thought she hated most. Somewhere, somehow, there had to have been something she could have done to prevent it all. It's all my fault, she thought, over and over again. He loved me; and I knew that; and if only I had told him I loved him, none of it would've happened. But I couldn't make up my mind, and I couldn't find the nerve to say *anything*; and so he died and went to heaven and I'm stuck down here without him. And it's gonna be that way for *ever*.

She wept then and went on for at least twenty minutes. There was nothing sadder to bring to mind. In fact she could not bring anything else to mind at all except how sad it was that there was no more Jon Cavaliere in the world. No-one would ever hear him play piano at a party or sing on stage, no-one would ever see him drive that car again or shoot billiards again, no-one would ever laugh at any more of his funny jokes in class, and no-one would ever be rescued by him, in the lake or at Snow Lodge or anywhere. The White Knight was gone.

And it was all so *stupid*! she wanted to cry aloud. It was all my *fault*! I'll *never* be able to live with myself again, just like he could never have lived without me. She began to cry again, willingly dwelling upon that one thought. He challenged Danny Harris to a duel, just like I knew he would, so they could decide which one of them could see me and which one would have to bow out. Jon wouldn't run Danny off the road just to win, because I was in the car, and because he's just too fair to do that. If the only way for him to win was to hit Danny's car, he would rather die. And so that's what he *did*.

It *was* honour, then, Jeanne realised; and her insides tingled with the notion. Just like Patti said. He was a man of honour, who would fight for the woman he loved and die rather than live without me. It was the most romantic concept Jeanne could behold; and she wanted to cry with the sweetness of the sentiment. He really and truly loved me.... I should always remember that. Only I can't *forget* it, Jeanne thought, because it's the part of it that means he's not *here* any more. And I'll always hate myself for that. It's the part I'll never get over.

She began to cry again and whimpered quietly in her bed for another half-hour. And, she thought, I bet he *would've* kept his part of the deal, too. I bet he *would've* bowed out gracefully, and wished me all the happiness in the world.... That's just how much of a gentleman he *is*. He has more honour than Danny could ever *dream* of having. He *is* the White Knight.

Wrong, Jeanne thought. It's 'was' now. He *was* that much of a gentleman. All those things you like to say about him, like about his honour and integrity and his talent and sincerity.... Well; he *was* all those things; but now he's not anything. The White Knight is *dead*.

Again she began to weep; and this time she vowed that she would never stop.

Her mother came up again, just before noon, and Jeanne was sitting up in her bed, leafing through last year's school yearbook. 'Well?' she asked cheerfully. 'How are you feeling now?'

'Okay,' said Jeanne, not looking up.

Mrs Banfield sat on the edge of the bed, as before, and put a hand to Jeanne's forehead. 'You do feel warm,' she worried. 'Why don't you let me take your temperature—'

'No,' said Jeanne. 'It's all right.'

Her mother looked at her for almost a full minute before speaking. 'Jeanne,' she asked seriously, 'is there something that's bothering you? Do you want to talk about it?'

'No,' Jeanne said shortly; and the brevity of her replies was what concerned her mother most. Normally Jeanne was full of words.

'Well; if you do, I'll listen. All right?'

'Okay.' Still Jeanne would not look up.

Mrs Banfield hesitated there for a moment and then went to the window to open the curtains. A cloud front had come in; there would be snow soon. 'Jeanne,' she asked, stopping by the door, 'is it anything about Danny?'

At that Jeanne looked up, as if fearfully. 'No. Why?'

'I don't know.... It's just a feeling I get from you when you're having boy problems.'

Jeanne shook her head and returned her eyes to the yearbook. 'I don't think you'd understand.'

Mrs Banfield smiled and came back to sit on the bed again. 'You forget that I was once a girl too, child. There's a lot you think I don't know.'

Jeanne made a little smile, albeit not a happy one. 'This,' she said with a sad sigh, 'I think, is beyond you.'

Mrs Banfield had a worry or two then. 'It's nothing that's happened to you physically–'

'*No*, Mom,' Jeanne said, as though that were truly a needless question.

'All right,' her mother said, and sighed a bit. 'Well; if you do want to talk about it....'

Jeanne said nothing. She only turned over the yearbook in her lap so her mother could see the page. Just above her fingertip was one smiling eleventh-grade face in the array of small portraits. Mrs Banfield leaned in to read the name beneath the photograph.

'Jon?' she wondered. 'The one from the lake–?'

Jeanne's eyes flooded at that memory in particular and she could not keep from wrinkling her pretty face with sorrow. 'Oh, Mom,' she cried, as her mother took a hold on her then, 'you wouldn't believe it; I swear you wouldn't *believe* it....'

It might have been easy, despite the heart-wrenching pain, to relate the whole story note-for-note. But though she and Jon had already dated, in the process admitting almost exactly the same feelings each had hoped to find in the other, no-one who had never known the depth of the unrequited love between them would ever understand the intensity of Jeanne's anguish now. Someday, in the far distant future, there might yet come a day when she could readily speak about it and admit at last how much of a void it had all left in her life. That is, thought Jeanne, if I ever live that long....

And so she would not tell her mother about her life's worst heartache. She wallowed alone, saying nothing of it to anyone, not even to Patti or PJ when they stopped by to call on her that weekend. She even considered taking her own life, just to be relieved of the hideous burden of emotional and psychological pain, but recognised a perfectly just torture in forcing herself to wait in dread anticipation of Fate's next hand. She was terrified to think she might be expected to find a new life after Jon Cavaliere; not once in over four years had she ever conceived of such a possibility. In any event she would have to accept responsibility for the fact that the race had been run and that an honourable young gentleman, whose life was only beginning, had died in a horrible car wreck. Morbidly taking heart, Jeanne came to cherish the notion of joining him in Heaven for ever, perhaps by simply taking a few too many sleeping-tablets and passing away in her bed; and yet, somewhere in the charred pit that had once been her heart, the tiniest ember still glowed to remind her that there might yet be something positive to come out of it all. Until then, she was sick in bed with a fever of one hundred point eight degrees Fahrenheit.

* * *

Outside, it was white. The snow had come in the night; Jeanne recalled her father remarking about the weather some time before midnight. Her father loved snow; probably it had been the reason why he had decided against an early retirement last autumn, in favour of another five years with the firm. Everyone would be expecting him to move to Florida when he retired.

Florida, Jeanne thought. The notion reminded her of summer; and summer instantly reminded her of Jon Cavaliere. Normally summer and Jon Cavaliere were two thoughts that could warm up any frozen winter's morning; but Jeanne was not ready to feel cheerful and warm after only five days. Patti and Anne giggled and chatted together, merrily tromping through the drifts at each street corner as though without a care to the contrary, whilst Jeanne moped along in silence two or three steps behind. Debbie joined them at the rear driveway, having walked with her brother and his friends only a block ahead. ''Morning, Jeannie!' she waved happily, as they all started up into the schoolyard.

'Hi, Debbie,' Jeanne said in obligatory fashion, her voice still hoarse and her throat still sore from the weekend's fever and cough. Debbie turned to Patti to ask about some assignment straight away. Jeanne wondered if she looked as dead as she felt. Her body ached from too much inactivity and bed rest, and her stomach was still queasy with apprehension about not having been able to keep anything down. The spark inside that had always kept her optimistic about each new day seemed as cold as the snow.

There between an old Mercury and a new orange Duster sat the Caprice, duly laden with snow like all the other cars. At the first glimpse of the right rear quarter, the bold monogram proclaiming the owner's initials stopped Jeanne dead in her tracks.

To the others it was only the same car they had become used to seeing just about every day; and so Jeanne's severity struck them as odd. 'Oh; okay, Jeannie,' Debbie said with a giggle, 'we all know you can get the real thing now without having to camp out at his car....'

The others all giggled. But Jeanne paid them no mind. 'It's *his car*,' she breathed, immeasurably awed by the realisation. 'It's *his car*.'

'Oh; mush mush,' teased Debbie; 'now here she goes....'

Patti, however, ever astute, had recognised the anxiety in Jeanne's reaction. 'Jeannie?' she asked with that pretty frown. 'What is it?''

Jeanne only stared at the car with a strange, shocked expression. 'Come on!' Debbie said. 'You've seen his car before. God! —like even—'

'But don't you *see?*' Jeanne said then. Patti and Anne frowned at her, whilst Debbie had wandered up to admire the car, as she often fancied it for herself. 'He's all *right*,' Jeanne insisted. 'It's like it never really—'

But what Debbie saw this morning made her gasp. 'Oh, my—'

Anne saw the damaged left rear panel too then. 'Oh my God,' she sighed. 'Look who got *clobbered....*'

Jeanne rushed round the Plymouth Duster then and up towards the front of the silver car and nearly dropped her books as she put a hand to her mouth. 'Oh, Jonny,' she whispered sadly, 'I am so *sorry....*'

They were all stunned by what they saw. The bumper had been fiercely struck about two feet from the left corner. The fibreglass bonnet was cracked and buckled halfway back to the windscreen, and the mesh grille was nearly all eradicated. One headlamp and one yellow fog-lamp were shattered, their shells staring blindly from behind a cage of icicles. Jeanne shivered to see the pretty red script of 'Spellbinder' had disappeared without a trace. Suddenly she felt faint.

The front right wing panel was badly scraped; and appalling stripes of cream-coloured paint hinted at something far more sinister than a collision with an innocent aluminium lamppost. Fortunately Anne and Debbie were over there on the left side, unable to see the colour that so unmistakably indicated another car. Jeanne felt a violent somersault in her stomach just then; and she knew it was only because she had not eaten in four days that she did not vomit on the spot. There was indeed something horrible in her past now, something no wishful thinking could ever erase. The thought of that was worse to consider than how awful her present had seemed, even a day ago.

'God,' Debbie was saying; 'like, this is really nasty. I bet this is why he hasn't been in school....'

'I wonder if he got hurt,' Anne said gravely; and she and Debbie both turned to Patti for some explanation. But Patti only glared stiffly at Jeanne. At once Jeanne turned away from their suspicion, aware she would have to answer to them all sooner or later about the car and her mysterious illness of the past week. She only hoped at least to put off them all until there was something somewhat more substantial to tell. The only advantage in all of what was now apparent, and it was a significant advantage at that, was that Jon Cavaliere was most certainly alive and well. That served as Jeanne's only hope to regain a positive outlook; and it accompanied her through every class in anticipation of the last period of the day.

She hurried to take her usual seat in Room 152. Still, Miss Simpson was a minute late and another minute getting to the roll book. At the first C she looked up and asked, 'Well; has anyone seen Jon today?'

'Oh; Cavaliere?' Art Donner laughed. 'Dude died. Kicked the old bucket.'

'Don't I wish,' mumbled someone behind Jeanne.

'Yeah; musta drove his car off the Curve,' said John Artis. 'Didja *see* it?'

'Probably high,' a girl supposed.

'Well,' said Miss Simpson cheerfully; 'I saw his car outside this morning, so I know he's here somewhere.'

Jeanne blanched. The teacher was using the same logic she had herself when she had seen the car outside too. God, I just hope that's right, she worried. I just hope I'm not completely wrong on this one....

'He's always here,' said the teacher, as though to reassure herself. 'I'm sure he'll be along in another minute.'

'If at *all*,' Paul Orwell said profoundly; and Jeanne looked over at him, sitting not in his usual place but two seats from the back in the first row. Even Cindy, who, though she was Jon's friend primarily, had still been friendly with her since the semester had begun, had not even turned round to say hello. Suddenly Jeanne felt terrified, as though everyone in the room knew more about it than she did. Perhaps she had indeed been absent from school for too long. Perhaps there was far more to the story than what she knew after all.

The lesson finally did commence about five or ten minutes later. The assignment from Wednesday had been to read the historical overview of William Shakespeare's plays and 'be able to discuss it in class'. Miss Simpson reiterated her point about the importance of history in studying literature; and within fifteen minutes the class was into one of their characteristically spirited and in-depth discussions of a minor point in the textbook. There were just about sixteen minutes left to the fifth and final period when Sylvia Monteone launched into a long-winded explanation as to why the late sixteenth-century was not a ripe audience for a new playwright. At exactly 12.01 the door opened.

He shuffled disdainfully into the room, dragging his heels and twirling his car keys by the key-ring in his left hand, dead to the world behind the dark mirrored sunglasses. The door swung closed by itself, very effectively announcing his entrance as unusually late and his attitude as arrogantly indifferent. Snowflakes from outside still garnished his hair and the shoulders of his leather flier's jacket. He had on the same old 'Wonderman' t-shirt he had worn on the first day of Composition class over a year ago and a pair of close-fitting, well-worn Levi's jeans. The heels of his shoes were the only sound as he strolled down the far right side of the room and took a seat behind where Paul now sat near the end of the first row, half the floor away from his ordinary place beside Jeanne.

The class remained eerily silent. Normally a tardy arrival, even one this late, went relatively unheralded. Sylvia, awed like everyone else, had broken off with all her reasons, having remembered them from the textbook anyway, but no-one seemed to care or even notice. Miss Simpson took a breath and addressed him. 'Well, Mr Cavaliere; as I see you don't have your book, are you at least accompanied by a late pass?'

'Me?' he asked dryly, barely looking up. 'A *pass*?'

This might have been the expected reply; many laughed. Miss Simpson smiled her usual dimply smile. 'I thought as much,' she said wryly, and noted an unexcused lateness in her book. 'How 'bout a pass for the three days you've been out?'

'Altogether, four,' Jon replied; 'but, who's counting?' He waited for a few chuckles, ever inclined towards playful banter with the teacher. 'And no; no pass. But I can get one.'

'I'm sure you can,' she said to him. 'Any last stabs at a believable alibi?'

'Well, I almost had to cancel; but rather than miss my *favourite class....*' He gave a shrug. 'McDonald's is too crowded during last period anyway.'

People laughed at that. 'Okay,' said the teacher, closing her roll book then. 'Uh, Sylvia? Where were we?'

The class had enjoyed this exchange; and Sylvia had forgotten what she had earlier been reciting almost verbatim. Miss Simpson posed a few new questions to other students and the late arrival of Jon Cavaliere drifted into the past.

Paul Orwell had been late to class as well; in fact he had been just a few yards ahead of Miss Simpson as she had come down the corridor. He turned about to Jon and whispered, 'So where were you?'

'Out cruisin'.'

'So how come you bothered with the last coupla minutes? I woulda went home.'

'Got bored,' Jon shrugged, and closed his eyes behind the sunglasses.

Paul laughed a little, under his breath, and turned forwards again.

Jeanne sat quietly in her seat, holding her open ring-binder with two hands and tapping it softly and steadily on the desktop. So why isn't he over *here*? she kept wondering. It's like he's avoiding me, like he's mad at me for something, and all I want to do is talk to him again.... I mean: maybe it is all my fault, but like if I could just *talk* to him about it....

Just three rows away, Jon laughed quietly to someone's whispered joke. He seemed much as he normally did, attractively cocky and amusingly naughty; but Jeanne was left feeling like she had missed part of the story. I just don't *get* it, she thought. I'm glad he's all right; I mean of *course* I'm glad about that, and I am sorry about his car; and I'd try to make it up to him somehow if he'd let me. And like maybe if we could just *talk*, we could at least say how we feel.... It's like we never dated, or talked, or *anything*. It's like nothing ever *happened*!

She got a sudden, ghastly chill all over and trembled feverishly in the chair. Oh, God! He's treating me like nothing ever happened! Like we never met, or talked, or never started that stupid race.... Like he's accepted that Danny *won*! Oh, God! –I just can't *believe* he would think that way! *I* know who won! Please, Jon, she thought, and wanted to yell across the room, I *swear*, Jon; just let us *talk* about it, and then I can tell you how I *really* feel! If you'd just give me a chance—

'Jeannie?'

She spun about and saw the teacher and half her classmates looking at her. There had been a question; and she had not even heard, let alone knew how to answer. 'What?'

Miss Simpson smiled pleasantly and crossed her legs, sitting up on top of the radiator. The radiator under the windows was her favourite spot, not merely because it was warm but because it made her feel more like a part of the class than its controller, although to most of the students she spoke from behind. 'Shakespeare's first theatre. What was it called?'

'Oh; um— The uh, *Globe* theatre.' Jeanne felt herself blushing beet-red.

'Okay; and what did the name have to do with it?'

'It was *round*,' someone spoke up.

'Okay; let's not call out while I'm calling on people. Jeannie, do you know *why* it was round?'

Jeanne swallowed and then said, 'So everyone could see the stage?'

A few people laughed; they may have thought she was joking. Miss Simpson scarcely minded that levity was more the norm than the exception in her classes. 'Okay; that's good, because the old Greek theatres were round, too. It was also *symbolic*, because it was intended to become the centre of English theatre, and eventually *world* theatre.'

Jeanne sighed in relief and tried to cool off. God, she thought, just get me through this day....

Not five minutes later the teacher called upon Jon. 'Okay; uh, Jon, do you know this material?'

'Ask Wonderman anything,' he replied, and the class all looked at him.

'Okay, then, Wonder-whatever-you-are,' she teased, and the others laughed along with her. 'Why don't you tell us why there weren't any women acting in Shakespeare's plays at this time?'

The question had not been covered in the assigned reading. But Miss Simpson expected more from Jon than a response straight out of the course text, and Jon would not evade the question. He made a little smirk and quickly stifled it; most did not notice. '*Logic*,' he said simply.

'Logic?' she asked him. His classmates were listening. 'What logic?'

'Real simple logic. Men can act better than women.'

The class broke up into laughter, with cheering from the boys and jeering from the offended girls. 'What a Chauvinist *pig*!' complained Karen.

'*Really*!' agreed another girl.

'Let's not leave out Ann-Margaret,' one boy called out.

'Diggit,' another agreed. 'Yo; didja hear she's gonna be in *Tommy?*'

'Okay, now he does have a point,' Miss Simpson said seriously, hoping that by explaining what she knew Jon had really meant she might chide both sexes into harmony. 'In Elizabethan times, even though the monarch was a woman, women as a part of society did not have the rights they have today.'

'Women as a *whole*,' Jon said quietly to Paul.

'They *still* don't have any rights,' Cindy said seriously.

Jon scoffed at that. 'Oh; you got all the rights you *need*.'

'Oh; come on, Jon,' she countered; 'get *real*! *You* know–'

'You get a bunch of dumb chicks holdin' political office, speakin' in Congress, runnin' for President–'

'So *what?*' Karen came back. 'Maybe it's about *time* we had a female President! And showed these cowards some *leadership!*'

'Yeah!' cheered Sylvia. 'Like how about that clumsy oaf who's in there *now?*'

'At least he's a *guy*,' Paul smirked.

'*Oooooogh!*' Cindy groaned angrily; and other girls voiced dissent as well.

'Go get 'em!' Jon called out over them all in a high falsetto. 'Burn those girdles and hit them with our purses!'

The class laughed riotously at him. 'So long as it's got a *brick* in it,' Cindy taunted him. Jon stuck out his tongue at her.

'Okay,' Miss Simpson called, worried about restoring order before her superiors came down the corridor; 'so much now for the *nineteen*-seventies. In the *fifteen*-seventies none of you girls would be able to speak out the way you can today. It was generally accepted by playwrights and other people of the day that women were not capable of deciding things for themselves, let alone able to act out a role, besides those of mother and housekeeper. So all of the parts were played by men.'

'*Romeo and Juliet* musta been a real winner,' Jon sided to Paul.

'But all of the *playwrights* were men!' Terri Milgram pointed out.

'Well; I guess they had it all planned,' Miss Simpson shrugged. 'Okay; it looks like we have only–' she glanced at the clock– 'four minutes left, so, let's all work on some homework, or read into the chapter…. I don't want to start on the play till Monday. Tomorrow we'll probably have a quiz on the sonnets and what we've covered so far.'

'A *quiz!*' someone complained.

'So,' said Miss Simpson; 'it's study time.' She got up off the radiator and went up to her desk.

'Okay dudes,' Jon addressed the class, 'let's all break out that homework now….'

'In other words, check into the latest gossip,' Terri said, and turned about to Karen's desk.

Jon made a partial smile. 'Diggit.'

At once the students set to the task of initiating as many separate conversations as possible. 'You know, Jon,' called the teacher from her desk, 'it isn't really so sunny in here. You could show us your eyes.'

He still had not taken off the sunglasses. 'Sorry. I couldn't handle this light right now. Anything brighter than the inside of a coffin....' He waited for her to laugh and then said quietly to himself, 'Which is about where I should be right now....'

Paul turned and leaned over the front of Jon's desk. 'So, hey, dude,' he said quietly, with the volume of others' talking masking his voice; 'so what's with you and, uh....' He nodded in the direction of Jeanne, who sat quietly, still tapping her notebook. 'I thought that, you know....'

Jon sighed a long sigh. It was perhaps the first time he would be straightforward all morning. 'Oh,' he said quietly; 'it's a long story. You don't really wanna know.'

'Hey, Jon,' a girl called over to him; 'so when you guys playin' the Riverfront again?'

'Next Wednesday,' Jon responded rather cheerfully; 'then not again for another couple weeks.'

'Solid,' she acknowledged, and resumed her own conversation.

'So does it have anything to do with your car?' Paul asked him in a soft voice, and tapped Jon's desktop with his fingernail.

Jon looked at him through the mirrored glasses and seemed to get a little sad, although maybe Paul only assumed he did. 'Well–' He cast a quick glance at Jeanne and then said, 'You know how it was with me and Harris; right?'

'Yeah....'

'I got really pissed-off about the whole thing; and so I called him out, to run up Slowham Road, you know, to see who would lay off....'

'Really?' Paul had not heard. Maybe no-one had. After all, thought Jon, only three people really know.... 'So what happened?'

'Some asshole drunk cut me off. I put the goddamn car into a lightpole about fifty feet from the finish line.'

'No shit!' He almost broke out of the whisper.

'Wasted the whole goddamn front end of the car, too. I think the frame's bent. It wobbles, somethin' fierce, at like seventy.'

'Damn....' Paul was reverently silent for a moment. 'Shit– what a bitch.'

'So,' Jon said, with a new breath; 'I have to lay off now. That was the arrangement.'

Paul looked at him. 'So you're gonna abide, yet? Do you really wanna do that?'

Jon shrugged, hating the question.   He thought about how many times he had asked himself the very same thing since Friday morning. 'I don't know,' he said, in a gentler tone. 'All I know is that she's worth a hell of a lot more than some asshole drag race. It was just a way to decide; and now that it's decided I say the hell with it. Better than to tear her all up inside, like; you know˜?'

'Yeah, yeah....' Paul could not disagree with that. He glanced over at Jeanne, sitting quietly, talking to no-one, still tapping the spine of her notebook binder on the desktop.   Jon slouched behind him, tapping his leather key tab in much the same way. 'She's been out since Friday,' Paul said quietly. 'Yesterday was the first day she was back.'

'It's the bug.' Jon was just as sure it was not. 'It's goin' around again, man. I was pukin' all Friday morning.'

'Really, man. My sister's got it too. I really feel for ya.'

'Don't bother,' Jon said.

'So hey,' Paul said brightly; 'what's shakin' with you tonight? Are you guys playin'?   I hear Carole Martin's got another party at her house. Me and some other dudes are gonna crash it about ten-o'clock. Whaddiya say?'

'Aaah; I doubt it. I'm really not in the mood. I gotta start figurin' out how I'm gonna fix the car.'

The bell rang. Jeanne rose with deliberation. Jon bolted up and dashed out of the room in a hurry; and then she made up her mind. She had her coat with her, owing to her illness, and so had no reason to stop at her locker. She had only to follow Jon out to his car and, summoning her very last bits of energy and courage, devise some opportunity to talk. Whatever little chance that gave her to make it up to him was probably all the chance she had left.

Ten paces up the corridor Jon was halted by DJ Berryfield. 'Say hey, JC! What's happenin'?'

Jeanne ducked into an open classroom doorway and waited, trying to listen. 'Aaah; you know, man; nothin' much.'

'So where the hell you *been*, man?   You've been a tough dude to track down, and doo.'

'Aaah; I've been sick, you know.'

'Serious, dude, I hear ya. You look like you lost some weight.'

'Yeah; a little, I think....'

'So hey, bro'; whaddiya say we take in Carole's party tonight? Mom and Dad will be *out*, and I hear Becky and some other people are bringin' over a coupla bottles of Comfort....'

'I doubt it, man, really–'

'Well shit, man; what the hell else are you gonna do? Tonight the whole *world* will be shakin'!'

'I said *pass*, man; really. I'm not in–'

'And some high-time chicks.... Southern Comfort comin' out the ass....'

'And out your *mouth*, too, when you puke it back up. All you *drunk* addicts, man....'

DJ laughed. 'Hah! Look who's talking! We'll all see you in hell!'

'*You* sure will,' Jon teased.

'Diggit. Well; I gotta shake it here. Later, dude.'

'Later.'

DJ went by her in the corridor; and Jeanne dashed back out into the fast-moving crowd, just catching a glimpse of Jon as he went round the far corner. She hurried after him, never one for fast walking herself and feeling ungainly at having to trot along with an armful of books just to keep up. By contrast Jon had a long, graceful stride and was keenly adroit at dodging his way through a crowd; it was like pursuing a badger through a dense wood. Jeanne tried to duck through the same openings in traffic and bumped hard into those who would not yield so graciously.

He was heading for the exit by the gymnasium, staying indoors as long as he could before going out into the weather. Poignantly she recalled the two times he had driven her home and tried her best to shake off the wave of emotion when she considered that such might never happen again. In the wider main galleries he had gained some distance on her; but, whether she feared looking conspicuous, especially by ignoring everyone who called hello to her, or simply hoped to postpone the inevitable, she was not sure. Jon reached the doors and pulled out his gloves from his back pockets. Without even slowing down he put up one foot to press the door's panic bar and started out into the snowfall.

The door banged closed. Jeanne hurried to it; but something made her stop there, her hand on the door bar, watching him walk away so obviously alone. Drained from six days of sickness and starvation and self-pity, she could formulate nothing profound or sincere or meaningful to say to him. She could only stand there, dazed, and watch what she wanted most in the world slipping away amidst the wide, soft snowflakes.

If only he would listen, she thought, it would not be so bad. We could talk, like maybe over some cocoa, and decide just where we stand. I could be all cool and rational about it, if he wanted me to be. All I want is a chance to talk about the truth....

Suddenly a warm and wonderful sensation came over her; and an excited tingle rocketed down her spine. As though boarding a rollercoaster ride, she was frightened and thrilled at the same time. It was nothing she had ever felt before; but she knew for certain that, if Jon Cavaliere had ever meant anything to her, nothing could keep her from riding home in that silver car today. If the truth was ever to come true, it had to start immediately.

With an anxious grunt she lunged into the door and ran headlong out into the snow. 'Jon!' she called after him. '*Jon!*'

For a short second he hesitated; but he may have simply slipped on the freezing pavement. He was not even sure himself; but he began to feel a little more in a hurry.

'Jon,' she called, 'uh, wait—' She caught up to him, stamping her feet on the perilously slippery pavement as she skidded to a slow walk beside him. 'Please, Jon; could you just wait—'

'It's okay, Jeanne,' he said, not looking at her. 'I'll be fine.'

'Jon....' Together they squeezed out the gate to the parking area. Jeanne slipped a little, walking half-sideways in the accumulating snow, and tried to close her unzipped coat with one hand. 'Well; I'm sure you'll be fine, Jon; I mean: I kind of wanted to—' It was discomforting to have to speak personally to someone walking so fast. 'Uh, Jon, could we like slow down, just a little, please—'

'Jeanne, it's okay. Please don't worry about it.'

Such distance and lack of warmth from him was alarming; she had never considered what it would be like if he did not care for her. It was exactly what she had never wanted. 'Uh, Jon, well; like I wanted to say that I kind of missed you, you know.... I was thinking about you, and— Hey; well; you know, like I kind of need a ride home, and no-one's here, and it is getting cold; and so.... Maybe we could like talk in your car....'

'No; not today. I'm sure Harris will be expecting to drive you home.'

'Well; um; he's not around, and— I had hoped that *you* would give me a ride today, Jon.'

'No,' he said, looking up at the dappled grey sky; 'it's okay. You don't have to worry about me bugging you any more.'

'Jon....' It saddened her to think he could feel that way. 'You've never bugged me....'

'Jeanne,' he said at last, almost looking at her, 'look. It's all okay now; okay? The whole thing is passed, and you know it and I know it. Even Harris knows it. You don't have to humour me over it. It was all a big mistake that was made; it was really *me* who made the mistake; and let's just get over all the stupid stuff and get on with life; okay? Just forgive me; and we'll forget the whole thing.'

'Oh, Jon.... *I* forgive you. I would forgive you for *anything*. It wasn't a mistake at all; it's just—'

'Yeah; it was a mistake; but it's all over. You go back to the one you should have, and I'll just stay as a memory from seventh grade; okay?'

Jeanne lowered her head then, recognising the moment at which she would have to give him the real truth, without pretending it was anything else. If it was going to work, only the truth would make it happen. 'I *have* gone to the one I should have, Jonny. You know it, and I know it.'

He must have heard this; he was right next to her, but he would say nothing. Rounding the corner of the old black Mercury beside his car, he got out his keys.

'Jon,' she said, standing at the rear of the Caprice, 'what's happening here? Can we at least *talk* about this, please?'

He shook his head, as though impatient, and unlocked the driver's door.

'Jon,' she tried, 'just wait, *please*? Don't leave, until we can talk....' Her eyes flooded with tears. 'I mean: it just can't *end* like this. It wasn't supposed to end at all....' She watched him dust away some wet snow, to open the door, and stamped her foot in frustration. 'Jonny, you *can't* go. You don't know how I *feel*. *I* didn't want you to get hurt. *I* didn't want the stupid drag race. Don't you *understand*, Jonny? It was all *my* fault. It wasn't what I wanted. It was just what *happened*. I just want the chance to make it up to you, because I *love* you.'

He paid her no mind and sat in the car.

'Jonny, I *love* you! Don't you understand? I've *always* loved you!'

The car door closed.

'Oh, *Jonny*!'

Jeanne broke down. She had done what she could; admitting her true feelings had done nothing. Everything she had dreamt for the last four years, the most precious years of her life, had finally amounted to nothing. There would be no spark inside tomorrow. There would be nothing to hope and nothing to dream and nothing to love again, nothing to excite her with chills in the corridors and nothing to keep her distracted with daydreams in class. It was all over, just as he had said.

'Ohhh!' she cried out, and spun herself about and went face-first into the pile of snow on the old Mercury's boot-lid, wailing aloud in her grief. 'God, he doesn't *love* me! Doesn't he *know*? Doesn't he *care*? Oh, God, what will I *do*? How could he not *want* me any more? How *could* he? What am I going to *do*?'

Other people walked by, students and teachers and classmates and friends, people for whom she had once kept up an attractive reputation but who would never understand what she felt now. Her reputation in front of those people meant nothing any more. It was all a different world now, the cold and the strangers and the books that slid into the snow on the ground. She put her face down in the snow on the back of some stranger's car, not caring that her glasses and her hair and her cheeks and her hands were all freezing wet and caring even less if the people passing by had begun to believe that their one and only universally-appealing Jeannie Banfield had turned into some kind of lunatic.

Jon turned the key. The parking-brake had not been released, the gearbox was still engaged, the chokes had not been set and the fuel was cold in the tank. The car gave merely a halfhearted 'clunk' and a weak jolt forwards and resigned without further ado. Jon took another jab at the key to switch it back to *off* and laid his head back in the seat in contemplation. With a mournful little sigh he yanked off his gloves, tossed his sunglasses up onto the dashboard and opened the door.

The tears rolled out and fell down her cheeks, mingling and freezing with the snow. It would not be so hard to just stay here, to allow the weather to take a final toll on her feebled body already undermined by lack of appetite and no sound sleep. Gradually she would grow colder and colder until her body temperature fell below healthy limits and she collapsed, hopefully ending up comatose beyond return. Possibly she would be saved by heroic doctors; but Jeanne knew she was destined to live on only as a walking shell with no more soul or emotion. It would be all too easy to just give up on everything now that it was all over. There was no spark of life left in her at all.

Someone touched her shoulder. She had felt so sure no-one could ever give her any comfort again; but, even so, she was compelled to lift her head up out of the snow. She coughed pitifully and tried to sniffle. Some warm, dry hand wiped snow away from the sides of her face and brushed back her hair. The fingers caressed her cheek and went inside her glasses to blot the wetness from her eyes. There was a voice, soothing and sincere. Her knees trembled; but she kept her eyes closed, summoning the last of her strength for the hope that perhaps there might yet be hope left, and maybe her homework and the stares of the people passing and the cold and dying inside to live on in an emotional coma were not all she had left. For once, maybe her hopes and Fate were on the same side.

'There, there, pretty Jeanne; please don't cry.'

She swallowed some tears and tried desperately to stand up straight. 'Oh, God,' she whimpered, feeling faint-headed, and her body went limp.

He caught her in his arms and turned her towards him; and she collapsed upon his chest with her head inside the collar of his jacket, where she allowed herself to cry unhindered. They were just like all the other tears, the ones of today and yesterday and last week and last year; and yet they were wonderful because there would be a rainbow just beyond them; for, when they had stopped, she might never have to cry again.

He patted her on the back, feeling awkward with holding a weeping girl in his arms, but just as glad she was his at last and belonged to no-one else. 'There, there,' he whispered softly beside her ear; 'it's all right now.... You don't have to cry. Everything is gonna be all right. Don't you see? Nothing is so bad now. You love me and I love you, and we've always known that; and we don't have to cry any more. It's all gonna be all right, Jeanne. We don't have to....' Suddenly he had to give up on being brave and buried his face into her neck to weep too.

'Oh, Jonny,' she cried, and neither of them thought it strange to hear her return to using the nickname she had for him when they had first met and become so fond of each other. Somehow it seemed perfectly fitting that she should now. 'God knows I've loved you....' She wiped her own eyes and then looked up to face him. He was unwilling to let her see him cry, but she looked at him anyway and wiped his eyes as he had done for her. 'Oh; I *do* love you, Jonny. Don't you know I do? I have always loved you. I was just so *afraid*....'

He sniffled, keeping his chin down, and nodded a little. 'I've always loved you too,' he admitted, and then turned away from her to weep again.

She pulled him towards herself and hugged him, and his arms went about her and hugged her even more tightly. After battling all his luck away he could see that she had always been right there, just an arm's-length away, refusing to get too far from him no matter what he had done or what he had become. It had only been his move to reach out and pull her close to him. Now that she was here there would be no letting go.

He looked at her then and she looked up at him, and they kissed, each of them going to gelatine inside and falling into each other. For what felt like hours on end they only stood there in the snow behind his car and held onto each other, the gentle bouquet of her perfume mingling with the hardy scent of his leather jacket; and the people walked by and the cars drove past and the snow came down all round. It was all going to be all right. Neither of them could think of anything else now, except that it was all going to be all right.

And so it was.

* * *

Lyrics credits

Used by arrangement

'Deirdre (Moonchild)'
J C
© 1985 Comet Songs
- epigram -

'Let's Pretend'
E Carmen
© 1972 Universal Songs of Polygram
Performed by The Strawberries

'Try It Out'
D Holloway, J Cavaliere
© 1974 Wilshire Songs
Performed by The Strawberries

'Lovely'
D Holloway, J Cavaliere
© 1974 Wilshire Songs
Performed by The Strawberries

'Band On The Run'
P McCartney, L McCartney
© 1973 MPL Communications
Performed by Paul McCartney & Wings

'Till There Was You'
M Willson
© 1961 Howard Music Co
Performed by The Strawberries

* * *

About Jonnie Comet

The Author spent the mid-1970s within the surfing community in the Atlantic Ocean resort of Surf City, New Jersey, serving as a guru and personal advisor to the teenaged locals and tourists. He performed as bass guitarist, vocalist and chief songwriter with the Shore-area outfit The Surf Rats before fronting The Jonnie Comet Band in the 1980s.

Influenced by an Anglo-European Christian artistic and academic ethic, the Author is educated in music, art, architecture, yacht design, sailing, flying, physics, philosophy, history, languages and literature. He has held professional capacities as a warehouseman, purchasing agent, customer-service consultant, hardware designer, literacy teacher, stage technician, truck driver, boatbuilder, and performing musician.

Jonnie Comet edited The Absolutist (1997-2007), a periodical in the Augustan tradition devoted to the conservation of philosophy and logic in social and academic discourse. His fiction tends to draw upon 18th-century models whilst involving modern, astute characters, exotic or fanciful settings and surreal social conditions.

As a single parent he raised two creative daughters, with whom he co-created and produced the original middle-school-age girls' comedy series *The Jarmman Show* for cable TV (2000-2001).

The Author lives on a yacht sailing the North American east coast.

Jonnie Comet fiction includes

East of the Sun (1982);
Jungleland (1984);
Best Friends; or: The Babysitter (1987);
The Seduction of Susie (1994);
Pamela; or: Virtue Reclaimed (2000);
Gothic Night (2004);
The Castle of The Seven Virgins (2010);
Sylvia; or: The Revenge of The Slave (2013);
the *Deirdre, the Wanderer* adventure saga (2002-);

… and *It's Only Love*; *All You Need Is Love*; and *The Love You Make*, the continuation of Jon and Jeanne's *Wilshire Tales*, extending into the *A Tale of Two Paradises* fantasy/fiction realm.

* * *